Critical accl...

'As always, Rankin p... own milieu. He br... Edinburgh deliciously... mainly in the confident way he weaves the ... threads into a cohesive whole' *Daily Mail*

'His novels flow as smoothly as the flooded Forth, and come peppered with three-dimensional characters who actually react to and are changed by events around them . . . This is Rankin at his raw-edged, page-turning best . . . With Rankin, you can practically smell the fag-smoke and whisky fumes'
Time Out

'A first-rate thriller' *Yorkshire Evening Post*

'The internal police politics and corruption in high places are both portrayed with bone-freezing accuracy. This novel should come with a wind-chill factor warning' *Daily Telegraph*

'Real life and fiction blur in this cynical, bleak tale. You'll love every second of it' *Daily Mirror*

'Rankin strips Edinburgh's polite façade to its gritty skeleton' *The Times*

'Rebus is the kind of detective who enjoys a deep dark mystery with a good moral conundrum'
New York Times

'Rankin writes laconic, sophisticated, well-paced thrillers' *Scotsman*

'First-rate plotting, dialogue and characterisations'
Literary Review

Born in the Kingdom of Fife in 1960, Ian Rankin graduated from the University of Edinburgh and has since been employed as grape-picker, swineherd, taxman, alcohol researcher, hi-fi journalist and punk musician. His first Rebus novel, *Knots & Crosses*, was published in 1987 and the Rebus books have now been translated into 26 languages. Ian Rankin has been elected a Hawthornden Fellow, and is a past winner of the prestigious Chandler-Fulbright Award, as well as two CWA short-story 'Daggers' and the 1997 CWA Macallan Gold Dagger for Fiction for *Black & Blue*, which was also shortlisted for the Mystery Writers of America 'Edgar' award for Best Novel. *Black & Blue*, *The Hanging Garden*, *Dead Souls* and *Mortal Causes* have been televised on ITV, starring John Hannah as Inspector Rebus. *Dead Souls*, the tenth novel in the series, was shortlisted for the CWA Gold Dagger Award in 1999. An Alumnus of the Year at Edinburgh University, he has also been awarded four honorary doctorates, from the University of Abertay Dundee in 1999, from the University of St Andrews in 2001, in 2003 from the University of Edinburgh and in 2005 from the Open University. In 2002 Ian Rankin was awarded an OBE for services to literature. In 2004 *Resurrection Men* won the Edgar Award for Best Novel. In 2005 *Fleshmarket Close* won the Crime Thriller of the Year award at the British Book Awards. Ian is the winner of the Crime Writers' Association Diamond Dagger 2005. In 2005 he was also awarded the Grand Prix du Littérature Policier (France), the Deutsche Krimi Prize (Germany) and the Icons of Scotland award. He lives in Edinburgh with his wife and two sons. Visit his website at www.ianrankin.net.

By Ian Rankin

The Inspector Rebus series
Knots & Crosses
Hide & Seek
Tooth & Nail
Strip Jack
The Black Book
Mortal Causes
Let It Bleed
Black & Blue
The Hanging Garden
Death Is Not The End (*novella*)
Dead Souls
Set in Darkness
The Falls
Resurrection Men
A Question of Blood
Fleshmarket Close

Other novels
The Flood
Watchman
Westwind

Writing as Jack Harvey
Witch Hunt
Bleeding Hearts
Blood Hunt

Short stories
A Good Hanging and Other Stories
Beggars Banquet

Omnibus editions
Rebus: The Early Years
(Knots & Crosses, Hide & Seek, Tooth & Nail)
Rebus: The St Leonard's Years
(Strip Jack, The Black Book, Mortal Causes)
Rebus: The Lost Years
(Let It Bleed, Black & Blue, The Hanging Garden)
Rebus: Capital Crimes (Dead Souls, Set in Darkness, The Falls)

All Ian Rankin's titles are available on audio. Also available:
Jackie Leven Said by Ian Rankin and Jackie Leven.

The Hanging Garden

—

Dead Souls

IAN RANKIN

ORION

The Hanging Garden
First published in Great Britain by Orion Books Ltd in 1998

Dead Souls
First published in Great Britain by Orion Books Ltd in 1999

This omnibus edition published in 2006
by Orion Books Ltd,
Orion House, 5 Upper St Martin's Lane,
London WC2H 9EA

A CIP catalogue record for this book is available from the British
Library.

ISBN 1 89880 194 0

Printed and bound in Great Britain by Mackays of Chatham plc

'If all time is eternally present
All time is unredeemable.'

T.S. Eliot, 'Burnt Norton'

'I went to Scotland and found nothing
there that looks like Scotland'

Arthur Freed, Producer *Brigadoon*

For Miranda

INTRODUCTION

Having lived in France for six years, in the autumn of 1996 I moved back to Edinburgh with my family. I had left Scotland ten years previously, newly married and fresh from university. I was returning with two children and a full-time career as a novelist. Okay, so I wasn't earning enough for the mortgage on a three-bedroom flat, but some of the uncertainties of the past had gone. I felt like a proper, grown-up writer, able to take on big moral themes under the guise of writing whodunits. Academe and literary circles might not take the form seriously, but I knew that the crime novel could say as much about human nature and the state of the world as any other branch of writerly endeavour. My next project was already well under way as we unpacked and started coming to terms with driving on the left (in our French-registered Peugeot). The genesis of this project had been a day-trip I'd made to a place called Oradour – a town which had, quite literally, died.

All the six years I'd spent in France, I'd heard of this place, knew it was just over an hour's drive away from our home in north-east Dordogne. Friends' children went there on school trips, but I'd never made the effort. Then I remembered London. We'd lived there for four years before making the move to France. After we'd left, I'd thought with regret of all the things I hadn't done, places I hadn't bothered to visit. So, towards the end of our time in France, I took the drive north to Oradour.

And was stunned.

The town has been kept as a shrine to its victims. No one knows how many died there, the day the 3rd Company of the SS 'Der Führer' Regiment marched in and started rounding people up. Not far short of a thousand, the histories say. Corpses were set alight, or dropped down wells. Men, women, children: almost no one escaped the slaughter. During my time there, peering through windows into kitchens and living rooms, passing burned-out cars and the rusty carcass of the local tram, the overcast sky gave way to steady rain. I sought shelter in the church, but its roof was missing – torched by the Nazis. I got in close to one of its walls, and realised there were bullet-holes in the plaster all around me. This was where the women had been brought, a machine-gun pointed at them. So I headed for the small museum instead, with its displays of everyday objects: hairbrushes, pairs of spectacles . . . mementoes of the dead.

But what really affected me about Oradour was the fact that the man responsible – the general who'd given the order for the massacre – had been captured by the Allies, but was then sent back to Germany to live out the rest of his days in industry and comfort. What sort of justice was that? There would be reasons for it, of course: probably to do with politics, with diplomacy, with secret deals and information traded. There were usually reasons for these things. I started doing some research, and along the way learned of a network called the Rat-Line (which you'll read about in this book). I also became intrigued that the lessons of the past had not been learned. Atrocities were a daily occurrence in ex-Yugoslavia at this time. The West knew the identities of the men responsible, the men in charge – they were on our TV screens nightly, going about their butchers' business. Yet little or nothing was being done to stop them.

This sense of history repeating would form the basis for *The Hanging Garden*. Most of the book was written in France, but when I arrived in Edinburgh I knew I needed to do some final research on war criminals and how we have dealt with them in the past. So I went to the National Library on Edinburgh's George IV Bridge – a place I'd haunted as a student, back when I'd been writing my first two novels – and did a search.

And found something.

Having decided, months before, that I wanted to write about Oradour, I'd scratched my head for a while. The sticking point was: how could I do so from the point of view of Detective Inspector John Rebus? The answer came eventually: I would have Rebus investigate an alleged Nazi war criminal who has been living quietly in Edinburgh for forty years or more. In this way, I could question the validity of prosecuting old men for their crimes of half a century before.

Perfect, I thought.

But that day in the National Library, I found information on an alleged war criminal . . . a real one . . . living quietly in Edinburgh. A TV documentary had been made about him, and he'd taken legal action against the producers. And though he hadn't been successful, I knew I would have to be careful that he couldn't see himself in *my* portrait of a suspected monster . . .

The book went on to win the Cognac Prix du Roman Policier – not bad, considering I hadn't managed to find a French publisher during my long sojourn in that country! It also sneaked on to the margins of the bestseller lists in the UK, and was the third biggest-selling title in Scotland in 1999 (after two of the Harry Potter instalments). Having managed critical success with *Black & Blue*, I was now beginning to see some sales success, too. The mortgage on that three-bedroom flat couldn't be too far away . . .

Having borrowed from a song by The Cure for the title of *The Hanging Garden*, I decided I wanted to preface each section of my book with a couple of lines from the song. I had no idea how to go about seeking permission, so turned to the band's fan club for help. Eventually, I received a phone call from someone on the management side. They had, they told me, talked it over with Robert – meaning Robert Smith, the band's lyricist. Robert said it would be okay, but of course there would be a fee. I sucked in some air and asked how much.

'A few signed copies when the book comes out.'

I laughed – from relief, but also because it showed what a gentleman Mr Smith was – and was quick to accept. Only later did it dawn on me that I had no address to send the books to, and no record of the name of the person who'd phoned me. So if anyone out there knows Robert Smith, tell him to get in touch. There's a first edition waiting here with his name on. I'd like him to see the book some time, if only for the smile it might raise when he finds out what I've done with other songs of his – most notably 'Fascination Street' and 'Mr Pink Eyes' . . .

Now read on . . .

May 2005

They were arguing in the living-room.

'Look, if your bloody job's so precious ...'

'What do you want from me?'

'You know bloody well!'

'I'm working my arse off for the three of us!'

'Don't give me that crap.'

And then they saw her. She was holding her teddy bear, Pa Broon, by one well-chewed ear. She was peering round the doorway, thumb in her mouth. They turned to her.

'What is it, sweetie?'

'I had a bad dream.'

'Come here.' The mother crouched down, opening her arms. But the girl ran to her father, wrapped herself around his legs.

'Come on, pet, I'll take you back to bed.'

He tucked her in, started to read her a story.

'Daddy,' she said, 'what if I fall asleep and don't wake up? Like Snow White or Sleeping Beauty?'

'Nobody sleeps forever, Sammy. All it takes to wake them up is a kiss. There's nothing the witches and evil queens can do about that.'

He kissed her forehead.

'Dead people don't wake up,' she said, hugging Pa Broon. 'Not even when you kiss them.'

1

John Rebus kissed his daughter.

'Sure you don't want a lift?'

Samantha shook her head. 'I need to walk off that pizza.'

Rebus put his hands in his pockets, felt folded banknotes beneath his handkerchief. He thought of offering her some money – wasn't that what fathers did? – but she'd only laugh. She was twenty-four and independent; didn't need the gesture and certainly wouldn't take the money. She'd even tried to pay for the pizza, arguing that she'd eaten half while he'd chewed on a single slice. The remains were in a box under her arm.

'Bye, Dad.' She pecked him on the cheek.

'Next week?'

'I'll phone you. Maybe the three of us ...?' By which she meant Ned Farlowe, her boyfriend. She was walking backwards as she spoke. One final wave, and she turned away from him, head moving as she checked the evening traffic, crossing the road without looking back. But on the opposite pavement she half-turned, saw him watching her, waved her hand in acknowledgement. A young man almost collided with her. He was staring at the pavement, the thin black cord from a pair of earphones dribbling down his neck. Turn round and look at her, Rebus commanded. Isn't she incredible? But the youth kept shuffling along the pavement, oblivious to her world.

And then she'd turned a corner and was gone. Rebus could only imagine her now: making sure the pizza box was secure beneath her left arm; walking with eyes fixed firmly ahead of her; rubbing a thumb behind her right ear, which she'd recently had pierced for the third time. He knew that her nose would twitch when she thought of something funny. He knew that if she wanted to concentrate, she might tuck the corner of one jacket-lapel into her mouth. He knew that she wore a bracelet of braided leather, three silver rings, a cheap watch with black plastic strap and indigo face. He knew that the brown of her hair was its natural colour. He knew she was headed for a Guy Fawkes party, but didn't intend staying long.

He didn't know nearly enough about her, which was why he'd wanted them to meet for dinner. It had been a tortuous process: dates rejigged, last-minute cancellations. Sometimes it was her fault, more often his. Even tonight he should have been elsewhere. He ran his hands down the front of his jacket, feeling the bulge in his inside breast pocket, his own little time-bomb. Checking his watch, he saw it was nearly nine o'clock. He could drive or he could walk – he wasn't going far.

He decided to drive.

Edinburgh on firework night, leaves blown into thick lines down the pavement. One morning soon he would find himself scraping frost from his car windscreen, feeling the cold like jabs to his kidneys. The south side of the city seemed to get the first frost earlier than the north. Rebus, of course, lived and worked on the south side. After a stint in Craigmillar, he was back at St Leonard's. He could make for there now – he was still on shift after all – but he had other plans. He passed three pubs on his way to his car. Chat at the bar, cigarettes and laughter, a fug of heat and alcohol: he knew these things better than he knew his own daughter. Two out of the three bars boasted 'doormen'. They didn't seem to be called bouncers these days. They were doormen or front-of-house managers, big guys with

4

short hair and shorter fuses. One of them wore a kilt. His face was all scar tissue and scowl, the scalp shaved to abrasion. Rebus thought his name was Wattie or Wallie. He belonged to Telford. Maybe they all did. Graffiti on the wall further along: Won't Anyone Help? Three words spreading across the city.

Rebus parked around the corner from Flint Street and started walking. The street was in darkness at ground level, except for a café and amusement arcade. There was one lamppost, its bulb dead. The council had been asked by police not to replace it in a hurry – the surveillance needed all the help it could get. A few lights were shining in the tenement flats. There were three cars parked kerbside, but only one of them with people in it. Rebus opened the back door and got in.

A man sat in the driver's seat, a woman next to him. They looked cold and bored. The woman was Detective Constable Siobhan Clarke, who had worked with Rebus at St Leonard's until a recent posting to the Scottish Crime Squad. The man, a Detective Sergeant called Claverhouse, was a Crime Squad regular. They were part of a team keeping twenty-four-hour tabs on Tommy Telford and all his deeds. Their slumped shoulders and pale faces bespoke not only tedium but the sure knowledge that surveillance was futile.

It was futile because Telford owned the street. Nobody parked here without him knowing who and why. The other two cars parked just now were Range Rovers belonging to Telford's gang. Anything but a Range Rover stuck out. The Crime Squad had a specially adapted van which they usually used for surveillance, but that wouldn't work in Flint Street. Any van parked here for longer than five minutes received close and personal attention from a couple

5

of Telford's men. They were trained to be courteous and menacing at the same time.

'Undercover bloody surveillance,' Claverhouse growled. 'Only we're not undercover and there's nothing to survey.' He tore at a Snickers wrapper with his teeth and offered the first bite to Siobhan Clarke, who shook her head.

'Shame about those flats,' she said, peering up through the windscreen. 'They'd be perfect.'

'Except Telford owns them all,' Claverhouse said through a mouthful of chocolate.

'Are they all occupied?' Rebus asked. He'd been in the car a minute and already his toes were cold.

'Some of them are empty,' Clarke said. 'Telford uses them for storage.'

'But every bugger in and out of the main door gets spotted,' Claverhouse added. 'We've had meter readers and plumbers try to wangle their way in.'

'Who was acting the plumber?' Rebus asked.

'Ormiston. Why?'

Rebus shrugged. 'Just need someone to fix a tap in my bathroom.'

Claverhouse smiled. He was tall and skinny, with huge dark bags under his eyes and thinning fair hair. Slow-moving and slow-talking, people often underestimated him. Those who did sometimes discovered that his nickname of 'Bloody' Claverhouse was merited.

Clarke checked her watch. 'Ninety minutes till the changeover.'

'You could do with the heating on,' Rebus offered. Claverhouse turned in his seat.

'That's what I keep telling her, but she won't have it.'

'Why not?' He caught Clarke's eyes in the rearview. She was smiling.

'Because,' Claverhouse said, 'it means running the

6

engine, and running the engine when we're not going anywhere is wasteful. Global warming or something.'

'It's true,' Clarke said.

Rebus winked at her reflection. It looked like she'd been accepted by Claverhouse, which meant acceptance by the whole team at Fettes. Rebus, the perennial outsider, envied her the ability to conform.

'Bloody useless anyway,' Claverhouse continued. 'The bugger knows we're here. The van was blown after twenty minutes, the plumber routine didn't even get Ormiston over the threshhold, and now here we are, the only sods on the whole street. We couldn't blend in less if we were doing panto.'

'Visible presence as a deterrent,' Rebus said.

'Aye, right, a few more nights of this and I'm sure Tommy'll be back on the straight and narrow.' Claverhouse shifted in his seat, trying to get comfortable. 'Any word of Candice?'

Sammy had asked her father the same thing. Rebus shook his head.

'You still think Tarawicz snatched her? No chance she did a runner?'

Rebus snorted.

'Just because you want it to be them doesn't mean it was. My advice: leave it to us. Forget about her. You've got that Adolf thing to keep you busy.'

'Don't remind me.'

'Did you ever track down Colquhoun?'

'Sudden holiday. His office got a doctor's line.'

'I think we did for him.'

Rebus realised one of his hands was caressing his breast pocket. 'So is Telford in the café or what?'

'Went in about an hour ago,' Clarke said. 'There's a room at the back, he uses that. He seems to like the arcade,

7

too. Those games where you sit on a motorbike and do the circuit.'

'We need someone on the inside,' Claverhouse said. 'Either that or wire the place.'

'We couldn't even get a plumber in there,' Rebus said. 'You think someone with a fistful of radio mikes is going to fare any better?'

'Couldn't do any worse.' Claverhouse switched on the radio, seeking music.

'Please,' Clarke pleaded, 'no country and western.'

Rebus stared out at the café. It was well-lit with a net curtain covering the bottom half of its window. On the top half was written 'Big Bites For Small Change'. There was a menu taped to the window, and a sandwich board on the pavement outside, which gave the café's hours as 6.30 a.m. – 8.30 p.m. The place should have been closed for an hour.

'How are his licences?'

'He has lawyers,' Clarke said.

'First thing we tried,' Claverhouse added. 'He's applied for a late-night extension. I can't see the neighbours complaining.'

'Well,' Rebus said, 'much as I'd love to sit around here chatting …'

'End of liaison?' Clarke asked. She was keeping her humour, but Rebus could see she was tired. Disrupted sleep pattern, body chill, plus the boredom of a surveillance you know is going nowhere. It was never easy partnering Claverhouse: no great fund of stories, just constant reminding that they had to do everything 'the right way', meaning by the book.

'Do us a favour,' Claverhouse said.

'What?'

'There's a chippy across from the Odeon.'

'What do you want?'

'Just a poke of chips.'

8

'Siobhan?'

'Irn-Bru.'

'Oh, and John?' Claverhouse added as Rebus stepped out of the car. 'Ask them for a hot-water bottle while you're at it.'

A car turned into the street, speeding up then screeching to a halt outside the café. The back door nearest the kerb opened, but nobody got out. The car accelerated away, door still hanging open, but there was something on the pavement now, something crawling, trying to push itself upright.

'Get after them!' Rebus shouted. Claverhouse had already turned the ignition, slammed the gear-shift into first. Clarke was on the radio as the car pulled away. As Rebus crossed the street, the man got to his feet. He stood with one hand against the café window, the other held to his head. As Rebus approached, the man seemed to sense his presence, staggered away from the café into the road.

'Christ!' he yelled. 'Help me!' He fell to his knees again, both hands scrabbling at his scalp. His face was a mask of blood. Rebus crouched in front of him.

'We'll get you an ambulance,' he said. A crowd had gathered at the window of the café. The door had been pulled open, and two young men were watching, like they were onlookers at a piece of street theatre. Rebus recognised them: Kenny Houston and Pretty-Boy. 'Don't just stand there!' he yelled. Houston looked to Pretty-Boy, but Pretty-Boy wasn't moving. Rebus took out his mobile, called in the emergency, his eyes fixing on Pretty-Boy: black wavy hair, eyeliner. Black leather jacket, black polo-neck, black jeans. Stones: 'Paint it Black'. But the face chalk-white, like it had been powdered. Rebus walked up to the door. Behind him, the man was beginning to wail, a roar of pain echoing into the night sky.

'We don't know him,' Pretty-Boy said.

'I didn't ask if you knew him, I asked for help.'

Pretty-Boy didn't blink. 'The magic word.'

Rebus got right up into his face. Pretty-Boy smiled and nodded towards Houston, who went to fetch towels.

Most of the customers had returned to their tables. One was studying the bloody palmprint on the window. Rebus saw another group of people, watching from the doorway of a room to the back of the café. At their centre stood Tommy Telford: tall, shoulders straight, legs apart. He looked almost soldierly.

'I thought you took care of your lads, Tommy!' Rebus called to him. Telford looked straight through him, then turned back into the room. The door closed. More screams from outside. Rebus grabbed the dishtowels from Houston and ran. The bleeder was on his feet again, weaving like a boxer in defeat.

'Take your hands down for a sec.' The man lifted both hands from his matted hair, and Rebus saw a section of scalp rise with them, like it was attached to the skull by a hinge. A thin jet of blood hit Rebus in the face. He turned away and felt it against his ear, his neck. Blindly he stuck the towel on to the man's head.

'Hold this.' Rebus grabbing the hands, forcing them on to the towel. Headlights: the unmarked police car. Claverhouse had his window down.

'Lost them in Causewayside. Stolen car, I'll bet. They'll be hoofing it.'

'We need to get this one to Emergency.' Rebus pulled open the back door. Clarke had found a box of paper hankies and was pulling out a wad.

'I think he's beyond Kleenex,' Rebus said as she handed them over.

'They're for you,' she said.

2

It was a three-minute drive to the Royal Infirmary. Accident & Emergency was gearing up for firework casualties. Rebus went to the toilets, stripped, and rinsed himself off as best he could. His shirt was damp and cold to the touch. A line of blood had dried down the front of his chest. He turned to look in the mirror, saw more blood on his back. He had wet a clump of blue paper towels. There was a change of clothes in his car, but his car was back near Flint Street. The door of the toilets opened and Claverhouse came in.

'Best I could do,' he said, holding out a black t-shirt. There was a garish print on the front, a zombie with demon's eyes, wielding a scythe. 'Belongs to one of the junior doctors, made me promise to get it back to him.'

Rebus dried himself off with another wad of towels. He asked Claverhouse how he looked.

'There's still some on your brow.' Claverhouse wiped the bits Rebus had missed.

'How is he?' Rebus asked.

'They reckon he'll be okay, if he doesn't get an infection on the brain.'

'What do you think?'

'Message to Tommy from Big Ger.'

'Is he one of Tommy's men?'

'He's not saying.'

'So what's his story?'

'Fell down a flight of steps, cracked his head at the bottom.'

'And the drop-off?'

'Says he can't remember.' Claverhouse paused. 'Eh, John ...?'

'What?'

'One of the nurses wanted me to ask you something.'

His tone told Rebus all he needed to know. 'AIDS test?'

'They just wondered.'

Rebus thought about it. Blood in his eyes, his ears, running down his neck. He looked himself over: no scratches or cuts. 'Let's wait and see,' he said.

'Maybe we should pull the surveillance,' Claverhouse said, 'leave them to get on with it.'

'And have a fleet of ambulances standing by to pick up the bodies?'

Claverhouse snorted. 'Is this sort of thing Big Ger's style?'

'Very much so,' Rebus said, reaching for his jacket.

'But not that nightclub stabbing?'

'No.'

Claverhouse started laughing, but there was no humour to the sound. He rubbed his eyes. 'Never got those chips, did we? Christ, I could use a drink.'

Rebus reached into his jacket for the quarter-bottle of Bell's.

Claverhouse didn't seem surprised as he broke the seal. He took a gulp, chased it down with another, and handed the bottle back. 'Just what the doctor ordered.'

Rebus started screwing the top back on.

'Not having one?'

'I'm on the wagon.' Rebus rubbed a thumb over the label.

'Since when?'

'The summer.'

'So why carry a bottle around?'

Rebus looked at it. 'Because that's not what it is.'

Claverhouse looked puzzled. 'Then what is it?'

'A bomb.' Rebus tucked the bottle back into his pocket. 'A little suicide bomb.'

They walked back to A&E. Siobhan Clarke was waiting for them outside a closed door.

'They've had to sedate him,' she said. 'He was up on his feet again, reeling all over the place.' She pointed to marks on the floor – airbrushed blood, smudged by footprints.

'Do we have a name?'

'He's not offered one. Nothing in his pockets to identify him. Over two hundred in cash, so we can rule out a mugging. What do you reckon for a weapon? Hammer?'

Rebus shrugged. 'A hammer would dent the skull. That flap looked too neat. I think they went for him with a cleaver.'

'Or a machete,' Claverhouse added. 'Something like that.'

Clarke stared at him. 'I smell whisky.'

Claverhouse put a finger to his lips.

'Anything else?' Rebus asked. It was Clarke's turn to shrug.

'Just one observation.'

'What's that?'

'I like the t-shirt.'

Claverhouse put money in the machine, got out three coffees. He'd called his office, told them the surveillance was suspended. Orders now were to stay at the hospital, see if the victim would say anything. The very least they wanted was an ID. Claverhouse handed a coffee to Rebus.

'White, no sugar.'

Rebus took the coffee with one hand. In the other he

held a polythene laundry-bag, inside which was his shirt. He'd have a go at cleaning it. It was a good shirt.

'You know, John,' Claverhouse said, 'there's no point you hanging around.'

Rebus knew. His flat was a short walk away across The Meadows. His large, empty flat. There were students through the wall. They played music a lot, stuff he didn't recognise.

'You know Telford's gang,' Rebus said. 'Didn't you recognise the face?'

Claverhouse shrugged. 'I thought he looked a bit like Danny Simpson.'

'But you're not sure?'

'If it's Danny, a name's about all we can hope to get out of him. Telford picks his boys with care.'

Clarke came towards them along the corridor. She took the coffee from Claverhouse.

'It's Danny Simpson,' she confirmed. 'I just got another look, now the blood's been cleaned off.' She took a swallow of coffee, frowned. 'Where's the sugar?'

'You're sweet enough already,' Claverhouse told her.

'Why did they pick on Simpson?' Rebus asked.

'Wrong place, wrong time?' Claverhouse suggested.

'Plus he's pretty low down the pecking order,' Clarke added, 'making it a gentle hint.'

Rebus looked at her. Short dark hair, shrewd face with a gleam to the eyes. He knew she worked well with suspects, kept them calm, listened carefully. Good on the street, too: fast on her feet as well as in her head.

'Like I say, John,' Claverhouse said, finishing his coffee, 'any time you want to head off ...'

Rebus looked up and down the empty corridor. 'Am I in the way or something?'

'It's not that. But your job's *liaison* – period. I know the way you work: you get attached to cases, maybe even over-attached. Look at Candice. I'm just saying ...'

'You're saying, don't butt in?' Colour rose to Rebus's cheeks: *Look at Candice*.

'I'm saying it's our case, not yours. That's all.'

Rebus's eyes narrowed. 'I don't get it.'

Clarke stepped in. 'John, I think all he means is –'

'Whoah! It's okay, Siobhan. Let the man speak for himself.'

Claverhouse sighed, screwed up his empty cup and looked around for a bin. 'John, investigating Telford means keeping half an eye on Big Ger Cafferty and his crew.'

'And?'

Claverhouse stared at him. 'Okay, you want it spelling out? You went to Barlinnie yesterday – news travels in our business. You met Cafferty. The two of you had a chinwag.'

'He asked me to go,' Rebus lied.

Claverhouse held up his hands. 'Fact is, as you've just said, he asked you and you went.' Claverhouse shrugged.

'Are you saying I'm in his pocket?' Rebus's voice had risen.

'Boys, boys,' Clarke said.

The doors at the end of the corridor had swung open. A young man in dark business suit, briefcase swinging, was coming towards the drinks machine. He was humming some tune. He stopped humming as he reached them, put down his case and searched his pockets for change. He smiled when he looked at them.

'Good evening.'

Early-thirties, black hair slicked back from his forehead. One kiss-curl looped down between his eyebrows.

'Anyone got change of a pound?'

They looked in their pockets, couldn't find enough coins.

'Never mind.' Though the machine was flashing EXACT

MONEY ONLY he stuck in the pound coin and selected tea, black, no sugar. He stooped down to retrieve the cup, but didn't seem in a hurry to leave.

'You're police officers,' he said. His voice was a drawl, slightly nasal: Scottish upper-class. He smiled. 'I don't think I know any of you professionally, but one can always tell.'

'And you're a lawyer,' Rebus guessed. The man bowed his head in acknowledgement. 'Here to represent the interests of a certain Mr Thomas Telford.'

'I'm Daniel Simpson's legal advisor.'

'Which adds up to the same thing.'

'I believe Daniel's just been admitted.' The man blew on his tea, sipped it.

'Who told you he was here?'

'Again, I don't believe that's any of your business, Detective …?'

'DI Rebus.'

The man transferred his cup to his left hand so he could hold out his right. 'Charles Groal.' He glanced at Rebus's t-shirt. 'Is that what you call "plain clothes", Inspector?'

Claverhouse and Clarke introduced themselves in turn. Groal made great show of handing out business cards.

'I take it,' he said, 'you're loitering here in the hope of interviewing my client?'

'That's right,' Claverhouse said.

'Might I ask why, DS Claverhouse? Or should I address that question to your superior?'

'He's not my –' Claverhouse caught Rebus's look.

Groal raised an eyebrow. 'Not your superior? And yet he manifestly is, being an Inspector to your Sergeant.' He looked towards the ceiling, tapped a finger against his cup. 'You're not strictly colleagues,' he said at last, bringing his gaze back down to focus on Claverhouse.

'DS Claverhouse and myself are attached to the Scottish Crime Squad,' Clarke said.

'And Inspector Rebus isn't,' Groal observed. 'Fascinating.'

'I'm at St Leonard's.'

'Then this is quite rightly part of your division. But as for the Crime Squad ...'

'We just want to know what happened,' Rebus went on.

'A fall of some kind, wasn't it? How is he, by the way?'

'Nice of you to show concern,' Claverhouse muttered.

'He's unconscious,' Clarke said.

'And likely to be in an operating theatre fairly soon. Or will they want to X-ray him first? I'm not very up on the procedures.'

'You could always ask a nurse,' Claverhouse said.

'DS Claverhouse, I detect a certain hostility.'

'Just his normal tone,' Rebus said. 'Look, you're here to make sure Danny Simpson keeps his trap shut. We're here to listen to whatever bunch of shite the two of you eventually concoct for our delectation. I think that's a pretty fair summary, don't you?'

Groal cocked his head slightly to one side. 'I've heard about you, Inspector. Occasionally stories can become exaggerated but not, I'm pleased to say, in your case.'

'He's a living legend,' Clarke offered. Rebus snorted and headed back into A&E.

There was a woolly-suit in there, seated on a chair, his cap on his lap and a paperback book resting on the cap. Rebus had seen him half an hour before. The constable was sitting outside a room with its door closed tight. Quiet voices came from the other side. The woolly-suit was called Redpath and he worked out of St Leonard's. He'd been in the force a bit under a year. Graduate recruit. They called him 'The Professor'. He was tall and spotty and had a shy look about him. He closed the book as Rebus approached, but kept a finger in his page.

'Science fiction,' he explained. 'Always thought I'd grow out of it.'

'There are a lot of things we don't grow out of, son. What's it about?'

'The usual: threats to the stability of the time contin-uum, parallel universes.' Redpath looked up. 'What do you think of parallel universes, sir?'

Rebus nodded towards the door. 'Who's in there?'

'Hit and run.'

'Bad?' The Professor shrugged. 'Where did it happen?'

'Top of Minto Street.'

'Did you get the car?'

Redpath shook his head. 'Waiting to see if she can tell us anything. What about you, sir?'

'Similar story, son. Parallel universe, you could call it.'

Siobhan Clarke appeared, nursing a fresh cup of coffee. She nodded a greeting towards Redpath, who stood up: a courtesy which gained him a sly smile.

'Telford doesn't want Danny talking,' she said to Rebus.

'Obviously.'

'And meantime he'll want to even the score.'

'Definitely.'

She caught Rebus's eyes. 'I thought he was a bit out of order back there.' Meaning Claverhouse, but not wanting to name names in front of a uniform.

Rebus nodded. 'Thanks.' Meaning: you did right not to say as much at the time. Claverhouse and Clarke were partners now. It wouldn't do for her to upset him.

A door slid open and a doctor appeared. She was young, and looked exhausted. Behind her in the room, Rebus could see a bed, a figure on the bed, staff milling around the various machines. Then the door slid closed.

'We're going to do a brain scan,' the doctor was telling Redpath. 'Have you contacted her family?'

'I don't have a name.'

'Her effects are inside.' The doctor slid open the door again and walked in. There was clothing folded on a chair, a bag beneath it. As the doctor pulled out the bag, Rebus saw something. A flat white cardboard box.

A white cardboard pizza box. Clothes: black denims, black bra, red satin shirt. A black duffel-coat.

'John?'

And black shoes with two-inch heels, square-toed, new-looking except for the scuff marks, like they'd been dragged along the road.

He was in the room now. They had a mask over her face, feeding her oxygen. Her forehead was cut and bruised, the hair pushed away from it. Her fingers were blistered, the palms scraped raw. The bed she lay on wasn't really a bed but a wide steel trolley.

'Excuse me, sir, you shouldn't be in here.'

'What's wrong?'

'It's this gentleman –'

'John? John, what is it?'

Her earrings had been removed. Three tiny pin-pricks, one of them redder than its neighbours. The face above the sheet: puffy blackened eyes, a broken nose, abrasions on both cheeks. Split lip, a graze on the chin, eyelids which didn't even flutter. He saw a hit and run victim. And beneath it all, he saw his daughter.

And he screamed.

Clarke and Redpath had to drag him out, helped by Claverhouse who'd heard the noise.

'Leave the door open! I'll kill you if you close that door!'

They tried to sit him down. Redpath rescued his book

from the chair. Rebus tore it from him and threw it down the hall.

'How could you read a fucking book?' he spat. 'That's Sammy in there! And you're out here reading a book!'

Clarke's cup of coffee had been kicked over, the floor slippy, Redpath going down as Rebus pushed at him.

'Can you jam that door open?' Claverhouse was asking the doctor. 'And what about a sedative?'

Rebus was clawing his hands through his hair, bawling dry-eyed, his voice hoarse and uncomprehending. Staring down at himself, he saw the ludicrous t-shirt and knew that's what he'd take away from this night: the image of an Iron Maiden t-shirt and its grinning bright-eyed demon. He hauled off his jacket and started tearing at the shirt.

She was behind that door, he thought, and I was out here chatting as casual as you like. She'd been in there all the time he'd been here. Two things clicked: a hit and run; the car speeding away from Flint Street.

He grabbed at Redpath. 'Top of Minto Street. You're sure?'

'What?'

'Sammy ... top of Minto Street?'

Redpath nodded. Clarke knew straight away what Rebus was thinking.

'I don't think so, John. They were headed the opposite way.'

'Could have doubled back.'

Claverhouse had caught some of the exchange. 'I just got off the phone. The guys who did Danny Simpson, we picked up the car. White Escort abandoned in Argyle Place.'

Rebus looked at Redpath. 'White Escort?'

Redpath was shaking his head. 'Witnesses say dark-coloured.'

Rebus turned to the wall, stood there with his palms

pressed to it. Staring at the paintwork, it was like he could see *inside* the paint.

Claverhouse put a hand on his shoulder. 'John, I'm sure she's going to be fine. The doctor's gone to fetch you a couple of tablets, but meantime what about one of these?'

Claverhouse with Rebus's jacket folded in the crook of his arm, the quarter-bottle in his hand.

The little suicide bomb.

He took the bottle from Claverhouse. Unscrewed its top, his eyes on the open doorway. Lifted the bottle to his lips.

Drank.

Book Two

'In the Hanging Garden/No one sleeps'

A seaside holiday: caravan park, long walks and sandcastles. He sat in a deck-chair, trying to read. Cold wind blowing, despite the sun. Rhona rubbed suntan lotion on Sammy, said you couldn't be too careful. Told him to keep an eye open, she was going back to the caravan for her book. Sammy was burying her father's feet in the sand.

He was trying to read, but thinking about work. Every day of the holiday, he sneaked off to a phone-box and called the station. They kept telling him to go and enjoy himself, forget about everything. He was halfway through a spy thriller. The plot had already lost him.

Rhona was doing her best. She'd wanted somewhere foreign, a bit of glamour and heat to go with the sunshine. Finances, however, were on his side. So here they were on the Fife coast, where he'd first met her. Was he hoping for something? Some memory rekindled? He'd come here with his own parents, played with Mickey, met other kids, then lost them again at the end of the fortnight.

He tried the spy novel again, but case-work got in the way. And then a shadow fell over him.

'Where is she?'

'What?' He looked down. His feet were buried in sand, but Sammy wasn't there. How long had she been gone? He stood up, scanned the seashore. A few tentative bathers, going in no further than their knees.

'Christ, John, where is she?'

He turned round, looked at the sand dunes in the distance.

'The dunes ...?'

They warned her. There were hollows in the dunes where the sand was eroding. Small dens had been created – a magnet for kids. Only they were prone to collapse. Earlier in the season, a ten-year-old boy had been dug out by frantic parents. He hadn't quite choked on the sand ...

They were running now. The dunes, the grass, no sign of her.

'Sammy!'

'Maybe she went into the water.'

'You were supposed to be keeping an eye on her!'

'I'm sorry. I ...'

'Sammy!'

A small shape in one of the dens. Hopping on its hands and knees. Rhona reached in, pulled her out, hugged her.

'Sweetie, we told you not to!'

'I was a rabbit.'

Rebus looked at the fragile roof: sand meshed with the roots of plants and grasses. Punched it with a fist. The roof collapsed. Rhona was looking at him.

End of holiday.

3

John Rebus kissed his daughter.

'See you later,' he said, watching her as she left the coffee shop. Espresso and a slice of caramel shortbread – that's all she'd had time for – but they'd fixed another date for dinner. Nothing fancy, just a pizza.

It was October 30th. By mid-November, if Nature were feeling bloody, it would be winter. Rebus had been taught at school that there were four distinct seasons, had painted pictures of them in bright and sombre colours, but his native country seemed not to know this. Winters were long, outstaying their welcome. The warm weather came suddenly, people stripping to t-shirts as the first buds appeared, so that spring and summer seemed entwined into a single season. And no sooner had the leaves started turning brown than the first frost came again.

Sammy waved at him through the cafe window then was gone. She seemed to have grown up all right. He'd always been on the lookout for evidence of instability, hints of childhood traumas or a genetic predisposition towards self-destruction. Maybe he should phone Rhona some day and thank her, thank her for bringing Samantha up on her own. It couldn't have been easy: that was what people always said. He knew it would be nice if he could feel some responsibility for the success, but he wasn't *that* hypocritical. The truth was, while she'd been growing up, he'd been elsewhere. It was the same with his marriage: even when in the same room as his wife, even out at the pictures or around the table at a dinner party ... the best part of him had been elsewhere, fixed on some case or other, some question that needed answering before he could rest.

Rebus lifted his coat from the back of his chair. Nothing left for it but to go back to the office. Sammy was headed back to her own office; she worked with ex-convicts. She had refused his offer of a lift. Now that it was out in the open, she'd wanted to talk about her man, Ned Farlowe. Rebus had tried to look interested, but found that his mind was half on Joseph Lintz – in other words, same problem as always. When he'd been given the Lintz case, he'd been told he was well-suited to it: his Army background for one thing; and his seeming affinity for historical cases – by which Farmer Watson, Rebus's chief superintendent, had meant Bible John – for another.

'With respect, sir,' Rebus had said, 'that sounds like a load of balls. Two reasons for me getting lumbered with this: one, no other bugger will touch it with a barge-pole; two, it'll keep me out of the way for a while.'

'Your remit,' the Farmer had said, unwilling to let Rebus rile him, 'is to sift through what there is, see if any of it amounts to evidence. You can interview Mr Lintz if it'll help. Do whatever you think necessary, and if you find enough to warrant a charge ...'

'I won't. You know I won't.' Rebus sighed. 'Sir, we've been through this before. It's the whole reason the War Crimes section was shut down. That case a few years back – lot of hoo-haa about bugger all.' He was shaking his head. 'Who wants it all dragged up, apart from the papers?'

'I'm taking you off the Mr Taystee case. Let Bill Pryde handle that.'

So it was settled: Lintz belonged to Rebus.

It had started with a news story, with documents handed over to a Sunday broadsheet. The documents had come from the Holocaust Investigation Bureau based in Tel Aviv.

They had passed on to the newspaper the name of Joseph Lintz, who had, they said, been living quietly in Scotland under an alias since the end of the war, and who was, in fact, Josef Linzstek, a native of Alsace. In June 1944, Lieutenant Linzstek had led the 3rd Company of an SS regiment, part of the 2nd Panzer Division, into the town of Villefranche d'Albarede in the Corrèze region of France. 3rd Company had rounded up everyone in the town – men, women, children. The sick were carried from their beds, the elderly pulled from their armchairs, babies hoisted from their cots.

A teenage girl – an evacuee from Lorraine – had seen what the Germans were capable of. She climbed into the attic of her house and hid there, watching from a small window in the roof-tiles. Everyone was marched into the village square. The teenager saw her schoolfriends find their families. She hadn't been in school that day: a throat infection. She wondered if anyone would tell the Germans …

There was a commotion as the mayor and other dignitaries remonstrated with the officer in charge. While machine guns were aimed at the crowd, these men – among them the priest, lawyer, and doctor – were set upon with rifle butts. Then ropes were produced, and strung over half a dozen of the trees which lined the square. The men were hauled to their feet, their heads pushed through the nooses. An order was given, a hand raised then dropped, and soldiers pulled on each rope, until six men were hanging from the trees, bodies writhing, legs kicking uselessly, the movements slowing by degrees.

As the teenager remembered it, it took an age for them to die. Stunned silence in the square, as if the whole village knew now, knew that this was no mere check of identity papers. More orders were barked. The men, separated from the women and children, were marched off to Prud-homme's barn, everyone else shepherded into the church. The square grew empty, except for a dozen or so soldiers, rifles slung over their shoulders. They chatted, kicked up dust and stones, shared jokes and cigarettes. One of them went into the bar and switched the radio on. Jazz music filled the air, competing with the rustle of leaves as a breeze twisted the corpses in the trees.

'It was strange,' the girl later said. 'I stopped seeing them as dead bodies. It was as if they'd become something else, parts of the trees themselves.'

Then the explosion, smoke and dust billowing from the church. A moment's silence, as though a vacuum had been created in the world, then screams, followed immediately by machine-gun fire. And when it finally stopped, she could still hear it. Because it wasn't just inside the church: it was in the distance, too.

Prudhomme's barn.

When she was finally found – by people from surround-ing villages – she was naked except for a shawl she had found in a trunk. The shawl had belonged to her grandmother, dead the previous year. But she was not alone in escaping the massacre. When the soldiers had opened fire in Prudhomme's barn, they'd aimed low. The first row of men to fall had been wounded in the lower body, and the bodies which fell on them shielded them from further fire. When straw was strewn over the mound and set alight, they'd waited as long as they could before starting to claw their way out from beneath, expecting at any moment to be shot. Four of them made it, two with their hair and clothes on fire, one dying later from his wounds.

Three men, one teenage girl: the only survivors.

The death toll was never finalised. No one knew how many visitors had been in Villefranche that day, how many refugees could be added to the count. A list was compiled of over seven hundred names, people who had most likely been killed.

Rebus sat at his desk and rubbed his eyes with his knuckles. The teenage girl was still alive, a pensioner now. The male survivors were all dead. But they'd been alive for the Bordeaux trial in 1953. He had summaries of their evidence. The summaries were in French. A lot of the material sitting on his desk was French, and Rebus didn't speak French. That was why he'd gone to the Modern Languages department at the university and found someone who could. Her name was Kirstin Mede, and she lectured in French, but also had a working knowledge of German, which was handy: the documents which weren't in French were in German. He had a one-page English summary of the trial proceedings, passed on from the Nazi hunters. The trial had opened in February 1953 and lasted just under a month. Of seventy-five men identified as having been part of the German force at Villefranche, only fifteen were present – six Germans and nine French Alsatians. Not one of them was an officer. One German received the death sentence, the others jail terms of between four and twelve years, but they were all released as soon as the trial finished. Alsace hadn't been enjoying the trial, and in a bid to unite the nation, the government had passed an amnesty. The Germans, meantime, were said to have already served their sentences.

The survivors of Villefranche had been horrified.

Even more extraordinary to Rebus's mind, the British had apprehended a couple of German officers involved in the massacre, but had refused to hand them over to the French authorities, returning them to Germany instead, where they lived long and prosperous lives. If Linzstek had been captured then, there would have been none of the present commotion.

Politics: it was all down to politics. Rebus looked up and

Kirstin Mede was standing there. She was tall, deftly constructed, and immaculately dressed. She wore make-up the way women usually did only in fashion adverts. Today she was wearing a check two-piece, the skirt just touching her knees, and long gold-coloured earrings. She had already opened her briefcase and was pulling out a sheaf of papers.

'Latest translations,' she said.

'Thanks.'

Rebus looked down at a note he'd made to himself: 'Corrèze trip necessary??' Well, the Farmer had said he could have whatever he wanted. He looked up at Kirstin Mede and wondered if the budget would stretch to a tour guide. She was sitting opposite him, putting on half-moon reading glasses.

'Can I get you a coffee?' he asked.

'I'm a bit pushed today. I just wanted you to see these.' She laid two sheets of paper on his desk so that they faced him. One sheet was the photocopy of a typed report, in German. The second sheet was her translation. Rebus looked at the German.

'– *Der Beginn der Vergeltungsmassnahmen hat ein merkbares Aufatmen hervorgerufen und die Stimmung sehr günstig beeinflusst.*'

'The beginning of reprisals,' he read, 'has brought about a marked improvement in morale, with the men now noticeably more relaxed.'

'It's supposed to be from Linzstek to his commander,' she explained.

'But no signature?'

'Just the typed name, underlined.'

'So it doesn't help us identify Linzstek.'

'No, but remember what we were talking about? It gives a reason for the assault.'

'A touch of R&R for the lads?'

Her look froze him. 'Sorry,' he said, raising his hands.

'Far too glib. And you're right, it's almost like the Lieutenant is trying to justify the whole thing in print.'

'For posterity?'

'Maybe. After all, they'd just started being the losing side.' He looked at the other papers. 'Anything else?'

'Some further reports, nothing too exciting. And some of the eyewitness testimony.' She looked at him with pale grey eyes. 'It gets to you after a while, doesn't it?'

Rebus looked at her and nodded.

The female survivor of the massacre lived in Juillac, and had been questioned recently by local police about the man in charge of the German troops. Her story hadn't changed from the one she'd told at the trial: she'd seen his face only for a few seconds, and looking down from the attic of a three-storey house. She'd been shown a recent photo of Joseph Lintz, and had shrugged.

'Maybe,' she'd said. 'Yes, maybe.'

Which would, Rebus knew, be turfed out by the Procurator-Fiscal, who knew damned well what any defence lawyer with half a brain would do with it.

'How's the case coming?' Kirstin Mede asked. Maybe she'd seen some look cross his face.

'Slowly. The problem is all this stuff.' He waved towards the strewn desk. 'On the one hand I've got all this, and on the other I've got a wee old man from the New Town. The two don't seem to go together.'

'Have you met him?'

'Once or twice.'

'What's he like?'

What was Joseph Lintz like? He was cultured, a linguist. He'd even been a Professor at the university, back in the early 70s. Only for a year or two. His own explanation: 'I was filling a vacuum until they could find someone of greater standing'. He'd been Professor of German. He'd lived in Scotland since 1945 or '46 – he was vague about

33

exact dates, blaming his memory. His early life was vague, too. He said papers had been destroyed. The Allies had had to create a duplicate set for him. There was only Lintz's word that these new papers were anything but an official record of lies he'd told and which had been believed. Lintz's story – birth in Alsace; parents and relatives all dead; forced enlistment in the SS. Rebus liked the touch about joining the SS. It was the sort of admission that would make officials decide: he's been honest about his involvement with that, so he's probably being honest about the other details. There was no actual record of a Joseph Lintz serving with any SS regiment, but then the SS had destroyed a lot of their own records once they'd seen the way the war was headed. Lintz's war record was vague, too. He mentioned shell-shock to explain the gaps in his memory. But he was vehement that he had never been called Linzstek and had never served in the Corrèze region of France.

'I was in the east,' he would say. 'That's where the Allies found me, in the east.'

The problem was that there was no convincing explanation as to how Lintz had found himself in the United Kingdom. He said he'd asked if he could go there and start a new life. He didn't want to return to Alsace, wanted to be as far away from the Germans as possible. He wanted water between him and them. Again, there was no documentation to back this up, and meantime the Holocaust investigators had come up with their own 'evidence', which pointed to Lintz's involvement in the 'Rat Line'.

'Have you ever heard of something called the Rat Line?' Rebus had asked at their first meeting.

'Of course,' Joseph Lintz had said. 'But I never had anything to do with it.'

Lintz: in the drawing-room of his Heriot Row home. An elegant four-storey Georgian edifice. A huge house for a man who'd never married. Rebus had said as much. Lintz had merely shrugged, as was his privilege. Where had the money come from?

'I've worked hard, Inspector.'

Maybe so, but Lintz had purchased the house in the late-1950s on a lecturer's salary. A colleague from the time had told Rebus everyone in the department suspected Lintz of having a private income. Lintz denied this.

'Houses were cheaper back then, Inspector. The fashion was for country properties and bungalows.'

Joseph Lintz: barely five foot tall, bespectacled. Parchment hands with liver spots. One wrist sported a pre-war Ingersoll watch. Glass-fronted bookcases lining his drawing-room. Charcoal-coloured suits. An elegant way about him, almost feminine: the way he lifted a cup to his lips; the way he flicked specks from his trousers.

'I don't blame the Jews,' he'd said. 'They'd implicate everyone if they could. They want the whole world feeling guilty. Maybe they're right.'

'In what way, sir?'

'Don't we all have little secrets, things we're ashamed of?' Lintz had smiled. 'You're playing their game, and you don't even know it.'

Rebus had pressed on. 'The two names are very similar, aren't they? Lintz, Linzstek.'

'Naturally, or they'd have absolutely no grounds for their accusations. Think, Inspector: wouldn't I have changed my name more radically? Do you credit me with a modicum of intelligence?'

'More than a modicum.' Framed diplomas on the walls, honorary degrees, photos taken with university chancellors, politicians. When the Farmer had learned a little more about Joseph Lintz, he'd cautioned Rebus to 'ca' canny'. Lintz was a patron of the arts – opera, museums, galleries – and a great giver to charities. He was a man with *friends*.

35

But also a solitary man, someone who was happiest when tending graves in Warriston Cemetery. Dark bags under his eyes, pushing down upon the angular cheeks. Did he sleep well?

'Like a lamb, Inspector.' Another smile. 'Of the sacrificial kind. You know, I don't blame you, you're only doing your job.'

'You seem to have no end of forgiveness, Mr Lintz.'

A careful shrug. 'Do you know Blake's words, Inspector? "And through all eternity/ I forgive you, you forgive me." I'm not so sure I can forgive the media.' This last word voiced with a distaste which manifested itself as a twist of facial muscles.

'Is that why you've set your lawyer on them?'

' "Set" makes me sound like a hunter, Inspector. This is a *newspaper*, with a team of expensive lawyers at its beck and call. Can an individual hope to win against such odds?'

'Then why bother trying?'

Lintz thumped both arms of his chair with clenched fists. 'For the principle, man!' Such outbursts were rare and short-lived, but Rebus had experienced enough of them to know that Lintz had a temper ...

'Hello?' Kirstin Mede said, angling her head to catch his gaze.

'What?'

She smiled. 'You were miles away.'

'Just across town,' he replied.

She pointed to the papers. 'I'll leave these here, okay? If you've any questions ...'

'Great, thanks.' Rebus got to his feet.

'It's okay, I know my way out.'

But Rebus was insistent. 'Sorry, I'm a bit ...' He waved his hands around his head.

'As I said, it gets to you after a while.'

As they walked back through the CID office, Rebus

36

could feel eyes following them. Bill Pryde came up, preening, wanting to be introduced. He had curly fair hair and thick blond eyelashes, his nose large and freckled, mouth small and topped with a ginger moustache – a fashion accessory he could well afford to lose.

'A pleasure,' he said, taking Kirstin Mede's hand. Then, to Rebus: 'Makes me wish we'd swopped.'

Pryde was working on the Mr Taystee case: an ice-cream man found dead in his van. Engine left running in a lock-up, looking initially like suicide.

Rebus steered Kirstin Mede past Pryde, kept them moving. He wanted to ask her out. He knew she wasn't married, but thought there might be a boyfriend in the frame. Rebus was thinking: what would she like to eat – French or Italian? She spoke both those languages. Maybe stick to something neutral: Indian or Chinese. Maybe she was vegetarian. Maybe she didn't like restaurants. A drink then? But Rebus didn't drink these days.

'... So what do you think?'

Rebus started. Kirstin Mede had asked him something. 'Sorry?'

She laughed, realising he hadn't been listening. He began to apologise, but she shook it off. 'I know,' she said, 'you're a bit ...' And she waved her hands around her head. He smiled. They'd stopped walking. They were facing one another. Her briefcase was tucked under one arm. It was the moment to ask her for a date, any kind of date – let *her* choose.

'What's that?' she said suddenly. It was a shriek, Rebus had heard it, too. It had come from behind the door nearest them, the door to the women's toilets. They heard it again. This time it was followed by some words they understood.

'Help me, somebody!'

Rebus pushed open the door and ran in. A WPC was pushing at a cubicle door, trying to force it with her shoulder. From behind the door, Rebus could hear choking noises.

'What is it?' he said.

'Picked her up twenty minutes ago, she said she needed the loo.' The policewoman's cheeks wore a flush of anger and embarrassment.

Rebus grabbed the top of the door and hauled himself up, peering over and down on to a figure seated on the pan. The woman there was young, heavily made-up. She sat with her back against the cistern, so that she was staring up at him, but glassily. And her hands were busy. They were busy pulling a streamer of toilet-paper from the roll, stuffing it into her mouth.

'She's gagging,' Rebus said, sliding back down. 'Stand back'. He shouldered the door, tried again. Stood back and hit the lock with the heel of his shoe. The door flew open, catching the seated woman on the knees. He pushed his way in. Her face was turning purple.

'Grab her hands,' he told the WPC. Then he started pulling the stream of white paper from her mouth, feeling like nothing so much as a cheap stage-show magician. There seemed to be half a roll in there, and as Rebus caught the WPC's eye, both of them let out a near-involuntary laugh. The woman had stopped struggling. Her hair was mousy-brown, lank and greasy. She wore a black skiing jacket and a tight black skirt. Her bare legs were mottled pink, bruising at one knee where the door had connected. Her bright red lipstick was coming off on Rebus's fingers. She had been crying, was crying still. Rebus, feeling guilty about the sudden laughter, crouched down so that he could look into her makeup-streaked eyes. She blinked, then held his gaze, coughing as the last of the paper was extracted.

'She's foreign,' the policewoman was explaining. 'Doesn't seem to speak English.'

'So how come she told you she needed the toilet?'

'There are ways, aren't there?'

'Where did you find her?'

'Down the Pleasance, brazen as you like.'

'That's a new patch on me.'

'Me, too.'

'Nobody with her?'

'Not that I saw.'

Rebus took the woman's hands. He was still crouching in front of her, aware of her knees brushing his chest.

'Are you all right?' She just blinked. He made his face show polite concern. 'Okay now?'

She nodded slightly. 'Okay,' she said, her voice husky. Rebus felt her fingers. They were cold. He was thinking: junkie? A lot of the working girls were. But he'd never come across one who couldn't speak English. Then he turned her hands, saw her wrists. Recent zigzag scar tissue. She didn't resist as he pushed up one sleeve of her jacket. The arm was a mass of similar inflictions.

'She's a cutter.'

The woman was talking now, babbling incoherently. Kirstin Mede, who had been standing back from proceedings, stepped forward. Rebus looked to her.

'It's not anything I understand … not quite. Eastern European.'

'Try her with something.'

So Mede asked a question in French, repeating it in three or four other languages. The woman seemed to understand what they were trying to do.

'There's probably someone at the uni who could help,' Mede said.

Rebus started to stand up. The woman grabbed him by the knees, pulled him to her so that he nearly lost his balance. Her grip was tight, her face resting against his legs. She was still crying and babbling.

'I think she likes you, sir,' the policewoman said. They

wrested her hands free, and Rebus stepped back, but she was after him at once, throwing herself forwards, like she was begging, her voice rising. There was an audience now, half a dozen officers in the doorway. Every time Rebus moved, she came after him on all fours. Rebus looked to where his exit was blocked by bodies. The cheap magician had become straight man in a comedy routine. The WPC grabbed her, pulled her back on to her feet, one arm twisted behind her back.

'Come on,' she said through gritted teeth. 'Back to the cell. Show's over, folks.'

There was scattered applause as the prisoner was marched away. She looked back once, seeking Rebus, her eyes pleading. For what, he did not know. He turned towards Kirstin Mede instead.

'Fancy a curry some time?'

She looked at him like he was mad.

'Two things: one, she's a Bosnian Muslim. Two, she wants to see you again.'

Rebus stared at the man from the Slavic Studies department, who'd come here at Kirstin Mede's request. They were talking in the corridor at St Leonard's.

'Bosnian?'

Dr Colquhoun nodded. He was short and almost spherical, with long black hair which was swept back either side of a bald dome. His puffy face was pockmarked, his brown suit worn and stained. He wore suede Hush Puppies – same colour as the suit. *This*, Rebus couldn't help feeling, was how dons were supposed to look. Colquhoun was a mass of nervous twitches, and had yet to make eye contact with Rebus.

'I'm not an expert on Bosnia,' he went on, 'but she says she's from Sarajevo.'

'Does she say how she ended up in Edinburgh?'

'I didn't ask.'

'Would you mind asking her now?' Rebus gestured back along the corridor. The two men walked together, Colquhoun's eyes on the floor.

'Sarajevo was hit hard in the war,' he said. 'She's twenty-two, by the way, she told me that.'

She'd looked older. Maybe she was; maybe she was lying. But as the door to the Interview Room opened and Rebus saw her again, he was struck by how unformed her face was, and he revised her age downwards. She stood up abruptly as he came in, looked like she might rush forward to him, but he held up a hand in warning, and pointed to the chair. She sat down again, hands cradling the mug of sweetened black tea. She never took her eyes off him.

'She's a big fan,' the WPC said. The policewoman – same one as the toilet incident – was called Ellen Sharpe. She was sitting on the room's other chair. There wasn't much space in the Interview Room: a table and two chairs just about filled it. On the table were twin video recorders and a twin cassette-machine. The video camera pointed down from one wall. Rebus gestured for Sharpe to give her seat to Colquhoun.

'Did she give you a name?' he asked the academic.

'She told me Candice,' Colquhoun said.

'You don't believe her?'

'It's not exactly ethnic, Inspector.' Candice said something. 'She's calling you her protector.'

'And what am I protecting her from?'

The dialogue between Colquhoun and Candice was gruff, guttural.

'She says firstly you protected her from herself. And now she says you have to continue.'

'Continue protecting her?'

'She says you own her now.'

Rebus looked at the academic, whose eyes were on

41

Candice's arms. She had removed her skiing jacket. Underneath she wore a ribbed, short-sleeved shirt through which her small breasts were visible. She had folded her bare arms, but the scratches and slashes were all too apparent.

'Ask her if those are self-inflicted.'

Colquhoun struggled with the translation. 'I'm more used to literature and film than ... um ...'

'What does she say?'

'She says she did them herself.'

Rebus looked at her for confirmation, and she nodded slowly, looking slightly ashamed.

'Who put her on the street?'

'You mean ...?'

'Who's running her? Who's her manager?'

Another short dialogue.

'She says she doesn't understand.'

'Does she deny working as a prostitute?'

'She says she doesn't understand.'

Rebus turned to WPC Sharpe. 'Well?'

'A couple of cars stopped. She leaned in the window to talk with the drivers. They drove off again. Didn't like the look of the goods, I suppose.'

'If she can't speak English, how did she manage to "talk" to the drivers?'

'There are ways.'

Rebus looked at Candice. He began to speak to her, very softly. 'Straight fuck, fifteen, twenty for a blow job. Unprotected is an extra fiver.' He paused. 'How much is anal, Candice?'

Colour flooded her cheeks. Rebus smiled.

'Maybe not university tuition, Dr Colquhoun, but someone's taught her a few words of English. Just enough to get her working. Ask her again how she got here.'

Colquhoun mopped his face first. Candice spoke with her head lowered.

'She says she left Sarajevo as a refugee. Went to Amsterdam, then came to Britain. The first thing she remembers is a place with lots of bridges.'

'Bridges?'

'She stayed there for some time.' Colquhoun seemed shaken by the story. He handed her a handkerchief so she could wipe her eyes. She rewarded him with a smile. Then she looked at Rebus.

'Burger chips, yes?'

'Are you hungry?' Rebus rubbed his stomach. She nodded and smiled. He turned to Sharpe. 'See what the canteen can come up with, will you?'

The WPC gave him a hard stare, not wanting to leave. 'Would you like anything, Dr Colquhoun?'

He shook his head. Rebus asked for another coffee. As Sharpe left, Rebus crouched down by the table and looked at Candice. 'Ask her how she got to Edinburgh.'

Colquhoun asked, then listened to what sounded like a long tale. He scratched some notes on a folded sheet of paper.

'The city with the bridges, she says she didn't see much of it. She was kept inside. Sometimes she was driven to some rendezvous … You'll have to forgive me, Inspector. I may be a linguist, but I'm no expert on colloquialisms.'

'You're doing fine, sir.'

'Well, she was used as a prostitute, that much I can infer. And one day they put her in the back of a car, and she thought she was going to another hotel or office.'

'Office?'

'From her descriptions, I'd say some of her … work … was done in offices. Also private apartments and houses. But mostly hotel rooms.'

'Where was she kept?'

43

'In a house. She had a bedroom, they kept it locked.'
Colquhoun pinched the bridge of his nose. 'They put her
in the car one day, and next thing she knew she was in
Edinburgh.'

'How long was the trip?'

'She's not sure. She slept part of the way.'

'Tell her everything's going to be all right.' Rebus
paused. 'And ask her who she works for now.'

The fear returned to Candice's face. She stammered,
shaking her head. Her voice sounded more guttural than
ever. Colquhoun looked like he was having trouble with the
translation.

'She can't tell you,' he said.

'Tell her she's safe.' Colquhoun did so. 'Tell her again,'
Rebus said. He made sure she was looking at him while
Colquhoun spoke. His face was set, a face she could trust.
She reached a hand out to him. He took it, squeezed.

'Ask her again who she works for.'

'She can't tell you, Inspector. They'd kill her. She's
heard stories.'

Rebus decided to try the name he'd been thinking of, the
man who ran half the city's working girls.

'Cafferty,' he said, watching for a reaction. There was
none. 'Big Ger. Big Ger Cafferty.' Her face remained
blank. Rebus squeezed her hand again. There was another
name ... one he'd been hearing recently.

'Telford,' he said. 'Tommy Telford.'

Candice pulled her hand away and broke into hysterics,
just as WPC Sharpe pushed open the door.

Rebus walked Dr Colquhoun out of the station, recalling
that just such a walk had got him into this in the first place.

'Thanks again, sir. If I need you, I hope you won't mind
if I call?'

'If you must, you must,' Colquhoun said grudgingly.

'Not too many Slavic specialists around,' Rebus said. He had Colquhoun's business card in his hand, a home phone number written on its back. 'Well,' Rebus put out his free hand, 'thanks again.' As they shook, Rebus thought of something.

'Were you at the university when Joseph Lintz was Professor of German?'

The question surprised Colquhoun. 'Yes,' he said at last.

'Did you know him?'

'Our departments weren't that close. I met him at a few social functions, the occasional lecture.'

'What did you think of him?'

Colquhoun blinked. He still wasn't looking at Rebus. 'They're saying he was a Nazi.'

'Yes, but back then …?'

'As I say, we weren't close. Are you investigating him?'

'Just curious, sir. Thanks for your time.'

Back in the station, Rebus found Ellen Sharpe outside the Interview Room door.

'So what do we do with her?' she asked.

'Keep her here.'

'You mean charge her?'

Rebus shook his head. 'Let's call it protective custody.'

'Does *she* know that?'

'Who's she going to complain to? There's only one bugger in the whole city can make out what she's saying, and I've just packed him off home.'

'What if her man comes to get her?'

'Think he will?'

She thought about it. 'Probably not.'

'No, because as far as he's concerned, all he has to do is wait, and we'll release her eventually. Meantime, she doesn't speak English, so what can she give us? And she's here illegally no doubt, so if she talks, all *we'd* probably do is kick her out of the country. Telford's clever … I hadn't realised it, but he is. Using illegal aliens as prossies. It's sweet.'

'How long do we keep her?'

Rebus shrugged.

'And what do I tell my boss?'

'Direct all enquiries to DI Rebus,' he said, going to open the door.

'I thought it was exemplary, sir.'

He stopped. 'What?'

'Your knowledge of the charge-scale for prostitutes.'

'Just doing my job,' he said, smiling.

'One last question, sir ... ?'

'Yes, Sharpe?'

'Why? What's the big deal?'

Rebus considered this, twitched his nose. 'Good question,' he said finally, opening the door and going in.

And he knew. He knew straight away. She looked like Sammy. Wipe away the make-up and the tears, get some sensible clothes on her, and she was the spitting image.

And she was scared.

And maybe he could help her.

'What can I call you, Candice? What's your real name?'

She took hold of his hand, put her face to it. He pointed to himself.

'John,' he said.

'Don.'

'John.'

'Shaun.'

'John.' He was smiling; so was she. 'John.'

'John.'

He nodded. 'That's it. And you?' He pointed at her now. 'Who are you?'

She paused. 'Candice,' she said, as a little light died behind her eyes.

4

Rebus didn't know Tommy Telford by sight, but he knew where to find him.

Flint Street was a passageway between Clerk Street and Buccleuch Street, near the university. The shops had mostly closed down, but the games arcade always did good business, and from Flint Street Telford leased gaming machines to pubs and clubs across the city. Flint Street was the centre of his eastern empire.

The franchise had until recently belonged to a man called Davie Donaldson, but he'd suddenly retired on 'health grounds'. Maybe he'd been right at that: if Tommy Telford wanted something from you and you weren't forthcoming, predictions of your future health could suddenly change. Donaldson was now in hiding somewhere: hiding not from Telford but from Big Ger Cafferty, for whom he had been holding the franchise 'in trust' while Cafferty bided his time in Barlinnie jail. There were some who said Cafferty ran Edinburgh as effectively from inside as he ever had done outside, but the reality was that gangsters, like Nature, abhorred a vacuum, and now Tommy Telford was in town.

Telford was a product of Ferguslie Park in Paisley. At eleven he'd joined the local gang; at twelve a couple of woolly-suits had visited him to ask about a spate of tyre slashings. They'd found him surrounded by other gang members, nearly all of them older than him, but he was at the centre, no doubt about it.

His gang had grown with him, taking over a sizeable chunk of Paisley, selling drugs and running prostitutes, doing a bit of extortion. These days he had shares in casinos and video shops, restaurants and a haulage firm, plus a property portfolio which made him landlord to several hundred people. He'd tried to make his mark in Glasgow, but had found it sealed down tight, so had gone exploring elsewhere. There were stories he'd become friendly with some big villain in Newcastle. Nobody could remember anything like it since the days when London's Krays had rented their muscle from 'Big Arthur' in Glasgow.

He'd arrived in Edinburgh a year ago, moving softly at first, buying a casino and hotel. Then suddenly he was inescapably *there*, like the shadow from a raincloud. With the chasing out of Davie Donaldson he'd given Cafferty a calculated punch to the gut. Cafferty could either fight or give up. Everyone was waiting for it to get messy …

The games arcade called itself Fascination Street. The machines were all flashing insistence, in stark contrast to the dead facial stares of the players. Then there were shoot-'em-ups with huge video screens and digital imprecations.

'Think you're tough enough, punk?' one of them challenged as Rebus walked past. They had names like Harbinger and NecroCop, this latter reminding Rebus of how old he felt. He looked at the faces around him, saw a few he recognised, kids who'd been pulled into St Leonard's. They'd be on the fringes of Telford's gang, awaiting the call-up, hanging around like foster children, hoping The Family would take them. Most of them came from families who weren't families, latchkey kids grown old before their time.

One of the staff came in from the café.

'Who ordered the bacon sarnie?'

Rebus smiled as the faces turned to him. Bacon meant

pig meant him. A moment's examination was all he warranted. There were more pressing demands on their attention. At the far end of the arcade were the really big machines: half-size motorbikes you sat astride as you negotiated the circuit on the screen in front of you. A small appreciative coterie stood around one bike, on which sat a young man dressed in a leather jacket. Not a market-stall jacket, something altogether more special. Quality goods. Shiny sharp-toed boots. Tight black denims. White polo neck. Surrounded by fawning courtiers. Steely Dan: 'Kid Charlemagne'. Rebus found a space for himself in the midst of the glaring onlookers.

'No takers for that bacon sarnie?' he asked.

'Who are you?' the man on the machine demanded.

'DI Rebus.'

'Cafferty's man.' Said with conviction.

'What?'

'I hear you and him go back.'

'I put him inside.'

'Not every cop gets visiting rights though.' Rebus realised that though Telford's gaze was fixed on the screen, he was watching Rebus in its reflection. Watching him, talking to him, yet still managing to control the bike through hairpin bends.

'So is there some problem, Inspector?'

'Yes, there's a problem. We picked up one of your girls.'

'My what?'

'She calls herself Candice. That's about as much as we know. But foreign lassies are a new one on me. And you're fairly new around here, too.'

'I'm not getting your drift, Inspector. I supply goods and services to the entertainment sector. Are you accusing me of being a pimp?'

Rebus stuck out a foot and pushed the bike sideways. On

the screen, it spun and hit a crash barrier. A moment later, the screen changed. Back to the start of the race.

'See, Inspector,' Telford said, still not turning round. 'That's the beauty of games. You can always start again after an accident. Not so easy in real life.'

'What if I cut the power? Game over.'

Slowly, Telford swivelled from the hips. Now he was looking at Rebus. Close up, he looked so young. Most of the gangsters Rebus had known, they'd had a worn look, undernourished but overfed. Telford had the look of some new strain of bacteria, not yet tested or understood.

'So what is it, Rebus? Some message from Cafferty?'

'Candice,' Rebus said quietly, the slight tremor in his voice betraying his anger. With a couple of drinks in him, he'd have had Telford on the floor by now. 'From tonight, she's off the game, understood?'

'I don't know any Candice.'

'Understood?'

'Hang on, let's see if I've got this. You want me to agree with you that a woman I've never met should stop touting her hole?'

Smiles from the spectators. Telford turned back to his game. 'Where's this woman from anyway?' he asked, almost casually.

'We're not sure,' Rebus lied. He didn't want Telford knowing any more than was necessary.

'Must have been a great little chat the two of you had.'

'She's scared shitless.'

'Me, too, Rebus. I'm scared you're going to bore me to death. This Candice, did she give you a taste of the goods? I'm betting it's not every scrubber would get you this het up.'

Laughter, Rebus its brunt.

'She's off the game, Telford. Don't think about touching her.'

'Not with a bargepole, pal. Myself, I'm a clean-living sort of individual. I say my prayers last thing at night.'

'And kiss your cuddly bear?'

Telford looked at him again. 'Don't believe all the stories, Inspector. Here, grab a bacon sarnie on your way out, I think there's one going spare.' Rebus stood his ground a few moments longer, then turned away. 'And tell the mugs out front I said hello.'

Rebus walked back through the arcade and out into the night, heading for Nicolson Street. He was wondering what he was going to do with Candice. Simple answer: let her go, and hope she had the sense to keep moving. As he made to pass a parked car, its window slid down.

'Fucking well get in,' a voice ordered from the passenger seat. Rebus stopped, looked at the man who'd spoken, recognised the face.

'Ormiston,' he said, opening the back door of the Orion. 'Now I know what he meant.'

'Who?'

'Tommy Telford. I'm to tell you he said hello.'

The driver stared at Ormiston. 'Rumbled again.' He didn't sound surprised. Rebus recognised the voice.

'Hello, Claverhouse.'

DS Claverhouse, DC Ormiston: Scottish Crime Squad, Fettes's finest. On surveillance. Claverhouse: as thin as 'twa ply o' reek', as Rebus's father would have said. Ormiston: freckle-faced and with Mick McManus's hair – slick, pudding-bowl cut, unfeasibly black.

'You were blown before I walked in there, if that's any consolation.'

'What the fuck were you doing?'

'Paying my respects. What about you?'

'Wasting our time,' Ormiston muttered.

The Crime Squad were out for Telford: good news for Rebus.

'I've got someone,' he said. 'She works for Telford. She's frightened. You could help her.'

'The frightened ones don't talk.'

'This one might.'

Claverhouse stared at him. 'And all we'd have to do is …?'

'Get her out of here, set her up somewhere.'

'Witness relocation?'

'If it comes to that.'

'What does she know?'

'I'm not sure. Her English isn't great.'

Claverhouse knew when he was being sold something. 'Tell us,' he said.

Rebus told them. They tried not to look interested.

'We'll talk to her,' Claverhouse said.

Rebus nodded. 'So how long has this been going on?'

'Ever since Telford and Cafferty squared off.'

'And whose side are we on?'

'We're the UN, same as always,' Claverhouse said. He spoke slowly, measuring each word and phrase. A careful man, DS Claverhouse. 'Meantime, you go charging in like some bloody mercenary.'

'I've never been a great one for tactics. Besides, I wanted to see the bastard close up.'

'And?'

'He looks like a kid.'

'And he's as clean as a whistle,' Claverhouse said. 'He's got a dozen lieutenants who'd take the fall for him.'

At the word 'lieutenants', Rebus's mind flashed to Joseph Lintz. Some men gave orders, some carried them out: which group was the more culpable?

'Tell me something,' he said, 'the teddy bear story … is it true?'

Claverhouse nodded. 'In the passenger seat of his Range

Rover. A fucking huge yellow thing, sort they raffle in the pub Sunday lunchtime.'

'So what's the story?'

Ormiston turned in his seat. 'Ever hear of Teddy Willocks? Glasgow hardman. Carpentry nails and a claw-hammer.'

Rebus nodded. 'You welched on someone, Willocks came to see you with the carpentry bag.'

'But then,' Claverhouse took over, 'Teddy got on the wrong side of some Geordie bastard. Telford was young, making a name for himself, and he very badly wanted an in with this Geordie, so he took care of Teddy.'

'And that's why he carries a teddy around with him,' Ormiston said. 'A reminder to everyone.'

Rebus was thinking. Geordie meant someone from Newcastle. Newcastle, with its bridges over the Tyne …

'Newcastle,' he said softly, leaning forward in his seat.

'What about it?'

'Maybe Candice was there. Her city of bridges. She might link Telford to this Geordie gangster.'

Ormiston and Claverhouse looked at one another.

'She'll need a safe place to stay,' Rebus told them. 'Money, somewhere to go afterwards.'

'A first-class flight home if she helps us nail Telford.'

'I'm not sure she'll want to go home.'

'That's for later,' Claverhouse said. 'First thing is to talk to her.'

'You'll need a translator.'

Claverhouse looked at him. 'And of course you know just the man … ?'

She was asleep in her cell, curled under the blanket, only her hair visible. The Mothers of Invention: 'Lonely Little Girl'. The cell was in the women's block. Painted pink and blue, a slab to sleep on, graffiti scratched into the walls.

'Candice,' Rebus said quietly, squeezing her shoulder. She started awake, as if he'd administered an electric shock. 'It's okay, it's me, John.'

She looked round blindly, focused on him slowly. 'John,' she said. Then she smiled.

Claverhouse was off making phone calls, squaring things. Ormiston stood in the doorway, appraising Candice. Not that Ormiston was known to be choosy. Rebus had tried Colquhoun at home, but there'd been no answer. So now Rebus was gesturing, letting her know they wanted to take her somewhere.

'A hotel,' he said.

She didn't like that word. She looked from him to Ormiston and back again.

'It's okay,' Rebus said. 'It's just a place for you to sleep, that's all, somewhere safe. No Telford, nothing like that.'

She seemed to soften, came off the bed and stood in front of him. Her eyes seemed to say, I'll trust you, and if you let me down I won't be surprised.

Claverhouse came back. 'All fixed,' he said, his examination falling on Candice. 'She doesn't speak any English?'

'Not as practised in polite society.'

'In that case,' Ormiston said, 'she should be fine with us.'

Three men and a young woman in a dark blue Ford Orion, heading south out of the city. It was late now, past midnight, black taxis cruising. Students were spilling from pubs.

'They get younger every year.' Claverhouse was never short of a cliché.

'And more of them end up joining the force,' Rebus commented.

Claverhouse smiled. 'I meant prossies, not students. We pulled one in last week, said she was fifteen. Turned out she was twelve, on the run. All grown up about it.'

Rebus tried to remember Sammy at twelve. He saw her

54

scared, in the clutches of a madman with a grievance against Rebus. She'd had lots of nightmares afterwards, till her mother had taken her to London. Rhona had phoned Rebus a few years later. She just wanted to let him know he'd robbed Sammy of her childhood.

'I phoned ahead,' Claverhouse said. 'Don't worry, we've used this place before. It's perfect.'

'She'll need some clothes,' Rebus said.

'Siobhan can fetch her some in the morning.'

'How is Siobhan?'

'Seems fine. Hasn't half cut into the jokes and the language though.'

'Ach, she can take a joke,' Ormiston said. 'Likes a drink, too.'

This last was news to Rebus. He wondered how much Siobhan Clarke would change in order to blend with her new surroundings.

'It's just off the bypass,' Claverhouse said, meaning their destination. 'Not far now.'

The city ended suddenly. Green belt, plus the Pentland Hills. The bypass was quiet, Ormiston doing the ton between exits. They came off at Colinton and signalled into the hotel. It was a motorist's stop, one of a nationwide chain: same prices, same rooms. The cars which crowded the parking area were salesmen's specials, cigarette packets littering the passenger seats. The reps would be sleeping, or lying in a daze with the TV remote to hand.

Candice seemed reluctant to get out of the car, until she saw that Rebus was coming, too.

'You light up her life,' Ormiston offered.

At reception, they signed her in as one half of a couple – Mrs Angus Campbell. The two Crime Squad cops had the routine off pat. Rebus watched the hotel clerk; but a wink from Claverhouse told him the man was okay.

'Make it the first floor, Malcolm,' Ormiston said. 'Don't want anyone peeking in the windows.'

Room number 20. 'Will someone be with her?' Rebus asked as they climbed the stairs.

'Right there in the room,' Claverhouse said. 'The landing's too obvious, and we'd freeze our bums off in the car. Did you give me Colquhoun's number?'

'Ormiston has it.'

Ormiston was unlocking the door. 'Who's on first watch?'

Claverhouse shrugged. Candice was looking towards Rebus, seeming to sense what was being discussed. She snatched at his arm, jabbering in her native tongue, looking first to Claverhouse and then to Ormiston, all the time waving Rebus's arm.

'It's okay, Candice, really. They'll take care of you.'

She kept shaking her head, holding him with one hand and pointing at him with the other, prodding his chest to make her meaning clear.

'What do you say, John?' Claverhouse asked. 'A happy witness is a willing witness.'

'What time's Siobhan expected?'

'I'll hurry her up.'

Rebus looked at Candice again, sighed, nodded. 'Okay.' He pointed to himself, then to the room. 'Just for a little while, okay?'

Candice seemed satisfied with this, and went inside. Ormiston handed Rebus the key.

'I don't want you young things waking the neighbours now ...'

Rebus closed the door on his face.

The room was exactly as expected. Rebus filled the kettle and switched it on, dumped a tea-bag into a cup. Candice pointed to the bathroom, made turning motions with her hands.

'A bath?' He gestured with his arm. 'Go ahead.'

The curtain over the window was closed. He parted it and looked out. A grassy slope, occasional lights from the bypass. He made sure the curtains were closed tight, then tried adjusting the heating. The room was stifling. There didn't seem to be a thermostat, so he went back to the window and opened it a fraction. Cold night air, and the swish of nearby traffic. He opened the pack of custard creams, two small biscuits. Suddenly he felt ravenous. He'd seen a snack machine in the lobby. Plenty of change in his pockets. He made the tea, added milk, sat down on the sofa. For want of any other distractions, he turned the TV on. The tea was fine. The tea was absolutely fine, no complaints there. He picked up the phone and called Jack Morton.

'Did I wake you?'

'Not really. How's it going?'

'I wanted a drink today.'

'So what's new?'

Rebus could hear his friend making himself comfortable. Jack had helped Rebus get off the booze. Jack had said he could phone any time he liked.

'I had to talk to this scumbag, Tommy Telford.'

'I know the name.'

Rebus lit a cigarette. 'I think a drink would have helped.'

'Before or after?'

'Both.' Rebus smiled. 'Guess where I am now?'

Jack couldn't, so Rebus told him the story.

'What's your angle?' Jack asked.

'I don't know.' Rebus thought about it. 'She seems to need me. It's been a long time since anyone's felt like that.' As he said the words, he feared they didn't tell the whole story. He remembered another argument with Rhona, her screaming that he'd exploited every relationship he'd ever had.

'Do you still want that drink?' Jack was asking.

'I'm a long way from one.' Rebus stubbed out his cigarette. 'Sweet dreams, Jack.'

He was on his second cup of tea when she came back in, wearing the same clothes, her hair wet and hanging in rat's-tails.

'Better?' he asked, making the thumbs-up sign. She nodded, smiling. 'Do you want some tea?' He pointed to the kettle. She nodded again, so he made her a cup. Then he suggested a trip to the snack machine. Their haul included crisps, nuts, chocolate, and a couple of cans of Coke. Another cup of tea finished off the tiny cartons of milk. Rebus lay along the sofa, shoes off, watching soundless television. Candice lay on the bed, fully-clothed, sliding the occasional crisp from its packet, flicking channels. She seemed to have forgotten he was there. He took this as a compliment.

He must have fallen asleep. The touch of her fingers on his knee brought him awake. She was standing in front of him, wearing the t-shirt and nothing else. She stared at him, fingers still resting on his knee. He smiled, shook his head, led her back to bed. Made her lie down. She lay on her back, arms stretched. He shook his head again and pulled the duvet over her.

'That's not you any more,' he told her. 'Goodnight, Candice.'

Rebus retreated to the sofa, lay down again, and wished she would stop saying his name.

The Doors: 'Wishful Sinful' ...

A tapping at the door brought him awake. Still dark outside. He'd forgotten to close the window, and the room was cold. The TV was still playing, but Candice was asleep, duvet kicked off, chocolate wrappers strewn around her bare legs and thighs. Rebus covered her up, then tiptoed to the door, peered through the spyhole, and opened up.

'For this relief, much thanks,' he whispered to Siobhan Clarke.

She was carrying a bulging polythene bag. 'Thank God for the twenty-four-hour shop.' They went inside. Clarke looked at the sleeping woman, then went over to the sofa and started unpacking the bag.

'For you,' she whispered, 'a couple of sandwiches.'

'God bless the child.'

'For sleeping beauty, some of my clothes. They'll do till the shops open.'

Rebus was already biting into the first sandwich. Cheese salad on white bread had never tasted finer.

'How am I getting home?' he asked.

'I called you a cab.' She checked her watch. 'It'll be here in two minutes.'

'What would I do without you?'

'It's a toss-up: either freeze to death or starve.' She closed the window. 'Now go on, get out of here.'

He looked at Candice one last time, almost wanting to wake her to let her know he wasn't leaving for good. But she was sleeping so soundly, and Siobhan could take care of everything.

So he tucked the second sandwich into his pocket, tossed the room-key on to the sofa, and left.

Four-thirty. The taxi was idling outside. Rebus felt hungover. He went through a mental list of all the places he could get a drink at this time of night. He didn't know how many days it had been since he'd had a drink. He wasn't counting.

He gave his address to the cabbie, and settled back, thinking again of Candice, so soundly asleep, and protected for now. And of Sammy, too old now to need anything from her father. She'd be asleep too, snuggling into Ned Farlowe. Sleep was innocence. Even the city looked innocent in sleep. He looked at the city sometimes and saw a beauty his cynicism couldn't touch. Someone in a bar – recently? years back? – had challenged him to define romance. How could he do that? He'd seen too much of love's obverse: people killed for passion and from lack of it. So that now when he saw beauty, he could do little but respond to it with the realisation that it would fade or be brutalised. He saw lovers in Princes Street Gardens and imagined them further down the road, at the crossroads where betrayal and conflict met. He saw valentines in the shops and imagined puncture wounds, real hearts bleeding.

Not that he'd voiced any of this to his public bar inquisitor.

'Define romance,' had been the challenge. And Rebus's response? He'd picked up a fresh pint of beer and kissed the glass.

He slept till nine, showered and made some coffee. Then he phoned the hotel, and Siobhan assured him all was well.

'She was a bit startled when she woke up and saw me instead of you. Kept saying your name. I told her she'd see you again.'

'So what's the plan?'

'Shopping – one quick swoop on The Gyle. After that, Fettes. Dr Colquhoun's coming in at noon for an hour. We'll see what we get.'

Rebus was at his window, looking down on a damp Arden Street. 'Take care of her, Siobhan.'

'No problem.'

Rebus knew there'd be no problem, not with Siobhan. This was her first real action with the Crime Squad, she'd be doing her damnedest to make it a success. He was in the kitchen when the phone rang.

'Is that Inspector Rebus?'

'Who's speaking?' A voice he didn't recognise.

'Inspector, my name is David Levy. We've never met. I

apologise for calling you at home. I was given this number by Matthew Vanderhyde.'

Old man Vanderhyde: Rebus hadn't seen him in a while. 'Yes?'

'I must say, I was astonished when it transpired he knew you.' The voice was tinged with a dry humour. 'But by now nothing about Matthew should surprise me. I went to him because he knows Edinburgh.'

'Yes?'

Laughter on the line. 'I'm sorry, Inspector. I can't blame you for being suspicious when I've made such a mess of the introductions. I am a historian by profession. I've been contacted by Solomon Mayerlink to see if I might offer assistance.'

Mayerlink ... Rebus knew the name. Placed it: Mayerlink ran the Holocaust Investigation Bureau.

'And exactly what "assistance" does Mr Mayerlink think I need?'

'Perhaps we could discuss it in person, Inspector. I'm staying in a hotel on Charlotte Square.'

'The Roxburghe?'

'Could we meet there? This morning, ideally.'

Rebus looked at his watch. 'An hour?' he suggested.

'Perfect. Goodbye, Inspector.'

Rebus called into the office, told them where he'd be.

5

They sat in the Roxburghe's lounge, Levy pouring coffee. An elderly couple in the far corner, beside the window, pored over sections of newspaper. David Levy was elderly, too. He wore black-rimmed glasses and had a small silver beard. His hair was a silver halo around a scalp the colour of tanned leather. His eyes seemed constantly moist, as if he'd just chewed on an onion. He sported a dun-coloured safari suit with blue shirt and tie beneath. His walking-stick rested against his chair. Now retired, he'd worked in Oxford, New York State, Tel Aviv itself, and several other locations around the globe.

'I never came into contact with Joseph Lintz, however. No reason why I should, our interests being different.'

'So why does Mr Mayerlink think you can help me?'

Levy put the coffee pot back on its tray. 'Milk? Sugar?' Rebus shook his head to both, then repeated his question.

'Well, Inspector,' Levy said, tipping two spoonfuls of sugar into his own cup, 'it's more a matter of moral support.'

'Moral support?'

'You see, many people before you have been in the same position in which you now find yourself. I'm talking about objective people, professionals with no axe to grind, and no real stake in the investigation.'

Rebus bristled. 'If you're suggesting I'm not doing my job ...'

A pained look crossed Levy's face. 'Please, Inspector,

I'm not making a very good job of this, am I? What I mean is that there will be times when you will doubt the validity of what you are doing. You'll doubt its worth.' His eyes gleamed. 'Perhaps you've already had doubts?'

Rebus said nothing. He had a drawerful of doubts, especially now that he had a real, living, breathing case – Candice. Candice, who might lead to Tommy Telford.

'You could say I'm here as your conscience, Inspector.' Levy winced again. 'No, I didn't put that right, either. You already have a conscience, that's not under debate.' He sighed. 'The question you've no doubt been pondering is the same one I've asked myself on occasions: can time wash away responsibility? For me, the answer would have to be no. The thing is this, Inspector.' Levy leaned forward. 'You are not investigating the crimes of an old man, but those of a young man who now happens to be old. Focus your mind on that. There have been investigations before, half-hearted affairs. Governments wait for these men to die rather than have to try them. But each investigation is an act of remembrance, and remembrance is never wasted. Remembrance is the only way we learn.'

'Like we've learned with Bosnia?'

'You're right, Inspector, as a species we've always been slow to take in lessons. Sometimes they have to be hammered home.'

'And you think I'm your carpenter? Were there Jews in Villefranche?' Rebus couldn't remember reading of any.

'Does it matter?'

'I'm just wondering, why the interest?'

'To be honest, Inspector, there is a slight ulterior motive.' Levy sipped coffee, considering his words. 'The Rat Line. We'd like to show that it existed, that it operated to save Nazis from possible tormentors.' He paused. 'That it worked with the tacit approval – the *more* than tacit approval – of several western governments and even the Vatican. It's a question of general complicity.'

'What you want is for everyone to feel guilty?'

'We want recognition, Inspector. We want the truth. Isn't that what you want? Matthew Vanderhyde would have me believe it is your guiding principle.'

'He doesn't know me very well.'

'I wouldn't be so sure of that. Meantime, there are people out there who want the truth to stay hidden.'

'The truth being …?'

'That known war criminals were brought back to Britain – and elsewhere – and offered new lives, new identities.'

'In exchange for what?'

'The Cold War was starting, Inspector. You know the old saying: My enemy's enemy is my friend. These murderers were protected by the secret services. Military Intelligence offered them jobs. There are people who would rather this did not become general knowledge.'

'So?'

'So a trial, an open trial, would expose them.'

'You're warning me about spooks?'

Levy put his hands together, almost in an attitude of prayer. 'Look, I'm not sure this has been a completely satisfactory meeting, and for that I apologise. I'll be staying here for a few days, maybe longer if necessary. Could we try this again?'

'I don't know.'

'Well, think about it, won't you?' Levy extended his right hand. Rebus took it. 'I'll be right here, Inspector. Thank you for seeing me.'

'Take care, Mr Levy.'

'*Shalom*, Inspector.'

At his desk, Rebus could still feel Levy's handshake. Surrounded by the Villefranche files, he felt like the curator of some museum visited only by specialists and cranks. Evil had been done in Villefranche, but had Joseph Lintz been responsible? And even if he had, had he perhaps atoned during the past half-century? Rebus phoned the Procurator-Fiscal's office to let them know how little progress he was making. They thanked him for calling. Then he went to see the Farmer.

'Come in, John, what can I do for you?'

'Sir, did you know the Crime Squad had set up a surveillance on our patch?'

'You mean Flint Street?'

'So you know about it?'

'They keep me informed.'

'Who's acting as liaison?'

The Farmer frowned. 'As I say, John, they keep me informed.'

'So there's no liaison at street level?' The Farmer stayed silent. 'By rights there should be, sir.'

'What are you getting at, John?'

'I want the job.'

The Farmer stared at his desk. 'You're busy on Villefranche.'

'I want the job, sir.'

'John, liaison means diplomacy. It's never been your strongest suit.'

So Rebus explained about Candice, and how he was already tied into the case. 'And since I'm already in, sir,' he concluded, 'I might as well act as liaison.'

'What about Villefranche?'

'That remains a priority, sir.'

The Farmer looked into his eyes. Rebus didn't blink. 'All right then,' he said at last.

'You'll let Fettes know?'

'I'll let them know.'

'Thank you, sir.' Rebus turned to leave.

'John …?' The Farmer was standing behind his desk. 'You know what I'm going to say.'

'You're going to tell me not to tread on too many toes, not to go off on my own little crusade, to keep in regular contact with you, and not betray your trust in me. Does that just about do it, sir?'

The Farmer shook his head, smiling. 'Bugger off,' he said.

Rebus buggered off.

When he walked into the room, Candice rose so quickly from her chair that it fell to the floor. She came forward and gave him a hug, while Rebus looked at the faces around them – Ormiston, Claverhouse, Dr Colquhoun, and a WPC.

They were in an Interview Room at Fettes, Lothian and Borders Police HQ. Colquhoun was wearing the same suit as the previous day and the same nervous look. Ormiston was picking up Candice's chair. He'd been standing against one wall. Claverhouse was seated at the table beside Colquhoun, a pad of paper in front of him, pen poised above it.

'She says she's happy to see you,' Colquhoun translated.

'I'd never have guessed.' Candice was wearing new clothes: denims too long for her and turned up four inches at the ankle; a black woollen v-neck jumper. Her skiing jacket was hanging over the back of her chair.

'Get her to sit down again, will you?' Claverhouse said. 'We're pushed for time.'

There was no chair for Rebus, so he stood next to Ormiston and the WPC. Candice went back to the story she'd been telling, but glanced regularly towards him. He noticed that beside Claverhouse's pad of paper sat a brown folder and an A4-sized envelope. On top of the envelope sat a black and white surveillance shot of Tommy Telford.

'This man,' Claverhouse asked, tapping the photo, 'she knows him?'

Colquhoun asked, then listened to her answer. 'She ...' He cleared his throat. 'She hasn't had any direct dealings with him.' Her two-minute commentary reduced to this. Claverhouse dipped into the envelope, spread more photos before her. Candice tapped one of them.

'Pretty-Boy,' Claverhouse said. He picked up the photo of Telford again. 'But she's had dealings with this man, too?'

'She's ...' Colquhoun mopped his face. 'She's saying something about Japanese people ... Oriental businessmen.'

Rebus shared a look with Ormiston, who shrugged.

'Where was this?' Claverhouse asked.

'In a car ... more than one car. You know, a sort of convoy.'

'She was in one of the cars?'

'Yes.'

'Where did they go?'

'They headed out of town, stopping once or twice.'

'Juniper Green,' Candice said, quite clearly.

'Juniper Green,' Colquhoun repeated.

'They stopped there?'

'No, they stopped before that.'

'To do what?'

Colquhoun spoke with Candice again. 'She doesn't know. She thinks one of the drivers went into a shop for some cigarettes. The others all seemed to be looking at a building, as if they were interested in it, but not saying anything.'

'What building?'

'She doesn't know.'

Claverhouse looked exasperated. She wasn't giving him much of anything, and Rebus knew that if there was nothing she could trade, Crime Squad would dump her

67

straight back on the street. Colquhoun was all wrong for this job, completely out of his depth.

'Where did they go after Juniper Green?'

'Just drove around the countryside. For two or three hours, she thinks. They would stop sometimes and get out, but just to look at the scenery. Lots of hills and ...' Colquhoun checked something. 'Hills and flags.'

'Flags? Flying from buildings?'

'No, stuck into the ground.'

Claverhouse gave Ormiston a look of hopelessness.

'Golf courses,' Rebus said. 'Try describing a golf course to her, Dr Colquhoun.'

Colquhoun did so, and she nodded agreement, beaming at Rebus. Claverhouse was looking at him, too.

'Just a guess,' Rebus said with a shrug. 'Japanese businessmen, it's what they like about Scotland.'

Claverhouse turned back to Candice. 'Ask her if she ... accommodated any of these men.'

Colquhoun cleared his throat again, colour flooding his cheeks as he spoke. Candice looked down at the table, moved her head in the affirmative, started to speak.

'She says that's why she was there. She was fooled at first. She thought maybe they just wanted a pretty woman to look at. They had a nice lunch ... the beautiful drive ... But then they came back into town, dropped the Japanese off at a hotel, and she was taken up to one of the hotel rooms. Three of them ... she, as you put it yourself, DS Claverhouse, she "accommodated" three of them.'

'Does she remember the name of the hotel?'

She didn't.

'Where did they have lunch?'

'A restaurant next to flags and ...' Colquhoun corrected himself. 'Next to a golf course.'

'How long ago was this?'

'Two or three weeks.'

'And how many of them were there?'

Colquhoun checked. 'The three Japanese, and maybe four other men.'

'Ask her how long she's been in Edinburgh,' Rebus asked.

Colquhoun did so. 'She thinks maybe a month.'

'A month working the street ... funny we haven't picked her up.'

'She was put there as a punishment.'

'For what?' Claverhouse asked. Rebus had the answer.

'For making herself ugly.' He turned to Candice. 'Ask her why she cuts herself.'

Candice looked at him and shrugged.

'What's your point?' Ormiston asked.

'She thinks the scars will deter punters. Which means she doesn't like the life she's been leading.'

'And helping us is her only sure ticket out?'

'Something like that.'

So Colquhoun asked her again, then said: 'They don't like that she does it. That's why she does it.'

'Tell her if she helps us, she won't ever have to do anything like that again.'

Colquhoun translated, glancing at his watch.

'Does the name Newcastle mean anything to her?' Claverhouse asked.

Colquhoun tried the name. 'I've explained to her that it's a town in England, built on a river.'

'Don't forget the bridges,' Rebus said.

Colquhoun added a few words, but Candice only shrugged. She looked upset that she was failing them. Rebus gave her another smile.

'What about the man she worked for?' Claverhouse asked. 'The one before she came to Edinburgh.'

She seemed to have plenty to say about this, and kept touching her face with her fingers while she talked.

Colquhoun nodded, made her stop from time to time so he could translate.

'A big man ... fat. He was the boss. Something about his skin ... a birthmark maybe, certainly something distinctive. And glasses, like sunglasses but not quite.'

Rebus saw Claverhouse and Ormiston exchange another look. It was all too vague to be much use. Colquhoun checked his watch again. 'And cars, a lot of cars. This man crashed them.'

'Maybe he got a scar on his face,' Ormiston offered.

'Glasses and a scar aren't going to get us very far,' Claverhouse added.

'Gentlemen,' Colquhoun said, while Candice looked towards Rebus, 'I'm afraid I'm going to have to leave.'

'Any chance of coming back in later, sir?' Claverhouse asked.

'You mean today?'

'I thought maybe this evening ...?'

'Look, I do have other commitments.'

'We appreciate that, sir. Meantime, DC Ormiston will run you back into town.'

'My pleasure,' Ormiston said, all charm. They needed Colquhoun, after all. They had to keep him sweet.

'One thing,' Colquhoun said. 'There's a refugee family in Fife. From Sarajevo. They'd probably take her in. I could ask.'

'Thank you, sir,' Claverhouse said. 'Maybe later on, eh?'

Colquhoun seemed disappointed as Ormiston led him away.

Rebus walked over to Claverhouse, who was shuffling his photos together.

'Bit of an oddball,' Claverhouse commented.

'Not used to the real world.'

'Not much help either.'

Rebus looked towards Candice. 'Mind if I take her out?'

'What?'

'Just for an hour.' Claverhouse stared at him. 'She's been cooped up here, and only her hotel room to look forward to. I'll drop her back there in an hour, hour and a half.'

'Bring her back in one piece, preferably with a smile on her face.'

Rebus motioned for Candice to join him.

'Japanese and golf courses,' Claverhouse mused. 'What do you think?'

'Telford's a businessman, we know that. Businessmen do deals with other businessmen.'

'He runs bouncers and slot machines: what's the Japanese connection?'

Rebus shrugged. 'I leave the hard questions to the likes of you.' He opened the door.

'And, John?' Claverhouse warned, nodding towards Candice. 'She's Crime Squad property, okay? And remember, *you* came to *us*.'

'No bother, Claverhouse. And by the way, I'm your B Division liaison.'

'Since when?'

'With immediate effect. If you don't believe me, ask your boss. This might be your case, but Telford works out of *my* territory.'

He took Candice by the arm and marched her from the room.

He stopped the car on the corner of Flint Street.

'It's okay, Candice,' he said, seeing her agitation. 'We're staying in the car. Everything's all right.' Her eyes were darting around, looking for faces she didn't want to see. Rebus started the car again and drove off. 'Look,' he told her, 'we're leaving.' Knowing she couldn't understand. 'I'm guessing this is where you started from that day.' He looked at her. 'The day you went to Juniper Green. The

Japanese would be staying in a central hotel, somewhere pricey. You picked them up, then headed east. Along Dalry Road maybe?' He was speaking for his own benefit. 'Christ, I don't know. Look, Candice, anything you see, anything that looks familiar, just let me know, okay?'

'Okay.'

Had she understood? No, she was smiling. All she'd heard was that final word. All she knew was that they were heading away from Flint Street. He took her down on to Princes Street first.

'Was it a hotel here, Candice? The Japanese? Was it here?' She gazed from the window with a blank look.

He headed up Lothian Road. 'Usher Hall,' he said. 'Sheraton ... Any of it ring a bell?' Nothing did. Out along the Western Approach Road, Slateford Road, and on to Lanark Road. Most of the lights were against them, giving her plenty of time to study the buildings. Each newsagent's they passed, Rebus pointed it out, just in case the convoy had paused there to buy cigarettes. Soon they were out of town and entering Juniper Green.

'Juniper Green!' she said, pointing at the signpost, delighted to have something to show him. Rebus attempted a smile. There were plenty of golf courses around the city. He couldn't hope to take her to every one of them, not in a week never mind an hour. He stopped for a few moments by the side of a field. Candice got out, so he followed, lit a cigarette. There were two stone gateposts next to the road, but no sign of a gate between them, or any sort of path behind them. Once there might have been a track, and a house at the end of it. Atop one of the pillars sat the badly worn representation of a bull. Candice pointed towards the ground behind the other pillar, where another lump of carved stone lay, half-covered by weeds and grass.

'Looks like a serpent,' Rebus said. 'Maybe a dragon.' He looked at her. 'It'll all mean something to somebody.' She looked back at him blankly. He saw Sammy's features, reminded himself that he wanted to help her. He was in danger of letting that slip, of focusing on how she might help them get to Telford.

Back in the car, he branched off towards Livingston, intending to head for Ratho and from there back into town. Then he noticed that Candice had turned to look out of the back window.

'What is it?'

She came out with a stream of words, her tone uncertain. Rebus turned the car anyway, and drove slowly back the way they'd just come. He stopped at the side of the road, opposite a low dry-stone wall, beyond which lay the undulations of a golf course.

'Recognise it?' She mumbled more words. Rebus pointed. 'Here? Yes?'

She turned to him, said something which sounded apologetic.

'It's okay,' he told her. 'Let's take a closer look anyway.' He drove to where a vast iron double-gate stood open. A sign to one side read POYNTINGHAME GOLF AND COUNTRY CLUB. Beneath it: 'Bar Lunches and A La Carte, Visitors Welcome'. As Rebus drove through the gates, Candice started nodding again, and when an oversized Georgian house came into view she almost bounced in her seat, slapping her hands against her thighs.

'I think I get the picture,' Rebus said.

He parked outside the main entrance, squeezing between a Volvo estate and a low-slung Toyota. Out on the course, three men were finishing their round. As the final putt went in, hands went to wallets and money changed hands.

Two things Rebus knew about golf: one, to some people it was a religion; two, a lot of players liked a bet. They'd bet on final tally, each hole, even every shot if they could.

And didn't the Japanese have a passion for gambling?

He took Candice's arm as he escorted her into the main building. Piano music from the bar. Panatella smoke and oak-panelling. Huge portraits of self-important unknowns. A few old wooden putters, framed behind glass. A poster advertised a Halloween dinner-dance for that evening. Rebus walked up to reception, explained who he was and what he wanted. The receptionist made a phone call, then led them to the Chief Executive's office.

Hugh Malahide, bald and thin, mid-forties, already had a slight stammer, which intensified when Rebus asked his first question. By throwing it back at the questioner, he seemed to be playing for time.

'Have we had any Japanese visitors recently? Well, we do get a few golfers.'

'These men came to lunch. Maybe a fortnight, three weeks back. There were three of them, plus three or four Scottish men. Probably driving Range Rovers. The table may have been reserved in the name of Telford.'

'Telford?'

'Thomas Telford.'

'Ah, yes ...' Malahide wasn't enjoying this at all.

'You know Mr Telford?'

'In a manner of speaking.'

Rebus leaned forward in his chair. 'Go on.'

'Well, he's ... look, the reason I seem so reticent is because we don't want this made common knowledge.'

'I understand, sir.'

'Mr Telford is acting as go-between.'

'Go-between?'

'In the negotiations.'

Rebus saw what Malahide was getting at. 'The Japanese want to buy Poyntinghame?'

'You understand, Inspector, I'm just the manager here. I mean, I run the day-to-day business.'

'But you're the Chief Executive.'

'With no personal share in the club. The actual owners were set against selling at first. But an offer has been made, and I believe it's a very good one. And the potential buyers ... well, they're persistent.'

'Have there been any threats, Mr Malahide?'

He looked horrified. 'What sort of threats?'

'Forget it.'

'The negotiations haven't been *hostile*, if that's what you mean.'

'So these Japanese, the ones who had lunch here ... ?'

'They were representing the consortium.'

'The consortium being ... ?'

'I don't know. The Japanese are always very secretive. Some big company or corporation, I'd guess.'

'Any idea why they want Poyntinghame?'

'I've wondered that myself.'

'And?'

'Everyone knows the Japanese love golf. It might be a prestige thing. Or it could be that they're opening a plant of some kind in Livingston.'

'And Poyntinghame would become the factory social club?'

Malahide shivered at the thought. Rebus got to his feet.

'You've been very helpful, sir. Anything else you can tell me?'

'Look, this has been off the record, Inspector.'

'I've no problem with that. I don't suppose you've got any names?'

'Names?'

'Of the diners that day.'

Malahide shook his head. 'I'm sorry, not even credit card details. Mr Telford paid cash as usual.'

'Did he leave a big tip?'

'Inspector,' smiling, 'some secrets are sacrosanct.'

'Let's keep this conversation that way, too, sir, all right?'

Malahide looked at Candice. 'She's a prostitute, isn't she? I thought as much the day they were here.' There was revulsion in his voice. 'Tarty little thing, aren't you?'

Candice stared at him, looked to Rebus for help, said a few words neither man understood.

'What's she saying?' Malahide asked.

'She says she once had a punter who looked just like you. He dressed in plus-fours and made her whack him with a mashie-niblick.'

Malahide showed them out.

6

Rebus telephoned Claverhouse from Candice's room.

'Could be something or nothing,' Claverhouse said, but Rebus could tell he was interested, which was good: the longer he stayed interested, the longer he'd want to hang on to Candice. Ormiston was on his way to the hotel to resume babysitting duties.

'What I want to know is, how the hell did Telford land something like this?'

'Good question,' Claverhouse said.

'It's way out of his previous sphere, isn't it?'

'As far as we know.'

'A chauffeur service for Jap companies ...'

'Maybe he's after the contract to supply their gaming machines.'

Rebus shook his head. 'I still don't get it.'

'Not your problem, John, remember that.'

'I suppose so.' There was a knock at the door. 'Sounds like Ormiston.'

'I doubt it. He's just left.'

Rebus stared at the door. 'Claverhouse, wait on the line.'

He left the receiver on the bedside table. The knock was repeated. Rebus motioned for Candice, who'd been flicking through a magazine on the sofa, to move into the bathroom. Then he crept up to the door and put his eye to the spy-hole. A woman: the day-shift receptionist. He unlocked the door.

'Yes?'

'Letter for your wife.'

He stared at the small white envelope which she was trying to hand him.

'Letter,' she repeated.

There was no name or address on the envelope, no stamp. Rebus took it and held it to the light. A single sheet of paper inside, and something flat and square, like a photograph.

'A man handed it in at reception.'

'How long ago?'

'Two, three minutes.'

'What did he look like?'

She shrugged. 'Tallish, short brown hair. He was wearing a suit, took the letter out of a briefcase.'

'How do you know who it's for?'

'He said it was for the foreign woman. He described her to a T.'

Rebus was staring at the envelope. 'Okay, thanks,' he mumbled. He closed the door, went back to the telephone.

'What is it?' Claverhouse asked.

'Someone's just dropped off a letter for Candice.' Rebus tore open the envelope, holding the receiver between shoulder and chin. There was a Polaroid photo and a single sheet, handwritten in small capitals. Foreign words.

'What does it say?' Claverhouse asked.

'I don't know.' Rebus tried a couple of words aloud. Candice had emerged from the bathroom. She snatched the paper from him and read it quickly, then fled back into the bathroom.

'It means something to Candice,' Rebus said. 'There's a photo, too.' He looked at it. 'She's on her knees gamming some fat bloke.'

'Description?'

'The camera's not exactly interested in his face. Claverhouse, we've got to get her away from here.'

'Hang on till Ormiston arrives. They might be trying to panic you. If they want to snatch her, one cop in a car isn't going to cause much of a problem. Two cops just might.'

'How did they know?'

'We'll think about that later.'

Rebus was staring at the bathroom door, remembering the locked cubicle at St Leonard's. 'I've got to go.'

'Be careful.'

Rebus put down the receiver.

'Candice?' He tried the door. It was locked. 'Candice?' He stood back and kicked. The door wasn't as strong as the one in St Leonard's; he nearly took it off its hinges. She was seated on the toilet, a plastic safety razor in her hand, slashing it across her arms. There was blood on her t-shirt, blood spraying the white tiled floor. She started screaming at him, the words collapsing into monosyllables. Rebus grabbed the razor, nicked his thumb in the process. He pulled her off the toilet, flushed the razor, and started wrapping towels around her arms. The note was lying in the bath. He waved it in her face.

'They're trying to scare you, that's all.' Not even half-believing it himself. If Telford could find her this quickly, if he had the means of writing to her in her own language, then he was much stronger, much cleverer than Rebus had suspected.

'It's going to be okay,' he went on. 'I promise. It's all okay. We'll look after you. We'll get you out of here, take you somewhere he can't get to you. I promise, Candice. Look, this is me talking.'

But she was bawling, tears dripping from her cheeks, head shaking from side to side. For a time, she'd actually believed in knights on white chargers. Now, she was realising how stupid she'd been ...

The coast seemed to be clear.

Rebus took her in his car, Ormiston tucked in behind. No other way to play it. It was a trade-off: a speedy exit versus hanging around for a cavalry escort. And the way Candice was bleeding, they couldn't afford to wait. The drive to the hospital was nerve-tingling, then there was the wait while her wounds were checked and some of them sewn up. Rebus and Ormiston waited in A&E, drinking coffee from beakers, asking one another questions they couldn't answer.

'How did he know?'

'Who did he get to write the note?'

'Why give us a warning? Why not just grab her?'

'What does the note say?'

It struck Rebus that they were near the university. He took Dr Colquhoun's card from his pocket and phoned his office. Colquhoun was in. Rebus read the message out to him, spelling some of the words.

'They sound like addresses,' Colquhoun said. 'Untrans-latable.'

'Addresses? Are any towns named?'

'I don't think so.'

'Sir, we'll be taking her to Fettes if she's well enough ... any chance you could meet us there? It's important.'

'Everything with you chaps is important.'

'Yes, sir, but this is *important*. Candice's life may be in danger.'

Colquhoun took time answering. 'I suppose in that case ...'

'I'll send a car for you.'

After an hour, she was well enough to leave. 'The cuts weren't too deep,' the doctor said. 'Not life-threatening.'

'They weren't meant to be.' Rebus turned to Ormiston. 'She thinks she's going back to Telford, that's why she did it. She *knows* she's going back to him.'

Candice looked as though all the blood had been drained

from her. Her face seemed more skeletal than before, and her eyes darker. Rebus tried to recall what her smile looked like. He doubted he'd be seeing one for a while. She kept her arms folded protectively in front of her, and wouldn't meet his eyes. Rebus had seen suspects act that way in custody: people for whom the world had become a trap.

At Fettes, Claverhouse and Colquhoun were already waiting. Rebus handed over the note and photo.

'As I said, Inspector,' Colquhoun stated, 'addresses.'

'Ask her what they mean,' Claverhouse demanded. They were in the same room as before. Candice knew her place, and was already seated, her arms still folded, showing cream-coloured bandages and pink plasters. Colquhoun asked, but it was as though he'd ceased to exist. Candice stared at the wall in front of her, unblinking, her only motion a slight rocking to and fro.

'Ask her again,' Claverhouse said. But Rebus interrupted before Colquhoun could start.

'Ask her if people she knows live there, people who are important to her.'

As Colquhoun formed the question, the rocking grew slightly in intensity. There were fresh tears in her eyes.

'Her mother and father? Brothers and sisters?'

Colquhoun translated. Candice tried to stop her mouth trembling.

'Maybe she left a kid behind ...'

As Colquhoun asked, Candice flew from her chair, shouting and screaming. Ormiston tried to grab her, but she kicked out at him. When she'd calmed, she subsided in a corner of the room, arms over her head.

'She's not going to tell us anything,' Colquhoun translated. 'She was stupid to believe us. She just wants to go now. There's nothing she can help us with.'

Rebus and Claverhouse shared a look.

'We can't hold her, John, not if she wants to leave. It's

been dodgy enough keeping her away from a lawyer. Once she starts asking to go ...' He shrugged.

'Come on, man,' Rebus hissed, 'she's shit-scared, and with good reason. And now you've got all you're going to get out of her, you're just going to hand her back to Telford?'

'Look, it's not a question of –'

'He'll kill her, you know he will.'

'If he was going to kill her, she'd be dead.' Claverhouse paused. 'He's cleverer than that. He knows damned well all he had to do was give her a fright. He *knows* her. It sticks in my craw, too, but what can we do?'

'Just keep her a few days, see if we can't ...'

'Can't what? You want to hand her over to Immigration?'

'It's an idea. Get her the hell away from here.'

Claverhouse pondered this, then turned to Colquhoun. 'Ask her if she wants to go back to Sarajevo.'

Colquhoun asked. She slurred some answer, choking back tears.

'She says if she goes back, they'll kill everyone.'

Silence in the room. They were all looking at her. Four men, men with jobs, family ties, men with lives of their own. In the scheme of things, they seldom realised how well off they were. And now they realised something else: how helpless they were.

'Tell her,' Claverhouse said quietly, 'she's free to walk out of here at any time, if that's what she really wants. If she stays, we'll do our damnedest to help her ...'

So Colquhoun spoke to her, and she listened, and when he'd finished she pushed herself back on to her feet and looked at them. Then she wiped her nose on her bandages, pushed the hair out of her eyes, and walked to the door.

'Don't go, Candice,' Rebus said.

She half-turned towards him. 'Okay,' she said.

Then she opened the door and was gone.

Rebus grabbed Claverhouse's arm. 'We've got to pull Telford in, warn him not to touch her.'

'You think he needs telling?'

'You think he'd listen?' Ormiston added.

'I can't believe this. He scared her half to death, and as a result we let her walk? I really can't get my head round this.'

'She could always have gone to Fife,' Colquhoun said. With Candice out of the room, he seemed to have perked up a bit.

'Bit late now,' Ormiston said.

'He beat us this time, that's all,' Claverhouse said, his eyes on Rebus. 'But we'll take him down, don't worry.' He managed a thin, humourless smile. 'Don't think we're giving up, John. It's not our style. Early days yet, pal. Early days ...'

She was waiting for him out in the car park, standing by the passenger-door of his battered Saab 900.

'Okay?' she said.

'Okay,' he agreed, smiling with relief as he unlocked the car. He could think of only one place to take her. As he drove through The Meadows, she nodded, recognising the tree-lined playing fields.

'You've been here before?'

She said a few words, nodded again as Rebus turned into Arden Street. He parked the car and turned to her.

'You've been *here*?'

She pointed upwards, fingers curled into the shape of binoculars.

'With Telford?'

'Telford,' she said. She made a show of writing something down, and Rebus took out his notebook and pen, handed them over. She drew a teddy bear.

'You came in Telford's car?' Rebus interpreted. 'And he

watched one of the flats up there?' He pointed to his own flat.

'Yes, yes.'

'When was this?' She didn't understand the question. 'I need a phrasebook,' he muttered. Then he opened his door, got out and looked around. The cars around him were all empty. No Range Rovers. He signalled for Candice to get out and follow him.

She seemed to like his living-room, went straight to the record collection but couldn't find anything she recognised. Rebus went into the kitchen to make coffee and to think. He couldn't keep her here, not if Telford knew about the place. Telford ... why had he been watching Rebus's flat? The answer was obvious: he knew the detective was linked to Cafferty, and therefore a potential threat. He thought Rebus was in Cafferty's pocket. Know your enemy: it was another rule Telford had learned.

Rebus phoned a contact from the *Scotland on Sunday* business section.

'Japanese companies,' Rebus said. 'Rumours pertaining to.'

'Can you narrow that down?'

'New sites around Edinburgh, maybe Livingston.'

Rebus could hear the reporter shuffling papers on his desk. 'There's a whisper going round about a microprocessor plant.'

'In Livingston?'

'That's one possibility.'

'Anything else?'

'Nope. Why the interest?'

'Cheers, Tony.' Rebus put down the receiver, looked across at Candice. He couldn't think where else to take her. Hotels weren't safe. One place came to mind, but it would be risky ... Well, not so very risky. He made the call.

'Sammy?' he said. 'Any chance you could do me a favour … ?'

Sammy lived in a 'colonies' flat in Shandon. Parking was almost impossible on the narrow street outside. Rebus got as close as he could.

Sammy was waiting for them in the narrow hallway, and led them into the cramped living-room. There was a guitar on a wicker chair and Candice lifted it, setting herself on the chair and strumming a chord.

'Sammy,' Rebus said, 'this is Candice.'

'Hello there,' Sammy said. 'Happy Halloween.' Candice was putting chords together now. 'Hey, that's Oasis.'

Candice looked up, smiled. 'Oasis,' she echoed.

'I've got the CD somewhere …' Sammy examined a tower of CDs next to the hi-fi. 'Here it is. Shall I put it on?'

'Yes, yes.'

Sammy switched the hi-fi on, told Candice she was going to make some coffee, and beckoned for Rebus to follow her into the kitchen.

'So who is she?' The kitchen was tiny. Rebus stayed in the doorway.

'She's a prostitute. Against her will. I don't want her pimp getting her.'

'Where's she from again?'

'Sarajevo.'

'And she doesn't have much English?'

'How's your Serbo-Croat?'

'Rusty.'

Rebus looked around. 'Where's your boyfriend?'

'Out working.'

'On the book?' Rebus didn't like Ned Farlowe. Partly it was that name: 'Neds' were what the *Sunday Post* called hooligans. They robbed old ladies of their pension books and walking-frames. Those were the Neds of this world. And Farlowe meant Chris Farlowe: 'Out of Time', a number one that should have belonged to the Stones. Farlowe was researching a history of organised crime in Scotland.

'Sod's law,' Sammy said. 'He needs money to buy the time to write the thing.'

'So what's he doing?'

'Just some freelance stuff. How long am I babysitting?'

'A couple of days at most. Just till I find somewhere else.'

'What will he do if he finds her?'

'I'm not that keen to find out.'

Sammy finished rinsing the mugs. 'She looks like me, doesn't she?'

'Yes, she does.'

'I've got some time off coming. Maybe I'll phone in, see if I can stay here with her. What's her real name?'

'She hasn't told me.'

'Has she any clothes?'

'At a hotel. I'll get a patrol car to bring them.'

'She's really in danger?'

'She might be.'

Sammy looked at him. 'But I'm not?'

'No,' her father said. 'Because it'll be our secret.'

'And what do I tell Ned?'

'Keep it short, just say you're doing your dad a favour.'

'You think a journalist's going to be content with that?'

'If he loves you.'

The kettle boiled, clicked off. Sammy poured water into three mugs. Through in the living-room, Candice's interest had shifted to a pile of American comic books.

Rebus drank his coffee, then left them to their music and their comics. Instead of going home, he made for Young Street and the Ox, ordering a mug of instant. Fifty pee.

86

Pretty good deal, when you thought about it. Fifty pence for … what, half a pint? A pound a pint? Cheap at twice the price. Well, one-point-seven times the price, which would take it to the price of a beer … give or take.

Not that Rebus was counting.

The back room was quiet, just somebody scribbling away at the table nearest the fire. He was a regular, a journalist of some kind. Rebus thought of Ned Farlowe, who would want to know about Candice, but if anyone could keep him at bay, Sammy could. Rebus took out his mobile, phoned Colquhoun's office.

'Sorry to bother you again,' he said.

'What is it now?' The lecturer sounded thoroughly exasperated.

'Those refugees you mentioned. Any chance you could have a word with them?'

'Well, I …' Colquhoun cleared his throat. 'Yes, I suppose I could talk to them. Does that mean …?'

'Candice is safe.'

'I don't have their number here.' Colquhoun sounded fuddled again. 'Can it wait till I go home?'

'Phone me when you've talked to them. And thanks.'

Rebus rang off, finished his coffee, and called Siobhan Clarke at home.

'I need a favour,' he said, feeling like a broken record.

'How much trouble will it get me in?'

'Almost none.'

'Can I have that in writing?'

'Think I'm stupid?' Rebus smiled. 'I want to see the files on Telford.'

'Why not just ask Claverhouse?'

'I'd rather ask you.'

'It's a lot of stuff. Do you want photocopies?'

'Whatever.'

'I'll see what I can do.' Voices were raised in the front bar. 'You're not in the Ox, are you?'

'As it happens, yes.'

'Drinking?'

'A mug of coffee.'

She laughed in disbelief and told him to take care. Rebus ended the call and stared at his mug. People like Siobhan Clarke, they could drive a man to drink.

7

It was 7 a.m. when the buzzer sounded, telling him there was someone at his tenement's main door. He staggered along the hall to the intercom, and asked who the bloody hell it was.

'The croissant man,' a rough English voice replied.

'The what?'

'Come on, dick-brain, wakey-wakey. Memory's not so hot these days, eh?'

A name tilted into Rebus's head. 'Abernethy?'

'Now open up, it's perishing down here.'

Rebus pushed the buzzer to let Abernethy in, then jogged back to the bedroom to put on some clothes. His mind felt numb. Abernethy was a DI in Special Branch, London. The last time he'd been in Edinburgh had been to chase terrorists. Rebus wondered what the hell he was doing here now.

When the doorbell sounded, Rebus tucked in his shirt and walked back down the hall. True to his word, Abernethy was carrying a bag of croissants. He hadn't changed much: same faded denims and black leather bomber, same cropped brown hair spiked with gel. His face was heavy, pockmarked, and his eyes an unnerving, psychopath's blue.

'How've you been, mate?' Abernethy slapped Rebus's shoulder and marched past him into the kitchen. 'Get the kettle on then.' Like they did this every day of the week. Like they didn't live four hundred miles apart.

'Abernethy, what the hell are you doing here?'

'Feeding you, of course, same thing the English have always done for the Jocks. Got any butter?'

'Try the butter-dish.'

'Plates?'

Rebus pointed to a cupboard.

'Bet you drink instant: am I right?'

'Abernethy ...'

'Let's get this ready first, then talk, okay?'

'The kettle boils quicker if you switch it on at the plug.'

'Right.'

'And I think there's some jam.'

'Any honey?'

'Do I look like a bee?'

Abernethy smirked. 'Old Georgie Flight sends his love, by the way. Word is, he'll be retiring soon.'

George Flight: another ghost from Rebus's past. Aberne-thy had unscrewed the top from the coffee jar and was sniffing the granules.

'How fresh is this?' He wrinkled his nose. 'No class, John.'

'Unlike you, you mean? When did you get here?'

'Hit town half an hour ago.'

'From London?'

'Stopped a couple of hours in a lay-by, got my head down. That A1 is murder though. North of Newcastle, it's like coming into a third-world country.'

'Did you drive four hundred miles just to insult me?'

They took everything through to the table in the living-room, Rebus shoving aside books and notepads, stuff about the Second World War.

'So,' he said, as they sat down, 'I'm assuming this isn't a social call?'

'Actually it is, in a way. I could have just telephoned, but I suddenly thought: wonder how the old devil's getting on?

Next thing I knew, I was in the car and heading for the North Circular.'

'I'm touched.'

'I've always tried to keep track of what you're up to.'

'Why?'

'Because last time we met ... well, you're different, aren't you?'

'Am I?'

'I mean, you're not a team player. You're a loner, bit like me. Loners can be useful.'

'Useful?'

'For undercover, jobs that are a bit out of the ordinary.'

'You think I'm Special Branch material?'

'Ever fancied moving to London? It's where the action is.'

'I get action enough up here.'

Abernethy looked out of the window. 'You couldn't wake this place with a fifty-megaton warhead.'

'Look, Abernethy, not that I'm not enjoying your company or anything, but why *are* you here?'

Abernethy brushed crumbs from his hands. 'So much for the social niceties.' He took a gulp of coffee, squirmed at its awfulness. 'War Crimes,' he said. Rebus stopped chewing. 'There's a new list of names. You know that, because you've got one of them living on your doorstep.'

'So?'

'So I'm heading up the London HQ. We've established a temporary War Crimes Unit. My job's to collate gen on the various investigations, create a central register.'

'You want to know what I know?'

'That's about it.'

'And you drove through the night to find out? There's got to be more to it.'

Abernethy laughed. 'Why's that?'

'There just has. A collator's job is for someone good at office work. That's not you, you're only happy in the field.'

'What about you? I'd never have taken you for a historian.' Abernethy tapped one of the books on the table.

'It's a penance.'

'What makes you think it's any different with me? So, what's the score with Herr Lintz?'

'There's no score. So far all the darts have missed the board. How many cases are there?'

'Twenty-seven originally, but eight of those are deceased.'

'Any progress?'

Abernethy shook his head. 'We got one to court, trial collapsed first day. Can't prosecute if they're ga-ga.'

'Well, for your information, here's where the Lintz case stands. I can't prove he was and is Josef Linzstek. I can't disprove his story of his participation in the war, or how he came to Britain.' Rebus shrugged.

'Same tale I've been hearing up and down the country.'

'What did you expect?' Rebus was picking at a croissant.

'Shame about this coffee,' Abernethy said. 'Any decent caffs in the neighbourhood?'

So they went to a café, where Abernethy ordered a double espresso, Rebus a decaf. There was a story on the front of the *Record* about a fatal stabbing outside a nightclub. The man reading the paper folded it up when he'd finished his breakfast and took it away with him.

'Any chance you'll be talking to Lintz today?' Abernethy asked suddenly.

'Why?'

'Thought I might tag along. It's not often you get to meet someone who might have killed seven hundred Frenchies.'

'Morbid attraction?'

'We're all a bit that way inclined, aren't we?'

'I've nothing new to ask him,' Rebus said, 'and he's already been muttering to his lawyer about harassment.'

'He's well-connected?'

Rebus stared across the table. 'You've done your reading.'

'Abernethy the Conscientious Cop.'

'Well, you're right. He has friends in high places, only a lot of them have been hiding behind the curtains since this all started.'

'Sounds like you think he's innocent.'

'Until proven guilty.'

Abernethy smiled, lifted his cup. 'There's a Jewish historian been going around. Has he contacted you?'

'What's his name?'

Another smile. 'How many Jewish historians have you been in touch with? His name's David Levy.'

'You say he's been going around?'

'A week here, a week there, asking how the cases are going.'

'He's in Edinburgh just now.'

Abernethy blew on his coffee. 'So you've spoken with him?'

'Yes, as it happens.'

'And?'

'And what?'

'Did he try his "Rat Line" story?'

'Again, why the interest?'

'He's tried it with everyone else.'

'What if he has?'

'Jesus, do you always answer a question with a question? Look, as collator, this guy Levy's name has popped up on my computer screen more than once. That's why I'm interested.'

'Abernethy the Conscientious Cop.'

'That's right. So shall we go see Lintz?'

'Well, seeing you've come all this way ...'

On the way back to the flat, Rebus stopped at a newsagent's and bought the *Record*. The stabbing had taken place outside Megan's Nightclub, a new establishment in Portobello. The fatality had been a 'doorman', William Tennant, aged 25. The story had made the front page because a Premier League footballer had been on the periphery of the incident. A friend who'd been with him had received minor cuts. The attacker had fled on a motorbike. The footballer had offered no comment to reporters. Rebus knew him. He lived in Linlithgow and a year or so back had been caught speeding in Edinburgh, with – in his own words – a 'wee bitty Charlie', meaning cocaine, on his person.

'Anything interesting?' Abernethy asked.

'Someone killed a bouncer. Quiet little backwater, eh?'

'A story like that, in London it wouldn't rate a column inch.'

'How long are you staying here?'

'I'll be off today, want to drop in on Carlisle. They're supposed to have another old Nazi. After that, it's Blackpool and Wolverhampton before home.'

'A sucker for punishment.'

Rebus drove them the tourist route: down The Mound and across Princes Street. He double parked in Heriot Row, but Joseph Lintz wasn't home.

'Never mind,' he said. 'I know where he'll probably be.' He took them down Inverleith Row and turned right into Warriston Gardens, stopping at the cemetery gates.

'What is he, a gravedigger?' Abernethy got out of the car and zipped his jacket.

'He plants flowers.'

'Flowers? What for?'

'I'm not sure.'

A cemetery should have been about death, but Warriston

didn't feel that way to Rebus. Much of it resembled a rambling park into which some statuary had been dropped. The newer section, with stone driveway, soon gave way to an earthen path between fading inscriptions. There were obelisks and Celtic crosses, lots of trees and birds, and the electric movements of squirrels. A tunnel beneath a walkway took you to the oldest part of the cemetery, but between tunnel and driveway sat the heart of the place, with its roll-call of Edinburgh's past. Names like Ovenstone, Cleugh, and Flockhart, and professions such as actuary, silk merchant, ironmonger. There were people who'd died in India, and some who'd died in infancy. A sign at the gate informed visitors that the place had been the subject of a compulsory purchase by the City of Edinburgh, because previous private owners had let it fall into neglect. But that same neglect was at least part of its charm. People walked their dogs here, or came to practise photography, or just mused among the tombstones. Gays came looking for company, others for solitude.

After dark, of course, the place had another reputation entirely. A Leith prostitute – a woman Rebus had known and liked – had been found murdered here earlier in the year. Rebus wondered if Joseph Lintz knew about that ...

'Mr Lintz?'

He was trimming the grass around a headstone, doing so with a half-sized pair of garden shears. There was a sheen of sweat on his face as he forced himself upright.

'Ah, Inspector Rebus. You have brought a colleague?'

'This is DI Abernethy.'

Abernethy was examining the headstone, which belonged to a teacher called Cosmo Merriman.

'They let you do this?' he asked, his eyes finally finding Lintz's.

'No one has tried to stop me.'

'Inspector Rebus tells me you plant flowers, too.'

'People assume I am a relative.'

'But you're not, are you?'

'Only in so far as we are the family of man, Inspector Abernethy.'

'You're a Christian then?'

'Yes, I am.'

'Born and bred?'

Lintz took out a handkerchief and wiped his nose. 'You're wondering if a Christian could commit an atrocity like Villefranche. It's perhaps not in my interest to say this, but I think it entirely possible. I've been explaining this to Inspector Rebus.'

Rebus nodded. 'We've had a couple of talks.'

'Religious belief is no defence, you see. Look at Bosnia, plenty of Catholics involved in the fighting, plenty of good Muslims, too. "Good" in that they are believers. And what they believe is that their faith gives them the right to kill.'

Bosnia: Rebus saw a sharp image of Candice escaping the terror, only to end up more terrified still, and more trapped than ever.

Lintz was stuffing the large white handkerchief into the pocket of his baggy brown cord trousers. In the outfit – green rubber overshoes, green woollen jersey, tweed jacket – he did look like a gardener. Little wonder he attracted so little attention in the cemetery. He blended in. Rebus wondered how artful it was, how deeply he'd learned the skill of invisibility.

'You look impatient, Inspector Abernethy. You're not a man for theories, am I right?'

'I wouldn't know about that, sir.'

'In that case, you must not know very much. Now Inspector Rebus, he listens to what I have to say. More than that, he looks *interested*. Whether he is or not, I can't judge, but his performance – if performance it be – is exemplary.' Lintz always spoke like this, like he'd been rehearsing each line. 'Last time he visited my home, we discussed human duality. Would you have any opinion on *that*, Inspector Abernethy?'

The look on Abernethy's face was cold. 'No, sir.'

Lintz shrugged: case against the Londoner proven. 'Atrocities, Inspector, occur by an effort of the collective will.' Spelling it out; sounding like the lecturer he had once been. 'Because sometimes all it takes to turn us into devils is the fear of being an outsider.'

Abernethy sniffed, hands in pockets. 'Sounds like you're justifying war crimes, sir. Sounds to me like you might even have been there yourself.'

'Do I need to be a spaceman to imagine Mars?' He turned to Rebus, gave him the fraction of a smile.

'Well, maybe I'm just a bit too simple, sir,' Abernethy said. 'I'm also a bit parky. Let's walk back to the car and carry on our discussion there, all right?'

While Lintz packed his few small tools into a canvas bag, Rebus looked around, saw movement in the distance, between headstones. The crouched figure of a man. Split-second glimpse of a face he recognised.

'What is it?' Abernethy asked.

Rebus shook his head. 'Nothing.'

The three men walked in silence back to the Saab. Rebus opened the back door for Lintz. To his surprise, Abernethy got into the back, too. Rebus took the driver's seat, felt warmth returning slowly to his toes. Abernethy had his arm along the back of the seat, his body twisted towards Lintz.

'Now, Herr Lintz, my role in all this is quite straightforward. I'm collating all the information on this latest outbreak of alleged old Nazis. You understand that with allegations such as these, very serious allegations, we have a duty to investigate?'

'Spurious allegations rather than "serious" ones.'

'In which case you've nothing to worry about.'

'Except my reputation.'

'When you're exonerated, we'll take care of that.'

Rebus was listening closely. None of this sounded like Abernethy. The hostile graveside tone had been replaced by something much more ambiguous.

'And meantime?' Lintz seemed to be picking up whatever the Londoner was saying between the lines. Rebus felt deliberately excluded from the conversation, which was why Abernethy had got into the back seat in the first place. He'd placed a physical barrier between himself and the officer investigating Joseph Lintz. There was something going on.

'Meantime,' Abernethy said, 'co-operate as fully as you can with my colleague. The sooner he's able to reach his conclusions, the sooner this will all be over.'

'The problem with conclusions is that they should be conclusive, and I have so little proof. This was wartime, Inspector Abernethy, a lot of records destroyed ...'

'Without proof either way, there's no case to answer.'

Lintz was nodding. 'I see,' he said.

Abernethy hadn't voiced anything Rebus himself didn't feel; the problem was, he'd voiced it to the suspect.

'It would help if your memory improved,' Rebus felt obliged to add.

'Well, Mr Lintz,' Abernethy was saying, 'thanks for your time.' His hand was on the elderly man's shoulder: protective, comforting. 'Can we drop you somewhere?'

'I'll stay here a little longer,' Lintz said, opening the door and easing himself out. Abernethy handed the bag of tools to him.

'Take care now,' he said.

Lintz nodded, gave a small bow to Rebus, and shuffled back towards the gate. Abernethy climbed into the passenger seat.

'Rum little bugger, isn't he?'

'You as good as told him he was off the hook.'

'Bollocks,' Abernethy said. 'I told him where he stands, let him know the score. That's all.' He saw the look on Rebus's face. 'Come on, do you really want to see him in court? An old professor who keeps cemeteries tidy?'

'It doesn't make it any easier if you sound like you're on his side.'

'Even supposing he *did* order that massacre – you think a trial and a couple of years in clink till he snuffs it is the answer? Better to just give them all a bloody good scare, stuff the trial, and save the taxpayer millions.'

'That's not our job,' Rebus said, starting the engine.

He took Abernethy back to Arden Street. They shook hands, Abernethy trying to sound like he wanted to stay a little longer.

'One of these days,' he said. And then he was gone. As his Sierra drew away, another car pulled into the space he'd just vacated. Siobhan Clarke got out, bringing with her a supermarket carrier-bag.

'For you,' she said. 'And I think I'm owed a coffee.'

She wasn't as fussy as Abernethy, accepted the mug of instant with thanks and ate a spare croissant. There was a message on the answering machine, Dr Colquhoun telling him the refugee family could take Candice tomorrow. Rebus jotted down the details, then turned his attention to the contents of Siobhan's carrier-bag. Maybe two hundred sheets of paper, photocopies.

'Don't get them out of order,' she warned. 'I didn't have time to staple them.'

'Fast work.'

'I went back into the office last night. Thought I'd get it done while no one was about. I can summarise, if you like.'

'Just tell me who the main players are.'

She came to the table and pulled a chair over beside him,

found a sequence of surveillance shots. Put names to the faces.

'Brian Summers,' she said, 'better known as "Pretty-Boy". He runs most of the working girls.' Pale, angular face, thick black lashes, a pouting mouth. Candice's pimp.

'He's not very pretty.'

Clarke found another picture. 'Kenny Houston.'

'From Pretty-Boy to Plug-Ugly.'

'I'm sure his mother loves him.' Prominent teeth, jaundiced skin.

'What does he do?'

'He runs the doormen. Kenny, Pretty-Boy and Tommy Telford grew up on the same street. They're at the heart of The Family.' She sifted through more photos. 'Malky Jordan ... he keeps the drugs flowing. Sean Haddow ... bit of a brainbox, runs the finances. Ally Cornwell ... he's muscle. Deek McGrain ... There's no religious divide in The Family, Prods and Papes working together.'

'A model society.'

'No women though. Telford's philosophy: relationships get in the way.'

Rebus picked up a sheaf of paper. 'So what have we got?'

'Everything but the evidence.'

'And surveillance is supposed to provide that?'

She smiled over the top of her mug. 'You don't agree?'

'It's not my problem.'

'And yet you're interested.' She paused. 'Candice?'

'I don't like what happened to her.'

'Well, just remember: you didn't get this stuff from me.'

'Thanks, Siobhan.' He paused. 'Everything going all right?'

'Fine. I like Crime Squad.'

'Bit livelier than St Leonard's.'

'I miss Brian.' Meaning her one-time partner, now out of the force.

'You ever see him?'

'No, do you?'

Rebus shook his head, got up to show her out.

He spent about an hour sifting through the paperwork, learning more about The Family and its convoluted workings. Nothing about Newcastle. Nothing about Japan. The core of The Family – eight or nine of them – had been at school together. Three of them were still based in Paisley, taking care of the established business. The rest were now in Edinburgh, and busy prying the city away from Big Ger Cafferty.

He went through lists of nightclubs and bars in which Telford had an interest. There were incident reports attached: arrests in the vicinity. Drunken brawls, swings taken at bouncers, cars and property damaged. Something caught Rebus's eye: mention of a hot-dog van, parked outside a couple of the clubs. The owner questioned: possible witness. But he'd never seen anything worth the recall. Name: Gavin Tay.

Mr Taystee.

Recent dodgy suicide. Rebus gave Bill Pryde a bell, asked how that investigation was going.

'Dead end street, pal,' Pryde said, not sounding too concerned. Pryde: too long the same rank, and not going anywhere. Beginning the long descent into retirement.

'Did you know he ran a hot-dog stall on the side?'

'Might explain where he got the cash from.'

Gavin Tay was an ex-con. He'd been in the ice-cream business a little over a year. Successful, too: new Merc parked outside his house. His financial records hadn't hinted at money to spare. His widow couldn't account for the Merc. And now: evidence of a job on the side, selling food and drink to punters stumbling out of nightclubs.

Tommy Telford's nightclubs.

Gavin Tay: previous convictions for assault and reset. A

persistent offender who'd finally gone straight ... The room began to feel stuffy, Rebus's head clotted and aching. He decided to get out.

Walked through The Meadows and down George IV Bridge, took the Playfair Steps down to Princes Street. A group was sitting on the stone steps of the Scottish Academy: unshaven, dyed hair, torn clothes. The city's dispossessed, trying their best not to be ignored. Rebus knew he had things in common with them. In the course of his life, he'd failed to fit several niches: husband, father, lover. He hadn't fit in with the Army's ideas of what he should be, and wasn't exactly 'one of the lads' in the police. When one of the group held out a hand, Rebus offered a fiver, before crossing Princes Street and heading for the Oxford Bar.

He settled into a corner with a mug of coffee, got out his mobile, and called Sammy's flat. She was home, all was well with Candice. Rebus told her he had a place for Candice, she could move out tomorrow.

'That's fine,' Sammy said. 'Hold on a second.' There was a rustling sound as the receiver was passed along.

'Hello, John, how are you?'

Rebus smiled. 'Hello, Candice. That's very good.'

'Thank you. Sammy is ... uh ... I am teaching how to ...' She broke into laughter, handed the receiver back.

'I'm teaching her English,' Sammy said.

'I can tell.'

'We started with some Oasis lyrics, just went from there.'

'I'll try to come round later. What did Ned say?'

'He was so shattered when he came home, I think he barely noticed.'

'Is he there? I'd like to talk to him.'

'He's out working.'

'What did you say he was doing again?'

'I didn't.'

'Right. Thanks again, Sammy. See you later.'

He took a swig of coffee, washed it around his mouth. Abernethy: he couldn't just let it go. He swallowed the coffee and called the Roxburghe, asked for David Levy's room.

'Levy speaking.'

'It's John Rebus.'

'Inspector, how good to hear from you. Is there something I can do?'

'I'd like to talk to you.'

'Are you in your office?'

Rebus looked around. 'In a manner of speaking. It's a two-minute walk from your hotel. Turn right out of the door, cross George Street, and walk down to Young Street. Far end, the Oxford Bar. I'm in the back room.'

When Levy arrived, Rebus bought him a half of eighty-bob. Levy eased himself into a chair, hanging his walking-stick on the back of it. 'So what can I do for you?'

'I'm not the only policeman you've spoken to.'

'No, you're not.'

'Someone from Special Branch in London came to see me today.'

'And he told you I'd been travelling around?'

'Yes.'

'Did he warn you against speaking to me?'

'Not in so many words.'

Levy took off his glasses, began polishing them. 'I told you, there are people who'd rather this was all relegated to history. This man, he came all the way from London just to tell you about me?'

'He wanted to see Joseph Lintz.'

'Ah.' Levy was thoughtful. 'Your interpretation, Inspector?'

'I was hoping for yours.'

'My utterly subjective interpretation?' Rebus nodded. 'He wants to be sure of Lintz. This man works for Special Branch, and as everyone knows Special Branch is the public arm of the secret services.'

'He wanted to be confident I wasn't going to get anything out of Lintz?'

Levy nodded, staring at the smoke from Rebus's cigarette. This case was like that: one minute you could see it, the next you couldn't. Like smoke.

'I have a little book with me,' Levy said, reaching into his pocket. 'I'd like you to read it. It's in English, translated from the Hebrew. It's about the Rat Line.'

Rebus took the book. 'Does it prove anything?'

'That depends on your terms.'

'Concrete proof.'

'Concrete proof exists, Inspector.'

'In this book?'

Levy shook his head. 'Under lock and key in Whitehall, kept from scrutiny by the Hundred Year Rule.'

'So there's no way to prove anything.'

'There's one way ...'

'What?'

'If someone talks. If we can get just *one* of them to talk ...'

'That's what this is all about: wearing down their resistance? Looking for the weakest link?'

Levy smiled again. 'We have learned patience, Inspector.' He finished his drink. 'I'm so grateful you called. This has been a much more satisfactory meeting.'

'Will you send your bosses a progress report?'

Levy chose to ignore this. 'We'll talk again, when you've read the book.' He stood up. 'The Special Branch officer ... I've forgotten his name?'

'I didn't give it.'

Levy waited a moment, then said, 'Ah, that explains it

then. Is he still in Edinburgh?' He watched Rebus shake his head. 'Then he's probably on his way to Carlisle, yes?'

Rebus sipped coffee, offered no comment.

'My thanks again, Inspector,' Levy said, undeterred.

'Thanks for dropping by.'

Levy took a final look around. 'Your office,' he said, shaking his head.

8

The Rat Line was an 'underground railway', delivering
Nazis – sometimes with the help of the Vatican – from their
Soviet persecutors. The end of the Second World War
meant the start of the Cold War. Intelligence was necessary,
as were intelligent, ruthless individuals who could provide a
certain level of expertise. It was said that Klaus Barbie, the
'Butcher of Lyons', had been offered a job with British
Intelligence. It was rumoured that high-profile Nazis had
been spirited away to America. It wasn't until 1987 that the
United Nations released its full list of fugitive Nazi and
Japanese war criminals, forty thousand of them.

Why so late in releasing the list? Rebus thought he could
understand. Modern politics had decreed that Germany
and Japan were part of the global brotherhood of capital-
ism. In whose interests would it be to reopen old wounds?
And besides, how many atrocities had the Allies themselves
hidden? Who fought a war with clean hands? Rebus, who'd
grown to adulthood in the Army, could comprehend this.
He'd done things ... He'd served time in Northern Ireland,
seen trust disfigured, hatred replace fear.

Part of him could well believe in the existence of a Rat
Line.

The book Levy had given him went into the mechanics
of how such an operation might have worked. Rebus
wondered: was it really possible to disappear completely, to
change identity? And again, the recurring question: did any
of it matter? There did exist sources of identification, and

there *had* been court cases – Eichmann, Barbie, Demjanjuk – with others ongoing. He read about war criminals who, rather than being tried or extradited, were allowed to return home, running businesses, growing rich, dying of old age. But he also read of criminals who served their sentences and became 'good people', people who *had* changed. These men said war itself was the real culprit. Rebus recalled one of his first conversations with Joseph Lintz, in the drawing-room of Lintz's home. The old man's voice was hoarse, a scarf around his throat.

'At my age, Inspector, a simple throat infection can feel like death.'

There didn't seem to be many photographs around. Lintz had explained that a lot had gone missing during the war.

'Along with other mementoes. I do have these photos though.'

He'd shown Rebus half a dozen framed shots, dating back to the 1930s. As he'd explained who the subjects were, Rebus had suddenly thought: what if he's making it up? What if these are just a bunch of old photos he picked up somewhere and had framed? And the names, the identities he now gave to the faces – had he invented them? He'd seen in that instant, for the first time, how easy it might be to construct another life.

And then, later in their conversation that day, Lintz, sipping honeyed tea, had started discussing Villefranche.

'I've been thinking a lot about it, Inspector, as you might imagine. This Lieutenant Linzstek, he was in charge on the day?'

'Yes.'

'But presumably under orders from above. A lieutenant is not so very far up the pecking order.'

'Perhaps.'

'You see, if a soldier is under orders … then they must carry out those orders, no?'

'Even if the order is insane?'

'Nevertheless, I'd say the person was at the very least *coerced* into committing the crime, and a crime that very many of us would have carried out under similar circumstances. Can't you see the hypocrisy of trying someone, when you'd probably have done the same thing yourself? One soldier standing out from the crowd … saying no to the massacre: would you have made that stand yourself?'

'I hope so.' Rebus thinking back to Ulster and the 'Mean Machine' …

Levy's book didn't prove anything. All Rebus knew was that Josef Linzstek's name was on a list as having used the Rat Line, posing as a Pole. But where had the list originated? In Israel. Again, it was highly speculative. It wasn't *proof*.

And if Rebus's instincts told him Lintz and Linzstek were one and the same, they were still failing to tell him whether it mattered.

He dropped the book back to the Roxburghe, asked the receptionist to see that Mr Levy got it.

'I think he's in his room, if you'd like to …'

Rebus shook his head. He hadn't left any message with the book, knowing Levy might interpret this as a message in itself. He went home for his car, drove down to Haymarket and along to Shandon. As usual, parking near Sammy's flat was a problem. Everyone was home from work and tucked in front of their televisions. He climbed the stone steps, wondering how treacherous they'd get when the frosts came, and rang the bell. Sammy herself led him into the living room, where Candice was watching a game show.

'Hello, John,' she said. 'Are you my wonderwall?'

'I'm nobody's wonderwall, Candice.' He turned to Sammy. 'Everything all right?'

'Just fine.'

At that moment, Ned Farlowe walked in from the kitchen. He was eating soup from a bowl, dunking a folded slice of brown bread into it.

'Mind if I have a word?' Rebus said.

Farlowe shook his head, then jerked it in the direction of the kitchen.

'Can I eat while we talk? I'm starving.' He sat down at the foldaway table, got another slice of bread from the packet and spread margarine on it. Sammy put her head round the doorway, saw the look on her father's face, and made a tactical retreat. The kitchen was about seven foot square and too full of pots and appliances. Swinging a cat, you could have done a lot of damage.

'I saw you today,' Rebus said, 'skulking in Warriston Cemetery. Coincidence?'

'What do you think?'

'I'm asking you.' Rebus leaned his back against the sink unit, folded his arms.

'I'm watching Lintz.'

'Why?'

'Because I'm being paid to.'

'By a newspaper?'

'Lintz's lawyer has interim interdicts flying around. Nobody can afford to be seen near him.'

'But they still want him watched?'

'If there's a court case coming, they want to know as much as possible, stands to reason.'

By court case, Farlowe didn't mean any trial of Lintz, but rather of the newspapers themselves, for libel.

'If he catches you ...'

'He doesn't know me from Adam. Besides, there'd

always be somebody to take my place. Now do I get to ask a question?'

'Let me say something first. You know I'm investigating Lintz?' Farlowe nodded. '"That means we're too close. If you find out anything, people might think it came from me.'

'I haven't told Sammy what I'm doing, *specifically* so there's no conflict of interests.'

'I'm just saying others might not believe it.'

'A few more days, I'll have enough money to fund the book for another month.' Farlowe had finished his soup. He carried the empty bowl over to the sink, stood next to Rebus.

'I don't want this to be a problem, but the bottom line is: what can you do about it?'

Rebus stared at him. His instinct was to stuff Farlowe's head into the sink, but how would that look with Sammy?

'Now,' Farlowe said, 'do I get to ask my question?'

'What is it?'

'Who's Candice?'

'A friend of mine.'

'So what's wrong with *your* flat?'

Rebus realised he was no longer dealing with his daughter's boyfriend. He was confronted with a journalist, someone with a nose for a story.

'Tell you what,' said Rebus, 'say I didn't see you in the cemetery. Say we didn't just have this little chat.'

'And I don't ask about Candice?' Rebus stayed quiet. Farlowe considered the deal. 'Say I get to ask you a few questions for my book.'

'What sort of questions?'

'About Cafferty.'

Rebus shook his head. 'I could talk about Tommy Telford though.'

'When?'

'When we've got him behind bars.'

Farlowe smiled. 'I could be on the pension by then.' He waited, saw Rebus was going to give him nothing.

'She's only here till tomorrow anyway,' Rebus said.

'Where's she off to?'

Rebus just winked. Left the kitchen, returned to the living-room. Talked to Sammy while Candice's game show reached its climax. Whenever she heard audience laughter, she joined in. Rebus made arrangements for the following day, then left. There was no sign of Farlowe. He'd either hidden himself in the bedroom or else gone back out. It took Rebus a few moments to remember where he'd parked his car. He drove home carefully; stopped for all the lights.

The parking spaces were all taken in Arden Street. He left the Saab on a yellow line. As he approached his tenement door, he heard a car door open and spun towards the sound.

It was Claverhouse. He was on his own. 'Mind if I come in?'

Rebus thought of a dozen reasons for saying yes. But he shrugged and made for the door. 'Any news of the stabbing at Megan's?' he asked.

'How did you know we'd be interested?'

'A bouncer gets stabbed, the attacker flees on a waiting motorbike. It was premeditated. And the majority of the bouncers work for Tommy Telford.'

They were climbing the stairs. Rebus's flat was on the second floor.

'Well, you're right,' Claverhouse said. 'Billy Tennant worked for Telford. He controlled the traffic in and out of Megan's.'

'Traffic as in dope?'

'The footballer's friend, the one who got wounded, he's a known dealer. Works out of Paisley.'

'Therefore connected to Telford, too.'

'We're speculating he was the target, Tennant just got in the way.'

'Leaving only one question: who was behind it?'

'Come on, John. It was Cafferty, obviously.'

'Not Cafferty's style,' Rebus said, unlocking his door.

'Maybe he's learned a thing or two from the Young Pretender.'

'Make yourself at home,' Rebus said, walking down the hall. The breakfast things were still on the dining table. Siobhan's bag of goodies was down the side of a chair.

'A guest.' Claverhouse had noticed the two mugs, two plates. He looked around. 'She's not here now though?'

'She wasn't here for breakfast either.'

'Because she's at your daughter's.'

Rebus froze.

'I went to settle up with the hotel. They said a police car had come and taken all her things away. So then I asked around, and the driver gave me Samantha's address as the drop-off.' Claverhouse sat down on the sofa, crossed one leg over the other. 'So what's the game, John, and how come you've seen fit to leave me on the bench?' He sounded calm now, but Rebus could tell there'd been a storm.

'Do you want a drink?'

'I want an answer.'

'When she walked out ... she waited beside my car. I couldn't think where to take her, so I brought her here. But she recognised the street. Telford had been watching my flat.'

Claverhouse looked interested. 'Why?'

'Maybe because I know Cafferty. I couldn't let Candice stay here, so I took her to Sammy's.'

'Is she still there?' Rebus nodded. 'So what happens now?'

'There's a place she can go, the refugee family.'

'For how long?'

'What do you mean?'

Claverhouse sighed. 'John, she's ... the only life she's known here is prostitution.'

Rebus went over to the hi-fi for something to do, looked through his tapes. He needed to do *something*.

'What's she going to do for money? Are you going to provide? What does that make you?'

Rebus dropped a CD, turned on his heels. 'Nothing like that,' he spat.

Claverhouse had his hands up, palms showing. 'Come on, John, you know yourself there's –'

'I don't know anything.'

'John ...'

'Look, get out, will you?' It wasn't just that it had been a long day, more that it felt like the day would never end. He could feel the evening stretch to infinity, no rest available to him. In his head, bodies were swaying gently from trees while smoke engulfed a church. Telford was on his arcade motorbike, cannoning off spectators. Abernethy was touching an old man's shoulder. Soldiers were rifle-butting civilians. And John Rebus ... John Rebus was in every frame, trying hard to remain an onlooker.

He put Van Morrison on the hi-fi: *Hardnose the Highway*. He'd played this music on East Neuk beaches and tenement stakeouts. It always seemed to heal him, or at least patch the wounds. When he turned back into the room, Claverhouse was gone. He looked out of his window. Two kids lived in the second-floor flat across from his. He'd watched them often from this window, and they never once saw him, for the simple reason that they never so much as glanced outside. Their world was complete and all-absorbing, anything outside their window an irrelevance. They were in bed now, their mother closing the shutters. Quiet city. Abernethy was right about that. There were large chunks of Edinburgh where you could live your whole life and never encounter a spot of bother. Yet the murder rate in Scotland was double that of its southern neighbour, and half those murders took place in the two main cities.

Not that the statistics mattered. A death was a death. Something unique had disappeared from the world. One murder or several hundred … they all meant something to the survivors. Rebus thought of Villefranche's sole existing survivor. He hadn't met her, probably never would. Another reason it was hard to get passionate about a historical case. In a contemporary one, you had many of the facts to hand, and could talk to witnesses. You could gather forensic evidence, question people's stories. You could measure guilt and grief. You became part of the whole story. This was what interested Rebus. The people interested him; their stories fascinated him. When part of their lives, he could forget his own.

He noticed the answering-machine was flashing: one message.

'Oh, hello there. I'm … um, I don't know how to put this …' Placed the voice: Kirstin Mede. She sighed. 'Look, I can't do this any more. So please don't … I'm sorry, I just can't. There are other people who can help you. I'm sure one of them …'

End of message. Rebus stared down at the machine. He didn't blame her. *I can't do this any more.* That makes two of us, Rebus thought. The only thing was, *he* had to keep going. He sat down at his table and pulled the Villefranche paperwork towards him: lists of names and occupations, ages and dates of birth. Picat, Mesplede, Rousseau, Deschamps. Wine merchant, china painter, cartwright, housemaid. What did any of it mean to a middle-aged Scot? He pushed it aside and lifted Siobhan's paperwork on to the table.

Off with Van the Man; on with side one of *Wish You*

Were Here. Scratched to hell. He remembered it had come in a black polythene wrapper. When opened, there'd been this smell, which afterwards he'd learned was supposed to be burning flesh …

'I need a drink,' he said to himself, sitting forward in his chair. 'I want a drink. A few beers, maybe with whiskies attached.' Something to smooth the edges …

He looked at his watch; not even near to closing time. Not that it mattered much in Edinburgh, the land that closing time forgot. Could he make it to the Ox before they shut up shop? Yes, too easily. It was nicer to have a challenge. Wait an hour or so and then repeat the debate.

Or call Jack Morton.

Or go out, right now.

The telephone rang. He picked it up.

'Hello?'

'John?' Making it sound like 'Sean'.

'Hello, Candice. What's up?'

'Up?'

'Is there a problem?'

'Problem, no. I just wanting … I say to you, see you tomorrow.'

He smiled. 'Yes, see you tomorrow. You speak very good English.'

'I was chained to a razor blade.'

'What?'

'Line from song.'

'Oh, right. But you're not chained to it now?'

She didn't seem to understand. 'I'm … uh …'

'It's okay, Candice. See you tomorrow.'

'Yes, see you.'

Rebus put down the receiver. Chained to a razor blade … Suddenly he didn't want a drink any more.

9

He picked Candice up the next afternoon. She had two carrier bags, her worldly belongings. She gave Sammy as much of a hug as her bandaged arms would allow.

'See you again, Candice,' Sammy said.

'Yes, see you. Thanks ...' Lost for an ending to the sentence, Candice opened her arms wide, bags swinging.

They stopped off at McDonald's (her choice) for something to eat. Zappa and the Mothers: 'Cruising for Burgers'. The day was bright and crisp, just right for crossing the Forth Bridge. Rebus took it slowly, so Candice could take in the view. He was heading towards Fife's East Neuk, a cluster of fishing villages popular with artists and holidaymakers. Out of season, Anstruther seemed practically deserted. Though Rebus had an address, he stopped to ask directions. Finally, he parked in front of a small terraced house. Candice stared at the red door until he gestured for her to follow him. He hadn't been able to make her understand what they were doing here. Hoped Mr and Mrs Drinic would make a better job of it.

The door was opened by a woman in her early forties. She had long black hair, and peered at him over half-moon glasses. Then her attention shifted to Candice, and she said something in a language both women understood. Candice replied, looking a little shy, not sure what was going on.

'Come in, please,' Mrs Drinic said. 'My husband is in the kitchen.'

They sat around the kitchen table. Mr Drinic was heavily

built, with a thick brown moustache and wavy brown and silver hair. A pot of tea was produced, and Mrs Drinic drew her chair beside Candice's and began talking again.

'She's explaining to the girl,' Mr Drinic said.

Rebus nodded, sipped the strong tea, listened to a conversation he could not understand. Candice, cautious at first, grew more animated as she told her story, and Mrs Drinic was a skilled listener, sympathising, showing shared horror and exasperation.

'She was taken to Amsterdam, told there would be a job there for her,' Mr Drinic explained. 'I know this has happened to other young women.'

'I think she left a child behind.'

'A son, yes. She's telling my wife about him.'

'What about you?' Rebus asked. 'How did you end up here?'

'I was an architect in Sarajevo. No easy decision, leaving your whole life behind.' He paused. 'We went to Belgrade first. A refugee bus brought us to Scotland.' He shrugged. 'That was nearly five years ago. Now I am a carpenter.' A smile. 'Distance no object.'

Rebus looked at Candice, who had started crying, Mrs Drinic comforting her.

'We will look after her,' Mrs Drinic said, staring at her husband.

Later, at the door, Rebus tried to give them some money, but they wouldn't take it.

'Is it all right if I come and see her sometime?'

'But of course.'

He stood in front of Candice.

'Her real name is Karina,' Mrs Drinic said quietly.

'Karina.' Rebus tried out the word. She smiled, her eyes softer than Rebus remembered them, as if some transformation were beginning. She bent forward.

'Kiss the girl,' she said.

A peck on both cheeks. Her eyes filling with tears again. Rebus nodded, to let her know he understood everything.

At his car, he waved once, and she blew him another kiss. Then he drove around the corner and stopped, gripping the steering-wheel hard. He wondered if she'd cope. If she'd learn to forget. He thought again of his ex-wife's words. What would she think of him now? Had he exploited Karina? No, but he wondered if that was only because she hadn't been able to give him anything on Telford. He felt he had somehow failed to do the right thing. So far, the only choice she'd had to make was when she'd waited for him by his car rather than going back to Telford. Before then and after, all the decisions had been taken for her. In a sense, she was still as trapped as ever, because the locks and chains were in her mind; they were what she expected from life. It would take time for her to change, to begin trusting the world again. The Drinics would help her.

Heading south down the coast, thinking about families, he decided to visit his brother.

Mickey lived on an estate in Kirkcaldy, his red BMW parked in the driveway. He was just home from work and suitably surprised to see Rebus.

'Chrissie and the kids are at her mum's,' he said. 'I was going to grab a curry for dinner. How about a beer?'

'Maybe just a coffee,' Rebus said. He sat in the lounge until Mickey returned, toting a couple of old shoe-boxes.

'Look what I dug out of the attic last weekend. Thought you might like a look. Milk and sugar?'

'A spot of milk.'

While Mickey went to the kitchen to fetch the coffee, Rebus examined the boxes. They were filled with packets of photographs. The packets had dates on them, some with questionmarks. Rebus opened one at random. Holiday snaps. A fancy dress parade. A picnic. Rebus didn't have any pictures of his parents, and the photos startled him. His mother had thicker legs than he remembered, but a tidy body, too. His father used the same grin in every shot, a grin Rebus shared with Mickey. Digging further into the box, he found one of himself with Rhona and Sammy. They were on a beach somewhere, the wind playing havoc. Peter Gabriel: 'Family Snapshot'. Rebus couldn't place it at all. Mickey came back through with a mug of coffee and a bottle of beer.

'There are some,' he said, 'I don't know who the people are. Relatives maybe? Grandma and Grandad?'

'I'm not sure I'd be much help.'

Mickey handed over a menu. 'Here,' he said, 'best Indian in town. Pick what you want.'

So Rebus chose, and Mickey phoned the order in. Twenty minutes till delivery. Rebus was on to another packet. These photos were older still, the 1940s. His father in uniform. The soldiers wore hats like McDonald's counter staff. They also wore long khaki shorts. 'Malaya' written on the backs of some, 'India' on the others.

'Remember, the old man got himself wounded in Malaya?' Mickey said.

'No, he didn't.'

'He showed us the wound. It was in his knee.'

Rebus was shaking his head. 'Uncle Jimmy told me it was a cut Dad got playing football. He kept picking the scab off, ended with a scar.'

'He told us it was a war wound.'

'He was fibbing.'

Mickey had started on the other box. 'Here, look at these ...' Handing over an inch-thick collection of post-cards and photographs, secured with an elastic band. Rebus pulled the band off, turned the cards over, saw his own writing. The photos were of him, too: posed snaps, badly taken.

'Where did you get these?'

'You always used to send me a card or a photo, don't you remember?'

They were all from Rebus's own Army days. 'I'd forgotten,' he said.

'Once a fortnight, usually. A letter to Dad, a card for me.'

Rebus sat back in his chair and started to go through them. Judging by the postmarks, they were in chronological sequence. Training, then service in Germany and Ulster, more exercises in Cyprus, Malta, Finland, and the desert of Saudi Arabia. The tone of each postcard was breezy, so that Rebus failed to recognise his own voice. The cards from Belfast consisted of almost nothing but jokes, yet Rebus remembered that as one of the most nightmarish periods of his life.

'I used to love getting them,' Mickey said, smiling. 'I'll tell you, you almost had me joining up.'

Rebus was still thinking of Belfast: the closed barracks, the whole compound a fortress. After a shift out on the streets, there was no way to let off steam. Booze, gambling and fights – all taking place within the same four walls. All culminating in the Mean Machine ... And here were these postcards, here was the image of Rebus's past life that Mickey had lived with these past twenty-odd years.

And it was all a lie.

Or was it? Where did the reality lie, other than in Rebus's own head? The postcards were fake documents, but they were also the only ones in existence. There was nothing to contradict them, nothing except Rebus's word. It was the same with the Rat Line, the same with Joseph Lintz's story. Rebus looked at his brother and knew he could break the spell right now. All he had to do was tell him the truth.

'What's the matter?' Mickey asked.

'Nothing.'

'Ready for that beer yet? The food'll be here any second.'

Rebus stared at the cooling mug of coffee. 'More than ready,' he said, putting the rubber band back around his past. 'But I'll stick to this.' He lifted the mug, toasted his brother.

10

Next morning, Rebus went to St Leonard's, telephoned the NCIS centre at Prestwick and asked if they had anything connecting British criminals to European prostitution. His reasoning: *someone* had brought Candice – she was still Candice to him – from Amsterdam to Britain, and he didn't think it was Telford. Whoever it was, Rebus would get to them somehow. He wanted to show Candice her chains could be broken.

He got NCIS to fax him what information they had. Most of it concerned the 'Tippelzone', a licensed car park where drivers went for sex. It was worked by foreign prostitutes mainly, most of them lacking work permits, many smuggled in from Eastern Europe. The main gangs seemed to be from former Yugoslavia. NCIS had no names for any of these kidnappers-cum-pimps. There was nothing about prostitutes making the trip from Amsterdam to Britain.

Rebus went into the car park to smoke his second cigarette of the day. There were a couple of other smokers out there, a small brotherhood of social pariahs. Back in the office, the Farmer wanted to know if there was any progress on Lintz.

'Maybe if I brought him in and slapped him around a bit,' Rebus suggested.

'Be serious, will you?' the Farmer growled, stalking back to his office.

Rebus sat down at his desk and pulled forward a file.

'Your problem, Inspector,' Lintz had said to him once, 'is that you're afraid of being taken seriously. You want to give people what you think they expect. I mention the Ishtar gate, and you talk of some Hollywood movie. At first I thought this was meant to rouse me to some indiscretion, but now it seems more a game you are playing against *yourself.*'

Rebus: seated in his usual chair in Lintz's drawing-room. The view from the window was of Queen Street Gardens. They were kept locked: you had to pay for a key.

'Do educated people frighten you?'

Rebus looked at the old man. 'No.'

'Are you sure? Don't you perhaps wish you were more like them?' Lintz grinned, showing small, discoloured teeth. 'Intellectuals like to see themselves as history's victims, prejudiced against, arrested for their beliefs, even tortured and murdered. But Karadzic thinks himself an intellectual. The Nazi hierarchy had its thinkers and philosophers. And even in Babylon ...' Lintz got up, poured himself more tea. Rebus declined a refill.

'Even in Babylon, Inspector,' Lintz continued, getting comfortable again, 'with its opulence and its artistry, with its enlightened king ... do you know what they did? Nebuchadnezzar held the Jews captive for seventy years. This splendid, awe-inspiring civilisation ... Do you begin to see the madness, Inspector, the flaws that run so deep in us?'

'Maybe I need glasses.'

Lintz threw his cup across the room. 'You need to listen and to learn! You need to understand!'

The cup and saucer lay on the carpet, still intact. Tea was soaking into the elaborate design, where it would become all but invisible ...

He parked on Buccleuch Place. The Slavic Studies

department was housed in one of the tenements. He tried the secretary's office first, asked if Dr Colquhoun was around.

'I haven't seen him today.'

When Rebus explained what he wanted, the secretary tried a couple of numbers but didn't find anyone. Then she suggested he take a look in their library, which was one floor up and kept locked. She handed him a key.

The room was about sixteen feet by twelve, and smelled stuffy. The shutters across the windows were closed, giving the place no natural light. A No Smoking sign sat on one of four desks. On another sat an ashtray with three butts in it. One entire wall was shelved, filled with books, pamphlets, magazines. There were boxes of press cuttings, and maps on the walls showing Yugoslavia's changing demarcation lines. Rebus lifted down the most recent box of cuttings.

Like a lot of people he knew, Rebus didn't know much about the war in ex-Yugoslavia. He'd seen some of the news reports, been shocked by the pictures, then had got on with his life. But if the cuttings were to be believed, the whole region was being run by war criminals. The Implementation Force seemed to have done its damnedest to avoid confrontation. There had been a few arrests recently, but nothing substantial: out of a meagre seventy-four suspects charged, only *seven* had been apprehended.

He found nothing about slave traders, so thanked the secretary and gave her back her key, then crawled through the city traffic. When the call came on his mobile, he nearly went off the road.

Candice had disappeared.

Mrs Drinic was distraught. They'd had dinner last night, breakfast this morning, and Karina had seemed fine.

'There was a lot she said she couldn't tell us,' Mr Drinic

said, standing behind his seated wife, hands stroking her shoulders. 'She said she wanted to forget.'

And then she'd gone out for a walk down to the harbour, and hadn't returned. Lost maybe, though the village was small. Mr Drinic had been working; his wife had gone out, asking people if they'd seen her.

'And Mrs Muir's son,' she said, 'he told me she'd been taken away in a car.'

'Where was this?' Rebus asked.

'Just a couple of streets away,' Mr Drinic said.

'Show me.'

Outside his home on Seaford Road, Eddie Muir, aged eleven, told Rebus what he'd seen. A car stopping beside a woman. A bit of chat, though he couldn't hear it. The door opening, the woman getting in.

'Which door, Eddie?'

'One of the back ones. Had to be, there were two of them in the car already.'

'Men?'

Eddie nodded.

'And the woman got in by herself? I mean, they didn't grab her or anything?'

Eddie shook his head. He was straddling his bike, keen to be going. One foot kept testing a pedal.

'Can you describe the car?'

'Big, a bit flash. Not from round here.'

'And the men?'

'Didn't really get a good look. Driver was wearing a Pars shirt.'

Meaning a football shirt, Dunfermline Athletic. Which would mean he was from Fife. Rebus frowned. A pick-up? Could that be it? Candice back to her old ways so soon? Not likely, not in a place like this, on a street like this. It was no chance encounter. Mrs Drinic was right: she'd been snatched. Which meant someone had known where to find her. Had Rebus been followed yesterday? If he had, they'd been invisible. Some device on his car? It seemed unlikely, but he checked wheel-arches and the underbody: nothing. Mrs Drinic had calmed a little, her husband having administered medicinal vodka. Rebus could use a shot himself, but turned down the offer.

'Did she make any phone calls?' he asked. Drinic shook his head. 'What about strangers hanging around the street?'

'I would have noticed. After Sarajevo, it's hard to feel safe, Inspector.' He opened his arms. 'And here's the proof – nowhere's safe.'

'Did you tell anyone about Karina?'

'Who would we tell?'

Who knew? That was the question. Rebus did. And Claverhouse and Ormiston knew about the place, because Colquhoun had mentioned it.

Colquhoun knew. The nervy old Slavic Studies specialist knew ... On the way back to Edinburgh, Rebus tried phoning him at office and home: no reply. He'd told the Drinics to let him know if Candice came back, but he didn't think she'd be coming back. He remembered the look she'd given him early on when he'd asked her to trust him. *I won't be surprised if you let me down.* Like she'd known back then that he'd fail. And she'd given him a second chance, waiting for him beside his car. And he'd let her down. He got back on his mobile and called Jack Morton.

'Jack,' he said, 'for Christ's sake, talk me out of having a drink.'

He tried Colquhoun's home address and the Slavic Studies office: both locked up tight. Then he drove to Flint Street and looked for Tommy Telford in the arcade. But Telford wasn't there. He was in the café's back office, surrounded as usual by his men.

'I want to talk to you,' Rebus said.

'So talk.'

'Without the audience.' Rebus pointed to Pretty-Boy. 'That one can stay.'

Telford took his time, but finally nodded, and the room began to empty. Pretty-Boy stood against a wall, hands behind his back. Telford had his feet up on his desk, leaning back in his chair. They were relaxed, confident. Rebus knew what *he* looked like: a caged bear.

'I want to know where she is.'

'Who?'

'Candice.'

Telford smiled. 'Still on about her, Inspector? How should I know where she is?'

'Because a couple of your boys grabbed her.' But as he spoke, Rebus realised he was making a mistake. Telford's gang was a *family*: they'd grown up together in Paisley. Not many Dunfermline supporters that distant from Fife. He stared at Pretty-Boy, who ran Telford's prostitutes. Candice had arrived in Edinburgh from a city of bridges, maybe Newcastle. Telford had Newcastle connections. And the Newcastle United strip – vertical black and white lines – was damned close to Dunfermline's. Probably only a kid in Fife could make the mistake.

A Newcastle strip. A Newcastle car.

Telford was talking, but Rebus wasn't listening. He walked straight out of the office and back to the Saab. Drove to Fettes – the Crime Squad offices – and started looking. He found a contact number for a DS Miriam Kenworthy. Tried the number but she wasn't there.

'Fuck it,' he told himself, getting back into his car.

The A1 was hardly the country's fastest road – Abernethy was right about that. Still, without the daytime traffic Rebus made decent time on his way south. It was late evening when he arrived in Newcastle, pubs emptying, queues forming outside clubs, a few United shirts on display, looking like prison bars. He didn't know the city. Drove around it in circles, passing the same signs and landmarks, heading further out, just cruising.

Looking for Candice. Or for girls who might know her.

After a couple of hours, he gave up, headed back into the centre. He'd had the idea of sleeping in his car, but when he found a hotel with an empty room, the thought of en-suite facilities suddenly seemed too good to miss.

He made sure there was no mini-bar.

A long soak with his eyes closed, mind and body still racing from the drive. He sat in a chair by his window and listened to the night: taxis and yells, delivery lorries. He couldn't sleep. He lay on the bed, watching soundless TV, remembering Candice in the hotel room, asleep under sweet wrappers. Deacon Blue: 'Chocolate Girl.'

He woke up to breakfast TV. Checked out of the hotel and had breakfast in a café, then called Miriam Kenworthy's office, relieved to find she was an early starter.

'Come right round,' she said, sounding bemused. 'You're only a couple of minutes away.'

She was younger than her telephone voice, face softer than her attitude. It was a milkmaid's face, rounded, the cheeks pink and plump. She studied him, swivelling slightly in her chair as he told her the story.

'Tarawicz,' she said when he'd finished. 'Jake Tarawicz. Real name Joachim, probably.' Kenworthy smiled. 'Some of us around here call him Mr Pink Eyes. He's had dealings – meetings anyway – with this guy Telford.' She opened the brown folder in front of her. 'Mr Pink Eyes has a lot of European connections. You know Chechnia?'

'In Russia?'

'It's Russia's Sicily, if you know what I mean.'

'Is that where Tarawicz comes from?'

'It's one theory. The other is that he's Serbian. Might explain why he set up the convoy.'

'What convoy?'

'Running aid lorries to former Yugoslavia. A real humanitarian, our Mr Pink.'

'But also a way of smuggling people out?'

Kenworthy looked at him. 'You've been doing your homework.'

'Call it an educated guess.'

'Well, it gets him noticed. He got a papal blessing six months ago. Married to an Englishwoman – not for love. She was one of his girls.'

'But it gives him residency here.'

She nodded. 'He hasn't been around that long, five or six years ...'

Like Telford, Rebus thought.

'But he's built himself a rep, muscled in where there used to be Asians, Turks ... Story is, he started with a nice line in stolen icons. A ton of stuff has been lifted out of the Soviet bloc. And when that operation started drying, he moved into prossies. Cheap girls, and he could keep them docile with a bit of crack. The crack comes up from London – the Yardies control that particular scene. Mr Pink spreads their goods around the north-east. He also deals heroin for the Turks and sells some girls to Triad brothels.' She looked at Rebus, saw she had his attention. 'No racial barriers when it comes to business.'

'So I see.'

'Probably also sells drugs to your friend Telford, who distributes them through his nightclubs.'

' "Probably"?'

'We've no hard proof. There was even a story going around that Pink wasn't selling to Telford, he was *buying*.'

Rebus blinked. 'Telford's not that big.'

She shrugged.

'Where would he get the stuff?'

'It was a story, that's all.'

But it had Rebus thinking, because it might help explain the relationship between Tarawicz and Telford …

'What does Tarawicz get out of it?' he asked, making his thoughts flesh.

'You mean apart from money? Well, Telford trains a good bouncer. Jock bouncers get respect down here. Then, of course, Telford has shares in a couple of casinos.'

'A way for Tarawicz to launder his cash?' Rebus thought about this. 'Is there anything Tarawicz *doesn't* have a finger in?'

'Plenty. He likes businesses which are fluid. And he's still a relative newcomer.'

Eagles: 'New Kid in Town'.

'We think he's been dealing arms: a lot of stuff crossing into Western Europe. The Chechens seem to have weaponry to spare.' She sniffed, gathered her thoughts.

'Sounds like he's one step ahead of Tommy Telford.' Which would explain why Telford was so keen to do business with him. He was on a learning curve, learning how to fit into the bigger picture. Yardies and Asians, Turks and Chechens, and all the others. Rebus saw them as spokes on a huge wheel which was trundling mercilessly across the world, breaking bones as it went.

'Why "Mr Pink Eyes"?' he asked.

She'd been awaiting the question, slid a colour photo towards him.

It was the close-up of a face, the skin pink and blistered, white lesions running through it. The face was puffy, bloated, and in its midst sat eyes hidden by blue-tinted glasses. There were no eyebrows. The hair above the jutting forehead was thin and yellow. The man looked like some monstrous shaved pig.

'What happened to him?' he asked.

'We don't know. That's the way he looked when he arrived.'

Rebus remembered the description Candice had given: sunglasses, looks like a car-crash victim. Dead ringer.

'I want to talk to him,' Rebus said.

But first, Kenworthy gave him a guided tour. They took her car, and she showed him where the street girls worked. It was mid-morning, no action to speak of. He gave her a description of Candice, and she promised she'd put the word out. They spoke with the few women they met. They all seemed to know Kenworthy, weren't hostile towards her.

'They're the same as you or me,' she told him, driving away. 'Working to feed their kids.'

'Or their habit.'

'That too, of course.'

'In Amsterdam, they've got a union.'

'Doesn't help the poor sods who're shipped there.' Kenworthy signalled at a junction. 'You're sure he has her?'

'I don't think Telford does. Someone knew addresses back in Sarajevo, addresses that were important to her. Someone shipped her out of there.'

'Sounds like Mr Pink all right.'

'And he's the only one who can send her back.'

She looked at him. 'Why would he do a thing like that?'

Just as Rebus was thinking their surroundings couldn't get any grimmer – all industrial decay, gutted buildings and pot-holes – Kenworthy signalled to turn in at the gates of a scrapyard.

'You're kidding?' he said.

Three Alsatians, tethered by thirty-foot chains, barked and bounded towards the car. Kenworthy ignored them, kept driving. It was like being in a ravine. Either side of them stood precarious canyon walls of car wrecks.

'Hear that?'

Rebus heard it: the sound of a collision. The car entered a wide clearing, and he saw a yellow crane, dangling a huge grab from its arm, pluck up the car it had dropped and lift it high, before dropping it again on to the carcass of another. A few men were standing at a safe distance, smoking cigarettes and looking bored. The grab dropped on to the roof of the top car, denting it badly. Glass shimmered on the oily ground, diamonds against black velvet.

Jake Tarawicz – Mr Pink Eyes – was in the crane, laughing and roaring as he picked up the car again, worrying it the way a cat might play with a mouse without noticing it was dead. If he'd seen the new additions to his audience, it didn't show. Kenworthy hadn't got out of her car immediately. First, she'd fixed on a face from her repertoire. When finally she was ready, she nodded to Rebus and they opened their doors simultaneously.

As Rebus stood upright, he saw that the grab had dropped the car and was swinging towards them. Kenworthy folded her arms and stood her ground. Rebus was reminded of those arcade games where you had to pick up a prize. He could see Tarawicz in the cab, manipulating the controls like a kid with a toy. He remembered Tommy Telford on his arcade bike, and saw at once something the two men had in common: neither had ever really grown up.

The motorised hum stopped suddenly, and Tarawicz dropped from the cab. He was wearing a cream suit and emerald shirt, open at the neck. He'd borrowed a pair of green wellies from somewhere, so as to keep his trousers clean. As he walked towards the two detectives, his men stepped into line behind him.

'Miriam,' he said, 'always a pleasure.' He paused. 'Or so

the rumour goes.' A couple of his men grinned. Rebus recognised one face: 'The Crab', that's what he'd been called in central Scotland. His grip could crush bones. Rebus hadn't seen him in a long time, and had never seen him so smartly groomed and dressed.

'All right, Crab?' Rebus said.

This seemed to disconcert Tarawicz, who half-turned towards his minion. The Crab stayed quiet, but colour had risen to his neck.

Up close, it was hard not to stare at Mr Pink Eyes's face. His eyes demanded that you meet them, but you really wanted to study the flesh in which they sat.

He was looking at Rebus now.

'Have we met?'

'No.'

'This is Detective Inspector Rebus,' Kenworthy explained. 'He's come all the way from Scotland to see you.'

'I'm flattered.' Tarawicz's grin showed small sharp teeth with gaps between them.

'I think you know why I'm here,' Rebus said.

Tarawicz made a show of astonishment. 'Do I?'

'Telford needed your help. He needed a home address for Candice, a note to her in Serbo–Croat ...'

'Is this some sort of riddle?'

'And now you've taken her back.'

'Have I?'

Rebus took a half-step forward. Tarawicz's men fanned out either side of their boss. There was a sheen on Tarawicz's face which could have been sweat or some medical cream.

'She wanted out,' Rebus told him. 'I promised I'd help her. I never break a promise.'

'She wanted out? She told you that?' Tarawicz's voice was teasing.

One of the men behind cleared his throat. Rebus had been wondering about this man, so much smaller and more reticent than the others, better dressed and with sad drooping eyes and sallow skin. Now he knew: lawyer. And the cough was his way of warning Tarawicz that he was saying too much.

'I'm going to take Tommy Telford down,' Rebus said quietly. 'That's my promise to you. Once he's in custody, who knows what he'll say?'

'I'm sure Mr Telford can look after himself, Inspector. Which is more than can be said for Candice.' The lawyer coughed again.

'I want her kept off the streets,' Rebus said.

Tarawicz stared at him, tiny black pupils like spots of absolute darkness.

'Can Thomas Telford go about his daily business unfettered?' he said at last. Behind him, the lawyer almost choked.

'You know I can't promise that,' Rebus said. 'It's not me he has to worry about.'

'Take a message to your friend,' Tarawicz said. 'And afterwards, stop being his friend.'

Rebus realised then: Tarawicz was talking about *Cafferty*. Telford had told him that Rebus was Cafferty's man.

'I think I can do that,' Rebus said quietly.

'Then do it.' Tarawicz turned away.

'And Candice?'

'I'll see what I can do.' He stopped, slid his hands into his jacket pockets. 'Hey, Miriam,' he said, his back still to them, 'I like you better in that red two-piece.'

Laughing, he walked away.

'Get in the car,' Kenworthy said through gritted teeth. Rebus got into the car. She looked nervous, dropped her keys, bent to retrieve them.

'What's wrong?'

'Nothing's wrong,' she snapped.

'The red two-piece?'

She glared at him. 'I don't have a red two-piece.' She did a three point-turn, hitting brakes and accelerator with a little more force than necessary.

'I don't get it.'

'Last week,' she said, 'I bought some red underwear ... bra and pants.' She revved the engine. 'Part of his little game.'

'So how does he know?'

'That's what I'm wondering.' She shot past the dogs and out of the gate. Rebus thought of Tommy Telford, and how he'd been watching Rebus's flat.

'Surveillance isn't always one-way,' he said, knowing now who'd taught Telford the skill. A little later he asked about the scrapyard.

'He owns it. He's got a compacter, but before the cars get squashed he likes to play with them. And if you cross him, he welds your seatbelt shut.' She looked at him. 'You become part of his game.'

Never get personally involved: it was *the* golden rule. And practically every case he worked, Rebus broke it. He sometimes felt that the reason he became so involved in his cases was that he had no life of his own. He could only live *through* other people.

Why had he become so involved with Candice? Was it down to her physical resemblance to Sammy? Or was it that she had seemed to need *him*? The way she'd clung to his leg that first day ... Had he wanted – just for a little while – to be someone's knight in shining armour, the real thing, not some mockery?

John Rebus: complete bloody sham.

He phoned Claverhouse from his car, filled him in. Claverhouse told him not to worry.

'Thanks for that,' Rebus said. 'I feel a whole lot better now. Listen, who's Telford's supplier?'

'For what? Dope?'

'Yes.'

'That's the real joker in the pack. I mean, he does business with Newcastle, but we can't be certain who's dealing and who's buying.'

'What if Telford's selling?'

'Then he's got a line from the continent.'

'What do Drugs Squad say?'

'They say not. If he's landing the stuff from a boat, it means transporting it from the coast. Much more likely he's buying from Newcastle. Tarawicz has the contacts in Europe.'

'Makes you wonder why he needs Tommy Telford at all ...'

'John, do yourself a favour, switch off for five minutes.'

'Colquhoun seems to be keeping his head down ...'

'Did you hear me?'

'I'll talk to you soon.'

'Are you heading back?'

'In a manner of speaking.' Rebus cut the call and drove.

11

'Strawman,' said Morris Gerald Cafferty, as he was escorted into the room by two prison guards.

Earlier in the year, Rebus had promised Cafferty he would put a Glasgow gangster, Uncle Joe Toal, behind bars. It hadn't worked, despite Rebus's best efforts. Toal, pleading old age and illness, was still a free man, like a war criminal excused for senility. Ever since then, Cafferty had felt Rebus owed him.

Cafferty sat down, rolled his neck a few times, loosening it.

'So?' he asked.

Rebus nodded for the guards to leave, waited in silence until they'd gone. Then he slipped a quarter-bottle of Bell's from his pocket.

'Keep it,' Cafferty told him. 'From the look of you, I'd say your need was greater than mine.'

Rebus put the bottle back in his pocket. 'I've brought a message from Newcastle.'

Cafferty folded his arms. 'Jake Tarawicz?'

Rebus nodded. 'He wants you to lay off Tommy Telford.'

'What does he mean?'

'Come on, Cafferty. That bouncer who got stabbed, the dealer wounded ... There's war breaking out.'

Cafferty stared at the detective. 'Not my doing.'

Rebus snorted, but looking into Cafferty's eyes, he found himself almost believing.

'So who was it?' he asked quietly.

'How do I know?'

'Nevertheless, war is breaking out.'

'That's as may be. What's in it for Tarawicz?'

'He does business with Tommy.'

'And to protect that, he needs to have *me* warned off by a cop?' Cafferty was shaking his head. 'You really buy that?'

'I don't know,' Rebus said.

'One way to finish this.' Cafferty paused. 'Take Telford out of the game.' He saw the look on Rebus's face. 'I don't mean top him, I mean put him away. That should be *your* job, Strawman.'

'I only came to deliver a message.'

'And what's in it for you? Something in Newcastle?'

'Maybe.'

'Are you Tarawicz's man now?'

'You know me better than that.'

'Do I?' Cafferty sat back in his chair, stretched out his legs. 'I wonder about that sometimes. I mean, it doesn't keep me awake at night, but I wonder all the same.'

Rebus leaned on the table. 'You must have a bit salted away. Why can't you just be content with that?'

Cafferty laughed. The air felt charged; there might have been only the two of them left in the world. 'You want me to retire?'

'A good boxer knows when to stop.'

'Then neither of us would be much cop in the ring, would we? Got any plans to retire, Strawman?'

Despite himself, Rebus smiled.

'Thought not. Do I have to say something for you to take back to Tarawicz?'

Rebus shook his head. 'That wasn't the deal.'

'Well, if he does come asking, tell him to get some life insurance, the kind with death benefits.'

Rebus looked at Cafferty. Prison might have softened him, but only physically.

'I'd be a happy man if someone took Telford out of the game,' Cafferty went on. 'Know what I mean, Strawman? It'd be worth a lot to me.'

Rebus stood up. 'No deal,' he said. 'Personally, I'd be happy if you wiped one another out. I'd be jumping for joy at ring-side.'

'Know what happens at ring-side?' Cafferty rubbed at his temples. 'You tend to get spattered with blood.'

'As long as it's someone else's.'

The laughter came from deep within Cafferty's chest. 'You're not a spectator, Strawman. It's not in your nature.'

'And you're some kind of psychologist?'

'Maybe not,' said Cafferty. 'But I know what gets people excited.'

Book Three

'Cover my face as the animals cry.'

Running through the hospital, stopping nurses to ask directions. Sweat dripping off him, tie hanging loose around his neck. Taking right turns, left turns, looking for signs. Whose fault? He kept asking himself that. A message which failed to reach him. Because he was on a surveillance. Because he wasn't in radio contact. Because the station didn't know how important the message was.

Now running, a stitch in his side. He'd run all the way from the car. Up two flights of stairs, down corridors. The place was quiet. Middle of the night.

'Maternity!' he called to a man pushing a trolley. The man pointed to a set of doors. He pushed through them. Three nurses in a glass cubicle. One of them came out.

'Can I help?'

'I'm John Rebus. My wife ...'

She gave him a hard look. 'Third bed along.' Pointing ... Third bed along, curtains closed around it. He pulled the curtains open. Rhona lay on her side, face still flushed, hair sticking to her brow. And beside her, nuzzling into her, a tiny perfection with wisps of brown hair and black, unfocused eyes.

He touched the nose, ran a finger round the curves of an ear. The face twitched. He bent past it to kiss his wife.

'Rhona ... I'm really sorry. They didn't get the message to me until ten minutes ago. How did it ... ? I mean ... he's beautiful.'

'He's a she,' his wife said, turning away from him.

12

Rebus was sitting in his boss's office. It was nine-fifteen and he had slept for probably forty-five minutes the previous night. There'd been the hospital vigil and Sammy's operation: something about a blood clot. She was still unconscious, still 'critical'. He'd called Rhona in London. She'd told him she'd catch the first train she could. He'd given her his mobile number, so she could let him know when she arrived. She'd started to ask … her voice had cracked. She'd put down the receiver. He'd tried to find some feeling for her. Richard and Linda Thompson: 'Withered and Died'.

He'd called Mickey, who said he'd drop by the hospital some time today. And that was it for the family. There were other people he could call, people like Patience, who had been his lover for a time, and Sammy's landlady until far more recently. But he didn't. He knew in the morning he'd call the office where Sammy worked. He wrote it in his notebook so he wouldn't forget. And then he'd called Sammy's flat and given Ned Farlowe the news.

Farlowe had asked a question nobody else had: 'How about you? Are you all right?'

Rebus had looked around the hospital corridor. 'Not exactly.'

'I'll be right there.'

So they'd spent a couple of hours in one another's company, not really saying very much at first. Farlowe smoked, and Rebus helped him empty the pack. He couldn't reciprocate with whisky – there was nothing in the bottle – but he'd bought the young man several cups of coffee, since Farlowe had spent nearly all his money on the taxi from Shandon ...

'Wakey-wakey, John.'

Rebus's boss was shaking him gently. Rebus blinked, straightened in his chair.

'Sorry, sir.'

Chief Superintendent Watson went around the desk and sat down. 'Hellish sorry to hear about Sammy. I don't really know what to say, except that she's in my prayers.'

'Thank you, sir.'

'Do you want some coffee?' The Farmer's coffee had a reputation throughout the station, but Rebus accepted a mug gladly. 'How is she anyway?'

'Still unconscious.'

'No sign of the car?'

'Not the last I heard.'

'Who's handling it?'

'Bill Pryde started the ball rolling last night. I don't know who's taken it from him.'

'I'll find out.' The Farmer made an internal call, Rebus watching him over the rim of his mug. The Farmer was a big man, imposing behind a desk. His cheeks were a mass of tiny red veins and his thin hair lay across the dome of his head like the lines of a well-furrowed field. There were photos on his desk: grandchildren. The photos had been taken in a garden. There was a swing in the background. One of the children was holding a teddy bear. Rebus felt his throat start to ache, tried to choke it back.

The Farmer put down the receiver. 'Bill's still on it,' he said. 'Felt if he worked straight through we might get a quicker result.'

'That's good of him.'

'Look, we'll let you know the minute we get something, but meantime you'll probably want to go home …'

'No, sir.'

'Or to the hospital.'

Rebus nodded slowly. Yes, the hospital. But not right this minute. He had to talk to Bill Pryde first.

'And meantime, I'll reassign your cases.' The Farmer started writing. 'There's this War Crimes thing, and your liaison on Telford. Are you working on anything else?'

'Sir, I'd prefer it if you … I mean, I want to keep working.'

The Farmer looked at him, then leaned back in his chair, pen balanced between his fingers.

'Why?'

Rebus shrugged. 'I want to keep busy.' Yes, there was that. And he didn't want anyone else taking his work. It was *his*. He owned it; it owned him.

'Look, John, you're going to want some time off, right?'

'I can handle things, sir.' His gaze met the Farmer's. 'Please.'

Across the hall in the CID room he nodded as everyone came up to say how sorry they were. One person stayed at their desk – Bill Pryde knew Rebus was coming to see him.

'Morning, Bill.'

Pryde nodded. They'd met in the wee small hours at the Infirmary. Ned Farlowe had been napping in a chair, so they'd stepped into the corridor to talk. Pryde looked tireder now. He had loosened the top button of his dark green shirt. His brown suit looked lived-in.

'Thanks for sticking with it,' Rebus said, drawing over a chair. Thinking: *I'd rather have had someone else, someone sharper* …

'No problem.'

'Any news?'

'A couple of good eyewitnesses. They were waiting to cross at the lights.'

'What's their story?'

Pryde considered his reply. He knew he was dealing with a father as well as a cop. 'She was crossing the road. Looked like she was heading down Minto Street, maybe making for the bus stop.'

Rebus shook his head. 'She was walking, Bill. Going to a friend's in Gilmour Road.'

She'd said as much over the pizza, apologising that she couldn't stay longer. Just one more coffee at the end of the meal … one more coffee and she wouldn't have been there at that moment. Or if she'd accepted his offer of a lift … When you thought about life, you thought of it as chunks of time, but really all it was was a series of connected moments, any one of which could change you completely.

'The car was heading south out of town,' Pryde went on. 'Looks like he ran a red light. Motorist sitting behind him seemed to think so.'

'Reckon he was drunk?'

Pryde nodded. 'Way he was driving. I mean, could be he just lost control, but in that case why didn't he stop?'

'Description?'

Pryde shook his head. 'We've got a dark car, a bit sporty. Nobody caught the licence plate.'

'It's a busy enough street, must've been other cars around.'

'A couple of people have called in.' Pryde flicked through his notes. 'Nothing helpful, but I'm going to interview them, see if I can jog a memory or two.'

'Could the car have been nicked? Maybe that's why he was in a hurry.'

'I can check.'

'I'll help you.'

Pryde considered this. 'You sure?'

'Try and stop me, Bill.'

'No skid marks,' Pryde said, 'no sign that he tried braking, either before or after.'

They were standing at the junction of Minto Street and Newington Road. The cross-streets were Salisbury Place and Salisbury Road. Cars, vans and buses queued at the traffic lights as pedestrians crossed the road.

It could have been any one of you, Rebus thought. Any one of them could have taken Sammy's place …

'She was about here,' Pryde went on, pointing to a spot where, just past the lights, a bus lane started. The carriageway was wide, a four-lane road. She hadn't crossed at the lights. She'd been lazy, carrying on down Minto Street a few strides, then crossing in a diagonal. When she'd been a child, they'd taught her about crossing the road. Green Cross Code, all of that. Drummed it into her. Rebus looked around. At the top of Minto Street were some private houses and Bed & Breakfasts. On one corner stood a bank, on another a branch of Remnant Kings, with a takeaway next door.

'The takeaway would have been open,' Rebus said, pointing. On the third corner stood a Spar. 'That place, too. Where did you say she was?'

'The bus lane.' She'd crossed three lanes, been only a yard or two from safety. 'Witnesses say she was nearly at the kerb when he hit her. I think he was drunk, lost it for a second.' Pryde nodded towards the bank. There were two phone boxes in front of it. 'Witness called from there.' The wall behind the phone boxes had a poster glued to it. Grinning maniac behind a steering-wheel, and some writing: 'So many pedestrians, so little time'. A computer game …

'It would have been so easy to avoid her,' Rebus said quietly.

'Sure you're okay? There's a café up the road.'

'I'm fine, Bill.' He looked around, took a deep breath. 'Looks like offices behind the Spar, doubtful anyone would have been there. But there are flats above Remnant Kings and the bank.'

'Want to talk to them?'

'And the Spar and the kebab shop. You take the B&Bs and the houses, meet back here in half an hour.'

Rebus talked to everyone he could find. In the Spar, there was a new shift on, but he got home phone numbers from the manager and called up the workers from the previous night. They hadn't seen or heard anything. First they'd known had been the flashing lights of the ambulance. The kebab shop was closed, but when Rebus banged on the door a woman came through from the back, wiping her hands on a tea-towel. He pressed his warrant card to the glass door, and she let him in. The shop had been busy last night. She didn't see the accident – she called it that, 'the accident'. And that's what it was: the word really hadn't sunk in until she said it. Elvis Costello: 'Accidents Will Happen'. Was the next line really 'It's only hit and run'?

'No,' the woman said, 'the first thing that caught my attention was the crowd. I mean, only three or four people, but I could see they were standing around something. And then the ambulance came. Will she be all right?'

The look in her eyes was one Rebus had encountered before. It almost wanted the victim dead, because then there was a story to be told.

'She's in hospital,' he said, unable to look at the woman any longer.

'Yes, but the paper said she's in a coma.'

'What paper?'

She brought him the first edition of the day's *Evening News*. There was a paragraph on one of the inside pages – 'Hit and Run Coma Victim'.

It wasn't a coma. She was unconscious, that was all. But Rebus was thankful for the story. Maybe someone would read it and come forward. Maybe guilt would begin to press down on the driver. Maybe there'd been a passenger ... It was hard to keep secrets, usually you told *some*one.

He tried Remnant Kings, but of course they had been closed last night, so he climbed to the flats above. There was no one home at the first flat. He wrote a brief message on the back of a business card and pushed it through the letterbox, then jotted down the surname on the door. If they didn't call him, he'd call them. A young man answered the second door. He was just out of his teens and pushed a thick lock of black hair away from his eyes. He wore Buddy Holly glasses and had acne scars around his mouth. Rebus introduced himself. The hand went to the hair again, a backward glance into the flat.

'Do you live here?' Rebus asked.

'Mm, yeah. Like, I'm not the owner. We rent it.'

There were no names on the door. 'Anyone else in at the moment?'

'Nope.'

'Are you all students?'

The young man nodded. Rebus asked his name.

'Rob. Robert Renton. What's this about?'

'There was an accident last night, Rob. A hit and run.' So many times he'd been in this situation, passing on the bland news of another changed life. It was a whole hour since he'd telephoned the hospital. In the end, they'd taken his mobile number, said it might be easier if they phoned him whenever there was news. They meant easier for them, not him.

'Oh, yes,' Renton was saying, 'I saw it.'

Rebus blinked. 'You saw it?'

Renton was nodding, hair bobbing in front of his eyes. 'From the window. I was up changing a CD, and –'

'Is it okay if I come in for a minute? I want to see what kind of view you had.'

Renton puffed out his cheeks, exhaled. 'Well, I suppose ...'

And Rebus was in.

The living-room was fairly tidy. Renton went ahead of him, crossed to where a hi-fi rack sat between two windows. 'I was putting on a new CD, and I looked out of the window. You can see the bus stop, and I wondered if I might catch Jane coming off a bus.' He paused. 'Jane's Eric's girlfriend.'

The words washed over Rebus. He was looking down on the street, where Sammy had been walking. 'Tell me what you saw.'

'This girl was crossing the road. She was nice-looking ... I thought so anyway. Then this car came through the lights, swerved and sent her flying.'

Rebus closed his eyes for a second.

'She must have gone ten feet in the air, hit that hedge, bounced back on to the pavement. She didn't move after that.'

Rebus opened his eyes. He was at the window, Renton standing just behind his left shoulder. Down on the street, people were crossing the road, walking over the spot where Sammy had been hit, the spot where she'd landed. Flicking ash on to the pavement where she'd lain.

'I don't suppose you saw the driver?'

'Not from this angle.'

'Any passengers?'

'Couldn't tell.'

He wears glasses, Rebus thought. How reliable is he?

'When you saw it happen, you didn't go down?'

'I'm not a medical student or anything.' He nodded towards an easel in the corner, and Rebus noticed a shelf of

151

paints and brushes. 'Someone ran to the phone box, so I knew help was coming.'

Rebus nodded. 'Anyone else see it?'

'They were in the kitchen.' Renton paused. 'I know what you're thinking.' Rebus doubted it. 'You're thinking I wear specs, so maybe I didn't see it right. But he definitely swerved. You know ... deliberately. I mean, like he was aiming for her.' He nodded to himself.

'*Aiming* for her?'

Renton made a movement with his hand, imitating a car gliding off one course and on to another. 'He steered straight for her.'

'The car didn't lose control?'

'That would have been jerkier, wouldn't it?'

'What colour was the car?'

'Dark green.'

'And the make?'

Renton shrugged. 'I'm hopeless with cars. Tell you what though ...'

'What?'

Renton took off his glasses, started polishing them. 'Why don't I try sketching it for you?'

He moved the easel over to the window and got to work. Rebus went into the hall and called the hospital. The person he got through to didn't sound too surprised.

'No change, I'm afraid. She's got a couple of visitors with her.'

Mickey and Rhona. Rebus terminated the call, made another to Pryde's mobile.

'I'm in one of the flats over Remnant Kings. I've got an eyewitness.'

'Yes?'

'He saw the whole thing. And he's an art student.'

'Yes?'

'Come on, Bill. Do you want me to draw it for you?'
There was silence for a moment, then Pryde said 'Ah'.

13

Rebus held the mobile to his ear as he walked through the hospital.

'Joe Herdman's put together a list,' Bill Pryde was saying. 'Rover 600 series, the newer Ford Mondeos, Toyota Celica, plus a couple of Nissans. Rank outsider is the BMW 5-series.'

'It narrows things down a bit, I suppose.'

'Joe says the Rover, Mondeo and Celica are favourites. He's given me a few more details – chrome around the number-plates, stuff like that. I'm going to call our artist friend, see if anything clicks.'

A nurse was glaring at Rebus as he walked towards her.

'Let me know what he says. Talk to you later, Bill.' Rebus slipped the phone back into his pocket.

'You're not supposed to use those things in here,' the nurse snapped.

'Look, I'm in a bit of a hurry …'

'They can interfere with the machines.'

Rebus pulled up, colour leaving his face. 'I forgot,' he said. He put a shaking hand to his forehead.

'Are you all right?'

'Fine, fine. Look, I won't do it again, okay?' He started to move off. 'You can rely on that.'

Rebus took a photocopy of Renton's drawing from his pocket. Joe Herdman was a desk sergeant who knew everything about cars. He'd been useful before, turning a vague description into something more concrete. Rebus looked at the drawing as he walked. All the details were there: buildings in the background, the hedge, the onlookers. And Sammy, caught at the point of impact. She'd half-turned, was stretching out her hands as if she could push the car to a stop. But Renton had drawn fine lines issuing from the back of the car, representing the air being pushed, representing speed. Where there should have been a face, he had left a blank oval. The back half of the car was very clearly defined, the front a blur of disappearing perspective. Renton said he'd left out anything he couldn't be sure of. He promised he hadn't let his imagination fill in the blanks.

It was the face, or the lack of it … it disturbed Rebus more than anything else in the picture. He drew himself into the scene, wondered what he'd have done. Would he have concentrated on the car, caught its licence plate? Or would his attention have been focused on Sammy? Which would have prevailed: cop instincts or fatherhood? Someone at the station had said, 'Don't worry, we'll get him.' Not, 'Don't worry, she'll be all right.' Which brought it all down to two things: him – meaning the driver – and retribution, rather than her – the victim – and recovery.

'I'd just have been another witness,' Rebus said quietly. Then he folded the drawing and put it away.

Sammy had a room to herself, all tubes and machinery, the way he'd seen it in films and on TV. Only here the room was dingier, paint flaking from the walls and around the window-frames. The chairs had metal legs and rubber feet and moulded plastic seats. A woman rose as he came in. They embraced. He kissed the side of her forehead.

Aiming for her. Didn't anyone say that?

'Hello, Rhona.'

'Hello, John.'

She looked tired, of course, but her hair was stylishly cut and dyed the colour of a dull golden harvest. Her clothes were smart and she wore jewellery. He studied her eyes. Their colour was wrong. Coloured contacts. Not even her eyes were going to betray her past.

'Christ, Rhona, I'm sorry.'

He was whispering, not wanting to disturb Sammy. Which was ludicrous, because right now all he wanted in the world was for her to wake up.

'How is she?' he asked.

'Much the same.'

Mickey stood up. There were three chairs arranged in a sort of semi-circle. Mickey and Rhona had been sitting with an empty chair between them. As Rhona broke from Rebus's embrace, his brother took her place.

'This is so fucking awful,' Mickey said, his voice low. He looked the same as ever: a party animal who'd stopped getting the invites.

Niceties dispensed with, Rebus went to Sammy's bedside. Her face was still bruised, and now he could place the probable cause of each abrasion: hedge, wall, pavement. One leg was broken, both arms heavily bandaged. A teddy bear, missing one ear, lay by her head. Rebus smiled.

'You brought Pa Broon.'

'Yes.'

'Do they know yet if there's any ... ?' His eyes were on Sammy as he spoke.

'What?' Rhona wanted him to spell it out. No hiding place.

'Brain damage,' he said.

'Nobody's told us anything,' she said, sounding snubbed.

Aiming for her. Didn't anyone say that? No, none of the other onlookers had even hinted as much, but then they hadn't had Renton's grandstand view.

'Has nobody been in?'

'Not since I got here.'

'And I was here before Rhona,' Mickey added. 'Haven't seen a soul.'

It was enough. Rebus strode from the room. A doctor and two nurses were standing chatting at the end of the corridor. One of the nurses was leaning against a wall.

'What's going on?' Rebus exploded. 'Nobody's been near my daughter all morning!'

The doctor was young, male. Blond hair cut short with a parting.

'We're doing everything we can.'

'What does that mean?'

'I can appreciate that you're –'

'Fuck you, pal. Why hasn't the big man been to look at her? Why's she just lying there like a –' Rebus choked back the words.

'Your daughter was seen by two specialists this morning,' the doctor said quietly. 'We're waiting for some test results to determine whether to operate again. There's some brain swelling. The tests take a little time to process, there's nothing we can do about it.'

Rebus felt cheated: still angry, but nothing to feel angry *about*, not here. He nodded, turned away.

Back in the room, he explained the situation to Rhona. A suitcase and large holdall were sitting behind one of the machines.

'Listen,' he told her, 'it'd make sense if you stayed at the flat. It's only ten minutes away, and I could let you have the car.'

She was shaking her head. 'We're booked into the Sheraton.'

'The flat's nearer, and I tend not to charge ...' *We?* Rebus looked at Mickey, whose eyes were on the bed. Then the door opened and a man came in. Short, thickly built, breathing hard. He was rubbing his hands to let everyone know he'd been to the toilet. Loose folds of flesh furrowed his brow and bulged from his shirt collar. His hair was thick and black, like an oil-slick. He stopped when he saw Rebus.

'John,' Rhona said, 'this is a friend of mine, Jackie.'

'Jackie Platt,' the man said, reaching out a plump hand. 'When Jackie heard, he insisted on driving me up.'

Platt shrugged, his head almost disappearing into his shoulders. 'Couldn't have her training it up on her ownio.'

'Hell of a drive,' Mickey said, his tone hinting at repetition.

'Could have done without the roadworks,' Jackie Platt agreed. Rebus's eyes caught Rhona's; she looked away quickly, dodging reproach.

To Rebus, this bulk didn't belong. It was as if a character had wandered on to the wrong set. Platt hadn't been in the script.

'She looks so peaceful, don't she?' the Londoner was saying, making for the bed. He touched her arm, Sammy's bandaged arm, grazing it with the back of his hand. Rebus's fingernails dug into his palms.

Then Platt yawned. 'You know, Rhona, it might not be good manners, but I think I'm about to crash. See you back at the hotel?' She nodded, relieved. Platt picked up the suitcase. As he passed her, his hand went into his trouser pocket, came out with a fold of banknotes.

'Get a cab back, all right?'

'All right, Jackie. See you later.'

'Cheers, pet.' And he squeezed her hand. 'Take care, Mickey. All the best, John.' A huge, face-creasing wink, then he was gone. They waited in silence for a few seconds. Rhona held up her free hand, the one without the wad of notes.

'Not a word, okay?'

'Furthest thing from my mind,' Rebus said, sitting down. ' "Think I'm about to crash". Tactful or what?'

'Come on, Johnny,' Mickey said. Johnny: only Mickey could do that, using the name so that the years fell from both of them. Rebus looked at his brother and smiled. Mickey was a therapist by profession; he knew the things to say.

'Why the cases?' Rebus asked Rhona.

'What?'

'You're going to a hotel, why not leave them in his car?'

'I thought about staying here. They said I could if I wanted to. Only then I saw her ... and I changed my mind.' Tears started down her face, smudging already-smudged mascara. Mickey had a handkerchief ready.

'John, what if she ... ? Oh, Jesus Christ, why did this have to happen?' She was wailing now. Rebus went over to her chair, crouched in front of it, his hands resting on hers. 'She's all we've got, John. She's all we ever had.'

'She's still here, Rhona. She's right here.'

'But why her? Why Samantha?'

'I'll ask him when I find him, Rhona.' He kissed her hair, his eyes on Mickey. 'And believe me, I'm going to find him.'

Later, when Ned Farlowe visited, Rebus took him outside. There was drizzle falling, but the air felt good.

'One of the eye-witnesses,' Rebus said, 'thinks it was deliberate.'

'I don't understand.'

'He thinks the driver meant to hit Sammy.'

'I still don't get it.'

'Look, there are two scenarios. One, he was intent on hitting a pedestrian, and anyone would have done. Two, Sammy was his target. He'd been following her, saw his chance when she crossed the road, only the lights were against him so he had to jump them. Then she was so close to the kerb he had to switch lanes.'

'But why?'

Rebus stared at him. 'This is Sammy's dad and her lover, right? For the purposes of what follows, I want you to stop being a reporter.'

Farlowe stared back, nodded slowly.

'I've had a few run-ins with Tommy Telford,' Rebus said. He was seeing teddy bears: Pa Broon, and the one Telford kept in his car. 'This might have been a message for me.' Telford or Tarawicz: flip a coin. 'Or for you, if you've been asking questions about Telford.'

'You think my book ...'

'I'm keeping an open mind. I've been working the Lintz case ... and so have you.'

'Someone warning us off Lintz?'

Rebus thought of Abernethy, shrugged. 'Then there's Sammy's job, working with ex-cons. Maybe one of them had a grudge.'

'Jesus.'

'She hadn't mentioned anyone following her? Nobody odd in the area?' Same question he'd put to the Drinics, only different victim ...

Farlowe shook his head. 'Look,' he said, 'until five minutes ago I thought this was an accident. Now you're saying it was attempted murder. Are you *sure*?'

'I'm trusting a witness.' But he knew what Bill Pryde thought: a drunk driver, a crazy man. And a grandstand spectator who wore glasses and had read it wrong. He took out the drawing again.

'What's that?'

Rebus handed it over. 'This is what someone saw last night.'

'What kind of car is it?'

'Rover 600, Ford Mondeo, something like that. Dark green. Ring any bells?'

Ned Farlowe shook his head, then looked at Rebus. 'Let me help. I can ask around.'

'One kid in a coma's enough.'

The rest of the office had packed up and gone home. Now there were only Rebus and Sammy's boss, a woman called Mae Crumley. The light from half a dozen desk-lamps illuminated the haphazard office, which was on the top floor of an old four-storey building off Palmerston Place. Rebus knew Palmerston Place: there was a church there where the AA held meetings. He'd been to a couple. He could still taste whisky at the back of his throat. Not that he'd had any so far today, not in daylight hours. But then he hadn't phoned Jack Morton either.

The address might have been posher than Rebus was expecting, but the accommodation was cramped. The office was in the eaves of the building, so that you couldn't stand up in half the available space, which hadn't stopped desks being sited in the most awkward corners.

'Which is hers?' Rebus asked. Mae Crumley pointed to the desk next to her own. There was a computer there somewhere, but only its screen was showing. Loose sheets of paper, books and pamphlets and reports, the whole lot spilled on to the chair and from there down on to the floor.

'She works too hard,' Crumley said. 'We all do.'

Rebus sipped the coffee she'd made him. Cafe Hag.

'When Sammy came here,' she went on, 'the first thing she said was that her father was CID. She never tried to hide it.'

'And you'd no qualms about taking her on?'

'None at all.' Crumley folded her arms. They were big arms; she was a big woman. Her hair was a fiery red, long and frizzy and tied back with a black ribbon. She wore an oatmeal linen shirt with a denim jacket over the top of it. Her eyebrows had been plucked into thin arches over pale grey eyes. Her desk was relatively tidy, but only, as she'd explained to Rebus, because she tended to stay later than anyone else.

'What about her clients?' Rebus asked. 'Could any of them have held a grudge?'

'Against her or against you?'

'Against me *through* her.'

Crumley considered this. 'To the extent that they'd run her over just to make a point? I very much doubt it.'

'I'd be interested to see her client list.'

She shook her head. 'Look … you shouldn't be doing this. It's too personal, you know that. I mean, who am I talking to here: Sammy's father, or a copper?'

'You think I've a score to settle?'

'Well haven't you?'

Rebus put down the coffee mug. 'Maybe.'

'And that's why you shouldn't be doing this.' She sighed. 'Number one on my wish list: Sammy back on her feet and back here. But what about if meantime I do a bit of poking around? I stand a better chance of getting them to talk than you do.'

Rebus nodded. 'I'd appreciate that.' He got to his feet. 'Thanks for the coffee.'

Outside, he checked the list the Juice Church had given him. He kept it in his pocket, didn't refer to it often. There was a meeting at Palmerston Place in about an hour and a half. No good. He knew he'd spend the time beforehand in a pub. Jack Morton had introduced him to Al-Anon, but Rebus hadn't really taken to it, though the stories had affected him.

'See,' one man had told the group, 'I had problems at work, problems with my wife, my kids. I had money problems and health problems and everything else. Practically the only problem I didn't have was with the drink. And that's because I was a drunk.'

Rebus lit himself a cigarette and drove home.

He sat in his chair and thought about Rhona. They'd shared so much over so many years ... and then it had all stopped. He'd chosen his job over his marriage, and that could not be forgiven. Last time he'd seen her had been in London, wearing her new life like armour. Nobody had warned him about Jackie Platt. His phone rang, and he snatched it from the floor.

'Rebus.'

'It's Bill.' Pryde sounded halfway to excited, which was as far as he ever ventured.

'What have you got?'

'Dark green Rover 600 – I think the owner called it "Sherwood Green" – stolen yesterday evening about an hour before the collision.'

'Where from?'

'Metered parking on George Street.'

'What do you reckon?'

'My advice is, keep an open mind. Having said that, at least now we've got a licence plate. Owner reported it at six-forty last night. It hasn't turned up anywhere, so I've upped the alert status.'

'Give me the reg.' Pryde read out the letters and numbers. Rebus thanked him and put down the phone. He was thinking of Danny Simpson, dumped outside Fascination Street around the time Sammy was being hit. Coincidence? Or a double message, Telford and Rebus. Which put Big Ger Cafferty in the frame. He called the hospital, was told there was no change. Farlowe was in visiting. The nurse said he had his laptop with him.

Rebus recalled Sammy growing up – a series of isolated images. He hadn't been there for her. He saw her in a series of fast jerky impressions, as if the film had been spliced. He tried not to think about the hell she had gone through at the hands of Gordon Reeve ...

He saw good people doing bad things and bad people doing good, and he tried dividing the two into groups. He saw Candice and Tommy Telford and Mr Pink Eyes. And encompassing it all, he saw Edinburgh. He saw the mass of the people just getting on with their lives, and he saluted them. They *knew* things and felt things, things he'd never feel. He used to think he knew things. As a kid, he'd known *everything*. Now he knew differently. The only thing you could be sure of was the inside of your head, and even that could deceive you. I don't even know myself, he thought. So how could he ever hope to know Sammy? And with each year, he understood less.

He thought of the Oxford Bar. Even on the wagon, he'd stayed a regular, drinking cola and mugs of coffee. A pub like the Ox was about so much more than just the hooch. It was therapy and refuge, entertainment and art. He checked his watch, thinking he could head down there now. Just a couple of whiskies and a beer, something to make him feel good about himself until the morning.

The phone rang again. He picked it up.

'Evening, John.'

Rebus smiled, leaned back in his chair. 'Jack, you must be a bloody mind reader ...'

14

Mid-morning, Rebus walked through the cemetery. He'd been to the hospital to check on Sammy – no change. Now, he felt he had time to kill ...

'A bit cooler today, Inspector.' Joseph Lintz rose from his knees and pushed his glasses back up to the bridge of his nose. There were damp patches on his trousers from where he'd been kneeling. He dropped his trowel on to a white polythene bag. Beside the bag stood pots of small green plants.

'Won't the frost get them?' Rebus asked. Lintz shrugged.

'It gets all of us, but we're allowed to bloom for a while.'

Rebus turned away. Today, he wasn't in the mood for games. Warriston Cemetery was vast. In the past, it had been a history lesson to Rebus – headstones telling the story of nineteenth-century Edinburgh – but now he found it a jarring reminder of mortality. They were the only living souls in the place. Lintz had pulled out a handkerchief.

'More questions?' he asked.

'Not exactly.'

'What then?'

'Truth is, Mr Lintz, I've got other things on my mind.'

The old man looked at him. 'Maybe all this archaeology is beginning to bore you, Inspector?'

'I still don't get it, planting things before the first frost?'

'Well, I can't plant very much afterwards, can I? And at my age ... any day now I could be lying in the ground. I like to think there might be a few flowers surviving above me.' He'd lived in Scotand the best part of half a century, but there was still something lurking beneath the local accent, peculiarities of phrasing and tone that would be with Joseph Lintz until he died, reminders of his far less recent history.

'So,' he said now, 'no questions today?' Rebus shook his head. 'You're right, Inspector, you do seem preoccupied. Is it something I can help with?'

'In what way?'

'I don't really know. But you've come here, questions or no. I take it there's a reason?'

A dog was bounding through the long grass, crunching on the fallen leaves, nose brushing the ground. It was a yellow labrador, short-haired and overweight. Lintz turned towards it and almost growled. Dogs were the enemy.

'I was just wondering,' Rebus was saying, 'what you're capable of.' Lintz looked puzzled. The dog began to paw at the ground. Lintz reached down, picked up a stone, and hurled it. It didn't reach the dog. The labrador's owner was rounding the corner. He was young, crop-haired and skinny.

'That thing should be kept on its lead!' Lintz roared.

'*Jawohl*!' the owner snapped back, clicking his heels. He was laughing as he passed them.

'I am a famous man now,' Lintz reflected, back to his old self after the outburst. 'Thanks to the newspapers.' He looked up at the sky, blinked. 'People send me hate by the Royal Mail. A car was parked outside my home the other night ... they put a brick through the windscreen. It wasn't my car, but they didn't know that. Now my neighbours keep clear of that spot, just in case.'

He spoke like the old man he was, a little tired, a little defeated.

'This is the worst year of my life.' He stared down at the border he'd been tending. The earth, newly turned, looked dark and rich, like crumbs of chocolate cake. A few worms and wood lice had been disturbed and were still looking for their old homes. 'And it's going to get worse, isn't it?'

Rebus shrugged. His feet were cold, the damp seeping in through his shoes. He was standing on the rough roadway, Lintz six inches above him on the grass. And still Lintz didn't reach his height. A little old man: that's what he was. And Rebus could study him, talk with him, go to his home and see what few photographs remained – according to Lintz – from the old days.

'What did you mean back there?' he said. 'What was it you said? Something about what I was capable of?'

Rebus stared at him. 'It's okay, the dog just showed me.'

'Showed you what?'

'What you're like with the enemy.'

Lintz smiled. 'I don't like dogs, it's true. Don't read too much into it, Inspector. That's the journalists' job.'

'Your life would be easier without dogs, wouldn't it?'

Lintz shrugged. 'Of course.'

'And easier without me, too?'

Lintz frowned. 'If it weren't you, it would be someone else, a boor like your Inspector Abernethy.'

'What do you think he was telling you?'

Lintz blinked. 'I'm not sure. Someone else came to see me. A man called Levy. I refused to talk to him – one privilege still open to me.'

Rebus shuffled his feet, trying to get some warmth into them. 'I have a daughter, did I ever tell you that?'

Lintz looked baffled. 'You might have mentioned it.'

'You know I have a daughter?'

'Yes … I mean, I think I knew before today.'

'Well, Mr Lintz, the night before last, someone tried to kill her, or at least do her some serious damage. She's in hospital, still unconscious. And *that* bothers me.'

'I'm so sorry. How did it … ? I mean, how do you … ?'

'I think maybe someone was trying to send me a message.'

Lintz's eyes widened. 'And you believe *me* capable of such a thing? My God, I thought we had come to understand one another, at least a little.'

Rebus was wondering. He was wondering how easy it would be to put on an act, when you'd spent half a century practising. He was wondering how easy it would be to steel yourself to killing an innocent … or at least ordering their death. All it took was an order. A few words to someone else who would carry out your bidding. Maybe Lintz had it in him. Maybe it wouldn't be any more difficult than it had been for Josef Linzstek.

'Something you should know,' Rebus said. 'Threats don't scare me off. Quite the opposite.'

'It's good that you are so strong.' Rebus looked for meaning behind the words. 'I'm on my way home. Can I offer you some tea?'

Rebus drove, and then sat in the drawing-room while Lintz busied himself in the kitchen. Started flicking through a pile of books on a desk.

'Ancient History, Inspector,' Lintz said, bringing in the tray – he always refused offers of help. 'Another hobby of mine. I'm fascinated by that intersection at which history and fiction meet.' The books were all about Babylonia. 'Babylon is an historical fact, you see, but what about the Tower of Babel?'

'A song by Elton John?' Rebus offered.

'Always making jokes.' Lintz looked up. 'What is it you're afraid of?'

Rebus took one of the cups. 'I've heard of the Gardens of Babylon,' he admitted, putting the book down. 'What other hobbies do you have?'

'Astrology, hauntings, the unknown.'

'Have you ever been haunted?'

Lintz seemed amused. 'No.'

'Would you like to be?'

'By seven hundred French villagers? No, Inspector, I wouldn't like that at all. It was astrology that first brought me to the Chaldeans. They came from Babylonia. Have you ever heard of Babylonian numbers ...?'

Lintz had a way of turning conversations in directions *he* wanted them to take. Rebus wasn't going to be deflected this time. He waited till Lintz had the cup to his lips.

'Did you try to kill my daughter?'

Lintz paused, then sipped, swallowed.

'No, Inspector,' he said quietly.

Which left Telford, Tarawicz and Cafferty. Rebus thought of Telford, surrounded by his Family but wanting to play with the big boys. How different was a gang war from any other kind? You had soldiers, and orders given to them. They had to prove themselves, or lose face, show themselves cowards. Shoot a civilian, run down a pedestrian. Rebus realised that he didn't want the driver as such – he wanted the person who'd *driven* them to do it. Lintz's defence of Linzstek was that the young lieutenant had been under orders, that war itself was the real culprit, as though humans had no say in the matter ...

'Inspector,' the old man was saying, 'do *you* think I'm Linzstek?'

Rebus nodded. 'I know you are.'

A wry smile. 'Then arrest me.'

'Here comes the blue-nose,' Father Conor Leary said. 'Out to steal Ireland's God-given Guinness.' He paused, eyes narrowing. 'Or are you still on that abstention kick?'

'I'm trying,' Rebus said.

'Well, I won't tempt you then.' Leary smiled. 'But you know me, John. I'm not one to judge, but a wee drop never harmed a soul.'

'Problem is, you put lots of wee drops together and you get a bloody big fall.'

Father Leary laughed. 'But aren't we all the fallen? Come away in.'

Father Leary was priest of Our Lady of Perpetual Help. Years back, someone had defaced the board outside to turn 'Help' into 'Hell'. The board had been corrected many times, but Rebus always thought of the place as 'Perpetual Hell': it was what the followers of Knox and Calvin would have believed. Father Leary took him through to the kitchen.

'Here, man, sit yourself down. I haven't seen you in so long, I thought you'd renounced me.' He went to the fridge and lifted out a can of Guinness.

'Are you operating a pharmacy on the side?' Rebus asked. Father Leary looked at him. Rebus nodded towards the fridge. 'The shelves of medicine.'

Father Leary rolled his eyes. 'At my age, you go to the doctor with angina and they dose you for every conceivable ailment. They think it makes old folk feel better.' He brought a glass to the table, placed it next to his can. Rebus felt a hand fall on his shoulder.

'I'm hellish sorry about Sammy.'

'How did you hear?'

'Her name was in one of the rags this morning.' Father Leary sat down. 'Hit and run, they said.'

'Hit and run,' Rebus echoed.

Father Leary shook his head wearily, one hand rubbing slowly over his chest. He was probably in his late-sixties, though he'd never said. Well-built, with a thatch of silver hair. Tufts of grey sprouted from his ears, nose and dog-collar. His hand seemed to smother the can of Guinness. But when he poured, he poured gently, almost with reverence.

'It's a terrible thing,' he said quietly. 'Coma, is it?'

'Not until the doctors say so.' Rebus cleared his throat. 'It's only been a day and a half.'

'You know what we believers say,' Father Leary went on. 'When something like this happens, it's a test for all of us. It's a way of making us stronger.' The head on his Guinness was perfect. He took a swallow, licked his lips thoughtfully. 'That's what we *say*; it may not be what we think.' He looked into his drink.

'It didn't make me strong. I went back to the whisky.'

'I can understand that.'

'Until a friend reminded me it was the lazy way out, the cowardly way.'

'And who's to say he's not right?'

' "Faint-Heart and the Sermon",' Rebus said with a smile.

'What's that?'

'A song. But maybe it's us, too.'

'Get away, we're just two old boys having a natter. So how are you holding up, John?'

'I don't know.' He paused. 'I don't think it was an accident. And the man I think is behind it ... Sammy isn't the first woman he's tried to destroy.' Rebus looked into the priest's eyes. 'I want to kill him.'

'But so far you haven't?'

'I haven't even talked to him.'

'Because you're worried what you might do?'

'Or not do.' Rebus's mobile sounded. He gave a look of apology and switched it on.

'John, it's Bill.'

'Yes, Bill?'

'Green Rover 600.'

'Yes?'

'We've got it.'

The car had been parked illegally on the street outside

Piershill Cemetery. There was a parking ticket on its windscreen, dated the previous afternoon. If anyone had checked, they'd have found the driver's-side door unlocked. Maybe someone had: the car was empty, no coins, no map-books or cassettes. The fascia had been removed from the radio/cassette. There were no keys in the ignition. A car transporter had arrived, and the Rover was being winched aboard.

'I called in a favour at Howdenhall,' Bill Pryde was saying, 'they've promised to fingerprint it today.'

Rebus was studying the front passenger side. No dents, nothing to suggest this car had been used as a battering-ram against his daughter.

'I think maybe we need your permission, John.'

'What for?'

'Someone should go to the Infirmary and print Sammy.'

Rebus stared at the front of the car, then got out the drawing. Yes, she'd put out a hand. Her prints might be there, invisible to him.

'Sure,' he said. 'No problem. You think this is it?'

'I'll tell you once we print it.'

'You steal a car,' Rebus said, 'then you hit someone with it, and leave it a couple of miles away.' He looked around. 'Ever been on this street before?' Pryde shook his head. 'Me neither.'

'Someone local?'

'I'm wondering why they stole it in the first place.'

'Stick false plates on and sell it,' Pryde suggested. 'Spot of joy-riding maybe.'

'Joy-riders don't leave cars looking like this.'

'No, but they'd had a fright. They'd just knocked someone down.'

'And they drove all the way over here before deciding to dump it?'

'Maybe it was stolen for a job, turn over a petrol station.

Then they hit Sammy and decide to jump ship. Maybe the job was this side of town.'

'Or Sammy *was* the job.'

Pryde put a hand on his shoulder. 'Let's see what the boffins turn up, eh?'

Rebus looked at him. 'You don't go for it?'

'Look, it's a feeling you've got, and that's fair enough, but right now all you've got is that student's word for it. There were other witnesses, John, and I asked them all again, and they told me the same thing: it looked like the driver lost control, that's all.'

There was an edge of irritation to Pryde's voice. Rebus knew why: long hours.

'Will Howdenhall let you know tonight?'

'They promised. And I'll phone you straight away, okay?'

'On my mobile,' Rebus said. 'I'm going to be on the move.' He looked around. 'There was something about Piershill Cemetery recently, wasn't there?'

'Kids,' Pryde said, nodding. 'They pushed over a load of gravestones.'

Rebus remembered now. 'Just the Jewish headstones, wasn't it?'

'I think so.'

And there, sprayed on the wall near the gates, the same piece of graffiti: Won't Anyone Help?

It was late evening, and Rebus was driving. Not the M90 into Fife: tonight, he was on the M8, heading west, heading for Glasgow. He'd spent half an hour at the hospital, followed by an hour and a half with Rhona and Jackie Platt, their guest for dinner at the Sheraton. He'd worn a fresh suit and shirt. He hadn't smoked. He'd drunk a bottle of Highland Spring.

They were planning yet more tests on Sammy. The

neurologist had taken them into his office and talked them through the procedures. There would probably be another operation at the end of it. Rebus could barely remember what the man had said. Rhona had asked for the occasional explanation, but these seemed no more lucid than what had gone before.

Dinner had been a subdued affair. Jackie Platt, it turned out, sold second-hand cars.

'See, John, where I really score is the obituaries. Check the local paper, hare round there and see if they've left a car behind. Quick cash offer.'

'Sammy doesn't drive, sorry,' Rebus had said, causing Rhona to drop her cutlery on to her plate.

At the end of the meal, she'd seen him out to his car, gripped one of his arms hard.

'Get the bastard, John. I want to look him in the face. Just get the bastard who did this to us.' Her eyes were blazing.

He nodded. Stones: 'Just Wanna See His Face'. Rebus wanted it, too.

The M8, which could be a nightmare at rush-hour, was a quiet drive in the evenings. Rebus knew he was making good time, and that he would soon see the outline of the Easterhouse estate against the sky. When his phone sounded, he didn't hear it at first: blame Wishbone Ash. As *Argus* finished, he picked up.

'Rebus.'

'John, it's Bill.'

'What've you got?'

'Forensics were good as gold. There are prints all over the car, interior and exterior. Several sets.' He paused, and Rebus thought the connection had gone. 'One good palm and finger set on the front of the bonnet ...'

'Sammy's?'

'For definite.'

'So we've got our car.'

'The owner's given us a set so we can eliminate him. When we've done that ...'

'We're still not home and dry, Bill. The car sat unlocked outside that cemetery, we don't know someone didn't clean it out.'

'Owner says the radio/cassette fascia was there when he left it. Also half a dozen tapes, a packet of Paracetamol, receipts for petrol and a road map. So someone cleaned it out, whether it's the bastard we want or just some scavenger.'

'At least we know it's the car.'

'I'll check again with Howdenhall tomorrow, collect any other prints and start trying to match them. Plus I'll ask around Piershill, see if anyone saw someone dumping it.'

'Meantime get some sleep, eh?'

'Try and stop me. What about you?'

'Me?' Two cups of espresso after dinner. And with the knowledge of what lay ahead. 'I'll get my head down soon enough, Bill. Talk to you tomorrow.'

On the outskirts of Glasgow, headed for Barlinnie Prison.

He'd phoned ahead, made sure they were expecting him. It was way outside any visiting hours, but Rebus had made up a story about a murder inquiry. 'Follow-up questions,' was what he'd said.

'At this time of night?'

'Lothian and Borders Police, pal. Motto: Justice Never Sleeps.'

Morris Gerald Cafferty probably didn't sleep much either. Rebus imagined him lying awake at night, hands under his head, staring into the darkness.

Scheming.

Running things through his mind: how to keep his

empire from falling, how best to combat threats like Tommy Telford. Rebus knew that Cafferty employed a lawyer – a middle-aged pinstripe from the New Town – to carry messages back to his gang in Edinburgh. He thought of Charles Groal, Telford's lawyer. Groal was young and sharp, like his paymaster.

'Strawman.'

He was waiting in the Interview Room, arms folded, chair set well away from the table. And of course his opening gambit was his nickname for Rebus.

'A lovely surprise, two visits in a week. Don't tell me you've another message from the Pole?'

Rebus sat down opposite Cafferty. 'Tarawicz isn't Polish.' He glanced towards the guard who stood by the door, lowered his voice. 'Another of Telford's boys got a doing.'

'How clumsy.'

'He was all but scalped. Are you looking for war?'

Cafferty drew his chair in to the table, leaned across towards Rebus. 'I've never backed down from a fight.'

'My daughter got hurt. Funny that, so soon after we'd had our little chat.'

'Hurt how?'

'Hit and run.'

Cafferty was thoughtful. 'I don't pick on civilians.'

Yes, Rebus thought, but she wasn't a civilian, because *he* had lured her on to the battlefield.

'Convince me,' Rebus said.

'Why should I bother?'

'The conversation we had … What you asked me to do.'

'Telford?' A whisper. Cafferty sat back for a moment to consider. When he leaned forward again, his eyes bored into Rebus's. 'There's something you've forgotten. I lost a son, remember. Think I could do that to another father? I'd do a lot of things, Rebus, but not that, never that.'

Rebus held the stare. 'All right,' he said.

'You want me to find who did it?'

Rebus nodded slowly.

'That's your price?'

Rhona's words: *I want to look him in the face.* Rebus shook his head. 'I want them *delivered* to me. I want you to do that, whatever it takes.'

Cafferty placed his hands on his knees, seemed to take his time positioning them just so. 'You know it's probably Telford?'

'Yes. If it's not you.'

'You'll be going after him then?'

'Any way I can.'

Cafferty smiled. 'But your ways aren't my ways.'

'You might get to him first. I want him *alive.*'

'And meantime, you're my man?'

Rebus stared at him. 'I'm your man,' he said.

15

Rebus got a phone call early the next morning from Leith CID, telling him Joseph Lintz was dead. The bad news was, it looked like murder: the body found hanging from a tree in Warriston Cemetery.

By the time Rebus appeared at the scene, they were cordoning it off, the doctor having concluded that most suicides wouldn't have bothered administering a violent blow to their own head before commencing with operations.

The corpse of Joseph Lintz was being zipped into a body bag. Rebus got a look at the face. He'd seen elderly corpses before, and mostly they'd looked wonderfully at peace, their faces shiny and child-like. But Joseph Lintz looked like he'd suffered. He didn't look to be at rest at all.

'You'll have come to thank us, no doubt,' a man said, walking towards Rebus. His shoulders were hunched inside a navy raincoat and he walked with head bowed, hands in pockets. His hair was thick and silver and wiry, his skin an almost jaundiced yellow – the remains of an autumn holiday tan.

'Hiya, Bobby,' Rebus said.

Bobby Hogan was Leith CID.

'To get back to my initial observation, John ...'

'What am I supposed to be thanking you for?'

Hogan nodded towards the body bag. 'Taking Mr Lintz off your hands. 'Don't tell me you were *enjoying* digging into all that?'

'Not exactly.'

'Any idea who might have wanted him dead?'

Rebus puffed out his cheeks. 'Where do you want me to start?'

'I mean, I'm right to rule out the usual, aren't I?' Hogan held up three fingers. 'It wasn't suicide, muggers aren't quite this creative, and it surely wasn't an accident.'

'Someone was making a point, no doubt about it.'

'But what sort of point?'

Scene of Crime officers were busying themselves, filling the *locus* with noise and movement. Rebus gestured for Hogan to walk with him. They were deep in the cemetery, the part Lintz had loved so much. As they walked, the place grew wilder, more overgrown.

'I was here with him yesterday morning,' Rebus said. 'I don't know if he had a routine exactly, but he came here most days.'

'We found a bag of gardening tools.'

'He planted flowers.'

'So if someone knew he'd be coming, they could have been waiting?'

Rebus nodded. 'An assassination.'

Hogan was thoughtful. 'Why hang him?'

'It's what happened at Villefranche. The town elders were strung up in the square.'

'Jesus.' Hogan stopped walking. 'I know you've got other stuff on the go, but can you help out on this, John?'

'Any way I can.'

'A list of possibles would do for a start.'

'How about an old woman living in France, and a Jewish historian who walks with a stick?'

'Is that all you've got?'

'Well, there's always me. Yesterday I as good as accused him of trying to kill my daughter.' Hogan stared at him. 'I don't think he did it.' Rebus paused, thinking of Sammy:

179

he'd called the hospital first thing. She was still unconscious; they still weren't using the word 'coma'. 'One more thing,' he said. 'Special Branch, a guy called Abernethy. He was here talking to Lintz.'

'What's the connection?'

'Abernethy's co-ordinating the various war crimes investigations. He's street-tough, not your typical desk-jockey.'

'A strange choice for the job?' Rebus nodded. 'Which hardly makes him a suspect.'

'I'm doing my best, Bobby. We could check Lintz's house, see if we can turn up any of the hate mail he claimed he'd been getting.'

' "Claimed"?'

Rebus shrugged. 'You were never sure where you were with Lintz. Do you have any idea what happened?'

'From what you've told me, I'd guess he came down here as usual to do his gardening stint – he's certainly dressed for it. Someone was waiting. They smacked him over the head, stuck his neck in a noose, and hauled him up into the tree. The rope was tied around a headstone.'

'Did the hanging kill him?'

'Doctor says yes. Haemorrhages in the eyes. What do you call them?'

'Tardieu spots.'

'That's it. The blow to the head was just to knock him out. Something else – bruising and cuts on the face. Looks like someone kicked him when he was down.'

'Knock him cold, thump him in the face, then string him up.'

'Big-time grudge.'

Rebus looked around. 'Someone with a flair for theatre.'

'And not afraid to take risks. This place might never get exactly crowded, but it's a public space and that tree's in open view. Anyone could have walked past.'

'What time are we talking about?'

'Eight, eight-thirty. I'm guessing Mr Lintz would have wanted to do his digging in daylight.'

'Could have been earlier,' Rebus suggested. 'A pre-arranged meeting.'

'Then why the tools?'

'Because by the time it got light, the meeting would be over.'

Hogan looked doubtful.

'And if it *was* a meeting,' Rebus said, 'there might be some record of it at Lintz's home.'

Hogan looked at him, nodded. 'My car or yours?'

'Better get his keys first.'

They started back up the slope.

'Searching through a dead man's pockets,' Hogan said to himself. 'Why is that never mentioned during recruitment?'

'I was here yesterday,' Rebus said. 'He invited me back for tea.'

'No family?'

'None.'

Hogan looked around the hallway. 'Big place. What happens to the money when it's sold?'

Rebus looked at him. 'We could split it two ways.'

'Or we could just move ourselves in. Basement and ground for me, you can have first and second.'

Hogan smiled, tried one of the doors off the hall. It opened on to an office. 'This could be my bedroom,' he said, going in.

'When I came here before, he always took me upstairs.'

'On you go. We'll take a floor each, then swop.'

Rebus headed up the staircase, running his hand over the varnished banister: not a speck of dust. Cleaning ladies could be invaluable informants.

'If you find a chequebook,' he called down to Hogan, 'look for regular payments to a Mrs Mop.'

Four doors led off the first-floor landing. Two were bedrooms, one a bathroom. The last door led into the huge drawing-room, where Rebus had asked his questions and listened to the stories and philosophy that Lintz had used in place of answers.

'Do you think guilt has a genetic component, Inspector?' he'd asked one time. 'Or are we taught it?'

'Does it matter, so long as it's there?' Rebus had said, and Lintz had nodded and smiled, as if the pupil had given some satisfactory answer.

The room was big, not too much furniture. Huge sash windows – recently cleaned – looked down on to the street. There were framed prints and paintings on the walls. They could have been priceless originals or junk-store stuff – Rebus was no expert. He liked one painting. It showed a ragged white-haired man seated on a rock, surrounded by a barren plain. He had a book open on his lap, but was staring skywards in horror or awe as a shining light appeared there, picking him out. It had a Biblical look, but Rebus couldn't quite place it. He knew the look on the man's face though. He'd seen it before when some suspect's carefully crafted alibi had suddenly come tumbling down.

Over the marble fireplace was a large gilt-framed mirror. Rebus studied himself in it. Behind him he could see the room. He knew he didn't fit here.

One bedroom was for guests, the other was Lintz's. A faint smell of embrocation, half a dozen medicine bottles on the bedside table. Books, too, a pile of them. The bed had been made, a dressing-gown draped across it. Lintz was a creature of habit; he'd been in no special hurry this morning.

The next floor up, Rebus found two further bedrooms and a toilet. There was a slight smell of damp in one room, and the ceiling was discoloured. Rebus didn't suppose Lintz got many visitors; no impetus to redecorate. Out on the landing again, he saw that one of the stair-rails was missing. It had been propped against the wall, awaiting repair. A house this size, things would always be going wrong.

He went back downstairs. Hogan was in the basement. The kitchen had a door on to a back garden – stone patio, lawn covered in rotting leaves, an ivy-covered wall giving privacy.

'Look what I found,' Hogan said, coming back from the utility room. He was holding a length of rope, frayed at one end where it had been cut.

'You think it'll match with the noose? That would mean the killer got it from here.'

'Meaning Lintz knew them.'

'Anything in the office?'

'It's going to take a bit of time. There's an address book, lots of entries, but most of them seem to go back a while.'

'How can you tell?'

'Old STD codes.'

'Computer?'

'Not even a typewriter. He used carbons. Lots of letters to his solicitor.'

'Trying to shut the media up?'

'You get a couple of mentions, too. Anything upstairs?'

'Go take a look. I'll check the office.'

Rebus climbed upstairs and stood in the office doorway, looking around. Then he sat down at the desk and imagined the room was his. What did he do here? He conducted his daily business. There were two filing-cabinets, but to get to them he'd have to stand up from the desk. And he was an old man. Say the cabinets were for dead correspondence. More recent stuff would be closer to hand.

He tried the drawers. Found the address book Hogan had mentioned. A few letters. A small snuff-box, its contents turned solid. Lintz hadn't even allowed himself that small vice. In a bottom drawer were some files. Rebus lifted out the one marked 'General/Household'. It comprised bills and guarantees. A large brown envelope was marked BT. Rebus opened it and took out the phone bills. They went back to the beginning of the year. The most recent bill was at the front. Rebus was disappointed to find that it wasn't itemised. Then he noticed that all the other statements *were*. Lintz had been meticulous, placing names beside calls made, double-checking British Telecom's totals at the foot of each page. The whole year was like that ... right up until recently. Frowning, Rebus realised that the penultimate statement was missing. Had Lintz mislaid it? Rebus couldn't see him mislaying anything. A missing bill would have hinted at chaos in his ordered world. No, it had to be somewhere.

But Rebus was damned if he could find it.

Lintz's correspondence was all business, either to lawyers or else to do with local charities and committees. He'd been resigning from his committees. Rebus wondered if pressure had been applied. Edinburgh could be cruel and cold that way.

'Well?' Hogan said, sticking his head round the door.

'I'm just wondering ...'

'What?'

'Whether to add on a conservatory and knock through from the kitchen.'

'We'd lose some garden space,' Hogan said. He came in, rested against the desk. 'Anything?'

'A missing phone bill, and a sudden change from being itemised.'

'Worth a call,' Hogan admitted. 'I found a chequebook in his bedroom. Stubs show payments of £60 a month to E. Forgan.'

'Where in the bedroom?'

'Marking his place in a book.' Hogan reached into the desk's top drawer, lifted out the address book.

Rebus got up. 'Pretty rich street this. Wonder how many of them do their own dusting.'

Hogan shut the book. 'No listing for an E. Forgan. Think the neighbours will know?'

'Edinburgh neighbours know *everything*. It's just that they most often keep it to themselves.'

16

Joseph Lintz's neighbours: an artist and her husband on one side; a retired advocate and his wife on the other. The artist used a cleaning lady called Ella Forgan. Mrs Forgan lived in East Claremont Street. The artist gave them a telephone number.

Conclusions drawn from the two interviews: shock and horror that Lintz was dead; praise for the quiet, considerate neighbour. A Christmas card every year, and an invitation to drinks one Sunday afternoon each July. Hard to tell when he'd been at home and when he'd been out. He went off on holiday without telling anyone except Mrs Forgan. Visitors to his home had been few – or few had been noticed, which wasn't quite the same thing.

'Men? Women?' Rebus had asked. 'Or a mixture?'

'A mixture, I'd say,' the artist had replied, measuring her words. 'Really, we knew very little about him, to say we've been neighbours these past twenty-odd years ...'

Ah, and that was Edinburgh for you, too, at least in this price bracket. Wealth was a very private thing in the city. It wasn't brash and colourful. It stayed behind its thick stone walls and was at peace.

Rebus and Hogan held a doorstep conference.

'I'll call the cleaning lady, see if I can meet her, preferably here.' Hogan looked back at Lintz's front door.

'I'd love to know where he got the money to buy this place,' Rebus said.

'That could take some excavating.'

Rebus nodded. 'Solicitor would be the place to start. What about the address book? Worth tracking down some of these elusive friends?'

'I suppose so.' Hogan looked dispirited at the prospect.

'I'll follow up on the phone bills,' Rebus said. 'If that'll help.'

Hogan was nodding. 'And remember to get me copies of your files. Are you busy otherwise?'

'Bobby, if time was money, I'd be in hock to every lender in town.'

Mae Crumley reached Rebus on his mobile.

'I thought you'd forgotten me,' he told Sammy's boss.

'Just being methodical, Inspector. I'm sure you'd want no less.' Rebus stopped at traffic lights. 'I've been in to see Sammy. Is there any news?'

'Nothing much. So you've talked to her clients?'

'Yes, and they all seemed genuinely upset and surprised. Sorry to disappoint you.'

'What makes you think I'm disappointed?'

'Sammy has a good rapport with all her clients. None of them would have wanted her hurt.'

'What about the ones who didn't want to be her clients?'

Crumley hesitated. 'There was one man ... When he was told Sammy had a police inspector for a father, he'd have nothing to do with her.'

'What's his name?'

'It couldn't have been him though.'

'Why not?'

'Because he killed himself. His name was Gavin Tay. He used to drive an ice-cream van ...'

Rebus thanked her for her call, and put down the phone. If someone had tried to kill Sammy on purpose, the question was: why? Rebus had been investigating Lintz; Ned Farlowe had been following him. Rebus had twice confronted Telford; Ned was writing a book about organised crime. Then there was Candice ... Could she have *told* Sammy something, something which might have threatened Telford, or even Mr Pink Eyes? Rebus just didn't know. He knew the most likely culprit – the most vicious – was Tommy Telford. He remembered their first meeting, and the young gangster's words to him: *That's the beauty of games. You can always start again after an accident. Not so easy in real life.* At the time it had sounded like bravado, a performance for the troops. But now it sounded like a plain threat.

And now there was Mr Taystee, connecting Sammy to Telford. Mr Taystee had worked Telford's clubs; Mr Taystee had rejected Sammy. Rebus knew he'd have to talk to the widow.

There was just the one problem. Mr Pink Eyes had intimated that if Telford wasn't left alone, Candice would suffer. He kept seeing images of Candice: torn from home and homeland; used and abused; abusing herself in the hope of respite; clinging to a stranger's legs ... He recalled Levy's words: *Can time wash away responsibility?* Justice was a fine and noble thing, but revenge ... revenge was an *emotion*, and so much stronger than an abstract like justice. He wondered if Sammy would want revenge. Probably not. She'd want him to help Candice, which meant yielding to Telford. Rebus didn't think he could do that.

And now there was Lintz's murder, unconnected but resonant.

'I've never felt comfortable with the past, Inspector,' Lintz had said once. Funny, Rebus felt the same way about the present.

Joanne Tay lived in Colinton: a newish three-bedroomed semi with the Merc still parked in the drive.

'It's too big for me,' she explained to Rebus. 'I'll have to sell it.'

He wasn't sure if she meant the house or the car. Having declined her offer of tea, he sat in the busy living-room, ornaments on every flat surface. Joanne Tay was still in mourning: black skirt and blouse, dark grooves beneath her eyes. He'd interviewed her back at the start of the inquiry.

'I still don't know why he did it,' she said now, reluctant to see her husband's death as anything other than suicide.

But the pathology and forensic tests had cast this into doubt.

'Have you ever heard,' Rebus asked, 'of a man called Tommy Telford?'

'He runs a nightclub, doesn't he? Gavin took me there once.'

'So Gavin knew him?'

'Seemed to.'

Yes: because no way was Mr Taystee setting up his hot-dog pitch outside Telford's premises without Telford's okay. And Telford's okay almost certainly meant payment of some kind. A percentage maybe … or a favour.

'The week before Gavin died,' Rebus went on, 'you said he'd been busy?'

'Working all hours.'

'Days as well as nights?' She nodded. 'The weather was lousy that week.'

'I know. I told him: you'll never get them buying ice-cream, a day like this. Pelting down outside. But still he went out.'

Rebus shifted in his chair. 'Did he ever mention SWEEP, Mrs Tay?'

'He had some woman would visit him … red hair.'

'Mae Crumley?'

She nodded, eyes staring at the coal-effect fire. She asked him again if he wanted some tea. Rebus shook his head and made to leave. Did pretty well: knocked over just the two ornaments on his way to the door.

*

The hospital was quiet. When he pushed open the door to Sammy's room, he saw that another bed had been added, a middle-aged woman sleeping in it. Her hands lay on the bedcovers, a white identity tag around one wrist. She was hooked up to a machine, and her head was bandaged.

Two women were sitting by Sammy's bed. Rhona, and Patience Aitken. Rebus hadn't seen Patience in a while. The women were sitting close together. Their whispered conversation stopped as he came in. He lifted a chair and placed it beside Patience's. She leaned over and squeezed his hand.

'Hello, John.'

He smiled at her, spoke to Rhona. 'How is she?'

'The specialist says those last tests were very positive.'

'What does that mean?'

'It means there's brain activity. She's not in deep coma.'

'Is that his version?'

'He thinks she'll come out of it, John.' Her eyes were bloodshot. He noticed a handkerchief gripped in one hand.

'That's good,' he said. 'Which doctor was it?'

'Dr Stafford. He's just back from holiday.'

'I can't keep track of them all.' Rebus rubbed his forehead.

'Look,' Patience said, checking her watch, 'I really should be going. I'm sure the two of you ...'

'Stay as long as you like,' Rebus told her.

'I'm already late for an appointment, actually.' She got to her feet. 'Nice to meet you, Rhona.'

'Thanks, Patience.' The two women shook hands a little awkwardly, then Rhona got up and they hugged, and the awkwardness vanished. 'Thanks for coming.'

Patience turned to Rebus. She looked radiant, he decided. Light really seemed to emanate from her skin. She was wearing her usual perfume, and had had her hair restyled.

'Thanks for looking in,' he said.

'She's going to be fine, John.' She took his hands in hers, leaned towards him. A peck on the cheek, a kiss between friends. Rebus saw Rhona watching them.

'John,' she said, 'see Patience out, will you?'

'No, that's all —'

'Of course, yes,' Rebus said.

They left the room together. Walked the first few steps in silence. Patience spoke first.

'She's great, isn't she?'

'Rhona?'

'Yes.'

Rebus was thoughtful. 'She's terrific. Have you met her paramour?'

'He's gone back to London. I've … I asked Rhona if she wanted to come stay with me. Hotels can be …'

Rebus smiled tiredly. 'Good idea. Then all you'd have to do is invite my brother over and you'd have the whole set.'

Her face cracked into an embarrassed grin. 'I suppose it must look a bit like I'm collecting you all.'

'The perfect hand of Unhappy Families.'

She turned to him. They were at the main doors of the hospital. She touched his shoulder. 'John, I'm really sorry about Sammy. Anything I can do, you've only got to ask.'

'Thanks, Patience.'

'But asking for things has never been your strong point, has it? You just sit in silence and hope they come to you.' She sighed. 'I can't believe I'm saying this, but I miss you. I think that's why I took in Sammy. If I couldn't be close to you, at least I could be close to someone who was. Does that make any sense? Is this where you say something about not deserving me?'

'You've seen the script.' He pulled back a little from her, just so he could look at her face. 'I miss you, too.'

All the nights slumped at the bar, or in his chair at home,

the long midnight drives so he could keep his restlessness alive. He'd have the TV and the hi-fi on at the same time, and the flat would still feel empty. Books he tried reading, finding he was ten pages in and couldn't remember anything. Gazing from his window at the darkened flats across the street, imagining lives at rest.

All because he didn't have *her*.

They embraced in silence for a while. 'You're going to be late,' he said.

'God, John, what are we going to do?'

'See one another?'

'That sounds like a start.'

'Tonight? Mario's at eight?' She nodded and they kissed again. He squeezed her hand. Her head was turned to look at him as she pushed open the doors.

Emerson, Lake and Palmer: 'Still ... You Turn Me On.'

Rebus felt a little giddy as he walked back to Sammy's room. Only it wasn't any more, wasn't 'Sammy's room'. Now there was another patient there. They'd said there was always that possibility – shortage of space, cutbacks. The woman was still asleep or unconscious, breathing noisily. Rebus ignored her and sat where Patience had been sitting.

'I've got a message for you,' Rhona said. 'From Dr Morrison.'

'Who's he when he's at home?'

'I've no idea. All he said was, could he have his t-shirt back?'

The ghoul with the scythe ... Rebus picked up Pa Broon, turned the bear in his hands. They sat in silence for a while, until Rhona shifted in her chair. 'Patience is really nice.'

'Did the two of you have a good chat?' She nodded. 'And you told her what a perfect husband I'd been?'

'You must be crazy, walking out on her.'

'Sanity's never exactly been my strong point.'

'But you used to know a good thing when you saw it.'

'Trouble is, that's never what I see when I look in the mirror.'

'What do you see?'

He looked at her. 'Sometimes I don't see anything at all.'

Later, they took a coffee-break, went to the machine.

'I lost her, you know,' Rhona said.

'What?'

'Sammy, I lost her. She came back here. She came back to you.'

'We hardly see one another, Rhona.'

'But she's *here*. Don't you get it? It's you she wants, not me.' She turned away from him, fumbled for her handkerchief. He stood close behind her, then couldn't think of anything to say. He was all out of words; every line of sympathy rang hollow to him, just another cliché. He touched the back of her neck, rubbed it. She lowered her head a little, didn't resist. Massage: there'd been a lot of massage early on in their relationship. By the end, he hadn't even given her time for a handshake.

'I don't know why she came back, Rhona,' he said at last. 'But I don't think she was running away, and I don't think it had much to do with seeing me.'

A couple of nurses ran past, urgency in their movements.

'I'd better get back,' Rhona said, rubbing a hand over her face, pulling it into something resembling composure.

Rebus went with her to the room, then said he had to be going. He bent down to kiss Sammy, feeling the breath from her nostrils against his cheek.

'Wake up, Sammy,' he cajoled. 'You can't stay in bed all your life. Time to get up.'

When there was no movement, no response, he turned and left the room.

17

David Levy was no longer in Edinburgh. At least, he wasn't at the Roxburghe Hotel. Rebus could think of only one way of contacting him. Seated at his desk, he called the Holocaust Investigation Bureau in Tel Aviv and asked to speak with Solomon Mayerlink. Mayerlink wasn't available, but Rebus identified himself and said he needed to contact him as a matter of urgency. He got a home telephone number.

'Is there news on Linzstek, Inspector?' Mayerlink's voice was a harsh rasp.

'Of a kind, yes. He's dead.'

Silence on the line, then a slow release of breath. 'That's a pity.'

'It is?'

'People die, a little bit of history dies with them. We would have preferred to see him in court, Inspector. Dead, he's worthless.' Mayerlink paused. 'I take it this ends your inquiry?'

'It changes the nature of the investigation. He was murdered.'

Static on the line; an eight-beat pause. 'How did it happen?'

'He was hung from a tree.'

There was a longer silence on the line. 'I see,' Mayerlink said at last. There was a slight echo on his voice. 'You think the allegations led to his murder?'

'What would you say?'

'I'm not a detective.'

But Rebus knew Mayerlink was lying: detection was *exactly* the role he'd chosen in life. A detective of history.

'I need to talk to David Levy,' Rebus said. 'Do you have his address and phone number?'

'He came to see you?'

'You know he did.'

'It's not that simple with David. He doesn't work for the Bureau. He's self-motivated. I ask him for help occasionally. Sometimes he helps, sometimes he doesn't.'

'But you do have some way of contacting him?'

It took Mayerlink a full minute to come up with the details. An address in Sussex, plus telephone number.

'Is David your number one suspect, Inspector?'

'Why do you ask?'

'I could tell you you're barking up the wrong tree.'

'The same tree Joseph Lintz swung from?'

'Can you really see David Levy as a murderer, Inspector?'

Safari suit, walking stick. 'It takes all sorts,' Rebus said, putting down the phone.

He tried Levy's number. It rang and rang. He gave it a couple of minutes, drank a coffee, tried again. Still no answer. He called British Telecom instead, explained what he needed, was finally put through to the right person.

'My name's Justine Graham, Inspector. How can I help?'

Rebus gave her Lintz's details. 'He used to get itemised bills, then he switched.'

He heard her fingers hammer a keyboard. 'That's right,' she told him. 'The customer asked for itemised billing to be discontinued.'

'Did he say why?'

'No record of that. You don't need to give an excuse, you know.'

'When was this?'

'A couple of months back. The customer had requested monthly billing several years previously.'

Monthly billing: because he was meticulous, kept his accounts by the month. A couple of months back – September – the Lintz/Linzstek story had blown up in the media. And, suddenly, he hadn't wanted his phone calls to be a matter of record.

'Do you have records of his calls, even the *un*itemised ones?'

'Yes, we should have that information.'

'I'd like to see a list. Everything from the first unitemised call through to this morning.'

'Is that when he died – this morning?'

'Yes.'

She was thoughtful. 'Well, I'll need to check.'

'Please do. But remember, Ms Graham, this is a murder inquiry.'

'Yes, of course.'

'And your information could be absolutely crucial.'

'I'm quite aware of –'

'So if I could have that by the end of today …?'

She hesitated. 'I'm not sure I can promise that.'

'And one last thing. The bill for September is missing. I'd like a copy of it. Let me give you the fax number here, speed things up.'

Rebus congratulated himself with another cup of coffee and a cigarette in the car park. She might or might not deliver later in the day, but he was confident she'd be trying her best. Wasn't that all you could ask of anybody?

Another call: Special Branch in London. He asked for Abernethy.

'I'll just put you through.'

Someone picked up: a grunt in place of an acknowledgement.

'Abernethy?' Rebus asked. He heard liquid being swallowed. The voice became clearer.

'He's not here. Can I help?'

'I really need to speak to him.'

'I could have him paged, if it's urgent.'

'My name's DI Rebus, Lothian and Borders Police.'

'Oh, right. Have you lost him or something?'

Rebus's expression turned quizzical. His voice carried a false note of humour. 'You know what Abernethy's like.'

A snort. 'Don't I just.'

'So any help appreciated.'

'Yeah, right. Look, give me your number. I'll get him to call you.'

Have you lost him or something? 'You've no idea where he is then?'

'It's your city, chum. Take your best shot.'

He's up here, Rebus thought. *He's right here.*

'I bet the office is quiet without him.'

Laughter on the line, then the sounds of a cigarette being lit. A long exhalation. 'It's like being on holiday. Keep him as long as you like.'

'So how long have you been without him?'

A pause. As the silence lengthened, Rebus could feel the change of atmosphere.

'What did you say your name was?'

'DI Rebus. I was only asking when he left London.'

'This morning, soon as he heard. So what have I won: the hatchback or the hostess trolley?'

Rebus's turn to laugh. 'Sorry, I'm just nosy.'

'I'll be sure to tell him that.' A single click, then the sound of an open line.

Later that afternoon, Rebus chased up British Telecom, then tried Levy's house again. This time he got through to a woman.

'Hello, Mrs Levy? My name's John Rebus. I was wondering if I could have a word with your husband?'

'You mean my father.'

'I'm sorry. Is your father there?'

'No, he's not.'

'Any idea when … ?'

'Absolutely none.' She sounded peeved. 'I'm just his cook and cleaner. Like I don't have a life of my own.' She caught herself. 'Sorry, Mr … ?'

'Rebus.'

'It's just that he never says how long he's going to be away.'

'He's away just now?'

'Has been for the best part of a fortnight. He rings two or three times a week, asks if there've been any calls or letters. If I'm lucky, he *might* remember to ask how *I'm* doing.'

'And how are you doing?'

A smile in her voice. 'I know, I know. I sound like I'm his mother or something.'

'Well, you know, fathers …' Rebus stared into the middle distance … 'if you don't tell them anything's wrong, they're happy to assume the best and hold their peace.'

'You speak from experience?'

'Too much experience.'

She was thoughtful. 'Is it something important?'

'Very.'

'Well, give me your name and number, and next time he calls I'll have him phone you.'

'Thanks.' Rebus reeled off two numbers: home and mobile.

'Got that,' she said. 'Any other message?'

'No, just have him call me.' Rebus thought for a moment. 'Has he had any other calls?'

'You mean, people trying to reach him? Why do you ask?'

'I just … no real reason.' He didn't want to say he was a policeman; didn't want her spooked. 'No reason,' he repeated.

As he came off the phone, someone handed him another coffee. 'That receiver must be red hot.'

He touched it with the tips of his fingers. It was pretty warm. Then it rang and he picked it up again.

'DI Rebus,' he said.

'John, it's Siobhan.'

'Hiya, how's tricks?'

'John, you remember that guy?' Her tone was warning him of something.

'What guy?' The humour was gone from his voice.

'Danny Simpson.' He of the flappy skull; Telford's lackey.

'What about him?'

'I've just found out he's HIV positive. His GP let the hospital know.'

Blood in Rebus's eyes, his ears, dribbling down his neck …

'Poor guy,' he said quietly.

'He should have said something at the time.'

'When?'

'When we got him to the hospital.'

'Well, he had other things on his mind, and some of them were in danger of falling off.'

'Christ, John, be serious for a minute!' Her voice was loud enough to have people glance up from their desks. 'You need to get a blood test.'

'Fine, no problem. How is he, by the way?'

'Back home but poorly. And sticking to his story.'

'Do I detect the influence of Telford's lawyer?'

'Charles Groal? That one's so slimy, he's practically primordial.'

'Saves you the cost of a valentine.'

'Look, just phone the hospital. Talk to a Dr Jones. She'll fix an appointment. They can do a test right away. Not that it'll be the last word – there's a three-month incubation.'

'Thanks, Siobhan.'

Rebus put down the receiver, drummed his fingers against it. Wouldn't *that* be a nice irony? Rebus out to get Telford, does the Good Samaritan bit for one of his men, gets AIDS and dies. Rebus stared at the ceiling.

Nice one, Big Man.

The phone rang again. Rebus snatched it up.

'Switchboard,' he said.

'Is that you, John?' Patience Aitken.

'The one and only.'

'Just wanted to check we're still on for tonight.'

'To be honest, Patience, I'm not sure I'll be at my most sparkling.'

'You want to cancel?'

'Absolutely not. But I have something to take care of. At the hospital.'

'Yes, of course.'

'No, I don't think you understand. It's not Sammy this time, it's me.'

'What's wrong?'

So he told her.

She went with him. Same hospital Sammy was in, different department. Last thing he wanted was to bump into Rhona, have to explain everything to her. Possibly HIV-infected: chances were, she'd red-card him from the bedside.

The waiting room was white, clean. Lots of information on the walls. Leaflets on every table, as if paperwork was the real virus.

'I must say, it's very pleasant for a leper colony.'

Patience didn't say anything. They were alone in the room. Someone on reception had dealt with him first, then a nurse had come out and taken some details. Now another door opened.

'Mr Rebus?'

A tall thin woman in a white coat, standing in the doorway: Dr Jones, he presumed. Patience took his arm as they walked towards her. Halfway across the floor, Rebus turned on his heels and bolted.

Patience caught up with him outside, asked what was wrong.

'I don't want to know,' he told her.

'But, John ...'

'Come on, Patience. All I got was a bit of blood splashed on me.'

She didn't look convinced. 'You need to take the test.'

He looked back towards the building. 'Fine.' Started walking away. 'But some other time, eh?'

It was one in the morning when he drove back into Arden Street. No dinner date with Patience: instead, they'd visited the hospital, sat with Rhona. He'd made a silent pact with the Big Man: bring her back and I'll keep off the booze. He'd driven Patience home. Her last words to him: 'Take that test. Get it over and done with.'

As he locked his car, a figure appeared from nowhere.

'Mr Rebus, long time no see.'

Rebus recognised the face. Pointy chin, misshapen teeth, the breathing a series of small gasps. The Weasel: one of Cafferty's men. He was dressed like a down-and-out, perfect camouflage for his role in life. He was Cafferty's eyes and ears on the street.

'We need to talk, Mr Rebus.' His hands were deep in the

pockets of a tweed coat meant for someone eight inches taller. He glanced towards the tenement door.

'Not in my flat,' Rebus stated. Some things were sacrosanct.

'Cold out here.'

Rebus just shook his head, and the Weasel sniffed hard.

'You think it was a hit?' he said.

'Yes,' Rebus answered.

'She was meant to die?'

'I don't know.'

'A pro wouldn't fuck up.'

'Then it was a warning.'

'We could do with seeing your notes.'

'Can't do that.'

The Weasel shrugged. 'Thought you wanted Mr Cafferty's help?'

'I can't give you the notes. What about if I summarise?'

'It'd be a start.'

'Rover 600, stolen from George Street that afternoon. Abandoned on a street by Piershill Cemetery. Radio and some tapes lifted – not necessarily by the same person.'

'Scavengers.'

'Could be.'

The Weasel was thoughtful. 'A warning ... That would mean a professional driver.'

'Yes,' Rebus said.

'And not one of ours ... Doesn't leave too many candidates. Rover 600 ... what colour?'

'Sherwood Green.'

'Parked on George Street?'

Rebus nodded.

'Thanks for that.' The Weasel made to turn away, then paused. 'Nice doing business with you again, Mr Rebus.'

Rebus was about to say something, then remembered he needed the Weasel more than the Weasel needed him. He wondered how much crap he'd take from Cafferty ... how long he'd have to take it. All his life? Had he made a contract with the devil?

For Sammy, he'd have done much, much worse ...

In his flat, he stuck on the CD of *Rock 'n' Roll Circus*, skipping to the actual Stones tracks. His answering machine was flashing. Three messages. The first: Hogan.

'Hello, John. Just thought I'd check, see if there's been any word from BT.'

Not by the time Rebus had left the office. Message two: Abernethy.

'Me again, bad penny and all that. Heard you've been trying to catch me. I'll call you tomorrow. Cheers.'

Rebus stared at the machine, willing Abernethy to say more, to give some hint of a location. But the machine was on to the final message. Bill Pryde.

'John, tried you at the office, left a message. But I thought you'd want to know, we've had final word on those prints. If you want to try me at home, I'm on ...'

Rebus took down the number. Two in the morning, but Bill would understand.

After a minute or so, a woman picked up. She sounded groggy.

'Sorry,' Rebus said. 'Is Bill there?'

'I'll get him.'

He heard background dialogue, then the receiver being hoisted.

'So what's this about prints?' he asked.

'Christ, John, when I said you could call, I didn't mean the middle of the night!'

'It's important.'

'Yes, I know. How's she doing anyway?'

'Still out cold.'

Pryde yawned. 'Well, most of the prints inside the car

belong to the owner and his wife. But we found one other set. Problem is, looks like they belong to a kid.'

'What makes you so sure?'

'The size.'

'Plenty of adults around with small hands.'

'I suppose so ...'

'You sound sceptical.'

'More likely to be one of two scenarios. One, Sammy was hit by a joyrider. I know what you think, but it does happen. Two, the prints belong to whoever rifled the car after it was left at the cemetery.'

'The kid who took the cassette player and tapes?'

'Exactly.'

'No other prints? Not even partials?'

'The car was clean, John.'

'Exterior?'

'Same three sets on the doors, plus Sammy's on the bonnet.' Pryde yawned again. 'So what about your grudge theory?'

'Still holds. A pro would be wearing gloves.'

'That's what I was thinking. Not too many pros out there though.'

'No.' Rebus was thinking of the Weasel: *I'm dealing with slime to catch a slug.* Nothing he hadn't done before, only this time there were personal reasons.

And he didn't think there'd be a trial.

18

Breakfast was on Hogan: bacon rolls in a brown paper bag. They ate them in the CID room at St Leonard's. A Murder Room had been established in Leith, and that's where Hogan should have been.

Only he wanted Rebus's files, and he knew better than to trust Rebus to deliver them.

'Thought I'd save you the hassle,' was what he said.

'You're a gentleman,' Rebus answered, examining the interior of his roll. 'Tell me, are pigs an endangered species?'

'I lifted half a slice from you.' Hogan pulled a string of fat from his mouth, tossed it into a bin. 'Thought I was doing you a favour: cholesterol and all that.'

Rebus put the roll to one side, took a swig from the can of Irn-Bru – Hogan's idea of a morning beverage – and swallowed. What was sugar consumption compared to HIV? 'What did you get from the cleaning lady?'

'Grief. Soon as she heard her employer was dead, the taps were on.' Hogan brushed flour from his fingers: mealtime over. 'She never met any of his friends, never had occasion to answer his telephone, hadn't noticed any change in him recently, and doesn't think he was a mass murderer. Quote: "If he'd killed that many people, I'd have known".'

'What is she, psychic or something?'

Hogan shrugged. 'About all I got from her was a glowing character reference and the fact that as she was paid in advance, she owes his estate a partial refund.'

'There's your motive.'

Hogan smiled. 'Speaking of motives …'

'You've got something?'

'Lintz's lawyer has come up with a letter from the deceased's bank.' He handed Rebus a photocopy. 'Seems our man made a cash withdrawal of five grand ten days ago.'

'*Cash?*'

'We found ten quid on his person, and about another thirty bar in the house. No five grand. I'm beginning to think blackmail.'

Rebus nodded. 'What about his address book?'

'Slow work. A lot of old numbers, people who've moved on or died. Plus a few charities, museums … an art gallery or two.' Hogan paused. 'What about you?'

Rebus opened his drawer, pulled out the fax sheets. 'Waiting for me this morning. The calls Lintz wanted kept secret.'

Hogan looked down the list. 'Calls plural, or one in particular?'

'I've just started going through them. Best guess: there'll be callers he spoke to regularly. Those numbers will show up on the other statements. We're looking for anomalies, one-offs.'

'Makes sense.' Hogan looked at his watch. 'Anything else I should know?'

'Two things. Remember I told you about the Special Branch interest?'

'Abernethy?'

Rebus nodded. 'I tried calling him yesterday.'

'And?'

'According to his office, he was on his way up here. He'd already heard the news.'

'So I've got Abernethy sniffing around, and you don't trust him? Terrific. What's the other thing?'

'David Levy. I spoke with his daughter. She doesn't know where he is. He could be anywhere.'

'With a grudge against Lintz?'

'It's possible.'

'What's his phone number?'

Rebus patted the topmost file on his desk. 'Ready for you to take away.'

Hogan studied the foot-high pile, looking glum.

'I whittled it down to what's absolutely necessary,' Rebus told him.

'There's a month's reading there.'

Rebus shrugged. 'My case is your case, Bobby.'

With Hogan gone, Rebus went back to the British Telecom list. It was as detailed as he could have wished for. Lots of calls to Lintz's solicitor, a few to one of the city's taxi firms. Rebus tried a couple of numbers, found himself connected to charity offices: Lintz would have been phoning to tender his resignation. There were a few calls that stood out from the crowd: the Roxburghe Hotel – duration four minutes; Edinburgh University – twenty-six minutes. The Roxburghe had to mean Levy. Rebus knew Levy had talked to Lintz – Lintz himself had admitted it. Talking to him – being confronted by him – was one thing; calling him at his hotel quite another.

The number for Edinburgh University connected Rebus to the main switchboard. He asked to be put through to Lintz's old department. The secretary was very helpful. She'd been in the job over twenty years, was due to retire. Yes, she remembered Professor Lintz, but he hadn't contacted the department recently.

'Every call that comes through here, I know about it.'

'He might have got straight through to a tutor though?' Rebus suggested.

'No one's mentioned speaking to him. There's nobody here from the Professor's day.'

'He doesn't keep in touch with the department?'

'I haven't spoken to him in years, Inspector. Too many years for me to remember ...'

So who had he been talking to for over twenty minutes? Rebus thanked the secretary and put down the phone. He went through the other numbers: a couple of restaurants, a wine shop, and the local radio station. Rebus told the receptionist what he was after, and she said she'd do her best. Then he went back to the restaurants, asked them to check if Lintz had been making a reservation.

Within half an hour, the calls started coming in. First restaurant: a booking for dinner, just the one cover. The radio station: they'd asked Lintz to appear on a programme. He'd said he'd consider it, then had called back to decline. Second restaurant: a lunch reservation, two covers.

'Two?'

'Mr Lintz and one other.'

'Any idea who the "other" might have been?'

'Another gentleman, quite elderly, I think ... I'm sorry, I don't really remember.'

'Did he walk with a stick?'

'I wish I could help, but it's a madhouse here at lunchtime.'

'You remember Lintz though?'

'Mr Lintz is a regular ... was a regular.'

'Did he usually eat alone, or with company?'

'Mostly alone. He didn't seem to mind. He'd bring a book with him.'

'Do you happen to recall any of his other guests?'

'I remember a young woman ... his daughter maybe? Or granddaughter?'

'So when you say "young" …?'

'Younger than him.' A pause. 'Maybe much younger.'

'When was this?'

'I really don't remember.' The voice impatient now.

'I appreciate your help, sir. Just one more minute of your time … This woman, did he bring her more than once?'

'I'm sorry, Inspector. The kitchen needs me.'

'Well, if you think of anything else …'

'Of course. Goodbye.'

Rebus put the phone down, made some notes. Just one number left. He waited for an answer.

'Yeah?' The voice grudging.

'Who's this?'

'This is Malky. Who the fuck are you?'

A voice in the background: 'Tommy says that new machine's fucked.' Rebus put the phone down. His hand was shaking. *That new machine* … Tommy Telford on his arcade motorbike. He remembered The Family mugshots: Malky Jordan. Tiny nose and eyes in a balloon of a face. *Joseph Lintz talking to one of Telford's men? Phoning Telford's office??* Rebus found the number of Hogan's mobile.

'Bobby,' he said. 'If you're driving, better slow down right now …'

Hogan's notion: five in cash was just Telford's style. Blackmail? But where was the connection? Something else …?

Hogan's play: he'd talk to Telford.

Rebus's notion: five was a bit steep for a hit-man. All the same, he wondered about Lintz … paying five thou' to Telford to set up the 'accident'. Motive: give Rebus a fright, scare him off? It put Lintz back in the frame, potentially.

Rebus had fixed up another meeting, one he didn't want

anyone knowing about. Haymarket Station was nice and anonymous. The bench on platform one, Ned Farlowe was already waiting. He looked tired: worry over Sammy. They talked about her for a couple of minutes. Then Rebus got down to business.

'You know Lintz has been murdered?'

'I didn't think this was a social call.'

'We're looking at a blackmail angle.'

Farlowe looked interested. 'And he didn't pay up?'

Oh, he paid up all right, Rebus thought. He paid up, and someone still took him out of the game.

'Look, Ned, this is *all* off the record. By rights I should take you in for questioning.'

'Because I followed him for a few days?'

'Yes.'

'And that makes me a suspect?'

'It makes you a possible witness.'

Farlowe thought about it. 'One evening. Lintz left his house, walked down the road, made a call from a phone-box, then went straight back home.'

Not wanting to use his home phone ... afraid it was bugged? Afraid of the number being traced? Telephone bugging: a favourite ploy of Special Branch.

'And something else,' Farlowe was saying. 'He met this woman on his doorstep. Like she was waiting for him. They had a few words. I think she was crying when she left.'

'What did she look like?'

'Tall, short dark hair, well-dressed. She had a briefcase with her.'

'Wearing?'

Farlowe shrugged. 'Skirt and jacket ... matching. Black and white check. You know ... elegant.'

He was describing Kirstin Mede. Her phone message to Rebus: *I can't do this any more ...*

'There's something I want to ask you,' Farlowe was saying. 'That girl Candice.'

'What about her?'

'You asked me if anything unusual had happened just before Sammy got hit.'

'Yes?'

'Well, *she* happened, didn't she?' Farlowe's eyes narrowed. 'Does she have anything to do with it?'

Rebus looked at Farlowe, who started nodding.

'Thanks for the confirmation. Who was she?'

'One of Telford's girls.'

Farlowe leaped to his feet, paced the platform. Rebus waited for him to sit down again. When he did, there could be no doubting the fury in his eyes.

'You hid one of Telford's girls with your own *daughter*?'

'I didn't have much choice. Telford knows where I live. I …'

'You were using us!' He paused. 'Telford did this, didn't he?'

'I don't know,' Rebus said. Farlowe leaped to his feet again. 'Look, Ned, I don't want you –'

'Quite frankly, *Inspector*, I don't think you're in any position to give advice.' He started walking, and though Rebus called after him, he never once looked back.

As Rebus walked into the Crime Squad office, a paper plane glided past and crashed into the wall. Ormiston had his feet up on the desk. Country and western music was playing softly in the background, its source a tape player on the window ledge behind Claverhouse's desk. Siobhan Clarke had pulled a chair over beside him. They were poring over some report.

'Not exactly the "A-Team" in here, is it?' Rebus retrieved the plane, straightened its crumpled nose, and sent it back to Ormiston, who asked what he was doing there.

'Liaising,' Rebus told him. 'My boss wants a progress report.'

Ormiston glanced towards Claverhouse, who was tipping himself back in his chair, hands behind his head.

'Want to take a guess at the headway we've made?'

Rebus sat down opposite Claverhouse, nodded a greeting to Siobhan.

'How's Sammy?' she asked.

'Just the same,' Rebus answered. Claverhouse looked abashed, and Rebus suddenly realised that he could use Sammy as a lever, play on people's sympathy. Why not? Hadn't he used her in the past? Wasn't Ned Farlowe on the nail there?

'We've pulled the surveillance,' Claverhouse said.

'Why?'

Ormiston snorted, but it was Claverhouse who answered.

'High maintenance, low returns.'

'Orders from above?'

'It isn't as if we were close to getting a result.'

'So we just let him get on with getting on?'

Claverhouse shrugged. Rebus wondered if news would get back to Newcastle. Jake Tarawicz would be happy. He'd think Rebus was fulfilling his part of the bargain. Candice would be safe. Maybe.

'Any news on that nightclub killing?'

'Nothing to link it to your chum Cafferty.'

'He's *not* my chum.'

'Whatever you say. Stick the kettle on, Ormie.' Ormiston glanced towards Clarke, then rose grudgingly from his chair. Rebus had thought the tension in the office was all to do with Telford. Not a bit of it. Claverhouse and Clarke close together, *involved*. Ormiston off on his own, a kid making paper planes, seeking attention. An old Status Quo song: 'Paper Plane'. But the status quo here had been disturbed: Clarke had usurped Ormiston. The office junior was absolved from making the tea.

Rebus could see why Ormiston was pissed off.

'I hear Herr Lintz was a bit of a swinger,' Claverhouse said.

'Now there's a joke I haven't heard before.' Rebus's pager sounded. The display gave him a number to call.

He used Claverhouse's phone. It sounded like he was connected to a pay-phone. Street sounds, heavy traffic close by.

'Mr Rebus?' Placed the voice at once: the Weasel.

'What is it?'

'A couple of questions. The tape player from the car, any idea of the make?'

'Sony.'

'The front bit detachable?'

'That's right.'

'So all they got was the front bit?'

'Yes.' Claverhouse and Clarke, back at their report, pretending they weren't listening.

'What about the tapes? You said some tapes got stolen?'

'Opera – *The Marriage of Figaro* and Verdi's *Macbeth*.' Rebus squeezed his eyes shut, thinking. 'And another tape with film music on it, famous themes. Plus Roy Orbison's *Greatest Hits*.' This last the wife's. Rebus knew what the Weasel was thinking: whoever took the stuff, they'd try flogging it round the pubs or at a car boot sale. Car boot sales were clearing houses for knock-off. But getting whoever had lifted the stuff from the unlocked car wasn't going to nail the driver ... Unless the kid – the one who'd lifted the stuff, whose prints were on the car – had *seen* something: been hanging around on the street, watched the car screeching to a stop, a man getting out and hoofing it ...

An eye witness, someone who could describe the driver.

'The only prints we got were small, maybe a kid's.'

'That's interesting.'

'Anything else I can do,' Rebus said, 'just let me know.' The Weasel hung up.

'Sony's a good make,' Claverhouse said, fishing.

'Some stuff lifted from a car,' Rebus told him. 'It might have turned up.'

Ormiston had made the tea. Rebus went to fetch himself a chair, saw someone walk past the open doorway. He dropped the chair and ran into the corridor, grabbed at an arm.

Abernethy spun quickly, saw who it was and relaxed.

'Nice one, son,' he said. 'You almost had knuckles for teeth.' He was working on a piece of chewing gum.

'What are you doing here?'

'Visiting.' Abernethy looked back at the open door, walked towards it. 'What about you?'

'Working.'

Abernethy read the sign on the door. 'Crime Squad,' he said, sounding amused, taking in the office and the people in it. Hands in pockets, he sauntered in, Rebus following.

'Abernethy, Special Branch,' the Londoner said by way of introduction. 'That music's a good idea: play it at interrogations, sap the suspect's will to live.' He was smiling, surveying the premises like he was thinking of moving in. The mug meant for Rebus was on the corner of the desk. Abernethy picked it up and slurped, made a face, started chewing again. The three Crime Squad officers were like a frozen tableau. Suddenly they looked like a unit: it had taken Abernethy to do that.

Had taken him all of ten seconds.

'What you working on?' No one answered. 'Must've got the sign on the door wrong,' Abernethy said. 'Should be Mime Squad.'

'Is there something we can do for you?' Claverhouse asked, his voice level, hostility in his eyes.

'I don't know. It was John pulled me in here.'

'And I'm pulling you out again,' Rebus said, taking his arm. Abernethy shrugged free, bunched his fists. 'A word in the corridor ... please.'

Abernethy smiled. 'Manners maketh the man, John.'

'What does that maketh you?'

Abernethy turned his head slowly, looked at Siobhan Clarke who'd just spoken.

'I'm just a regular guy with a heart of gold and twelve big inches of ability.' He grinned at her.

'To go with your twelve big points of IQ,' she said, going back to the report. Ormiston and Claverhouse weren't trying too hard to conceal their laughter as Abernethy stormed out of the room. Rebus hung back long enough to watch Ormiston pat Clarke on the back, then headed off after the Special Branch man.

'What a bitch,' Abernethy said. He was making for the exit.

'She's a friend of mine.'

'And they say you can choose your friends ...' Abernethy shook his head.

'What brings you back?'

'You have to ask?'

'Lintz is dead. Case closed as far as you're concerned.' They emerged from the building.

'So?'

'So,' Rebus persisted, 'why come all the way back here? What is there that couldn't be done with a phone or fax?'

Abernethy stopped, turned to face him. 'Loose ends.'

'What loose ends?'

'There aren't any.' Abernethy gave a cheerless smile and took a key from his pocket. As they approached his car, he used the remote to unlock it and disable the alarm.

'What's going on, Abernethy?'

'Nothing to worry your pretty little head about.' He opened the driver's-side door.

'Are you glad he's dead?'

'What?'

'Lintz. How do you feel about him being murdered?'

'I've no feelings either way. He's dead, which means I can cross him off my list.'

'That last time you came up here, you were warning him.'

'Not true.'

'Was his phone bugged?' Abernethy just snorted. 'Did you know he might be killed?'

Abernethy turned on Rebus. 'What's it to you? I'll tell you: nothing. Leith CID are on the murder, and you're out of it. End of story.'

'Is it the Rat Line? Too embarrassing if it all came to light?'

'Christ, what *is* it with you? Just give it a rest.' Abernethy got into the car, closed the door. Rebus didn't move. The engine turned and caught, Abernethy's window slid down. Rebus was ready.

'They sent you four hundred miles just to check there were no loose ends.'

'So?'

'So there's rather a large loose end, isn't there?' Rebus paused. 'Unless you know who Lintz's killer was.'

'I leave that sort of thing to you guys.'

'Heading down to Leith?'

'I have to talk to Hogan.' Abernethy stared at Rebus. 'You're a hard bastard, aren't you? Maybe even a bit selfish.'

'How's that?'

'If I'd a daughter in hospital, police work would be the last thing on my mind.'

As Rebus lunged towards the open window, Abernethy gunned the car. Footsteps behind: Siobhan Clarke.

'Good riddance,' she said, watching the car speed off. A finger appeared from Abernethy's window. She gave a two-fingered reply. 'I didn't want to say anything in the office ...' she began.

'I took the test yesterday,' Rebus lied.

'It'll be negative.'

'Are you positive?'

She smiled a little longer than the joke merited. 'Ormiston chucked your tea away, said he was going to disinfect the mug.'

'Abernethy has that effect on people.' He looked at her. 'Remember, Ormiston and Claverhouse go back years.'

'I know. I think Claverhouse has a crush on me. It'll pass, but until it does ...'

'Tread carefully.' They started walking back towards the main entrance. 'And don't let him tempt you into the broom cupboard.'

19

Rebus went back to St Leonard's, saw that the office was coping quite well without him, and headed over to the hospital with Dr Morrison's Iron Maiden t-shirt in a plastic bag. A third bed had been moved into Sammy's room. An elderly woman lay in it. Though awake, she stared fixedly at the ceiling. Rhona was at Sammy's bedside, reading a book.

Rebus stroked his daughter's hair. 'How is she?'

'No change.'

'Any more tests planned?'

'Not that I know of.'

'That's it then? She just stays like this?'

He lifted a chair over, sat down. It had turned into a sort of ritual now, this bedside vigil. It felt almost … the word he wanted to use was 'comfortable'. He squeezed Rhona's hand, sat there for twenty minutes, saying almost nothing, then went to find Kirstin Mede.

She was in her office at the French Department, marking scripts. She sat at a big desk in front of the window, but moved from this to a coffee-table with half a dozen chairs arranged around it.

'Sit down,' she said. Rebus sat down.

'I got your message,' he told her.

'Hardly matters now, does it? The man's dead.'

'I know you spoke with him, Kirstin.'

She glanced towards him. 'I'm sorry?'

'You waited for him outside his house. Did the two of you have a nice chat?'

Colour had risen to her cheeks. She crossed her legs, tugged the hem of her skirt towards her knee. 'Yes,' she said at last, 'I went to his house.'

'Why?'

'Because I wanted to see him close up.' Her eyes were on his now, challenging him. 'I thought maybe I could tell from his face ... the look in his eyes. Maybe something in his tone of voice.'

'And could you?'

She shook her head. 'Not a damned thing. No window to the soul.'

'What did you say to him?'

'I told him who I was.'

'Any reaction?'

'Yes.' She folded her arms. 'His words: "My dear lady, will you kindly piss off".'

'And did you?'

'Yes. Because I knew then. Not whether he was Linzstek or not, but something else.'

'What?'

'That he was at the end of his tether.' She was nodding. 'Absolutely at breaking point.' She looked at Rebus again. 'And capable of anything.'

The problem with the Flint Street surveillance was that it had been so open. A hidden operation – deep cover – that's what was needed. Rebus had decided to scout out the territory.

The tenement flats across the road from Telford's café and arcade were served by a single main door. It was locked, so Rebus chose a buzzer at random – marked HETHERINGTON. Waited, pushed again. An elderly voice came on the intercom.

'Who is it, please?'

'Mrs Hetherington? Detective Inspector Rebus, I'm your Community CID officer. Can I talk to you about home security? There've been a few break-ins around here, especially with elderly victims.'

'Gracious, you'd better come up.'

'Which floor?'

'The first.' The door buzzed, and Rebus pushed it open.

Mrs Hetherington was waiting for him in her doorway. She was tiny and frail-looking, but her eyes were lively and her movements assured. The flat was small, well-maintained. The sitting-room was heated by a two-bar electric fire. Rebus wandered over to the window, found himself looking down on to the arcade. Perfect location for a surveillance. He pretended to check her windows.

'These seem fine,' he said. 'Are they always locked?'

'I open them a bit in the summer,' Mrs Hetherington said, 'and when they need washing. But I always lock them again afterwards.'

'One thing I should warn you about, and that's bogus officials. People coming to your door, telling you they're so-and-so. Always ask to see some ID, and don't open up until you're satisfied.'

'How can I see it without opening the door?'

'Ask them to push it through the letterbox.'

'I didn't see *your* identification, did I?'

Rebus smiled. 'No, you didn't.' He took it out and showed her. 'Sometimes the fake stuff can look pretty convincing. If you're unsure, keep the door locked and call the police.' He looked around. 'You have a phone?'

'In the bedroom.'

'Any windows in there?'

'Yes.'

'Can I take a look?'

The bedroom window also looked out on to Flint Street.

Rebus noticed travel brochures on the dressing-table, a small suitcase standing near the door.

'Off on holiday, eh?' With the flat empty, maybe he could move the surveillance in.

'Just a long weekend,' she said.

'Somewhere nice?'

'Holland. Wrong time of year for the bulb-fields, but I've always wanted to go. It's a nuisance flying from Inverness, but so much cheaper. Since my husband died ... well, I've done a bit of travelling.'

'Any chance of taking me with you?' Rebus smiled. 'This window's fine, too. I'll just check your door, see if it could do with more locks.' They went into the narrow hall.

'You know,' she said, 'we've always been very lucky here, no break-ins or anything like that.'

Hardly surprising with Tommy Telford as proprietor.

'And with the panic button, of course ...'

Rebus looked at the wall next to the front door. A large red button. He'd assumed it was for the stairhead lights or something.

'Anyone who calls, anyone at all, I'm supposed to press it.'

Rebus opened the door. 'And do you?'

Two very large men were standing right outside.

'Oh, yes,' Mrs Hetherington said. 'I always do.'

For thugs, they were very polite. Rebus showed them his warrant card and explained the nature of his visit. He asked them who they were, and they told him they were 'representatives of the building's owner'. He knew the faces though: Kenny Houston, Ally Cornwell. Houston – the ugly one – ran Telford's doormen; Cornwell, with his wrestler's bulk, was general muscle. The little charade was carried out with humour and good nature on both sides. They accompanied him downstairs. Across the street,

Tommy Telford was standing in the café doorway, wagging his finger. A pedestrian crossed Rebus's line of vision. Too late, Rebus saw who it was. Had his mouth open to shout something, then saw Telford hang his head, hands going to his face. Screeching.

Rebus ran across the road, pulled the pedestrian round: Ned Farlowe. A bottle dropped from Farlowe's hand. Telford's men were closing in. Rebus held tight to Farlowe.

'I'm placing this man under arrest,' he said. 'He's *mine*, understood?'

A dozen faces glaring at him. And Tommy Telford down on his knees.

'Get your boss to the hospital,' Rebus said. 'I'm taking this one to St Leonard's ...'

Ned Farlowe sat on the ledge in one of the cells. The walls were blue, smeared brown near the toilet-pan. Farlowe was looking pleased with himself.

'Acid?' Rebus said, pacing the cell. '*Acid?* All this research must have gone to your head.'

'It's what he deserved.'

Rebus glared at him. 'You don't know what you've done.'

'I know *exactly* what I've done.'

'He'll kill you.'

Farlowe shrugged. 'Am I under arrest?'

'You'd better believe it, son. I want you kept out of harm's way. If I hadn't been there ...' But he didn't want to think about that. He looked at Farlowe. Looked at Sammy's lover, who'd just staged a full-frontal assault on Telford, the kind of assault Rebus knew wouldn't work.

Now Rebus would have to redouble his efforts. Because otherwise, Ned Farlowe was a dead man ... and when Sammy came round, he didn't want news like that to be waiting for her.

*

He drove back towards Flint Street, parked at a distance from it, and headed there on foot. Telford had the place sewn up, no doubt about it. Letting his flats to old folk might have been a charitable act but he'd made damned sure it served its purpose. Rebus wondered if, given the same circumstances, Cafferty would have been clever enough to think of panic-buttons. He suspected not. Cafferty wasn't thick, but most of what he did he did by instinct. Rebus wondered if Tommy Telford had ever made a rash move in his life.

He was staking out Flint Street because he needed an *in*, needed to find the weak link in the chain around Telford. After ten minutes of windchill, he thought of a better idea. On his mobile, he called one of the city's taxi firms. Identified himself and asked if Henry Wilson was on shift. He was. Rebus told the switchboard to put a call out to Henry. It was as simple as that.

Ten minutes later, Wilson turned up. He drank in the Ox occasionally, which was his problem really. Drunk in charge of a taxi-cab. Luckily Rebus had been around to smooth things over, as a result of which Wilson owed him a lifetime of favours. He was tall, heavily built, with short black hair and a long black beard. Ruddy-faced, and he always wore check shirts. Rebus thought of him as 'The Lumberjack'.

'Need a lift?' Wilson said, as Rebus got into the front passenger-seat.

'First thing I need is a blast of the heater.' Wilson obliged. 'Second thing I need is to use your taxi as cover.'

'You mean, sit here?'

'That's what I mean.'

'With the meter running?'

'You've got an engine problem, Henry. Your cab's out of the game for the rest of the afternoon.'

'I'm saving up for Christmas,' Wilson complained.

Rebus stared him out. The big man sighed and lifted a newspaper from the side of his seat. 'Help me pick a few winners then,' he said, turning to the racing pages.

They sat for over an hour at the end of Flint Street, and Rebus stayed in the front of the cab. His reasoning: a cab parked with a passenger in the back looked suspicious. A cab parked with two guys in the front, and you'd just think they were on their break, or at shift's end – two cabbies sharing stories and a flask of tea.

Rebus took one sip from the plastic cup and winced. Half a bag of sugar in the flask.

'I've always had a sweet tooth,' Wilson explained. He had a packet of crisps open on his lap: pickled onion flavour.

Finally, Rebus saw two Range Rovers being driven into Flint Street. Sean Haddow – Telford's money man – was driving the lead car. He got out and went into the arcade. On the passenger seat, Rebus could see a huge yellow teddy bear. Haddow was coming out again, bringing Telford with him. Telford: back from the hospital already, hands bandaged, gauze patches on his face like he'd had a particularly ropey shave. But not about to let a little thing like an acid attack get in the way of business. Haddow held the back door open, and Telford got in.

'This is us, Henry,' Rebus said. 'You're going to be following those two Range Rovers. Stay back as far as you like. Those things are so high off the ground, we'll be able to see them over anything smaller than a double-decker.'

Both Range Rovers headed out of Flint Street. The second car carried three of Telford's 'soldiers'. Rebus recognised Pretty-Boy. The other two were younger recruits, well-dressed with groomed hair. One hundred percent business.

The convoy headed for the city centre, stopped outside a

hotel. Telford had a word with his men, but entered the building alone. The cars stayed where they were.

'Are you going in?' Wilson asked.

'I think I'd be noticed,' Rebus said. The drivers of both Range Rovers had got out and were enjoying a smoke, but keeping a keen eye on people entering and leaving the hotel. A couple of prospects looked into the cab, but Wilson shook his head.

'I could be making a mint here,' he muttered. Rebus offered him a Polo. Wilson accepted with a snort.

'Brilliant,' Rebus said. Wilson looked back towards the hotel. A parking warden was talking to Haddow and Pretty-Boy. She had her notebook out. They were tapping their watches, attempting charm. Double yellow lines kerbside: no parking any time.

Haddow and Pretty-Boy held up their hands in surrender, had a quick confab, then it was back into the Range Rovers. Pretty-Boy made circling motions with one hand, letting his passengers know they were going to circle the block. The warden stood her ground till they'd moved off. Haddow was on his mobile: doubtless letting his boss know the score.

Interesting: they hadn't tried to strongarm the warden, or bribe her, nothing like that. Law-abiding citizens. Telford's rules, no doubt. Again, Rebus couldn't see any of Cafferty's men giving in so quickly.

'You going in then?' Wilson asked.

'Not much point, Henry. Telford will already be in a bedroom or somebody's suite. If he's doing business, it'll be behind closed doors.'

'So that was Tommy Telford?'

'You've heard of him?'

'I'm a taxi driver, we hear things. He's after Big Ger's cab business.' Wilson paused. 'Not that Big Ger *has* a cab business, you understand.'

'Any idea how Telford plans to wrest it away from Cafferty?'

'Scare off the drivers, or get them to switch sides.'

'What about your company, Henry?'

'Honest, legal and decent, Mr Rebus.'

'No approach by Telford?'

'Not yet.'

'Here they come again.' They watched as the two Range Rovers turned back into the street. There was no sign of the warden. A couple of minutes later, Telford emerged from the hotel, bringing with him a Japanese man with spiky hair and a shiny aquamarine suit. He carried a briefcase but didn't look like a businessman. Maybe it was the sunglasses, worn in late-afternoon twilight; maybe it was the cigarette slouching from the corner of the downturned mouth. Both men got into the back of the lead car. The Japanese leaned forward and ruffled the teddy bear's ears, making some joke. Telford didn't look amused.

'Do we follow them?' Wilson asked. He saw the look on Rebus's face, turned the key in the ignition.

They were heading west out of town. Rebus already had an inkling of their ultimate destination, but he wanted to know what route they'd take. Turned out it was much the same route he'd taken with Candice. She hadn't recognised anything until Juniper Green, but it wasn't as if there were many landmarks. On Slateford Road the back car signalled that it was pulling over.

'What do I do?' Wilson asked.

'Keep going. Make the first left you can, and turn the cab round. We'll wait for them to go past us.'

Haddow had gone into a newspaper shop. Same story as with Candice. Strange, during what was a business trip, that Telford would allow a stop. And what about the building which, according to Candice, he'd seemed so interested in? There it was: an anonymous brick edifice. A warehouse maybe? Rebus could think of reasons why a warehouse might be of interest to Tommy Telford. Haddow stayed in the shop three minutes – Rebus timed him. No one else came out, so it wasn't as if he'd had to queue. Back into the car, and the little convoy set off again. They were heading for Juniper Green, and after that Poyntinghame Country Club. Little point in tagging along: the further they got out of town, the more conspicuous the cab would be. Rebus told Henry to turn around.

He got the cabbie to drop him off at the Oxford Bar. Wilson slid down his window as he was about to move off.

'Are we square now?' he called.

'Till next time, Henry.' Rebus pushed open the door and walked into the pub.

Perched on a stool, daytime TV and Margaret the barmaid for company, Rebus ordered a mug of coffee and a corned beef and beetroot roll. For his main course Margaret suggested a bridie.

'Excellent choice,' Rebus agreed. He was thinking about the Japanese businessman. Who hadn't really looked like a businessman at all. He'd been all sharp edges, chiselled face. Fortified, Rebus walked from the Ox back to the hotel, and kept watch on it from an overpriced bar across the street. He passed the time making calls on his mobile. By the time the battery died, he'd spoken with Hogan, Bill Pryde, Siobhan Clarke, Rhona and Patience, and had been about to call Torphichen cop-shop, see if anyone there could identify the building on Slateford Road. Two hours crawled by. He broke his 'personal best' for slow drinking: two Cokes. The bar wasn't exactly crowded; no one seemed to mind. The music was on a tape-loop. 'Psycho Killer' was coming round for the third time when the Range Rovers stopped outside the hotel. Telford and the Jap shook hands, made slight bows. Telford and his men drove off.

Rebus left the bar, crossed the road, and entered the

hotel. The lift doors were closing on Mr Aquamarine.
Rebus walked up to reception, showed his ID.

'The guest who just came in, I need his name.'

The receptionist had to check. 'Mr Matsumoto.'

'First name?'

'Takeshi.'

'When did he arrive?'

She checked the register again. 'Yesterday.'

'How long's he staying?'

'Three more days. Look, I should call my supervisor ...'

Rebus shook his head. 'That's all I needed to know,
thanks. Mind if I sit in the lounge for a while?'

She shook her head, so Rebus wandered into the
residents' lounge. He settled on a sofa – perfect view of the
reception area through the glass double-doors – and picked
up a newspaper. Matsumoto was in town on Poyntinghame
business, but Rebus had a whiff of something altogether
less savoury. Hugh Malahide's story had been that a
corporation wanted to buy the club, but Matsumoto didn't
look like he worked in any above-board business. When he
finally emerged into reception, he'd changed into a white
suit, black open-necked shirt, and Burberry trenchcoat,
topped off with a woollen tartan scarf. He had a cigarette in
his mouth, but didn't light it until he was outside the hotel.
With the collar of his coat turned up, he started walking.
Rebus followed him for the best part of a mile, and kept
checking that no one was following *him*. It was possible,
after all, that Telford would want to keep tabs on
Matsumoto. But if there was surveillance, it was excep-
tional. Matsumoto wasn't playing the tourist, wasn't
dawdling. He kept his head down, protecting his face from
the wind, and seemed to have some destination in mind.

When he disappeared into a building, Rebus paused,
studying the glass door behind which stood a flight of red-
carpeted stairs. He knew where he was, didn't need the sign

above the door to tell him. He was outside the Morvena Casino. The place used to be owned by a local villain called Topper Hamilton and managed by a man called Mandelson. But Hamilton was in retirement, and Mandelson had scarpered. The new owner was still an unknown quantity – or had been till now. Rebus guessed he wouldn't be far wrong if he placed Tommy Telford and his Japanese friends in the frame. He looked around, checking the parked cars: no Range Rovers.

'What the hell,' he said to himself, pushing open the door and starting to climb the stairs.

In the upstairs foyer he was eyeballed by security: two of them looking uncomfortable in their black suits and bowties, white shirts. One skinny – he'd be all about speed and manoeuvres; one a real heavyweight – slow muscle to back up the fast moves. Rebus seemed to pass whatever test they'd just given him. He bought a twenty's worth of chips and walked into the gaming room.

At one time, it would have been the drawing-room of a Georgian house. There were two huge bay windows, and ornate cornicing connected the twenty-foot-high cream walls to the pastel-pink ceiling. Now it was home to gaming tables: blackjack, dice, roulette. Hostesses moved between the tables, taking orders for drinks. There was very little noise: the gamblers took their work seriously. Rebus wouldn't have called the place busy, but what clientele there was comprised a veritable United Nations. Matsumoto's coat had disappeared into the cloakroom, and he was seated at the roulette table. Rebus sat down beside two men at the blackjack table, nodded a greeting. The dealer – young, but obviously sure of himself – smiled. Rebus won with his first hand. Lost with his second and third. Won again with his fourth. There was a voice just behind his right ear.

'Something to drink, sir?'

The hostess had bent forward to speak to him, showing plenty of cleavage.

'Coke,' he told her. 'Ice and lemon.' He pretended to watch her move away. Really, he was scoping the room. He'd sat in on the game quickly: walking around the room would have attracted everyone's interest, and he couldn't be sure if there'd be anyone here who'd know him.

He needn't have worried. The only person he recognised was Matsumoto, rubbing his hands as the croupier pushed chips towards him. Rebus stuck on eighteen. The dealer got twenty. Rebus had never been a great gambler. He'd tried the football pools, sometimes the horses, and now occasionally the lottery. But fruit machines didn't interest him; the poker sessions organised in the office didn't interest him. He had other ways of losing money.

Matsumoto lost and gave what sounded like a curse, a little bit louder than the room liked. The skinny security ape put his head around the door, but Matsumoto ignored him, and when Mr Skinny saw who was making the noise, he retreated fast. Matsumoto laughed: he might not have much English, but he knew he had power in this place. He told everyone something in a stream of Japanese, nodding, trying for eye contact. Then a hostess brought him a big tumbler of whisky and ice. He handed her a couple of chips as a tip. The croupier was telling everyone to place their bets. Matsumoto quietened down and went back to work.

Rebus's drink was a while coming, Coke the unlikely beverage of the high roller. He'd won a couple of hands, felt a bit better. Stood up to accept the drink. The table knew to leave him out of the next deal.

'Where are you from?' he asked the hostess. 'I can't place your accent.'

'I am from Ukraine.'

'You speak good English.'

'Thank you.' She turned away. Conversation was not house policy, it kept the punters away from their games. Ukraine: Rebus wondered if she was another of Tarawicz's imports. Like Candice ... A few things seemed clear to him. Matsumoto was comfortable here, therefore known. And the staff were wary of him, therefore he had clout, had Telford behind him. Telford wanted him kept sweet. It wasn't much return for all Rebus's work, but it was something.

Then someone walked in. Someone Rebus knew. Dr Colquhoun. He saw Rebus immediately and fear jumped into his face. Colquhoun: with his sick line to the university; his enforced holiday; no forwarding address. Colquhoun: who'd known Rebus was taking Candice to the Drinics.

Rebus watched him back towards the doors. Watched him turn and run.

Options: go after him, or stay with Matsumoto? Which was the more important to him now, Candice or Telford? Rebus stayed. But now Colquhoun was back in town, he'd track him down.

For definite.

After an hour and a quarter's play, he was considering cashing a cheque for more chips. Twenty quid down in a little over an hour, and Candice fighting for some space in his crowded head. He took a break, moved to a row of fruit machines, but the lights and buttons defeated him. He wasted three nudges and ran out of time on some accumulator. Another two quid gone – this time in a couple of minutes. Little wonder clubs and pubs wanted slot machines. Tommy Telford was in the right business. His hostess came to see him again, asked if he wanted another drink.

'I'm fine,' he said. 'Not much action tonight.'

'It's early,' she told him. 'Wait till after midnight ...'

No way was he sticking around that long. But Matsumoto surprised him, threw up his hands and came out with another rush of Japanese, nodding and grinning, gathering up his chips. He cashed them and left the casino. Rebus waited all of thirty seconds, then followed. He said a breezy goodnight to the security men, felt their eyes on him all the way back down the stairs.

Matsumoto was buttoning his coat, wrapping the scarf tight around his neck. He was headed back in the direction of the hotel. Rebus, suddenly bone-tired, stopped in his tracks. He was thinking of Sammy and Lintz and the Weasel, thinking of all the time he seemed to be wasting.

'Fuck this for a game of soldiers.'

Turned on his heels and went to collect his car. Ten Years After: 'Goin' Home'.

It was a twenty-minute walk to Flint Street, a lot of it uphill and with the wind doing nobody any favours. The city was quiet: people huddled at bus stops; students munching on baked potatoes, chips with curry sauce. A few souls marching home with the concentrated tread of the sozzled. Rebus stopped, frowned, looked around. This was where he'd left the Saab. He was positive ... no, not 'positive' – the word had taken on malign overtones. He was *sure*, yes, sure he'd left the Saab right here. Where now a black Ford Sierra was parked, and behind that a Mini. But no sign of Rebus's car.

'Aw, Christ,' he exploded. There were no signs of glass by the roadside, which meant they hadn't taken a brick to one of his windows. Oh, there'd be jokes in the office about this though, whether he got the car back or not. A taxi came along and he flagged it down, then remembered he'd no cash, so waved it off again.

His flat in Arden Street wasn't that far off, but had he been a camel, he'd have been keeping well clear of any straw.

20

He was asleep in his chair by the living-room window, duvet pulled up to his neck, when the buzzer sounded. He couldn't remember setting the alarm. Consciousness brought the dawning realisation that it was his door. He staggered to his feet, found his trousers and put them on.

'All right, all right,' he called, heading for the hall. 'Keep your hair on.'

He opened the door and saw Bill Pryde.

'Jesus, Bill, is this some sort of twisted revenge?' Rebus looked at his watch: two-fifteen.

'Afraid not, John,' Pryde said. His face and voice told Rebus something bad had happened.

Something very bad indeed.

'I've been off the booze for weeks.'

'Sure about that?'

'Definite.' Rebus's eyes burned into those of DCI Gill Templer. They were in her office at St Leonard's. Pryde was there, too. His jacket was off and his sleeves rolled up. Gill Templer looked bleary from interrupted sleep. Rebus was pacing what floor there was, unable to stay seated.

'I've had nothing to drink all day but coffee and Coke.'

'Really?'

Rebus ran his hands through his hair. He felt groggy, and his head was throbbing. But he couldn't ask for Paracetamol and water: they'd assume hangover.

'Come on, Gill,' he said, 'I'm being shafted here.'

'Who authorised your surveillance?'

'Nobody. I did it in my own time.'

'How do you work that out?'

'The Chief Super said I could take a bit of time off.'

'He meant so you could visit your daughter.' She paused.
'Is that what this was all about?'

'Maybe.'

'This Mr …' she checked her notes '… Matsumoto, he
was connected to Thomas Telford. And your theory is that
Telford was behind the attack on your daughter?'

Rebus thumped the wall with his fists. 'It's a set-up,
oldest trick in the book. I've yet to see one perfected.
There's got to be something at the scene … something out
of kilter.' He turned to his colleagues. 'You've got to let me
go there, take a look around.'

Templer looked to Bill Pryde. Pryde folded his arms,
shrugged assent. But it was Templer's play, she was the
senior officer here. She tapped her pen against her teeth,
then dropped it on to the desk.

'Will you submit to a blood test?'

Rebus swallowed. 'Why not?' he said at last.

'Come on then,' she said, getting to her feet.

The story was: Matsumoto had been on his way back to his
hotel. Crossing the road, he'd been hit by a car travelling at
speed. The driver hadn't stopped, not right away. But the
car had travelled only another couple of hundred yards
before mounting the pavement with its front wheels. It had
been abandoned there, driver's door open.

A Saab 900, its identity known to half the Lothian and
Borders force.

The interior reeked of whisky, the screw-top from a
bottle lying on the passenger seat. No sign of the bottle, no
sign of the driver. Just the car, and two hundred yards

further back, the body of the Japanese businessman, growing cold by the roadside.

Nobody had seen anything. Nobody had heard anything. Rebus could believe it: never one of the city centre's busier routes, at this hour the place was dead.

'When I followed him from his hotel, he didn't come this way,' Rebus told Templer. She stood with shoulders hunched, hands deep in her coat pockets, keeping out the cold.

'So?' she asked.

'Long way round for a short-cut.'

'Maybe he wanted to see the sights,' Pryde suggested.

'What time's this supposed to have happened?' Rebus asked.

Templer hesitated. 'There's a margin of error.'

'Look, Gill, I know this is awkward. You shouldn't have brought me here, you shouldn't answer my questions. I'm the number one suspect, after all.' Rebus knew how much she had to lose. Over two hundred male Chief Inspectors in Scotland; only *five* women. Bad odds, and a lot of people waiting for her to fail. He held up his hands. 'Look, if I was blind drunk and I hit somebody, think I'd leave the car at the scene?'

'You might not know you'd hit anyone. You hear a thunk, lose control and mount the kerb, and some survival instinct tells you it's time to get out and walk.'

'Only I hadn't been drinking. I left the car near Flint Street, and that's where they took it from. Any signs it was broken into?'

She didn't say anything.

'I'll guess not,' Rebus went on. 'Because professionals don't leave marks. But to get it started, they must have wired it or got into the steering column. That's what you should be looking for.'

The car had been towed. First thing in the morning, forensics would be all over it.

Rebus laughed, shaking his head. 'It's nice though, isn't it? First they make Sammy look like a hit and run, and now they try to pin me for the same thing.'

'Who's "they"?'

'Telford and his men.'

'I thought you said they were doing business with Matsumoto?'

'They're all gangsters, Gill. Gangsters fall out.'

'What about Cafferty?'

Rebus frowned. 'What about him?'

'He's got an old grudge against you. This way, he stitches you up *and* annoys Telford.'

'So you do think I'm being stitched up?'

'I'm giving you the benefit of the doubt.' She paused. 'Not everyone will. What was Matsumoto's business with Telford?'

'Something to do with a country club – on the surface at least. Some Japanese were buying it, and Telford was clearing the way.' He shivered: should have worn a coat over his jacket. He rubbed his arm where the blood sample had been taken to test his alcohol level. 'Of course, a check of the deceased's hotel room might throw up something.'

'We've already been there,' Pryde said. 'Nothing out of the ordinary.'

'Which deadbeat did you send?'

'I went myself,' Gill Templer said, voice as icy as the wind. Rebus bowed his head in apology. She had a point though: Matsumoto and Telford had been doing business. There had been nothing about their farewell to one another to suggest a break-up, and Matsumoto had seemed happy and confident at the casino. What had Telford to gain by bumping him off?

Apart from maybe getting Rebus off his back.

Templer had mentioned Cafferty: was Big Ger capable of such a move? What did *he* stand to gain? Apart from settling a long-held grudge against Rebus, giving Telford a headache, and maybe gaining Poyntinghame and the Japanese deal for himself.

Balance the two – Telford against Cafferty. Cafferty's side tipped, went clunk as it hit the ground.

'Let's get back to the station,' Templer said. 'I'm reaching the early stages of frostbite.'

'Can I go home then?'

'We're not done with you yet, John,' she said, getting into the car. 'Not by a long chalk.'

But eventually they had to let him go. He wasn't being charged, not yet. There was work still to be done. He knew they could make a case against him if they wanted to, knew it only too well. *He'd* followed Matsumoto out of the club. *He* was the one with the grudge against Telford. *He* was the one who'd see poetic justice in sending Telford a message by driving over one of his associates.

He, John Rebus, was firmly in the frame. It was tightly constructed and quite elegant in its way. The scales suddenly tipped back towards Telford again, so much subtler than Cafferty.

Telford.

Rebus visited Farlowe in his cell. The reporter wasn't asleep.

'How long do I have to stay here?' he asked.

'As long as possible.'

'How's Telford?'

'Minor burns. Don't expect him to press charges. He'll want you on the outside.'

'Then you'll have to let me go.'

'Don't bet on it, Ned. *We* can press charges. We don't need Telford.'

Farlowe looked at him. 'You're going to prosecute me?'

'I saw the whole thing. Unwarranted attack on an innocent man.'

Farlowe snorted, then smiled. 'Ironic, isn't it? Charging me for my own good.' He paused. 'I won't be able to see Sammy, will I?'

Rebus shook his head.

'I didn't think of that. Fact is, I didn't *think*.' He looked up from his ledge. 'I just did. And right up until the moment I did it, it felt … brilliant.'

'And afterwards?'

Farlowe shrugged. 'What does afterwards matter? It's only the rest of my life.'

Rebus didn't go home, knew he wouldn't sleep. And he'd no car, so he couldn't go driving. Instead, he visited the hospital, sat down by Sammy's bedside. He took her hand, rested it against his face.

When a nurse came in and asked if he wanted anything, he asked if she'd any Paracetamol.

'In a hospital?' she said, smiling. 'I'll see what I can do.'

21

Rebus was due for further questioning at St Leonard's at ten o'clock, so when his pager sounded at eight-fifteen, he assumed it was a reminder. But the phone number it wanted him to call was the mortuary down in the Cowgate. He called from the hospital payphone, and was put through to Dr Curt.

'Looks like I've drawn the short straw,' Curt told him.

'You're about to start work on Matsumoto?'

'For my sins. Look, I've heard the stories ... don't suppose there's any truth in them?'

'I didn't kill him.'

'Glad to hear it, John.' Curt seemed to be struggling to say something. 'There are questions of ethics, of course, so I can't suggest that you come down here ...'

'There's something you think I should see?'

'That I can't say.' Curt cleared his throat. 'But if you happened to be here ... and the place is always very quiet this time of the morning ...'

'I'm on my way.'

The Infirmary to the mortuary: a ten-minute walk. Curt himself was waiting to lead Rebus to the body.

The room was all white tile, bright light and stainless steel. Two of the dissecting-tables lay empty. Matsumoto's naked body lay on the third. Rebus walked around it, stunned by what he saw.

Tattoos.

And not just the kilted piper on a sailor's arm. These

were works of art, and they were massive. A scaly green dragon, breathing pink and red fire, covered one shoulder and crept down the arm towards the wrist. Its back legs reached around the body's neck, while its front ones rested on the chest. There were other smaller dragons, and a landscape – Mount Fuji reflected in water. There were Japanese symbols and the visored face of a kendo champion. Curt put on rubber gloves, and had Rebus do the same. Then the two men rolled the body over, displaying a further gallery across Matsumoto's back. A masked actor, something out of a Noh play, and a warrior in full armour. Some delicate flowers. The effect was mesmerising.

'Stunning, aren't they?' Curt said.

'Phenomenal.'

'I've visited Japan a few times, given papers at conferences.'

'So you recognise some of these?'

'A few of the references, yes. Thing is, tattoos – especially on this scale – usually mean you're a gang member.'

'Like the Triads?'

'The Japanese are called Yakuza. Look here.' Curt held up the left hand. The pinkie had been severed at the first joint, the skin healed in a rough crust.

'That's what happens when they screw up, isn't it?' Rebus said, the word 'Yakuza' bouncing around in his head. 'Someone cuts off a finger every time.'

'I think so, yes,' Curt said. 'Just thought you might like to know.'

Rebus nodded, eyes glued to the corpse. 'Anything else?'

'Well, I haven't started on him yet, really. All looks fairly standard: evidence of impact with a moving vehicle. Crushed ribcage, fractures to the arms and legs.' Rebus noticed that a bone was protruding from one calf, obscenely white against the skin. 'There'll be a lot of internal damage.

Shock probably killed him.' Curt was thoughtful. 'I must let Professor Gates know. Doubt he'll have seen anything like it.'

'Can I use your phone?' Rebus asked.

He knew one person who might know about the Yakuza – she'd seemed knowledgeable about every other country's criminal gangs. So he spoke to Miriam Kenworthy in Newcastle.

'Tattoos and missing fingers?' she said.

'Bingo.'

'That's Yakuza.'

'Actually, it's only the top bit missing from one little finger. That's done to them when they step out of line, isn't it?'

'Not quite. They do it to *themselves* as a way of saying they're sorry. I'm not sure I know much more than that.' There was the sound of papers being shifted. 'I'm just looking for my notes.'

'What notes?'

'When I was connecting all these gangs, different cultures, I did some research. Might be something on the Yakuza ... Look, can I call you back?'

'How long?'

'Five minutes.'

Rebus gave her Curt's number, then sat and waited. Curt's room wasn't so much an office as a walk-in cupboard. Files were stacked high on his desk, and a dictaphone lay on top of them, along with a fresh pack of tapes. The room reeked of cigarettes and bad ventilation. On the walls: schedules of meetings, postcards, a couple of framed prints. The place was a bolt-hole, a necessity; Curt spent most of his time elsewhere.

Rebus took out Colquhoun's business card, tried home

and office. As far as his secretary was concerned, Dr Colquhoun was still off sick.

Maybe, but he was well enough to visit a casino. One of Telford's casinos. No coincidence surely ...

Kenworthy was good as gold.

'Yakuza,' she said, sounding like she was lifting from her script. 'Ninety thousand members split into something like two and a half thousand groupings. Utterly ruthless, but also highly intelligent and sophisticated. Very hierarchical structure, almost impenetrable to outsiders. Like a secret society. They even have a sort of middle management level, called the Sokaiya.'

Rebus was writing it all down. 'How do you spell that?'

She told him. 'Back in Japan they run *pachinko* parlours – that's a sort of gaming thing – and have fingers in most other illegal pies.'

'Unless they've lopped them off. What about outside Japan?'

'Only thing I've got down here is that they ship expensive designer stuff back home to sell on the black market, also stolen art, ship it back to wealthy buyers ...'

'Wait a minute, you told me Jake Tarawicz started out smuggling icons out of Russia.'

'You're saying Pink Eyes might connect to the Yakuza?'

'Tommy Telford's been chauffeuring them around. There's a warehouse everyone seems interested in, plus a country club.'

'What's in the warehouse?'

'I don't know yet.'

'Maybe you should find out.'

'It's on my list. Something else, these *pachinko* parlours ... would those be like amusement arcades?'

'Pretty much.'

'Another connection with Telford: he puts gaming machines into half the pubs and clubs on the east coast.'

'You think the Yakuza saw someone they could do a deal with?'

'I don't know.' He tried stifling a yawn.

'Too early in the morning for big questions?'

He smiled. 'Something like that. Thanks for your help, Miriam.'

'No problem. Keep me posted.'

'Sure. Anything new on Tarawicz?'

'Nothing I've heard. No sign of Candice either, sorry.'

'Thanks again.'

''Bye.'

Curt was standing in the doorway. He'd stripped off gown and gloves, and his hands smelled of soap.

'Not much I can do till my assistants get in.' He looked at his watch. 'Fancy a spot of breakfast?'

'You have to appreciate how this looks, John. The media could be all over us. I can think of a few journalists who'd give their drinking-arm to nail you.'

Chief Superintendent Watson was in his element. Seated behind his desk, hands folded, he had the serenity of a large stone Buddha. The occasional crises with which John Rebus presented him had hardened the Farmer to life's lesser knocks and taught him calm acceptance.

'You're going to suspend me,' Rebus stated with conviction – he'd been here before. He finished the coffee his boss had given him, but kept his hands locked around the mug. 'Then you're going to open an investigation.'

'Not straight away,' Watson surprised him by saying. 'What I want first of all is your statement – and I mean a full and frank explanation – of your recent movements, your interest in Mr Matsumoto and Thomas Telford. Bring in anything you want about your daughter's accident, any suspicions you've had, and above all the *validity* of those suspicions. Telford already has a lawyer asking awkward questions about our Japanese friend's untimely end. The lawyer ...' Watson looked to Gill Templer, seated by the door, mouth a thin unimpressed line.

'Charles Groal,' she said flatly.

'Groal, yes. He's been asking at the casino. He got a description of a man who came in just after Matsumoto, and left immediately after him. He seems to think it's you.'

'Are you telling him otherwise?' Rebus asked.

'We're telling him nothing, not until our own inquiries have established ... et cetera. But I can't hold him off forever, John.'

'Have you asked anyone what Matsumoto was doing here?'

'He works for a firm of management consultants. He was here at a client's behest, finalising the takeover of a country club.'

'With Tommy Telford in tow.'

'John, let's not lose sight of ...'

'Matsumoto was a member of the Yakuza, sir. The closest I've come to one of those before has been on a TV screen. Now suddenly they're in Edinburgh.' Rebus paused. 'Don't you find that just a *wee* bit curious? I mean, doesn't it worry you at all? I don't know, maybe I'm getting my priorities all wrong, but it seems to me we're splashing about in puddles while a tidal wave's coming in!'

The pressure of his hands around the mug had been increasing by degrees. Now the thing broke, a piece falling to the floor as Rebus winced. He picked one ceramic shard out of his palm. Drops of blood hit the carpet. Gill Templer had come forward, was reaching for his hand.

'Here, let me.'

He spun away from her. 'No!' Way too loud. Fumbling in his pocket for a handkerchief.

'I've got some paper ones in my bag.'

'It's all right.' Blood dripping on to his shoes. Watson

was saying something about the mug having a crack; Templer was staring at him. He wrapped white cotton around the wound.

'I'll go wash it,' he said. 'With your permission, sir?'

'On you go, John. Sure you're all right?'

'I'll be fine.'

It wasn't a bad cut. Cold water helped. He dried off with paper towels, which he flushed down the toilet, waiting to see they'd gone. A first aid box next: half a dozen plasters, cover the nick good and proper. He bunched his fist, saw no sign of leakage. Had to be content with that.

Back at his desk, he started on his memoirs – as ordered by Watson. Gill Templer came past, decided he needed a few soft words.

'None of us thinks you did it, John. But something like this ... questions being asked by the Japanese consul ... it has to be done by the book.'

'It all comes down to politics in the end, eh?' He was thinking of Joseph Lintz.

At lunchtime he dropped in on Ned Farlowe, asked him if he needed anything. Farlowe wanted sandwiches, books, newspapers, company. He looked drawn, weary of imprisonment. Maybe soon he'd think to ask for a lawyer. A lawyer – any lawyer – would get him out.

Rebus handed his report to Watson's secretary and headed out of the station. He'd gone fifty yards when a car pulled up alongside. Range Rover. Pretty-Boy telling him to get in. Rebus looked into the back of the car.

Telford. Ointment on his blistered face. Looking like a scaled-down Jake Tarawicz ...

Rebus hesitated. The cop shop was a short sprint away.

'Get in,' Pretty-Boy repeated. Sucker for a free offer, Rebus got in.

Pretty-Boy turned the car. The giant yellow teddy had been strapped into the passenger seat.

'I don't suppose,' Rebus said, 'it's worth my while asking you to leave Ned Farlowe be?'

Telford's mind was on other things. 'He wants war, he's going to get war.'

'Who?'

'Your boss.'

'I don't work for Cafferty.'

'Don't give me that.'

'I'm the one who put him inside.'

'And you've been snuggling up ever since.'

'I didn't kill Matsumoto.'

Telford looked at him for the first time, and Rebus could see he was itching for violence.

'You know I didn't,' Rebus went on.

'What do you mean?'

'Because you did it, and you want me to –'

Telford's hands were around Rebus's neck. Rebus shrugged them off, tried pinning Telford down. Impossible with the car in motion, cramped in the back seat. Pretty-Boy stopped the car and got out, opened Rebus's door and dragged him on to the pavement. Telford followed, face beetroot-red, eyes bulging.

'You're not going to pin this on me!' he roared. Drivers slowed to watch. Pedestrians crossed the road to safety.

'Who else?' Rebus's voice was shaky.

'Cafferty!' Telford screeched. 'It's you and Cafferty, trying to shut me down!'

'I'm telling you, I didn't do it.'

'Boss,' Pretty-Boy was saying, 'let's screw the head, eh?' He was looking around, nervous of the attention they were attracting. Telford saw his point, let his shoulders relax a little.

'Get in the car,' he said to Rebus. Rebus just stared at

him. 'It's okay. Just get in. I want to show you a couple of things.'

Rebus, world's craziest cop, got back in.

There was silence for a couple of minutes, Telford rearranging the dressings on his fingers, which had come loose during the fight.

'I don't think Cafferty wants war,' Rebus said.

'What makes you so sure?'

Because I've done a deal with him – it's me who's going to shut you down. They were heading west. Rebus tried not to think about possible destinations.

'You were in the Army, weren't you?' Telford asked.

Rebus nodded.

'Paratroops, then the SAS.'

'I didn't get past training.' Rebus thinking: he's well-informed.

'So you decided to become a cop instead.' Telford was completely calm again. He'd brushed down his suit and checked the knot in his tie. 'Thing is, working for structures like those – Army, cops – you need to obey orders. I hear you're not very good at it. You wouldn't last long with me.' He looked out of the window. 'What's Cafferty planning?'

'No idea.'

'Why were you watching Matsumoto?'

'Because he tied into you.'

'Crime Squad pulled their surveillance.' Rebus said nothing. 'But you kept yours going.' Telford turned towards him. 'Why?'

'Because you tried to kill my daughter.'

Telford stared at him, unblinking. 'Is that what this is about?'

'It's why Ned Farlowe tried to blind you. He's her boyfriend.'

Telford choked out a disbelieving laugh, started to shake

his head. 'I'd nothing to do with your daughter. Where's the reason?'

'To get at me. Because she helped me with Candice.'

Telford was thoughtful. 'Okay,' he said, nodding, 'I can see your thinking, and I don't suppose my word's going to count for much, but for what it's worth, I know absolutely nothing about your daughter.' He paused. Rebus could hear sirens nearby. 'Is that what took you to Cafferty?'

Rebus said nothing, which seemed, to Telford's mind, to confirm his suspicions. He smiled again.

'Pull over,' Telford said. Pretty-Boy stopped the car. The road ahead was blocked anyway, police diverting traffic down side-streets. Rebus realised he'd been smelling smoke for some time. The tenements had hidden it from view, but now he could see the fire. It was in the lot where Cafferty kept his taxis. The shed used as an office had been reduced to ash. The garage behind, where the cabs were worked on and cleaned up, was about to lose its corrugated roof. A row of vehicles was burning nicely.

'We could have sold tickets,' Pretty-Boy said. Telford turned from the spectacle to Rebus.

'Fire Brigade's going to be stretched. Two of Cafferty's offices are spontaneously combusting ...' he checked his watch ... 'right about now, as is that beautiful house of his. Don't worry, we waited till his wife was out shopping. Final ultimatums have been delivered to his men – they can shuffle out of town or off this mortal coil.' He shrugged. 'Makes no odds to me. Go tell Cafferty: he's finished in Edinburgh.'

Rebus licked his lips. 'You've just said I'm wrong about you, that you had nothing to do with my daughter. What if *you're* wrong about Cafferty?'

'Wake up, will you? The stabbing at Megan's, then Danny Simpson ... Cafferty's not exactly subtle.'

'Did Danny say it was Cafferty's men?'

'He knows, same as I do.' Telford tapped Pretty-Boy's shoulder. 'Back to base.' To Rebus: 'Another little message for you to take to Barlinnie. Here's what I told Cafferty's men – any of them left in this city after midnight are fair game ... and I don't take prisoners.' He sniffed, seemed pleased with himself, settled back in the seat. 'You won't mind if I drop you at Flint Street? Only I've a business meeting in fifteen minutes.'

'With Matsumoto's bosses?'

'If they want Poyntinghame, they'll keep dealing with me.' He looked at Rebus. 'You should deal with me, too. Think about this: who'd want you pissed off with me? It comes back to Cafferty: hitting your daughter, setting up Matsumoto ... It *all* comes back to Cafferty. Think it over, then maybe we should talk again.'

After a couple of minutes, Rebus broke the silence.

'You know a man called Joseph Lintz?'

'Bobby Hogan mentioned him.'

'He phoned your office in Flint Street.'

Telford shrugged. 'I'll tell you what I told Hogan. Maybe it was a wrong number. Whatever it was, *I* didn't speak to any old Nazi.'

'You're not the only one uses that office though.' Rebus saw Pretty-Boy watching him in the rearview mirror. 'What about you?'

'Never heard of the cat.'

A car was parked in Flint Street – a huge white limousine with blackened windows. There was a TV aerial on the boot, and the hubcaps were painted pink.

'Christ,' Telford said in amusement, 'look at his latest toy.' He seemed to have forgotten all about Rebus. He was out of the car and loping towards the man who was emerging from the back of the limo. White suit, panama hat, big cigar, and a bright red paisley shirt. None of which stopped you staring at the scarred face and blue-tinted glasses. Telford was commenting on the attire, the car, the audacity, and Mr Pink Eyes was loving it. He put a hand around Telford's shoulder, steering him towards the amusement arcade. But then he stopped, clicked his fingers, turned back to the limo and reached out a hand.

And now a woman was emerging. Short black dress and black tights, fur jacket keeping out the chills. Tarawicz rubbed a hand over her backside; Telford kissed her on the neck. She smiled, eyes slightly glazed. Then Tarawicz and Telford turned towards the Range Rover. They were both staring at Rebus.

'Trip's over, Inspector,' Pretty-Boy said, telling Rebus it was time to get out. He did so, his eyes on Candice. But she wasn't looking at him. She was snuggling into Mr Pink Eyes, head on his chest. He was still rubbing her backside, the dress rising and falling. He was watching Rebus, eyes alight, face pulled into a latex grin. Rebus walked over to them, and now Candice saw him, and looked frightened.

'Inspector,' Tarawicz said, 'good to see you again. Come to whisk the damsel away to safety?'

Rebus ignored him. 'Come on, Candice.' His hand, not quite steady, held out towards her.

She looked at him and shook her head. 'Why would I want that?' she said, and was rewarded with another kiss from Tarawicz.

'You were abducted. You can press charges.'

Tarawicz was laughing, leading her into the café.

'Candice.' Rebus reached for her arm, but she pulled away and followed her master inside.

Two of Telford's men were blocking the door. Pretty-Boy was behind Rebus.

'No cheap heroics?' he asked, making to pass the policeman.

Back at St Leonard's, Rebus took Farlowe his food and

newspapers, then hitched a lift in a patrol car to Torphichen. The man he wanted was DI 'Shug' Davidson, and
Davidson was in the CID office, looking frazzled.

'Somebody torched a taxi rank,' he told Rebus.

'Any idea who?'

Davidson's eyes narrowed. 'The rank was owned by Jock
Scallow. Is there something you're trying to tell me?'

'Who really owned the outfit, Shug?'

'You know damned well.'

'And who's muscling in on Cafferty's patch?'

'I've heard rumours.'

Rebus rested against Davidson's desk. 'Tommy Telford's going into combat, unless we can stop him.'

' "We"?'

'I want you to take me somewhere,' Rebus said.

Shug Davidson was happily married to an understanding
wife, and had kids who didn't see as much of him as they
deserved. A year back, he'd won forty grand on the
Lottery. Everyone in his station got a drink. The rest of the
money had been salted away.

Rebus had worked with him before. He wasn't a bad cop,
maybe lacking a little in imagination. They had to work
their way around the scene of the fire. A further mile and a
half on, Rebus told him to stop.

'What is it?' Davidson asked.

'That's what I want you to tell me.' Rebus was looking
towards the brick building, the same one which so
interested Tommy Telford.

'It's Maclean's,' Davidson said.

'And what's Maclean's when it's at home?'

Davidson smiled. 'You really don't know?' He opened
his car door. 'Come on, I'll show you.'

They had to have their identities checked at the main
entrance. Rebus noticed a lot of security, albeit subtle:

cameras trained down from the corners of the building, catching every angle of approach. A phone call was made, and a man in a white coat came down to sign them in. They pinned visitor's badges to their jackets, and the tour began.

'I've been here before,' Davidson confided. 'If you ask me, it's the best kept secret in the city.'

They climbed steps, walked down passageways. Everywhere there was security: guards checked their badges; doors had to be unlocked; cameras charted their progress. Which puzzled Rebus, for it was such an unassuming building, really. And nothing spectacular was happening.

'What is it, Fort Knox?' he asked. But then their guide handed them white coats to put on, before pushing open the door to a laboratory, and Rebus started to understand.

People were working with chemicals, examining test-tubes, writing notes. There were all sorts of weird and wonderful machines, but in essence it was a school chemistry-lab on a slightly grander scale.

'Welcome,' Davidson said, 'to the world's biggest drugs factory.'

Which wasn't quite correct, for Maclean's was only the world's largest *legal* producer of heroin and cocaine, something the guide explained.

'We're licensed by the government. Back in 1961 there was an international agreement: every country in the world was allowed just one producer, and we're it for Britain.'

'So what do you make?' Rebus was staring at the rows of locked fridges.

'All sorts of things: methadone for heroin addicts, pethedine for women in labour. Diamorphine to ease terminal illnesses and cocaine for use in medical procedures. The company started out supplying laudanum to the Victorians.'

'And these days?'

'We produce about seventy tonnes of opiates a year,' the

guide said. 'And around two million pounds' worth of pure cocaine.'

Rebus rubbed his forehead. 'I begin to see the need for security.'

The guide smiled. 'The MoD has asked us for advice – that's how good our security is.'

'No break-ins?'

'A couple of attempts, nothing we couldn't deal with.'

No, Rebus thought, but then you've never had to deal with Tommy Telford and the Yakuza ... not yet.

Rebus walked around the lab, smiled and nodded at a woman who just seemed to be standing there, not doing anything.

'Who's she?' he asked the guide.

'Our nurse. She's on stand-by.'

'What for?'

The guide nodded towards where a man was operating one of the machines. 'Etorphine,' he said. 'Forty thousand pounds a kilo, and extremely potent. The nurse has the antidote, just in case.'

'So what's it used for, this etorphine?'

'Knocking out rhinos,' the guide said, like the answer should have been obvious.

The cocaine was produced from coca leaves flown in from Peru. The opium came from plantations in Tasmania and Australia. The pure heroin and cocaine were kept in a strongroom. Each lab had its share of locked safes. The storage warehouse boasted infrared detectors and move-ment sensors. Five minutes in the place told Rebus *exactly* why Tommy Telford was interested in Maclean's. And he'd brought the Yakuza in on the plan either because he needed their help – which was unlikely – or to brag about the exploit.

Back at the car, Davidson asked the obvious question. 'What's this all about, John?'

Rebus pinched the bridge of his nose. 'I think Telford's planning to hit this place.'

Davidson snorted. 'He'd never get in. Like you said yourself, it's Fort bloody Knox.'

'It's a prestige thing, Shug. If he can empty the place, it'll make his name. He'll have beaten Cafferty hands down.' It was the same with the fire-bombings: they weren't just a message to Cafferty, but a sort of 'red carpet' for Mr Pink Eyes – welcome to Edinburgh, and look what I can do.

'I'm telling you,' Davidson said, 'there's no way in. Christ, that's cheap!' Davidson's attention had been diverted by signs on the window of the corner shop. Rebus looked, too. Cut-price cigarettes. Cheap sandwiches and hot rolls. Plus five pence off any morning paper.

'Competition around here must be crippling,' Davidson said. 'Fancy a roll?'

Rebus was watching workers leaving the gates of Maclean's. Afternoon break maybe. Saw them cross the road, dodging traffic. Counting small change from their pockets as they pushed open the door to the shop.

'Yes,' Rebus said quietly, 'why not?'

The small shop was packed out. Davidson got in the queue, while Rebus looked at the rack of papers and magazines. The workers were sharing jokes and gossip. Two staff worked behind the counter – young males, mixing banter with less-than-efficient service.

'What do you fancy, John? Bacon?'

'Fine,' Rebus said. Remembered he hadn't had lunch. 'Make it two.'

Two bacon rolls came in at one pound exactly. They sat in the car to eat.

'You know, Shug, the usual ploy with a shop like that is to take a beating on one or two necessities to get the punters in.' Davidson nodded, attacked his roll. 'But that place looked like Bargain City.' Rebus had stopped eating. 'Do us both a favour: find out the shop's history, who owns it, who those two are behind the counter.'

Davidson's chewing slowed. 'You think ... ?'

'Just check it out, all right?'

22

Back at St Leonard's, his telephone was ringing. He sat down and prised the lid from a beaker of coffee. On the drive back he'd been thinking about Candice. Two swigs of coffee and he lifted the receiver.

'DI Rebus,' he said.

'What the fuck is that little shite up to?' The voice of Big Ger Cafferty.

'Where are you?'

'Where do you think I am?'

'Sounds like a mobile.'

'Amazing the things that find their way into Barlinnie. Now tell me, what is happening over there?'

'You've heard then.'

'He torched my house! My *house*! Am I supposed to let him get away with that?'

'Look, I think I may have found a way to get to him.' Cafferty calmed a little. 'Tell me?'

'Not yet, I want to –'

'And all my taxis,' Cafferty exploded again. 'The little bastard!'

'Look, the point is: what's he expecting you to do? He's waiting for instant retaliation.'

'And he's going to get it.'

'He'll be ready. Wouldn't it be better to catch him off-guard?'

'That little bastard hasn't been off-guard since he was lifted from the cradle.'

'Shall I tell you why he did it?'

Cafferty's anger ebbed again. 'Why?'

'Because he says you killed Matsumoto.'

'Who?'

'A business acquaintance. Whoever did it made it look like I was behind the wheel.'

'It wasn't me.'

'Try telling Telford that. He thinks you ordered me to do it.'

'We know differently.'

'That's right. *We* know someone was setting me up, trying to get me out of the way.'

'What was his name again, the dead one?'

'Matsumoto.'

'Is that Japanese?'

Rebus wished he could see Cafferty's eyes. Even then, it was hard to tell when the man was playing games.

'He was Japanese,' Rebus stated.

'What the hell did he have to do with Telford?'

'Sounds to me like your intelligence has gone to pot.'

There was silence on the line. 'About your daughter ...'

Rebus froze. 'What about her?'

'A secondhand shop in Porty.' Meaning Portobello. 'The owner bought some stuff from a seller. Including opera tapes and Roy Orbison. Stuck in his mind. They don't naturally go together.'

Rebus's hand tightened on the receiver. 'Which shop? What did the seller look like?'

Cold laughter. 'We're working on it, Strawman, just leave everything to us. Now, about this Japanese fellow ...?'

'I said *I'd* put Telford out of the game. That was the agreement.'

'I've yet to see any action.'

'I'm working on it!'

'I want to hear about him anyway.'

Rebus paused.

'How is Samantha anyway?' Cafferty asked. 'That's her name, isn't it?'

'She's …'

'Because it looks like I'll be fulfilling *my* side of our bargain any day. While you, on the other hand …'

'Matsumoto was Yakuza: heard of them?'

A moment's silence. 'I've heard of them.'

'Telford's helping them buy a country club.'

'What in God's name do they want with that?'

'I'm not sure.'

Cafferty was silent again. Rebus almost thought his mobile had died. Then: 'He's got big ideas, hasn't he?' Like there was just a touch of respect there, battling the sense of territorial breach.

'We've both seen people overreach themselves.' An idea formed in Rebus's mind, a sudden notion of where everything was headed.

'Looks like Telford's got plenty of stretch left in him though,' Cafferty was saying. 'And me, I'm not even halfway through *my* stretch.'

'Know something, Cafferty? Every time you start to sound beaten, that's when I know you're just coming to the boil.'

'You know I'm going to have to retaliate, whether I want to or not. A little ritual we have to go through, like shaking hands.'

'How many men have you got?'

'More than enough.'

'Listen, one last thing …' Rebus couldn't believe he was telling his arch-enemy this. 'Jake Tarawicz arrived here today. I think the fireworks were meant to impress him.'

'Telford torched my house just so he'd have something to show that ugly Russian bastard?'

Like a kid showing off to his elders, Rebus was thinking. Overreaching himself ...

'That's it, Strawman!' Cafferty was back to being furious. 'All bets are off. Those two want to get dirty with Morris Gerald Cafferty, I'll give them both anthrax. I'll infect the pair of them. They'll think they've caught full-blown fucking AIDS by the time I'm finished!'

Which was about as much as Rebus could take. He put down the phone, drank his cold coffee, checked his messages. Patience wondered if he could make it to supper. Rhona said they'd carried out another scan. Bobby Hogan wanted a word.

He called the hospital first. Rhona said something about a new scan to assess the amount of damage done to the brain.

'Then why the hell didn't they give her *that* scan straight away?'

'I don't know.'

'Did you ask?'

'Why don't *you* come down here? Why don't *you* ask? Seems like when I'm not here, you're happy enough spending time with Samantha, even sleeping in the chair. What is it – do I scare you off?'

'Look, Rhona, I'm sorry. It's been a rough day.'

'For you and everyone else.'

'I know. I'm a selfish bastard.'

The rest of their conversation was predictable. It was a relief to say goodbye. He tried Patience, got her answering machine, and told it he'd be happy to accept the invitation. Then he called Bobby Hogan.

'Hiya, Bobby, what've you got?'

'Not much. I had a word with Telford.'

'I know, he told me.'

'You've been speaking to him?'

'Says he never knew Lintz. Did you talk to The Family?'

'The ones who frequent the office. Same story.'

'Did you mention the five thou'?'

'Think I'm stupid? Listen, I thought you might be able to help me.'

'Fire away.'

'Lintz's address book, I found a couple of addresses for a Dr Colquhoun. Thought at first it must be his GP.'

'He's a Slavic Studies lecturer.'

'Only Lintz seems to have been keeping track of him. Three changes of address, going back twenty years. First two addresses have phone numbers with them, but not the most recent. I checked, and Colquhoun's only been at this latest address three years.'

'So?'

'So Lintz didn't have his home phone number. So if he wanted to speak to him ...'

Rebus twigged. 'He'd phone the university.' The call on Lintz's bill: twenty-odd minutes. Rebus was remembering what Colquhoun had said about Lintz.

I met him at a few social functions ... our departments weren't that close ... As I say, we weren't close ...

'They weren't in the same department,' Rebus said. 'Colquhoun told me they'd barely met ...'

'So how come Lintz has been keeping up with Colquhoun's various moves around the city?'

'Beats me, Bobby. Have you asked him?'

'No, but I intend to.'

'He's lying low. I've been trying to talk to him for a week.' Last seen at the Morvena: did Colquhoun link Telford to Lintz?

'Well, he's back now.'

'What?'

'I've an appointment with him at his office.'

'Count me in,' Rebus said, getting to his feet.

*

As Rebus parked in Buccleuch Place – he was in an unmarked Astra, courtesy of St Leonard's – he saw the car in the neighbouring bay make to leave. He waved, but Kirstin Mede didn't see him, and by the time he'd found the horn, she'd pulled away. He wondered how well she knew Colquhoun. After all, she'd been the one to suggest him as a translator …

Hogan, standing by the railings, had seen Rebus's attempts at communication.

'Someone you know?'

'Kirstin Mede.'

Hogan placed the name. 'The one who did those translations?'

Rebus looked up at the Slavic Studies building. 'Have you tracked down David Levy?'

'Daughter still hasn't heard from him.'

'How long has that been?'

'Long enough to seem suspicious in itself, only she doesn't seem too bothered.'

'How do you want to play this?' Rebus asked.

'Depends what he's like.'

'You ask your questions. Me, I just want to be there.'

Hogan looked at him, then shrugged and pushed open the door. They started to climb the worn stone steps. 'Hope they haven't put him in the penthouse.'

Colquhoun's name was on a piece of card stuck to a door on the second floor. They pushed it open, and were confronted with a short hallway and another five or six doors. Colquhoun's office was first on the right, and he was already standing in the doorway.

'Thought I heard you. Sound carries in this place. Come in, come in.' He wasn't expecting Hogan to have company. His words dried up when he saw Rebus. He walked back into his office, motioned for both officers to sit, then fussed about moving their chairs around so they'd be facing his desk.

'Terrible muddle,' he said, kicking over a pile of books.

'Know the feeling, sir,' Hogan said.

Colquhoun peered in Rebus's direction. 'My secretary says you used the library.'

'Filling in some of the gaps, sir.' Rebus kept his voice level.

'Yes, Candice ...' Colquhoun was thoughtful. 'Is she ... ? I mean, did she ... ?'

'But today, sir,' Hogan interrupted, 'we want to talk to you about Joseph Lintz.'

Colquhoun sat down heavily in his wooden chair, which creaked under the weight. Then he sprang to his feet again. 'Tea, coffee? You must excuse the mess. Not normally this disorganised ...'

'Not for us, sir,' Hogan said. 'If you'd just take a seat?'

'Of course, of course.' Again, Colquhoun collapsed on to his chair.

'Joseph Lintz, sir,' Hogan prompted.

'Terrible tragedy ... terrible. They think it's murder, you know.'

'Yes, sir, we do know.'

'Of course you do. Apologies.'

The desk in front of Colquhoun was venerable and spotted with woodworm. The shelves were bowed under the weight of textbooks. There were old framed prints on the walls, and a blackboard with the single word CHARACTER on it. University paperwork was piled on the window ledge, all but blacking out the bottom two panes. The smell in the room was that of intellect gone awry.

'It's just that Mr Lintz had your name in his address book, sir,' Hogan continued. 'And we're talking to all his friends.'

'Friends?' Colquhoun looked up. 'I wouldn't call us

"friends" exactly. We were colleagues, but I don't think I met him socially more than three or four times in twenty-odd years.'

'Funny, he seems to have taken an interest in you, sir.' Hogan flipped open his notebook. 'Starting with your address in Warrender Park Terrace.'

'I haven't lived there since the seventies.'

'He also has your telephone number there. After that, it's Currie.'

'I thought I was ready for the rural life …'

'In Currie?' Hogan sounded sceptical.

Colquhoun tipped his head. 'I eventually realised my mistake.'

'And moved to Duddingston.'

'Not at first. I rented a few properties while I was looking for a place to buy.'

'Mr Lintz has your telephone number in Currie, but not for the Duddingston address.'

'Interesting. I went ex-directory when I moved.'

'Any reason for that, sir?'

Colquhoun swayed in his chair. 'Well, I'm sure it sounds awful …'

'Try us.'

'I didn't want students bothering me.'

'Did they do that?'

'Oh, yes, phoning to ask questions, advice. Worried about exams or wanting deadlines extended.'

'Do you remember giving Mr Lintz your address, sir?'

'No, I don't.'

'You're sure of that?'

'Yes, but it wouldn't have been hard for him to find out. I mean, he could just have asked one of the secretaries.'

Colquhoun was beginning to look more agitated than ever. The little chair could barely contain him.

'Sir,' Hogan said, 'is there anything you want to tell us about Mr Lintz, anything at all?'

Colquhoun just shook his head, staring at the surface of his desk.

Rebus decided to use their joker. 'Mr Lintz made a phone call to this office. He was talking for over twenty minutes.'

'That's ... simply not true.' Colquhoun mopped his face with a handkerchief. 'Look, gentlemen, I'd like to help, but the fact is, I barely knew Joseph Lintz.'

'And he didn't phone you?'

'No.'

'And you've no idea why he'd keep note of your Edinburgh addresses for the past three decades?'

'No.'

Hogan sighed theatrically. 'Then we're wasting your time and ours.' He got to his feet. 'Thank you, Dr Colquhoun.'

The look of relief on the old academic's face told both detectives all they needed to know.

They said nothing as they walked back downstairs – like Colquhoun had said, sound could travel. Hogan's car was nearest. They rested against it as they talked.

'He was worried,' Rebus said.

'Hiding something. Think we should go back up?'

Rebus shook his head. 'Let him sweat for a day or so, then hit him.'

'He didn't like the fact you were there.'

'I noticed.'

'That restaurant ... Lintz dining with an elderly gent.'

'We could tell him we've got a description from the restaurant staff.'

'Without going into specifics?'

Rebus nodded. 'See if it flushes him out.'

'What about the other person Lintz took to lunch, the young woman?'

'No idea.'

'Posh restaurant, old man, young woman ...'

'A call girl?'

Hogan smiled. 'Do they still call them that?'

Rebus was thoughtful. 'It might explain the phone call to Telford. Only I doubt Telford's daft enough to discuss business like that from his office. Besides, his escort agency runs from another address.'

'Fact is, he called Telford's office.'

'And nobody's owned up to talking to him.'

'Escort agency stuff, could be very innocent. He doesn't want to eat alone, hires some company. Afterwards, a peck on the cheek and separate taxis.' Hogan exhaled. 'This one's running in circles.'

'I know the feeling, Bobby.'

They looked up at the second-floor windows. Saw Colquhoun staring down, handkerchief to his face.

'Let's leave him to it,' Hogan said, unlocking his car.

'I've been meaning to ask: how did you get on with Abernethy?'

'He didn't give me too much trouble.' Hogan avoided Rebus's eyes.

'So he's gone?'

Hogan had disappeared into the driver's seat. 'He's gone. See you, John.'

Leaving Rebus on the pavement, a frown on his face. He waited till Hogan's car had turned the corner, then went back into the stairwell and climbed the steps again.

Colquhoun's office door was open, the old man fidgeting behind his desk. Rebus sat down opposite him, said nothing.

'I've been ill,' Colquhoun said.

'You've been hiding.' Colquhoun started shaking his

head. 'You told them where to find Candice.' Head still shaking. 'Then you got worried, so they hid you away, maybe in a room at the casino.' Rebus paused. 'How am I doing?'

'I've no comment to make,' Colquhoun snapped.

'What if I just keep talking then?'

'I want you to leave now. If you don't go, I'll have to call my lawyer.'

'Name of Charles Groal?' Rebus smiled. 'They might have spent the last few days tutoring you, but they can't change what you've done.' Rebus stood up. '*You* sent Candice back to them. *You* did that.' He leaned down over the desk. 'You knew all along who she was, didn't you? That's why you were so nervous. How come you knew who she was, Dr Colquhoun? How come you're so chummy with a turd like Tommy Telford?'

Colquhoun picked up the receiver, his hands shaking so badly he kept missing the digits.

'Don't bother,' Rebus said. 'I'm going. But we'll talk again. And you *will* talk. You'll talk because you're a coward, Dr Colquhoun. And cowards always talk eventually …'

23

The Crime Squad office at Fettes: home of country and western; Claverhouse terminating a phone call. No sign of Ormiston and Clarke.

'They're out on a call,' Claverhouse said.

'Any progress on that stabbing?'

'What do you think?'

'I think there's something you should know.' Rebus seated himself behind Siobhan Clarke's desk, admiring its tidy surface. He opened a drawer: it was tidy, too. Compartments, he thought to himself. Clarke was very good at dividing her life into separate compartments. 'Jake Tarawicz is in town. He's got this outrageous white limo, hard to miss.' Rebus paused. 'And he's brought Candice with him.'

'What's he doing here?'

'I think he's here for the show.'

'What show?'

'Cafferty and Telford, fifteen rounds of bare-knuckle and no referee.' Rebus leaned forward, arms on the desk. 'And I've got an idea where it's headed.'

Rebus went home, called Patience and told her he might be late.

'How late?' she asked.

'How late can I be without us falling out?'

She thought about it. 'Half-nine.'

'I'll be there.'

He checked his answering machine: David Levy, saying he could be reached at home.

'Where the hell have you been?' Rebus asked, when Levy's daughter had put her father on.

'I had business elsewhere.'

'You know your daughter's been worried. You might have phoned her.'

'Does this counselling service come free?'

'My fee cancels out when you answer a few questions. You know Lintz is dead?'

'I've heard.'

'Where were you when you *heard*?'

'I've told you, I had business ... Inspector, am I a suspect?'

'Practically the only one we've got.'

Levy gave a harsh laugh. 'This is preposterous. I'm not a ...' He couldn't say the word. Rebus guessed his daughter was within hearing distance. 'Hold on a moment, please.' The receiver was muffled: Levy ordering his daughter out of the room. He came back on, voice lower than before.

'Inspector, for the record, I feel I must let you know how *angry* I felt when I heard the news. Justice may have been done or not done – I can't argue those points just now – but what is absolutely certain is that history has been cheated here!'

'Of the trial?'

'Of course! And the Rat Line, too. With each suspect who dies, we're that much less likely to prove its existence. Lintz isn't the first, you know. One man, the brakes failed on his car. Another fell from an upstairs window. There've been two apparent suicides, six more cases of what look like natural causes.'

'Am I going to get the full conspiracy theory?'

'This isn't a joke, Inspector.'

'Did you hear me laughing? What about you, Mr Levy? When did you leave Edinburgh?'

'Before Lintz died.'

'Did you see him?' Rebus knowing he had, but seeking a lie.

Levy paused. '*Confronted* would be a more apposite term.'

'Just the once?'

'Three times. He wasn't keen to talk about himself, but I stated my case nonetheless.'

'And the phone call?'

Levy paused. 'What phone call?'

'When he called you at the Roxburghe.'

'I wish I'd recorded it for posterity. Rage, Inspector. Foul-mouthed rage. I'm positive he was mad.'

'Mad?'

'You didn't hear him. He's very good at seeming perfectly normal – he must be, or he wouldn't have gone undetected for so long. But the man is ... was ... mad. Truly mad.'

Rebus was remembering the crooked little man in the cemetery, and how he'd suddenly let fly at a passing dog. Poise, to rage, to poise again.

'The story he told ...' Levy sighed.

'Was this in the restaurant?'

'What restaurant?'

'Sorry, I thought the two of you went out to lunch.'

'I can assure you we didn't.'

'So what story is this then?'

'These men, Inspector, they come to justify their actions by blanking them out, or by transference. Transference is the more common.'

'They tell themselves someone else did it?'

'Yes.'

'And that was Lintz's story?'

'Less believable than most. He said it was all a case of mistaken identity.'

'And who did he think you were mistaking him for?'
'A colleague at the university ... a Dr Colquhoun.'

Rebus called Hogan, gave him the story.
'I told Levy you'd want to speak to him.'
'I'll phone him right now.'
'What do you think?'
'Colquhoun a war criminal?' Hogan snorted.
'Me, too,' Rebus said. 'I asked Levy why he didn't think any of this worth telling us.'
'And?'
'He said as he gave it no credence, it was worthless.'
'All the same, we'd better talk to Colquhoun again. Tonight.'
'I've other plans for tonight, Bobby.'
'Fair enough, John. Look, I really appreciate all your help.'
'You're going to talk to him alone?'
'I'll have someone with me.'
Rebus hated being left out. If he cancelled that late supper ...
'Let me know how you get on.' Rebus put the telephone down. On the hi-fi: Eddie Harris, upbeat and melodic. He went and soaked in a bath, facecloth across his eyes. Everyone, it seemed to him, lived their lives out of little boxes, opening different ones for different occasions. Nobody ever gave their whole self away. Cops were like that, each box a safety mechanism. Most people you met in the course of your life, you never even learned their names. Everybody was boxed off from everybody else. It was called society.

He was wondering about Joseph Lintz, always questioning, turning every conversation into a philosophy lesson. Stuck in his own little box, identity blocked off elsewhere, his past a necessary mystery ... Joseph Lintz, furious when cornered, possibly clinically mad, driven there by … what? Memories? Or the lack of them? Driven there by other people?

The Eddie Harris CD was on its last track by the time he emerged from the bathroom. He put on the clothes he'd be wearing to Patience's. Only he had a couple of stops to make first: check on Sammy at the hospital, and then a meeting at Torphichen.

'The gang's all here,' he said, walking into the CID room.

Shug Davidson, Claverhouse, Ormiston, and Siobhan Clarke, all seated around the one big desk, drinking coffee from identical Rangers mugs. Rebus pulled a chair over.

'Have you filled them in, Shug?'

Davidson nodded.

'What about the shop?'

'I was just getting to that.' Davidson picked up a pen, played with it. 'The last owner went out of business, not enough passing trade. The shop was shut the best part of a year, then suddenly reopened – under new management and with prices that stopped the locals looking elsewhere.'

'And got the workers at Maclean's interested, too,' Rebus added. 'So how long's it been going?'

'Five weeks, selling cut-price everything.'

'No profit motive, you see.' Rebus looked around the table. This was mostly for the benefit of Ormiston and Clarke; he'd given Claverhouse the story already.

'And the owners?' Clarke asked.

'Well, the shop's *run* by a couple of lads called Declan Delaney and Ken Wilkinson. Guess where they come from?'

'Paisley,' Claverhouse said, keen to hurry things on.

'So they're part of Telford's gang?' Ormiston asked.

'Not in so many words, but they're connected to him, no doubt about that.' Davidson blew his nose loudly. 'Of course, Dec and Ken are running the shop, but they don't own it.'

'Telford does,' Rebus stated.

'Okay,' Claverhouse said. 'So we've got Telford owning a loss-making business, in the hope of gathering intelligence.'

'I think it goes further than that,' Rebus said. 'I mean, listening in on gossip is one thing, but I don't suppose any of the workers are standing around talking about the various security systems and how to beat them. Dec and Ken are garrulous, perfect for the job Telford's given them. But it's going to look suspicious if they start asking too many questions.'

'So what's Telford looking for?' Ormiston asked. Siobhan Clarke turned to him.

'A mole,' she said.

'Makes sense,' Davidson went on. 'That place *is* well-protected, but not impregnable. We all know any break-in's going to be a lot easier with someone on the inside.'

'So what do we do?' Clarke asked.

'We fight Telford's sting with our own,' Rebus explained. 'He wants a man on the inside, *we* give him one.'

'I'm seeing the head of Maclean's later on tonight,' Davidson said.

'I'll come with you,' Claverhouse said, keen not to be left out.

'So we put someone of our own inside the factory.' Clarke was working it out for herself. 'And they shoot their mouth off in the shop, making them an attractive proposition. And we sit and pray that Telford approaches *them* rather than anyone else?'

'The less luck we have to rely on the better,' Claverhouse said. 'Got to do this right.'

'Which is why we work it like this.' Rebus said. 'There's a bookie called Marty Jones. He owes me one big favour.

Say our man's just been into Telford's shop. As he's coming out, a car pulls up. Marty and a couple of his men. Marty wants some bets paid off. Big argy-bargy, and a punch in the guts as warning.'

Clarke could see it. 'He stumbles back into the shop, sits down to catch his breath. Dec and Ken ask him what's going on.'

'And he gives them the whole sorry story: gambling debts, broken marriage, whatever.'

'To make him more attractive still,' Davidson said, 'we make him a security guard.'

Ormiston looked at him. 'You think Maclean's will go for it?'

'We'll persuade them,' Claverhouse said quietly.

'More importantly,' Clarke asked, 'will *Telford* go for it?'

'Depends how desperate he is,' Rebus answered.

'A man on the inside ...' Ormiston's eyes were alight. 'Working for Telford – it's what we've always wanted.'

Claverhouse nodded. 'Just one thing.' He looked at Rebus and Davidson. 'Who's it going to be? Telford knows us.'

'We get someone from outside,' Rebus said. 'Someone I've worked with before. Telford won't have heard of him. He's a good man.'

'Is he willing?'

There was silence around the table.

'Depends who's asking,' a voice called from the doorway. A stocky man with thick, well-groomed hair and narrow eyes. Rebus got up, shook Jack Morton's hand, made the introductions.

'I'll need a history,' Morton said, all business. 'John's explained the deal, and I like it. But I'll need a flat, something scruffy and local.'

'First thing tomorrow,' Claverhouse said. 'Look, we need to talk to our bosses about this, make sure it's cleared.'

He looked at Morton. 'What did you tell your own boss, Jack?'

'I've got a few days off, didn't think it was worth mentioning.'

Claverhouse nodded. 'I'll talk to him as soon as we get the go-ahead.'

'We need that go-ahead *tonight*,' Rebus said. 'Telford's men may already have lined someone up. If we hang around, we might lose it.'

'Agreed,' Claverhouse said, checking his watch. 'I'll make a few phone calls, interrupt a few post-prandial whiskies.'

'I'll back you up if need be,' Davidson said.

Rebus looked at Jack Morton – his friend – and mouthed the word 'thanks'. Morton shrugged it off. Then Rebus got to his feet.

'I'm going to have to leave you to it,' he told the assembly. 'You've got my pager number and mobile if you need me.'

He was halfway down the hall when Siobhan Clarke caught him.

'I just wanted to say thanks.'

Rebus blinked. 'What for?'

'Ever since you got Claverhouse excited, the tape machine's stayed off.'

24

Supper was fine. He talked to Patience about Sammy, Rhona, his obsession with sixties music, his ignorance of fashion. She talked about work, an experimental cookery class she'd been taking, a trip to Orkney she was thinking of. They ate fresh pasta with a homemade mussel and prawn sauce, and shared a bottle of Highland Spring. Rebus tried his damnedest to forget about the sting operation, Tarawicz, Candice, Lintz ... She could see at least half his mind was elsewhere; tried not to feel betrayed. She asked him if he was going home.

'Is that an invitation?'

'I'm not sure ... I suppose so.'

'Let's pretend it wasn't, then I won't feel like complete scum when I turn it down.'

'That sounds reasonable. Things on your mind?'

'I'm surprised you can't see them leaking out of my ears.'

'Do you want to talk about any of it? I mean, you may not have noticed, but we've talked about practically everything tonight except *us*.'

'I don't think talking would help.'

'But bottling it up does?' She threw out an arm. 'Behold the Scottish male, at his happiest when in denial.'

'What am I denying?'

'For a start, you're denying *me* access to your life.'

'Sorry.'

'Christ, John, get the word put on a t-shirt.'

'Thanks, maybe I will.' He got up from the sofa.

'Oh, hell, I'm sorry.' She smiled. 'Look, you've got me at it now.'

'Yes, it's catching, all right.'

She stood up, touched his arm. 'You're worried about taking the test?'

'Right now, believe it or not, that's the least of my worries.'

'It should be. Everything's going to be fine.'

'Hunky dory.'

'Hunky dory,' she repeated, smiling again. She pecked him on the cheek. 'You know, I've never quite understood what that meant.'

'*Hunky Dory?*'

She nodded.

'It's a David Bowie album.' He kissed her brow.

He would never know what instinct made him decide on the detour, but he was glad he'd made it. For there, parked outside the Morvena casino, stood the white stretch limo. The driver leaned against it, smoking a cigarette, looking bored. From time to time he took out a mobile phone and had a short conversation. Rebus stared at the Morvena, thinking: Tommy Telford has a slice of the place; the hostesses come from Eastern Europe, provided by Mr Pink Eyes. Rebus wondered how closely entwined the two empires – Telford's and Tarawicz's – really were. And add a third strand: the Yakuza. Something refused to add up.

What was Tarawicz getting out of it?

Miriam Kenworthy had suggested muscle: Scottish hardmen trained in Telford's organisation then shipped south. But it wasn't *enough* of a trade. There had to be more. Was Mr Pink Eyes due a share of the Maclean's pay-out? Was Telford tempting him with some Yakuza action? What about the theory that Telford was Tarawicz's supplier?

At quarter to midnight, another phone call had the driver springing into action. He flicked his cigarette on to the road, started opening doors. Tarawicz and his entourage breezed out of the casino looking like they owned the world. Candice was wearing a black full-length coat over a shimmering pink dress which didn't quite reach her knees. She was carrying a bottle of champagne. Rebus counted three of Tarawicz's men, remembering them from the scrapyard. Two no-shows: the lawyer, and the Crab. Telford was there, too, with a couple of minders, one of them Pretty-Boy. Pretty-Boy was making sure his jacket hung right, trying to decide whether it would look better buttoned. But his eyes raked the darkened street. Rebus had parked away from the street-lights, confident he was invisible. They were piling into the limo. Rebus watched it move off, waited until it had signalled and turned a corner before switching on his own headlamps and starting the engine.

They drove to the same hotel Matsumoto had stayed at. Telford's Range Rover was parked outside. Pedestrians – late-night couples hurrying home from the pub – turned to stare at the limo. Saw the entourage spill out, probably mistook them for pop stars or film people. Rebus as casting director: Candice's starlet being mauled by sleazy producer Tarawicz. Telford a sleek young operator on his way up, looking to learn from the producer before toppling him. The others were bit players, except maybe Pretty-Boy, who was hanging on to his boss's coattails, maybe readying himself for his own big break ...

If Tarawicz had a suite, there might be room for them all. If not, they'd be in the bar. Rebus parked, followed them inside.

The lights hurt his eyes. The reception area was all mirrors and pine, brass and pot-plants. He tried to look like he'd been left behind by the party. They were settling down in the bar, through a double set of swing-doors with glass panels. Rebus hung back. Sitting target in the empty reception; bigger target in the bar. Retreat to the car? Someone was standing up, shrugging off a long black coat. Candice. Smiling now, saying something to Tarawicz, who was nodding. Took her hand and planted a kiss in the palm. Went further: a slow lick across the palm and up her wrist. Everyone laughing, whistling. Candice looking numb. Tarawicz got to the inside of her elbow and took a bite. She squealed, pulled back, rubbed her arm. Tarawicz had his tongue out, playing to the gallery. Give Tommy Telford credit: he wasn't grinning along with everyone else.

Candice stood there, a stooge to her owner's little act. Then he waved her off with a flick of his hand. Permission granted, she started for the doors. Rebus moved back into a recess where the public telephones sat. She turned right out of the doors, disappeared into the ladies'. At the table, they were busy ordering more champagne – and an orange juice for Pretty-Boy.

Rebus looked around, took a deep breath. Walked into the ladies' toilets like it was the most natural thing in the world.

She was splashing her face with water. A little brown bottle sat next to the sink. Three yellow tablets lying ready. Rebus swept them on to the floor.

'Hey!' She turned, saw him, put a hand to her mouth. She tried backing away, but there was nowhere to go.

'Is this what you want, Karina?' Using her real name as a weapon: friendly fire.

She frowned, shook her head: incomprehension on her face. He grabbed her shoulders, squeezed.

'Sammy,' he hissed. 'Sammy's in hospital. Very ill.' He pointed towards the hotel bar. '*They* tried to kill her.'

The gist got through. Candice shook her head. Tears were smudging her mascara.

'Did you tell Sammy anything?'

She frowned again.

'Anything about Telford or Tarawicz? Did you talk to Sammy about them?'

A slow, determined shake of the head. 'Sammy ... hospital?'

He nodded. Turned his hands into a steering-wheel, made engine noises, then slammed a fist into his open palm. Candice turned away, grabbed the sink. She was crying, shoulders jerking. She scrabbled for more tablets. Rebus tore them from her hand.

'You want to blank it all out? Forget it.' He threw them on to the floor, crushed them under his heel. She crouched down, licked a finger and dabbed at the powder. Rebus hauled her to her feet. Her knees wouldn't lock; he had to keep holding her upright. She wouldn't look him in the eyes.

'It's funny, we first met in a toilet, remember? You were scared. You hated your life so much you'd slashed your arms.' He touched her scarred wrists. 'That's how much you hated your life. And now you're straight back in it.'

Her face was against his jacket, tears dropping on to his shirt.

'Remember the Japanese?' he cooed. 'Remember Juniper Green, the golf club?'

She drew back, wiped her nose on her bare wrist. 'Juniper Green,' she said.

'That's right. And a big factory ... the car stopped, and everyone looked at the factory.'

She was nodding.

'Did anyone talk about it? Did they say *anything*?'

She was shaking her head. 'John ...' Her hands on his lapels. She sniffed, swiped at her nose again. She slid down his jacket, his shirt. She was on her knees, looking up at him, blinking tears, while her damp fingers scored white powder from the tiles. Rebus crouched down in front of her.

'Come with me,' he said. 'I'll help you.' He pointed towards the door, towards the world outside, but she was busy in her own world now, fingers going to her mouth. Someone pushed open the door. Rebus looked up.

A woman: young, drunk, hair falling into her eyes. She stopped and studied the two people on the floor, then smiled and headed for a cubicle.

'Save some for me,' she said, sliding the lock.

'Go, John.' There was powder at the corners of Candice's mouth. A tiny piece of tablet had lodged between her front two teeth. 'Please, go now.'

'I don't want you getting hurt.' He sought her hands, squeezed them.

'I do not hurt any more.'

She got to her feet and turned from him. Checked her face in the mirror, wiped away the powder and dabbed at her mascara. Blew her nose and took a deep breath.

Walked out of the toilets.

Rebus waited a moment, time enough for her to reach the table. Then he opened the door and made his exit. Walked back to his car on legs that seemed to belong to someone else.

Drove home, not quite crying.

But not quite not.

25

Four in the morning, the blessed telephone pulled him out of a nightmare.

Prison-camp prostitutes with teeth filed to points were kneeling in front of him. Jake Tarawicz, in full SS regalia, held him from behind, telling him resistance was useless. Through the barred window, Rebus could see black berets – the *maquis*, busy freeing the camp but leaving his billet till last. Alarm bells ringing, everything telling him that salvation was at hand ...

... alarm becoming his telephone ... he staggered from his chair, picked it up.

'Yes.'

'John?' The Chief Super's voice: Aberdonian, instantly recognisable.

'Yes, sir?'

'We've got a spot of bother. Get down here.'

'What kind of bother?'

'I'll tell you when you get here. Now *shift*.'

Night shift, to be precise. The city asleep. St Leonard's was lit up, the tenements around it dark. No sign of the Farmer's 'spot of bother'. The Chief Super's office: the Farmer in conference with Gill Templer.

'Sit down, John. Coffee?'

'No, thanks, sir.'

While Templer and the Chief Super were deciding who should speak, Rebus helped them out.

'Tommy Telford's businesses have been hit.'

Templer blinked. 'Telepathy?'

'Cafferty's offices and taxis got firebombed. So did his house.' Rebus shrugged. 'We knew there'd be payback.'

'Did we?'

What could he say? *I did, because Cafferty told me.* He didn't think they'd like that. 'I just put two and two together.'

The Farmer poured himself a mug of coffee. 'So now we've got open war.'

'What got hit?'

'The arcade on Flint Street,' Templer said. 'Not too much damage: the place has a sprinkler system.' She smiled: an amusement arcade with a sprinkler system ... not that Telford was careful or anything.

'Plus a couple of nightclubs,' the Farmer added. 'And a casino.'

'Which one?'

The Chief Super looked to Templer, who answered: 'The Morvena.'

'Any injuries?'

'The manager and a couple of friends: concussion and bruising.'

'Which they got ...?'

'Falling over each other as they ran down the stairs.'

Rebus nodded. 'Funny how some people have trouble with stairs.' He sat back. 'So what does all this have to do with me? Don't tell me: having disposed of Telford's Japanese partner, I decided to take up fire-raising?'

'John ...' The Farmer got up, rested his backside against the desk. 'The three of us, we know you had nothing to do with that. Tell me, we found an untouched half-bottle of malt under your driver's seat ...'

Rebus nodded. 'It's mine.' Another of his little suicide bombs.

'So why would you be drinking a supermarket blend?'

'Is that what the screw-top was? The cheap bastards.'

'No alcohol in your blood either. Meantime, as you say, Cafferty's in the frame for this. And Cafferty and you ...'

'You want me to talk to him?'

Gill Templer leaned forward in her chair. 'We don't want war.'

'Takes two to make a ceasefire.'

'I'll talk to Telford,' she said.

'He's a sharp little bugger, watch out for him.'

She nodded. 'Will you talk to Cafferty?'

Rebus didn't want a war. It would take Telford's mind off the Maclean's heist. He'd need all the troops he could get; the shop might even have to close. No, Rebus didn't want a war.

'I'll talk to him,' he said.

Breakfast-time at Barlinnie.

Rebus jangling after the drive, knowing a whisky would smooth out his nerve-endings. Cafferty waiting for him, same room as before.

'Top of the morning, Strawman.' Arms folded, looking pleased with himself.

'You've had a busy night.'

'On the contrary, I slept as well as I ever have done in this place. What about you?'

'I was up at four o'clock, checking damage reports. I could have done without driving all the way here. Maybe if you gave me the number of your mobile ...?'

Cafferty grinned. 'I hear the nightclubs were gutted.'

'I think your boys are making themselves look good.'

Cafferty's grin tightened. 'Telford's premises seem to have state of the art fire prevention. Smoke sensors, sprinklers, fire-doors. The damage was minimal.'

'This is just the start,' Cafferty said. 'I'll have that little arse-wipe.'

'I thought that was supposed to be *my* job?'

'I've seen precious little from you, Strawman.'

'I've got something in the pipeline. If it comes off, you'll like it.'

Cafferty's eyes narrowed. 'Give me details. Make me believe you.'

But Rebus was shaking his head. 'Sometimes, you just have to have faith.' He paused. 'Deal?'

'I must have missed something.'

Rebus spelled it out. 'Back off. Leave Telford to me.'

'We've been through this. He hits me and I do nothing, I look like something you'd step around on the pavement.'

'We're talking to him, warning him off.'

'And meantime I'm supposed to trust you to get the job done?'

'We shook hands on it.'

Cafferty snorted. 'I've shaken hands with a lot of bastards.'

'And now you've met an exception to the rule.'

'You're an exception to a lot of rules, Strawman.' Cafferty looked thoughtful. 'The casino, the clubs, the arcade … they weren't badly hit?'

'My guess is the sprinklers will have done as much damage as anything.'

Cafferty's jaw hardened. 'Makes me look even more of a mug.'

Rebus sat in silence, waiting for him to finish whatever chess-game was being played inside his head.

'Okay,' the gangster said at last, 'I'll call off the troops. Maybe it's time to do some recruiting anyway.' He looked up at Rebus. 'Time for some fresh blood.'

Which reminded Rebus of another job he'd been putting off.

*

Danny Simpson lived at home with his mother in a terraced house in Wester Hailes.

This bleak housing-scheme, designed by sadists who'd never had to live anywhere near it, had a heart which had shrivelled but refused to stop pumping. Rebus had a lot of respect for the place. Tommy Smith had grown up here, practising with socks stuffed into the mouth of his sax, so as not to disturb the neighbours through the thin walls of the high-rise. Tommy Smith was one of the best sax players Rebus had ever heard.

In a sense, Wester Hailes existed outside the real world: it wasn't on a route from anywhere to anywhere. Rebus had never had cause to drive *through* it – he only went there if he had business there. The city bypass flew past it, offering many drivers their only encounter with Wester Hailes. They saw: high-rise blocks, terraces, tracts of unused playing field. They didn't see: people. Not so much concrete jungle as concrete vacuum.

Rebus knocked on Danny Simpson's door. He didn't know what he was going to say to the young man. He just wanted to see him again. He wanted to see him without the blood and the pain. Wanted to see him whole and of a piece.

Wanted to see him.

But Danny Simpson wasn't in, and neither was his mother. A neighbour, lacking her top set of dentures, came out and explained the situation.

The situation took Rebus to the Infirmary, where, in a small, gloomy ward not easily found, Danny Simpson lay in bed, head bandaged, sweating like he'd just played a full ninety minutes. He wasn't conscious. His mother sat beside him, stroking his wrist. A nurse explained to Rebus that a hospice would be the best place for Danny, supposing they could find him a bed.

'What happened?'

'We think infection must have set in. When you lose your resistance … the world's a lethal place.' She shrugged, looked like she'd been through it all once too often. Danny's mother had seen them talking. Maybe she thought Rebus was a doctor. She got up and came towards him, then just stood there, waiting for him to speak.

'I came to see Danny,' he said.

'Yes?'

'The night he … the night of his accident, I was the one who brought him here. I just wondered how he was doing.'

'See for yourself.' Her voice was breaking.

Rebus thought: a five-minute walk from here, he'd be in Sammy's room. He'd thought her situation unique, because it was unique to *him*. Now he saw that within a short radius of Sammy's bed, other parents were crying, and squeezing their children's hands, and asking why.

'I'm really sorry,' he said. 'I wish …'

'Me, too,' the woman said. 'You know, he's never been a bad laddie. Cheeky, but never bad. His problem was, he was always itching for something new, something to stop him getting bored. We all know where that can lead.'

Rebus nodded, suddenly not wanting to be here, not wanting to hear Danny Simpson's life story. He had enough ghosts to contend with as it was. He squeezed the woman's arm.

'Look,' he said, 'I'm sorry, but I have to go.'

She nodded distractedly, wandered off in the direction of her son's bed. Rebus wanted to curse Danny Simpson for the mere *possibility* that he'd passed on the virus. He realised now that if they'd met on the doorstep, that's the way their conversation would have gone, and maybe Rebus would have gone further.

He wanted to curse him … but he couldn't. It would be every bit as efficacious as cursing the Big Man. A waste of time and breath. So instead he went to Sammy's room, to find that she was back on her own. No other patients, no nursing staff, no Rhona. He kissed her forehead. It tasted salty. Sweat: she needed wiping down. There was a smell he hadn't noticed before. Talcum powder. He sat down, took her warm hands in his.

'How are you doing, Sammy? I keep meaning to bring in some Oasis, see if that would bring you round. Your mum sits here listening to classical. I wonder if you can hear it. I don't even know if you like that sort of stuff. Lots of things we've never got round to talking about.'

He saw something. Stood up to be sure. Movement behind her eyelids.

'Sammy? Sammy?'

He hadn't seen her do that before. Pushed the button beside her bed. Waited for a nurse to come. Pushed it again.

'Come on, come on.'

Eyelids fluttering … then stopping.

'Sammy!'

Door opening, nurse coming in.

'What is it?'

Rebus: 'I thought I saw … she was moving.'

'Moving?'

'Just her eyes, like she was trying to open them.'

'I'll fetch a doctor.'

'Come on, Sammy, try again. Wakey-wakey, sweetheart.' Patting her wrists, then her cheeks.

The doctor arrived. He was the same one Rebus had shouted at that first day. Lifted her eyelids, shone a thin torch into them, pulling it away, checking her pupils.

'If you saw it, I'm sure it was there.'

'Yes, but does it mean anything?'

'Hard to say.'

'Try anyway.' Eyes boring into the doctor's.

'She's asleep. She has dreams. Sometimes when you dream you experience REM: Rapid Eye Movement.'

'So it could be ...' Rebus sought the word '... involuntary?'

'As I say, it's hard to tell. Latest scans show definite improvement.' He paused. '*Minor* improvement, but certainly there.'

Rebus nodding, trembling. The doctor saw it, asked if he needed anything. Rebus shaking his head. The doctor checking his watch, other places to be. The nurse shuffling her feet. Rebus thanked them both and headed out.

HOGAN: You agree to this interview being taped, Dr Colquhoun?

COLQUHOUN: I've no objections.

HOGAN: It's in your interests as well as ours.

COLQUHOUN: I've nothing to hide, Inspector Hogan. (*Coughs.*)

HOGAN: Fine, sir. Maybe we'll just start then?

COLQUHOUN: Might I ask a question? Just for the record, you want to ask me about Joseph Lintz – nothing else?

HOGAN: What else might there be, sir?

COLQUHOUN: I just wanted to check.

HOGAN: You wish to have a solicitor present?

COLQUHOUN: No.

HOGAN: Right you are, sir. Well, if I can begin ... it's really just a question of your relationship with Professor Joseph Lintz.

COLQUHOUN: Yes.

HOGAN: Only, when we spoke before, you said you didn't know Professor Lintz.

COLQUHOUN: I think I said I didn't know him very well.

HOGAN: Okay, sir. If that's what you said ...

COLQUHOUN: It is, to the best of my recollection.

HOGAN: Only, we've had some new information ...

COLQUHOUN: Yes?

HOGAN: That you knew Professor Lintz a little better than that.

COLQUHOUN: And this is according to ...?

HOGAN: New information in our possession. The informant tells us that Joseph Lintz accused you of being a war criminal. Anything to say to that, sir?

COLQUHOUN: Only that it's a lie. An outrageous lie.

HOGAN: He didn't think you were a war criminal?

COLQUHOUN: Oh, he thought it all right! He told me to my face on more than one occasion.

HOGAN: When?

COLQUHOUN: Years back. He got it into his head ... the man was mad, Inspector. I could see that. Driven by demons.

HOGAN: What did he say exactly?

COLQUHOUN: Hard to remember. This was a long time ago, the early 1970s, I suppose.

HOGAN: It would help us if you could ...

COLQUHOUN: He came out with it in the middle of a party. I believe it was some function to welcome a visiting professor. Anyway, Joseph insisted on taking me to one side. He looked feverish. Then he came out with it: I was some sort of Nazi, and I'd come to this country by some circuitous route. He kept on about it.

HOGAN: What did you do?

COLQUHOUN: Told him he was drunk, babbling.

HOGAN: And?

COLQUHOUN: And he was. Had to be taken home in a taxi. I said no more about it. In academic circles, one becomes used to a certain amount of ... eccentric behaviour. We're obsessive people, it can't be helped.

HOGAN: But Lintz persisted?

COLQUHOUN: Not really, no. But every few years ... there'd ... he'd say something, allege some atrocity ...

HOGAN: Did he approach you outside the university?

COLQUHOUN: For a time, he telephoned my home.

HOGAN: You moved?

COLQUHOUN: Yes.

HOGAN: To an unlisted phone number?

COLQUHOUN: Eventually.

HOGAN: To stop him calling you?

COLQUHOUN: I suppose that was part of it.

HOGAN: Did you speak to anyone about Lintz?

COLQUHOUN: You mean the authorities? No, no one. He was a nuisance, nothing more.

HOGAN: And then what happened?

COLQUHOUN: Then these stories started appearing in the papers, saying Joseph might be a Nazi, a war criminal. And suddenly he was on my back again.

HOGAN: He phoned you at your office?

COLQUHOUN: Yes.

HOGAN: You lied to us about that?

COLQUHOUN: I'm sorry. I panicked.

HOGAN: What was there to panic about?

COLQUHOUN: Just ... I don't know.

HOGAN: So you met him? To straighten things out?

COLQUHOUN: We had lunch together. He seemed ... lucid. Only what he was saying, it was the stuff of madness. He had a whole history mapped out, only it wasn't mine. I kept saying to him, 'Joseph, when the war ended I wasn't out of my teens.' Besides, I was born and raised here. It's all on record.

HOGAN: What did he say to that?

COLQUHOUN: He said records could be faked.

HOGAN: Faked records ... one way Josef Linzstek could have gone undetected.

COLQUHOUN: I know.

HOGAN: You think Joseph Lintz was Josef Linzstek?

COLQUHOUN: I don't know. Maybe the stories got to him ... he started to believe ... I don't know.

HOGAN: Yes, but these accusations, they began before the media circus – decades before.

COLQUHOUN: That's true.

HOGAN: So he was hounding you. Did he say he would go to the media with his version of events?

COLQUHOUN: He may have ... I can't remember.

HOGAN: Mmm.

COLQUHOUN: You're looking for a motive, aren't you? You're looking for reasons why I'd want him dead.

HOGAN: Did you kill him, Dr Colquhoun?

COLQUHOUN: Emphatically not.

HOGAN: Any idea who did?

COLQUHOUN: No.

HOGAN: Why didn't you tell us? Why tell lies?

COLQUHOUN: Because I knew this would happen. These suspicions. Stupidly, I thought I could circumvent them.

HOGAN: Circumvent?

COLQUHOUN: Yes.

HOGAN: A young woman was seen dining with Lintz, same restaurant he took you to. Any idea who she might be?

COLQUHOUN: None.

HOGAN: You knew Professor Lintz a long time ... what did you think were his sexual proclivities?

COLQUHOUN: Never thought about it.

HOGAN: No?

COLQUHOUN: No.

HOGAN: What about yourself, sir?

COLQUHOUN: I don't see what that ... well, for the record, Inspector, I'm monogamous and heterosexual.

HOGAN: Thank you, sir. I appreciate your frankness.

Rebus switched off the tape.

'I'll bet you did.'

'What do you think?' Bobby Hogan asked.

'I think you mistimed the did-you-do-it. Otherwise, not bad.' Rebus tapped the tape machine. 'Is there much more?'

'Not a lot.'

Rebus switched it back on.

HOGAN: When you met in the restaurant, it was the same routine as before?

COLQUHOUN: Oh, yes. Names, dates ... countries I was taken through on my way into Britain from the continent.

HOGAN: He told you how this was achieved?

COLQUHOUN: He called it the Rat Line. Said it was operated by the Vatican, if you can believe that. And all the western governments were in cahoots to get the top Nazis – the scientists and intellectuals – away from the Russians. I mean, really ... it's Ian Fleming meets John Le Carré, isn't it?

HOGAN: But he was very detailed?

COLQUHOUN: Yes, but it can be that way with obsessives.

HOGAN: There have been books written alleging the same thing Professor Lintz was talking about.

COLQUHOUN: Have there?

HOGAN: Nazis smuggled overseas ... war criminals rescued from the gallows.

COLQUHOUN: Well, yes, but those are just stories. You don't seriously think ...?

HOGAN: I'm just collecting information, Dr Colquhoun. In my job, we don't throw anything away.

COLQUHOUN: Yes, I can see that. The problem is, sorting out the wheat from the chaff.

HOGAN: You mean the truths from the lies? Yes, that's one problem.

COLQUHOUN: I mean, the stories you hear about Bosnia

and Croatia ... slaughterhouses, mass torture, the guilty being spirited away ... It's hard to know what's *true*.

HOGAN: Just before we finish ... any idea what happened to the money?

COLQUHOUN: What money?

HOGAN: The withdrawal Lintz made from his bank. Five thousand pounds in cash.

COLQUHOUN: This is the first I've heard of it. Another motive?

HOGAN: Thank you for your time, Dr Colquhoun. It might be necessary for us to talk again. I'm sorry, but you shouldn't have lied to us, it makes our job that much more difficult.

COLQUHOUN: I'm sorry, Inspector Hogan. I quite understand, but I hope you can comprehend why I did it.

HOGAN: My mum always told me never to lie, sir. Thanks again for your time.

Rebus looked at Hogan. 'Your mum?'

Hogan shrugged. 'Maybe it was my granny.'

Rebus drained his coffee. 'So we know one of Lintz's mealtime companions.'

'And we know he was hounding Colquhoun.'

'Is he a suspect?'

'I'm not exactly snowed under with them.'

'Fair point, but all the same ...'

'You think he's on the level?'

'I don't know, Bobby. He sounded like he had it rehearsed. And he was relieved at the end.'

'You don't think I got it all? I could bring him in again.'

Rebus was thinking: *stories you hear ... the guilty being spirited away*. Not stories you *read*, but ones you *hear* ... Who might he have heard them from? Candice? Jake Tarawicz?

Hogan rubbed the bridge of his nose. 'I need a drink.'

Rebus dropped his beaker into a waste-bin. 'Message received and understood. By the way, any word from Abernethy?'

'He's a bloody nuisance,' Hogan said, turning away.

26

'He's in place,' Claverhouse said, when Rebus phoned him to ask about Jack Morton. 'Got him a little one-bedroom shit-hole in Polwarth. Measured him up for his uniform, and he's now officially a member of on-site security.'

'Is anyone else in on it?'

'Just the big boss. His name's Livingstone. We had a long session with him last night.'

'Won't the other security men find it a bit odd, a stranger arriving in their midst?'

'It's down to Jack to put them at ease. He was pretty confident.'

'What's his cover?'

'Secret drinker, open gambler, busted marriage.'

'He doesn't drink.'

'Yes, he told me. Doesn't matter, so long as everyone *thinks* he does.'

'Is he in character?'

'Getting there. He's going to be working double shifts. That way he makes more trips to the shop, some in the evening when the place is quieter. More chance to get to know Ken and Dec. We've no contact with him during the day. Debriefing takes place once he's reached home. Telephone only, can't risk too many meetings.'

'You think they'll watch him?'

'If they're being thorough. And *if* they fall for the plan.'

'Did you talk to Marty Jones?'

'That's set for tomorrow. He'll bring a couple of heavies, but they'll go easy on Jack.'

'Isn't tomorrow a bit soon?'

'Can we afford to wait? They might already have someone in mind.'

'We're asking a lot of him.'

'He was *your* idea.'

'I know.'

'You don't think he's up to it?'

'It's not that … but he's stepping into a war.'

'Then get the ceasefire sorted out.'

'It is.'

'That's not what I hear …'

Rebus heard it too, as soon as he got off the phone. He knocked on the Chief Super's door. The Farmer was in conference with Gill Templer.

'Did you talk to him?' the Farmer asked.

'He agreed to a ceasefire,' Rebus said. He was looking at Templer. 'What about you?'

She took a deep breath. 'I spoke to Mr Telford – his solicitor was present throughout. I kept telling him what we wanted, and the lawyer kept telling me I was blackening his client's name.'

'And Telford?'

'Just sat there, arms folded, smiling at the wall.' Colour was creeping up her face. 'I don't think he looked at me once.'

'But you gave him the message?'

'Yes.'

'You said Cafferty would comply?'

She nodded.

'Then what the hell's happening?'

'We can't let it get out of control,' the Farmer said.

'Looks to me like it already is.'

The latest score-line: two of Cafferty's men, their faces mashed to something resembling fruit-pulp.

'Lucky they're not dead,' the Farmer went on.

'You know what's happening?' Rebus said. 'It's Tarawicz, *he's* the problem. Tommy's playing up to him.'

'It's times like this you yearn for independence,' the Farmer agreed. 'Then we could just extradite the bugger.'

'Why don't we?' Rebus suggested. 'Tell him his presence here is no longer acceptable.'

'And if he stays?'

'We shadow him, make sure everyone knows we're doing it. We make *nuisances* of ourselves.'

'You think that would work?' Gill Templer sounded sceptical.

'Probably not,' Rebus agreed, slumping into a chair.

'We've no real leverage,' the Farmer said, glancing at his watch. 'Which isn't going to please the Chief Constable. He wants me in his office in half an hour.' He got on the phone, ordered a car, rose to his feet.

'Look, see if you can thrash something out between you.'

Rebus and Templer exchanged a look.

'I'll be back in an hour or two.' The Farmer looked around, as if he were suddenly lost. 'Lock the door when you leave.' With that and a wave of his hand, he left. There was silence in the room.

'Has to keep his office locked,' Rebus said, 'to stop people stealing the secret of his terrible coffee.'

'Actually, it's been getting better recently.'

'Maybe your taste buds are being corroded. So, Chief Inspector ...' Rebus turned his chair to face hers. 'What about thrashing it out then, eh?'

She smiled. 'He thinks he's losing it.'

'Is he in for a bollocking?'

'Probably.'

'So it's down to us to come to the rescue?'

'I don't really see us as the Dynamic Duo, do you?'

'No.'

'Then there's always that part of you that says, let them tear each other apart. So long as no civilians get caught in the crossfire.'

Rebus thought of Sammy, of Candice. 'Thing is,' he said, 'they always do.'

She looked at him. 'How are you doing?'

'Same as ever.'

'As bad as that?'

'It's my calling.'

'You're done with Lintz though?'

Rebus shook his head. 'There's half a chance he ties in to Telford.'

'You still think Telford was behind the hit-and-run?'

'Telford or Cafferty.'

'Cafferty?'

'Setting up Telford, the way someone tried to set *me* up for Matsumoto.'

'You know you're not out of the woods?'

He looked at her. 'An internal inquiry? The men with rubber soles?' She nodded. 'Bring them on.' He sat forward in his chair, rubbed his temples. 'No reason they should be left out of the party.'

'What party?'

'The one inside my head. The party that never stops.' Rebus leaned across the desk to answer the phone. 'No, he's not here. Can I take a message? This is DI Rebus.' A pause; he was looking at Gill Templer. 'Yes, I'm working that case.' He found pen and paper, started writing. 'Mmm, I see. Yes, sounds like. I'll let him know when he gets back.' Eyes *boring into* hers. Then the punchline: 'How many did you say were dead?'

Just the one. Another fled the scene, holding his arm, all

but severed from the shoulder. He turned up at a local hospital later, needing surgery and a huge transfusion of blood.

In broad daylight. Not in Edinburgh, but Paisley. Telford's hometown, the town he still ruled. Four men, dressed in council work jackets, like a road team. But in place of picks and shovels, they'd toted machetes and a large-calibre revolver. They'd chased two men into a housing scheme. Kids playing on tricycles; kicking a ball up the street. Women hanging out of their windows. And grown men itching to hurt one another. A machete swung overhead, coming down hard. The wounded man kept running. His friend tried hurdling a fence, wasn't agile enough. Three inches higher and he'd have made it. As it was, his toe caught, and he fell. He was pushing himself back up when the barrel of the gun touched the back of his head. Two shots, a fine drizzle of blood and brain. The children not playing any more, the women screaming for them to run. But something had been satisfied by those two shots. The chase was over. The four men turned and jogged back down the street, towards a waiting van.

A public execution, in Tommy Telford's heartland.

The two victims: known money-lenders. The one in hospital was called 'Wee' Stevie Murray, age twenty-two. The one in the mortuary was Donny Draper – known since childhood as 'Curtains'. They'd be making jokes about that. Curtains was two weeks shy of his twenty-fifth birthday. Rebus hoped he'd made the most of his short time on the planet.

Paisley police knew about Telford's move to Edinburgh, knew there were some problems there. A courtesy call had been placed to Chief Superintendent Watson.

The caller said: the men were two of Telford's brightest and best.

The caller said: descriptions of the attackers were vague.

The caller said: the children weren't talking. They were being shielded by their parents, fearful of reprisals. Well, they might not be talking to the *police*, but Rebus doubted they'd be so reticent when Tommy Telford came calling, armed with his own questions and determined to have answers.

This was bad. This was *escalation*. Fire-bombings and beatings: these could be remedied. But murder ... murder put the grudge-match on to a much higher plane.

'Is it worth talking to them again?' Gill Templer asked. They were in the canteen, sandwiches untouched in front of them.

'What do you think?'

He knew what she thought. She was talking because she thought talking was better than doing nothing. He could have told her to save her breath.

'They used a machete,' he said.

'Same thing they took to Danny Simpson's scalp.' Rebus nodded. 'I've got to ask ...' she said.

'What?'

'About Lintz ... what you said?'

He drained the last inch of his cold coffee. 'Fancy another?'

'John ...'

He looked at her. 'Lintz had some phone calls he was trying to hide. One of them was to Tommy Telford's office in Flint Street. We don't know how it ties in, but we think it *does* tie in.'

'What could Lintz and Telford have had in common?'

'Maybe Lintz went to him for help. Maybe he rented prossies off him. Like I say, we don't *know*. Which is why we're keeping it under the table.'

'You want Telford very badly, don't you?'

Rebus stared at her, thought about it. 'Not as much as I did. He's not enough any more.'

'You want Cafferty, too?'

'And Tarawicz … and the Yakuza … and anybody else who's along for the ride.'

She nodded. 'This is the party you were talking about?'

He tapped his head. 'They're all in here, Gill. I've tried kicking them out, but they won't leave.'

'Maybe if you stopped playing their kind of music?'

He smiled tiredly. 'Now there's an idea. What do you reckon: ELP? The Enid? How about a Yes triple album?'

'Your department, not mine, thank God.'

'You don't know what you're missing.'

'Yes, I do: I was there first time round.'

Old Scottish proverb: he who has had knuckles rapped will want to rap someone else's. Which is why Rebus found himself back in Watson's office. The Farmer's cheeks were still red from his meeting with the Chief Constable. When Rebus made to sit, Watson told him to get back on his feet.

'You'll sit when you're told and not before.'

'Thank you, sir.'

'What the bloody hell's going on, John?'

'Pardon, sir?'

The Farmer looked at the note Rebus had left on his desk. 'What's this?'

'One dead, one seriously wounded in Paisley, sir. Telford's men. Cafferty's hitting him where it hurts. Probably reckons that Telford's territory's spun a bit thin. Leaves him open to breaches.'

'Paisley.' The Farmer stuffed the note in his drawer. 'Not our problem.'

'It will be, sir. When Telford hits back, it'll be right here.'

'Never mind that, Inspector. Let's talk about Maclean's Pharmaceuticals.'

Rebus blinked, relaxed his shoulders. 'I was going to tell you, sir.'

'But instead I had to hear it from the Chief Constable?'

'Not really my baby, sir. Crime Squad are pushing the pram.'

'But who put the baby *in* the pram?'

'I was going to tell you, sir.'

'Know how it makes me look? I walk into Fettes and I don't know something one of my junior officers knows? I look like a mug.'

'With respect, sir, I'm sure that's not the case.'

'I look like a *mug*!' The Farmer slammed the desk with both palms. 'And it's not as though this was the first time. I've always tried to do my best for you, you know that.'

'Yes, sir.'

'Always been fair.'

'Absolutely, sir.'

'And you pay me back like this?'

'It won't happen again, sir.'

The Farmer stared at him; Rebus held it, returned it.

'I bloody well hope not.' The Farmer leaned back in his chair. He'd calmed down a little. Bollocking as therapy. 'Nothing else you want to tell me, is there, while I've got you here?'

'No, sir. Except ... well ...'

'Go on.' The Farmer sat forward again.

'It's the man in the flat above me, sir,' Rebus said. 'I think he might be Lord Lucan.'

27

Leonard Cohen: 'There is a War'.

They were waiting for Telford's retaliatory strike. The Chief Constable's idea: 'visible presence as deterrent'. It came as no surprise to Rebus: probably even less so to Telford, who had Charles Groal ready, claiming harassment the minute the patrol cars turned up in Flint Street. How was his client supposed to carry on with his legitimate and substantial business interests, as well as his many community developments, under the pressure of unwarranted and intrusive police surveillance? 'Community developments' meaning the pensioners and their rent-free flats: Telford wouldn't hesitate to use them as pawns. The media would love it.

The patrol cars would be pulled, it was just a matter of time. And afterwards: firework night all over again. That's what everyone was expecting.

Rebus went to the hospital, sat with Rhona. The room, so familiar to him now, was an oasis where calm and order reigned, where each hour of the day brought its comforting rituals.

'They've washed her hair,' he said.

'She's had another scan,' Rhona explained. 'They had to get the gunk off afterwards.' Rebus nodded. 'They said you'd noticed eye movement?'

'I thought I did.'

Rhona touched his arm. 'Jackie says he might manage to come up again at the weekend. Call this fair warning.'

'Received and understood.'

'You look tired.'

He smiled. 'One of these days someone's going to tell me how terrific I'm looking.'

'But not today,' Rhona said.

'Must be all the booze, clubbing and women.'

Thinking: Coke, the Morvena Casino, and Candice.

Thinking: why do I feel like piggy in the middle? Are Cafferty and Telford *both* playing games with me?

Thinking: I hope Jack Morton's okay.

The phone was ringing when he got back to Arden Street. He picked up just as the answering machine was cutting in.

'Hold on till I stop this thing.' Found the right button and hit it.

'Technology, eh, Strawman?'

Cafferty.

'What do you want?'

'I've heard about Paisley.'

'You mean you've been talking to yourself?'

'I had nothing to do with it.'

Rebus laughed out loud.

'I'm telling you.'

Rebus fell into his chair. 'And I'm supposed to believe you?' Games, he was thinking.

'Whether you believe me or not, I wanted you to know.'

'Thanks, I'm sure I'll sleep better for that.'

'I'm being set up, Strawman.'

'Telford doesn't *need* to set you up.' Rebus sighed, stretched his neck to left and right. 'Look, have you considered another possibility?'

'What?'

'Your men have lost it. They're going behind your back.'

'I'd know.'

'You'd know what your own lieutenants tell you. What if

they're lying? I'm not saying it's the whole gang, could be just two or three gone rogue.'

'I'd know.' The emotion had drained from Cafferty's voice. He was thinking it over.

'Fine, okay, you'd know: who'd be the first to tell you? Cafferty, you're on the other side of the country. You're in *prison*. How hard would it be to keep stuff from you?'

'These are men I'd trust with my life.' Cafferty paused. 'They'd tell me.'

'*If* they knew. *If* they hadn't been warned not to tell you. See what I'm saying?'

'Two or three gone rogue ...' Cafferty echoed.

'You must have candidates?'

'Jeffries would know.'

'Jeffries? Is that the Weasel's name?'

'Don't let him hear you call him that.'

'Give me his number. I'll talk to him.'

'No, but I'll get him to call you.'

'And if he's part of the breakaway?'

'We don't know there is one.'

'But you admit it makes sense?'

'I admit Tommy Telford's trying to put me in a box.' Rebus stared from his window. 'You mean literally?'

'I've heard word of a contract.'

'But you've got protection?'

Cafferty chuckled. 'Strawman, you almost sound concerned.'

'You're imagining things.'

'Look, there are only two ways out of this. One, *you* deal with Telford. Two, *I* deal with him. Are we agreed on that? I mean, I'm not the one who went poaching players and territory and putting out frighteners.'

'Maybe he's just more ambitious than you. Maybe he reminds you of the way you used to be.'

'Are you saying I've gone soft?'

'I'm saying it's adapt or die.'

'Have *you* adapted, Strawman?'

'Maybe a little.'

'Aye, a fucking speck, if that.'

'We're not talking about me though.'

'You're as involved as anyone. Remember that, Strawman. And sweet dreams.'

Rebus put down the phone. He felt exhausted, and depressed. The kids across the way were in bed, shutters closed. He looked around the room. Jack Morton had helped him paint it, back when Rebus was thinking of selling. Jack had helped him off the sauce, too …

He knew he wouldn't be able to sleep. Got back into the car and headed for Young Street. The Oxford Bar was quiet. A couple of philosophers in the corner, and through in the back-room three musicians who'd packed up their fiddles. He drank a couple of cups of black coffee, then drove to Oxford Terrace. Parked the car outside Patience's flat, turned off the ignition and sat there for a while, jazz on the radio. He hit a good streak: Astrid Gilberto, Stan Getz, Art Pepper, Duke Ellington. Told himself he'd wait till a bad record came on, then go knock on Patience's door.

But by then it was too late. He didn't want to turn up unannounced. It would be … it wouldn't look right. He didn't mind that it smacked of desperation, but he didn't want her to think he was pushing. He started the engine again and moved off, drove around the New Town and down to Granton. Sat by the edge of the Forth, window down, listening to water and the nighttime traffic of HGVs.

Even with eyes closed, he couldn't shut out the world. In fact, in those moments before sleep came, his images were at their most vivid. He wondered what Sammy dreamed about, or even if she dreamed at all. Rhona said that Sammy had come north to be with him. He couldn't think what he'd done to deserve her.

Back into town for an espresso at Gordon's Trattoria, then the hospital: easy to find a parking space this time of night. A taxi was idling outside the entrance. He made his way to Sammy's room, was surprised to see someone there. His first thought: Rhona. The only illumination in the room was that given through the closed curtains. A woman, kneeling by the bed, head resting on the covers. He walked forwards. She heard him, turned, face glistening with tears.

Candice.

Her eyes widened. She stumbled to her feet.

'I wanting see her,' she said quietly.

Rebus nodded. In shadows, she looked even more like Sammy: same build, similar hair and shape to her face. She wore a long red coat, fished in the pocket for a paper hankie.

'I like her,' she said. He nodded again.

'Does Tarawicz know where you are?' he asked.

She shook her head.

'The taxi outside?' he guessed.

She nodded. 'They went casino. I said sore head.' She spoke falteringly, checking each word was right before using it.

'Will he find out you've gone?'

She thought about it, shook her head.

'You sleep in the same room?' Rebus asked.

She shook her head again, smiled. 'Jake not liking women.'

This was news to Rebus. Miriam Kenworthy had said something about him marrying an Englishwoman ... but put that down to immigration. He remembered the way Tarawicz had pawed Candice, realised now it had been for *Telford's* benefit. He'd been showing Telford that he could control his women. While Telford ... well, Telford had let her get arrested, then be taken in by the Crime Squad. A small sign of rivalry between the two partners. Something to be exploited?

'Is she ... will she ...?'

Rebus shrugged. 'We hope so, Candice.'

She looked down at the floor. 'My name is Karina.'

'Karina,' he echoed.

'Sarajevo was ...' She looked up at him. 'You know, like *really*. I was escaping ... lucky. They all said to me: "You lucky, you lucky".' She stabbed at her chest with a finger. 'Lucky. Survivor.' She broke down again, and this time he held her.

The Stones: 'Soul Survivor'. Only sometimes it was the body alone that survived, the soul eaten into, chewed up by experience.

'Karina,' he said, repeating her name, reinforcing her true identity, trying to get through to the one part of her she'd kept hidden since Sarajevo. 'Karina, sshhh. It's going to be all right. Sshhh.' And stroking her hair, her face, his other hand on her back, feeling her tremble. Blinking back his own tears, and watching Sammy's body. The atmosphere in the room crackled like electricity: he wondered if any part of it was reaching Sammy's brain.

'Karina, Karina, Karina ...'

She pulled away, turned her back on him. He wouldn't let her go. Walked up to her and rested his hands on her shoulders.

'Karina,' he said, 'how did Tarawicz find you?' She seemed not to understand. 'In Anstruther, his men found you.'

'Brian,' she said quietly.

Rebus frowned. 'Brian Summers?' Pretty-Boy ...

'He tell Jake.'

'He told Tarawicz where you were?' But why not just take her back to Edinburgh? Rebus thought he knew: she was too dangerous; she'd been too close to the police. Best get her out of the way. Not a killing: that would have implicated all of them. But Tarawicz could control her. Mr Pink Eyes bailing out his friend one more time ...

'He brought you here so he could gloat over Telford.' Rebus was thoughtful. He looked at Candice. What could he do with her? Where would be safe? She seemed to sense his thoughts, squeezed his hand.

'You know I have a ...' She made a cradling motion with her hands.

'A boy,' Rebus said. She nodded. 'And Tarawicz knows where he is?'

She shook her head. 'The lorries ... they took him.'

'Tarawicz's refugee lorries?' She nodded again. 'And you don't know where he is?'

'Jake knows. He says his man ...' she made scuttling motions with her hands '... will kill my boy if ...'

Scuttling motions: the Crab. Something struck Rebus. 'Why isn't the Crab up here with Tarawicz?' She was looking at him. 'Tarawicz here,' he said, 'Crab in Newcastle. Why?'

She shrugged, looked thoughtful. 'He don't come.' She was remembering some snippet of conversation. 'Danger.'

'Dangerous?' Rebus frowned. 'Who for?'

She shrugged again. Rebus took her hands.

'You can't trust him, Karina. You have to leave him.'

She smiled up at him, eyes glinting. 'I tried.'

They looked at one another, held one another for a while. Afterwards, he walked her back out to her taxi.

28

In the morning he called the hospital, found out how Sammy was doing, then asked to be transferred.

'How's Danny Simpson getting on?'

'I'm sorry, are you family?'

Which told him everything. He identified himself, asked when it had happened.

'In the night,' the nurse said.

Body at its lowest ebb: the dying hours. Rebus called the mother, identified himself again.

'Sorry to hear the news,' he said. 'Is the funeral …?'

'Just family, if you don't mind. No flowers. We're asking for donations to be sent to an … to a charity. Danny was well thought of, you know.'

'I'm sure.'

Rebus took down details of the charity – an AIDS hospice; the mother couldn't bring herself to say the word. Terminated the call. Got an envelope out and put in ten pounds, plus a note: 'In memory of Danny Simpson'. He wondered about going for that test … His phone rang and he picked it up.

'Hello?'

Lots of static and engine noise: car-phone, on the move at speed.

'This takes persecution to new levels.' *Telford.*

'What do you mean?' Rebus trying to compose himself.

'Danny Simpson's been dead six hours, and already you're on the phone to his mum.'

'How do you know?'

'I was *there*. Paying my respects.'

'Same reason I phoned then. Know what, Telford? I think *you're* taking persecution complexes to new levels.'

'Yes, and Cafferty's not out to shut me down.'

'He says he didn't have anything to do with Paisley.'

'I bet you believed in the Tooth Fairy when you were a kid.'

'I still do.'

'You'll need more than a good fairy if you side with Cafferty.'

'Is that a threat? Don't tell me: Tarawicz is in the car with you?' Silence. Bingo, Rebus thought. 'You think Tarawicz will respect you because you bad-mouth cops? He's got no respect for you whatsoever – look how he's waving Candice in your face.'

Mixing levity with fury: 'Hey, Rebus, you and Candice in that hotel – what was she like? Jake tells me she's vindaloo.' Background laughter: Mr Pink Eyes, who, according to Candice, had never touched her. For 'laughter' read 'bravado'. Telford and Tarawicz, playing games between themselves, playing games with the world.

Rebus found the tone of voice he wanted. 'I tried to help her. If she's too stupid to know that, she deserves the likes of you and Tarawicz.' Telling them he had no further interest in her. 'Anyway, Tarawicz didn't have any trouble taking her off *your* hands.' Rebus jabbing away, looking for gaps in the armour of the Telford/Tarawicz relationship.

'What if Cafferty wasn't behind Paisley?' he asked into the silence.

'It was his men.'

'Gone rogue.'

'He can't control them, that's his look-out. He's a *joke*, Rebus. He's finished.'

Rebus didn't say anything; listened instead to a muted

conversation. Then Telford again: 'Mr Tarawicz wants a word.' The phone was handed over.

'Rebus? I thought we were civilised men?'

'In what way?'

'When we met in Newcastle ... I thought we came to an understanding?'

The unspoken agreement: leave Telford alone, have nothing more to do with Cafferty, and Candice and her son would be safe. What was Tarawicz getting at?

'I've kept my side.'

A forced chuckle. 'You know what Paisley represents?'

'What?'

'The beginning of the end of Morris Gerald Cafferty.'

'And I bet you'd send flowers to the grave.'

Dead flowers at that.

Rebus went into St Leonard's, got settled in front of his computer screen, and took a look at the Crab.

The Crab: William Andrew Colton. Plenty of form. Rebus decided he'd like to read the files. Phoned in and requested them, backed up the request in writing. Buzzed from downstairs: a man to see him, no name supplied. Description: the Weasel.

Rebus went downstairs.

The Weasel was outside, smoking a cigarette. He was wearing a green waxed jacket, torn at both pockets. A lumberjack hat with its flaps down protected his ears from the wind.

'Let's walk,' Rebus said. The Weasel got into step with him. They wandered through an estate of new flats: satellite dishes and windows picked from Lego boxes. Behind the flats sat Salisbury Crags.

'Don't worry,' Rebus said, 'I'm not in the mood for rock-climbing.'

'I'm in the mood for indoors.' The Weasel tucked his chin into the upturned collar of his coat.

'What's the news on my daughter?'

'We're close, I told you.'

'How close?'

The Weasel measured his response. 'We've got the tapes from the car, the guy who sold them. He says he got them from another party.'

'And he is …?'

A sly smile: the Weasel knew he had control over Rebus. He'd play it out as long as possible.

'You're going to be meeting him fairly shortly.'

'Even so … say the tapes got taken from the car after it was abandoned?'

The Weasel was shaking his head. 'That's not how it was.'

'Then how was it?' He wanted to pull his tormentor down on to the ground and start hammering his skull on the pavement.

'Give us a day or two, we'll have everything you need.' The wind gusted some grit towards them. They turned their faces. Rebus saw a heavy-set man loitering sixty yards behind.

'Don't worry,' the Weasel said, 'he's with me.'

'Getting jittery?'

'After Paisley, Telford's out for blood.'

'What do you know about Paisley?'

The Weasel's eyes became slits. 'Nothing.'

'No? Cafferty's beginning to suspect some of his own men might have gone rogue.' Rebus watched the Weasel shake his head.

'I don't know the first thing about it.'

'Who's your boss's main man?'

'Ask Mr Cafferty.' The Weasel was looking around, as if bored by the conversation. He made a signal to the back-marker, who passed it along. Seconds later, a newish Jaguar – arterial-red paint-job – cruised to a stop beside them. Rebus saw: a driver itching for a less sedentary occupation; cream leather interior; the back-marker jogging forwards, opening the door for the Weasel.

'It's you,' Rebus said. The Weasel: Cafferty's eyes and ears on the street; the man with the look and dress-code of a down-and-out. The Weasel was running the show. All the lieutenants in the various outposts ... all the tailor-made suits ... the collective which, according to police intelligence, ran Cafferty's kingdom in their master's absence ... they were a smokescreen. The hunched man pulling off his lumberjack hat, the man with bad teeth and a blunt razor, *he* was in charge.

Rebus actually laughed. The bodyguard got into the car's passenger seat, having made sure his boss was comfortable in the back. Rebus tapped on the window. The Weasel lowered it.

'Tell me,' Rebus asked, 'have you got the bottle to wrest it away from him?'

'Mr Cafferty trusts me. He knows I'll do right by him.'

'What about Telford?'

The Weasel stared at him. 'Telford's not my concern.'

'Then who is?'

But the window was rising again, and the Weasel – Cafferty had called him Jeffries – had turned his face away, dismissing Rebus from his mind.

He stood there, watching the car drive off. Was Cafferty making a big mistake, putting the Weasel in charge? Was it just that his best men had scarpered or gone over to the other side?

Or was the Weasel every bit as sly, clever and vicious as his namesake?

Back at the station, Rebus sought out Bill Pryde. Pryde was

shrugging his shoulders even before Rebus had reached his desk.

'Sorry, John, no news.'

'Nothing at all? What about the stolen tapes?' Pryde shook his head. 'That's funny, I've just been talking to someone who claims to know who sold them on, and who *he* got them from.'

Pryde sat back in his chair. 'I wondered why you hadn't been chasing me up. What've you done, hired a private eye?' Blood was rising to his face. 'I've been working my arse off on this, John, you know I have. Now you don't trust me to do the job?'

'It's not like that, Bill.' Rebus suddenly found himself on the defensive.

'Who've you got working for you, John?'

'Just people on the street.'

'Well-connected people by the sound of it.' He paused. 'Are we talking villains?'

'My daughter's in a coma, Bill.'

'I'm well aware of that. Now answer my question!'

People around them were staring. Rebus lowered his voice. 'Just a few of my grasses.'

'Then give me their names.'

'Come on, Bill ...'

Pryde's hands gripped the table. 'These past days, I've been thinking you'd lost interest. Thinking maybe you didn't *want* an answer.' He was thoughtful. 'You wouldn't go to Telford ... Cafferty?' His eyes widened. 'Is that it, John?'

Rebus turned his head away.

'Christ, John ... what's the deal here? He hands over the driver, what do *you* hand *him*?'

'It's not like that.'

'I can't believe you'd trust Cafferty. You put him away, for Christ's sake!'

'It's not a question of trust.'

But Pryde was shaking his head. 'There's a line we don't cross.'

'Get a grip, Bill. There's no line.' Rebus spread his arms. 'If there is, show me it.'

Pryde tapped his forehead. 'It's up here.'

'Then it's a fiction.'

'You really believe that?'

Rebus sought an answer, slumped against the desk, ran his hands over his head. He remembered something Lintz had once said: *when we stop believing in God, we don't suddenly believe in 'nothing' ... we believe anything.*

'John?' someone called. 'Phone call.'

Rebus stared at Pryde. 'Later,' he said. He walked across to another desk, took the call.

'Rebus here.'

'It's Bobby.' Bobby Hogan.

'What can I do for you, Bobby?'

'For a start, you can help get that Special Branch arsehole off my back.'

'Abernethy?'

'He won't leave me alone.'

'Keeps phoning you?'

'Christ, John, aren't you listening? He's *here.*'

'When did he get in?'

'He never went away.'

'Whoah, hold on.'

'And he's driving me round the twist. He says he knows you from way back, so how about having a word?'

'Are you at Leith?'

'Where else?'

'I'll be there in twenty minutes.'

'I got so pissed off, I went to my boss – and that's something I seldom have to resort to.' Bobby Hogan was drinking coffee like it was something best taken intravenously. The top button of his shirt was undone, tie hanging loose.

'Only,' he went on, '*his* boss had a word with my *boss's* boss, and I ended up with a warning: co-operate or else.'

'Meaning?'

'I wasn't to tell anyone he was still around.'

'Thanks, pal. So what's he actually doing?'

'What *isn't* he doing? He wants to be in on any interviews. He wants copies of tapes and transcripts. He wants to see all the paperwork, wants to know what I'm planning to do next, what I had for breakfast ...'

'I don't suppose he's managing to be helpful in any shape or form?'

Hogan's look gave Rebus his answer.

'I don't mind him taking an interest, but this verges on the obstructive. He's slowing the case to a dead stop.'

'Maybe that's his plan.'

Hogan looked up from his cup. 'I don't get it.'

'Neither do I. Look, if he's being obstructive, let's put on a show, see how he reacts.'

'What sort of show?'

'What time will he be in?'

Hogan checked his watch. 'Half an hour or so. That's when my work stops for the day, while I fill him in.'

'Half an hour's enough. Mind if I use your phone?'

29

When Abernethy arrived, he didn't manage not to look surprised. The space put aside for the investigation – Hogan's space – now contained three bodies, and they were working at the devil's own pace.

Hogan was on the telephone to a librarian. He was asking for a run-down of books and articles about the 'Rat Line'. Rebus was sorting through paperwork, putting it in order, cross-referencing, laying aside anything he didn't think useful. And Siobhan Clarke was there, too. She appeared to be on the phone to some Jewish organisation, and was asking them about lists of war criminals. Rebus nodded towards Abernethy, but kept on working.

'What's going on?' Abernethy asked, taking off his raincoat.

'Helping out. Bobby's got so many leads to work on ...' He nodded towards Siobhan. 'And Crime Squad are interested, too.'

'Since when?'

Rebus waved a piece of paper. 'This might be bigger than we think.'

Abernethy looked around. He wanted to speak to Hogan, but Hogan was still on the phone. Rebus was the only one with time to talk.

Which was just the way Rebus had planned it.

He'd only had five minutes in which to brief Siobhan, but she was a born actress, even holding a conversation with the dialling tone. Hogan's fantasy librarian, meantime, was asking him all the right questions. And Abernethy was looking glazed.

'What do you mean?'

'In fact,' Rebus said, putting down a file, 'you might be able to help.'

'How?'

'You're Special Branch, and Special Branch has access to the secret services.' Rebus paused. 'Right?'

Abernethy licked his lips and shrugged.

'See,' Rebus went on, 'we're beginning to wonder something. There could be a dozen reasons why someone would want to kill Joseph Lintz, but the one we've been practically ignoring' (ignoring at Abernethy's suggestion, according to Hogan) 'is the one that just might provide the answer. I'm talking about the Rat Line. What if Lintz's murder had something to do with that?'

'How could it?'

It was Rebus's turn to shrug. 'That's why we need your help. We need any and all information we can get on the Rat Line.'

'But it never existed.'

'Funny, a lot of books seem to say it did.'

'They're wrong.'

'Then there are all these survivors ... except they haven't survived. Suicides, car crashes, a fall from a window. Lintz is just one of a long line of dead men.'

Siobhan Clarke and Bobby Hogan had finished their calls and were listening.

'You're climbing the wrong tree,' Abernethy said.

'Well, you know, if you're in a forest, climbing any tree will give you a better view.'

'There is no Rat Line.'

'You're an expert?'

'I've been collating ...'

'Yes, yes, all the investigations. And how far have you got? Is any one of them going to make it to trial?'

'It's too early to tell.'

'And soon it may be too late. These men aren't getting any younger. I've seen the same thing all around Europe: delay the trial until the defendants are so old they snuff it or go doolally. Result's the same: no trial.'

'Look, this has nothing to do with ...'

'Why are you here, Abernethy? Why did you come up that time to speak to Lintz?'

'Look, Rebus, it's not ...'

'If you can't tell us, talk to your boss. Get *him* to do it. Otherwise, the way we're digging, we're bound to throw up an old bone sooner or later.'

Abernethy stood back a pace. 'I think I get it,' he said. And he began to smile. 'You're trying to stiff me.' He was looking at Hogan. 'That's what this is.'

'Not at all,' Rebus answered. 'What I'm saying is: we'll redouble our efforts. We'll sniff into every little corner. The Rat Line, the Vatican, turning Nazis into cold war spies for the allies ... it could all count as evidence. The other men on your list, the other suspects ... we'll need to talk to all of them, see if they knew Joseph Lintz. Maybe they met him on the trip over.'

Abernethy was shaking his head. 'I'm not going to let you do that.'

'You're going to obstruct the investigation?'

'That's not what I said.'

'No, but it's what you'll *do*.' Rebus paused. 'If you think we're climbing the wrong tree – and, incidentally, that should be *barking up* – go ahead and prove it. Give us everything you've got on Lintz's past.'

Abernethy's eyes were fierce.

'Or we go on digging and sniffing.' Rebus opened another file, lifted out the first sheet. Hogan picked up his telephone, made another call. Siobhan Clarke looked at a list of numbers and chose one.

'Hello, is that the City Synagogue?' Hogan was saying. 'Yes, it's Detective Inspector Hogan here, Leith CID. Do you by any chance have information on a Joseph Lintz?'

Abernethy grabbed his coat, turned on his heels and left. They waited thirty seconds, then Hogan put the receiver down.

'He looked nettled.'

'That's one Christmas wish I can chalk off,' Siobhan Clarke said.

'Thanks for your time, Siobhan,' Rebus said.

'Happy to oblige. But why did it have to be me?'

'Because he knows you're Crime Squad. I wanted him to think interest was escalating. And because the two of you didn't exactly hit it off last time you met. Antagonism always helps.'

'And what did we accomplish?' Bobby Hogan asked, beginning to gather together the files, half of which belonged to other cases.

'We rattled his cage,' Rebus said. 'He's not up here for the good of his health – or yours, come to that. He's here because Special Branch in London want to know all about the investigation. And to me, that means they're scared of something.'

'The Rat Line?'

'That would be my guess. Abernethy's been keeping an eye on all the new cases nationwide. Someone in London is getting a bit sweaty.'

'They're worried this Rat Line will connect to whoever killed Lintz?'

'I'm not sure it goes that far,' Rebus said.

'Meaning?'

He looked at Clarke. 'Meaning I'm not sure it goes that far.'

'Well,' Hogan said, 'looks like he's off my back for a little while at least, for which I'm grateful.' He got to his feet. 'Get anyone a coffee?'

Clarke checked her watch. 'Go on then.'

Rebus waited till Hogan was gone, then thanked Siobhan again. 'I wasn't sure you'd be able to spare the time.'

'We're giving Jack Morton a wide berth,' she explained. 'Nothing to do but bite our fingernails and wait. What about you, what are you up to?'

'Keeping my nose clean.'

She smiled. 'I'll bet.'

Hogan came back with three coffees. 'Powdered milk, sorry.'

Clarke wrinkled her nose. 'Actually, I've got to be getting back.' She stood up and put on her coat.

'That's one I owe you,' Hogan said, shaking her hand.

'I won't let you forget.' She turned to Rebus. 'See you later.'

'Cheers, Siobhan.'

Hogan put her cup beside his own. 'So we got Abernethy off my back, but did we get anything else?'

'Wait and see, Bobby. I didn't exactly have much time to devise a strategy.'

The phone rang, just as Hogan took a mouthful of scalding coffee. Rebus picked up.

'Hello?'

'Is that you, John?' Country and western twanging in the background: Claverhouse.

'You've just missed her,' Rebus told him.

'It's not Clarke I wanted, it's you.'

'Oh?'

'Something I thought you might be interested in. It's just filtered down from NCIS.' Rebus heard Claverhouse pick up a sheet of paper. 'Sakiji Shoda ... I think I've pronounced that right. Flew into Heathrow from Kansai

Airport yesterday. South-East Regional Crime Squad were apprised.'

'Terrific.'

'He didn't hang around, caught a connection to Inverness. Stayed the night in a local hotel, and now I hear he's in Edinburgh.'

Rebus looked out of the window. 'Not exactly golfing weather.'

'I don't think he's up here for the golf. According to the original report, Mr Shoda is a high-ranking member of the ... can't make it out on the fax. Socky-something.'

'Sokaiya?' Rebus sat up.

'That looks about right.'

'Where is he now?'

'I tried a couple of hotels. He's staying at the Caly. What's the Sokaiya?'

'It's the upper echelons of the Yakuza.'

'How does it read to you?'

'I was going to suggest he's Matsumoto's replacement, but it sounds to me like he's a few grades higher.'

'Matsumoto's boss?'

'Which means he's probably here to find out what happened to his boy.' Rebus tapped a pen against his teeth. Hogan was listening, but not getting any of it. 'Why Inverness? Why not direct to Edinburgh?'

'I've been wondering that.' Claverhouse sneezed. 'How pissed off will he be?'

'Somewhere between "mildly" and "very". More importantly, how are Telford and Mr Pink Eyes going to react?'

'You think Telford will drop Maclean's?'

'On the contrary, I think he'll want to show Mr Shoda that he can do *some* things right.' Rebus thought back to something Claverhouse had said. 'South-East Crime Squad?'

'Yes.'

'Rather than Scotland Yard?'

'Maybe the two are the same?'

'Maybe. Do you have a contact number?'

Claverhouse gave it to him.

'You'll speak to Jack Morton tonight?' Rebus asked.

'Yes.'

'Better tell him about this.'

'Talk to you again.'

Rebus put down the receiver, picked it up again, got an outside line and made the call. Explained his reason for calling and asked if there was anyone who could help him.

He was told to hold.

'Is this to do with Telford?' Hogan asked. Rebus nodded.

'Hey, Bobby, did you ever talk to Telford again?'

'I tried a couple of times. He just kept saying: "It must've been a wrong number".'

'And this was echoed by his staff?'

Hogan nodded, smiled. 'Tell you a funny thing. I walked into Telford's office, and someone was at his desk, back to me. I apologised, said I'd come back when he'd finished with the lady. Well, the "lady" turns, face like fury ...'

'Pretty-Boy?'

Hogan nodded. 'And pretty fucking angry the last I saw him.' Hogan laughed.

'Putting you through,' the switchboard told Rebus.

'How can I help you?' The voice sounded Welsh.

'My name's DI Rebus, Scottish Crime Squad.' Rebus winked at Hogan: the lie would give him more clout.

'Yes, Inspector?'

'And you are ...?'

'DI Morgan.'

'We had this message this morning ...'

'Yes?'

'Concerning Sakiji Shoda.'

'That would be my boss has sent you that.'

'What I'm wondering is, what's your interest?'

'Well, Inspector, I'm more of an expert on *vory v zakone*.'

'That clears things up then.'

Morgan chuckled. ' "Thieves within the code". Meaning *mafiya*.'

'Russian mafia?'

'That's it.'

'You'll have to help me here. What's that got to do with ...?'

'Why do you want to know?'

Rebus took a sip of coffee. 'We've had a spot of bother with the Yakuza up here. One victim so far. My guess is that Shoda is the victim's boss.'

'And he's up there for a sort of unofficial committal?'

'We don't have the committal stage in Scotland, DI Morgan.'

'Well, pardon me for breathing.'

'Thing is, we've also got a Russian gangster up here. I say he's Russian, word is he's Chechen.'

'Is it Jake Tarawicz?'

'You've heard of him?'

'That's my job, sonny boy.'

'Well, anyway, with the Yakuza and the Chechens in town ...'

'You've got a nightmare scenario. Understood. Well, look ... What about if you give me your number there, and I'll call back in five minutes? Need to put some facts together first.'

Rebus gave him the number, then waited ten minutes for the call back.

'You were checking me out,' he told the Welshman.

'Got to be careful. Bit naughty of you to say you were Crime Squad.'

'Let's just say I'm the next best thing. So is there anything you can tell me?'

Morgan took a deep breath. 'We've been chasing a lot of dirty money around the world.'

Rebus couldn't find a clean sheet of paper to write on. Hogan gave him a pad.

'See,' Morgan was saying, 'the old Soviet Asia is now the biggest supplier of raw opium in the world. And wherever there's drugs, there's money needs laundering.'

'And this money makes its way to Britain?'

'On its way elsewhere. Companies in London, private banks in Guernsey ... the money gets filtered down, getting cleaner all the time. Everyone wants to do business with the Russians.'

'Why?'

'Because they make everyone money. Russia's one giant bazaar. You want weapons, counterfeit goods, money, fake passports, even plastic surgery? You want any of that, it's in Russia. The place has open borders, airports nobody knows exist ... it's ideal.'

'If you happen to be an international mobster.'

'Exactly. And the *mafiya* have made links with their Sicilian cousins, with the Camorra, the Calabrians ... I could go on forever. British villains go shopping there. They all love the Russians.'

'And now they're here?'

'Oh, they're here all right. Running protection and prossies, dealing drugs ...'

Prostitutes, drugs: Mr Pink Eyes's territory; Telford's territory.

'Any evidence of a hook-up with the Yakuza?'

'Not that I know of.'

'But if they moved into Britain ...?'

'They'd be trying to control drugs and prostitution. They'd be laundering money.'

Ways to launder money: through legitimate businesses such as country clubs and the like; by swopping dirty money for casino chips at an establishment like the Morvena.

Rebus already knew that the Yakuza liked to smuggle artworks back into Japan. Rebus already knew Mr Pink had made his early money smuggling icons out of Russia. Put the two together.

Then add Tommy Telford to the equation.

Did they need the haul from Maclean's? It didn't sound to Rebus like they did. So why was Tommy Telford doing it? Two possible reasons: one, to show off; two, *because they'd told him to*. Some rite of passage ... If he wanted to play with the big boys, he had to prove himself. He had to wipe out Cafferty, and pull off what would be the biggest heist in Scottish history.

Something hit Rebus between the eyes.

Telford wasn't meant to succeed. Telford was meant to fail.

Telford was being set up by Tarawicz and the Yakuza.

Because he had something they wanted: a steady supply of drugs; a kingdom waiting to be plucked from his grasp. Miriam Kenworthy had said as much: rumour was, the drugs were going south from Scotland. Which meant Telford had a supply ... something *nobody* knew about.

With Cafferty out of the way, there'd be no competition. The Yakuza would have their British base – solid, respectable, reliable. The electronics factory would act as perfect cover, maybe even as a laundering operation itself. Every way Rebus looked at it, Telford was unnecessary to the equation, like a zero that could be safely cancelled out.

Which was where Rebus wanted Telford ... only not at the price being asked.

'Thanks for your help,' he said. He noticed that Hogan

had stopped listening and was staring into space. Rebus put the phone down.

'Sorry to have bored you.'

Hogan blinked. 'No, nothing like that. It's just that I thought of something.'

'What?'

'Pretty-Boy. I mistook him for a woman.'

'You're probably not the first.'

'Exactly.'

'I'm not sure I follow you?'

'In the restaurant ... Lintz and a young woman.' Hogan shrugged. 'It's a long shot.'

Rebus saw it. 'Talking business?'

Hogan nodded. 'Pretty-Boy runs Telford's stable.'

'And takes a personal interest in the higher-price models. It's worth a try, Bobby.'

'What do you think – bring him in?'

'Definitely. Beef up the restaurant angle. Say there's a positive ID. See what he says to that.'

'Same gag we pulled with Colquhoun? Pretty-Boy's bound to deny it.'

'Doesn't mean it ain't so.' Rebus patted Hogan on the shoulder.

'What about your call?'

'My call?' Rebus looked at his scrawled notes. Gangsters preparing to carve up Scotland. 'It wasn't the worst news I've ever had.'

'And is that saying much?'

'Afraid not, Bobby,' Rebus said, putting on his jacket. 'Afraid not.'

30

By the end of play, Rebus still hadn't received the files on the Crab, but he had fielded a frank and foul-mouthed call from Abernethy, accusing him of everything from obstruction – which was pretty rich, considering – to racism, which Rebus thought nicely ironic.

They'd given him back his car. Someone had run their finger through the dirt crusted on the boot, creating two messages: TERMINAL CASE, and WASHED BY STEVIE WONDER. The Saab, affronted, started first time and seemed to have shrugged off some of its repertoire of clanks and thunks. On the drive home, Rebus kept the windows open so he wouldn't smell the whisky that had soaked into the upholstery.

The evening had turned out fine, the sky clear, temperature dropping sharply. The low red sun, curse of the city's drivers, had disappeared behind the rooftops. Rebus left his coat unbuttoned as he walked down to the chip shop. He bought a fish supper, two buttered rolls, and a couple of cans of Irn-Bru, then returned to the flat. Nothing on the TV, so he put on a record. Van Morrison: *Astral Weeks*. The record had more scratches than a dog with eczema.

The opening track contained the refrain 'To be born again'. Rebus thought of Father Leary, shored up by a fridge full of medicine. Then he thought of Sammy, crowned with electrodes, machines rising either side of her, like she was being offered to them in sacrifice. Leary often talked of faith, but it was hard to have faith in a human race that never learned, that seemed ready to accept torture, murder, destruction. He opened his newspaper: Kosovo, Zaire, Rwanda. Punishment beatings in Northern Ireland. A young girl found murdered in England, another girl's disappearance termed 'a cause for concern'. The predators were out there, no doubt about it. Strip the veneer, and the world had moved only a couple of steps from the cave.

To be born again ... But sometimes only after a baptism of fire.

Belfast, 1970. A sniper's bullet blew open the skull of a British squaddie. The victim was nineteen, came from Glasgow. Back in the barracks, there'd been little mourning, just an overspill of anger. The assassin would never be caught. He'd slipped back into the shadows of a tower-block, and from there deep into the Catholic housing estate.

Leaving one more newspaper story, one early statistic in the 'Troubles'.

And anger.

The ring-leader went by the nickname of 'Mean Machine'. He was a lance-corporal, came from somewhere in Ayrshire. Cropped blond hair, looked like he'd played rugby, liked to work out, even if it was just press-ups and sit-ups in the barracks. He started the campaign for retribution. It was to be covert – meaning behind the backs of the 'brass'. It was to be a release-valve for the frustration, the pressure that was building in the cramped confines of the barracks. The world outside was enemy terrain, everyone a potential foe. Knowing there was no way to punish the sniper, Mean Machine had decided to hold the entire community to blame: collective responsibility, for which there would be collective justice.

The plan: a raid on a known IRA bar, a place where sympathisers drank and colluded. The pretext: a man with a handgun, chased into the bar, necessitating a search.

Maximum harassment, ending with the beating of the local IRA fundraiser.

And Rebus went along with it ... because it *was* collective. You were either part of the team, or you were dead meat. And Rebus wasn't in the market for pariah status.

But all the same, he knew the line between 'good guys' and 'bad guys' had become blurred. And during the incursion, it disappeared altogether.

Mean Machine went in hardest, teeth bared, eyes ablaze. He swung with his rifle, cracking skulls. Tables flew, pint glasses shattered. Initially the other soldiers seemed shocked by the sudden violence. They looked to each other for guidance. Then one of them lashed out, and the others fell in beside him. A mirror dissolved into glittering stars, stout and lager washed over the wooden floor. Men were shouting, begging, crawling on hands and knees across the glass minefield. Mean Machine had the IRA man pinned to a wall, kneeing him in the groin. He twisted his body, threw him to the floor, then started pummelling him with the rifle-butt. More soldiers were pouring into the drinking-club: armoured cars arriving outside. A chair crashed into the row of optics. The smell of whisky was almost overpowering.

Rebus tried to shut it out, his own teeth bared not in anger but anguish. Then he aimed his rifle at the ceiling and let loose a single shot, and everything froze ... A final kick to the bloodied figure on the floor and Mean Machine turned and walked out of the club. The others hesitated again, then followed. He'd proved something to the other men: for all his lowly rank, he'd become their leader.

They enjoyed themselves that night in the barracks, chiding Rebus for letting his trigger-finger slip. They cracked open cans of beer and told stories, stories which were already being exaggerated, turning the event into a myth, giving it a grandeur it had lacked.

Turning it into a lie.

A few weeks later, the same IRA man was found shot dead in a stolen car south of the city, on a farm road with a view of hills and grazing land. Protestant paramilitaries took the blame, but Mean Machine, though he admitted nothing, would wink and grin when the incident was mentioned. Bravado or confession – Rebus was never sure. All he knew was that he wanted out, away from Mean Machine's newly minted code of ethics. So he did the one thing he could – applied to join the SAS. Nobody would think him a coward or a turncoat for applying to join the elite.

To be born again.

Side one had finished; Rebus turned the record over, switched off the lights and went to sit in his chair. He felt a chill run through him. Because he *knew* how events like Villefranche could come to be. Because he *knew* how the world's continuing horrors could come to be perpetrated at the cusp of the twentieth century. He knew that mankind's instinct was raw, that every act of bravery and kindness was countered by so many acts of savagery.

And he suspected that if his daughter had been that sniper's victim, he'd have run into the bar with his trigger-finger already working.

Telford's gang ran in a pack, too, trusted their leader. But now *he* wanted to run with an even bigger gang …

The phone rang and he picked up.

'John Rebus,' he said.

'John, it's Jack.' Jack Morton. Rebus put down his can.

'Hello, Jack. Where are you?'

'In the poky one-bedroomed flat our friends at Fettes so graciously provided.'

'It has to fit the image.'

'Aye, I suppose so. Got a phone though. Coin job, but you can't have everything.' He paused. 'You okay, John? You sound ... not all there.'

'That just about sums me up, Jack. What's it like being a security guard?'

'A dawdle, pal. Should have taken it up years ago.'

'Wait till your pension's safe.'

'Aye, right.'

'And it went okay with Marty Jones?'

'Oscars all round. They were just heavy enough. I stumbled back into the shop, said I had to sit down. The Gruesome Twosome were very solicitous, then started asking me all these questions ... Not very subtle.'

'You don't think they twigged?'

'Like you, I was a bit dubious about setting it up so fast, but I think they fell for it. Whether their boss goes along is a different story.'

'Well, he's under a lot of pressure.'

'With the war going on?'

'I don't think that's the whole story, Jack. I think he's under pressure from his partners.'

'The Russian and the Japs?'

'I think they're setting him up for a fall, and Maclean's is the precipice.'

'Evidence?'

'Gut feeling.'

Jack was thoughtful. 'So where do I stand?'

'Just ca' canny, Jack.'

'I never thought of that.'

Rebus laughed. 'When do you think they'll make contact?'

'They followed me home – that's how desperate they are. They're sitting outside right now.'

'They must think you're a good thing.'

Rebus could see the way it was going. Dec and Ken

getting panicky, needing a quick result – feeling vulnerable so far away from Flint Street, not knowing if they'd be Cafferty's next victims. Telford, pressure applied by Tarawicz, and now with the Yakuza boss in town ... needing a result, something to show he was top dog.

'What about you, John? It's been a while.'

'Yes.'

'How are you holding up?'

'I'm on soft drinks only, if that's what you mean.' And a car doused in whisky ... he could taste it in his lungs.

'Hang on,' Jack said. 'Someone's at the door. I'll call you back.'

'Be careful.'

The phone went dead.

Rebus gave it an hour. When Jack hadn't called, he got on the blower to Claverhouse.

'It's okay,' Claverhouse told him from his mobile. 'Tweedledee and Tweedledum came calling, took him off somewhere.'

'You're watching the flat?'

'Decorator's van parked down the street.'

'So you've no idea where they've taken him?'

'I'd guess he's at Flint Street.'

'With no back-up?'

'That's how we all wanted it.'

'Christ, I don't know ...'

'Thanks for the vote of confidence.'

'It's not you in the firing line. And I'm the one who volunteered him.'

'He knows the score, John.'

'So now you wait for him either to come home or end up on a slab?'

'Christ, John, Calvin was Charlie Chester compared to you.' Claverhouse had lost all patience. Rebus tried to think of a comeback, slammed the phone down instead.

Suddenly he couldn't be doing with Van the Man; put on Bowie instead, *Aladdin Sane*: nicely discordant, Mike Garson's piano in key with his thoughts.

Empty juice cans and a dead pack of cigarettes stared up at him. He didn't know Jack's address. The only person who'd give it to him was Claverhouse, and he didn't want to pick up their conversation. He took Bowie off halfway through side one, substituted *Quadrophenia*. Liner notes: 'Schizophrenic? I'm bleeding Quadrophenic'. Which was just about right.

Quarter past midnight, the phone rang. It was Jack Morton.

'Back home safe and sound?' Rebus asked.

'Right as nails.'

'Have you spoken to Claverhouse?'

'He can wait his turn. I said I'd phone you back.'

'So what did you get?'

'The third degree, basically. Some guy with dyed black hair, frizzy ... tight jeans.'

'Pretty-Boy.'

'Wears mascara.'

'Looks like. So what was the gist?'

'Second hurdle passed. Nobody's mentioned what the job is yet. Tonight was a sort of preface. Wanted to know all about me, told me my money worries could be over. If I could help them with a "little problem" – Pretty-Boy's words.'

'You asked what the problem was?'

'He wasn't saying. If you ask me, he goes to Telford, talks it through. Then there's another meeting, and that's where they tell me the plan.'

'And you'll be miked up?'

'Yes.'

'And if they strip you?'

'Claverhouse has access to some miniaturised stuff, cuff-links and the like.'

'And your character would obviously wear cuff-links.'

'True enough. Maybe fit a transmitter into a bookie's pencil.'

'Now you're thinking.'

'I'm thinking I'm wiped out.'

'What was the mood like?'

'Fraught.'

'Any sign of Tarawicz or Shoda?'

'Nope, just Pretty-Boy and the Gruesome Twosome.'

'Claverhouse calls them Tweedledum and Tweedledee.'

'He's obviously classically educated.' Morton paused. 'You've spoken to him?'

'When you didn't call back.'

'I'm touched. Do you think he's up to it?'

'Claverhouse?' Rebus thought about it. 'I'd feel better if *I* was in charge. But that probably puts me in a minority.'

'I didn't say that.'

'You're a pal, Jack.'

'They're running a check on me. But that's all in place. With luck, I'll pass.'

'What did they say to your sudden arrival at Maclean's?'

'I've been transferred from another plant. If they go looking, I'm in the personnel files.' Morton paused again. 'One thing I want to know …'

'What?'

'Pretty-Boy handed me a hundred quid on account: what do I do with it?'

'That's between you and your conscience, Jack. See you soon.'

'Night, John.'

For the first time in a while, Rebus actually made it as far as his bed. His sleep was deep and dreamless.

31

Doctors in white coats were doing things to Sammy when Rebus arrived at the hospital next morning: taking her pulse, shining lights in her eyes. They were setting up another scanner, a nurse trying to untangle the thin coloured leads. Rhona looked like she'd lost some sleep. She jumped up and ran towards him.

'She woke up!'

It took him a second to take it in. Rhona was holding his arms, shaking him.

'She woke *up*, John!'

He pushed his way to the bedside.

'When?'

'Last night.'

'Why didn't you phone me?'

'I tried three, four times. You were engaged. I tried Patience, but there was no answer there.'

'What happened?' To him, Sammy looked the same as ever.

'She just opened her eyes … No, first off, it was like she was moving her eyeballs. You know, with her eyelids closed. Then she opened her eyes.'

Rebus could see that the medical personnel were finding their work hampered. Half of him wanted to lash out – *We're her fucking parents!* The other half wanted them to do all they could to bring her round again. He took Rhona by the shoulder and guided her out into the hallway.

'Did she … Did she look at you? Did she say anything?'

'She was just staring at the ceiling, where the strip-light is. Then I thought she was going to blink, but she closed her eyes again and they stayed shut.' Rhona burst into tears. 'It was like ... I lost her all over again.'

Rebus took her in his arms. She hugged him back.

'She did it once,' he whispered into her ear, 'she'll do it again.'

'That's what one of the doctors said. He said they're "very hopeful". Oh, John, I wanted to tell you! I wanted to tell *everyone*!'

And he'd been busy with work: Claverhouse, Jack Morton. And he'd got Sammy into all this in the first place. Sammy and Candice – pebbles dropped into a pool. And now the ripples had grown so that he'd all but forgotten about the centre, the starting point. Just like when he was married, work consuming him, becoming an end in itself. And Rhona's words: *You've exploited every relationship you ever had.*

To be born again ...

'I'm sorry, Rhona,' he said.

'Can you let Ned know?' She started crying again.

'Come on,' he said, 'let's get some breakfast. Have you been here all night?'

'I couldn't leave.'

'I know.' He kissed her cheek.

'The person in the car ...'

'What?'

She looked at him. 'I don't care any more. I don't care who they were or whether they get caught. All I want is for her to wake up.'

Rebus nodded, told her he understood. Told her breakfast was on him. He kept the talk going, his mind not really on it. Instead, her words bounced around in his head: *I don't care who they were or whether they get caught ...*

Whichever stress he put on it, he couldn't make it sound like surrender.

At St Leonard's, he broke the news to Ned Farlowe. Farlowe wanted to go to the hospital, but Rebus shook his head. Farlowe was crying as Rebus left his cell. Back at his desk, the files on the Crab were waiting.

The Crab: real name, William Andrew Colton. He had form going back to his teens, celebrated his fortieth birthday on Guy Fawkes Day. Rebus hadn't had many dealings with him during his time in Edinburgh. Looked like the Crab had lived in the city for a couple of years in the early-80s, and again in the early-90s. 1982: Rebus gave evidence against him in a conspiracy trial. Charges dropped. 1983: he was in trouble again – a fight in a pub left one man in a coma and his girlfriend needing sixty stitches to her face. Sixty stitches: you could knit a pair of mittens with less.

The Crab had held various jobs: bouncer, bodyguard, general labourer. The Inland Revenue had a go at him in 1986. By '88, he was on the West Coast, which was presumably where Tommy Telford had found him. Knowing good muscle when he saw it, he'd put the Crab on the doors of his club in Paisley. More blood-spilling; more accusations. Nothing came of them. The Crab had lived a charmed life, the sort of life that niggled at cops the world over: witnesses too scared to testify; withdrawing or refusing to give evidence. The Crab didn't often make it to trial. He'd served three adult sentences – a total of twenty-seven months – in a career that was now entering its fourth decade. Rebus went through the paperwork again, picked up the phone and called CID in Paisley. The man he wanted to speak to had been transferred to Motherwell. Rebus made the call, eventually got through to Detective Sergeant Ronnie Hannigan, and explained his interest.

'It's just that reading between the lines, you suspected the Crab of a lot more than ever got put down on paper.'

'You're right.' Hannigan cleared his throat. 'Never got close to proving anything though. You say he's south of the border now?'

'Telford placed him with a gangster in Newcastle.'

'Have criminal tendencies, will travel. Well, let's hope they keep him. He was a one-man reign of terror, and that's no exaggeration. Probably why Telford palmed him off on someone else: the Crab was getting out of control. My theory is, Telford tried him out as a hit-man. Crab wasn't suitable, so Telford needed to jettison him.'

'What was the hit?'

'Down in Ayr. Must've been ... four years ago? Lot of drugs swilling around, most of them inside a dance-club ... can't remember its name. I don't know what happened: maybe a deal went sour, maybe someone was skimming. Whatever, there was a hit outside the club. Guy got his face half torn off with a carving knife.'

'You put the Crab in the frame?'

'He had an alibi, of course, and the eye-witnesses all seemed to have suffered temporary blindness. Could be a plot for the *X-Files* in that.'

A knife attack outside a nightclub ... Rebus tapped his desk with a pen. 'Any idea how the attacker got away?'

'On a motorbike. The Crab likes bikes. Crash helmet makes a good disguise.'

'We had an almost identical attack recently. Guy on a motorbike went for a drug dealer outside one of Tommy Telford's nightclubs. Killed a bouncer instead.'

And Cafferty denied any involvement ...

'Well, like you say, the Crab's in Newcastle.'

Yes, and staying put ... *scared* to come north. Warned off by Tarawicz. Because Edinburgh was too dangerous ... people might *remember* him.

'Do you know how far away Newcastle is?'

'A couple of hours?'

'No distance at all by bike. Anything else I should know?'

'Well, Telford tried the Crab in the van, but he wasn't much good.'

'What van?'

'The ice-cream van.'

Rebus nearly dropped the phone. 'Explain,' he said.

'Easy: Telford's boys were selling dope from an ice-cream van. The "five-pound special", they called it. You handed over a fiver and got back a cone or wafer with a wee plastic bag tucked inside …'

Rebus thanked Hannigan and terminated the call. Five-pound specials: Mr Taystee with his clients who ate ice-cream in all weathers. His daytime pitches: near schools. His nighttime pitches: outside Telford's clubs. Five-pound specials on the menu, Telford taking his cut … The new Merc: Mr Taystee's big mistake. Telford's moneymen wouldn't have taken long to work out their boy was skimming. Telford would have decided to turn Mr Taystee into a lesson …

It was coming together. He spun his pen, caught it, and made another call, this time to Newcastle.

'Nice to hear from you,' Miriam Kenworthy said. 'Any sign of your lady friend?'

'She's turned up here.'

'Great.'

'In tow with Mr Pink Eyes.'

'Not so great. I wondered where he'd gone.'

'And he's not here to see the sights.'

'I'll bet he isn't.'

'Which is really why I'm calling.'

'Mmm?'

341

'I'm just wondering if he's ever been linked to machete attacks.'

'Machetes? Let me think ...' She was so quiet for so long, he thought the connection had failed. 'You know, that *does* ring a bell. Let me put it up on the screen.' Clackety-clack of her keyboard. Rebus was biting his bottom lip, almost drawing blood.

'God, yes,' she said. 'A year or so back, a battle on an estate. Rival gangs, that was the story, but everyone knew what was behind it: namely, drugs and pitch incursions.'

'And where there's drugs, there's Tarawicz?'

'There was a rumour his men were involved.'

'And they used machetes?'

'One of them did. His name's Patrick Kenneth Moyni-han, known to all and sundry as "PK".'

'Can you give me a description?'

'I can fax you his picture. But meantime: tall, heavy build, curly black hair and a black beard.'

He wasn't part of the Tarawicz retinue. Two of Mr Pink's best muscle-men had been left behind in Newcastle. For safety's sake. Rebus put PK down as one of the Paisley attackers – Cafferty again in the clear.

'Thanks, Miriam. Listen, about that rumour ...'

'Remind me.'

'Telford supplying Tarawicz rather than the other way round: anything to back it up?'

'We tracked Pink Eyes and his men. A couple of jaunts to the continent, only they came back clean.'

'Leading you up the garden path?'

'Which made us start reassessing.'

'Where would Telford be getting the stuff?'

'We didn't reassess that far.'

'Well, thanks again ...'

'Hey, don't leave me hanging: what's the story?'

'Morning Glory. Cheers, Miriam.'

Rebus went and got a coffee, put sugar in it without realising, had finished half the cup before he noticed. Tarawicz was attacking Telford. Telford was blaming Cafferty. The resulting war would destroy Cafferty and weaken Telford. Then Telford would pull off the Maclean's break-in but be grassed up ...

And Tarawicz would fill the vacuum. That had been the plan all along. Bluesbreakers: 'Double-Crossing Time'. Christ, it was beautiful: set the two rivals against one another and wait for the carnage to end ...

The prize: something Rebus didn't yet know. There had to be something big. Tarawicz, the theory went, was sourcing his drugs not from London but from Scotland. From Tommy Telford.

What did Telford know? What was it that made *his* supply so valuable? Did it have something to do with Maclean's? Rebus got another coffee, washed down three Paracetamol with it. His head felt ready to explode. Back at his desk, he tried Claverhouse, couldn't get him. Paged him instead, and got an immediate call back.

'I'm in the van,' Claverhouse said.

'I've something to tell you.'

'What?'

Rebus wanted to know what was happening. Wanted in on the action. 'It's got to be face to face. Where are you parked?'

Claverhouse sounded suspicious. 'Down from the shop.'

'White decorator's van?'

'This definitely isn't a good idea ...'

'You want to hear what I've got?'

'Sell me the idea.'

'It clears everything up,' Rebus lied.

Claverhouse waited for more, but Rebus wasn't obliging. Theatrical sigh: life was hard on Claverhouse.

'I'll be there in half an hour,' Rebus said. He put down

the phone, looked around the office. 'Anyone got a set of overalls?'

'Nice disguise,' Claverhouse said, as Rebus squeezed into the front seat.

Ormiston was in the driver's seat, plastic piece-box open in front of him. A flask of tea had been opened, steaming up the windscreen. The back of the van was full of paint-tins, brushes and other paraphernalia. A ladder was strapped to the roof, and another was leaning against the wall of the tenement beside which the van had been parked. Claverhouse and Ormiston were in white overalls, daubed with swatches of old paint. The best Rebus could come up with was a blue boilersuit, tight at the waist and chest. He pulled the first few studs open as he settled in.

'Anything happening?'

'Jack's been in twice this morning.' Claverhouse looked towards the shop. 'Once for ciggies and a paper, once for a can of juice and a filled roll.'

'He doesn't smoke.'

'He does for this operation: perfect excuse to nip to the shop.'

'He hasn't given you any signal?'

'You expecting him to put the flags out?' Ormiston exhaled fish-paste.

'Just asking.' Rebus checked his watch. 'Either of you want a break?'

'We're fine,' Claverhouse said.

'What's Siobhan up to?'

'Paperwork,' Ormiston said with a smile. 'Ever come across a woman house painter?'

'Done much house painting yourself, Ormie?'

This brought a smile from Claverhouse. 'So, John,' he said, 'what is it you've got for us?'

344

Rebus filled them in quickly, noting Claverhouse's mounting interest.

'So Tarawicz is planning to double-cross Telford?' Ormiston said at the end.

Rebus shrugged. 'That's my guess.'

'Then why the hell are we bothering to set up a sting? Just let them get on with it.'

'That wouldn't give us Tarawicz,' Claverhouse said, his eyes slitted in concentration. 'If he sets up Telford for a fall, *he's* home and dry. Telford gets put away, and all we've done is replace one villain with another.'

'And an altogether nastier species at that,' Rebus said.

'What? And Telford's Robin Hood?'

'No, but at least with him, we know what we're dealing with.'

'And the old dears in his flats love him,' Claverhouse said.

Rebus thought of Mrs Hetherington, readying herself for her trip to Holland. The only drawback: she had to fly from Inverness ... Sakiji Shoda had flown from London to Inverness ...

Rebus started laughing.

'What's so funny?'

He shook his head, still laughing, wiping his eyes. It wasn't funny, not really.

'We could let Telford know what we know,' Claverhouse said, studying Rebus. 'Set him against Tarawicz, let them eat each other alive.'

Rebus nodded, took a deep breath. 'That's certainly one option.'

'Give me another.'

'Later,' Rebus said. He opened the door.

'Where are you off to?' Claverhouse asked.

'Got to fly.'

32

But in fact he was driving. A long drive, too. North through Perth and from there into the Highlands, taking a route which could be cut off during the worst of the winter. It wasn't a bad road, but traffic was heavy. He'd get past one slow-moving lorry only to catch up with another. He knew he should be thankful for small mercies: in the summer, caravans could end up fronting mile-long tail-backs.

He did pass a couple of caravans outside Pitlochry. They were from the Netherlands. Mrs Hetherington had said it was out of season for a trip to Holland. Most people her age would go in the spring, ready to fill their senses with the bulb-fields. But not Mrs Hetherington. Telford's offer: go when I say. Telford probably provided spending money, too. Told her to have a good time, not worry about a thing . . .

As he neared Inverness, Rebus hit dual carriageway again. He'd been on the road well over two hours. Sammy might be coming round again; Rhona had his mobile number. Inverness Airport was signposted from the road into town. Rebus parked and got out, stretched his legs and arched his back, feeling the vertebrae pop. He went into the terminal and asked for security. He got a small balding man with glasses and a limp. Rebus introduced himself. The man offered coffee, but Rebus was jumpy enough after the drive. Hungry though: no lunch. He gave the man his story, and eventually they tracked down a representative of

Her Majesty's Customs. During his tour of the facilities, Rebus got the impression of a low-key operation. The Customs official was in her early thirties, rosy-cheeked and with black curly hair. There was a purple birthmark, the size of a small coin, in the middle of her forehead, looking for all the world like a third eye.

She took Rebus into the Customs area and found a room they could use for their conversation.

'They've just started direct international flights,' she said, in answer to his question. 'It's shocking really.'

'Why?'

'Because at the same time, they've cut back on manpower.'

'You mean in Customs?'

She nodded.

'You're worried about drugs?'

'Of course.' She paused. 'And everything else.'

'Are there flights to Amsterdam?'

'There will be.'

'But as of now ... ?'

She shrugged. 'You can fly to London, make the connection there.'

Rebus was thoughtful. 'There was a guy a few days ago, flew from Japan to Heathrow, then got a flight to Inverness.'

'Did he stop off in London?'

Rebus shook his head. 'Caught the first connection.'

'That counts as an international connection.'

'Meaning?'

'His luggage would be put on the plane in Japan, and he wouldn't see it again until Inverness.'

'So you'd be the first Customs point?'

She nodded.

'And if his flight came in at some horrible hour ...?'

She shrugged again. 'We do what we can, Inspector.'

Yes, Rebus could imagine: a lone, bleary-eyed Customs official, wits not at their sharpest …

'So the bags change planes at Heathrow, but no one checks them there?'

'That's about it.'

'And if you were flying from Holland to Inverness via London?'

'Same deal.'

Rebus knew now, knew the brilliance of Tommy Telford's thinking. *He* was supplying drugs for Tarawicz, and Christ knew how many others. His little old ladies and men were bringing them in past early-morning or late-night Customs posts. How difficult would it be to slip something into a piece of luggage? Then Telford's men would be on hand to take everyone back to Edinburgh, carry their luggage upstairs … and surreptitiously remove each package.

Old age pensioners as unwitting drugs couriers. It was stunning.

And Shoda hadn't flown into Inverness so he could check out the local tourist amenities. He'd flown in so he could see how easy it was, what a brilliant route Telford had found, quick and efficient with a minimum of risk. Rebus had to laugh again. The Highlands had its own drugs problem these days: bored teenagers and cash-rich oil-workers. Rebus had smashed one north-east ring back in early summer, only to have Tommy Telford come along …

Cafferty would never have thought of it. Cafferty would never have been so daring. But Cafferty would have kept it quiet. He wouldn't have sought to expand, wouldn't have brought partners into the scheme.

Telford was still a kid in some respects. The passenger-seat teddy bear was proof of that.

Rebus thanked the Customs official and went in search of food. Parked in the middle of town and grabbed a burger, sat at a window table and thought it all through. There were still aspects that didn't make sense, but he could cope with that.

He made two calls: one to the hospital; one to Bobby Hogan. Sammy hadn't woken up again. Hogan was interviewing Pretty-Boy at seven o'clock. Rebus said he'd be there.

The weather was kind on the trip south, the traffic manageable. The Saab seemed to enjoy long drives, or maybe it was just that at seventy miles an hour the engine noise disguised all the rattles and bumps.

He drove straight to Leith cop-shop, looked at his watch and found he was quarter of an hour late. Which didn't matter, since they were just starting the interview. Pretty-Boy was there with Charles Groal, all-purpose solicitor. Hogan was sitting with another CID officer, DC James Preston. A tape-recorder had been set up. Hogan looked nervous, realising how speculative this whole venture was, especially with a lawyer present. Rebus gave him a reassuring wink and apologised for having been detained. The burger had given him indigestion, and the coffee he'd had with it had done nothing for his frayed nerves. He had to shake his head clear of Inverness and all its implications and concentrate on Pretty-Boy and Joseph Lintz.

Pretty-Boy looked calm. He was wearing a charcoal suit with a yellow t-shirt, black suede winkle-picker boots. He smelt of expensive aftershave. In front of him on the desk: a pair of tortoiseshell Ray-Bans and his car keys. Rebus knew he'd own a Range Rover – it was mandatory for Telford employees – but the key-ring boasted the Porsche marque, and on the street outside Rebus had parked behind a cobalt blue 944. Pretty-Boy showing a touch of individuality …

Groal had his briefcase open on the floor beside him. On the desk in front of him: an A4 pad of ruled paper, and a fat black Mont Blanc pen.

Lawyer and client oozed money easily made and just as easily spent. Pretty-Boy used his money to buy class, but Rebus knew his background: working-class Paisley, a granite-hard introduction to life.

Hogan identified those present for the benefit of the tape-recorder, then looked at his own notes.

'Mr Summers ...' Pretty-Boy's real name: Brian Summers. 'Do you know why you're here?'

Pretty-Boy made an O of his glossy lips and stared ceilingwards.

'Mr Summers,' Charles Groal began, 'has informed me that he is willing to co-operate, Inspector Hogan, but that he'd like some indication of the accusations against him and their validity.'

Hogan stared at Groal, didn't blink. 'Who said he's accused of anything?'

'Inspector, Mr Summers works for Thomas Telford, and your police force's harassment of that individual is on record ...'

'Nothing to do with me, Mr Groal, or this station.' Hogan paused. 'Nothing at all to do with my present inquiries.'

Groal blinked half a dozen times in quick succession. He looked at Pretty-Boy, who was now studying the tips of his boots.

'You want me to say something?' Pretty-Boy asked the lawyer.

'I'm just ... I'm not sure if ...'

Pretty-Boy cut him off with a wave of his hand, then looked at Hogan.

'Ask away.'

Hogan made show of studying his notes again. 'Do you know why you're here, Mr Summers?'

'General vilification as part of your witch-hunt against my employer.' He smiled at the three CID men. 'Bet you didn't think I'd know a word like "vilification".' His gaze rested on Rebus, then he turned to Groal.

'DI Rebus isn't based at this station.'

Groal took the hint. 'That's true, Inspector. Might I ask by what authority you've been allowed to sit in on this interview?'

'That will become clear,' Hogan said, '*if* you'll allow us to begin?'

Groal cleared his throat, but said nothing. Hogan let the silence lie for a few moments, then began.

'Mr Summers, do you know a man called Joseph Lintz?'

'No.'

The silence stretched out. Summers recrossed his feet. He looked up at Hogan, and blinked, the blink deteriorating into a momentary twitch of one eye. He sniffed, rubbed at his nose – trying to make out that the twitch meant nothing.

'You've never met him?'

'No.'

'The name means nothing to you?'

'You've asked me about him before. I'll tell you same as I told you then: I never knew the cat.' Summers sat up a bit straighter in his chair.

'You've never spoken to him by telephone?'

Summers looked at Groal.

'Hasn't my client made himself clear, Inspector?'

'I'd like an answer.'

'I don't know him,' Summers said, forcing himself to relax again, 'I've never spoken to him.' He gave Hogan his stare again, and this time held it. There was nothing behind the eyes but naked self-interest. Rebus wondered how anyone could ever think him 'pretty', when his whole outlook on life was so fundamentally ugly.

'He didn't phone you at your ... business premises?'

'I don't have any business premises.'

'The office you share with your employer.'

Pretty-Boy smiled. He liked those phrases: 'business premises'; 'your employer'. They all knew the truth, yet played this little game … and he liked playing games.

'I've already said, I never spoke to him.'

'Funny, the phone company says differently.'

'Maybe they made a mistake.'

'I doubt that, Mr Summers.'

'Look, we've been through this before.' Summers sat forward in his chair. 'Maybe it was a wrong number. Maybe he spoke to one of my associates, and they *told* him he had a wrong number.' He opened his arms. 'This is going nowhere.'

'I agree with my client, Inspector,' Charles Groal said, scribbling something down. 'I mean, is this leading anywhere?'

'It's leading, Mr Groal, to an identification of Mr Summers.'

'Where and by whom?'

'In a restaurant with Mr Lintz. The same Mr Lintz he claims never to have met, never to have spoken to.'

Rebus saw hesitation cross Pretty-Boy's face. *Hesitation*, rather than surprise. He made no immediate denial.

'An identification made by a member of staff at the restaurant,' Hogan continued. 'Corroborated by another diner.'

Groal looked to his client, who wasn't saying anything, but the way he was staring at the table, Rebus wondered a smoking hole didn't start appearing in it.

'Well,' Groal went on, 'this is fairly irregular, Inspector.'

Hogan wasn't interested in the lawyer. It was Pretty-Boy and him now.

'What about it, Mr Summers? Care to revise your version of events? What were you talking about with Mr

Lintz? Was he looking for female company? I believe that's your particular area of expertise.'

'Inspector, I must insist …'

'Insist away, Mr Groal. It won't change the facts. I'm just wondering what Mr Summers will say in court when he's asked about the phone call, the meeting … when the witnesses identify him. I'm sure he's got a fund of stories, but he'll have to find a bloody good one.'

Summers slapped the desk with both palms, half-rose to his feet. There wasn't an ounce of fat on him. Veins stood out on the backs of his hands.

'I told you, I've never met him, never talked to him. Period, end of story, finito. And if you've got witnesses, they're lying. Maybe *you've* told them to lie. And that's all I've got to say.' He sat back down, put his hands in his pockets.

'I've heard,' Rebus said, as though attempting to liven up a flagging conversation between friends, 'that you run the more upmarket girls, the three-figure jobs rather than the gam-and-bam merchants.'

Summers snorted and shook his head.

'Inspector,' Groal said, 'I can't allow these accusations to continue.'

'Was that what Lintz wanted? Did he have expensive tastes?'

Summers continued shaking his head. He seemed about to say something, but caught himself, laughed instead.

'I would like to remind you,' Groal went on, unheeded by anyone, 'that my client has co-operated fully throughout this outrageous …'

Rebus caught Pretty-Boy's eyes, held their stare. There was so much he wasn't telling … so much he very nearly *wanted* to tell. Rebus thought of the length of rope in Lintz's house.

'He liked to tie them up, didn't he?' Rebus asked quietly.

Groal stood up, yanking Summers to his feet.

'Brian?' Rebus asked.

'Thank you, gentlemen,' Groal said. He was stuffing his notepad into his case, closing its brass locks. 'If you should find yourselves with any questions worth my client's time, we'll be pleased to assist. But otherwise, I'd advise you to ...'

'Brian?'

DC Preston had turned off the tape recorder and gone to open the door. Summers picked up his car keys, slipped his sunglasses on.

'Gentlemen,' he said, 'it's been educational.'

'S&M,' Rebus persisted, getting in Pretty-Boy's face. 'Did he tie them up?'

Pretty-Boy snorted, shook his head again. He paused as his lawyer led him past Rebus.

'It was for *him*,' he said in an undertone.

It was for him.

Rebus drove to the hospital. Sat with Sammy for twenty minutes. Twenty minutes of meditation and head-clearing. Twenty reviving minutes, at the end of which he squeezed his daughter's hand.

'Thanks for that,' he said.

Back at the flat, he thought of ignoring the answering-machine until after he'd had a bath. His shoulders and back were aching from the drive to Inverness. But something made him press the button. Jack Morton's voice: 'I'm on for a meeting with TT. Let's meet after. Half-ten at the Ox. I'll aim for that, but can't promise. Wish me luck.'

He walked in at eleven.

There was folk music in the back room. The front would have been quiet if it weren't for two loud-mouths who looked like they'd been at it since their office closed for the night. They still wore work-suits, newspapers rolled in their pockets. They were drinking G&T.

Rebus asked Jack Morton what he wanted.

'A pint of orange and lemonade.'

'So how did it go?' Rebus ordered the drink. In forty minutes, he'd managed to put away two Cokes, and was now on coffee.

'They seem keen.'

'So who was at the meeting?'

'My sponsors from the shop, plus Telford and a couple of his men.'

'The transmitter worked okay?'

'Sound as a pound.'

'Did they search you?'

Morton shook his head. 'They were sloppy, seemed really sweaty about something. Want to hear the plan?' Rebus nodded. 'Middle of the night, truck arrives at the factory, and I let it through the gates. My story is, I had a phone call from the boss okaying the delivery. So I wasn't suspicious.'

'Only your boss never made the call?'

'That's right. So I was duped by a voice. And that's all I need to tell the police.'

'We'd sweat the truth out of you.'

'Like I say, John, the whole plan's half-baked. I'll give them this though – they did check my background. Seemed satisfied.'

'Who's going to be in the truck?'

'Ten men, armed to the teeth. I'm to get a rough plan of the place to Telford tomorrow, let him know how many people will be around, what the alarm system's like ...'

'What's in it for you?'

'Five grand. He's judged that right: five gets my debts repaid and puts a wedge in my pocket.'

Five grand: the amount Joseph Lintz had taken out of his bank ...

'Your story's holding?'

'They've staked out my flat.'

'And they didn't follow you here?'

Morton shook his head, and Rebus filled him in on what he'd learned and what he suspected. While Morton was taking it in, Rebus threw a question at him,

'How does Claverhouse want to play it?'

'The tape evidence is good: Telford talking, me making sure I called him "Mr Telford" and "Tommy" a few times. It's obviously him on the recording. But ... Claverhouse wants Telford's crew caught red-handed.'

' "Got to do it right".'

'That seems to be his catch-phrase.'

'Is there a date?'

'Saturday, all being well.'

'What's the betting we get a tip-off on Friday?'

'If your theory's right.'

'If I'm right,' he agreed.

33

The tip-off didn't come until Saturday lunchtime, but when it did, Rebus knew his hunch had been right.

Claverhouse was the first to congratulate him, which surprised Rebus, because Claverhouse had a lot on his plate and had acted very casually when the call had come. Pinned to the walls of the Crime Squad office were detailed maps of the drugs plant, along with staff rosters. Coloured stickers showed where personnel would be stationed. During the night, it was security only, unless some big order was demanding overtime. Tonight, the usual security staff would be augmented by Lothian & Borders Police. Twenty people inside the plant, with marksmen stationed on roofs and at certain key windows. A dozen cars and vans as back-up. It was the biggest operation of Claverhouse's career; a lot was expected of him. He kept saying 'it has to be done right'. He said he would leave 'nothing to chance'. Those two phrases had become his mantra.

Rebus had listened to a recording of the snitch call: 'Be at Maclean's factory in Slateford tonight. Two in the morning, it's going to be turned over. Ten men, tooled up, driving a lorry. If you're canny, you can catch all of them.'

Scots accent, but sounding long distance. Rebus smiled, looked at the turning spools, and said 'Hello again, Crab' out loud.

No mention of Telford, which was interesting. Telford's men were loyal: they'd go down without saying a word. And Tarawicz wasn't grassing up Telford. He couldn't know the police already had taped evidence of Telford's involvement. Which meant he was planning on letting Telford go … No, think it through. With the plan dead in the water and ten of his best men in custody, Tarawicz didn't *need* Telford under lock and key. He wanted him out in the open and worried, Yakuza breathing down his neck, all his frailties exposed. He could be picked off at any time, or made to hand over *everything*. No blood-letting required; it would be a simple business proposition.

'It has to be …'

'Done right,' Rebus said. 'Claverhouse, we *know*, okay?'

Claverhouse lost it. 'You're only here because I tolerate you! So let's get that straight for a start. I snap my fingers and you're out of the game, understood?'

Rebus just stared at him. A line of sweat was running down Claverhouse's left temple. Ormiston was looking up from his desk. Siobhan Clarke, briefing another officer beside a wall-chart, stopped talking.

'I promise I'll be a good boy,' Rebus said quietly, 'if you'll promise to stop with the broken record routine.'

Claverhouse's jaw was working, but eventually he produced a near-smile of apology.

'Let's get on with it then.'

Not that there was much for them to do. Jack Morton was working a double shift, wouldn't start till three o'clock. They'd be watching the place from then on, just in case Telford changed the game-plan. This meant personnel were going to miss the big match: Hibs against Hearts at Easter Road. Rebus had his money on a 3–2 home win.

Ormiston's summing-up: 'Easiest quid you'll ever lose.'

Rebus retired to one of the computers and got back to work. Siobhan Clarke had already come round snooping.

'Writing it up for one of the tabloids?'

'No such luck.'

He tried to keep it simple, and when he was happy with

the finished product he printed off two copies. Then he went out to buy a couple of nice, bright folders …

He dropped off one of the folders, then returned home, too restless to be much use at Fettes. Three men were waiting in his tenement stairwell. Two more came in behind him, blocking the only escape route. Rebus recognised Jake Tarawicz and one of his muscle-men from the scrapyard. The others were new to him.

'Up the stairs,' Tarawicz ordered. Rebus was a prisoner under escort as they climbed the steps.

'Unlock the door.'

'If I'd known you were coming, I'd have got in some beers,' Rebus said, searching his pockets for keys. He was wondering which was safer: let them in, or keep them out? Tarawicz made the decision for him, nodded some signal. Rebus's arms were grabbed, hands went into his jacket and trousers, found his keys. He kept his face blank, eyes on Tarawicz.

'Big mistake,' he said.

'In,' Tarawicz ordered. They pushed Rebus into the hallway, walked him to the living room.

'Sit.'

Hands pushed Rebus on to the sofa.

'At least let me make a pot of tea,' he said. Inside he was trembling, knowing everything he couldn't afford to give away.

'Nice place,' Mr Pink Eyes was saying. 'Lacks the feminine touch though.' He turned to Rebus. 'Where is she?' Two of the men had peeled off to search the place.

'Who?'

'I mean, who else would she turn to? Not your daughter … not now she's in a coma.'

Rebus stared at him. 'What do you know about that?' The two men returned, shook their heads.

'I hear things.' Tarawicz pulled out a dining-chair and sat down. There were two men behind the sofa, two in front.

'Make yourselves at home, lads. Where's the Crab, Jake?' Reasoning: a question he might be expected to ask.

'Down south. What's it to you?'

Rebus shrugged.

'Shame about your daughter. Going to make a recovery, is she?' Rebus didn't answer. Tarawicz smiled. 'National Health Service ... I wouldn't trust it myself.' He paused. 'Where is she, Rebus?'

'Using my finely honed detective's skills, I'll assume you mean Candice.' Meaning she'd done a runner. Trusting to herself for once. Rebus was proud of her.

Tarawicz snapped his fingers. Arms grabbed Rebus from behind, pinning back his shoulders. One man stepped forward and punched him solidly on the jaw. Stepped back again. Second man forward: gut punches. A hand tugged his hair, forcing his eyes up to the ceiling. He didn't see the flat-handed chop aiming for his throat. When it came, he thought he was going to cough out his voice-box. They let him go, and he pitched forward, hands going to his throat, retching for breath. A couple of teeth felt loose, and the skin inside his cheek had burst. He got out a handkerchief, spat blood.

'Unfortunately,' Tarawicz was saying, 'I have no sense of humour. So I hope you'll understand I'm not joking when I say that I'll kill you if I have to.'

Rebus shook his head free of all the secrets he knew, all the power he held over Tarawicz. He told himself: *you don't know anything.*

He told himself: *you're not going to die.*

'Even ... if ... I did know ...' Fighting for breath. 'I wouldn't tell you. If the two of us were standing in a minefield, I wouldn't let you know. Want me … to tell you why?'

'Sticks and stones, Rebus.'

'It's not because of *who* you are, it's *what* you are. You trade in human beings.' Rebus dabbed at his mouth. 'You're no better than the Nazis.'

Tarawicz put a hand to his chest. 'I'm struck to the quick.'

'Chance would be a fine thing.' Rebus coughed again. 'Tell me, why do you want her back?' Rebus knowing the answer: because he was about to head south, leaving Telford in Shit Street. Because to return to Newcastle without her was a small but palpable defeat. Tarawicz wanted it *all*. He wanted every last crumb on the plate.

'My business,' Tarawicz said. Another signal, and the hands grabbed him again, Rebus resisting this time. Packing-tape was being wound around his mouth.

'Everybody tells me how *genteel* Edinburgh is,' Tarawicz was saying. 'Can't have the neighbours complaining about the screams. Put him on a chair.'

Rebus was lifted up. He struggled. A kidney punch buckled his knees. They forced him down on to a dining-chair. Tarawicz was removing his jacket, undoing gold cufflinks so he could roll up the sleeves of his pink and blue striped shirt. His arms were hairless, thick, and the same mottled colour as his face.

'A skin complaint,' he explained, removing his blue-tinted glasses. 'Some distant cousin of leprosy, they tell me.' He loosened his top button. 'I'm not as pretty as Tommy Telford, but I think you'll find me his master in every other respect.' A smile to his troops, a smile Rebus wasn't supposed to understand. 'We can start anywhere you want, Rebus. And *you* get to choose when we stop. Just nod your head, tell me where she is, and I walk out of your life forever.'

He got in close to Rebus, the sheen on his face like a protective seal. His pale blue eyes had tiny black pupils. Rebus thought: consumer as well as pusher. Tarawicz waited for a nod which didn't come, then retreated. Found an anglepoise lamp next to Rebus's chair. Planted both feet on its base and yanked on the mains cable, ripping it free.

'Bring him over here,' he ordered. Two men pulled both Rebus and chair over towards where Tarawicz was checking that the cable was plugged into the wall and that the socket was switched on. Another man closed the curtains: no free show for the kids across the way. Tarawicz was dangling the cable, letting Rebus see the loose wires – the very *live* wires. Two-hundred-and-forty volts just waiting to make his acquaintance.

'Believe me,' Tarawicz said, 'this is nothing. The Serbs had torture down to a fine art. Much of the time, they weren't even looking for a confession. I've helped a few of the more intelligent ones, the ones who knew when it was time to run. There was money to be made in the early days, power for the taking. Now the politicians are moving in, bringing trial-judges with them.' He looked at Rebus. 'The intelligent ones always know when it's time to quit. One last chance, Rebus. Remember, a nod of the head …' The wires were inches from his cheek. Tarawicz changed his mind, moved them towards his nostrils, then his eyeballs.

'A nod of the head …'

Rebus was twisting, arms holding him down – his legs, arms, shoulders. Hands holding his head, chest. Wait! The shock would pass straight through Tarawicz's men! Rebus saw it for a bluff. His eyes met Tarawicz's, and they both knew. Tarawicz pulled back.

'Tape him to the chair.' Two-inch-wide runs of tape, fixing him in place.

'This time for real, Rebus.' To his men: 'Hold him till I get close. Pull away when I say.'

Rebus thinking: there'd be a split-second after they let go ... A moment in which to break free. The tape wasn't the strongest he'd seen, but there was plenty of it. Maybe too much. He flexed his chest against it, felt no sign that it would break.

'Here we go,' Tarawicz said. 'First the face ... then the genitals. You *will* tell me, we both know it. How much bravado you want to show is up to you, but don't think it means anything.'

Rebus said something behind the gag.

'No point talking,' Tarawicz said. 'The only thing I want from you is a nod, understood?'

Rebus nodded.

'Was that a nod?'

Forcing a smile, Rebus shook his head.

Tarawicz didn't look impressed. His mind was on business. That was all Rebus was to him. He aimed the wire at Rebus's cheek.

'Let go!'

The pressure on Rebus fell away. He pushed against his bonds, couldn't budge them. Electricity flashed through his nervous system, and he went rigid. His heart felt like it had doubled in size, his eyeballs bulged, tongue pushing against the gag. Tarawicz lifted the cable away.

'Hold him.'

Arms fell on Rebus again, finding less resistance than before.

'Doesn't even leave a mark,' Tarawicz said. 'And the real beauty is, you end up paying for it from your own electric bill.'

His men laughed. They were beginning to enjoy themselves.

Tarawicz crouched down, face to face. His eyes sought Rebus's.

'For your information, that was a five-second jolt.

Things only start to get interesting at the half-minute mark. How's your heart? For your sake, I hope it's in good condition.'

Rebus felt like he'd just mainlined adrenaline. Five seconds: it had seemed much longer. He was changing strategies, trying to think up some new lies Mr Pink might believe, anything to get him out of the flat ...

'Undo his trousers,' Tarawicz was saying. 'Let's see what a jolt down there will do.'

Behind the gag, Rebus started screaming. His tormentor was looking around the room again.

'Definitely lacks the feminine touch.'

Hands were loosening his trouser-belt. They stopped when a buzzer sounded. There was someone at the main door.

'Just wait,' Tarawicz said quietly. 'They'll go away.'

The buzzer sounded again. Rebus wrestled with his bonds. Silence. Then the buzzer again, more insistent now. One of the men went for the window.

'Don't!' Tarawicz snapped.

Buzzer again. Rebus hoped it would go on forever. Couldn't think who it might be: Rhona? Patience? A sudden thought ... what if they persisted, and Tarawicz decided to allow them inside? Rhona or Patience ...

Time stretched. No more buzzing. They'd gone away. Tarawicz was beginning to relax, focusing his mind on his work once more.

Then there was a knock at the flat door. The person had got into the tenement. Now they were on the landing outside. Knocking again. Lifting the flap of the letterbox.

'Rebus!'

A male voice. Tarawicz looked to his men, nodded another signal. Curtains were opened; Rebus's bonds cut; the tape ripped from his face. Tarawicz rolled down his sleeves, put his jacket back on. Left the flex lying on the floor. One last word to Rebus: 'We'll speak again.' Then he marched his men to the door, opened it.

'Excuse us.'

Rebus was left sitting on the chair. He couldn't move, felt too shaky to stand up.

'Hang on a minute, chief!'

Rebus placed the voice: Abernethy. It didn't sound as if Tarawicz was heeding the Special Branch man.

'What's the score?' Now Abernethy was in the living-room, looking around.

'Business meeting,' Rebus croaked.

Abernethy came forward. 'Funny old business where you have to unzip your flies.'

Rebus looked down, started to make repairs.

'Who was that?' Abernethy persisted.

'A Chechen from Newcastle.'

'Likes to travel mob-handed, does he?' Abernethy walked around the room, found the bare flex and tut-tutted, unplugged it at the socket. 'Fun and games,' he said.

'Don't worry,' Rebus told him, 'it's under control.'

Abernethy laughed.

'What do you want anyway?'

'Brought someone to see you.' He nodded towards the doorway. A distinguished-looking man was standing there, dressed in three-quarter-length black woollen coat and white silk scarf. He was completely bald, with a huge dome of a head and cheeks reddened from cold. He had a sniffle, and was wiping his nose with a handkerchief.

'Thought we might pop out somewhere,' the man said, locution impeccable, his eyes everywhere but on Rebus. 'Get a spot to eat, if you're hungry.'

'I'm not,' Rebus said.

'Something to drink then.'

'There's whisky in the kitchen.'

The man looked reluctant.

'Look, pal,' Rebus told him, 'I'm staying right here. You can join me or you can bugger off.'

'I see,' the man said. He put the handkerchief away and stepped forward, stretched out a hand. 'Name's Harris, by the way.'

Rebus took the hand, expecting sparks to leap from his fingertips.

'Mr Harris, let's sit at the dining-table.' Rebus got to his feet. He was shaky, but his knees held till he'd crossed the floor. Abernethy appeared from the kitchen with the bottle and three glasses. Left again, and returned with a milk-jug of water.

Ever the host, Rebus poured, sizing up the trembling in his right arm. He felt disoriented. Adrenaline and electricity coursing through him.

'*Slainte*,' he said, lifting the glass. But he paused with it at his nostrils. Pact with the Big Man: no drinking, and Sammy back. His throat hurt when he swallowed, but he put the glass down untouched. Harris was pouring too much water into his own glass. Even Abernethy looked disapproving.

'So, Mr Harris,' Rebus said, rubbing his throat, 'just who the hell are you?'

Harris affected a smile. He was playing with his glass.

'I'm a member of the intelligence community, Inspector. I know what that probably conjures up in your mind, but I'm afraid the reality is far more prosaic. Intelligence-gathering means just that: lots of paperwork and filing.'

'And you're here because of Joseph Lintz?'

'I'm here because DI Abernethy says you're determined to link the murder of Joseph Lintz with the various accusations which have been made against him.'

'And?'

'And that, of course, is your prerogative. But there are

matters not necessarily germane which might prove ... embarrassing, if brought into the open.'

'Such as that Lintz really was Linzstek, and was brought to this country by the Rat Line, probably with help from the Vatican?'

'As to whether Lintz and Linzstek were the same man ... I can't tell you. A lot of the documentation was destroyed just after the war.'

'But "Joseph Lintz" was brought to this country by the Allies?'

'Yes.'

'And why did we do that?'

'Lintz was useful to this country, Inspector.'

Rebus poured a fresh whisky for Abernethy. Harris hadn't touched his. 'How useful?'

'He was a reputable academic. As such he was invited to attend conferences and give guest lectures all round the world. During this time, he did some work for us. Translation, intelligence-gathering, recruitment ...'

'He recruited people in other countries?' Rebus stared at Harris. 'He was a *spy*?'

'He did some dangerous and ... influential work for this country.'

'And got his reward: the house in Heriot Row?'

'He earned every penny in the early days.'

Harris's tone told Rebus something. 'What happened?'

'He became ... unreliable.' Harris lifted the glass to his nose, sniffed it, but put it down again untouched.

'Drink it before it evaporates,' Abernethy chided. Harris looked at him, and the Londoner mumbled an apology.

'Define "unreliable",' Rebus said, pushing aside his own glass.

'He began to ... fantasise.'

'He thought a colleague at the university had been in the Rat Line?'

Harris was nodding. 'He became obsessed with the Rat Line, began to imagine that everyone around him had been involved in it, that we were *all* culpable. Paranoia, Inspector. It affected his work and eventually we had to let him go. This was years back. He hasn't worked for us since.'

'So why the interest? What does it matter if any of this comes out?'

Harris sighed. 'You're right, of course. The problem is not the Rat Line *per se*, or the notion of Vatican involvement or any of the other conspiracy theories.'

'Then what is …?' Rebus broke off, realised the truth. 'The problem is the personnel,' he stated. 'The other people brought in by the Rat Line.' He nodded to himself. 'Who are we talking about? Who might be implicated?'

'Senior figures,' Harris admitted. He'd stopped playing with the glass. His hands were flat on the table. He was telling Rebus: this is *serious*.

'Past or present?'

'Past … plus people whose children have gone on to achieve positions of power.'

'MPs? Government ministers? Judges?'

Harris was shaking his head. 'I can't tell you, Inspector. I haven't been trusted with that knowledge myself.'

'But you could hazard a guess.'

'I don't deal in guesswork.' He looked at Rebus. There was steel behind the eyes. 'I deal in known quantities. It's a good maxim – one you should try.'

'But whoever killed Lintz did so *because* of his past.'

'Are you sure?'

'It doesn't make sense otherwise.'

'DI Abernethy tells me there's a link with some criminal elements in Edinburgh, perhaps a question of prostitution. It all sounds sordid enough to be believable.'

'And if it's believable, that's good enough for you?'

Harris stood up. 'Thank you for listening.' He blew his nose again, looked to Abernethy. 'Time to go, I believe. DI Hogan is waiting for us.'

'Harris,' Rebus said, 'you said yourself, Lintz had gone loopy, become a liability. Who's to say *you* didn't have him killed?'

Harris shrugged. 'If we'd arranged it, his demise would not have been quite so obvious.'

'Car crash, suicide, falling from a window ...?'

'Goodbye, Inspector.'

As Harris walked to the door, Abernethy stood up and locked eyes with Rebus. He didn't say anything, but the message was there.

This is deeper water than either of us wants to be in. So do yourself a favour, swim for shore.

Rebus nodded, reached out a hand. The two men shook.

34

Two in the morning.

Frost on the car windscreens. They couldn't clear them: had to blend in with the other cars on the street. Back-up – four units – parked in a builder's yard just round the corner. Bulbs had been removed from street-lights, leaving the area in almost total darkness. Maclean's was like a Christmas tree: security lights, every window blazing, same as every other night.

No heating in the unmarked cars: heat would melt the frost; exhaust fumes a dead giveaway.

'This all seems very familiar,' Siobhan Clarke said. The surveillance on Flint Street seemed a lifetime ago to Rebus. Clarke was in the driving seat, Rebus in the back. Two to each car. That way, they had space to duck should anyone come snooping. Not that they expected anyone to do that: the whole heist was half-baked. Telford desperate *and* with his mind on other things. Sakiji Shoda was still in town – a quiet word with the hotel manager had revealed a Monday morning check-out. Rebus was betting Tarawicz and his men had already gone.

'You look pretty snug,' Rebus said, referring to her padded ski-jacket. She brought a hand out of her pocket, showed him what it was holding. It looked like a slim lighter. Rebus lifted it from her palm. It was warm.

'What the hell is it?'

Clarke smiled. 'I got it from one of those catalogues. It's a handwarmer.'

'How does it work?'

'Fuel rods. Each one lasts up to twelve hours.'

'So you've got one warm hand?'

She brought her other hand out, showed him an identical rod. 'I bought two,' she said.

'You might have said.' Rebus closed his fingers around the handwarmer, stuck it deep into his pocket.

'That's not fair.'

'Call it a privilege of rank.'

'Lights,' she warned. They dived for cover, surfaced again when the car had sped past: false alarm.

Rebus checked his watch. Jack Morton had been told to expect the truck some time between one-thirty and two-fifteen. Rebus and Clarke had been in the car since just after midnight. The snipers on the roof, poor bastards, had been in position since one o'clock. Rebus hoped they had a good supply of fuel rods. He still felt jittery from the afternoon's events. He didn't like that he owed Abernethy such a huge favour; indeed, maybe owed him his life. He knew he could cancel it out by agreeing – along with Hogan – to soft-pedal on the Lintz inquiry. He didn't like the idea, but all the same ... And the day's silver lining: Candice had made the break from Tarawicz.

Clarke's police radio was silent. They had maintained silence since before midnight. Claverhouse's words: 'The first person to speak will be me, understood? Anyone uses a radio before me, they're in farmyard shit. And I won't utter a sound until the truck's entered the compound. Is that clear?' Nods all around. 'They could be listening in, so this is *important*. We've got to do this *right*.' Averting his eyes from Rebus as he said it. 'I'd wish us all luck, but the less luck's involved the better I'll like it. A few hours from now, if we stick to the plan, we should have broken up Tommy Telford's gang.' He paused. 'Just let that sink in. We'll be heroes.' He swallowed, realising the immensity of the prize.

Rebus couldn't get so excited. The whole enterprise had shown him a simple truth: no vacuum. Where you had society, you had criminals. No belly without an underbelly.

Rebus knew his own criteria came cheaply: his flat, books, music and clapped-out car. And he realised that he had reduced his life to a mere shell in recognition that he had completely failed at the important things: love, relationships, family life. He'd been accused of being in thrall to his career, but that had never been the case. His work sustained him only because it was an easy option. He dealt every day with strangers, with people who didn't mean anything to him in the wider scheme. He could enter their lives, and leave again just as easily. He got to live other people's lives, or at least portions of them, experiencing things at one remove, which wasn't nearly as challenging as the real thing.

Sammy had brought home to him these essential truths: that he was not only a failed father but a failed human being; that police work kept him sane, yet was a substitute for the life he could have had, the kind of life everyone else seemed to lead. And if he became obsessed with his casework, well, that was no different from being obsessed with train numbers or cigarette cards or rock albums. Obsession came easy – especially to men – because it was a cheap way of achieving *control*, albeit control over something practically worthless. What did it matter if you could reel off the track listing to every '60s Stones album? It didn't matter a damn. What did it matter if Tommy Telford got put away? Tarawicz would take his place, and if he didn't, there was always Big Ger Cafferty. And if not Cafferty, then someone else. The disease was endemic, no cure in sight.

'What are you thinking about?' Clarke asked, switching her rod from left hand to right.

'My next cigarette.' Patience's words: *happiest when in denial* …

They heard the truck before they saw it: changing gears noisily. Slid down into their seats, then up again as it made to pull into Maclean's. A wheeze of air-brakes as it jolted to a stop at the gates. A guard came out to talk to the driver. He carried a clip-board.

'Jack really suits a uniform,' Rebus said.

'Clothes maketh the man.'

'You reckon your boss has got it right?' He meant Claverhouse's plan: when the truck was in the compound, they'd use a megaphone and show the marksmen to whoever was in the driver's cab, tell them to come out. The rest of the men could stay locked in the back of the vehicle. They'd have them toss out any arms and then come out one at a time.

It was either that or wait until they were *all* out of the truck. Merit of this second plan: they'd know what they were dealing with. Merit of the first: most of the gang would be nicely stowed in the truck, and could be dealt with as and when.

Claverhouse had plumped for plan one.

Marked and unmarked cars were to move in as soon as the truck had come to a stop – engine off – in the compound. They would block the exit, then watch from safety while Claverhouse, at a first-floor window with his megaphone, and the marksmen (roof; ground-floor windows) did their stuff. 'Negotiation with force' was how Claverhouse had described it.

'Jack's opening the gates,' Rebus said, peering through the side window.

Engine roar, and the truck jerked forward.

'Driver seems a bit nervous,' Clarke commented.

'Or isn't used to HGVs.'

'Okay, they're in.'

Rebus stared at the radio, willing it to burst into life. Clarke had turned the ignition one click away from starting.

Jack Morton was watching the truck move into the compound. He turned his head towards the line of cars parked across the way.

'Any second ...'

The truck's brake-lights came on, then went off again. Air-brakes sounded.

The radio fizzed a single word: '*Now!*'

Clarke turned the engine, revved hard. Five other cars did the same. Exhaust smoke billowed suddenly into the night air. The noise was like the start of a stock-car race. Rebus wound his window down, the better to hear Claverhouse's megaphone diplomacy. Clarke's car leaped forward, first to the gates. Both she and Rebus jumped out, keeping their heads down, the car a shield between themselves and the truck.

'Engine's still running,' Rebus hissed.

'What?'

'The truck. Its engine's still running!'

Claverhouse's voice, warbling – partly nerves, partly megaphone quality: 'Armed police. Open the cab doors slowly and come out one at a time, hands held high. I repeat: armed police. Discard weapons before coming out. I repeat: discard weapons.'

'Do it!' Rebus hissed. Then: 'Tell them to switch off the bloody engine!'

Claverhouse: 'The gate is blocked, there's no escape, and we don't want anyone getting hurt.'

'Tell them to throw out the keys.' Cursing, Rebus dived back into the car, grabbed the handset. 'Claverhouse, tell them to ditch the bloody keys!'

Windscreen frosted over; he couldn't see a thing. Heard Clarke's yell: '*Get out!*'

Saw: dim white lights. The truck was reversing. At speed. A roar from its engine, veering crazily but heading for the gates.

Heading straight for him.

An explosion: bricks flying from the factory's front wall. Rebus dropped the handset, got his arm stuck in the seatbelt. Clarke was screaming as he leaped clear.

A second later, truck and car connected in a rending of metal and smashing of glass. Domino effect: Clarke's car hit the one behind, throwing officers off balance. The road was like a skating rink, the truck pushing one car, two cars, then three cars back on to the highway.

Claverhouse was on the megaphone, choking on dust: 'No shooting! Officers too close! Officers too close!'

Yes, all they needed now was to be pinned down by sniper fire. Men and women were slipping, losing their footing, clambering from their cars. Some of them armed, but dazed. The truck's back doors, buckled by the initial collision, flew open, seven or eight men hit the ground running. Two of them had handguns, and loosed off three or four shots apiece.

Shouts, screams, the megaphone. The glass wall of the gatehouse exploded as a bullet hit it. Rebus couldn't see Jack Morton ... couldn't see Siobhan. He was lying on his front on a section of grass verge, hands over his head: classic defence/defeat posture and bloody useless with it. The whole area was picked out by floodlights, and one of the gunmen – Declan from the shop – was now aiming at those. Other members of the gang had headed out into the street and were running for it. They carried shotguns, pickaxe handles. Rebus recognised a few more faces: Ally Cornwell, Deek McGrain. The streetlights were dead, of course, giving them all the cover they could want. Rebus hoped the backup cars from the builder's yard were coming.

Yes: turning the corner now, all lights blazing, sirens howling. Tenement curtains were twitching, palms rubbing at windows. And right in front of Rebus, about an inch from his nose, a thickly rimed blade of grass. He could make out each sliver of frost, and the complex patterns which had formed. But he realised it was melting fast as his breath hit it. And his front was growing cold. And the marksmen were running from the building, lit up like a firing-range.

And Siobhan Clarke was safe: he could see her lying beneath a car. Good girl.

And one policewoman, also lying low, had been wounded in the knee. She kept touching it with her hand, then pulling the hand away to stare at the blood.

And there was still no sign of Jack Morton.

The gunmen were returning fire, scattering shots, smashing windscreens. Uniforms were ordered out of the front back-up car. Four of the gang got in.

Second car: uniforms out, three of the gang got in. No windscreens, but they were rolling. Yelling and whooping, waving their weapons. The two remaining gunmen were cool. They were taking a good look round, assessing the situation. Did they want to be here when the marksmen arrived? Maybe they did. Maybe they fancied their chances in that arena, too. Their luck had held *this* far, after all. Claverhouse: *the less luck's involved, the better I'll like it.*

Rebus got on to his knees, then his feet, staying at a crouch. He felt moderately safe. After all, *his* luck had held today, too.

'You okay, Siobhan?' Voice low, eyes on the gunmen. The two getaway cars added up to seven men. Two still left. Where was number ten?

'Fine,' Clarke said. 'What about you?'

'I'm okay.' Rebus left her, worked his way round to the front of the truck. The driver was unconscious behind his wheel, head bleeding where it had connected after the collision. There was some kind of grenade launcher on the seat beside him. It had left a bloody great hole in the wall of

Maclean's. Rebus checked the driver for firearms, found none. Then checked the pulse: steady. Recognised the face: one of the arcade regulars; looked about nineteen, twenty. Rebus took out his handcuffs, hooked the driver to the steering-wheel, threw the grenade launcher on to the road.

Then headed for the gatehouse. Jack Morton, in uniform but missing his cap, prone on the floor, covered by a glass shroud. The bullet had pierced his right breast-pocket. Pulse was weak.

'Christ, Jack …'

There was a telephone in the booth. Rebus punched 999 and asked for ambulances.

'Police officers down at the Maclean's factory on Slateford Road!' Staring down at his friend.

'Whereabouts on Slateford Road?'

'Believe me, they won't be able to miss it.'

Five marksmen, dressed in black, aimed rifles at Rebus from outside. Saw him on the phone, saw him shake his head, moved on. Saw their targets out on the road, getting into a patrol car. Yelled the order to stop, warning that they would fire.

Response: muzzle-flash. Rebus ducked again. Fire was returned, the noise deafening but momentary.

Shouts from the road: 'Got them!'

A plaintive wail: one of the gunmen wounded. Rebus looked. The other was lying quite still on the road. Marksmen yelling to the wounded man: 'Drop the weapon, turn on to your front, hands behind your back.'

Response: 'I'm shot!'

Rebus to himself: 'Bastard's only wounded. Finish him off.'

Jack Morton unconscious. Rebus knew better than to move him. He could staunch the bleeding, that was all. Removed his jacket, folded it and pressed it to his friend's chest. Must've hurt, but Jack was out of it. Rebus dug the fuel rod out of his own pocket, the tiny canister still warm. Pressed it into Jack's right hand, curled the fingers around it.

'Stick around, pal. Just keep sticking around.'

Siobhan Clarke at the doorway, tears welling in her eyes.

Rebus pushed past her, slid his way across the road to where the Armed Response Team were cuffing the wounded man. Nobody much bothering with his dead partner. A little group of onlookers, keeping their distance. Rebus walked right up to the corpse, prised the handgun from its fingers, walked back around the front of the car. Heard someone call out: 'He's got a gun!'

Rebus bending down until the barrel of the gun touched the back of the wounded man's neck. Declan from the shop: breath coming in short gasps, hair matted with sweat, burrowing his face into the tarmac.

'John ...'

Claverhouse. No megaphone needed. Standing right behind him. 'You really want to be like them?'

Like them ... Like Mean Machine. Like Telford and Cafferty and Tarawicz. He'd crossed the line before, made several trips forth and back. His foot was on Declan's neck, the gun barrel so hot it was singeing nape-skin.

'Please, no ... oh, Christ, please ... don't ... don't ...'

'Shut up,' Rebus hissed. He felt Claverhouse's hand close over his, flick on the safety.

'My responsibility, John. My fuck-up, don't make it yours, too.'

'Jack ...'

'I know.'

Rebus's vision blurred. 'They're getting away.'

Claverhouse shook his head. 'Road blocks. Back-up are already on it.'

'And Telford?'

Claverhouse checked his watch. 'Ormie will be picking him up right about now.'

Rebus grabbed Claverhouse's lapels. 'Nail him!'

Sirens nearing. Rebus shouted for the drivers to move their cars, make room for the ambulance. Then he ran back to the gatehouse. Siobhan Clarke was kneeling beside Jack, stroking his forehead. Her face was streaked with tears. She looked up at Rebus and shook her head.

'He's gone,' she said.

'No.' But he knew the truth. Which didn't stop him saying the word over and over again.

35

They divided the gang between two different locations –
Torphichen and Fettes – and took Telford and a few of his
'lieutenants' to St Leonard's. Result: a logistical nightmare.
Claverhouse was washing Pro-Plus down with double-
strength coffee, part of him wanting to do things right, the
other part knowing he was answerable for the blood-bath at
Maclean's. One officer dead, six wounded or otherwise
injured – one of them seriously. One gunman dead, one
wounded – not seriously enough to some people's minds.

The getaway cars had been apprehended and arrests
made – shots exchanged but no bloodshed. None of the
gang was saying anything, not a single damned word.

Rebus was sitting in an empty Interview Room at St
Leonard's, arms on the table, head resting on arms. He'd
been sitting there for a while, just thinking about loss,
about how suddenly it could strike. A life, a friendship, just
snatched away.

Irretrievable.

He hadn't cried, and didn't think he would. Instead, he
felt numb, as if his soul had been spiked with novocaine.
The world seemed to have slowed, like the mechanism was
running down. He wondered if the sun would have the
energy to rise again.

And I got him into it.

He had wallowed before in feelings of guilt and
inadequacy, but nothing to measure up to this. This was
overwhelming. Jack Morton, a copper with a quiet patch in

Falkirk ... murdered in Edinburgh because a friend had asked a favour. Jack Morton, who'd brought himself back to life by swearing off cigarettes and booze, getting into shape, eating right, taking *care* of himself ... Lying in the mortuary, deep-body temperature dropping.

And I put him there.

He jumped up suddenly, threw the chair at the wall. Gill Templer walked into the room.

'All right, John?'

He wiped his mouth with the back of his hand.

'Fine.'

'My office is empty if you want to get your head down.'

'No, I'll be fine. Just ...' He looked around. 'Is this place needed?'

She nodded.

'Right. Okay.' He picked up the chair. 'Who is it?'

'Brian Summers,' she said.

Pretty-Boy. Rebus straightened his back.

'I can make him talk.'

Templer looked sceptical.

'Honest, Gill.' Hands trembling. 'He doesn't know what I've got on him.'

She folded her arms. 'And what's that?'

'I just need ...' He checked his watch. 'An hour or so; two hours tops. Bobby Hogan needs to be here. And I want Colquhoun brought in pronto.'

'Who's he?'

Rebus found the business card and handed it over. 'Pronto,' he repeated. He worked at his tie, making himself presentable. Smoothed back his hair. Said nothing.

'John, I'm not sure you're in any state to ...'

He pointed at her, turned it into a wagging finger. 'Don't presume, Gill. If I say I can break him, I mean it.'

'No one else has said a single word.'

'Summers will be different.' He stared at her. 'Believe me.'

Looking back at him, she believed. 'I'll hold him back till Hogan gets here.'

'Thanks, Gill.'

'And, John?'

'Yes?'

'I'm really sorry about Jack Morton. I didn't know him, but I've heard what everyone's saying.'

Rebus nodded.

'They're saying he'd be the last one to blame you.'

Rebus smiled. 'Right at the back of the queue.'

'There's only one person in the queue, John,' she said quietly. 'And you're it.'

Rebus phoned the night-desk at the Caledonian Hotel, learned that Sakiji Shoda had checked out unexpectedly, less than two hours after Rebus had dropped off the green folder which had cost him fifty-five pence at a stationer's on Raeburn Place. Actually, the folders had come in three-packs at one sixty-five. He had the other two in his car, only one of them empty.

Bobby Hogan was on his way. He lived in Portobello. He said to give him half an hour. Bill Pryde came over to Rebus's desk and said how sorry he was about Jack Morton, how he knew the two of them had been old friends.

'Just don't get too close to me, Bill,' Rebus told him. 'The people closest to me tend to lose their health.'

He got a message from reception: someone there to see him. He headed downstairs, found Patience Aitken.

'Patience?'

She had all her clothes on, but not necessarily in the right order, like she'd dressed in a power-cut.

'I heard on the radio,' she said. 'I couldn't sleep, so I had the radio on, and they said about this police raid and how people were dead … And you weren't in your flat, so I …'

He hugged her. 'I'm okay,' he whispered. 'I should have called you.'

'It's my fault, I …' She looked at him. 'You were there, I can see it on your face.' He nodded. 'What happened?'

'I lost a friend.'

'Oh, Christ, John.' She hugged him again. She was still warm from the bedclothes. He could smell shampoo on her hair, perfume on her neck. *The people closest to me* … He pulled away gently, planted a kiss on her cheek.

'Go get some sleep,' he told her.

'Come for breakfast.'

'I just want to go home and crash.'

'You could sleep at my place. It's Sunday. We could stay in bed.'

'I don't know what time I'll finish here.'

She found his eyes. 'Don't feed on it, John. Don't keep it all inside.'

'Okay, Doc.' He pecked her cheek again. 'Now vamoose.'

He managed a smile and a wink: both felt treacherous. He stood at the door and watched her leave. A lot of times while he'd been married, he'd thought of just walking. There were times when all the responsibilities and the shite at work and the pressure and the *need* would make him dream of escape.

He was tempted again now. Push open the door and head off to somewhere that wasn't here, to do something that wasn't this. But that, too, would be treachery. He had scores to settle, and a reason to settle them. He knew Telford was somewhere in the building, probably consulting with Charles Groal, saying nothing to anyone else. He wondered how the team were playing it. When would they let Telford know about the tape? When would they tell him the security guard had been a plant? When would they tell him that same man was now dead?

He hoped they were being clever. He hoped they were rattling Telford's cage.

He couldn't help wondering – and not for the first time – if it was all worth it. Some cops treated it like a game, others like a crusade, and for most of the rest it was neither, just a way of earning their daily bread. He asked himself why he'd invited Jack Morton in. Answers: because he'd wanted a *friend* involved, someone who'd keep *him* in the game; because he'd thought Jack was bored, and would enjoy the challenge; because tactics had demanded an outsider. There were plenty of reasons. Claverhouse had asked if Morton had any family, anyone who should be informed. Rebus had told him: divorced, four kids.

Did Rebus blame Claverhouse? Easy to be wise after the event, but then Claverhouse's reputation had been built on being wise *before* the event. And he'd failed ... monumentally.

Icy roads: they'd needed the gates closed. The blockade had been too easy to move with the horsepower available to a truck.

Marksmen in the building: fine in the enclosed space of the yard, but they'd failed to keep the truck there, and the marksmen had been ineffectual once the truck had reversed out.

More armed officers *behind* the truck: producing little but a crossfire hazard.

Claverhouse should have got them to turn off the ignition, or – better still – waited for it to be turned off before making his presence known.

Jack Morton should have kept his head down.

And Rebus should have warned him.

Only, a shout would have turned the gunmen's attention towards him. Cowardice: was that what was at the bottom of his feelings? Simple human cowardice. Like in the bar in Belfast, when he hadn't said anything, fearing Mean Machine's wrath, fearing a rifle-butt turned on *him*. Maybe that was why – no, *of course* that was why – Lintz had got beneath Rebus's skin. Because when it came down to it, if Rebus had been in Villefranche ... drunk on failure, the dream of conquest over ... if he'd been under orders, just a lackey with a gun ... if he'd been primed by racism and the loss of comrades ... who was to say what he'd have done?

'Christ, John, how long have you been out here?'

It was Bobby Hogan, touching his face, prising the folder from frozen fingers.

'You're like ice, man, let's get you inside.'

'I'm fine,' Rebus breathed. And it had to be true: how else to explain the sweat on his back and his brow? How else to explain that he only started shivering *after* Bobby led him indoors?

Hogan got two mugs of sweet tea into him. The station was still buzzing: shock, rumour, theories. Rebus filled Hogan in.

'They'll have to let Telford walk, if nobody talks.'

'What about the tape?'

'They'll want to spring that later ... if they're being canny.'

'Who's in with him?'

Rebus shrugged. 'Farmer Watson himself, last time I heard. He was doing a double-act with Bill Pryde, but I saw Bill later, so they've either taken a break or else done a swop.'

Hogan shook his head. 'What a fucking business.'

Rebus stared at his tea. 'I hate sugar.'

'You drank the first mug all right.'

'Did I?' He took a mouthful, squirmed.

'What the hell did you think you were doing out there?'

'Catching a breath.'

'Catching your death more like.' Hogan patted down an unruly clump of hair. 'I had a visit from a man called Harris.'

'What are you going to do?'

Hogan shrugged. 'Let it go, I suppose.'

Rebus stared at him. 'You might not have to.'

36

Colquhoun didn't look happy to be there.

'Thanks for coming in,' Rebus told him.

'I didn't have much choice.' He had a solicitor sitting beside him, a middle-aged man: one of Telford's? Rebus couldn't have cared less.

'You might have to get used to not having choices, Dr Colquhoun. Know who else is in here tonight? Tommy Telford; Brian Summers.'

'Who?'

Rebus shook his head. 'You're getting your script wrong. It's okay for you to know who they are: we talked about them in front of Candice.'

Colquhoun's face flushed.

'You remember Candice, don't you? Her real name's Karina: did I ever tell you that? She's got a son somewhere, only they took him away. Maybe she'll find him one day, maybe not.'

'I don't see what this –'

'Telford and Summers are going to be spending a while behind bars.' Rebus sat back. 'If I want to, I could have a damned good go at putting you in there with them. How would you like that, Dr Colquhoun? Conspiracy to pervert, et cetera.'

Rebus could feel himself relaxing into his work; doing it for Jack.

The solicitor was about to say something, but Colquhoun got in first. 'It was a mistake.'

'A mistake?' Rebus hooted. 'One way of putting it, I suppose.' He sat forward, resting his elbows on the table. 'Time to talk, Dr Colquhoun. You know what they say about confession ...'

Brian 'Pretty-Boy' Summers looked immaculate.

He had a lawyer with him, too, a senior partner who looked like an undertaker and wasn't taking kindly to being kept waiting. As they settled at the table in the Interview Room, and Hogan slotted tapes into cassette machine and video recorder, the lawyer started the protest he'd spent the past hour or two preparing in his head.

'On behalf of my client, Inspector, I feel duty bound to say that this is some of the most appalling behaviour I've –'

'You think you've seen appalling behaviour?' Rebus answered. 'In the words of the song, you ain't seen nothing yet.'

'Look, it's clear to me that you –'

Rebus ignored him, slapped the folder down on to the table, slid it towards Pretty-Boy.

'Take a look.'

Pretty-Boy was wearing a charcoal suit and purple shirt, open at the neck. No sunglasses or car-keys. He'd been brought in from his flat in the New Town. Comment from one of the men who'd gone to fetch him: 'Biggest hi-fi I've seen in my life. Bugger was wide awake, listening to Patsy Cline.'

Rebus started whistling 'Crazy': that got Pretty-Boy's attention and a wry smile, but he kept his arms folded.

'I would if I were you,' Rebus said.

'Ready,' Hogan said, meaning he had the tapes running. They went through the formalities: date and time, location, individuals present. Rebus looked towards the lawyer and smiled. He looked pretty expensive. Telford would have ordered the best, same as always.

'Know any Elton John, Brian?' Rebus asked. 'He's got this song: "Someone Saved My Life Tonight". You'll be singing it to me once you've looked inside.' He tapped the folder. 'Go on, you know it makes sense. I'm not playing some trick, and you don't have to say anything. But you really should do yourself a favour ...'

'I've got nothing to say.'

Rebus shrugged. 'Just open the folder, take a look.'

Pretty-Boy looked to his lawyer, who seemed uncertain.

'Your client won't be incriminating himself,' Rebus explained. 'If you want to read what's in there first, that's fine. It might not mean much to you, but go ahead.'

The lawyer opened the folder, found a dozen sheets of paper.

'Sorry in advance for any mistakes,' Rebus said. 'I typed it in a bit of a rush.'

Pretty-Boy didn't so much as glance towards the material. He kept his eyes on Rebus, while the lawyer sifted through the papers.

'These allegations,' the lawyer finally said, 'you must realise they're worthless?'

'If that's your opinion, fair enough. I'm not asking Mr Summers to admit or deny anything. Like I said, he can do a deaf and dumb routine for all I care, so long as he uses his *eyes*.'

A smile from Pretty-Boy, then a glance towards his lawyer, who shrugged his shoulders, saying there was nothing here to fear. A glance back at Rebus, and Pretty-Boy unfolded his arms, picked up the first sheet, and started reading.

'Just so we have a record for the tape,' Rebus said, 'Mr Summers is now reading a draft report prepared by myself earlier today.' Rebus paused. 'Actually, I mean yesterday, Saturday. He's reading my interpretation of recent events in and around Edinburgh, events concerning his employer,

Thomas Telford, a Japanese business consortium – which is really, in my opinion, a Yakuza front – and a gentleman from Newcastle by the name of Jake Tarawicz.'

He paused. The lawyer said: 'Agreed, thus far.' Rebus nodded and continued.

'My version of events is as follows. Jake Tarawicz became an associate of Thomas Telford only because he wanted something Telford had: namely, a slick operation to bring drugs into Britain without raising suspicion. Either that or it was only later on, once their relationship had become established, that Tarawicz decided he could move in on Telford's turf. To facilitate this, he manufactured a war between Telford and Morris Gerald Cafferty. This was easily accomplished. Telford had moved in aggressively on Cafferty's territory, probably with Tarawicz egging him on. All Tarawicz had to do was make sure things escalated. To this end, he had one of his men attack a drug dealer outside one of Telford's night-clubs, Telford immediately placing the blame on Cafferty. He also had some of his men attack a Telford stronghold in Paisley. Meanwhile, there were attacks on Cafferty's territory and associates, retaliation by Telford for perceived wrongs.'

Rebus cleared his throat, took a sip of tea – a fresh cup, no sugar.

'Does this sound familiar, Mr Summers?' Pretty-Boy said nothing. He was busy reading. 'My guess is that the Japanese were never meant to become involved. In other words, they had no knowledge of what was happening. Telford was showing them around, easing the way for them as they tried to buy a country club. Rest and recreation for their members, plus a good way of laundering money – less suspect than a casino or similar operation, especially when an electronics factory is about to open, so that the Yakuza slip into the country as just a few more Japanese businessmen.

'I think when Tarawicz saw this, he began to worry. He didn't want to get rid of Tommy Telford just to leave the way open for other competitors to muscle in. So he decided they'd have to become part of his plan. He had Matsumoto followed. He had him killed, and in a nice twist made *me* the chief suspect. Why? Two reasons. First, Tommy Telford had me pegged as Cafferty's man, so by fingering me, Tarawicz was fingering Cafferty. Second, he wanted me out of the game, because I'd gone to Newcastle, and had met one of his men, a guy called William 'The Crab' Colton. I knew the Crab of old, and it so happened Tarawicz had used him for the hit on the drug dealer. He didn't want me putting two and two together.'

Rebus paused again. 'How's it sounding, Brian?'

Pretty-Boy had finished reading. His arms were folded again, eyes on Rebus.

'We've yet to see any evidence, Inspector,' the lawyer said.

Rebus shrugged. 'I don't need evidence. See, the same file you've got there, I delivered a copy to a Mr Sakiji Shoda at the Caledonian Hotel.' Rebus watched Pretty-Boy's eyelids flutter. 'Now, the way I see it, Mr Shoda is going to be a bit pissed off. I mean, he's already pissed off, that's why he was here. He'd seen Telford screw up, and wanted to see if he could do anything *right*. I don't suppose the raid on Maclean's will have given him any renewed sense of confidence. But he was also here to find out why one of his men had been killed, and who was responsible. This report tells him Tarawicz was behind it, and if he chooses to believe that, he'll go after Tarawicz. In fact, he checked out of his hotel yesterday evening – seems he was in a bit of a rush. I'm wondering if he was on his way home via Newcastle. Doesn't matter. What matters is that he'll *still* be pissed off at Telford for letting it happen. And meantime Jake Tarawicz is going to be wondering who shopped him to Shoda. The Yakuza are not nice people, Brian. You lot are nursery school by comparison.' Rebus sat back in his chair.

'One last point,' he said. 'Tarawicz's base is Newcastle. I'm betting he had eyes and ears here in Edinburgh. In fact, I know he did. I've just been having a chat with Dr Colquhoun. You remember him, Brian? You'd heard about him from Lintz. Then when Tarawicz offered East Europeans as working girls, you reckoned maybe Tommy should have a few foreign phrases to hand. Colquhoun did the teaching. You told him stories about Tarawicz, about Bosnia. Catch was, he's the only person round these parts who knew the subject, so when we picked up Candice, we ended up using him, too. Colquhoun sussed straight off what was happening. He wasn't sure if he had anything to fear: he'd never met her, and her answers were reassuringly vague – or he kept them that way. All the same, he came to you. Your solution: ship Candice to Fife, then snatch her, and take Colquhoun out of the game till the heat died.'

Rebus smiled. 'He told *you* about Fife. Yet it was *Tarawicz* who got Candice. I think Tommy will find that a bit odd, don't you? So, here we sit. And I can tell you that the minute you walk out of here, you're going to be a marked man. Could be the Yakuza, could be Cafferty, could be your own boss or Tarawicz himself. You haven't got any friends, and nowhere's safe any more.' Rebus paused. 'Unless *we* help you. I've talked to Chief Superintendent Watson, and he's agreeing to witness protection, new identity, whatever you want. There may be a short sentence to serve – just so it looks right – but it'll be a soft option, room of your own, no other prisoners allowed near. And afterwards, you'll be home and dry. That's a big commitment on our part, and we'll need a big commitment from *you*. We'll want everything.' Rebus counted off on his fingers. 'The drug shipments, the war with Cafferty, the

Newcastle connection, the Yakuza, the prostitutes.' He paused again, drained his tea. 'Tall order, I know. Your boss had a meteoric rise, Brian, and he nearly made it. But that's all over. Best thing you can do now is talk. It's either that or spend the rest of your days waiting for the bullet or the machete to strike ...'

The lawyer started to protest. Rebus held up a hand.

'We'll need all of it, Brian. Including Lintz.'

'Lintz,' Pretty-Boy said dismissively. 'Lintz is nothing.'

'So where's the harm?'

The look in Pretty-Boy's eyes was a mix of anger, fear and disorientation. Rebus stood up.

'I need something else to drink. What about you gentlemen?'

'Coffee,' the lawyer said, 'black, no sugar.'

Pretty-Boy hesitated, then said, 'Get me a Coke.' And at that point – for the very first time – Rebus knew a deal might be done. He stopped the interview, Hogan switched off the tapes, and both men left the room. Hogan patted him on the back.

Farmer Watson was coming along the corridor towards them. Rebus moved to meet him, leading them away from the door.

'I think we might be in with a shout, sir,' Rebus said. 'He'll try to twist the deal, give us less than we want, but I think there's a chance.'

Watson beamed a smile, as Rebus leaned against the wall, eyes closed. 'I feel about a hundred years old.'

'Experience tells,' Hogan said.

Rebus growled at him, then they went to fetch the drinks.

'Mr Summers,' the lawyer said, as Rebus handed him his cup, 'would like to tell you the story of his relationship with Joseph Lintz. But first we'll need some assurances.'

'What about everything else I mentioned?'

'These can be negotiated.'

Rebus stared at Pretty-Boy. 'You don't trust me?'

Pretty-Boy picked up his can, said 'No', and drank.

'Fine.' Rebus walked over to the far wall. 'In that case, you're free to go.' He checked his watch. 'Soon as you've finished your drinks, I want you out of here. Interview Rooms are at a premium tonight. DI Hogan, mark up the tapes, will you?'

Hogan ejected both cassettes. Rebus sat down beside him and they started discussing work, as though Pretty-Boy had been dismissed from their minds. Hogan examined a sheet of paper, checking who was due to be interviewed next.

From the corner of his eye, Rebus saw Pretty-Boy leaning in towards his lawyer, whispering something. He turned on them.

'Can you do that outside, please? We need to vacate this room.'

Pretty-Boy *knew* Rebus was bluffing ... knew the policeman needed him. But he realised, too, that Rebus was *not* bluffing about giving the file to Shoda, and he was far too intelligent not to be scared. He didn't move from the chair, and held his lawyer's arm so he had to stay and listen. Eventually the lawyer cleared his throat.

'Inspector, Mr Summers is willing to answer your questions.'

'*All* my questions?'

The lawyer nodded. 'But I must insist on hearing more of the "deal" you're proposing.'

Rebus looked at Hogan. 'Go get the Chief Super.'

Rebus left the room, stood in the hallway while Hogan was away. Cadged a cigarette off a passing uniform. He'd just got it lit when Farmer Watson came barrelling towards him, Hogan behind as though attached to Watson by an invisible leash.

'No smoking, John, you know that.'

'Yes, sir,' Rebus said, crimping the tip. 'I was just holding it for Inspector Hogan.'

Watson nodded towards the door. 'What do they want?'

'We've been talking possible immunity from prosecution. At the very least, he'll want a soft sentence, and a safe one, plus new ID afterwards.'

Watson was thoughtful. 'We haven't had a cheep out of any of them. Not that it matters greatly. There's the gang we caught red-handed, plus Telford on the audio tape ...'

'Summers is a real insider, knows Telford's organisation.'

'So how come he's willing to spill?'

'Because he's scared, and his fear is overwhelming his loyalty. I'm not saying we'll get every last detail out of him, but we'll probably get enough to start pressing the other members. Once they know someone's yapping, they'll all want a trade.'

'What's his lawyer like?'

'Expensive.'

'No point shilly-shallying then.'

'I couldn't have put it better myself, sir.'

The Chief Super pinned back his shoulders. 'All right, let's do a deal.'

'When did you first meet Joseph Lintz?'

Pretty-Boy's arms were no longer folded. He was resting them on the desk, head in his hands. His hair flopped forward, making him look younger than ever.

'About six months ago. We'd spoken on the phone before that.'

'He was a punter?'

'Yes.'

'Meaning what exactly?'

Pretty-Boy looked at the turning spools. 'You want me to explain for all our listeners?'

'That's right.'

'Joseph Lintz was a client of the escort service for which I worked.'

'Come on, Brian, you were a bit more than a flunkey. You ran it, didn't you?'

'If you say so.'

'Anytime you want to walk, Brian ...'

Eyes burning. 'Okay, I *ran* it for my employer.'

'And Mr Lintz phoned wanting an escort?'

'He wanted one of our girls to go to his home.'

'And?'

'And that was it. He'd sit there opposite her and just stare for half an hour.'

'Both of them fully clothed?'

'Yes.'

'Nothing else?'

'Not at first.'

'Ah.' Rebus paused. 'You must have been curious.'

Pretty-Boy shrugged. 'Takes all sorts, doesn't it?'

'I suppose it does. So how did your business relationship progress?'

'Well, on a gig like that, there's always a chaperone.'

'Yourself?'

'Yes.'

'You didn't have better things to do?'

Another shrug. 'I was curious.'

'About what?'

'The address: Heriot Row.'

'Mr Lintz had ... class?'

'Coming out his ears. I mean, I've met plenty fat cats, corporate types looking for a shag in their hotel, but Lintz was a long way from that.'

'He just wanted to look at the girls.'

'That's right. And this huge house he had …'

'You went in? You didn't just wait in the car?'

'Told him it was company policy.' A smile. 'Really, all I wanted was to snoop.'

'Did you talk to him?'

'Later, yes.'

'You became friends?'

'Not really … maybe. He knew things, had a real brain on him.'

'You were impressed.'

Pretty-Boy nodded. Yes, Rebus could imagine. His previous role model had always been Tommy Telford, but Pretty-Boy had aspirations. He *wanted* class. He wanted people to acknowledge him for his mind. Rebus knew how seductive Lintz's storytelling could be. How much more seductive would Pretty-Boy have found it?

'Then what happened?'

Pretty-Boy shifted. 'His tastes changed.'

'Or his real tastes started to emerge?'

'That's what I wondered.'

'So what did he want?'

'He wanted the girls … he had this length of rope … he'd made it into a noose.' Pretty-Boy swallowed. His lawyer had stopped writing, was listening intently. 'He wanted the girls to slip it over their heads, then lie down like they were dead.'

'Dressed or naked?'

'Naked.'

'And?'

'And he'd … he'd sit on his chair and get off. Some of the girls wouldn't go along. He wanted the works: bulging eyes, tongue sticking out, neck twisted …' Pretty-Boy rubbed his hands through his hair.

'Did you ever talk about it?'

'With him? No, never.'

'So what did you talk about?'

'All sorts of things.' Pretty-Boy looked up at the ceiling, laughed. 'He told me once, he believed in God. Said the problem was, he wasn't sure God believed in him. That seemed clever at the time ... he always managed to get me thinking. And this was the same guy who tossed himself off over bodies with ropes round their necks.'

'All this personal attention you were giving him,' Rebus said, 'you were sizing him up, weren't you?'

Pretty-Boy looked into his lap, nodded.

'For the tape, please.'

'Tommy always wanted to know if a punter was worth squeezing.'

'And ... ?'

Pretty-Boy shrugged. 'We found out about the Nazi stuff, realised we couldn't hurt him any more than he was already being hurt. Turned into a bit of a joke. There we were, thinking of threatening him with exposure as a perv, and at the same time the papers were saying he was a mass murderer.' He laughed again.

'So you dropped that idea?'

'Yes.'

'But he paid you five grand?' Rebus fishing.

Pretty-Boy licked his lips. 'He'd tried topping himself. He told me that. Tying the rope to the top of his banister and jumping off. Only it didn't work. Banister snapped and he fell half a flight.'

Rebus remembering: the broken stair-rail.

Rebus remembering: Lintz with a scarf around his neck, his voice hoarse. Telling Rebus he had a throat bug.

'He told you this?'

'He phoned the office, said we had to meet. That was unusual. In the past, he'd always used phone boxes and got me on my mobile. Safe old bugger, I'd always thought. Then he calls from home, right to the office.'

'Where did you meet?'

'In a restaurant. He bought me lunch.' The young woman … 'Told me he'd tried killing himself and couldn't do it. He kept saying he'd proved himself a "moral coward", whatever that means.'

'So what did he want?'

Pretty-Boy stared up at Rebus. 'He needed someone to help him.'

'You?'

Pretty-Boy shrugged.

'And the price was right?'

'No haggling necessary. He wanted it done in Warriston Cemetery.'

'Did you ask him why?'

'I knew he liked the place. We met at his house, really early. I drove him down there. He seemed the same as ever, except he kept thanking me for my "resolve". I wasn't sure what he meant by that. To me, Resolve is something you take after a hard night.'

Rebus smiled, as was expected. 'Go on,' he said.

'Not much more to tell, is there? *He* put the noose over his head. *He* told me to pull on the rope. I had a last go at talking him out of it, but the bugger was determined. It's not murder, is it? Assisted suicide: a lot of places, it's legal.'

'How did the dunt get on his head?'

'He was heavier than I thought. First time I hauled him up, the rope slipped and he fell, thumped himself on the ground.'

Bobby Hogan cleared his throat. 'Brian, did he say anything … right at the end?'

'Famous last words and all that?' Pretty-Boy shook his head. 'All he said was "thank you". Poor old sod. One thing: he wrote it all down.'

'What?'

'About me helping him. A sort of insurance, in case

anyone ever linked us. Letter says he paid me, begged me to help.'

'Where is this?'

'In a safe. I can get it for you.'

Rebus nodded, stretched his back. 'Did you ever talk about Villefranche?'

'A little bit, mostly about the way the papers and TV were hounding him, how difficult it made it when he wanted … company.'

'But not the massacre itself?'

Pretty-Boy shook his head. 'Know something else? Even if he *had* told me, I wouldn't tell you.'

Rebus tapped his pen against the desk. He knew the Lintz story was as closed as it was ever going to be. Bobby Hogan knew it, too. They had the secret at last, the story of how Lintz had died. They knew he'd been helped by the Rat Line, but they'd never know whether he'd been Josef Linzstek or not. The circumstantial evidence was over-whelming, but so was the evidence that Lintz had been hounded to death. He'd started putting the escorts into nooses only *after* the accusations had been made.

Hogan caught Rebus's eye and shrugged, as if to say: what does it matter? Rebus nodded back. Part of him wanted to take a break, but now that Pretty-Boy was rolling it was important to keep up the steam.

'Thanks for that, Mr Summers. We may come back to Mr Lintz if we think of any more questions. But meantime, let's move on to the relationship between Thomas Telford and Jake Tarawicz.'

Pretty-Boy shifted, as if trying to get comfortable. 'This could take a while,' he said.

'Take as long as you like,' Rebus told him.

37

They got it all, in time.

Pretty-Boy had to rest, and so did they. Other teams came in, worked on different areas. The tapes were filling up, being listened to elsewhere, notes and transcripts made. Back-up questions were forwarded to the Interview Room. Telford wasn't talking. Rebus went and took a look at him, sat across from him. Telford didn't blink once. He sat ramrod-straight, hands on knees. And all the while, Pretty-Boy's confession was being used to squeeze other gang members – without letting slip who was singing.

The ranks broke, slowly at first and then in a cataract of accusation, self-defence and denial. And they got it all.

Telford and Tarawicz: European prostitutes heading north; muscle and dope heading south.

Mr Taystee: taking more than his fair share; dealt with accordingly.

The Japanese: using Telford as their introduction to Scotland, finding it a good base of operations.

Only now Rebus had scuppered that. In his folder to Shoda he'd warned the gangster to leave Poyntinghame alone, or he'd be 'implicated in ongoing criminal investigations'. The Yakuza weren't stupid. He doubted they'd be back ... for a while at least.

His last trip of the night: Rebus went down to the cells, unlocked one of the doors and told Ned Farlowe he was free. Told him he had nothing to fear ...

Unlike Mr Pink Eyes. The Yakuza had a score to settle.

And it didn't stay unsettled long. He was found in his car-crusher, seatbelt welded shut. His men had started running.

Some of them were running still.

Rebus sat in his living-room, staring at the door Jack Morton had stripped and varnished. He was thinking about the funeral, about how the Juice Church would be there in force. He wondered if they'd blame him. Jack's kids would be there, too. Rebus had never met them; didn't think he wanted to see them.

Wednesday morning, he was back in Inverness, meeting Mrs Hetherington off her flight. She'd been delayed in Holland, answering Customs questions. They'd laid a little trap, caught a man called De Gier – a known trafficker – planting the kilo package of heroin in Mrs Hetherington's luggage: a secret compartment in her suitcase, the suitcase itself a gift from her landlord. Several of Telford's other elderly tenants were enjoying short breaks in Belgium. They'd be questioned by local police.

Home again, Rebus telephoned David Levy.

'Lintz committed suicide,' he told him.

'That's your conclusion?'

'It's the truth. No conspiracy, no cover-up.'

A sigh. 'It's of little consequence, Inspector. What matters is that we've lost another one.'

'Villefranche doesn't mean a thing to you, does it? The Rat Line, that's all you care about.'

'There's nothing we can do about Villefranche.'

Rebus took a deep breath. 'A man called Harris came to see me. He works for British Intelligence. They're protecting some big names, high-level people. Rat Line survivors, maybe their children. Tell Mayerlink to keep digging.'

There was silence for a moment. 'Thank you, Inspector.'

Rebus was in a car. It was the Weasel's Jag. The Weasel

was in the back with him. Their driver was missing a big chunk of his left ear. The shape made him resemble a pixie – but only from the side, and you wouldn't want to tell him to his face.

'You did well,' the Weasel was saying. 'Mr Cafferty's pleased.'

'How long have you been holding him?'

The Weasel smiled. 'Nothing gets past you, Rebus.'

'Rangers have offered me a trial in goal. How long have you had him?'

'A few days. Had to be sure we had the right one, didn't we?'

'And now you're sure?'

'Absolutely positive.'

Rebus looked out of the window at the passing parade of shops, pedestrians, buses. The car was heading down towards Newhaven and Granton. 'You wouldn't be setting up some loser to take the blame?'

'He's genuine.'

'You could have spent the past few days making sure he was going to say the right things.'

The Weasel seemed amused. 'Such as?'

'Such as that he was in Telford's pay.'

'Rather than Mr Cafferty's, you mean?' Rebus glared at the Weasel, who laughed. 'I think you'll find him a pretty convincing candidate.'

The way he said it made Rebus shiver. 'He's still alive, isn't he?'

'Oh, yes. How long he remains so is entirely up to you.'

'You think I want him dead?'

'I know you do. You didn't go to Mr Cafferty because you wanted justice. You went out of *revenge*.'

Rebus stared at the Weasel. 'You don't sound like yourself.'

'You mean I don't sound like my persona – different thing entirely.'

'And do many people get behind the persona?' The Who: 'Can You See the Real Me?'

The Weasel smiled again. 'I thought you deserved it, after all the trouble you've gone to.'

'I didn't break Telford just to please your boss.'

'Nevertheless ...' The Weasel slid across his seat towards Rebus. 'How's Sammy, by the way?'

'She's fine.'

'Recuperating?'

'Yes.'

'That's good news. Mr Cafferty will be pleased. He's disappointed you haven't been to see him.'

Rebus took a newspaper from his pocket. It was folded at a story: FATAL STABBING AT JAIL.

'Your boss?' he said, handing the paper over.

The Weasel made show of reading it. ' "Aged twenty-six, from Govan ... stabbed through the heart in his cell ... no witnesses, no weapon recovered despite a thorough search." ' He tutted. 'Bit careless.'

'He'd taken up the contract on Cafferty?'

'Had he?' The Weasel looked amazed.

'Fuck off,' Rebus said, turning back to his window.

'By the way, Rebus, if you decide not to go to trial with the driver ...' The Weasel was holding something out. A homemade screwdriver, filed to a point, grip covered in packing-tape. Rebus looked at it in disgust.

'I washed the blood off,' the Weasel assured him. Then he laughed again. Rebus felt like he was being ferried straight to hell. In front of him he could see the grey expanse of the Firth of Forth, and Fife beyond it. They were coming into an area of docks, gas-plant and warehouses. It had been earmarked for a development spill-over from Leith. The whole city was changing. Traffic routes and priorities were altered overnight, cranes were kept busy on building-sites, and the council, who always complained about being broke, had all manner of schemes underway to further alter the shape and scope of his chosen home.

'Nearly there,' the Weasel said.

Rebus wondered if there'd be any turning back.

They stopped at the gates to a warehouse complex. The driver undid the padlock, pulled the chain free. The gates swung open. In they went. The Weasel ordered the driver to park around the back. There was a plain white van there, more rust than metal. Its back windows had been painted over, turning it into a suitable hearse should occasion demand.

They got out into a salt wind. The Weasel shuffled over towards a door and banged once. The door was pushed open from within. They stepped inside.

A huge open space, filled with only a few packing cases, a couple of pieces of machinery covered with oil-cloth. And two men: the one who'd let them in, and another at the far end. This man was standing in front of a wooden chair. There was a figure tied to the chair, half-hidden by the man. The Weasel led the procession. Rebus tried to control his breathing, which was growing painfully shallow. His heart was racing, nerves jangling. He pushed back the anger, wasn't sure he could hold it.

When they were eight feet from the chair, the Weasel nodded and the man stood away, revealing to Rebus the terrified figure of a kid.

A boy.

Nine or ten, no older.

One black eye, nose caked with blood, both cheeks bruised and a graze on his chin. Burst lip beginning to heal, trousers torn at the knees, one shoe missing.

And a smell, as if he'd wet himself, maybe even worse.

'What the hell is this?' Rebus asked.

'This,' the Weasel said, 'is the little bastard who stole the car. This is the little bastard who lost his nerve at a red light and gunned through it, losing control of the pedals because he could barely reach them. This ...' The Weasel stepped forward, planted a hand on the kid's shoulder. 'This is the culprit.'

Rebus looked at the faces around him. 'Is this your idea of a joke?'

'No joke, Rebus.'

He looked at the boy. Dried tear-tracks. Eyes bloodshot from crying. Shoulders trembling. They'd tied his arms behind him. Tied his ankles to the chair-legs.

'Puh–please, mister ...' Dry, cracked voice. 'I ... help me, puh–please ...'

'Nicked the car,' the Weasel recited, 'then did the hit and run, got scared, and dumped the car near where he lives. Took the cassette and the tapes. He wanted the car for a race. That's what they do, race cars around the schemes. This little runt can start an engine in ten seconds flat.' He rubbed his hands together. 'So ... here we all are.'

'Help me ...'

Rebus recalling the city's graffiti: Won't Anyone Help? The Weasel nodding towards one of his men, the man producing a pickaxe-handle.

'Or the screwdriver,' the Weasel said. 'Or whatever you like, really. We are at your command.' And he gave a little bow.

Rebus could hardly speak. 'Cut the ropes.'

Silence in the warehouse.

'*Cut those fucking ropes!*'

A sniff from the Weasel. 'You heard the man, Tony.'

Ca-chink of a flick-knife opening. Ropes severed like cutting through butter. Rebus walked to within inches of the boy.

'What's your name?'

'J-Jordan.'

'Is that your first name or your second?'

The boy looked at him. 'First.'

'Okay, Jordan.' Rebus leaned down. The boy flinched, but did not resist as Rebus picked him up. He weighed almost nothing. Rebus started walking with him.

'What now, Rebus?' the Weasel asked. But Rebus didn't answer. He carried the boy to the threshold, kicked open the door, stepped out into sunshine.

'I'm … I'm really sorry.' The boy had a hand across his eyes, unused to the light. He was starting to cry.

'You know what you did?'

Jordan nodded. 'I've been … ever since that night. I knew it was bad …' Now the tears came.

'Did they say who I was?'

'Please don't kill me.'

'I'm not going to kill you, Jordan.'

The boy blinked, trying to clear tears from his eyes, the better to know whether he was being lied to.

'I think you've been through enough, pal,' Rebus said. Then added: 'I think we both have.'

So after everything, it had come to this. Bob Dylan: 'Simple Twist of Fate'. Segue to Leonard Cohen: 'Is This What You Wanted?'

Rebus didn't know the answer to that.

38

Clean and sober, he went to the hospital. An open ward this time, set hours for visitors. No more darkened vigils. No return visit by Candice, though nurses spoke of regular phone calls by someone foreign-sounding. No way of knowing where she was. Maybe out there searching for her son. It didn't matter, so long as she was safe. So long as she was in control.

When he reached the ward's far end, two women rose from their chairs so he could kiss them: Rhona and Patience. He had a carrier-bag with him, magazines and grapes. Sammy was sitting up, supported by three pillows, Pa Broon propped beside her. Her hair had been washed and brushed, and she was smiling at him.

'Women's magazines,' he said, shaking his head. 'They should be on the top-shelf.'

'I need a few fantasies to sustain me in here,' Sammy said. Rebus beamed at her, said hello, then bent down and kissed his daughter.

The sun was shining as they walked through The Meadows – a rare day off for both. They held hands and watched people sunbathing and playing football. He knew Rhona was excited, and thought he knew why. But he wasn't going to spoil things with speculation.

'If you had a daughter, what would you call her?' she asked.

He shrugged. 'Haven't really thought about it.'

'What about a son?'

'I quite like Sam.'

'Sam?'

'When I was a kid, I had a bear called Sam. My mum knitted it for me.'

'Sam ...' She tried the name out. 'It would work both ways, wouldn't it?'

He stopped, circled his arms around her waist. 'How do you mean?'

'Well, it could be Samuel or Samantha. You don't get many of those – names that work both ways.'

'I suppose not. Rhona, is there ...?'

She put a finger to his lips, then kissed him. They walked on. There didn't seem to be a cloud in the whole damned sky.

Afterword

My fictional French village of Villefranche d'Albarede owes its existence to the real village of Oradour-sur-Glâne, which was the subject of an attack by the 3rd Company of the SS 'Der Führer' regiment.

On the afternoon of Saturday 10 June 1944, 3rd Company – known as 'Das Reich' – entered the village and rounded up everyone. The women and children were herded into the church, while the men were split into groups and marched to various barns and other buildings around the village. Then the slaughter began.

Some 642 victims have been accounted for, but the estimate is that up to a thousand people may have perished that day. Only fifty-three corpses were ever identified. One boy from Lorraine, having first-hand knowledge of SS atrocities, managed to flee when the troops entered the village. Five men escaped the massacre in Laudy's barn. Wounded, they were able to crawl from the burning building and hide until the next day. One woman escaped from the church, climbing out of a window after playing dead beside the corpse of her child.

Soldiers went from house to house, finding villagers too sick or elderly to leave their beds. These people were shot and their houses set alight. Some of the bodies were hidden in mass graves, or dumped down wells and in bread ovens.

General Lammerding was the commanding officer. On 9 June he'd ordered the deaths of ninety-nine hostages in Tulle. He also gave the order for the Oradour massacre.

Later on in the war, Lammerding was captured by the British, who refused his extradition to France. Instead, he was returned to Düsseldorf, where he ran a successful company until his death in 1971.

In the general euphoria of the Normandy landings, the tragedy at Oradour went almost unnoticed. Eventually, in January 1953, the trial opened in Bordeaux of sixty-five men identified as having been involved in the massacre. Of these sixty-five, only twenty-one were present: seven Germans, and fourteen natives of French Alsace. None of the men was of officer rank.

Every individual found guilty at the Bordeaux trial left court a free man. A special Act of Amnesty had been passed, in the interests of national unity. (People in Alsace were disgruntled that their countrymen had been picked out for condemnation.) Meantime, the Germans were said to have already served their terms.

As a result, Oradour broke off all relations with the French state, a rupture which lasted seventeen years.

In May 1983, a man stood trial in East Berlin, charged with having been a lieutenant in 'Das Reich' during the Oradour massacre. He admitted everything, and was sentenced to life imprisonment.

In June 1996, it was reported that around 12,000 foreign volunteers to the Waffen SS are still receiving pensions from the Federal German government. One of these pensioners, a former Obersturmbannführer, was a participant at Oradour ...

Oradour still stands as a shrine. The village has been left just the way it was on that day in June 1944.

DEAD SOULS

To my long-suffering editor, Caroline Oakley

The world is full of missing persons, and their numbers increase all the time. the space they occupy lies somewhere between what we know about the ways of being alive and what we hear about the ways of being dead. They wander there, unaccompanied and unknowable, like shadows of people.

Andrew O'Hagan, *The Missing*

Once I caught a train to Cardenden by mistake . . . When we reached Cardenden we got off and waited for the next train back to Edinburgh. I was very tired and if Cardenden had looked more promising, I think I would have simply stayed there. And if you've ever been to Cardenden you'll know how bad things must have been.

Kate Atkinson, *Behind the Scenes at the Museum*

INTRODUCTION

Dead Souls was wholly conceived and written in Edinburgh – the first time this had happened since Rebus's initial outing in *Knots & Crosses*. The intervening novels had been written during my four-year stint in London, or else in the further six years spent in rural France. Now I was back in Edinburgh . . . and worried that I would no longer be able to write about the place. This was a realistic fear, too: I had used geographical distance to help me recreate Edinburgh as a fictionalised city. How would I cope now that I could take a short stroll and see what I'd been getting wrong all those years?

I needn't have worried.

Dead Souls is named after a song by Joy Division. As its title might suggest, it's not a number you would dance to at weddings, unless you count the Addams Family among your in-laws. I was aware, of course, of Joy Division's source material – the unfinished novel *Dead Souls* by Russian writer Nikolai Gogol. The phrase 'tortured genius' might have been coined with Gogol in mind. Having published the first half of *Dead Souls*, he ended up burning the drafts of its second half. Later on, he started work on the book again, until his religious teacher persuaded him to renounce literature altogether. So the latest version of the second half went up in flames again, and Gogol died ten days later.

My own book is divided into two parts, entitled 'Lost' and 'Found'. Both begin with an italicised quotation from Gogol's work, the one accompanying 'Found' being the last words recorded by him. The title of the book came to me early. I knew I wanted to write about MisPers – missing persons. I had become interested in them when doing research for *Black & Blue*. In a non-fiction work entitled *The Missing* (which I had read because it contained passages about the Bible John murders), journalist Andrew O'Hagan had discussed the phenomenon of loss and the hole left in the fabric of our lives when someone vanishes. Inspired by O'Hagan's work, I'd written a seventy-page novella called *Death Is Not The End* (itself a Bob Dylan title, but known to me through a contemporary reworking by Nick Cave). This novella had been written at the behest of an American publisher, who then seemed to find no immediate market for it. Worried that it might never see the light of day, I decided to 'cannibalise' parts of the story for my next full-length novel – which is why two versions of the story exist, albeit with different outcomes.

Okay, so I was ready to rework my novella into a novel. But another real-life story had caught my eye in the interim. On a rough housing estate in Stirling, the locals had been roused by news that a convicted paedophile was living quietly in their midst. The vigilante instinct took over, and the man was chased out. Two things struck me about this. One was that it continued the theme I'd touched on in my previous novel *The Hanging Garden* – namely, how do we begin to measure right and wrong? The other was that Rebus's knee-jerk reaction to news of a 'hidden' paedophile would be the same as that of many people of his generation, class and philosophy: he'd 'out' the bugger, and damn the consequences. Well, I've seldom shirked a challenge: I wanted to see if I could change his mind about a few things . . .

I also wanted to take him home, back to where he grew up in central Fife. Although many of my books have had cause to send Rebus to Fife, *Dead Souls* is my most personal investigation of my own background. When high-school 'flame' Janice reminisces with Rebus, she is using my own memories and anecdotes. We learn more, too, about Rebus's childhood, including that he was born in a pre-fab (as I was) but soon moved to a terraced house in a cul-de-sac (as I did). We find out that, like me, he drank in his home town's Goth pub (Goth being short for Gothenburg), and that his father brought a silk scarf back from World War II (as did mine). Much of this is reflected in the names I give to Rebus's school friends: Brian and Janice Mee. They're 'me', you see, as are characteristics of many of my other creations, Rebus chief among them.

There are plenty of in-jokes in the book, despite the sombre tone of its material. We meet Harry, 'the rudest barman in Edinburgh' (who, in real life, is now landlord of the Oxford Bar and can afford to be rude only to a select few of us who expect no less of him). The nightclub in the book is called Gaitano's, after the American crime writer Nick Gaitano, who also wrote under his real name of Eugene Izzi. He'd been found dead shortly before I started work on the book, in what appeared, at least initially, to be mysterious circumstances. The headless coachman mentioned at the start of the book (and later on, as the name of a pub) is actually Major Weir, a real-life character from Edinburgh's dark side. Weir and his sister were accused in 1678 of being warlock and witch. Both were eventually executed, despite having lived lives of exemplary piety, and with only the Major's rambling and befuddled confession as 'proof'.

The modern equivalent of a witch-hunt? Look no further than the popular media's treatment of suspected paedophiles . . .

Dead Souls was a landmark of sorts for me, being the first time I had allowed a charity to auction off the right for someone to appear as a character in one of my books. These days, I do this up to six times per book, but there was just the one instance in *Dead Souls*. The prize was won by a friend, but she didn't want the honour for herself. Oh no, she wanted it for another of her friends in the USA, a woman called Fern Bogot.

'It doesn't sound very Scottish,' I complained.

In the end, I decided that 'Fern' sounded like an assumed name. Who might not want to use their real name as they went about their business? Of course: a prostitute! So it was, and with some little reluctance on her part, that clean-living Fern Bogot became an Edinburgh hooker . . .

One last thing about *Dead Souls*. A fan at a question-and-answer session once picked me up on my use of the phrase 'trellis tables' when what I actually meant was 'trestle tables'. She was right, and I've left the error intact for your enjoyment. But she also told me that I use trestle tables a lot in my books . . . and in rereading the series as preparation for writing all the new introductions, I can confirm that she was right in this particular also. Don't ask me what it is about them; I just can't stop writing the words down . . .

Trestle tables.

There, I did it again.

May 2005

Prologue

From this height, the sleeping city seems like a child's construction, a model which has refused to be constrained by imagination. The volcanic plug might be black Plasticine, the castle balanced solidly atop it a skewed rendition of crenellated building bricks. The orange street lamps are crumpled toffee-wrappers glued to lollipop sticks.

Out in the Forth, the faint bulbs from pocket torches illuminate toy boats resting on black crêpe paper. In this universe, the jagged spires of the Old Town would be angled matchsticks, Princes Street Gardens a Fuzzy-Felt board. Cardboard boxes for the tenements, doors and windows painstakingly detailed with coloured pens. Drinking straws could become guttering and downpipes, and with a fine blade – maybe a scalpel – those doors could be made to open. But peering inside ... peering inside would destroy the effect.

Peering inside would change *everything*.

He shoves his hands in his pockets. The wind is stropping his ears. He can pretend it is a child's breath, but the reality chides him.

I am the last cold wind you'll feel.

He takes a step forward, peers over the edge and into darkness. Arthur's Seat crouches behind him, humped and silent as though offended by his presence, coiled to pounce. He tells himself it is papier-mâché. He smooths his hands over strips of newsprint, not reading the stories, then realises he is stroking the air and withdraws his hands, laughing guiltily. Somewhere behind him, he hears a voice.

3

In the past, he'd climbed up here in daylight. Years back, it would have been with a lover maybe, climbing hand in hand, seeing the city spread out like a promise. Then later, with his wife and child, stopping at the summit to take photos, making sure no one went too close to the edge. Father and husband, he would tuck his chin into his collar, seeing Edinburgh in shades of grey, but getting it into perspective, having risen above it with his family. Digesting the whole city with a slow sweep of his head, he would feel that all problems were containable.

But now, in darkness, he knows better.

He knows that life is a trap, that the jaws eventually spring shut on anyone foolish enough to think they could cheat their way to a victory. A police car blares in the distance, but it's not coming for him. A black coach is waiting for him at the foot of Salisbury Crags. Its headless driver is becoming impatient. The horses tremble and whinny. Their flanks will lather on the ride home.

'Salisbury Crag' has become rhyming slang in the city. It means skag, heroin. 'Morningside Speed' is cocaine. A snort of coke just now would do him the world of good, but wouldn't be enough. Arthur's Seat could be made of the stuff: in the scheme of things, it wouldn't matter a damn.

There is a figure behind him in the darkness, drawing nearer. He half-turns to confront it, then quickly looks away, suddenly fearful of meeting the face. He begins to say something.

'I know you'll find it hard to believe, but I've . . .'

He never finishes the sentence. Because now he's sailing out across the city, jacket flying up over his head, smothering a final, heartfelt cry. As his stomach surges and voids, he wonders if there really is a coachman waiting for him.

And feels his heart burst open with the knowledge that he'll never see his daughter again, in this world or any other.

Part One
Lost

We commit all sorts of injustices at every step without the slightest evil intention. Every minute we are the cause of someone's unhappiness . . .

1

John Rebus was pretending to stare at the meerkats when he saw the man, and knew he wasn't the one.

For the best part of an hour, Rebus had been trying to blink away a hangover, which was about as much exercise as he could sustain. He'd planted himself on benches and against walls, wiping his brow even though Edinburgh's early spring was a blood relative of midwinter. His shirt was damp against his back, uncomfortably tight every time he rose to his feet. The capybara had looked at him almost with pity, and there had seemed a glint of recognition and empathy behind the long-lashed eye of the hunched white rhino, standing so still it might have been a feature in a shopping mall, yet somehow dignified in its very isolation.

Rebus felt isolated, and about as dignified as a chimpanzee. He hadn't been to the zoo in years; thought probably the last time had been when he'd brought his daughter to see Palango the gorilla. Sammy had been so young, he'd carried her on his shoulders without feeling the strain.

Today, he carried nothing with him but a concealed radio and set of handcuffs. He wondered how conspicuous he looked, walking such a narrow ambit while shunning the attractions further up and down the slope, stopping now and then at the kiosk to buy a can of Irn-Bru. The penguin parade had come and gone and seen him not leaving his perch. Oddly, it was when the visitors moved on, seeking excitement, that the first of the meerkats appeared, rising on its hind legs, body narrow and wavering, scouting the territory. Two more had appeared from their burrow, circling, noses to the ground. They paid little attention to the silent figure seated on the low wall of their enclosure; passed him time and again as they explored the same orbit of hard-packed earth, jumping back only when he lifted a handkerchief to his face. He was feeling the poison fizz in his veins: not the booze, but an early-morning double espresso from one of the converted police boxes near The Meadows. He'd been on his way to work, on his way to learning that today was zoo patrol. The mirror in the cop-shop toilet had lacked any sense of diplomacy.

Greenslade: 'Sunkissed You're Not'. Segue to Jefferson Airplane: 'If You Feel Like China Breaking'.

But it could always be worse, Rebus had reminded himself, applying his thoughts instead to the day's central question: who was poisoning the zoo animals of Edinburgh? The fact of the matter was, some individual was to blame. Somebody cruel and calculating and so far missed by surveillance cameras and keepers alike. Police had a vague description, and spot-checks were being made of visitors' bags and coat pockets, but what everyone really wanted – except perhaps the media – was to have someone in custody, preferably with the tainted tidbits locked away as evidence.

Meantime, as senior staff had indicated, the irony was that the poisoner had actually been good for business. There'd been no copycat offences yet, but Rebus wondered how long that would last . . .

The next announcement concerned feeding the sea-lions. Rebus had sauntered past their pool earlier, thinking it not overly large for a family of three. The meerkat den was surrounded by children now, and the meerkats themselves had disappeared, leaving Rebus strangely pleased to have been accorded their company.

He moved away, but not too far, and proceeded to untie and tie a shoelace, which was his way of marking the quarter-hours. Zoos and the like had never held any

8

fascination for him. As a child, his roll-call of pets had seen more than its fair share of those listed 'Missing in Action' or 'Killed in the Line of Duty'. His tortoise had absconded, despite having its owner's name painted on its shell; several budgies had failed to reach maturity; and ill-health had plagued his only goldfish (won at the fair in Kirkcaldy). Living as he did in a tenement flat, he'd never been tempted in adulthood by the thought of a cat or dog. He'd tried horse-riding exactly once, rubbing his inside legs raw in the process and vowing afterwards that the closest he'd come in future to the noble beast would be on a betting slip.

But he'd liked the meerkats for a mixture of reasons: the resonance of their name; the low comedy of their rituals; their instinct for self-preservation. Kids were dangling over the wall now, legs kicking in the air. Rebus imagined a role reversal – cages filled with children, peered at by passing animals as they capered and squealed, loving the attention. Except the animals wouldn't share a human's curiosity. They would be unmoved by any display of agility or tenderness, would fail to comprehend that some game was being played, or that someone had skinned a knee. Animals would not build zoos, would have no need of them. Rebus was wondering why humans needed them.

The place suddenly became ridiculous to him, a chunk of prime Edinburgh real estate given over to the unreal . . . And then he saw the camera.

Saw it because it replaced the face that should have been there. The man was standing on a grassy slope sixty-odd feet away, adjusting the focus on a sizeable telescopic lens. The mouth below the camera's body was a thin line of concentration, rippling slightly as forefinger and thumb fine-tuned the apparatus. He wore a black denim jacket, creased chinos, and running shoes. He'd removed a faded blue baseball cap from his head. It dangled from a free finger as he took his pictures. His hair was thinning and brown, forehead wrinkled. Recognition came as soon as he lowered the camera. Rebus looked away, turning in the direction of the photographer's subjects: children. Children leaning into the meerkat enclosure. All you could see were shoe-soles and legs, girls' skirts and the smalls of backs where T-shirts and jerseys had ridden up.

Rebus knew the man. Context made it easier. Hadn't seen him in probably four years but couldn't forget eyes like that, the hunger shining on cheeks whose suffused redness highlighted old acne scars. The hair had been longer four years ago, curling over misshapen ears. Rebus sought for a name, at the same time reaching into his pocket for his radio. The photographer caught the movement, eyes turning to match Rebus's gaze, which was already moving elsewhere. Recognition worked both ways. The lens came off and was stuffed into a shoulder-bag. A lens-cap was clipped over the aperture. And then the man was off, walking briskly downhill. Rebus yanked out his radio.

'He's heading downhill from me, west side of the Members' house. Black denim jacket, light trousers . . .' Rebus kept the description going as he followed. Turning back, the photographer saw him and broke into a trot, hindered by the heavy camera bag.

The radio burst into life, officers heading for the area. Past a restaurant and cafeteria, past couples holding hands and children attacking ice-creams. Peccaries, otters, pelicans. It was all downhill, for which Rebus was thankful, and the man's unusual gait – one leg slightly shorter than the other – was helping close the gap. The walkway narrowed just at the point where the crowd thickened. Rebus wasn't sure what was causing the bottleneck, then heard a splash, followed by cheers and applause.

'Sea-lion enclosure!' he yelled into his radio.

The man half-turned, saw the radio at Rebus's mouth,

looked ahead of him and saw heads and bodies, camou-
flaging the approach of any other officers. There was fear
in his eyes now, replacing the earlier calculation. He had
ceased to be in control of events. With Rebus just about
within grabbing distance, the man pushed two spectators
aside and clambered over the low stone wall. On the other
side of the pool was a rock outcrop atop which stood the
female keeper, stooping over two black plastic pails. Rebus
saw that there were hardly any spectators behind the
keeper, since the rocks obstructed any view of the sea-
lions. By dodging the crowd, the man could clamber back
over the wall at the far side and be within striking
distance of the exit. Rebus cursed under his breath, lifted a
foot on to the wall, and hauled himself over.

The onlookers were whistling, a few even cheering as
video cameras were hoisted to record the antics of two
men cautiously making their way along the sharp slopes.
Glancing towards the water, Rebus saw rapid movement,
and heard warning yells from the keeper as a sea-lion
slithered up on to the rocks near her. Its sleek black body
rested only long enough for a fish to be dropped
accurately into its mouth, before turning and slipping
back into the pool. It looked neither too big nor too fierce,
but its appearance had rattled Rebus's quarry. The man
turned back for a moment, his camera bag sliding down
his arm. He moved it so it was hanging around his neck.
He looked ready to retreat, but when he saw his pursuer,
he changed his mind again. The keeper had reached for a
radio of her own, alerting security. But the pool's
occupants were becoming impatient. The water beside
Rebus seemed to flex and sway. A wave foamed against
his face as something huge and ink-black rose from the
depths, obliterating the sun and slapping itself down on
the rocks. The crowd screamed as the male sea-lion, easily
four or five times the size of its offspring, landed and
looked around for food, loud snorts belching from its nose.
As it opened its mouth and let out a ferocious wail, the

photographer yelped and lost his balance, plunging into the pool and taking the camera bag with him.

Two shapes in the pool – mother and child – nosed towards him. The keeper was blowing the whistle strung around her neck, for all the world like the referee at a Sunday kickabout faced with a conflagration. The male sea-lion looked at Rebus a final time and plunged back into its pool, heading for where its mate was prodding the new arrival.

'For Christ's sake,' Rebus shouted, 'chuck in some fish!'

The keeper got the message and kicked a pail of food into the pool, at which all three sea-lions sped towards the scene. Rebus took his chance and waded in, closing his eyes and diving, grabbing the man and hauling him back towards the rocks. A couple of spectators came to help, followed by two plain-clothes detectives. Rebus's eyes stung. The scent of raw fish was heavy in the air.

'Let's get you out,' someone said, offering a hand. Rebus let himself be reeled in. He snatched the camera from around the drenched man's neck.

'Got you,' he said. Then, kneeling on the rocks, starting to shiver, he threw up into the pool.

2

Next morning, Rebus was surrounded by memories.

Not his own, but those of his Chief Super: framed photographs cluttering the tight space of the office. The thing with memories was, they meant nothing to the outsider. Rebus could have been looking at a museum display. Children, lots of children. The Chief Super's kids, their faces ageing over time, and then grandchildren. Rebus got the feeling his boss hadn't taken the photos. They were gifts, passed on to him, and he'd felt it necessary to bring them here.

The clues were all in their situation: the photos on the desk faced out from it, so anyone in the office could see them with the exception of the man who used the desk every day. Others were on the window-ledge behind the desk – same effect – and still more on top of a filing cabinet in the corner. Rebus sat in Chief Superintendent Watson's chair to confirm his theory. The snapshots weren't for Watson; they were for visitors. And what they told visitors was that Watson was a family man, a man of rectitude, a man who had achieved something in his life. Instead of humanising the drab office, they sat in it with all the ease of exhibits.

A new photo had been added to the collection. It was old, slightly out of focus as though smeared by a flicker of camera movement. Crimped edges, white border, and the photographer's illegible signature in one corner. A family group: father standing, one hand proprietorially on the shoulder of his seated wife, who held in her lap a toddler. The father's other hand gripped the blazered shoulder of a young boy, cropped hair and glaring eyes. Some pre-sitting tension was evident: the boy was trying to pull his shoulder from beneath his father's claw. Rebus took the photo over to the window, marvelled at the starched solemnity. He felt starched himself, in his dark woollen suit, white shirt and black tie. Black socks and shoes, the latter given a decent polish first thing this morning. Outside it was overcast, threatening rain. Fine weather for a funeral.

Chief Superintendent Watson came into the room, lazy progress belying his temperament. Behind his back they called him 'the Farmer', because he came from the north and had something of the Aberdeen Angus about him. He was dressed in his best uniform, cap in one hand, white A4 envelope in the other. He placed both on his desk, as Rebus replaced the photograph, angling it so it faced the Farmer's chair.

'That you, sir?' he asked, tapping the scowling child.

'That's me.'

'Brave of you to let us see you in shorts.'

But the Farmer was not to be deflected. Rebus could think of three explanations for the red veins highlighted on Watson's face: exertion, spirits, or anger. No sign of breathlessness, so rule out the first. And when the Farmer drank whisky, it didn't just affect his cheeks: his whole face took on a roseate glow and seemed to contract until it became puckish.

Which left anger.

'Let's get down to it,' Watson said, glancing at his watch. Neither man had much time. The Farmer opened the envelope and shook a packet of photographs on to his desk, then opened the packet and tossed the photos towards Rebus.

'Look for yourself.'

Rebus looked. They were the photos from Darren Rough's camera. The Farmer reached into his drawer to pull out a file. Rebus kept looking. Zoo animals, caged and

14

behind walls. And in some of the shots – not all of them, but a fair proportion – children. The camera had focused on these children, involved in conversations among themselves, or chewing sweets, or making faces at the animals. Rebus felt immediate relief, and looked to the Farmer for a confirmation that wasn't there.

'According to Mr Rough,' the Farmer was saying, studying a sheet from the file, 'the photos comprise part of a portfolio.'

'I'll bet they do.'

'Of a day in the life of Edinburgh Zoo.'

'Sure.'

The Farmer cleared his throat. 'He's enrolled in a photography night-class. I've checked and it's true. It's also true that his project is the zoo.'

'And there are kids in almost every shot.'

'In fewer than half the shots, actually.'

Rebus slid the photos across the desk. 'Come on, sir.'

'John, Darren Rough has been out of prison the best part of a year and has yet to show any sign of reoffending.'

'I heard he'd gone south.'

'And moved back again.'

'He ran for it when he saw me.'

The Farmer just stared the comment down. 'There's nothing here, John,' he said.

'A guy like Rough, he doesn't go to the zoo for the birds and the bees, believe me.'

'It wasn't even his choice of project. His tutor assigned it.'

'Yes, Rough would have preferred a play-park.' Rebus sighed. 'What does his lawyer say? Rough was always good at roping in a lawyer.'

'Mr Rough just wants to be left in peace.'

'The way he left those kids in peace?'

The Farmer sat back. 'Does the word "atonement" mean anything to you, John?'

Rebus shook his head. 'Not applicable.'

'How do you know?'

'Ever seen a leopard change its spots?'

The Farmer checked his watch. 'I know the two of you have a history.'

'I wasn't the one he made the complaint against.'

'No,' the Farmer said, 'Jim Margolies was.'

They left that in the air for a moment, lost in their own thoughts.

'So we do nothing?' Rebus queried at last. The word "atonement" was flitting about inside his skull. His friend the priest had been known to use it: reconciliation of God and man through Christ's life and death. A far cry from Darren Rough. Rebus wondered what Jim Margolies had been atoning for when he'd pitched himself off Salisbury Crags . . .

'His sheet's clean.' The Farmer reached into his desk's deep bottom drawer, pulled out a bottle and two glasses. Malt whisky. 'I don't know about you,' he said, 'but I need one of these before a funeral.'

Rebus nodded, watching the man pour. Cascading sound of mountain streams. *Usquebaugh* in the Gaelic. *Uisge*: water; *beatha*: life. Water of life. *Beatha* sounding like 'birth'. Each drink was a birth to Rebus's mind. But as his doctor kept telling him, each drop was a little death, too. He lifted the glass to his nose, nodded appreciation.

'Another good man gone,' the Farmer said.

And suddenly there were ghosts swirling around the room, just on the periphery of Rebus's vision, and chief amongst them Jack Morton. Jack, his old colleague, now three months dead. The Byrds: 'He Was a Friend of Mine'. A friend who refused to stay buried. The Farmer followed Rebus's eyes, but saw nothing. Drained his glass and put the bottle away again.

'Little and often,' he said. And then, as though the whisky had opened some bargain between them: 'There are ways and means, John.'

'Of what, sir?' Jack had melted into the windowpanes.

'Of coping.' Already the whisky was working on the Farmer's face, turning it triangular. 'Since what happened to Jim Margolies . . . well, it's made some of us think more about the stresses of the job.' He paused. 'Too many mistakes, John.'

'I'm having a bad patch, that's all.'

'A bad patch has its reasons.'

'Such as?'

The Farmer left the question unanswered, knowing perhaps that Rebus was busy answering it for himself: Jack Morton's death; Sammy in a wheelchair.

And whisky a therapist he could afford, at least in monetary terms.

'I'll manage,' he said at last, not even managing to convince himself.

'All by yourself?'

'That's the way, isn't it?'

The Farmer shrugged. 'And meantime we all live with your mistakes?'

Mistakes: like pulling men towards Darren Rough, who wasn't the man they wanted. Allowing the poisoner open access to the meerkats – an apple tossed into their enclosure. Luckily a keeper had walked past, picked it up before the animals could. He'd known about the scare, handed it in for testing.

Positive for rat poison.

Rebus's fault.

'Come on,' the Farmer said, after a final glance at his watch, 'let's get moving.'

So that once again Rebus's speech had gone unspoken, the one about how he'd lost any sense of vocation, any feeling of optimism about the role – the very existence – of policing. About how these thoughts scared him, left him either sleepless or scarred by bad dreams. About the ghosts which had come to haunt him, even in daytime.

About how he didn't want to be a cop any more.

*

17

Jim Margolies had had it all.

Ten years younger than Rebus, he was being tipped for accelerated advancement. They were waiting for him to learn the final few lessons, after which the rank of detective inspector would have been shed like a final skin. Bright, personable, a canny strategist with an eye to internal politics. Handsome, too, keeping fit playing rugby for his old school, Boroughmuir. He came from a good background and had connections to the Edinburgh establishment, his wife charming and elegant, his young daughter an acknowledged beauty. Liked by his fellow officers, and with an enviable ratio of arrests to convictions. The family lived quietly in The Grange, attended a local church, seemed the perfect little unit in every way.

The Farmer kept the commentary going, voice barely audible. He'd started on the drive to the church, kept it up during the service, and was closing with a graveside peroration.

'He had it all, John. And then he goes and does something like that. What makes a man . . . I mean, what goes through his head? This was someone even older officers looked up to – I mean the cynical old buggers within spitting distance of their pension. They've seen everything in their time, but they'd never seen anyone quite like Jim Margolies.'

Rebus and the Farmer – their station's representatives – were towards the back of the crowd. And it was a good crowd, too. Lots of brass, alongside rugby players, churchgoers, and neighbours. Plus extended family. And standing by the open grave, the widow dressed in black, managing to look composed. She'd lifted her daughter off the ground. The daughter in a white lace dress, her hair thick and long and ringlet-blonde, face shining as she waved bye-bye to the wooden casket. With the blonde hair and white dress, she looked like an angel. Perhaps that had been the intention. Certainly, she stood out from the crowd.

Margolies' parents were there, too. The father looking ex-forces, stiff-backed as a grandfather clock but with both trembling hands gripping the silver knob of a walking-stick. The mother teary-eyed, fragile, a veil falling to her wet mouth. She'd lost both her children. According to the Farmer, Jim's sister had killed herself too, years back. History of mental instability, and she'd slashed her wrists. Rebus looked again at the parents, who had now outlived both their offspring. His mind flashed to his own daughter, wondering how scarred *she* was, scarred in places you couldn't see.

Other family members nestled close to the parents, seeking comfort or ready to offer support – Rebus couldn't tell which.

'Nice family,' the Farmer was whispering. Rebus almost perceived a whiff of envy. 'Hannah's won competitions.'

Hannah being the daughter. She was eight, Rebus learned. Blue-eyed like her father and perfect-skinned. The widow's name was Katherine.

'Dear Lord, the sheer waste.'

Rebus thought of the Farmer's photographs, of the way individuals met and interlaced, forming a pattern which drew in others, colours merging or taking on discernible contrasts. You made friends, married into a new family, you had children who played with the children of other parents. You went to work, met colleagues who became friends. Bit by bit your identity became subsumed, no longer an individual and yet stronger somehow as a result.

Except it didn't always work that way. Conflicts could arise: work perhaps, or the slow realisation that you'd made a wrong decision some time back. Rebus had seen it in his own life, had chosen profession over marriage, pushing his wife away. She'd taken their daughter with her. He felt now that he'd made the right choice for the wrong reasons, that he should have owned up to his failings from the start. His work had merely given him a reasonable excuse for bailing out.

He wondered about Jim Margolies, who had thrown himself to his death in the dark. He wondered what had driven him to that final stark decision. No one seemed to have a clue. Rebus had come across plenty of suicides over the years, from bungled to assisted and all points in between. But there had always been some kind of explanation, some breaking point reached, some deep-seated sense of loss or failure or foreboding. Leaf Hound: 'Drowned My Life in Fear'.

But when it came to Jim Margolies . . . nothing clicked. There was no sense to it. His widow, parents, workmates . . . no one had been able to offer the first hint of an explanation. He'd been declared A1 fit. Things had been fine on the work front and at home. He loved his wife, his daughter. Money was not a problem.

But something had been a problem.

Dear Lord, the sheer waste.

And the cruelty of it: to leave everyone not only grieving but questioning, wondering if they were some-how to blame.

To erase your own life when life was so precious.

Looking towards the trees, Rebus saw Jack Morton standing there, seeming as young as when the two had first met.

Earth was being tossed down on to the coffin lid, a final futile wake-up call. The Farmer started walking away, hands clasped behind his back.

'As long as I live,' he said, 'I'll never understand it.'

'You never know your luck,' said Rebus.

3

He stood atop Salisbury Crags. There was a fierce wind blowing, and he turned up the collar of his coat. He'd been home to change out of his funeral clothes and should have been heading back for the station – he could see St Leonard's from here – but something had made him take this detour.

Behind and above him, a few hardy souls had achieved the summit of Arthur's Seat. Their reward: the panoramic view, plus ears that would sting for hours. With his fear of heights, Rebus didn't get too close to the edge. The landscape was extraordinary. It was as though God had slapped his hand down on to Holyrood Park, flattening part of it but leaving this sheer face of rock, a reminder of the city's origins.

Jim Margolies had jumped from here. Or a sudden gust had taken him: that was the less plausible, but more easily digested alternative. His widow had stated her belief that he'd been 'walking, just walking', and had lost his footing in the dark. But this raised unanswerable questions. What would take him from his bed in the middle of the night? If he had worries, why did he need to think them out at the top of Salisbury Crags, several miles from his home? He lived in The Grange, in what had been his wife's parents' house. It was raining that night, yet he didn't take the car. Would a desperate man notice he was getting soaked . . . ?

Looking down, Rebus saw the site of the old brewery, where they were going to build the new Scottish parliament. The first in three hundred years, and sited next to a theme park. Nearby stood the Greenfield housing scheme, a compact maze of high-rise blocks and sheltered accommodation. He wondered why the Crags should be so much more impressive than the man-made ingenuity of high-rises, then reached into his pocket for a folded piece of paper. He checked an address, looked back down on to Greenfield, and knew he had one more detour to make.

Greenfield's flat-roofed tower blocks had been built in the mid-1960s and were showing their age. Dark stains bloomed on the discoloured harling. Overflow pipes dripped water on to cracked paving slabs. Rotting wood was flaking from the window surrounds. The wall of one ground-floor flat, its windows boarded up, had been painted to identify the one-time tenant as 'Junky Scum'.

No council planner had ever lived here. No director of housing or community architect. All the council had done was move in problem tenants and tell everyone central heating was on its way. The estate had been built on the flat bottom of a bowl of land, so that Salisbury Crags loomed monstrously over the whole. Rebus rechecked the address on the paper. He'd had dealings in Greenfield before. It was far from the worst of the city's estates, but still had its troubles. It was early afternoon now, and the streets were quiet. Someone had left a bicycle, missing its front wheel, in the middle of the road. Further along stood a pair of shopping trolleys, nose to nose as though deep in local gossip. In the midst of the six eleven-storey blocks stood four neat rows of terraced bungalows, complete with pocket-handkerchief gardens and low wooden fences. Net curtains covered most of the windows, and above each door a burglar alarm had been secured to the wall.

Part of the tarmac arena between the tower blocks had been given over to a play area. One boy was pulling another along on a sledge, imagining snow as the runners scraped across the ground. Rebus called out the words 'Cragside Court' and the boy on the sledge waved in the direction of one of the blocks. When Rebus got up close to it, he saw that a sign on the wall identifying the building had been defaced so that 'Cragside' read 'Crap-site'. A window on the second floor swung open.

'You needn't bother,' a woman's voice boomed. 'He's not here.'

Rebus stood back and angled his head upwards.

'Who is it I'm supposed to be looking for?'

'Trying to be smart?'

'No, I just didn't know there was a clairvoyant on the premises. Is it your husband or your boyfriend I'm after?'

The woman stared down at him, made up her mind that she'd spoken too soon. 'Never mind,' she said, pulling her head back in and closing the window.

There was an intercom system, but only the numbers of flats, no names. He pulled at the door; it was unlocked anyway. He waited a couple of minutes for the lift to come, then let it shudder its way slowly up to the fifth floor. A walkway, open to the elements, led him past the front doors of half a dozen flats until he was standing outside 5/14 Cragside Court. There was a window, but curtained with what looked like a frayed blue bedsheet. The door showed signs of abuse: failed break-ins maybe, or just people kicking at it because there was no bell or knocker. No nameplate, but that didn't matter. Rebus knew who lived here.

Darren Rough.

The address was new to Rebus. When he'd helped build the case against Rough four years before, Rough had been living in a flat on Buccleuch Street. Now he was back in Edinburgh, and Rebus was keen for him to know just how welcome he was. Besides, he had a couple of questions for Darren Rough, questions about Jim Margolies . . .

The only problem was, he got the feeling the flat was empty. He tried one half-hearted thump at both door and window. When there was no response, he leaned down to peer through the letterbox, but found it had been blocked from inside. Either Rough didn't want anyone looking in, or else he'd been getting unwelcome deliveries. Straightening up, Rebus turned and rested his arms on the balcony railing. He found himself staring straight down on to the kids' playground. Kids: an estate like Greenfield would be full of kids. He turned back to study Rough's abode. No graffiti on walls or door, nothing to identify the tenant as 'Pervo Scum'. Down at ground level, the sledge had taken a corner too fast, throwing off its rider. A window below Rebus opened noisily.

'I saw you, Billy Horman! You did that on purpose!' The same woman, her words aimed at the boy who'd been pulling the sledge.

'Never did!' he yelled back.

'You fucking did! I'll murder you.' Then, tone changing: 'Are you all right, Jamie? I've told you before about playing with that wee bastard. Now get in here!'

The injured boy rubbed a hand beneath his nose – as close as he was going to get to defiance – then made his way towards the tower block, glancing back at his friend. Their shared look lasted only a second or two, but it managed to convey that they were still friends, that the adult world could never break that bond.

Rebus watched the sledge-puller, Billy Horman, shuffle away, then walked down three floors. The woman's flat was easy to find. He could hear her shouting from thirty yards away. He wondered if she constituted a problem tenant; got the feeling few would dare to complain to her face . . .

The door was solid, recently painted dark blue, and boasting a spy-hole. Net curtains at the window. They twitched as the woman checked who her caller was. When she opened the door, her son darted back out and along the walkway.

'Just going to the shop, Mum!'

'Come back here, you!'

But he was pretending not to have heard; disappeared around a corner.

'Give me the strength to wring his neck,' she said.

'I'm sure you love him really.'

She stared hard at him. 'Do we have any business?'

'You never answered my question: husband or boyfriend?'

She folded her arms. 'Eldest son, if you must know.'

'And you thought I was here to see him?'

'You're the police, aren't you?' She snorted when he said nothing.

'Should I know him then?'

'Calumn Brady,' she said.

'You're Cal's mum?' Rebus nodded slowly. He knew Cal Brady by reputation: regal chancer. He'd heard of Cal's mother, too.

She stood about five feet eight in her sheepskin slippers. Heavily built, with thick arms and wrists, her face had decided long ago that make-up wasn't going to cure anything. Her hair, thick and platinum-coloured, brown at the roots, fell from a centre parting. She was dressed in regulation satin-look shell suit, blue with a silver stripe up the arms and legs.

'You're not here for Cal then?' she said.

Rebus shook his head. 'Not unless you think he's done something.'

'So what *are* you doing here?'

'Ever have any dealings with one of your neighbours, youngish lad called Darren Rough?'

'Which flat's he in?' Rebus didn't answer. 'We get a lot of coming and going. Social Work stuff them in here for a couple of weeks. Christ knows what happens to them, they go AWOL or get shifted.' She sniffed. 'What's he look like?'

'Doesn't matter,' Rebus said. Jamie was back down in the playground, no sign of his friend. He ran in circles, pulling the sledge. Rebus got the idea he could run like that all day.

'Jamie's not in school today?' he asked, turning back towards the door.

'None of your bloody business,' Mrs Brady said, closing it in his face.

4

Back at St Leonard's police station, Rebus looked up Calumn Brady on the computer. At age seventeen, Cal already had impressive form: assault, shoplifting, drunk and disorderly. There was no sign as yet that Jamie was following in his footsteps, but the mother, Vanessa Brady, known as 'Van', had been in trouble. Disputes with neighbours had become violent, and she'd been caught giving Cal a false alibi for one of his assault charges. No mention anywhere of a husband. Whistling 'We Are Family', Rebus went to ask the desk sergeant if he knew who the community officer was for Greenfield.

'Tom Jackson,' he was told. 'And I know where he is, because I saw him not two minutes ago.'

Tom Jackson was in the car park at the back of the station, finishing a cigarette. Rebus joined him, lit one for himself and made the offer. Jackson shook his head.

'Got to pace myself, sir,' he said.

Jackson was in his mid-forties, barrel-chested and silver-haired with matching moustache. His eyes were dark, so that he always looked sceptical. He saw this as a decided bonus, since all he had to do was keep quiet and suspects would offer up more than they wanted to, just to appease that look.

'I hear you're still working Greenfield, Tom.'

'For my sins.' Jackson flicked ash from his cigarette, then brushed a few flecks from his uniform. 'I was due a transfer in January.'

'What happened?'

'The locals needed a Santa for their Christmas do. They

27

have one every year at the church. Underprivileged kids. They asked muggins here.'

'And?'

'And I did it. Some of those kids . . . poor wee bastards. Almost had me in tears.' The memory stopped him for a moment. 'Some of the locals came up afterwards, started whispering.' He smiled. 'It was like the confessional. See, the only way they could think to thank me was to furnish a few tip-offs.'

Rebus smiled. 'Shopping their neighbours.'

'As a result of which, my clear-up rate got a sudden lift. Bugger is, they've decided to keep me there, seeing how I'm suddenly so clever.'

'A victim of your own success, Tom.' Rebus inhaled, holding the smoke as he examined the tip of his cigarette. Exhaling, he shook his head. 'Christ, I love smoking.'

'Not me. Interviewing some kid, warning him off drugs, and all the time I'm gasping for a draw.' He shook his head. 'Wish I could give it up.'

'Have you tried patches?'

'No good, they kept slipping off my eye.'

They shared a laugh at that.

'I'm assuming you'll get round to it eventually,' Jackson said.

'What, trying a patch?'

'No, telling me what it is you're after.'

'Am I that transparent?'

'Maybe it's just my finely honed intuition.'

Rebus flicked ash into the breeze. 'I was out at Greenfield earlier. You know a guy called Darren Rough?'

'Can't say I do.'

'I had a run-in with him at the zoo.'

Jackson nodded, stubbed out his cigarette. 'I heard about it. Paedophile, yes?'

'And living in Cragside Court.'

Jackson stared at Rebus. 'That I didn't know.'

'Neighbours don't seem to know either.'

'They'd murder him if they did.'

'Maybe someone could have a word . . .'

Jackson frowned. 'Christ, I don't know about that. They'd string him up.'

'Bit of an exaggeration, Tom. Run him out of town maybe.'

Jackson straightened his back. 'And that's what you want?'

'You really want a paedophile on your beat?'

Jackson thought about it. He brought out his pack of cigarettes and was reaching into it when he checked his watch: ciggie break over.

'Let me think on it.'

'Fair enough, Tom.' Rebus flicked his own cigarette on to the tarmac. 'I bumped into one of Rough's neighbours, Van Brady.'

Jackson winced. 'Don't get on the wrong side of that one.'

'You mean she has a *right* side?'

'Best seen when retreating.'

Back at his desk, Rebus put a call in to the council offices and was eventually put through to Darren Rough's social worker, a man called Andy Davies.

'Do you think it was a wise move?' Rebus asked.

'Care to give me some clue what you're talking about?'

'Convicted paedophile, council flat in Greenfield, nice view of the children's playground.'

'What's he done?' Sounding suddenly tired.

'Nothing I can pin him for.' Rebus paused. 'Not yet. I'm phoning while there's still time.'

'Time for what?'

'To move him.'

'Move him where exactly?'

'How about Bass Rock?'

'Or a cage at the zoo maybe?'

Rebus sat back in his chair. 'He's told you.'

'Of course he's told me. I'm his social worker.'

'He was taking photos of kids.'

'It's all been explained to Chief Superintendent Watson.'

Rebus looked around the office. 'Not to my satisfaction, Mr Davies.'

'Then I suggest you take it up with your superior, Inspector.' No hiding the irritation in the voice.

'So you're going to do nothing?'

'It was your lot wanted him here in the first place!'

Silence on the line, then Rebus: 'What did you just say?'

'Look, I've nothing to add. Take it up with your Chief Superintendent. OK?'

The connection was broken. Rebus tried Watson's office, but his secretary said he was out. He chewed on his pen, wishing plastic had a nicotine content.

It was your lot wanted him here.

DC Siobhan Clarke was at her desk, busy on the phone. He noticed that on the wall behind her was pinned up a postcard of a sea-lion. Walking up to it, he saw someone had added a speech balloon, issuing from the creature's mouth: 'I'll have a Rebus supper, thanks.'

'Ho ho,' he said, pulling the card from the wall. Clarke had finished her call.

'Don't look at me,' she said.

He scanned the room. DC Grant Hood reading a tabloid, DS George Silvers frowning at his computer screen. Then DI Bill Pryde walked into the office, and Rebus knew he had his man. Curly fair hair, ginger moustache: a face just made for mischief. Rebus waved the card at him and watched Pryde's face take on a look of false wounded innocence. As Rebus walked towards him, a phone began sounding.

'That's yours,' Pryde said, retreating. On his way to the phone, Rebus tossed the card into a bin.

'DI Rebus,' he said.

'Oh, hello. You probably won't remember me.' A short

laugh on the line. 'That used to be a bit of a joke at school.'

Rebus, immune to every kind of crank, rested against the edge of the desk. 'Why's that?' he asked, wondering what kind of punch-line he was walking into.

'Because it's my name: Mee.' The caller spelled it for him. 'Brian Mee.'

Inside Rebus's head, a fuzzy photograph began to develop – mouthful of prominent teeth; freckled nose and cheeks; kitchen-stool haircut.

'Barney Mee?' he said.

More laughter on the line. 'I never knew why everyone called me that.'

Rebus could have told him: after Barney Rubble in *The Flintstones*. He could have added: because you were a dense wee bastard. Instead, he asked Mee what he could do for him.

'Well, Janice and me, we thought . . . well, it was my mum's idea actually. She knew your dad. Both my parents knew him, only my dad passed away, like. They all drank at the Goth.'

'Are you still in Bowhill?'

'Never quite escaped. I work in Glenrothes though.'

The photo had become clearer: decent footballer, bit of a terrier, the hair reddish-brown. Dragging his satchel along the ground until the stitching burst. Always with some huge hard sweet in his mouth, crunching down on it, nose running.

'So what can I do for you, Brian?'

'It was my mum's idea. She remembered you were in the police in Edinburgh, thought maybe you could help.'

'With what?'

'It's our son. Mine and Janice's. He's called Damon.'

'What's he done?'

'He's vanished.'

'Run away?'

31

'More like a puff of smoke. He was in this club with his pals, see—'

'Have you tried calling the police?' Rebus caught himself. 'I mean Fife Constabulary.'

'Thing is, the club's in Edinburgh. Police there say they looked into it, asked a few questions. See, Damon's nineteen. They say that means he's got a right to bugger off if he wants.'

'They've got a point, Brian. People run away all the time. Girl trouble maybe.'

'He was engaged.'

'Maybe he got scared.'

'Helen's a lovely girl. Never a raised voice between them.'

'Did he leave a note?'

'I went through this with the police. No note, and he didn't take any clothes or anything.'

'You think something's happened to him?'

'We just want to know he's all right . . .' The voice fell away. 'My mum always speaks well of your dad. He's remembered in this town.'

And buried there, too, Rebus thought. He picked up his pen. 'Give me a few details, Brian, and I'll see what I can do.'

A little later, Rebus visited Grant Hood's desk and retrieved the discarded newspaper from the bin. Turning the pages, he found the editorial section. At the bottom, in bold script, were the words 'Do you have a story for us? Call the newsroom day or night.' They'd printed the telephone number. Rebus jotted it into his notebook.

5

The silent dance resumed. Couples writhed and shuffled, threw back their heads or ran hands through their hair, eyes seeking out future partners or past loves to make jealous. The video monitor gave a greasy look to everything.

No sound, just pictures, the tape cutting from dancefloor to main bar to second bar to toilet hallway. Then the entrance foyer, exterior front and back. Exterior back was a puddled alley boasting rubbish bins and a Merc belonging to the club's owner. The club was called Gaitano's, nobody knew why. Some of the clientele had come up with the nickname 'Guiser's', and that was the name by which Rebus knew it.

It was on Rose Street, started to get busy around ten thirty each evening. There'd been a stabbing in the back alley the previous summer, the owner complaining of blood on his Merc.

Rebus was seated in a small uncomfortable chair in a small dimly lit room. In the other chair, hand on the video's remote, sat DC Phyllida Hawes.

'Here we go again,' she said. Rebus leaned forward a little. The view jumped from back alley to dancefloor. 'Any second.' Another cut: main bar, punters queuing three deep. She froze the picture. It wasn't so much black and white as sepia, the colour of dead photographs. Interior light, she'd explained earlier. She moved the action along one frame at a time as Rebus moved in on the screen, bending so one knee touched the floor. His finger touched a face.

'That's him,' she agreed.

On the desk was a slim file. Rebus had taken from it a photograph, which he now held to the screen.

'All right,' he said. 'Forward at half-speed.'

The security camera stayed with the main bar for another ten seconds, then switched to second bar and all points on the compass. When it returned to the main bar, the crush of drinkers seemed not to have moved. She froze the tape again.

'He's not there,' Rebus said.

'No chance he got served. The two ahead of him are still waiting.'

Rebus nodded. 'He should be there.' He touched the screen again.

'Next to the blonde,' Hawes said.

Yes, the blonde: spun-silver hair, dark eyes and lips. While those around her were intent on catching the eyes of the bar staff, she was looking off to one side. There were no sleeves to her dress.

Twenty seconds of footage from the foyer showed a steady stream entering the club, but no one leaving.

'I went through the whole tape,' Hawes said. 'Believe me, he's not on it.'

'So what happened to him?'

'Easy, he walked out, only the cameras didn't pick him up.'

'And left his pals gasping?'

Rebus studied the file again. Damon Mee had been out with two friends, a night in the big city. It had been Damon's shout – two lagers and a Coke, this last for the designated driver. They'd waited for him, then gone looking. Initial reaction: he'd scored and slunk off without telling them. Maybe she'd been a dinosaur, not something to brag about. But then he hadn't turned up at home, and his parents had started asking questions, questions no one could answer.

Simple truth: Damon Mee had, as the timer on the

camera footage showed, vanished from the world between 11.44 and 11.45 p.m. the previous Friday night.

Hawes switched off the machine. She was tall and thin and knew her job; hadn't liked Rebus appearing at Gayfield cop shop like this; hadn't liked the implication.

'There's no hint of foul play,' she said defensively. 'Quarter of a million MisPers every year, most turn up again in their own sweet time.'

'Look,' Rebus assured her, 'I'm doing this for an old friend, that's all. He just wants to know we've done all we can.'

'What's to do?'

Good question, and one Rebus was unable to answer right that minute. Instead, he brushed dust from the knees of his trousers and asked if he could look at the video one last time.

'And something else,' he said. 'Any chance we can get a print-out?'

'A print-out?'

'A photo of the crush at the bar.'

'I'm not sure. It's not going to be much use though, is it? And we've decent photos of Damon as it is.'

'It's not him I'm interested in,' Rebus said as the tape began to play. 'It's the blonde who watched him leave.'

That evening, he drove north out of Edinburgh, paid his toll at the Forth Road Bridge, and crossed into Fife. The place liked to call itself 'the Kingdom' and there were those who would agree that it was another country, a place with its own linguistic and cultural currency. For such a small place, it seemed almost endlessly complex, had seemed that way to Rebus even when he'd been growing up there. To outsiders the place meant coastal scenery and St Andrews, or just a stretch of motorway between Edinburgh and Dundee, but the west central Fife of Rebus's childhood had been very different, ruled by coal mines and linoleum, dockyard and chemical plant, an

35

industrial landscape shaped by basic needs and producing people who were wary and inward-looking, with the blackest humour you'd ever find.

They'd built new roads since Rebus's last visit, and knocked down a few more landmarks, but the place didn't feel so very different from thirty-odd years before. It wasn't such a great span of time after all, except in human terms, and maybe not even then. Entering Cardenden – Bowhill had disappeared from road-signs in the 1960s, even if locals still knew it as a village distinct from its neighbour – Rebus slowed to see if the memories would turn out sweet or sour. Then he caught sight of a Chinese takeaway and thought: both, of course.

Brian and Janice Mee's house was easy enough to find: they were standing by the gate waiting for him. Rebus had been born in a pre-fab but brought up in a terrace much like this one. Brian Mee practically opened the car door for him, and was trying to shake his hand while Rebus was still undoing his seat-belt.

'Let the man catch his breath!' his wife snapped. She was still standing by the gate, arms folded. 'How have you been, Johnny?'

And Rebus realised that Brian had married Janice Playfair, the only girl in his long and trouble-strewn life who'd ever managed to knock John Rebus unconscious.

The narrow low-ceilinged room was full to bursting – not just Rebus, Brian and Janice, but Brian's mother and Mr and Mrs Playfair, plus a billowing three-piece suite and assorted tables and units. Introductions had to be made and Rebus guided to 'the seat by the fire'. The room was overheated. A pot of tea was produced, and on the table by Rebus's armchair sat enough slices of cake to feed a football crowd.

'He's a brainy one,' Janice's mother said, handing Rebus a framed photograph of Damon Mee. 'Plenty of certificates from school. Works hard. Saving to get married.'

The photo showed a smiling imp, not long out of school.

'We gave the most recent pictures to the police,' Janice explained. Rebus nodded: he'd seen them in the file. All the same, when a packet of holiday snaps was handed to him, he went through them slowly: it saved having to look at the expectant faces. He felt like a doctor, expected to produce both immediate diagnosis and remedy. The photos showed a face more careworn than in the framed print. The impish smile remained, but noticeably older: some effort had gone into it. There was something behind the eyes, disenchantment maybe. Damon's parents were in a few of the photos.

'We all went together,' Brian explained. 'The whole family.'

Beaches, a big white hotel, poolside games. 'Where is it?'

'Lanzarote,' Janice said, handing him his tea. 'Do you still take sugar?'

'Haven't done for years,' Rebus said. In a couple of the pictures she was wearing her bikini: good body for her age, or any age come to that. He tried not to linger.

'Can I take a couple of the close-ups?' he asked. Janice looked at him. 'Of Damon.' She nodded and he put the other photos back in the packet.

'We're really grateful,' someone said: Janice's mum? Brian's? Rebus couldn't tell.

'You said his girlfriend's called Helen?'

Brian nodded. He'd lost some hair and put on weight, his face jowly. There was a row of cheap trophies above the mantelpiece: darts and pool, pub sports. He reckoned Brian kept in training most nights. Janice . . . Janice looked the same as ever. No, that wasn't strictly true. She had wisps of grey in her hair. But all the same, talking to her was like stepping back into a previous age.

'Does Helen live locally?' he asked.

'Practically round the corner.'

'I'd like to talk to her.'

'I'll give her a bell.' Brian got to his feet, left the room.

'Where does Damon work?' Rebus asked, for want of a better question.

'Same place as his dad,' Janice said, lighting a cigarette. Rebus raised an eyebrow: at school, she'd been anti-tobacco. She saw his look and smiled.

'He got a job in packaging,' her dad said. He seemed frail, chin quivering. Rebus wondered if he'd had a stroke. One side of his face looked slack. 'He's learning the ropes. It'll be management soon.'

Working-class nepotism, jobs handed down from father to son. Rebus was surprised it still existed.

'Lucky to find any work at all around here,' Mrs Playfair added.

'Are things bad?'

She made a tutting sound, dismissing the question.

'Remember the old pit, John?' Janice asked.

Of course he remembered it, and the bing and the wilderness around it. Long walks on summer evenings, stopping for kisses that seemed to last hours. Wisps of coal-smoke rising from the bing, the dross within still smouldering.

'It's all been levelled now, turned into parkland. They're talking about building a mining museum.'

Mrs Playfair tutted again. 'All it'll do is remind us what we once had.'

'Job creation,' her daughter said.

'They used to call Cowdenbeath the Chicago of Fife,' Brian Mee's mother added.

'The Blue Brazil,' Mr Playfair said, giving a croaking laugh. He meant Cowdenbeath football club, the nick-name a self-imposed piece of irony. They called themselves the Blue Brazil because they were rubbish.

'Helen'll be here in a minute,' Brian said, coming back in.

'Are you not eating any cake, Inspector?' added Mrs Playfair.

On the drive back to Edinburgh, Rebus thought back to his chat with Helen Cousins. She hadn't been able to add much to Rebus's picture of Damon, and hadn't been there the night he'd vanished. She'd been out with friends. It was a Friday ritual: Damon went out with 'the lads', she went out with 'the girls'. He'd spoken with one of Damon's companions; the other had been out. He'd learned nothing helpful.

As he crossed the Forth Road Bridge, he thought about the symbol Fife had decided upon for its 'Welcome to Fife' signs: the Forth Rail Bridge. Not an identity so much as an admission of failure, recognition that Fife was for many people a conduit or mere adjunct to Edinburgh.

Helen Cousins had worn black eyeliner and crimson lipstick and would never be pretty. Acne had carved cruel lines into her sallow face. Her hair had been dyed black and fell to a gelled fringe. When asked what she thought had happened to Damon, she'd just shrugged and folded her arms, crossing one leg over the other in a refusal to take any blame he might be trying to foist on her.

Joey, who'd been at Guiser's that night, had been similarly reticent.

'Just a night out,' he'd said. 'Nothing unusual about it.'

'And nothing different about Damon?'

'Like what?'

'I don't know. Was he maybe preoccupied? Did he look nervous?'

A shrug: the apparent extent of Joey's concern for his friend . . .

Rebus knew he was headed home, meaning Patience's flat. But as he stop-started between the lights on Queensferry Road, he thought maybe he'd go to the Oxford Bar. Not for a drink, maybe just for a cola or a coffee, and some company. He'd drink a soft drink and listen to the gossip.

So he drove past Oxford Terrace, stopped at the foot of Castle Street. Walked up the slope towards the Ox. Edinburgh Castle was just over the rise. The best view you could get of it was from a burger place on Princes Street. He pushed open the door to the pub, feeling heat and smelling smoke. He didn't need cigarettes in the Ox: breathing was like killing a ten-pack. Coke or a coffee, he was having trouble making up his mind. Harry was on duty tonight. He lifted an empty pint glass and waved it in Rebus's direction.

'Aye, OK then,' Rebus said, like it was the easiest decision he'd ever made.

He got in at quarter to midnight. Patience was watching TV. She didn't say much about his drinking these days: silence every bit as effective as lectures had ever been. But she wrinkled her nose at the cigarette smoke clinging to his clothes, so he dumped them in the washing basket and took a shower. She was in bed by the time he got out. There was a fresh glass of water his side of the bed.

'Thanks,' he said, draining it with two paracetamol.

'How was your day?' she asked: automatic question, automatic response.

'Not so bad. Yours?'

A sleepy grunt in reply. She had her eyes closed. There were things Rebus wanted to say, questions he'd like to ask. What are we doing here? Do you want me out? He thought maybe Patience had the same questions or similar. Somehow they never got asked; fear of the answers, perhaps, and what those answers would mean. Who in the world relished failure?

'I went to a funeral,' he told her. 'A guy I knew.'

'I'm sorry.'

'I didn't really know him that well.'

'What did he die of?' Head still on the pillow, eyes closed.

'A fall.'

'Accident?'

She was drifting away from him. He spoke anyway. 'His widow, she'd dressed their daughter to look like an angel. One way of dealing with it, I suppose.' He paused, listening to Patience's breathing grow regular. 'I went to Fife tonight, back to the old town. Friends I haven't seen in years.' He looked at her. 'An old flame, someone I could have ended up married to.' Touched her hair. 'No Edinburgh, no Dr Patience Aitken.' His eyes turned towards the window. No Sammy . . . maybe no job in the police either.

No ghosts.

When she was asleep, he went back through to the living room and plugged headphones into the hi-fi. He'd added a record deck to her CD system. In a bag under the bookshelf he found his last purchases from Backbeat Records: Light of Darkness and Writing on the Wall, two Scottish bands he vaguely remembered from times past. As he sat to listen, he wondered why it was he was only ever happy on rewind. He thought back to times when he'd been happy, realising that at the time he hadn't felt happy: it was only in retrospect that it dawned on him. Why was that? He sat back with eyes closed. Incredible String Band: 'The Half-Remarkable Question'. Segue to Brian Eno: 'Everything Merges with the Night'. He saw Janice Playfair the way she'd been the night she'd laid him out, the night that had changed everything. And he saw Alec Chisholm, who'd walked away from school one day and never been seen again. He didn't have Alec's face, just a vague outline and a way of standing, of composing himself. Alec the brainy one, the one who was going to go far.

Only nobody'd expected him to go the way he did.

Without opening his eyes, Rebus knew Jack Morton was seated in the chair across from him. Could Jack hear the music? He never spoke, so it was hard to know if sounds meant anything to him. He was waiting for the track called 'Bogeyman'; listening and waiting . . .

It was nearly dawn when, on her way back from the toilet, Patience removed the headphones from his sleeping form and threw a blanket over him.

6

There were three men in the room, all in uniform, all wanting to hit Cary Oakes. He could see it in their eyes, in the way they stood half-tensed, cheekbones working at wads of gum. He made a sudden movement, but only stretching his legs out, shifting his weight on the chair, arching his head back so it caught the full glare of the sun, streaming through the high window. Bathed in heat and light, he felt the smile stretch across his face. His mother had always told him, 'Your face *shines* when you smile, Cary.' Crazy old woman, even back then. She'd had one of those double sinks in the kitchen, with a mangle you could fix between them. Wash the clothes in one sink, then through the mangle into the other. He'd stuck the tips of his fingers against the rollers once, started cranking the handle until it hurt.

Three prison guards: that's what they reckoned Cary Oakes was worth. Three guards, and chains for his legs and arms.

'Hey, guys,' he said, pointing his chin at them. 'Take your best shot.'

'Can it, Oakes.'

Cary Oakes grinned again. He'd forced a reaction: of such small victories were his days made. The guard who'd spoken, the one with the tag identifying him as SAUNDERS, did tend towards the excitable. Oakes narrowed his eyes and imagined the moustached face pressed against a mangle, imagined the strength needed to force that face all the way through. Oakes rubbed his stomach; not so much as an ounce of flab there, despite the food they tried

43

to serve him. He stuck to vegetables and fruit, water and juices. Had to keep the brain in gear. A lot of the other prisoners, they'd slipped into neutral, engines revving but heading nowhere. A stretch of confinement could do that to you, make you start believing things that weren't true. Oakes kept up with events, had magazine and newspaper subscriptions, watched current affairs on TV and avoided everything else, except maybe a little sport. But even sport was a kind of novocaine. Instead of watching the screen, he watched the other faces, saw them heavy-lidded, no need to concentrate, like babies being spoon-fed contentment, bellies and brains filled to capacity with warmed-over gunk.

He started whistling a Beatles song: 'Good Day, Sunshine', wondering if any of the guards would know it. Potential for another reaction. But then the door opened and his attorney came in. His fifth lawyer in sixteen years, not a bad average, batting .300. This lawyer was young – mid-twenties – and wore blue blazers with cream slacks, a combination which made him look like a kid trying on his dad's clothes. The blazers had brass-effect buttons and intricate designs on the breast pocket.

'Ahoy, shipmate!' Oakes cried, not shifting in his chair.

His lawyer sat down opposite him at the table. Oakes put his hands behind his head, rattling the chains.

'Any chance of removing those from my client?' the lawyer asked.

'For your own protection, sir.' The stock response.

Oakes used both hands to scratch his shaved head. 'Know those divers and spacemen? Use weighted boots, necessary tool of the trade. I reckon when I lose these chains, I'm going to float up to the ceiling. I can make my living in freak shows: the human fly, see him scale the walls. Man, imagine the possibilities. I can float up to second-floor windows and watch all the ladies getting ready for bed.' He turned his head to the guards. 'Any of you guys married?'

The lawyer was ignoring this. He had his job to do, opening the briefcase and lifting out the paperwork. Wherever lawyers went, paper went with them. Lots of paper. Oakes tried not to look interested.

'Mr Oakes,' the lawyer said, 'it's just a matter of detail now.'

'I've always enjoyed detail.'

'Some papers that have to be signed by various officials.'

'See, guys,' Oakes called to the guards, 'I told you no prison could hold Cary Oakes! OK, so it's taken me fifteen years, but, hey, nobody's perfect.' He laughed, turning to his lawyer. 'So how long should all these . . . details take?'

'Days rather than weeks.'

Inside, Oakes's heart was pumping. His ears were hissing with the intensity of it, the swell of apprehension and anticipation. *Days* . . .

'But I haven't finished painting my cell. I want it left pretty for the next tenant.'

Finally the attorney smiled, and Oakes knew him in that instant: working his way up in Daddy's practice; reviled by his elders, mistrusted by his peers. Was he spying on them, reporting back to the old man? How could he prove himself? If he joined them for drinks on a Friday night, loosening his tie and mussing up his hair, they felt uncomfortable. If he kept his distance, he was a cold fish. And what about the father? The old man couldn't have anyone accusing him of nepotism, the boy had to learn the hard way. Give him the shitty-stick cases, the no-hopers, the ones that left you needing a shower and change of clothes. Make him prove himself. Long hours of thankless toil, a shining example to everyone else in the firm.

All this discerned from a single smile, the smile of a half-shy, self-conscious drone who dreamt of being King Bee, who perhaps even harboured little fantasies of patricide and succession.

'You'll be deported, of course,' the prince was saying now.

'What?'

'You were in this country illegally, Mr Oakes.'

'I've been here nearly half my life.'

'Nevertheless . . .'

Nevertheless . . . His mother's word. Every time he had an excuse prepared, some story to explain the situation, she'd listen in silence, then take a deep breath, and it was like he could see the word forming in the air that issued from her mouth. During his trial, he'd rehearsed little conversations with her.

'*Mother, I've been a good son, haven't I?*'

'*Nevertheless . . .*'

'*Nevertheless, I killed two people.*'

'*Really, Cary? You're sure it was only two . . . ?*'

He sat up in his chair. 'So let them deport me, I'll come straight back.'

'It won't be so easy. I can't see you securing a tourist visa this time, Mr Oakes.'

'I don't need one. You're behind the times.'

'Your name will be on record . . .'

'I'll walk across from Canada or Mexico.'

The lawyer shifted in his seat. He didn't like to hear this.

'I have to come back and see my pals,' nodding towards the guards. 'They'll miss me when I'm gone. And so will their wives.'

'Fuck you, slime.' Saunders again.

Oakes beamed at his lawyer. 'Isn't that nice? We have nicknames for each other.'

'I don't think any of this is very helpful, Mr Oakes.'

'Hey, I'm the model prisoner. That's the way it works, right? I learned a fast lesson: use the same system they used to put you where you are. Read up on the law, go back over everything, know the questions to ask, the objections that should have been made at the original trial. The lawyer they had representing me, I'll tell you, he

46

couldn't have presented a school prize, never mind my case.' He smiled again. 'You're better than him. You're going to be all right. Remember that next time your pop is chewing you out. Just say to yourself: I'm better than that, I'm going to be all right.' He winked. 'No charge for my time, son.'

Son: as if he was fifty rather than thirty-eight. As if the knowledge of the ages was his for the dispensing.

'So I get a free flight back to London?'

'I'm not sure.' The lawyer looked through his notes. 'You're from Lothian originally?' Pronouncing it *loathing*.

'As in Edinburgh, Scotland.'

'Well, you might end up back there.'

Cary Oakes rubbed at his chin. Edinburgh might do for a while. He had unfinished business in Edinburgh. Was going to leave it till the heat had died down, but nevertheless . . . He leaned forward over the table.

'How many murders did they pin on me?'

The lawyer blinked, sat there with palms flat on the table. 'Two,' he said at last.

'How many did they start with?'

'I believe it was five.'

'Six actually.' Oakes nodded slowly. 'But who's counting, eh?' A chuckle. 'They ever catch anyone for the others?'

The lawyer shook his head. There were beads of perspiration at his temples. He'd be making a detour home for a shower and fresh clothes.

Cary Oakes sat back again and angled his face into the sun, turning his head so every part felt the warmth. 'Two's not much of a tally, is it, in the scheme of things? You kill your old man, you'll only be one behind.'

He was still chuckling to himself as his lawyer was led out of the room.

7

Younger runaways tended to take the same few routes: by bus, train or hitching, and to London, Glasgow or Edinburgh. There were organisations who would keep an eye open for runaways, and even if they wouldn't always reveal their whereabouts to the anxious families, at least they could confirm that someone was alive and unharmed.

But a nineteen-year-old, someone with money to hand ... could be anywhere. No destination was too distant – his passport hadn't turned up. He took it with him to clubs as proof of age. Damon had a current account at the local bank, complete with cashcard, and an interest-bearing account with a building society in Kirkcaldy. The bank might be worth trying. Rebus picked up the telephone.

The manager at first insisted that he'd need something in writing, but relented when Rebus promised to fax him later. Rebus held while the manager went off to check, and had doodled half a village, complete with stream, parkland and pit-head, by the time the man came back.

'The most recent withdrawal was a cash machine in Edinburgh's West End. One hundred pounds on the fifteenth.'

The night Damon had gone to Gaitano's. A hundred seemed a lot to Rebus, even for a good night out.

'Nothing since then?'

'No.'

'How up to date is that?'

'Up to the close of play yesterday.'

'Could I ask you a favour, sir? I'd like tabs kept on that

48

account. Any new withdrawals, I'd like to know about them pronto.'

'I'd need that in writing, Inspector. And I'd probably also need the approval of my head office.'

'I'd appreciate it, Mr Brayne.'

'It's Bain,' the bank manager said coldly, putting down the phone.

Rebus called the building society and endured the same rigmarole before learning that Damon hadn't touched his account in more than a fortnight. He made one last call to Gayfield police station and asked for DC Hawes. She didn't sound too thrilled when he identified himself.

'What's the word on Gaitano's?' he asked.

'Everyone calls it Guiser's. Pretty choice establishment. Two stabbings last year, one in the club itself, one in the alley out back. Been quieter this year, which is probably down to a stricter door policy.'

'You mean bigger bouncers.'

'Front-of-house managers, if you please. Locals still complain about the noise at chucking-out time.'

'Who owns it?'

'Charles Mackenzie, nicknamed "Charmer".'

A couple of uniforms had talked to Mackenzie about Damon Mee, and he'd offered up the security tape which had languished in Gayfield ever since.

'Know how many MisPers there are every year?' Hawes said with a sigh.

'You told me.'

'Then you should know that if there's no suspicion of foul play, they're not exactly a white-hot priority. God knows there are times I've felt like doing a runner myself.'

Rebus thought of his night-time car-rides, long, directionless hours, just filling in the blank spaces of his life. 'Haven't we all?' he said.

'Look, I know you're doing this as a favour . . .'

'Yes?'

'But we've done all we can, haven't we?'

'Pretty much.'

'So what's the point?'

'I'm not sure.' Rebus could have told her that it had to do with the past, with some debt he felt he owed to Janice Playfair and Barney Mee – and to the memory of a friend he'd once had called Mitch. Somehow, he didn't think explaining it to an outsider would help. 'One last thing,' he asked instead. 'Did you get me a still of that woman?'

Gaitano's was little more than a solid black door with a neon sign above it, flanked either side by pubs and with a hi-fi shop across the road. There were valve amplifiers and an outsized record deck in the shop window. The deck had an outsized price-tag to match. One of the pubs was called The Headless Coachman. It had changed its name a couple of years back and was touting for tourists.

Rebus pushed the door-buzzer to Gaitano's and a woman opened it for him. She was the cleaner, and Rebus didn't envy her the job. Glasses had been cleared from the tables, but the place still looked like a wreck. There was an industrial vacuum cleaner on the carpet which encircled the dance floor. The floor was littered with cigarette stubs, cellophane, the occasional empty bottle. She'd finished cleaning the foyer, but was only halfway through the main dance area. There were mirrors on all the walls, and in the right light the place would look many times its actual size. In bare white light and with no music, no punters, it looked and felt desolate. There was a fug of stale sweat and beer in the air. Rebus saw a security camera in one corner and gave it a wave.

'Inspector Rebus.'

The man walking towards him across the dancefloor was about five feet four inches and as thin as a swizzle-stick. Rebus placed him in his mid-fifties. He wore a powder-blue suit and open-necked white shirt to show off his suntan and gold jewellery. His hair was silver and thinning, but as well-cut as the suit. They shook hands.

'Do you want a drink?'

He was leading Rebus towards the bar. Rebus looked at the row of optics.

'No thank you, sir.'

Charmer Mackenzie went behind the bar and poured himself a cola.

'Sure?' he said.

'Same as you're having,' Rebus said. He examined one of the bar stools for cigarette ash, then pulled himself up on to it. They faced one another across the bar.

'Not your normal tipple?' Mackenzie guessed. 'In my trade, you get a nose for these things.' And he tapped his nose for effect. 'The kid hasn't turned up then?'

'No, sir.'

'Sometimes they get a notion . . .' He shrugged, dismissing the foibles of a generation.

'I've got a photograph.' Rebus reached into his pocket, handed it over. 'The missing person is second row.'

Mackenzie nodded, not really interested.

'See just behind him?'

'Is that his doll?'

'Do you know her?'

Mackenzie snorted. 'Wish I did.'

'You haven't seen her before?'

'Picture's not the best, but I don't think so.'

'What time do the staff clock on?'

'Not till tonight.'

Rebus took the photo back, put it in his pocket.

'Any chance of getting my video back?' Mackenzie asked.

'Why?'

'Those things cost money. Overheads, that's what can cripple a business like this, Inspector.'

Rebus wondered how he'd merited the nickname 'Charmer'. He had all the charm of sandpaper. 'We wouldn't want that now, would we, Mr Mackenzie?' he said, getting to his feet.

*

51

Back at the office, he played the tape again, watching the blonde. The way her head was angled, strong jawline, mouth open slightly. Could she be saying something to Damon? A minute later, he was gone. Had she said she'd meet him somewhere? After he'd gone, she'd stayed at the bar, ordering a drink for herself. At dead on midnight, fifteen minutes after Damon had vanished, she'd left the nightclub. The final shot was from a camera mounted on the club's exterior wall. It showed her turning left along Rose Street, watched by a few drunks who were trying to get into Gaitano's.

Someone put their head round the door and told him he had a call. It was Mairie Henderson.

'Thanks for getting back to me,' he said.

'I take it you've a favour to ask?'

'Quite the reverse.'

'In that case, lunch is on me. I'm in the Engine Shed.'

'How convenient.' Rebus smiled: the Engine Shed was just behind St Leonard's. 'I'll be there in five minutes.'

'Make it two, or all the meatballs will have gone.'

Which was a joke of sorts, in that there was no meat in the meatballs. They were savoury balls of mushroom and chickpea with a tomato sauce. Though a one-minute walk from his office, Rebus had never eaten in the Engine Shed. Everything about it was too healthy, too nutritious. The drink of the day was organic apple juice, and smoking was strictly forbidden. He knew it was run by some sort of charity, and staffed by people who needed a job more than most. Typical of Mairie to choose it for a meeting. She was seated by a window, and Rebus joined her with his tray.

'You look well,' he said.

'It's all this salad.' She nodded towards her plate.

'Lifestyle still suit you?'

He meant her decision to quit the local daily paper and go freelance. They'd helped one another out on occasion, but Rebus was aware he owed her more brownie points

52

than she owed him. Her face was all clean, sharp lines, her eyes quick and dark. She'd restyled her hair to early Cilla Black. On the table beside her sat her notebook and cellphone.

'I get the occasional story picked up by the London papers. Then my old paper has to run its own version the next day.'

'That must annoy them.'

She beamed. 'Have to let them know what they're missing.'

'Well,' Rebus said, 'they've been missing a story that's right under their noses.' He pushed another forkful of food into his mouth, having to admit to himself that it wasn't at all bad. Looking around the other tables, he realised all the other diners were women. Some of them were tending to kids in high chairs, some were involved in quiet gossip. The restaurant wasn't big, and Rebus kept his voice down when he spoke.

'What story's that?' Mairie said.

Rebus's voice went lower. 'Paedophile living in Green-field.'

'Convicted?'

Rebus nodded. 'Served his time, now they've plonked him in a flat with a lovely view of a kids' play-park.'

'What's he been up to?'

'Nothing yet, nothing I can pin him for. Thing is, his neighbours don't know what's living next door to them.'

She was staring at him.

'What is it?' he said.

'Nothing.' She munched on more salad, chewing slowly. 'So where's the story?'

'Come on, Mairie . . .'

'I know what you want me to do. She pointed her fork at him. 'I know why you want it.'

'And?'

'And what has he done?'

'Christ, Mairie, do you know what the reoffending rate

53

is? It's not something you cure by slapping them in prison for a few years.'

'We've got to take a chance.'

'*We?* It's not us he'll be after.'

'All of us, we've all got to give them a chance.'

'Look, Mairie, it's a good story.'

'No, it's your way of getting to him. Does this all come back to Shiellion?'

'It's got bugger all to do with Shiellion.'

'I hear they've got you down to give evidence.' She stared at him again, but all he did was shrug. 'Only,' she went on, 'the knives are out as it is. If I do a story on a paedophile living in Greenfield of all places . . . it'd be incitement to murder.'

'Come on, Mairie . . .'

'Know what I think, John?' She put down her knife and fork. 'I think something's gone bad inside you.'

'Mairie, all I want . . .'

But she was on her feet, unhooking her coat from the back of the chair, collecting her phone, notebook, bag.

'I don't have much of an appetite any more,' she said.

'Time was, you'd have gnawed a story like this to the bone.'

She looked thoughtful for a moment. 'Maybe you're right,' she said. 'I hope to God you're not, but maybe you are.'

She walked the length of the restaurant's wooden floorboards on noisy heels. Rebus looked down at his lunch, at the untouched glass of juice. There was a pub not three minutes away. He pushed the plate away. He told himself Mairie was wrong: it had nothing to do with Shiellion. It was down to Jim Margolies, to the fact that Darren Rough had once made a complaint against him. Now Jim was dead, and Rebus wanted something back. Could he lay Jim's ghost to rest by tormenting Jim's tormentor? He reached into his pocket, found the sliver of paper there, the telephone number still perfectly legible.

I think something's gone bad inside you.

Who was he to disagree?

8

Four years before, Jim Margolies had been passing through St Leonard's, seconded to help with a staff shortfall. Three of the CID were down with flu, and another was in hospital for a minor op. Margolies, whose usual beat was Leith, came highly recommended, which made his new colleagues wary. Sometimes a recommendation was made so a station could offload dead weight elsewhere. But Margolies had proved himself quickly, handling a paedophile inquiry with dedication and tact. Two boys had been interfered with on The Meadows during, of all things, a children's festival. Darren Rough was already in police files. At twelve, he'd interfered with a neighbour's son, aged six at the time. He'd had counselling, and spent time in a children's home. At fifteen, he'd been caught peeping in at windows at the student residences in Pollock Halls. More counselling. Another mark in his police file.

The schoolboys' description of their attacker had taken police to the house Rough shared with his father. At nine in the morning, the father was drunk at the kitchen table. The mother had died the previous summer, which looked to be the last time the house had been cleaned. Soiled clothes and mouldy dishes were everywhere. It looked like nothing ever got thrown out: burst and rotting binbags stood inside the kitchen door; mail was piled high in a corner of the front hall, where damp had turned it into a single sodden mass. In Darren Rough's bedroom, Jim Margolies found clothing catalogues, crude penned additions made to the child models. There were collections of teen magazines under the bed, stories about – and pictures of – teenage girls and boys. And best of all from the police point of view, tucked under a corner of rotting carpet was Darren's 'Fantasy League', detailing his sexual proclivities and wish lists, with his Meadows exploit dated and signed.

For all of which the Procurator Fiscal was duly grateful. Darren Rough, by now twenty years old, was found guilty and sent to jail. A crate of beer was opened at St Leonard's, and Jim Margolies sat at the top of the table.

Rebus was there, too. He'd been part of the shift team interviewing Rough. He'd spent enough time with the prisoner to know that they were doing the right thing locking him up.

'Not that it ever helps with those bastards,' DI Alistair Flower had said. 'Reoffend as soon as they're out.'

'You're suggesting treatment replaces incarceration?' Margolies had asked.

'I'm suggesting we throw away the fucking key!' To which there had been cheers of agreement. Siobhan Clarke had been too canny to add her own view, but Rebus knew what she'd been thinking. Nothing was said of the complaint Rough had made. Bruising to his face and body: he'd told his solicitor Jim Margolies had given him a beating. No witnesses. Self-inflicted was the consensus. Rebus knew he'd felt like giving Rough a couple of slaps himself, but Margolies had no history of aggression against suspects.

There'd been an internal inquiry. Margolies had denied the accusation. A medical examination had been unable to determine whether Rough's bruises were self-inflicted. And that's where it had ended, with the faintest of blots on Margolies' record, the faintest doubt hanging over the rest of his career.

Rebus closed the case file and walked back to the vault with it.

Mairie: *I think something's gone bad inside you.*

Rough's social worker: *Your lot wanted him here.*

Rebus went to the Farmer's office, knocked on the door, entered when told.

'What can I do for you, John?'

'I had a word with Darren Rough's social worker, sir.'

The Farmer looked up from his paperwork. 'Any particular reason?'

'Just wanted to know why Rough had been given a flat with a view of a kiddies' playground.'

'I bet they loved you for that.' Not sounding disapproving. Social workers rated only a rung or two above paedophiles on the Farmer's moral stepladder.

'They told me that we wanted him here in the first place.'

The Farmer's face furrowed. 'Meaning what?'

'They suggested I ask you.'

'I haven't the faintest idea.' The Farmer sat back in his chair. '*We* wanted him here?'

'That's what they said.'

'Meaning Edinburgh?'

Rebus nodded. 'I've just been through the file on Rough. He was in a children's home for a while.'

'Not Shiellion?' The Farmer was looking interested.

Rebus shook his head. 'Callstone House, other side of the city. Just for a short spell. Both parents were alcoholic, neglecting him. There was nowhere else for him to go.'

'What happened?'

'Mother dried out, Rough went back home. Then, later on, she was diagnosed with liver disease, only nobody bothered moving Rough.'

'Why?'

'Because by that time, he was looking after his father.'

The Farmer looked towards his collection of family snaps. 'The way some people live . . .'

'Yes, sir,' Rebus agreed.

'So where's this leading?'

'Only this: Rough comes back to Edinburgh, apparently

58

because we want him here. Next thing, the officer who put him away ends up walking off Salisbury Crags.'

'You're not suggesting a connection?'

Rebus shrugged. 'Jim goes out to dinner at some friends' with his wife and kid. Drives home. Goes to bed. Next morning he's dead. I'm looking for reasons why Jim Margolies would take his own life. Thing is, I'm not finding any. And I'm also wondering who'd want Darren Rough back here and why.'

The Farmer was thoughtful. 'You want me to talk to Social Work?'

'They wouldn't talk to me.'

The Farmer reached for paper and a pen. 'Give me a name.'

'Andy Davies is Rough's social worker.'

The Farmer underlined the words. 'Leave it with me, John.'

'Yes, sir. Meantime, I'd like to take a look at Jim's suicide.'

'Mind if I ask why?'

'To see if it *does* tie in with Rough.' And maybe, he could have added, to satisfy his own curiosity.

The Farmer nodded. 'On the subject of Shiellion ... when do you give evidence?'

'Tomorrow, sir.'

'Got your spiel rehearsed?'

Rebus nodded.

'Remember the secret of a good court appearance, John.'

'Presentation, sir?'

The Farmer shook his head. 'Make sure you take plenty of reading matter with you.'

That evening, on his way home, he dropped in to see his daughter. Sammy had moved out of her first-floor colony flat into a newish ground-floor flat in a brick-built block off Newhaven Road.

59

'Downhill all the way to the coast,' she'd told her father. 'And you should see this thing with the brakes off.'

Referring to her wheelchair. Rebus had wanted to put his hand in his pocket for a motorised one, but she'd waved away the offer.

'I'm building up my muscles,' she'd said. 'And besides, I won't be in this thing for long.'

Perhaps not, but the road back to full mobility was proving hard going. She was receiving physio only twice a week, spending the rest of her time concentrating on home exercises. It was as if the accident had affected both her spine and her legs.

'My brain tells them what to do, but they don't always listen.'

There was a little wooden ramp at the main door to her block. A friend of a friend had constructed it for her. One of the bedrooms in the flat had been turned into a makeshift gym, a large mirror placed against one wall, and parallel bars taking up most of the available space. The doorways were narrow, but Sammy had proved adept at manoeuvring her wheelchair in and out without grazing knuckles or elbows.

When Rebus arrived, Ned Farlowe opened the door. He had a job subbing for one of the local freesheets. The hours were short, which gave him time to help Sammy with her workouts. The two men still didn't trust one another – did fathers ever really come to trust the men who were sleeping with their daughters? – but Ned seemed to be doing his damnedest for Sammy.

'Hi there,' he said. 'She's working out. Fancy a cuppa?'

'No thanks.'

'I'm just making some dinner.' Ned was already retreating to the long, narrow kitchen. Rebus knew he'd only be in the way.

'I'll just go and . . .'

'Fine.'

The smells from the kitchen were like those in the

Engine Shed: aromatic and vegetarian. Rebus walked down the hall, noting graze-marks on the walls where the wheelchair had connected. Music was coming from the spare bedroom, a disco beat. Sammy was lying on the floor in her black leotard and tights, trying to get her legs to do things. Her face was flushed with effort, hair matted to her forehead. When she saw her father, she rested her head against the floor.

'Turn that thing off, will you?' she said.

'I could just watch.'

But she shook her head. She didn't like him watching her at work. This was *her* fight, a private battle with her own body. Rebus switched off the tape machine.

'Recognise it?' she asked.

'Chic, "Le Freak". I went to enough bad discos in the seventies.'

'I can't imagine you in flares.'

'Distress flares.'

She had pushed herself up to sitting. He made just the one step forward to help her, knowing if he got any closer she'd shoo him away.

'How's your claim for disability going?'

She rolled her eyes, reached a hand out for a towel, starting wiping her face. 'I thought I knew all about bureaucracy. Thing is, I'm going to get better.'

'Sure.'

'So there are all kinds of complications. Plus my job at SWEEP's still open.'

'But the office is three floors up.' He sat on the floor beside her.

'I can work from home.'

'Really?'

'Only I don't want to. I don't want to become dependent on just these four walls.'

Rebus nodded. 'If there's anything you need . . .'

'Got any disco tapes?'

He smiled. 'I was more Rory Gallagher and John Martyn.'

'Well, nobody's perfect,' she said, wrapping the towel around her neck. 'Speaking of which, how's Patience?'

'She's fine.'

'I talk to her on the phone.'

'Oh?'

'She says I speak to her more than you do.'

'I don't think that's true.'

'Don't you?'

Rebus looked at his daughter. Had she always had this edge to her? Was it something to do with the accident?

'We get along fine,' he said.

'On whose terms?'

He stood up. 'I think your dinner's nearly ready. Want me to help you into the chair?'

'Ned likes to do it.'

He nodded slowly.

'You didn't answer my question.'

'I'm a policeman. Usually *we* ask the questions.'

She draped the towel over her head. 'Is it because of me?'

'What?'

'Ever since . . .' She looked down at her legs. 'It's like you blame yourself.'

'It was an accident.' He wasn't looking at her.

'It pushed the two of you back together. Do you see what I'm saying?'

'You're saying I'm busy blaming myself for your accident, while you're busy blaming yourself for Patience and me.' He glanced towards her. 'Does that just about sum it up?'

She smiled. 'Stay and have something to eat.'

'Don't you think I should head home to Patience?'

She lifted the towel from her eyes. 'Is that where you're going?'

'Where else?' He gave her a wave as he left the room.

9

Being down Newhaven Road, he stopped off at a couple of waterfront bars, a pint in one, nip of whisky in the other. Plenty of water in the whisky. It was dark, but he could see streetlights across the Forth in Fife. He thought of Janice and Brian Mee, who had never left their home town. He wondered how he'd have turned out if he'd stayed. He thought again of Alec Chisholm, the boy who had never been found. They'd scoured the countryside, sent men down into disused coal-shafts, dredged the river. A long hot summer, the Beatles and the Stones on the café jukebox, ice-cold bottles of Coke from the machine. Glass coffee cups topped with frothed milk. And questions about Alec, questions which showed that none of them had ever really known him, not deep down, not the way they thought they knew each other. And Alec's parents and grandparents, walking the streets late at night, stopping to ask strangers the same thing: have you seen our boy? Until the strangers became acquaintances, and they ran out of people to stop.

Now Damon Mee had stepped away from the world, or had been yanked out of it by some irresistible force. Rebus got back in his car and drove along the coast, came up on to the Forth Bridge, and headed into Fife. He tried telling himself he wasn't escaping – from Sammy's words and Patience and Edinburgh, from all the ghosts. From thoughts of paedophiles and suicide leaps.

When he got to Cardenden, he slowed the car, finally coming to a stop on the main drag. There seemed to be flyers in every shop window: Damon's picture and the word MISSING. There were more taped to lamp-posts and the bus shelter. Rebus started the car again and headed for Janice's house. But there was no one at home. A neighbour supplied the information Rebus needed, information which sent him straight back to Edinburgh and Rose Street, where he found Janice and Brian sticking more flyers on to lamp-posts and walls, pushing them through letterboxes. Photocopied sheets of A4. Holiday photo of Damon, and handwritten plea: DAMON MEE IS MISSING: HAVE YOU SEEN HIM? Physical description, including the clothes he'd been wearing, and the Mees' telephone number.

'We've covered the pubs,' Brian Mee said. He looked tired, eyes dark, face unshaven. The roll of sellotape he held was nearly finished. Janice leaned against a wall. Looking at the pair of them was far from like stepping into the past – present worries had scarred them.

'The one place they don't want to know,' Janice said, 'is that club.'

'Gaitano's?'

She nodded. 'Bouncers wouldn't let us in. Wouldn't even take flyers from us. I stuck one on the door but they took it down.' She was almost in tears. Rebus looked back along the street towards the flashing neon sign above Gaitano's.

'Come on,' he said. 'Let's try the magic word this time.'

And when he got to the door, he flashed his ID and said, 'Police.' The three were ushered inside while someone got on the phone to Charmer Mackenzie. Rebus looked to Janice and winked.

'Open Sesame,' he said. She was looking at him as if he'd done something wonderful.

'Mr Mackenzie's not here,' one of the bouncers said.

'So who's in charge?'

'Archie Frost. He's assistant manager.'

'Lead me to him.'

The bouncer looked unhappy. 'He's having a drink at the bar.'

'No problem,' Rebus said. 'We know our way.'

Bass music was pulsing, the club's interior dark and hot. Couples were hitting the dancefloor, others smoking furiously, knees pumping as they scanned the dimness for action. Rebus leaned towards Janice, so his mouth was an inch from her ear.

'Go round the tables, ask your questions.'

She nodded, passed the message along to Brian, who was looking uncomfortable with the noise.

Rebus walked towards the bar, walked through beams of indigo light. There were people waiting for drinks, but only two men actually drinking at the bar. Well, one of them was drinking. The other – who looked thirsty – was listening to what was being said to him.

'Sorry to butt in,' Rebus said.

The speaker turned to him. 'You will be in a minute.'

Maybe twenty or twenty-one, black hair pulled back into a ponytail. Stocky, wearing a suit with no lapels and a dazzling white T-shirt. Rebus pushed his warrant card into the face, identified himself.

'Been taking charm-school lessons from your boss?' he asked. Archie Frost said nothing, just finished his drink. 'I want a word, Mr Frost.'

'They don't look like polis,' Frost said, nodding towards where Janice and Brian Mee were working the room.

'That's because they're not. Their son went missing. Disappeared from here, in fact.'

'I know.'

'Well then, you'll know why I'm here.' Rebus brought out the photograph of the mystery blonde. 'Seen her before?'

Frost shook his head automatically.

'Take a closer look.'

Frost took the photo grudgingly, and angled it towards

the light. Then he shook his head and tried handing it back.

'What about your pal?'

'What about him?'

The 'pal' in question, the young man without a drink, had half-turned from them, so he was watching the dancefloor.

'He's not in here much,' Frost said.

'All the same,' Rebus persisted. So Frost stuck the photo in front of his friend's nose. An immediate shake of the head.

'I'm going to take this around your punters,' Rebus said, lifting the photo from Frost's hand, 'see if their memories are any better.' He wasn't looking at Frost; he was looking at his companion. 'Do I know you from somewhere, son? Your face looks familiar.'

The young man snorted, kept his eyes on the dancing.

'I'll let you get back to your business then,' Rebus said. He did a circuit of the room, following behind Janice and Brian. They'd left flyers on most of the tables. A couple had already been crumpled up. Rebus fixed the culprits with a stare. He wasn't faring any better with his own picture, but saw that ahead of him Janice and Brian had seated themselves at a table and were deep in conversation with two girls there. Eventually, he caught up with them. Janice looked up at him.

'They say they saw Damon,' she yelled, fighting the music.

'He was getting into a taxi,' one of the girls repeated for the newcomer's benefit.

'Where?' Rebus asked.

'Outside The Dome.'

'Other side of the road,' her friend corrected. They were wearing too much make-up, trying for a look they'd probably call 'sophisticated', trying to look older than their years. Soon enough, they'd be reversing the process. They wore incredibly short skirts. Rebus could see Brian trying not to stare.

66

'What time was this?'

'About quarter past twelve. We were late for a party.'

'You're sure about the date?' Rebus asked. Janice looked at him accusingly, not wanting this fragile bubble to burst.

One girl got a diary out of her handbag, tapped a page. 'That's the party.'

Rebus looked: it was the same date Damon had disappeared. 'How come you noticed him?'

'We'd seen him in here earlier.'

'Just standing at the bar,' her friend added. 'Not dancing or anything.'

A couple of young men, still in their day-job suits, had peeled off from an office party and were approaching, ready to ask for a dance. The girls tried to look disinterested, but a glower from Rebus sent the suitors back in the direction they'd come.

'We were after a taxi ourselves,' one girl explained. 'Saw them waiting across the road. Only they got lucky, we ended up walking.'

' "They"?'

'Him and his girl.'

Rebus looked to Janice, then handed over the photo.

'Yeah, that looks like her.'

'Blonde out of a bottle,' the other agreed.

Janice took the photo from them, looked at it herself.

'Who is she, John?'

Rebus shook his head, telling her he didn't know. Glancing towards the bar, he saw two things. One was that Archie Frost was watching him intently over the rim of a fresh glass. The other was that his non-drinking friend had gone.

'Maybe they've run off together,' one of the girls was saying, trying hard to be helpful. 'That would be romantic, wouldn't it?'

*

67

Janice and Brian hadn't eaten, so Rebus took them to an Indian on Hanover Street, where he explained the little he knew about the woman in the photograph. Janice kept the photo in one hand as she ate.

'It's a start, isn't it?' Brian said, pulling apart a nan bread.

Rebus nodded agreement.

'I mean,' Brian went on, 'we know now he left with someone. He's probably still with her.'

'Only he didn't go off with her,' Janice said. 'John's already told us, Damon left on his own.'

In fact, Rebus hadn't even gone that far. They only had the girls' word for it that Damon had left the club at all . . .

'Well,' Brian stumbled on, 'thing is, he wouldn't want his mates seeing them together, not when he was supposed to be engaged.'

'I can't believe it of Damon.' Janice's eyes were on Rebus. 'He loves Helen.'

Rebus nodded. 'But it happens, doesn't it?'

She gave a rueful smile. Brian saw a look passing between them, but chose to ignore it.

'Anyone want any more rice?' he asked instead, lifting the salver from its hotplate.

'We should be getting home,' his wife said. 'Damon might have tried phoning.' She was getting to her feet. Rebus gestured towards the photo, and she handed it back. It was smudged, creased at the corners. Brian was looking down at the food still on his plate.

'Brian . . .' Janice said. He sniffed and got up from his chair. 'Get the bill, will you?'

'This is on me,' Rebus said. 'They'll stick it on my tab.'

'Thanks again, John.' She held out her hand and he took it. It was long and slender. Rebus remembered holding it when they danced, remembered the way it would be warm and dry, unlike other girls' hands. Warm and dry, and his heart pounding in his chest. She'd been so slender at the waist, he'd felt he could encircle her with just his hands.

'Yes, thanks, Johnny.' Brian Mee laughed. 'You don't mind me calling you Johnny?'

'Why should I mind?' Rebus said, still looking into Janice's eyes. 'It's my name, isn't it?'

10

First thing, Rebus looked through the newspapers, but he didn't find anything to interest him.

He headed down to Leith police station, where Jim Margolies had been stationed. He'd told the Farmer he was looking for a connection between Rough's reappearance and Jim's death, but he wasn't particularly confident of finding one. Still, he really *did* want to know why Jim had done it, had done something Rebus had thought about doing more than once – taking the high walk. He was met in Leith by a wary Detective Inspector Bobby Hogan.

'I know I owe you a favour or two, John,' Hogan began. 'But do you mind telling me what it's all about? Margolies was a good man, we're missing him badly.'

They were walking through the station, making for CID. Hogan was a couple of years younger than Rebus, but had been on the force for longer. He could take retirement any time he wanted, but Rebus doubted the man would ever want it.

'I knew him, too,' Rebus was saying. 'I'm probably just asking myself the same question all of you have been asking.'

'You mean why?'

Rebus nodded. 'He was headed for the top, Bobby. Everyone knew it.'

'Maybe he got vertigo.' Hogan shook his head. 'The notes aren't going to tell you anything, John.'

They had stopped outside an interview room.

'I just need to see them, Bobby.'

Hogan stared at him, then nodded slowly. 'This makes us even, pal.'

Rebus touched him on the shoulder, walked into the room. The manila file was sitting on the otherwise empty desk. There were two chairs in the room.

'Thought you'd like some privacy,' Hogan said. 'Look, if anyone wonders . . .'

'My lips are sealed, Bobby.' Rebus was already sitting down. He examined the folder. 'This won't take long.'

Hogan fetched a cup of coffee, then left him to it. It took Rebus precisely twenty minutes to sift through everything: initial report and back-up, plus Jim Margolies' history. Twenty minutes wasn't long for a CV. Of course, there was little about his home life. Speculation was for after-work drinks, for cigarette breaks and coffee-machine meetings. The bare facts, set down between double margins, gave no clues at all. His father was a doctor, now retired. Comfortable upbringing. The sister who'd committed suicide in her teens . . . Rebus wondered if his sister's death had been at the back of Jim Margolies' mind all these years. There was no mention of Darren Rough, no mention of Margolies' short time at St Leonard's. His last night on earth, Jim had been out to dinner at some friends' house. Nothing out of the ordinary. But afterwards, in the middle of the night, he'd slipped from his bed, got dressed again, and gone walking in the rain. All the way to Holyrood Park . . .

'Anything?' Bobby Hogan asked.

'Not a sausage,' Rebus admitted, closing the file.

Walking in the rain . . . A long walk, from The Grange to Salisbury Crags. No one had come forward to say they'd seen him. Inquiries had been made, cabbies questioned. Perfunctory for the most part: you didn't want to linger over a suicide. Sometimes you could find out things that were better left undisturbed.

Rebus drove back into town, parked in the car park behind St Leonard's and went into the station. He knocked on Farmer Watson's door, obeyed the command to enter. Watson looked like the day had started badly.

'Where have you been?'

'I had a bit of business down at D Division, looking at Jim Margolies' file.' Rebus watched the Farmer pace behind his desk. He cradled a mug of coffee in both hands. 'Did you speak to Andy Davies, sir?'

'Who?'

'Andy Davies. Darren Rough's social worker.'

The Farmer nodded.

'And, sir?'

'And he told me I'd have to speak to his boss.'

'What did his boss say?'

The Farmer swung round. 'Christ, John, give me time, will you? I've got more to deal with than your little . . .' He exhaled, his shoulders slumping. Then he mumbled an apology.

'No problem, sir. I'll just . . .' Rebus headed for the door.

'Sit down,' the Farmer ordered. 'Now you're here, let's see if you can come up with any clever ideas.'

Rebus sat down. 'To do with what, sir?'

The Farmer sat too, then noticed that his mug was empty. He got up again to fill it from the pot, pouring for Rebus too. Rebus examined the dark liquid suspiciously. Over the years, the Farmer's coffee had definitely improved, but there were still days . . .

'To do with Cary Dennis Oakes.'

Rebus frowned. 'Should I know him?'

'If you don't, you soon will.' The Farmer tossed a newspaper in Rebus's direction. It fell to the floor. Rebus picked it up, saw that it was folded to a particular story, a story Rebus had missed because it wasn't the one he'd been looking for.

KILLER IS SENT 'HOME'.

'Cary Oakes,' Rebus read, 'convicted of two murders in Washington State, USA, will today board a flight back to the United Kingdom after serving a fifteen-year sentence

72

in a maximum-security prison in Walla Walla, Washington. It is believed that Oakes will make his way back to Edinburgh, where he lived for several years before going to the United States.'

There was a lot more. Oakes had flown to the States toting a rucksack and a tourist visa, and then had simply stayed put, taking a series of short-term jobs before embarking on a mugging and robbery spree which had climaxed with two killings, the victims clubbed and strangled to death.

Rebus put down the paper. 'Did you know?'

The Farmer slammed his fists down on the table. 'Of course I didn't know!'

'Shouldn't we have been told?'

'Think about it, John. You're a cop in Wallumballa or whatever it's called. You're sending this murderer back to *Scotland*. Who do you tell?'

Rebus nodded. 'Scotland Yard.'

'Not realising for one minute that Scotland Yard might actually be in another country altogether.'

'And the brainboxes in London decided not to pass the message on?'

'Their version is, they got their wires crossed, thought Oakes was only travelling as far as *their* patch. In fact, his ticket only goes as far as London.'

'So he's their problem.' But the Farmer was shaking his head. 'Don't tell me,' Rebus said, 'they've had a whip-round and added the fare to Edinburgh?'

'Bingo.'

'So when does he get here?'

'Later on today.'

'And what do we do?'

The Farmer stared at Rebus. He liked that *we*. A problem shared – even if with a thorn like Rebus – was a problem that could be dealt with. 'What would you suggest?'

'High-visibility surveillance, let him know we're watching. With any luck he'll get fed up and slope off somewhere else.'

The Farmer rubbed at his eyes. 'Take a look,' he said, sliding a folder across the desk. Rebus looked: sheets of fax paper, about twenty of them. 'The Met took pity on us at the last, sent what they'd been sent by the Americans.'

Rebus started reading. 'How come he's been released? I thought in America "life" meant till death.'

'Some technicality to do with the original trial. So arcane, even the American authorities aren't sure.'

'But they're letting him go?'

'A retrial would cost a fortune, plus there's the problem of tracing the original witnesses. They offered him a deal. If he gave it up, signed away the right to any retrial or compensation, they'd fly him home.'

'In the news story, "home" had inverted commas.'

'He hasn't spent much time in Edinburgh.'

'So why here?'

'His choice, apparently.'

'But why?'

'Maybe the fax will tell you.'

The message of the fax was clear and simple. It said Cary Oakes would kill again.

The psychologist had warned the authorities of this. The psychologist said, Cary Oakes has little concept of right and wrong. There were lots of psychological terms applied to this. The word 'psychopath' wasn't used much any more by the experts, but reading between the lines and the jargon, Rebus knew that was what they were dealing with. Anti-social tendencies ... deep-seated sense of betrayal ...

Oakes was thirty-eight years old. There was a grainy photo of him included with the file. His head had been shaved. The forehead was large and jutting, the face thin and angular. He had small eyes, like little black beads, and

74

a narrow mouth. He was described as above-average intelligence (self-taught in prison), interested in health and fitness. He'd made no friends during his incarceration, kept no pictures on his walls, and his only correspondence was with his team of lawyers (five different sets in total).

The Farmer was on the telephone, finding out Oakes's flight schedule, liaising with the Assistant Chief Constable at Fettes. When he'd finished, Rebus asked what the ACC thought.

'He thinks we should ca' canny.'

Rebus smiled: it was a typical response.

'He's right in a way,' the Farmer continued. 'The media will be all over this. We can't be seen to be harassing the man.'

'Maybe we'll get lucky and the reporters will scare him off.'

'Maybe.'

'It says here he was originally questioned about another four murders.'

The Farmer nodded, but seemed distracted. 'I don't need this,' he said at last, staring at his desk. The desk was a measure of the man: always carefully ordered, reflecting the room as a whole. No piles of paperwork, no mess or clutter, not so much as a single stray paperclip on the carpet.

'I've been at this job too long, John.' The Farmer sat back in his chair. 'You know the worst kind of officers?'

'You mean ones like me, sir?'

The Farmer smiled. 'Quite the opposite. I mean the ones who're biding their time till pension day. The clock-watchers. Recently, I've been turning into one. Another six months, that's what I was giving myself. Six more months till retirement.' He smiled again. 'And I wanted them quiet. I've been praying for them to be quiet.'

'We don't know this guy's going to be a problem. We've been here before, sir.'

The Farmer nodded: so they had. Men who'd done time

75

in Australia and Canada, and hardmen from Glasgow's Bar-L, all of them settling in Edinburgh, or just passing through. All of them with pasts carved into their faces. Even when they weren't a problem, they were still a problem. They might settle down, live quietly, but there were people who knew who they were, who knew the reputation they carried with them, something they'd never shake off. And eventually, after too many beers down the pub, one of these people would decide it was time to test himself, because what the hardman brought with him was a parameter, something you could measure yourself against. It was pure Hollywood: the retired gunslinger challenged by the punk kid. But to the police, all it was was trouble.

'Thing is, John, can we afford to play a waiting game? The ACC says we can have funding for partial surveillance.'

'How partial?'

'Two teams of two, maybe a fortnight.'

'That's big of him.'

'The man likes a nice tight budget.'

'Even when this guy might kill again?'

'Even murder has a budget these days, John.'

'I still don't get it.' Rebus picked up the fax. 'According to the notes, Oakes wasn't born here, doesn't have family here. He lived here for, what, four or five years. Went to the States at twenty, he's been almost half his life there. What's for him back here?'

The Farmer shrugged. 'A fresh start?'

A fresh start: Rebus was thinking of Darren Rough.

'There has to be more to it than that, sir,' Rebus said, picking up the file again. 'There has to be.'

The Farmer looked at his watch. 'Aren't you due in court?'

Rebus nodded agreement. 'Waste of time, sir. They won't call me.'

'All the same, Inspector . . .'

Rebus got up. 'Mind if I take this stuff?' Waving the sheets of fax paper. 'You told me I should take something to read.'

11

Rebus sat with other witnesses, other cases, all of them waiting to be called to give evidence. There were uniforms, attentive to their notebooks, and CID officers, arms folded, trying to be casual about the whole thing. Rebus knew a few faces, held quiet conversations. The members of the public sat there with hands clasped between knees, or with heads angled to the ceiling, bored out of their minds. Newspapers – already read, crosswords finished – lay strewn around the room. A couple of dog-eared paperbacks had attracted interest, but not for long. There was something about the atmosphere that sucked all the enthusiasm out of you. The lighting gave you a headache, and all the time you were wondering why you were here.

Answer: to serve justice.

And one of the court officers would wander in and, looking at a clipboard, call your name, and you'd creak your way to the court, where your numbed memory would be poked and prodded by strangers playing to a judge, jury, and public gallery.

This was justice.

There was one witness, seated directly across from Rebus, who kept bursting into tears. He was a young man, maybe mid-twenties, corpulent and with thin strands of black hair plastered to his head. He kept emptying his nose loudly into a stained handkerchief. One time, when he looked up, Rebus gave him a reassuring smile, but that only started him off again. Eventually, Rebus had to get out. He told one of the uniforms that he was going for a ciggie.

'I'll join you,' the uniform said.

Outside, they smoked furiously and in silence, watching the ebb and flow of people from the building. The High Court was tucked in behind St Giles' Cathedral, and occasionally tourists would wander towards it, wondering what it was. There were few signs about, just Roman numerals above the various heavy wooden doors. A guard on the car park would sometimes point them back towards the High Street. Though members of the public could enter the court building, tourists were actively discouraged. The Great Hall was enough of a cattle market as it was. But Rebus liked it: he liked the carved wooden ceiling, the statue of Sir Walter Scott, the huge stained-glass window. He liked peering through the glass door into the library where the lawyers sought precedents in large dusty tomes.

But he preferred the fresh air, setts below him and grey stone above, and the inhalation of nicotine, and the illusion that he could walk away from all this if he chose. For the thing was, behind the splendour of the architecture, and the weight of tradition, and the high concepts of justice and the law, this was a place of immense and continual human pain, where brutal stories were wrenched up, where tortured images were replayed as daily fare. People who thought they'd put the whole thing behind them were asked to delve into the most secret and tragic moments of their past. Victims rendered their stories, the professionals laid down cold facts over the emotions of others, the accused wove their own versions in an attempt to woo the jury.

And while it was easy to see it as a game, as some kind of cruel spectator sport, still it could not be dismissed. Because for all the hard work Rebus and others put into a case, this was where it sank or swam. And this was where all policemen learned an early lesson that truth and justice were far from being allies, and that victims were something more than sealed bags of evidence, recordings and statements.

It had probably all been simple enough once upon a time; the concept still was fairly simple. There is an accused, and a victim. Lawyers speak for both sides, presenting the evidence. A judgment is made. But the whole thing was a matter of words and interpretation, and Rebus knew how facts could be twisted, misrepresented, how some evidence sounded more eloquent than others, how juries could decide from the off which way they'd vote, based on the manner or styling of the accused. And so it turned into theatre, and the cleverer the lawyers became, the more arcane became their games with language. Rebus had long since given up fighting them on their own terms. He gave his evidence, kept his answers short, and tried not to fall for any of the tried and tested tricks. Some of the lawyers could see it in his eyes, could see that he'd been here too often before. They detained him only briefly, before moving on to more amenable subjects.

That was why he didn't think they'd call him today. But all the same, he had to sit it out, had to waste his time and energy in the great name of justice.

One of the guards came out. Rebus knew him, and offered a cigarette. The man took it with a nod, accepting Rebus's box of matches.

'Fucking awful in there today,' the guard said, shaking his head. All three men were staring across the car park.

'We're not allowed to know,' Rebus reminded him with a sly smile.

'Which court are you in?'

'Shiellion,' Rebus said.

'That's the one I'm talking about,' the guard said. 'Some of the testimony . . .' And he shook his head, a man who'd heard more horror stories than most in his working life.

Suddenly, Rebus knew why the man across from him

had been crying. And if he couldn't put a name to the man, at least now he knew who he was: he was one of the Shiellion survivors.

Shiellion House lay just off the Glasgow Road at Ingliston Mains. Built in the 1820s for one of the city's Lord Provosts, after his death and various family wranglings it had passed into the care of the Church of Scotland. As a private residence it was found to be too big and draughty, its isolation – distant farms its only neighbours – driving away most of its residents. By the 1930s it had become a children's home, dealing with orphans and the impoverished, teaching them Christianity with hard lessons and early rises. Shiellion had finally closed the previous year. There was talk of it becoming a hotel or a country club. But in its later years, Shiellion had garnered something of a reputation. There had been accusations from former residents, similar stories told by different intakes about the same two men.

Stories of abuse.

Physical and mental abuse to be sure, but eventually sexual abuse too. A couple of cases had come to the attention of the police, but the accusations were one-sided – the word of aggressive children against their quietly spoken carers. The investigations had been half-hearted. The Church had carried out its own internal inquiries, which had shown the children's stories to be tissues of vindictive lies.

But these inquiries, it now transpired, had been fixed from the start, comprising little more than cover-ups. Something *had* been happening in Shiellion. Something bad.

The survivors formed a pressure group, and got some media interest. A fresh police investigation was implemented, and it had led to this – the Shiellion trial; two men up on charges ranging from assault to sodomy. Twenty-eight counts against either man. And meantime, the victims were readying to sue the Church.

Rebus didn't wonder that the guard was pale-faced. He'd heard whispers about the stories being retold in court number one. He'd read some of the original transcripts, details of interviews held at police stations up and down the country, as children who'd been held in Shiellion were traced – adults now – and questioned. Some of them had refused to have anything to do with it. 'That's all behind me,' was an oft-used excuse. Only it was more than an excuse: it was the simple truth. They'd worked hard to lock out the nightmares from their childhood: why would they want to relive them? They had whatever peace would ever be available to them in life: why change that?

Who would face terror across a courtroom, if they could choose to avoid it?

Who indeed.

The survivors' group comprised eight individuals who had chosen the more difficult path. They were going to see to it that after all these years justice was finally done. They were going to lock away the two monsters who'd ripped apart their innocence, monsters who were still there in the world whenever they woke from their nightmares.

Harold Ince was fifty-seven, short and skinny and bespectacled. He had curly hair, turning grey. He had a wife and three grown children. He was a grandfather. He hadn't worked in seven years. He had a dazed look to him in all the photographs Rebus had seen.

Ramsay Marshall was forty-four, tall and broad, hair cut short and spiky. Divorced, no children, had until recently been living and working (as a chef) in Aberdeen. Photographs showed a scowling face, jutting chin.

The two men had met at Shiellion in the early 1980s, formed a friendship or at the very least an alliance. Found they shared a common interest, one that could, it seemed, be carried out with impunity in Shiellion House.

Abusers. Rebus was sickened by them. They couldn't be cured or changed. They just went on and on. Released

82

into the community, they'd soon revert to type. They were control junkies, weak-minded, and just awful. They were like addicts who couldn't be weaned off their fix. There were no prescription drugs, and no amount of psychotherapy seemed to work. They saw weakness and had to exploit it; saw innocence and had to explore it. Rebus had had a bellyful of them.

Like with Darren Rough. Rebus knew he'd snapped in the zoo because of Shiellion, because of the way it wasn't going away. The trial had lasted two weeks so far, heading into week three, and still there were stories to be told, still there were people crying in the waiting room.

'Chemical castration,' the guard said, stubbing out his cigarette. 'It's the only way.'

Then there was a cry from the courthouse door: one of the ushers.

'Inspector Rebus?' she called. Rebus nodded, flicked his cigarette on to the setts.

'You're up,' she called. He was already moving towards her.

Rebus didn't know why he was here. Except that he'd interviewed Harold Ince. Which was to say, he'd been part of the team interviewing Ince. But only for one day – other work had pulled him away from Shiellion. Only for one day, early on in the inquiry. He'd shared the sessions with Bill Pryde, but it wasn't Bill Pryde the defence wanted to examine. It was John Rebus.

The public gallery was half-empty. The jury of fifteen sat with glazed expressions, the effect of sharing someone else's nightmare, day in, day out. The judge was Lord Justice Petrie. Ince and Marshall sat in the dock. Ince leaned forward, the better to hear the evidence, his hands twisting the polished brass rail in front of him. Marshall leaned back, looking bored by proceedings. He examined his shirt-front, then would turn his neck from side to side, cracking it. Clear his throat and click his tongue and go back to studying himself.

The defence lawyer was Richard Cordover, Richie to his friends. Rebus had had dealings with him before; he'd yet to be invited to call the lawyer 'Richie'. Cordover was in his forties, hair already grey. Medium height and with a muscular neck, face tanned. Health club regular, Rebus guessed. Prosecution was a fiscal-depute nearly half Rebus's age. He looked confident but careful, browsing through his case notes, jotting points down with a fat black fountain pen.

Petrie cleared his throat, reminding Cordover that time was passing. Cordover bowed to the judge and approached Rebus.

'Detective Inspector Rebus . . .' Pausing immediately for effect. 'I believe you interviewed one of the suspects.'

'That's right, sir. I was present at the interview of Harold Ince on October the twentieth last year. Others present included—'

'This was where exactly?'

'Interview Room B, St Leonard's police station.'

Cordover turned away from Rebus, walked slowly towards the jury. 'You were part of the investigating team?'

'Yes, sir.'

'For how long?'

'Just over a week, sir.'

Cordover turned to Rebus. 'How long did the investigation last in total, Inspector?'

'A matter of some months, I believe.'

'Some months, yes . . .' Cordover went as if to check his notes. Rebus noticed a woman seated on a chair near the door. She was a CID detective called Jane Barbour. Though she sat with arms folded and legs crossed, she looked as tense as Rebus felt. Normally, she worked out of Fettes, but halfway through Shiellion she'd been put in charge: after Rebus's time; he hadn't had any dealings with her.

'Eight and a half months,' Cordover was saying. 'A decent period of gestation.' He smiled coldly at Rebus, who said nothing. He was wondering where this was leading; knew now that the defence had some bloody good reason for bringing him here. Only he didn't yet know what.

'Were you pulled from the inquiry, Inspector Rebus?' Asked casually, as if to satisfy curiosity only.

'Pulled? No, sir. Something else came up—'

'And someone was needed to deal with it?'

'That's right.'

'Why you, do you think?'

'I've no idea, sir.'

'No?' Cordover sounded surprised. He turned towards the jury. 'You've no idea why you were pulled from that inquiry after just one—'

The prosecution counsel was on his feet, arms spread. 'The detective inspector has already stated that the word "pulled" is an inaccuracy, Your Honour.'

'Well then,' Cordover went on quickly, 'let's say you were *transferred*. Would that be more accurate, Inspector?'

Rebus just shrugged, unwilling to agree to anything. Cordover was persistent.

'Yes or no will do.'

'Yes, sir.'

'Yes, you were transferred from a major inquiry after one week?'

'Yes, sir.'

'And you've no idea why?'

'Because I was needed elsewhere, sir.' Rebus was trying not to look towards the fiscal-depute: any glance in that direction would have Cordover scenting blood, scenting someone who needed rescuing. Jane Barbour was shifting in her seat, still with arms folded.

'You were needed elsewhere,' Cordover repeated in a

flat tone of voice. He returned to his notes. 'How's your disciplinary record, Inspector?'

The fiscal-depute was on his feet. 'Inspector Rebus is not on trial here, Your Honour. He has come to give evidence, and so far I can't see any point to the—'

'I withdraw the remark, Your Honour,' Cordover said airily. He smiled at Rebus, approached again. 'You conducted how many interviews with Mr Ince?'

'Two sessions over a single day.'

'Did they go well?' Rebus looked blank. 'Did my client co-operate?'

'His answers were deliberately obtuse, sir.'

'"Deliberately"? Are you some kind of expert, Inspector?'

Rebus fixed his eyes on the advocate. 'I can tell when someone's being evasive.'

'Really?' Cordover was making for the jury again. Rebus wondered how many miles of floor he covered in a day. 'My client is of the opinion that you were "a threatening presence" – his words, not mine.'

'The interviews were recorded, sir.'

'Indeed they were. And videotaped, too. I've watched them several times, and I think you'd have to agree that your method of questioning is *aggressive*.'

'No, sir.'

'No?' Cordover raised his eyebrows. 'My client was obviously terrified of you.'

'The interviews followed every procedure, sir.'

'Oh, yes, yes,' Cordover said dismissively, 'but let's be honest here, Inspector.' He was in front of Rebus now, close enough to hit. 'There are ways and ways, aren't there? Body language, gestures, ways of phrasing a question or statement. You may or may not be expert at divinating obtuse answers, but you're certainly a ruthless questioner.'

The judge peered over the top of his glasses. 'Is this

leading somewhere, other than to an attempt at character assassination?'

'If you'll bear with me a moment longer, Your Honour.' Cordover bowed again, consummate showman. Not for the first time, Rebus was struck by the utter ridiculousness of the whole enterprise: a game played by well-paid lawyers using real lives as the pieces.

'A few days ago, Inspector,' Cordover went on, 'were you part of a surveillance team at Edinburgh Zoo?'

Oh, hell. Rebus knew now *exactly* where Cordover was leading, and like a bad chess-player put against a master, he could do little to forestall the conclusion.

'Yes, sir.'

'You ended up in pursuit of a member of the public?'

The fiscal-depute was on his feet again, but the judge waved him aside.

'I did, yes.'

'You were part of an undercover team trying to catch our notorious poisoner?'

'Yes, sir.'

'And the man you chased . . . I believe it was into the sea-lion enclosure?' Cordover looked up for confirmation. Rebus nodded dutifully. 'Was this man the poisoner?'

'No, sir.'

'Did you suspect him of being the poisoner?'

'He was a convicted paedophile . . .' There was anger in Rebus's voice, and he knew his face had reddened. He broke off, but too late. He'd given the defence lawyer everything he wanted.

'A man who had served his sentence and been released into the community. A man who has not reoffended. A man who was enjoying the pleasures of a trip to the zoo until *you* recognised him and chased after him.'

'He ran first.'

'He ran? From *you*, Inspector? Now why would he do a thing like that?'

All right, you sarky bastard, get it over with.

'The point I'm making,' Cordover said to the jury, approaching them with something close to reverence, 'is that there is prejudice against anyone even *suspected* of crimes against children. The Inspector happened to catch sight of a man who had served a single custodial sentence, and immediately suspected the worst, and *acted* on that suspicion – quite wrongly, as it turned out. No charges were made, the poisoner struck again, and I believe the innocent party is considering suing the police for wrongful arrest.' He nodded. 'Your tax money, I'm afraid.' He took a deep breath. 'Now, it may be that we can all understand the Inspector's feelings. The blood rises where children are involved. But I'd ask you: is it morally right? And does it contaminate the entire case against my clients, seeping down through the tools of the investigation, coming to rest with the very officers who conducted the inquiry?' He pointed towards Rebus, who felt now that he was in the dock rather than the witness box. Seeing his discomfort, Ramsay Marshall's eyes were twinkling with pleasure. 'Later, I shall produce further evidence that the initial police investigation was flawed from the outset, and that Detective Inspector Rebus here was not the only culprit.' He turned to Rebus. 'No more questions.'

And Rebus was dismissed.

'That was a tough one.'

Rebus looked up at the figure walking slowly towards him. He was lighting a cigarette, inhaling deeply. He offered one over, but she shook her head.

'Have you come across Cordover before?' Rebus asked.

'We've had our run-ins,' Jane Barbour said.

'Sorry I couldn't . . .'

'Not much you could have done about it.' She exhaled noisily, clutching a briefcase to her chest. They were outside the court building. Rebus felt gritty and exhausted. He noticed she was looking pretty tired herself.

'Fancy a drink?'

She shook her head. 'Things to do.'

He nodded. 'Think we'll win?'

'Not if Cordover has anything to do with it.' She scraped the heel of one shoe across the ground. 'I seem to be losing more than I'm winning lately.'

'You still at Fettes?'

She nodded. 'Sex Offences.'

'Still a DI?'

She nodded again. Rebus remembered a rumour about a promotion. So Gill Templer remained the only female chief inspector in Lothian. Rebus studied her from behind his cigarette. She was tall, what his mother would have called 'big-boned'. Shoulder-length brown hair fashioned into waves. Mustard-coloured two-piece with a light silk blouse. She sported a mole on one cheek and another on her chin. Mid-thirties . . . ? Rebus was hopeless with ages.

'Well . . .' she said, ready to leave but looking for an excuse not to.

'Goodbye then.' A voice sounded behind them. They turned and watched Richard Cordover walking to his car. It was a red TVR with personalised plate. By the time he was unlocking the car, he seemed to have forgotten about them.

'One cold bastard,' Barbour muttered.

'Must have saved him a few bob.'

She looked at Rebus. 'How's that?'

'He could skip the TVR's air-conditioning option. Sure about that drink? There's something I wanted to ask you . . .'

They bypassed Deacon Brodie's – too many 'clients' drank there – and headed for the Jolly Judge. Rebus had once had a drink there with an advocate who drank advocaat. Now Rangers had signed a Dutch manager called Advocaat and the jokes were being dusted off . . . He bought a Virgin Mary for Barbour and a half of Eighty for himself. They sat at a table below the stairs, well out of the way.

'Cheers,' she said.

Rebus raised his glass to her, then to his lips.

'So what can I do for you?'

He put down the glass. 'Just some background. You used to work MisPers, didn't you?'

'For my sins, yes.'

'What did you do exactly?'

'Collect, collate, stick them all into filing cabinets and computer memories. A bit of liaison, punting our MisPers to other forces and receiving theirs in return. Lots of meetings with the various charities . . .' She puffed out her cheeks. 'Lots of meetings with families, too, trying to help them understand what had happened.'

'Job satisfaction?'

'Up there with sewing mailbags. Why the interest?'

'I've got a missing person.'

'How old?'

'He's nineteen. Still lives at home; his parents are worried.'

She was shaking her head. 'Needle in a haystack.'

'I know.'

'Did he leave a note?'

'No, and they say he'd no reason to leave.'

'Sometimes there aren't reasons, not any that would make sense to the family.' She straightened in her chair. 'Here's the checklist.' She counted fingers as she spoke. 'Bank accounts, building society, anything like that. You're looking for withdrawals.'

'Done.'

'Check with hostels. Local, plus the usual cities – anything between Aberdeen and London. Some of them have charities who deal with the homeless and runaways: Centrepoint in London, for example. Get a description out. Then there's the National Missing Persons Bureau in London. Fax any details to them. You might ask the Sally Army to keep their eyes open too. Soup kitchens, night shelters, you never know who'll turn up.'

Rebus was jotting in his notebook. He looked up, watched her shrug.

'That's about it.'

'Is it a big problem?'

She smiled. 'Thing is, it's not a problem *at all*, not unless you're the one who's lost somebody. A lot of them turn up, some don't. Last estimate I saw said there could be as many as a quarter of a million MisPers out there. People who've just dropped out, changed their identity, or been dumped by the so-called "caring" services.'

'Care in the community?'

She gave her bitter smile again, drank some of her drink, checked her watch.

'I can see Shiellion must have come as a welcome break.'

She snorted. 'Oh yes, like a camping trip. Abuse cases are always a breeze.' She turned thoughtful. 'I had a double rapist a few weeks back, he ended up walking. Crown cocked it up, prosecuted it as a summary case.'

'Maximum sentence three months?'

She nodded. 'He wasn't up for rape this time, just indecent exposure. The Sheriff was furious. By the time remand was taken into account, the bastard had under two weeks to serve, so the Sheriff put him back on the streets.' She looked at Rebus. 'Psych report said he'd do it again. Probation and community service, with a bit of counselling thrown in. And he'll do it again.'

He'll do it again. Rebus was thinking of Darren Rough, but of Cary Oakes too. He checked his own watch. Soon Oakes would be touching down at Turnhouse. Soon he'd be a problem . . .

'Sorry I can't be more help about your MisPer,' she said, beginning to stand. 'Is it someone you know?'

'Son of some friends.' She was nodding. 'How did you know?'

91

'No offence, John, but you probably wouldn't be bothering otherwise.' She lifted up her briefcase. 'He's one out of quarter of a million. Who's got the time?'

12

There were reporters waiting inside the terminal building. Most carried mobile phones with which they kept in touch with the office. Photographers chatted to each other about lenses and film speeds and the impact digital cameras would eventually have. There were three TV crews: Scottish, BBC and Edinburgh Live. Everyone seemed to know everyone else; they were all pretty relaxed, maybe even looking a bit tired by the wait.

The flight was subject to a twenty-minute delay.

Rebus knew the reason why. The reason was that the Met officers at Heathrow had taken their time transferring Cary Oakes. Oakes had spent over an hour in Heathrow. He'd visited the toilet, had a drink in one of the bars, bought a newspaper and a couple of magazines, and taken a telephone call.

The telephone call had intrigued Rebus.

'He was paged,' the Farmer had informed him. 'Someone got a call through to him.'

'Who would that be?'

The Farmer had shaken his head.

Now Oakes was bound for Edinburgh. Detectives had accompanied him on to the flight, then had left again, keeping their eyes on the plane right up until it left London air space. Then they'd called their colleagues at Lothian and Borders HQ.

'He's all yours,' was the message.

The ACC (Crime) was putting the Farmer in charge. The Farmer didn't usually stray from his office: he was happy to delegate; trusted his team. But tonight . . . tonight was a bit special. So he was seated alongside Rebus in the squad car. DC Siobhan Clarke sat in the back. It was a marked car: they wanted Oakes to know about it. Rebus had been out to recce the scene, reporting back with news of the journos.

'Anyone we know?' Clarke asked.

'Usual faces,' Rebus said, accepting another piece of chewing gum from her. This was the bargain they'd made: he wouldn't smoke so long as she bought the gum. His reconnaissance had been an excuse for a ciggie.

The dashboard clock said the plane would be touching down any minute. They heard it before they saw it: a dull whine, lights flashing in the dark sky. They had one window down, stopping the car from steaming up.

'Could be the one,' the Farmer stated.

'Could be.'

Siobhan Clarke had all the paperwork beside her; she'd been doing her reading on Cary Dennis Oakes. She wasn't sure that they were serving any purpose here other than curiosity. Still, she *was* curious.

'Shouldn't take long,' she said.

'Don't bet on it,' Rebus said, opening his door again. He was digging in his pocket for a cigarette as he made towards the terminal doors.

He circumvented the huddle of pressmen and made for a No Entry sign. Showing his ID, he made his way towards the arrivals hall. He'd already had a word, and Customs and Immigration were waiting for him. He knew what happened with international transfers: there were no checks at Heathrow. Often, there were no checks at Edinburgh either: it depended on staff rotas; the cutbacks had bitten hard. But there'd be the full panoply of checks tonight. Rebus watched as the passengers from the Heathrow flight filtered into the terminal and began the wait for baggage. Businessmen mostly, carrying briefcases and newspapers. Half the flight carried hand-luggage only. They made their way briskly through Customs, cars waiting in the car park, families waiting at home.

Then there was the man wearing casual clothes: denims and trainers, red and black check shirt, white baseball cap. He carried a sports holdall. It didn't look particularly full. Rebus nodded to the Customs officer, who stepped out and stopped the man, bringing him over to the counter.

'Passport, please,' the Immigration officer said.

The man dug into his shirt-breast pocket and produced a new-looking passport. It had been applied for over a month back, when the Americans had known they'd be freeing him. The Immigration officer flipped through it, finding little but empty pages.

'Where are you travelling from, sir?'

Cary Oakes's eyes were on the man in the background, the man who'd arranged all this.

'United States,' he said. His voice was an odd mix of transatlantic inflexions.

'And what were you doing there, sir?'

Oakes smirked. He had the face of a weathered schoolboy, the classroom joker. 'Passing time,' he said.

The Customs officer had decanted the contents of his bag on to the counter. Washbag, change of clothes, a couple of razzle mags. A manila folder was full of drawings and photos clipped from magazines. They looked like they'd been pinned to a wall for a long time. There was a good luck card, too, telling him to 'fly high and straight' and signed by 'your buddies on the wing'. Another folder contained trial notes and newspaper court reports. There were two paperback books, one a Bible, the other a dictionary. Both looked well-used.

'Travel light, that's my motto,' Oakes informed them.

The Customs officer looked to Rebus, who nodded, keeping his stare fixed on Oakes. Everything was put back into the bag.

'This is actually pretty low-key,' Oakes said. 'And don't

think I don't appreciate it. Quiet life's going to suit me for a while.' He was nodding to himself.

'Don't plan on sticking around,' Rebus said quietly.

'I don't think we've been introduced, Officer.' Oakes thrust out a hand. Rebus saw that the back of it was dotted with ink tattoos: initials, crosses, a heart. After a moment, Oakes withdrew the hand, laughing to himself. 'Not so easy to make new friends, I guess,' he mused. 'I've lost the old social skills.'

The Customs officer was zipping the holdall. Oakes grabbed its handles.

'Now, gentlemen, if you've had your fun . . . ?'

'Where are you headed?' the Immigration man asked.

'A nice hotel in the city. Hotels for me from now on. They wanted to put me in some palace out in the country, but I said no, I want lights and action. I want some *buzz*.' He laughed again.

'Who's they?' Rebus couldn't help asking.

Oakes just grinned and winked. 'You'll find out, partner. Won't even have to do much detecting.' He hefted the bag and slung it over his shoulder, whistling as he walked away, joining the throng headed for the exit.

Rebus followed. The reporters outside were getting their photos and footage, even if Oakes had slid the baseball cap down over his face. Questions were hurled at him. And then an overweight man was pushing his way through, cigarette dangling from his mouth. Rebus recognised him: Jim Stevens. He worked for one of the Glasgow tabloids. He grabbed Oakes by the arm and said something into his ear. They shook hands, and then Stevens was in charge, manoeuvring Oakes through the huddle, proprietorial hand on his shoulder.

'Oh, Jim, for Christ's sake,' one of the other reporters cried.

'No comment,' Stevens said, the cigarette flapping at one corner of his mouth. 'But you can read our exclusive serialisation, starting tomorrow.'

And with a final wave, he was through the doors and off. Rebus made for another exit, got into the car beside the Farmer.

'Looks like he's made a friend,' Siobhan Clarke commented, watching Stevens put Oakes's bag into the boot of a Vauxhall Astra.

'Jim Stevens,' Rebus told her. 'He works out of Glasgow.'

'And Oakes is now his property?' she guessed.

'So it would seem. I think they're heading into town.'

The Farmer slapped the dashboard. 'Should have guessed one of the papers would nab him.'

'They won't hang on to him forever. Soon as the story's done . . .'

'But till then, they've got their lawyers.' The Farmer turned to Rebus. 'So we can't do *anything* that could be construed as harassment.'

'As you wish, sir,' Rebus said, starting the engine. He turned to the Farmer. 'So do we head home now?'

The Farmer nodded. 'Just as soon as we've tailed them. Let Stevens know the score.'

'There's a cop car after us,' Cary Oakes warned.

Jim Stevens reached for the cigarette lighter. 'I know.'

'Welcoming committee at the airport, too.'

'He's called Rebus.'

'Who is?'

'Detective Inspector John Rebus. I've had a few run-ins with him. What did he say to you?'

Oakes shrugged. 'Just stood there trying to look mean. Guys I met in prison, they'd have given him a nervous breakdown.'

Stevens smiled. 'Save it till the recorder's running.'

Oakes had the passenger-side window open all the way, angling his head into the fierce cold air.

'Does smoking bother you?' Stevens said.

'No.' Oakes moved his head to and fro, as if under a hair dryer. 'Clever of you to have me paged at Heathrow.'

'I wanted to be the first to make you an offer.'

'Ten grand, right?'

'I think we can manage ten.'

'Exclusive rights?'

'Got to be, for that price.'

Oakes brought his head back into the car. 'I'm not sure how good I'll be.'

'You'll be fine. You're a Scot, aren't you? We're born storytellers.'

'I guess Edinburgh's changed.'

'You've been away a while.'

'Oh, yes.'

'Do you still know anyone here?'

'I can think of a couple of names.' Oakes smiled. 'Jim Stevens, John Rebus. That's two, and I've only been in the country half an hour.' Jim Stevens started to laugh. Oakes rolled the window back up, leaned down to switch off the music. Turned in his seat so Stevens had his full attention. 'So tell me about Rebus. I'd like to get to know him.'

'Why?'

Oakes's eyes never left the reporter's. 'Someone takes an interest in me,' he said, 'I take an interest back.'

'Does that put me in the frame too?'

'You never know your luck, Jim. You just never know your luck.'

Stevens had wanted Oakes out of Edinburgh. He'd wanted him in seclusion for as long as it took to do the interviews. But Oakes had told him on the phone: it has to be Edinburgh. It just has to be. So Edinburgh it was; a discreet hotel in a New Town terrace. Stevens had to smile at 'New Town': everywhere else in Scotland, it meant the likes of Glenrothes and Livingston, places built from nothing in the fifties and sixties. But in Edinburgh, the New Town dated back to the eighteenth century. That was about as new as the city liked things. The hotel would have been a private residence at one time, spread over four floors. Understated elegance; a quiet street. Oakes took one look at it and decided it wouldn't do. He didn't say why, just stood on the steps outside, taking in the air, while Stevens made a couple of frantic calls on his mobile.

'It would help if I knew what you wanted.'

Oakes just shrugged. 'I'll know when I see it.' He waved a little wave towards where the police car had parked, its lights still on.

'Right,' Stevens said at last. 'Back in the motor.'

They headed down Leith Walk, towards the port of Leith itself.

'This still a rough part of town?' Oakes said.

'It's changing. New developments, Scottish Office. New restaurants and a couple of hotels.'

'But it's still Leith, right?'

Stevens nodded. 'Still Leith,' he conceded. But when they hit the waterfront and Oakes saw their hotel, he started nodding straight away.

'Atmosphere,' he said, looking out across the docks. There was a container ship tied up there, arc lights on as men worked around it. A couple of pubs, both with restaurants attached. Across the basin was a permanent mooring, a boat which had become a floating nightclub. New flats being built across there too.

'Scottish Office is just down there,' Stevens said, pointing.

'How long do you think they'll keep this up?' Oakes asked, watching the police car come to a stop.

'Not long. If they try it on, I'll phone our lawyers. I need to call them anyway, get your contract sorted.'

'Contract.' Oakes tried out the word. 'Long time since I've had a job.'

'Just talking into a microphone, posing for a few pictures.'

Oakes turned to him. 'For ten thou, I'll do re-enactments for you.'

Some of the colour slid from Stevens' face. Oakes was watching him intently, measuring the reaction.

'That probably won't be necessary,' Stevens said.

Oakes laughed, liking that 'probably'.

Inside the hotel, he approved of his room. Stevens couldn't get one next door, had to settle for down the hall. Stuck the rooms on plastic and said they'd need them for a few days. He found Oakes lying on the bed in his room, shoes still on, holdall on the bed beside him. He'd taken one item from it: a battered Bible. It lay on the bedside table. Nice touch: Stevens would use it in his intro.

'You a religious man, Jim?' Oakes asked.

'Not especially.'

'Shame on you. Bible'll teach you a lot of things. I got my first taste in prison. Time was, I'd no time for the Good Book.'

'Did you go to church?'

Oakes nodded, seeming distracted. 'We had Sunday service in the jail. I was a regular.' He looked to Stevens. 'I'm not a prisoner, right? I mean, I can come and go?'

'Last thing I want is for you to feel like a prisoner.'

'Makes two of us.'

'But there are a few rules, so long as *I'm* paying your way. If you go out, I want to know. In fact, I'd like to tag along.'

'Afraid the competition will hook me?'

'Something like that.'

Oakes turned his head, grinned. 'Supposing I want a woman? You going to be sitting in the corner while I hump her?'

'Listening at the door will be fine,' Stevens said.

Oakes laughed, wriggled on the mattress. 'Softest bed I ever had. Smells nice too.' He lay a moment longer, then swung swiftly to his feet. Stevens was surprised at the turn of speed.

'Come on then,' Oakes told him.

'Where?'

'Out, man. But don't fret, I'm not going more than fifty yards.'

Stevens followed him outside, but stayed by the hotel, could see where Oakes was headed.

The police car; lights still on; three figures inside. Oakes peered through the windscreen, headed for the driver's side, tapped on the glass. The one he now knew as Rebus wound down the window.

'Hey,' Oakes said by way of greeting, nodding his head to the other two – young woman, and a senior-looking man with a huge scowl on his face. He gestured towards the hotel. 'Nice place, huh? Any of you ever stay someplace like that?' They said nothing. He leaned one arm on the roof of the car, the other on the door panel.

'I was . . .' All at once he looked a little shy. 'Yeah,' knowing now how to put it, 'I was real sorry to hear about your daughter. Man, that's got to be a bitch.' Looking at Rebus with liquid, soulless eyes. 'One of the killings they pinned me for, girl would have been about the same age. I mean, same age as your daughter. Sammy, that's her name, right?'

Rebus pushed open his door so hard, it propelled Oakes back almost to the water's edge. The other man – Rebus's boss – was calling out a warning; the young woman was coming out of the car behind Rebus. Rebus himself was up in Cary Oakes's face. Jim Stevens was sprinting from the hotel.

Oakes had his hands raised high over his head. 'You touch me, it's assault.'

'You're a liar.'

'Say again?'

'They didn't charge you with anybody my daughter's age.'

Oakes laughed, rubbed his chin. 'Well, you've got

101

something there. Guess that gives you the first round, huh?'

The woman officer was gripping one of Rebus's arms. Jim Stevens was panting after the short jog. The chief stayed sitting in the car, watching.

Oakes bent a little to peer in. 'Too important for all this, huh? Or no stomach for it? Your call, man.'

Stevens grabbed him by the shoulder. 'Come on.'

Oakes shrugged free. 'Nobody touches me, that's rule one.' But he allowed himself to be steered back across the road towards the hotel. Stevens turned round, found Rebus staring at him hard, knowing who'd told Oakes about him, about his family.

Oakes started laughing, laughed all the way to the hotel's glass doors. He stood on the inside, looking out.

'That Rebus,' he said quietly. 'He's not exactly what you'd call a slow burner, now is he?'

Back at Patience's flat in Oxford Terrace, Rebus poured himself a whisky and added water from a bottle in the fridge. She came through from the bedroom, eyes slanted in the sudden light, a pale yellow nightdress falling to her ankles.

'Sorry if I woke you,' Rebus said.

'I wanted a drink anyway.' She took grapefruit juice from the fridge door, poured herself a large glass. 'Good day?'

Rebus didn't know whether to laugh or cry. They took the drinks into the living room, sat together on the sofa. Rebus picked up a copy of *The Big Issue*: Patience always bought it, but he was the one who read it. Inside, there were fresh appeals for MisPer information. He knew if he turned on the TV and went to Teletext, there was a listing for missing persons. He'd watched it from time to time, scanning a few pages. It was run by the National MisPer Helpline. Janice had said she'd contact them . . .

'What about you?' he asked.

102

Patience tucked her feet beneath her. 'Same old story. Sometimes, I almost think a robot could do the work. Same symptoms, same prescriptions. Tonsils, measles, dizzy spells . . .'

'Maybe we could go away.' She looked at him. 'Just for a weekend.'

'We tried it, remember? You got bored.'

'Ach, that was the country.'

'So which romantic interlude did you have in mind? Dundee? Falkirk? Kirkcaldy?'

He got up for a refill, asked her if she wanted one. She shook her head, her eyes on his empty glass.

'Second one today,' he said, making for the kitchen.

'What's brought this on anyway?' She was following him.

'What?'

'The sudden notion of a holiday.'

He glanced towards her. 'I went to see Sammy yesterday. She said she speaks to you more than I do.'

'A bit of an exaggeration . . .'

'That's what I said. But she has a point all the same.'

'Oh?'

He poured less water into the glass this time. And maybe a drop more whisky too. 'I mean, I know I can be . . . distracted. I know I'm a pretty lousy proposition.' He closed the fridge, turned to her and shrugged. 'That's about it, really.'

Kept his eyes on the glass as he spoke, wondering why it was that as he said the words, a holiday snap of Janice Mee flashed across his mind.

'I keep thinking you'll come back,' Patience said. He looked at her. She tapped her own head. 'From wherever it is you've gone.'

'I'm right here.'

She shook her head. 'No you're not. You're not really here at all.' She turned away, walked back through to the living room.

103

A little later, she went to bed. Rebus said he'd stay up a bit longer. Flipped TV channels, finding nothing. Went to Teletext, page 346. Stuck the headphones on so he could listen to Genesis: 'For Absent Friends'. Jack Morton sitting on the arm of the sofa as screen after screen of missing persons appeared. No sign of Damon yet. Rebus lit a cigarette, blew smoke at the television, watching it dissolve. Then remembered this was Patience's flat, and she didn't like smoking. Back into the kitchen to extinguish his guilty pleasure. After Genesis, he switched to Family: 'Song for Sinking Loves'.

Something's gone bad inside you.

It was your lot wanted him here.

Saw two men in the dock, their lawyer working on the jury. Saw Cary Oakes leaning into the car.

He'll do it again.

Saw Jim Margolies take that final flight into darkness. Maybe there was no way to understand any of it. He turned to Jack. Often he'd phoned Jack – didn't matter what time of night it was, Jack never complained. They'd talk around subjects, share worries and depressions.

'How could you do that to me, Jack?' Rebus said quietly, drinking his drink as the room filled with ghosts.

It was late, but Jim Stevens knew his editor wouldn't mind. He tried the mobile number first. Bingo: his boss was at a dinner party in Kelvingrove. Politicos, the usual movers and shakers. Stevens's boss liked all that crowd. Maybe he was the wrong man for a tabloid.

Or maybe, all these years down the road, it was Jim Stevens who was out of touch. He seemed surrounded by journalists younger, brighter, and keener than him. These days, you could be washed up at fifty. He wondered how long it would be till the cheque for services rendered was being countersigned at his editor's desk, how long before the young bloods in the office were having a whip-round to see off 'good old Jim'. He knew the drill, even knew the speeches they'd make – stuff any self-respecting sub would block and delete. He knew because he'd been there himself, back in the days when *he'd* been a young blood and the old-timers had been complaining about falling standards and the changing world of journalism.

Soon as Jim had heard about Cary Oakes, he'd taken his boss aside for a private word, then had checked flight schedules, brown-nosing Heathrow Information so they'd page the prodigal son.

'It's yours, Jim,' his editor had said, but with a warning finger. 'Could be the cream on the cake. Just make sure it doesn't turn sour.'

Now the boss was giving him a couple of snippets of gossip from the dinner party. He'd obviously had a few drinks. They wouldn't stop him heading into the news-room afterwards. Twelve-hour days: a while since Jim Stevens had worked any of those.

'So what can I do you for, Jim?'

At last. Stevens took a deep breath. 'I've got us settled in at the hotel.'

'How does he seem?'

'All right.'

'Not a slavering monster or anything?'

'No, pretty quiet really.' Stevens deciding his boss needn't know about the blow-up with Rebus.

'And ready to give us the exclusive?'

'Yes.' Stevens lit a cigarette for himself.

'You might try to sound a bit more enthusiastic.'

'Just been a long day, boss, that's all.'

'Sure you've got the stamina, Jim? I could lend you one of the newsroom crew . . . ?'

'Thanks but no thanks.' Stevens heard his boss laughing. Ha bloody ha. 'That's not the kind of back-up that worries me.'

'You mean corroboration?'

'Lack of it, more like.'

'Mmm.' Thoughtful now. 'Got a game plan?'

105

'You worked for a year or two in the States, didn't you?'

'While back.'

'Still got friends there?'

'Might have one or two.'

'I need to hook up with someone on a Seattle paper, see if I can talk to one of the cops who worked the Oakes case.'

'One guy I knew now works news for CBS.'

'That'd be a start.'

'Soon as I get to the office, OK, Jim?'

'Thanks.'

'And Jim? Don't worry too much about confirmation. First thing you need to get from our friend Oakes is a bloody good story. Whatever it takes.'

Stevens put the phone down, lay back on his bed. Part of him wanted to chuck the job right now. But the other part was still hungry. It *wanted* those kids in the office to stare at him, wondering if they'd ever be as good, as sharp. It wanted Oakes's story. Afterwards, he could walk away if he liked: crowning glory and all that. He thought again of Rebus. Wondered what Oakes had to gain from sparring with him. From what Stevens knew, no one had ever got into the ring with Rebus and come away without at least a few cuts and bruises. And sometimes ... sometimes there'd be traction and a hospital waiting.

But Oakes had looked keen. Oakes had looked ready, *making* Rebus come at him like that.

Jim Stevens was supposed to be Oakes's baby-sitter. But it seemed to him that Oakes had either an agenda or a death wish. Difficult to baby-sit either one.

'This is your last job, Jim,' Stevens promised himself. Decided a raid on the mini-bar would seal the contract.

13

The surveillance budget was so tight, they were reduced to singles. Four in the morning, Rebus couldn't sleep, so he drove down to the waterfront, stopping off at an all-night garage. Siobhan Clarke was in an unmarked Rover 200. She'd dressed for a mountain trek: trousers tucked into thick socks and climbing boots; thermal jacket and bobble hat. On the passenger seat: notebook and pen; three empty packets of lo-fat crisps; two flasks. Rebus climbed into the back and offered a microwaved pasty and beaker of coffee.

'Cheers,' she said.

Rebus looked out at the hotel. 'Any movement?'

She shook her head, chewed and swallowed. 'I'm a bit worried though. There are service exits to the back of the building. No way I can cover those.'

'He's probably jet-lagged anyway.'

'Meaning awake all night, asleep all day?'

'I hadn't thought of that.' Rebus leaned forward. 'He hasn't been out *at all*?'

She shook her head. 'All those years in jail, maybe he's turned agoraphobic.'

'Maybe.' Rebus knew she might have a point. He'd known ex-cons who just couldn't cope with the outside world – all that space and light. They ended up reoffending, only way they could get put away again.

'He ate dinner in the restaurant.' She nodded towards the plate-glass windows of the hotel's dining room.

'Did he spot you?'

'Not sure. His room's on the second floor. That window at the far end.'

Rebus looked. Twelve small square panes of glass. The window was open an inch at the bottom. 'How do you know?'

'I asked the manager.'

Rebus nodded: orders from the Farmer – no need to be subtle. 'How did the manager take it?'

'He seemed uncomfortable.' She took a final bite of pasty.

'Don't want to make Oakes's stay too pleasant, do we?'

'No, sir,' Clarke said.

Rebus opened his door. 'Just going for a recce.' He paused. 'What do you do when you need to . . . ?'

She lifted one of the flasks, reached to the floor for a kitchen funnel.

'And what if . . . ?'

'Self-control, sir.'

He nodded. 'Don't get your flasks mixed up, will you?'

Outside, the air was fresh. Sounds of night traffic at the port, the occasional taxi cruising past the end of the road. Taxis: he had to ask them about Damon and the woman. He walked around the side of the hotel, wandered into the car park. The service exits were locked. Beside them were four rubbish skips, separated by a high wooden fence from the guests' cars. Jim Stevens's Astra was easy to spot. Rebus tore a page from his notebook, scribbled a couple of words, folded the sheet and fixed it beneath a wiper blade. Back at the service doors, Rebus checked they couldn't be opened from outside. He left satisfied that even if Oakes used them to get out of the hotel, he'd have to use the front entrance to get back in.

Always supposing he'd come back. Maybe he'd just scarper: wasn't that what they wanted? No, not exactly: they wanted to be *certain* he'd left Edinburgh. Oakes missing from his hotel wasn't quite the same thing. Rebus went back to Clarke's car, got out his mobile and made a call. Hotel reception answered.

'Good evening,' Rebus said. 'Could you put me through to Mr Oakes's room, please?'

'One moment.'

Rebus winked at Clarke. He held the mobile between them so she could listen. A buzzing noise repeated three or four times. Then the pick-up.

'Yeah? What is it?' Sounding authentically groggy.

'Tommy, is that you?' Mock-Glaswegian. 'We're having a bit of a bevvy in my room. Thought you were coming up.'

Silence for a moment. Then: 'What room is it again?'

Rebus pondered an answer, cut the connection instead. 'At least we know he's there.'

'And awake now.'

Rebus checked his watch. 'Your shift ends at six.'

'If Bill Pryde doesn't sleep in.'

'I'll give him an alarm call for you.' Rebus made to leave the car again.

'Look, sir.' Clarke was nodding towards the hotel.

Rebus looked: second-floor window, right at the far end. No light on, but curtains open and a face at the window, peering out. Looking straight at them. Rebus gave Cary Oakes a wave as he made for his own car.

No need to be subtle.

At eight sharp he was in the office, typing up details of Damon Mee, preparing a blitz on charities, hostels and organisations for the homeless. At nine there was a message from the front desk. Someone to see him.

Janice.

'You must be psychic,' Rebus told her. 'I was just working on Damon. Any news?'

He was guiding her down Rankeillor Street. They'd find a café on Clerk Street. He didn't want to talk to her in the cop-shop. A bundle of motives: didn't want anyone to suspect he was working on a case that wasn't official L&B business; didn't want her seeing some of the stuff in St Leonard's – photos of MisPers and suspects, cases dealt with without emotion or (often) enthusiasm; and maybe, just maybe, he didn't want to share her. Didn't want the part of her that belonged to his past intruding on his here and now, his workplace.

'No news,' she said. 'I thought I'd spend the day in Edinburgh, see if I couldn't . . . I don't know. I have to do *something*.'

Rebus nodded. There were dark half-moons beneath her eyes. 'Are you getting much sleep?' he asked.

'The doctor gave me some pills.'

Rebus remembered the way her replies to questions could sometimes only *seem* to be answers.

'Do you take them?' She smiled, glanced at him. 'Thought not,' he said. It wasn't that Janice would lie to you, but you had to know how to phrase a question to make sure of getting a truthful response.

'We used to have these conversations all the time, didn't we?'

She was right, they did. Rebus wondering if she fancied any of his friends, trying to find ways of asking without seeming jealous. She telling him versions of her life before they'd started dating. Dialogues of the left-unsaid.

He guided her into the café. They took a corner table. The owner, recently arrived, had only unlocked the door because he recognised Rebus.

'I can't cook anything,' he warned them.

'Coffee's fine for me,' Rebus said. He looked to Janice, who nodded. Their eyes stayed on one another as the café owner walked away.

'Have you ever forgiven me?' she asked.

'For what?'

'I think you know.'

He nodded. 'But I want to hear you say it.'

She smiled. 'For knocking you out.'

110

He looked around. 'Keep your voice down, someone might hear.'

She laughed, the way he'd meant her to. 'You were always the joker, Johnny.'

'Was I?' He tried to remember.

'Did you keep in touch with Mitch?'

He puffed out his cheeks. 'Now there's a name from the past.'

'The two of you were like this.' She twisted two fingers together.

'I'm not sure that's legal these days.'

She smiled, looked down at the tabletop. 'Always the joker.' There were spots of red high on her cheeks. Yes, he'd been able to make her blush back then too.

'What about you?' he asked.

'What about me?'

'You and Barney.'

'Nobody calls him Barney these days.' She sat back in her chair. 'We were just friendly, stayed that way for a few years. One night he asked me out. Started seeing one another.' She shrugged. 'That's how it works sometimes. No Cupid's arrow, no fireworks. Just . . . nice.' She looked up at him, smiled again. 'As for the rest of the crew . . . Billy and Sarah are still around. They got married but split up, three kids. Tom's still around, got some industrial injury, hasn't been back to work in years. Cranny – you remember her?' Rebus nodded. 'Some moved away . . . a few died.'

'Died?'

'Car smashes, accidents. Wee Paula got cancer. Midge had a heart attack.' She paused as their coffees arrived, topped with a froth of milk.

'I've got some biscuits . . . ?' the café owner suggested. They shook their heads.

Janice blew on the coffee, sipped. 'Then there was Alec . . .'

'Never turned up?' Alec Chisholm, who'd gone to play football. Alec, who'd never reached the park.

'His mum's still alive, you know. She's in her eighties. Still wonders what happened to him.'

Rebus said nothing. He could see what she was thinking: *maybe that's my future too.* He leaned across the table, squeezed her hand. It was warm, pliant.

'You can help me,' he said.

She looked in her bag for a handkerchief. 'How?'

Rebus took out the list he'd printed that morning. 'Hostels and charities,' he told her. She blew her nose and examined the list. 'They all need contacting. I was going to do it myself, but we'd save time if you made a start.'

'OK.'

'Then there are the taxis. That means putting the word out, visiting each rank and letting them know what we need. Damon and the blonde, across the road from The Dome.'

Janice was nodding. 'I can do that,' she said.

'I'll give you a list of where to find them.'

The café owner was standing by the counter, smoking a breakfast cigarette and opening the morning's paper. Rebus caught a headline, knew he had to buy the paper for himself. Janice was checking in her purse.

'I'll get these,' Rebus told her.

'I'll need coins for the phone,' she said.

Rebus thought for a moment. 'Why not use my flat as a base? It's not that much more comfortable than most phone boxes, but at least you can sit down, have a cup of coffee . . .' He held out a bunch of keys to her. She looked at him.

'Are you sure?'

'Sure I'm sure.' He wrote his address on a page of his notebook, added his work and mobile phone numbers, tore the page out and handed it to her. She studied it.

'No secrets there you don't want anyone to see?'

112

He smiled. 'I don't use the place much, to be honest. There's a couple of local shops if you need—'

'So where do you usually stay?'

He cleared his throat. 'With a friend.'

Her turn to smile. 'That's nice.'

Why had he said 'friend' rather than 'lover'? Rebus wondered if they sounded as awkward as he felt: kids again, language the clumsiest form of communication.

'I'll give you a lift,' he said.

'Remember the list of taxi ranks,' she told him. 'And an A to Z if you've got one.'

Rebus went to pay. The owner rang it up on the till. His paper was open at a court headline: previous day's testimony from the Shiellion case. KIDS' BOSS BRANDED MONSTER. There was a photograph of Harold Ince being led to a police van by the court guard Rebus had shared a smoke with. Ince looked tired, ordinary.

That was the trouble with monsters. They could be every bit as ordinary as anyone else.

Jim Stevens couldn't hide the relief on his face when he walked into the dining room. He made for one of the window tables. A couple of guests nodded and smiled at him as he passed them. He got the idea they'd been in the bar last night.

'Morning, Jim,' Cary Oakes said, wiping egg yolk from the corners of his mouth. He gazed out of the window. 'Grey old day, just the way I remember.' He picked up the last triangle of fried bread and started working on it. 'Cops are still out there.'

Jim Stevens looked out of the window. An unmarked car, but unmistakable. A man in the driver's seat, chewing on a roll.

'How long do you think they'll keep it up?' Oakes asked.

Stevens looked at him. 'I tried phoning your room.'

'When?'

'Fifteen, twenty minutes ago.'

'I was down here, partner, soaking up the *ambience.*'

Stevens looked around for a waiter.

'You help yourself to fruit juices and cereals,' Oakes explained, nodding towards a self-serve area. 'Then they take your order for the hot breakfast.'

Stevens looked at Oakes's greasy plate. 'After last night, I think I'll stick to orange juice and coffee.'

Oakes laughed. 'That's why I don't drink.' Last night he'd been on pints of orange and lemonade: Stevens remembered now. 'Besides,' Oakes said, leaning over the table towards the reporter, 'when I drink I do crazy things.'

'Save it for the tape machine, Cary.'

When the waiter came, Oakes asked if he could have another cooked breakfast. 'Just the bits I missed out on last time.' He studied the menu. 'Uh, how about fried liver, some onions and maybe some fried haggis and black pudding.' He patted his stomach, smiling at Stevens. 'Just today, you understand. The fitness regime recommences tomorrow.'

When the food arrived, Stevens, who'd been knocking back orange juice and trying to steel himself for toast, took one look at the plate and made his excuses. He drifted outside, lit a cigarette. There was a cold breeze blowing in from the docks. Just through the dock gates, he could see the Scot FM building. Turning his head, he saw the cop in the car watching him. He didn't recognise the face. Through the dining room window, Oakes was tucking in with exaggerated relish, teasing the detective. Smiling, Stevens walked around to the car park, examined the executive motors: Beamers, Rover 600s, an Audi. Noticed something on the windscreen of his own car. At first he took it for a piece of rubbish, gusted there. Then thought maybe it was a flyer for a carpet sale or antique show. But when he unfolded it, he knew who it was from. Two words:

DROP HIM.

Stevens tucked the note in his pocket, headed back to the hotel. Oakes had finished breakfast and was sitting on one of the sofas in reception, flicking through a newspaper: one of the broadsheets.

'I'm hurt,' he said. 'After that scrum at the airport . . .'

'Try the tabloids,' Stevens said, sitting down opposite him. 'Plenty of coverage there. I think my favourite is "Killer Cary Comes Home".'

'Well, isn't that nice?' Oakes tossed the paper aside. 'So when do we get down to work?'

'Let's say fifteen minutes in your room?'

'Fine by me. Before that, though, I've another favour to ask.'

'What?'

'Someone I want to find. His name's Archibald.'

'Plenty of those around.'

'That's his surname. First name, Alan.'

'Alan Archibald? Should I know him?'

Oakes shook his head.

'Care to tell me who he is?'

'He was a policeman – maybe still is. Got to be getting on a bit, though.'

'And?'

Oakes shrugged. 'For now, that's all you need. If you're a good boy, I'll maybe tell you the story.'

'For what we're paying you, we want *all* the stories.'

'Just find him, Jim. You'll make me happy.'

Stevens studied his charge, wondering just who was pulling the strings. He knew it should be him. But all the same . . .

'I can make a couple of calls,' he conceded.

'That's my boy.' Oakes got to his feet. 'Fifteen minutes in my room. Bring all the papers with you. I like being the day's news.'

And with that he set off towards the stairs.

14

It was Jamie's job to fetch milk, papers and breakfast rolls from the shop. He'd turned it into an art, skimming cash by lying about the prices. His mum complained, knew they could be found cheaper elsewhere, but 'elsewhere' wasn't walking distance for Jamie. She didn't like him straying too far. That was fine: whenever he wanted to wander the city, he had Billy Boy to say he'd been round at his house.

Jamie thought he was pretty smart.

He stopped outside the shop for a cigarette. He didn't buy them there – it was against the law and the Paki owner wouldn't let him. Instead, he had a deal with an older kid at school, who supplied packets of twenty in exchange for scud mags. Jamie got the mags from under Cal's bed. There were so many of them, Cal never seemed to notice. Even in freezing weather, Jamie liked his smoke outside the shop. Early-rise kids on their way to school would stare at him. Friends would sometimes join him. He got noticed.

A neighbour once told his mum, and she'd tried whacking him, but he was super-fast and dodged beneath her arm, spinning out of the door, laughing at her curses. One time she'd really gone for him had been when the school had sent the letter home. He'd been skiving, whole weeks at a time. His mum had belted him purple and sent him crying to his room, face red with shame at his own tears.

He'd probably go to school some time today. Cal was good at forging letters. He'd been doing it so long, the school thought *his* signature was their mum's, and when she'd signed some note about going on a school trip, the headmaster had quizzed Jamie about its origins. He'd even picked up the phone to talk to Jamie's mum, which had made Jamie smile: they didn't have a telephone in the flat. About two dozen ashtrays, most of them from holidays or nicked from pubs, but no telephone. Cal had a mobile, and that's what they used in emergencies – when Cal was in a mood to let them.

That was the problem with Cal. He could be great . . . and then he could lose the rag. Boom: like a bottle exploding against a wall. Or he'd get all quiet and lock himself in his room and refuse to write notes to the school. Jamie would go out and get him something, maybe nick it from a shop: peace offerings for some wrong he hadn't done. On good days, Cal would rub knuckles hard against Jamie's head, tell him he was the peacemaker: Jamie liked the sound of that. Cal would say he was the United Nations, sustaining an uneasy truce. He got stuff like that from the papers: 'United Nations'; 'uneasy truce'. Jamie asked him once: 'If nations are supposed to be united, how come we want to split away?'

'How do you mean, pal?'

'Split from England.'

Cal had folded the newspaper on his lap, flicked ash into an ashtray on the arm of his chair. 'Because we don't like the English.'

'How no?'

'Because they're *English*.' An edge to Cal's voice, telling Jamie to back off.

'We've got cousins in England, haven't we? We don't hate them, do we, Cal?'

'Look . . .'

'And fighting the Germans, we fought with the English, didn't we?'

'Look, Jamie, we want to run our own country, OK? That's all it is. Scotland's a country, isn't it?' He'd waited for Jamie's nod. 'Then who should be in charge of it? London or Edinburgh?'

'Edinburgh, Cal.'

'Right then.' Picking up the paper: discussion adjourned.

Jamie had a lot more questions, but never seemed to get answers. His mum was useless: 'Don't talk to me about politics,' she'd say. Or 'Don't talk to me about religion.' Or anything, really. As if she'd done all the hard thinking in her life, found satisfactory answers, and wasn't about to start over again for *his* benefit.

'That's why you've got teachers,' she'd say.

Which was fair enough, but at school Jamie had a rep to maintain. He was *Cal Brady's brother*. He couldn't go asking the teachers questions. They'd begin to wonder about him. Cal had told him a long time ago: 'With school, Jamie, it's definitely "us" and "them", know what I mean? A battlefield, pal, take no prisoners, understood?'

And Jamie had nodded, understanding nothing.

As he stood at the shop, tapping the toe of one shoe against a rubbish bin, along came Billy Horman. Jamie straightened a bit.

'All right, Billy Boy?'

'No' bad. Got a fag?'

Jamie handed over one of his precious cigarettes.

'See the football last night?'

Jamie shook his head, sniffed. 'Not bothered,' he said.

'Hearts, ya beauties.' The way Billy looked at him as he said this, seeking approval or something, Jamie knew Billy had heard it from someone else, maybe his mum's boyfriend, and wasn't sure about it.

'They're doing OK,' Jamie conceded as Billy mimed a blazing shot at goal.

'You going home?' Billy asked.

Jamie tapped the paper and rolls, held under one of his arms.

'Wait a minute, I'll come with you.' Billy marched into

the shop, came out again with milk and a carton of marge. 'Mum went spare this morning. Her new man got in from the pub and had about ten slices of toast.' He tossed the marge and caught it. 'Finished the tub.'

Jamie didn't say anything. He was thinking about fathers, how it was funny neither Billy nor he had one. Jamie wondered where his was, which story about him to believe.

'Who was that you were with yesterday?' he asked as they began walking.

'Eh?'

'Bottom of St Mary's Street. An uncle or somebody?'

'Aye, that's it. My Uncle Bill.'

But Billy Boy was lying. His ears always went red when he lied . . .

Back at the flat, Jamie took the paper into Cal's bedroom.

'About fucking time, wee man.' Cal lying in bed, portable telly on. The room smelled stale. Jamie sometimes tried to hold his breath. Cal had a mug of tea on the floor beside his ashtray.

'Switch the channel, will you?'

The TV was on a chest of drawers at the bottom of the bed. It didn't have a remote. Cal had just brought it home one night, said he won it in a bet at the pub. There was a little square beside the panel of buttons. It said 'Remote Sensor'. So Jamie knew there should be a remote with it. He had to jump over a pile of Cal's clothes on the floor to get to the TV. Pressed the button for Channel 4. You got some dolls on the breakfast show – Cal had taught him the word: dolls.

Jamie leapt back over the clothes and fled the room, letting out a huge exhalation in the hallway. Twenty-five seconds: not even near his record for breath-holding. His mum was buttering rolls at the kitchen table. She handed him one. He got himself a mug of milk and sat down. He'd told his mum that because of cutbacks, his school didn't

119

start till half past nine. Either she'd believed him, or hadn't been up to arguing. She looked tired, his mum, looked like she needed a treat. But he knew looks could deceive: she could go from tired to mental in two seconds flat. He'd seen her do it with one of the old hoors from upstairs who'd come to complain about the noise. Pure mental. Same thing with the old guy who'd complained of the ball landing in his garden.

'Next time I'll put a garden fork through it, so help me.'

'Do that,' Jamie's mum had said, 'and I'll take your fucking fork and stick it through your balls.' Right up close to him, growing huge as he seemed to shrink.

Jamie had a lot of respect for his mum. Last time she'd clipped him, it had been because he'd tried calling her Van. Cal called her Van, but that was all right because he was grown up, same as she was. Jamie couldn't wait to grow up.

With a mug of tea in her hand, his mum went through her morning ritual: trying to remember where she'd put her cigarettes.

'Maybe Cal's got them,' Jamie suggested.

'Finish what's in your mouth before you speak.' She yelled towards Cal's room, got a yelled denial back. In the living room, she pulled cushions off the sofa and chair, kicked the pile of car and music magazines sitting on the floor. Found half a packet on top of the hi-fi. The top of the flip-pack was missing. Cal used them for his 'special roll-ups'. His mum pulled out a cigarette, but most of it was missing too. She sighed heavily, stuck it in her mouth anyway and lit it with the lighter she found inside the packet.

She didn't have any pockets, so put the cigarettes on the arm of her chair. She was wearing silver-grey shell-suit bottoms with a purple zip-up jogging top. The top was old, the lettering on its back – SPORTING NATION – cracked and peeling. Jamie wondered if Sporting Nation meant Scotland.

120

Roll and milk finished, he slid off his chair. He had plans for today: Princes Street maybe, or a bus out to The Gyle. On his own, or with anyone he could round up. Problem with The Gyle was, it was in the middle of nowhere. There was a games arcade on Lothian Road, he liked it there, but there were other regulars who were better than him at the games, and even if he didn't want to play against them, they'd stand and watch him on his machine, then tell him what mistakes he was making and say they could do better with their wrists in plaster.

Just as well, he knew he should tell them, *because the way you're going, your whole body's going to end up in plaster.* But he never did: most of them were bigger than him. And they didn't know Cal, so he was no use as a threat. Which was why Jamie didn't go in there so much any more . . .

Cal's bedroom door flew open and he stalked into the kitchen. He had his jeans on, but had forgotten to zip them up or buckle his belt. No shoes or socks, no T-shirt. He had nicks and bruises on his chest and arms. You could see the muscles moving beneath his skin. He flung the paper on to the table and slapped a hand down on it.

'Look at this,' he hissed, face pink with anger. 'Just take a look at this.'

Jamie looked: double-page story. SEX OFFENDER WITH PLAYGROUND VIEW. There were photos. One showed a block of flats, an arrow pointing to one of the storeys. The other showed a patch of tarmac and a couple of kids playing.

'That's here,' he said, amazed. He'd never seen Greenfield in the papers before, never seen photos of the place. His mum came over.

'What is it?' she asked.

'Fucking pervert living right under our noses,' Cal spat. 'Nobody told us.' He stabbed the paper. 'Says so right here. Nobody bothered to tell us.'

Van studied the story. 'There's no picture of him.'

'No, but they as good as point at the bastard's door.'

She remembered something. 'Cops came round the other day. I thought they were looking for you.'

'What did they want?'

'Just the one of them. Asked if I knew somebody called . . .' She squeezed shut her eyes. 'Darren something-or-other.'

'Darren Rough,' Jamie said. Cal stared at him.

'You know him?'

Jamie didn't know what answer would please Cal. He shrugged. 'Seen him around the place.'

'How do you know his name?' Eyes burning into him.

'He . . . I don't know.'

'He what?' Cal was facing him now, fists bunched. 'Which flat's he in?' Jamie started to tell him, but Cal snatched the neck of his shirt. 'Better still, show me.'

But as they walked along the landing to Darren Rough's flat, they saw that others had the same idea. A group of seven or eight residents stood outside Rough's door. Most of them had the morning paper with them, rolled up and brandished like a weapon. Cal was disappointed they weren't the first.

'Is he no' in?'

'No' answering anyway.'

Cal kicked at the door, saw from the looks around him that they were impressed. Stood back and shouldered the door, kicked it again. Two locks: Yale and mortice. No way to see inside: letterbox was blocked up; a sheet pinned across the window. Everyone was talking about it.

'Wake up, ya bastardin' pervert!' Cal Brady shouted at the window. 'Come and meet your fan club!' There were smiles around him.

'Maybe he works shifts,' someone offered. Cal couldn't think of a smart remark to make back. He thumped on the window instead, then went back to kicking the door. A few more residents arrived, but more began to drift away. Soon there were just a couple of kids, plus Cal and Jamie.

'Jamie,' Cal said, 'go get me a spray can. Try under my bed.'

Jamie already knew there were a couple of cans under there. 'Blue or black?' he asked, before he realised what he'd done.

But Cal didn't notice. He was busy staring at the door. 'Doesn't matter,' he said. Jamie went off to fetch the can. His mum was outside, arms folded, talking with a couple of women from the landing. Jamie trotted past them.

'Well?' his mum said.

'Nobody's in.'

She turned back to her friends. 'Could be anywhere. Scum like that, there's no telling.'

'What we need's a petition,' one of the women said.

'Aye, get the council to rehouse him.'

'Think they'll listen to us?' Van said. 'Direct action, that's what we want. Our problem, we deal with it, never mind what anyone else says.'

'People's Republic of Greenfield,' another woman offered.

'I'm serious, Michele,' Van said, 'deadly serious.' Behind her, Jamie disappeared into the flat.

15

'Mum and me, we seemed to move around a lot in the early days.'

Cary Oakes was in a chair by his bedroom window, feet up on the table in front of him. Jim Stevens sat on a corner of the bed, holding the tape recorder at arm's length.

'Places? Dates?'

Oakes looked at him. 'I don't remember the names of towns, people we stayed with. When you're a kid, that sort of thing doesn't matter, does it? I had my own life, my own little fantasy world. I'd be a soldier or a fighter pilot. Scotland would be full of aliens, and I'd be out to get them, a vigilante sort of scenario.' He gazed out of the window. 'Because we moved so much, I never really made any friends. Not close friends.' He saw that Stevens was about to interrupt. 'Again, I can't give any names. I remember coming to Edinburgh, though.' He paused, stretched to rub his thumb across the toe of one shoe, removing a trace of dirt. 'Yes, Edinburgh sticks in my mind. We stayed with family. My aunt and her husband. Don't remember which part of town they lived in. There was a park nearby. I went there a lot. Maybe we could get a picture of me there.'

Stevens nodded. 'If you can remember where it is.'

Oakes smiled. 'Any park would do, wouldn't it? We'd just pretend. That's what I did in that park. It was my universe. *Mine*. I could do whatever the hell I liked there. I was God.'

'So what did you do?' Stevens was thinking: this is easy, fluid. Oakes was either a born storyteller or else . . . or else

he'd been rehearsing. But something had jarred, something about family: *my aunt and her husband.* A strange
way of putting it.

'What did I do? I played games, same as every other kid.
I had an imagination, I'll tell you that. When you're a kid,
nobody minds if you run around shooting up the world,
know what I'm saying? In your head, you can kill whole
populations. I'll bet there isn't one damned person on this
planet hasn't thought about murdering someone at *some*
time. I'll bet you have.'

'I'll show you my collection of voodoo dolls.'

Oakes smiled. 'My mum, she did her best for me.' He
paused. 'I'm sure of that.'

'What happened to her?'

'She died, man.' His eyes bored into the reporter's. 'But
then everybody dies.'

'You played these games by yourself?'

Oakes shook his head. 'The other kids got to know me. I
joined a gang, rose through the ranks.'

'See much action?'

Oakes shrugged. 'There were a few fights. Mostly we
just played football and glowered at strangers. Offed a few
of the neighbourhood cats too.'

'How?'

'Sprayed them with lighter fluid, torched them.' Oakes's
eyes fixed on Stevens. 'Typical start to your basic serial
killer. I read about it in jail. Loner who torches animals.'

'But you weren't alone, you were with your gang.'

Oakes smiled again. 'But I was the one with the lighter,
Jim. And that made all the difference.'

When they took a break, Stevens returned to his own
room. Two sachets of coffee into a cup of boiling water.
He'd been wakened at four that morning by the telephone. His boss had worked a miracle, and Stevens found
himself speaking to a Seattle journalist who'd followed the
Oakes case all the way along. The journalist, Matt Lewin,

confirmed that Oakes had attended regular Sunday services in the Walla Walla penitentiary.

'A lot of them do, doesn't mean they've seen the light.'

Now Stevens lay back on the bed and sipped his coffee. He wanted to track down Oakes's teenage gang. It would be good background, another insight into Cary Oakes. If they ran the story, maybe someone from the gang would read it and come forward. Then Stevens could interview them for the book. He'd asked Matt Lewin if any American publishers would be interested.

'Not when he's not one of ours. We like home-grown product. Besides, Jim, serial killers went out of fashion a while back.'

Stevens was hoping for a fashion revival. The book deal would be his gold watch, a little retirement gift to himself. He knew he should do some research, try to check the stories Oakes had been telling. But he felt so tired, and his boss had told him: get the story first, confirm it later. He finished his coffee and reached for a cigarette. Swung his legs off the bed.

Showtime.

Janice Mee took a break, ate at the restaurant at the top of John Lewis's. From one window, the view was of Calton Hill. They'd climbed it with Damon one day, back when he was seven or eight. She had photos of the trip in one of her albums: Calton Hill, the Castle, Museum of Childhood . . . There were dozens of albums. She kept them in the bottom of the wardrobe. She'd taken them out recently, brought the whole lot downstairs so she could go through them, reviving memories of holiday camps and days at the seaside, birthday parties and sports days. From one of the restaurant's other windows, she had a good view of the Fife coastline. She couldn't see as far inland as her home town. There were times in the course of her life when she'd contemplated a move: south to Edinburgh, north to Dundee. But there was something comfortable about the place where you were born, where your family and friends were. Her parents and grandparents had been born in Fife, the history of the place inextricably linked to her own. Her mother had been a little girl at the time of the General Strike, but remembered them putting up barricades around Lochgelly. Her father had clung to a lamp-post to watch Johnny Thomson's funeral. The way a family stretched back in time could be measured. But that sense of history misled you into thinking the future would be the same. As Janice was finding out, the thread of continuity could be snapped at any point along the way.

She ate the roll, filled with prawn mayonnaise, without any pleasure or sense of taste. She knew she'd drunk her coffee only because the cup was empty. One pale prawn sat on the rim of the plate, where it had fallen from the roll. She left it where it was and got up from the table.

Outside the St James' Centre she crossed Princes Street and headed for Waverley Station. A line of taxi cabs snaked from the underground concourse back up on to Waverley Bridge. The drivers sat behind their wheels, some reading or eating or listening to their radios. Others staring into space or sharing news with fellow drivers. She started at the back of the queue and worked her way forwards. John Rebus had given her some names. One of them was Henry Wilson. The drivers all seemed to know him, called him 'The Lumberjack'. They put out a call to him. Meantime, she showed them her pictures of Damon and explained that he'd been picked up on George Street.

'Anyone with him, love?' one driver asked.

'A woman . . . short blonde hair.'

The driver shook his head. 'I've a good memory for blondes,' he said, handing back the flyer.

The problem was, a couple of trains had just arrived – London and Glasgow. The taxis were moving faster than she could, heading down to where their passengers waited. She looked back up the slope. More taxis were joining the back of the queue. She couldn't tell who she'd talked to and who was new. Engines were starting, fumes getting into her lungs. Cars sounding their horns as they moved past her, heading down into the station, wondering what she was doing on the roadway when there was a pavement the other side. Day-trippers looked at her, too. They knew she'd never get a taxi here, knew the system: you queued at the rank.

Her mouth felt sour and gritty. The coffee had been strong: she could feel her heart pounding. And then another car sounded its horn.

'All right, all right,' she said, passing down the line to the next taxi, which was already moving off. The car-horn sounded again: right behind her. She turned on it, glowering, saw it was another black cab, window open. Nobody in the back, just the driver, leaning towards her. Short black hair, long black beard, green tartan shirt.

'Lumberjack?' she said.

He nodded. 'That's what they call me.'

She smiled. 'John Rebus gave me your name.' Cars were held up behind him. One flashed its lights.

'You better get in,' he said. 'Before they have my licence off me for obstruction.'

Janice Mee got in.

The taxi went down into the station, and took the exit ramp back up, then turned right and crossed the traffic, settling at the back of the queue of cabs. Henry Wilson pulled on the handbrake and turned in his seat.

'So what does the Inspector want this time?'

And Janice Mee told him.

It had to be serious: instead of summoning him, the Farmer had come looking for Rebus, who was out in the car park having a cigarette and thinking about Janice Playfair aged fifteen . . .

'Is it the surveillance?' Rebus asked, thinking maybe something had happened.

'No, it bloody well isn't.' The Farmer stuck his hands in his pockets: he meant business.

'What have I done this time?'

'The press have got hold of Darren Rough. One paper printed the story this morning, the rest are busy catching up. My secretary's fielded so many calls, she doesn't know if she's in St Leonard's or St Pancras.'

'How did they get the story?' Rebus asked, ditching his cigarette.

The Farmer narrowed his eyes. 'That's what Rough's social worker wants to know. He's ready to make a formal complaint.'

Rebus rubbed at his nose. 'He thinks I did it?'

'John, I know bloody well you did it.'

'With respect, sir—'

'John, just shut up, will you? The reporter you spoke to, first thing he did when you'd put the phone down was hit 1471. He got the number you were calling from.'

'And?'

'And it was The Maltings.' Public house: almost directly across the street from St Leonard's. 'But better than that, our intrepid reporter asked the punter who answered about the person who'd last used the phone. Want me to read you the description?'

'Male, white, middle-aged?' Rebus guessed. 'Could be a thousand blokes.'

'Could be. Which hasn't stopped Rough's social worker thinking it's you.'

Rebus looked out towards Salisbury Crags. 'I'm glad somebody shopped him.' He paused. 'If that was what it was going to take.'

'Take to do what? To run him out of town? To get a mob baying for his blood? John, I'd hate to see what you'd do to Ince and Marshall.'

Ince and Marshall: the Shiellion accused.

'You wouldn't have to watch,' Rebus said. He squared up to his boss. 'What do you want me to do?'

'Steer clear of Rough, that's number one. Stay on the Oakes surveillance, at least that way you'll keep out of trouble for six hours at a stretch. And give Jane Barbour a bell.' He handed Rebus a slip of paper with a phone number on it.

'Barbour? What does she want?'

'No idea. Probably something to do with Shiellion House.'

Rebus stared at the phone number. 'Probably,' he said.

The Farmer left him to it, and instead of going back into the station, Rebus walked down the lane towards the main road, checked for traffic and walked briskly across. Stepped into The Maltings. It was quiet most daytimes. When he'd made the call, there'd only been one other drinker in the place. A minute after opening time, the same man was alone at the bar with a half-pint and a whisky in front of him.

'Alexander,' Rebus said, 'a word with you, please.' He pulled the drinker by his arm towards the gents' toilets: didn't want the barmaid listening in.

'Christ, man, what is it?' The drinker's name was Alexander Jessup. He didn't like Alex or Alec or Sandy or Eck: it had to be Alexander. He'd run his own business at one time: a printer's. Did headed paper, account books, raffle tickets and the like. Sold it on and was quietly drinking the proceeds away. As a man about town, he heard things, but never gave Rebus much that proved useful. He did like to talk though; he'd talk to anyone who'd listen.

'Any reporters been after you?' Rebus asked.

Jessup looked at him with rheumy eyes, like those of an old dog. He shook his head. His face was a mess of puffiness and burst capillaries.

'You spoke to one on the phone,' Rebus reminded him.

'Was he a reporter?' Jessup looked stung. 'He never said.'

'You gave him my description.'

'I might've done.' He thought about it, nodded, then held up a finger. 'But no names, you know me, John. I never gave him your name.'

Rebus kept his voice low. 'If anyone comes looking, keep the description as vague as you can, understood? You never saw the guy on the phone before, he's not a regular.' He waited for the message to sink in. Jessup gave him an enormous wink.

'Message received.'

'And understood?'

'And understood,' Jessup confirmed. 'I didn't get you into trouble, did I?' Dying to know. 'You know I'd never do something like that.'

Rebus patted his shoulder. 'I know, Alexander. Just remember who brings you your breakfast when they've put you in the cells for the night.'

'Right enough, John.' Jessup gave an 'OK' sign with his hand. 'Sorry if I got you into any bother.'

Rebus pulled open the door. 'Here, let me buy you one, eh?'

'Only if you'll take one back.'

'It's tempting,' Rebus said, as they headed for the bar. 'I'd be lying if I said that it wasn't.'

'Have you been drinking?' Janice Mee asked.

Rebus didn't reply straight away; he was too busy looking around his living room. Janice laughed.

'Sorry,' she said. 'Couldn't help myself.'

The place had been tidied: newspapers and magazines now took up space on the bottom bookshelf. Books which had been scattered across the floor were on the second and third shelves up. Mugs and plates had vanished into the kitchen, takeaway wrappers and beer cans deposited in the bin. Even the ashtray had been cleaned. Rebus picked it up.

'I think that's the first time I've been able to make out what it says.'

It was lifted from a pub, advertising some new beer which hadn't made the grade.

Janice smiled. 'It's something I do when I'm nervous.'

'You should be nervous round here more often.'

She gave him a punch.

'Careful,' he said, 'last time you tried that, I was out cold for ten minutes.'

'I bought teabags and milk while I was out,' she told him, making for the kitchen. 'Do you want a cup?'

'Please.' He followed the trail of her perfume. He hadn't brought Patience here in over a year; had never entertained many women here. 'So how did it go?'

'I liked The Lumberjack.'

'But was he any help?'

She made herself busy with the kettle. 'Oh, you know . . .'

'Did you get round all the cab ranks?'

'Your friend said I didn't need to. He'd do it for me.'

'Which left you feeling useless again?'

She tried to smile. 'I thought . . . I thought coming here I could . . .' She bowed her head, voice dropping to a whisper. 'I'd have been better off staying at home.'

'Janice.' He turned her so she was facing him. 'You're doing your best.' Her height, her softness and slenderness. They stood as close together now as they had done when they'd danced at the school leaving party, their last night as a couple. Formal dances: waltzes and military two-steps and the Gay Gordons. She wanting each dance to last; he wanting to take her round the back of the school, to their secret place – the same secret place everyone else used.

'You're doing your best,' he repeated.

'But it's not helping. Know what I found myself thinking today? I thought: I'll kill him for putting me through this.' Bitter twist of a smile. 'Then I thought: what if he's already dead?'

'He's not dead,' Rebus said. 'Trust me on this. He's not.'

They took the tea through to the living room, sat at the dining table.

'What time are you headed back?' he asked.

'I thought six. There's a train around then.'

'I'll drive you.'

She shook her head. 'Even a country girl like me knows what the traffic's like that time of day. I'd be quicker on the train.'

Which was true. 'I'll run you to the station then.' What else had he to do before his shift started, other than try to doze for a while?

She placed her hands around the mug. 'Why a policeman, Johnny?'

'Why?' He tried to form an answer she'd accept. 'I'd been in the army, didn't like it, didn't know what I wanted to do.'

'It's not exactly the kind of job you drift into.'

'For some of us it is. See, I really got into it.'

'And you're good at what you do?'

He shrugged. 'I get results.'

'Is that not the same thing?'

'Not exactly. Keeping your head down and your nose clean, being good at the office politics . . . I fall down there.' He shifted in his chair. 'You always said you were going to be a teacher.'

'I was a teacher . . . for a while.'

Rebus refrained from saying that his ex-wife had been a teacher too.

'Then you married Brian?' he asked instead.

'The two aren't connected.' She looked down into her tea, seemed relieved when the phone rang. Rebus picked it up.

'Evening, Mr Rebus.'

'Henry,' Rebus said for Janice's benefit, 'got anything for us?'

'Might have. Two fares, picked up on George Street.

Driver remembered the blonde. Distinctive face, he said. Kind of hard. Cold eyes. He thought maybe she was a pro.'

'Where did he take them?' Rebus looking at Janice, who had stood up, still clutching the mug.

'Down to Leith, dropped them by The Shore.'

Leith: where the city's working girls plied their trade. The Shore: where Cary Oakes's hotel was.

'Did he see where they went?'

'The lad wasn't a big tipper. My mate got straight back on the road. Someone had tried flagging him down on Bernard Street. Not many places they could have been going. That time of night, the pubs would be on last orders if they weren't already shut. There are flats down there, though.'

Rebus agreed. Flats . . . and the hotel.

'Unless they were going to that boat,' Wilson said.

'What boat?'

'The one that's tied up down there.' Yes: Rebus had seen it, looked like a semi-permanent mooring. 'They use it for parties,' Wilson was saying. 'Not that I've ever been to one . . .'

He dropped Janice off at Waverley's concourse. They'd arranged to meet the next afternoon, go look at the boat.

'May be something or nothing,' Rebus had felt obliged to warn her.

'I'll settle for that,' she'd said.

As she made to leave the car, she hesitated, then leaned towards him and planted a kiss on his cheek.

'What, no tongues?' he said, smiling. She made to thump his arm, thought better of it. 'Say hello to Brian from me.'

'I will. If he's not out with his pals.' Something in her tone made Rebus want to pursue the subject, but she was out of the car, closing the door. She waved, blew him a kiss, turned and walked towards her platform with the look of a woman who knows she's being watched. Rebus realised he had one hand on his door handle.

'Forget it,' he told himself. Instead, he picked up his mobile, told Patience's machine that he was on night shift and was headed back to his own flat for a bit of kip.

But first, a pit-stop at the Oxford Bar: whisky with plenty of water. Just the one: responsible car-driver. He caught up on the gossip, adding little to the conversation. George Klasser chastised him for a lapse of faith.

'You're becoming an irregular regular, John.'

'I always was, Doc.'

Further along the bar, a rugby argument was developing, drawing other drinkers in. Everyone had an opinion, everyone but Rebus himself. He stared at a print on the wall: portrait of Robert Burns. There was another on the far wall: Burns meeting a young Walter Scott. It looked like a fairly awkward affair, the artist working with benefit of hindsight. It was as if Burns knew the child before him was destined to outsell him, knew the runt would get a knighthood, build Abbotsford and cosy up to the King.

It was a great thing, hindsight.

He looked into his glass and saw the leavers' dance. Saw a gangly kid called Johnny leading his girlfriend out of the hall, out the school doors and down the steps. Making like it was a game, but tugging her hard by both hands. Both of them pretending it was all right, because that was part of the whole ritual. And back in the hall, Johnny's pal Mitch – best friends; always sticking up for one another – not realising he was being stalked by three boys who'd become his enemies. Boys who knew this might be their last chance for revenge. Revenge for what? They probably didn't know themselves. Maybe for some ugly feeling that life had already short-changed them; that people like Mitch were going to succeed where they'd taste only failure.

Three against one.

While Johnny Rebus played out another fate entirely.

Rebus finished his drink, drove home. Sank into his chair, a double malt in his fist. Listened to Tommy Smith, *The Sound of Love*. Pondered whether or not you really could *hear* love.

Fell asleep in the orange sodium glow of the streetlights. As close to being at peace as he got.

It had taken them a while to find a church with an unlocked door.

'No one has any trust these days,' Cary Oakes had said, 'not even God.'

They'd walked through Leith and up the Walk to Pilrig. It was a Catholic church, nobody around but them. Cool and dark inside. There were plenty of windows, but the church was surrounded on three sides by tenement buildings. Time was, as Stevens recalled, you weren't allowed to build anything higher than a church. Oakes was sitting in a pew near the front, head bowed. He didn't look exactly peaceful or contemplative: his neck and shoulders were tensed, his breathing fast and shallow. Stevens wasn't comfortable. The door might not have been locked, but he felt like a trespasser. A Catholic church, too: he didn't think he'd been in one of those his whole life. Didn't look much different from the Presbyterian model: no smell of incense. Confession boxes, but he'd seen those before in films. One of them, the curtain was open. He glanced in, trying not to think that it looked like a Photo-Me booth. He tried to take soundless steps; didn't want a priest appearing, having to explain what they were doing there.

Oakes's request: 'I'd like to go to church.'

Stevens: 'Can't it wait till Sunday?'

But Oakes's eyes had told him it was no joking matter. So they'd headed off on foot, the surveillance car following at a crawl, drawing attention to itself and to them.

'They want to play it that way,' Oakes had said, 'that's fine by me.'

136

Ten, fifteen minutes passed. Stevens wondered if maybe Oakes had nodded off. He walked down the aisle, stopped beside him. Oakes looked up.

'A couple more minutes, Jim.' Oakes motioned with his head. 'Take a break, if you like.'

Stevens didn't need telling twice. Stepped outside for a cigarette. Cop car parked at the end of the street, driver watching him. He'd just got one lit when the thought struck him: you're a reporter on a story. You should be in there, trying to find an angle, running phrases through your head. Oakes in church: it could open one of the book chapters. So he nipped the cigarette, slipped it back into the packet. Pushed open the door and went inside.

There was no sign of Oakes in any of the pews. Sound of running water. Stevens peered into the gloom, eyes adjusting slowly. A shape over by the confessional. Oakes standing there, looking over his shoulder towards Stevens, body arched as he urinated through the curtain. Oakes grinned, winked. Finished his business and zipped himself up. He was walking back up the aisle, back to where Stevens stood, face failing to disguise his shock. Oakes pointed up towards the ceiling.

'Got to remind Him just who's boss, Jim.' He moved past Stevens and out into daylight. Stevens stood there a moment longer. Pissing into the confessional: a message to God, or to the reporter himself? Stevens turned and left the church, wondering how the hell his world had come to this.

16

A young DS called Roy Frazer was the fourth member of
the surveillance team. He'd arrived at St Leonard's the
previous month, a rare recruit from F Division, based in
Livingston. Edinburgh city cops knew the Livingston
operation as 'F Troop'. They'd had a few digs at Frazer,
but he'd been able – or at least willing – to take them. The
Farmer had chosen Frazer for the team. The Farmer
thought Frazer was a bit special.

Rebus sat beside him in the Rover, listening to his
report.

'Only real highlight,' Frazer was saying, 'that restaurant next to the pub back there, they took pity on me,
brought me out a meal.'

'You're kidding.' Rebus looked back towards the pub in
question. Just past closing time, and drinkers were taking
their grudging leave.

'Carrot soup, then some chicken thing in puff pastry.
Wasn't bad at all.'

Rebus looked down at the carrier bag he'd brought with
him: flask of strong coffee; two filled rolls (corned beef and
beetroot); chocolate and crisps; some tapes and his
Walkman; an evening paper and a couple of books.

'Brought it out on a tray, came back half an hour later
with some coffee and mints.'

'You want to be careful, son,' Rebus cautioned. 'No
such thing as a free dinner. Once you start taking
bribes . . .' He shook his head ruefully. 'I mean, it might
have been the done thing in Livingston, but you're not in
the sticks now.'

Frazer saw at last that he was joking, produced a grin which was two parts relief to one part humour. He was strong-looking, played rugby for the police team. Cropped black hair, square-jawed. When he'd arrived at St Leonard's, he'd sported a thick moustache, but had shaved it off for some reason. The skin beneath still looked pink and delicate. Rebus knew he came from farming stock – somewhere between West Calder and the A70. His father still farmed there. Something he had in common with The Farmer, whose family had worked the land around Stonehaven. Another thing the two men shared: regular church-going. Rebus, too, went to churches, but seldom on a Sunday. He liked them empty except for his thoughts.

'Have you got the log?' Rebus asked. Frazer produced the A4-sized notebook. Bill Pryde had taken over from Siobhan Clarke at 6 a.m., recorded that Oakes and Stevens had stayed in the hotel until eleven. Up till then, they hadn't come downstairs – he'd checked with the front desk. Morning coffee for two had been ordered for Oakes's room. Pryde's interpretation: they were working. A cab had arrived at eleven, and both men had come out of the hotel. Stevens had handed a large envelope to the cabbie, who'd driven off again. Pryde's guess: tape of first interview, heading for the newspaper office.

With the taxi gone, Stevens and Oakes had walked into Leith Docks, Pryde following on foot. They looked like they were killing time, taking a breather. Then it was back to the hotel. Siobhan Clarke took over at noon: Rebus had persuaded her to change shifts with him. Not that it had been difficult: 'I like my own bed at night,' she'd admitted.

The afternoon had gone much as the morning: the two men ensconced in the hotel; taxi taking delivery of an envelope; the two men taking a break. Except this time they'd headed into town, stopping at a church in Pilrig. Rebus looked at Frazer.

'A church?'

Frazer just shrugged. After the church, they'd headed to the top of the Walk and John Lewis's, where they shopped for clothes for Oakes. New shoes, too. Stevens put everything on his plastic. Then they'd hit a couple of pubs: the Café Royal, Guildford Arms. Clarke had stayed outside: 'Didn't know whether to go in or not. It's not as if they didn't know I was there.'

Back to the hotel, Oakes giving her a wave as she pulled up outside.

Relieved by Frazer at 6 p.m. The two men, Stevens and Oakes, had walked to one of the new restaurants built facing the Scottish Office. One wall was all glass, affording them a view of Frazer as he kicked his heels outside. Apart from his own surprise dinner – not mentioned in the notebook – that was about it.

'Would I be right in thinking this is a complete waste of time?' Frazer stated when Rebus had finished reading.

'Depends on your parameters,' Rebus said. He'd lifted the line from a training course at Tulliallan.

'Well, they're obviously here for the duration, aren't they?'

'We just want Oakes to know.'

'Yes, but surely the time to let him know is when he's left to his own devices. Once he's found himself a place to live, and all the media stuff's finished.'

Frazer had a point. Rebus conceded as much with a slow nod of his head. 'Don't tell me,' he said, 'tell the Chief Super.'

'That's just what I did.' Rebus looked at him, waiting for more. 'He turned up about nine o'clock, wanting to know how things were going.'

'And you told him?'

Frazer nodded; Rebus laughed.

'What did he say?'

'He said to give it a few more days.'

'You know they think Oakes might kill again?'

140

'Only person within range at the moment is that reporter. Anything happened to him, I'd be heartbroken.'

Rebus burst out laughing again. 'Know something, Roy? You're going to be all right.'

'The power of prayer, sir.'

Rebus had been in the car by himself for an hour, cold seeping inside his three pairs of socks, when he saw someone push open the door of the hotel and step outside. The hotel bar was still open, wouldn't close till the last guest had had enough. Stevens wore his tie loose around his neck, top two shirt buttons open. He was blowing cigarette smoke up into the sky, shuffling his feet to keep his balance. Been there, done that, Rebus thought. Eventually, Stevens focused on the police car, seemed to find it amusing. Chuckled to himself, bending forward at the waist, shaking his head slowly. Came walking towards the car. Rebus got out, waited for him.

'So we meet at last, Moriarty,' Stevens said. Rebus folded his arms, leaned against the car.

'How's the baby-sitting?'

Stevens puffed out his cheeks. 'To tell you the truth, I'm having trouble getting a handle on him.'

'How do you mean?'

'All that time behind bars – no pun intended – you'd think he might want to celebrate.'

'I'm guessing he doesn't drink.'

'Your guess is correct. Says drink contaminates his mind, makes him feel dangerous.' A humourless laugh.

'How much longer?' Rebus could smell the whisky on Stevens' breath. Give him a minute or two, he'd place the brand.

'Couple more days. It's good stuff, wait till you read it.'

'Know what the Yanks told us? They said he'll kill again.'

'Really?'

'Has he said anything?'

141

Stevens nodded. 'Gave me a list of his next victims. Nice tie-in with the story.' Stevens grinned lopsidedly, saw the look on Rebus's face. 'Sorry, sorry. Not in very good taste. I've got a publisher interested, did I tell you? Coming back to me tomorrow or the day after with an offer.'

'How can you do it?' Rebus asked quietly.

Stevens got his balance back. 'Do what?'

'Do what you do.'

'Sounds like a Motown line.' He sniffed, coughed. 'It's an interesting story, Rebus. That's what he means to me: a story. What does he mean to you?' He awaited a response, didn't get one, wagged a finger. 'That note you left me: "Drop him". Think I'd suddenly see the light, hand him over to somebody else, some other paper? No chance, pal. This isn't the Damascus Road.'

'I'd noticed.'

'And my boy's not the only ex-offender in the news, is he? I see someone outed a paedophile. Word is, it was a cop.' He tutted, wagged his finger again. 'Any comment to make, Inspector?'

'Go fuck yourself, Stevens.'

'Ah, now there's another thing. Guy's been in the nick fourteen years, and here we are in Leith, Edinburgh's knocking-shop, and he's not interested. Can you credit that?'

'Maybe he's got other things on his mind.'

'Wouldn't bother me if he preferred chickens, just so long as he gets me a book deal.' He rubbed his hands together. 'Look at us, eh? You out here, me in that big hotel. Makes you think.'

'Go to bed, Stevens. You need all the beauty sleep you can get.'

Stevens turned away, remembered something and turned back. 'OK for a wee photo-shoot tomorrow night? Photographer's coming anyway, and I thought it'd make a nice sidebar: cop who'll never sleep while killer's at large.'

Rebus said nothing, waited till the reporter had turned away again. 'What did he want in the church?' The question stopped Stevens cold. Rebus repeated it. Stevens half-turned towards him, shook his head slowly, then walked back across the road. There was something tired in the walk now, something Rebus couldn't interpret. He reached into the car for his cigarettes, lit one. Closed the driver's door and walked fifty yards to the end of the road, then across the bridge to the other side of the basin, where a boat was moored. There was a sign telling patrons to respect the neighbours and keep the noise down late at night. But the boat wasn't being used tonight, no private party or celebration. Nearby, they were building more 'New York loft-style apartments' for young professionals, part of Leith's revival. Rebus crossed back to the pub, but it was closed now. The bar staff would probably be inside, enjoying a drink as they replayed the evening's highlights. Rebus walked back to the car.

An hour later, a taxi pulled up outside the hotel. His first thought: another tape for the newspaper. But someone was in the taxi. They paid the driver, got out. Rebus checked his watch. Two fifteen. One of the guests who'd been out on the town. He took a nip from his quarter-bottle, slipped the headphones back on to his ears. String Driven Thing: 'Another Night in This Old City'.

That's all it ever was . . .

Forty minutes later, the man from the taxi exited the hotel. He waved back to the night porter. Window down, Rebus heard him say, 'Good night.' He stood outside, glanced at his watch, looked up and down the street. Looking for a taxi, Rebus thought. Who would be visiting a hotel this time of night? *Who* would he be visiting?

The man's gaze fell on the police car. Rebus wound the window down further, flicked ash on to the roadway. The man was making his way towards the car. Rebus opened his door, got out.

'Inspector Rebus?' The man held out his hand. Rebus

gave him a once-over. Late fifties, well-dressed. Didn't look the type to pull a stunt, but you could never be sure. The man read his thoughts, smiled.

'I don't blame you. Middle of the night, stranger wants to make friends, already knows your name . . .'

Rebus narrowed his eyes. 'We've met before, haven't we?'

'A while back. You've got a good memory. My name's Archibald. Alan Archibald.'

Rebus nodded, finally shook Archibald's hand. 'You had a posting at Great London Road.'

'For a couple of months, yes. Before I retired, I was based at Fettes, pushing paper around a desk.'

Alan Archibald: tall, cropped salt-and-pepper hair. A face full of strong features, a body resisting the ageing process.

'I heard you'd retired.'

Archibald shrugged. 'Twenty years in, I thought it was time.' His look said: what about you? Rebus's mouth twitched.

'It's warmer in the car. I can't offer you a lift, but I could probably . . .'

'I know,' Alan Archibald was saying. 'Cary Oakes told me.'

'He what?'

Archibald nodded towards the car. 'I'll take you up on your offer, though. I'm not used to night shifts these days.'

So they got into the car, Archibald tucking his black woollen overcoat around him. Rebus ran the engine, stuck the heating on, offered Archibald a cigarette.

'I don't, thanks all the same. But don't let me stop you.'

'You'd need heavy artillery to stop me,' Rebus said, lighting another for himself. 'So what's the story with Oakes?'

Archibald touched his fingers to the dashboard. 'He called me, told me where he was.' He looked at Rebus. 'He knows all about you.'

144

Rebus shrugged. 'That's the point.'

'Yes, he knows that too. But he knew *you* were on the late shift.'

'Not difficult. He can see me from his bedroom window.' Rebus pointed towards it. 'Or maybe his minder told him.'

'The journalist? I didn't meet him.'

'Probably in bed.'

'Yes, I had to ring up to Oakes's bedroom. He wasn't sleeping, though, told me it's jet-lag.'

'How did he get your number?'

'It's unlisted.' Archibald paused. 'I'm guessing the journalist pulled a few strings.'

Rebus inhaled smoke, let it pour down his nostrils. 'So what's the story?'

'My guess is, Oakes wants to play some game.'

Rebus looked at his passenger. 'What sort of game?'

'The sort that gets me out of bed at one in the morning. That's when he phoned, said we had to meet now or never at all.'

'What about?'

'The murder.'

Rebus frowned. 'Murder singular?'

'Not one of the ones he committed in the States. This happened right here in Edinburgh. More specifically, out at Hillend.'

Hillend: at the northern tip of the Pentland Hills – hence the name. Known locally for its artificial ski-slope. From the bypass, you could see the lights at night. Suddenly, Rebus remembered the case. An outcrop of rocks, a woman's body. Young woman: student at a teacher-training college. Rebus had helped with the initial search. The search had taken him from Hillend to Swanston Cottages, an extraordinary cluster of homes, seemingly untouched by modernity. All at once he'd wanted to buy a place there, but it had been too isolated for his wife – and outwith their means anyway.

'This was fifteen years ago?' Rebus said.

145

Archibald shook his head. He'd slipped his hands into his pockets, was staring at the windscreen. 'Seventeen years,' he told Rebus. 'Seventeen years this month. Her name was Deirdre Campbell.'

'Were you on the case?'

Archibald shook his head again. 'Wasn't possible at the time.' He took a deep breath. 'Never found the killer.'

'She was strangled?'

'Beaten about the head, then strangled.'

Rebus remembered Oakes's *modus operandi*. Again, it was as if Archibald could read his mind.

'Similar,' he said.

'Was Oakes here at the time?'

'It was just before he left for the States.'

Rebus gave a low whistle. 'He's owned up?'

Archibald shifted in his seat. 'Not exactly. When he was arrested in the States, I followed his trial, noticed similarities. I went out there to interview him.'

'And?'

'And he played his little games. Hints, smiles and half-truths and stories. He led me a merry little dance.'

'I thought you weren't on the case?'

'I wasn't. Not officially.'

'I don't get it.'

Archibald examined his fingertips. 'All these years he's been inside, we've played his games. Because I know I can wear him down. He doesn't know how persistent I can be.'

'And now he phones you in the middle of the night?'

'And feeds me more stories.' A half-smile. 'But he doesn't seem to realise, the gameboard has changed. He's in Scotland now. *My* rules.' A pause. 'I've asked him to come out to Hillend with me.'

Rebus stared at Archibald. 'The man's a killer. Psych reports say he'll do it again.'

'He kills the weak. I'm not weak.'

Rebus wondered about that. 'Maybe he's switched games,' he said.

Archibald shook his head. He looked like a man obsessed. Jesus, Rebus could write the book on that one: cases which grabbed you and wouldn't let go; unsolveds which stayed with you all the long sleepless nights. You sifted through them time and again, examining the grains of sand, seeking anomalies . . .

'I still don't get it,' Rebus said. 'You weren't on the original case . . . how come you're . . . '

Then he remembered. It should have come to him sooner. The story had gone around at the time, had been passed between the searchers on the hillside.

'Oh shit,' Rebus said. 'She was your niece . . .'

17

It had been easy, finding an unoccupied room in the hotel. Simplicity itself to pick the door lock. So it was that Cary Oakes sat in darkness at the window, a window unwatched by Detective Inspector John Rebus. He had to smile: the watcher had become the watched, without realising it.

There was an *A–Z* on his lap. He'd told Stevens he needed it so he could reacquaint himself with his city. Earlier, Stevens had let slip that Rebus used to live in Arden Street, and maybe still did. Arden Street in Marchmont. Page 15, square 6G. Alan Archibald lived in Corstorphine, or had done when he'd written to Oakes in prison. All those letters, he'd never once let the prisoner know his phone number. It had taken Oakes less than a day to discover it. Strength in knowledge; always surprise your opponent – that's how games were played.

Oakes watched the two men talking in the car. He felt a certain pride, almost like running a dating agency. He'd brought the two of them together; he felt sure they'd get along. They sat there for an hour, even sharing a hot drink from a flask. Then a patrol car turned up – Rebus must have radioed for it. Wasn't that thoughtful: a free ride home for the retired detective. Archibald had aged well, maybe out of spite. Oakes knew *he* didn't look as fresh as the day he'd been incarcerated. Flesh sagged from his face, and there was a dead look to his eyes, despite the regular vitamins and exercise regime.

He slipped a hand into his pocket, felt a fold of banknotes there. He'd been drinking at the bar, spinning a line to some business types, Stevens his quiet partner. Stevens had given up eventually, left them to it. Oakes had learned many trades during his time inside. Lock-picking was one; pocket-picking another. He'd left the credit cards alone: that was the sort of thing that could be traced, get him in trouble. He let cash alone be his guide. He knew Stevens wanted him to be dependent on the paper, knew that was why Stevens was holding back payment. Well, for now he needed Stevens, but that would change. And meantime, he had work to do.

And the money would be his means.

He left the room and made his way down the stairs to the first-floor landing. At the end was a window which opened on to a line of lock-up garages. Eight-foot drop to the roof of the nearest garage. He crouched on the windowledge, waited for the taxi to come. Heard its engine as it rolled towards the hotel. He'd given the name and room number of one of his drinking companions. He listened for the moment when the taxi would pass Rebus's car, the moment when the detective would be least likely to hear anything, then dropped through the darkness on to the roof, sliding down and on to solid tarmac. Not even pausing for breath or to dust himself off, immediately jogging towards the wall which would take him into the lane, the lane which would take him away from the hotel.

With any luck, he'd pick up a taxi. There'd be one coming along in a minute, its driver disgruntled and seeking a fare . . .

Four in the morning, Darren Rough reckoned it would be safe. Everyone would be asleep. He counted himself lucky: out late the night before this, picking up an early edition of his paper on the way home, seeing his story twisted there. He'd been in the flat, Radio Two playing quietly so as not to disturb the neighbours: they had kids, kids needed sleep, everyone knew that. Radio barely audible, tea and toast, sitting by the gas fire.

Then coming upon those pages. Reading just the first couple of paragraphs, enough to make him screw the paper up, pace the floor, start hyperventilating. He breathed into a paper bag until the attack passed. Felt weak, crawling into the bathroom on hands and knees. Splashed water from the toilet on to his face and neck. Hauled himself up on to the pan, sat there for a while, head bowed under its massive weight. When he got back the use of his legs, he uncrumpled the paper, spread it out on the floor. Read the story through.

So it starts again, he thought to himself.

Knew he had to get out before morning. Spent the rest of the night walking the streets, bones cold and aching with tiredness. A café first thing for breakfast. His social worker didn't get into the office till nine, said he'd talk to a solicitor, see what grounds they had for a complaint. Said everything would be fine.

'We just have to ride it out.'

Easy words from a warm office; warm family probably waiting at home too. The car his social worker drove was an estate; kids' football boots in the back. Family man, doing his nine-to-five.

The rest of that day, Darren kept his distance from Greenfield. Walked as far as the Botanics, pretended to be interested in the plants. Kept warm in the hothouses: did about a dozen circuits. Back into town, Princes Street Gardens: he managed an hour's kip on a bench, until a policeman told him to move on. His plight was remarked on by a group of travellers. They offered him cigarettes and strong lager. He stayed with them for an hour, but didn't like them: too scruffy; not his kind of people at all.

Art galleries; churches: there was a lot that was free in Edinburgh. By evening, he reckoned he could write his own guidebook. Ate in a fast-food restaurant, taking as long as he could over the meal. Then a pub on Broughton Street. Waiting for a day to pass ... it made you realise why people needed goals, needed work. He liked a structure to his day. Liked not to feel hunted.

After closing time, he'd met some more travellers, listened to more of their stories. Then had made his way carefully back towards Greenfield, turning away three times before finally confronting his own fear and overcoming it. Goal achieved.

He crept up the stairwell, expecting at every turn to find a waiting face, a knife-blade. Nothing. Just shadows. Along the landing, past closed doors, sleeping windows. His key sounded like a wood-saw as he slipped it into the lock. Then he noticed his hands were sticky. Stood back, noticed for the first time that his door was smeared with mud . . . No, not mud: excrement. He could smell it on the back of his hand, his knuckles, fingers. And beneath the shit, something in black paint, some writing. He crouched, wiped his hands on the concrete flooring, looked up at the message.

MONSTER YOU DIE.

The word DIE was underlined twice, just so he wouldn't miss it.

This was the park.

It hadn't changed. They'd installed some swings and a roundabout, but the roundabout was gone, leaving only a metal stump. The swings were thick rubber tyres. Tarmac underfoot, playing field off to the left. Trees had been planted, but looked stunted. His aunt's house . . . you could see a thin vertical slice of the park from the upstairs bathroom window, peering between two blocks of terraced housing. The house was still there, in darkness, curtains closed. He'd shared a bedroom with his mother at the back of the house, with a view down on to a small neglected garden, the hut which had become his refuge.

There hadn't been much refuge in the park. The local gang hung out there, and Cary was never allowed to join. He was an 'incomer', an 'outsider', the two terms

151

sounding like opposites. He stayed on the periphery, clinging to the park railings, until one of them, fed up of cursing him, would come over to administer a kicking.

And he'd take it. Because it was better than nothing.

The one time he'd stalked a cat, squirting lighter fluid on it, watching the tail catch fire . . . there'd been no one there to see him. Police had questioned the gang, but no one had bothered with Cary Oakes. No one had bothered to ask 'the runt'.

He stood by the fence now. Half of it was missing. Middle of the night, no one was about. No cars passed. No one to see him as his hands worked at the rusted railings, turning them in their sockets.

Then a sound: drunken laughter. Three of them, young, wandering, not bothered who heard them, whose sleep they might be disturbing. The teenage Cary had lain awake late into the night, hearing above his mother's breathing the sounds of revellers as they headed home, some singing songs about King Billy and the Sash.

Three of them, not worried about waking anyone because *they* ruled this place. They ran in the local gang. *They* were all that mattered.

They were on the other side of the road, but saw Oakes, saw him looking at them.

'What you staring at?'

No answer. They started a conversation among themselves, didn't seem to be stopping.

'One of them paedophiles.'

'Always hang out in parks.'

'Or maybe a poof like.'

'This time of night, just standing there . . .'

Now they'd stopped. Turning back, crossing the road. Three of them.

Excellent odds.

'Hiy, pal, what you up to, eh?'

'Thinking about things,' Oakes said quietly, one hand still working at the railing. The three youths looked at each other. They'd spent the night in town, pubbing and clubbing. Booze and some drugs maybe. A mix to up the aggression and confidence. While they were still considering what to do with this stranger, and which one of them should take the lead, Oakes hauled the steel rail up out of the fence and swung it. Caught the first one across the nose, which burst open like a flower in one of those speeded-up film jobs. Hands went to face as the young man screeched and dropped to his knees. As the rail finished one arc, Oakes swung it back again, pendulum-style, caught number two on the ear. Number three swung a kick, but the rail whacked against his shin, then swung upwards to smash into his mouth, breaking teeth. Oakes dropped the weapon. Broken Nose he felled with a kick to the throat. Eardrum he smashed with his fist. Shin and Teeth was limping away, but Oakes walked after him, tripped him, then sent a flurry of kicks to his head.

He stood up straight afterwards, got his breathing under control. Looked around at the houses he remembered so well. No one had moved from bed. No one had seen him in his moment of victory. He wiped the toes of his shoes against the prone figure's shirt, examined them to make sure they hadn't been scuffed in the fight. Walked over to Eardrum and pulled him up by the hair. Another squeal. Oakes put his lips close to the ear that wasn't bleeding.

'This is *my* place now, understood? Anyone fucks with me gets tenfold back.'

'We didn't—'

Oakes pressed his thumb hard against the bleeding ear.

'None of you would ever listen.' He was looking towards the gap in the terrace, where his aunt's house stood. He threw the youth's head hard against the ground. Patted it once, then turned to walk away.

At twenty past six, Rebus crept into Patience's flat on Oxford Terrace, armed with bread still warm from the oven, fresh milk and newspaper. He made himself a mug of tea and sat in the kitchen, reading the sports pages. At six forty-five he put the radio on, just as the central heating was kicking in. Made a fresh pot of tea, poured out a glass of orange juice for Patience. Sliced the bread and got a tray ready. Took it into the bedroom. Patience peered at him with one eye.

'What's this?'

'Breakfast in bed.'

She sat up, arranged the pillows behind her. He laid the tray on her lap.

'Have I forgotten some anniversary?'

He pushed a strand of hair back from her eyes. 'I just didn't want you oversleeping.'

'Why not?'

'Because as soon as you get up, I'm into that bed and asleep.'

He dodged the butter-knife as she swiped it at him. They were both laughing as he started to unbutton his shirt.

Jim Stevens went down to breakfast, expecting to find Cary Oakes halfway through another fry-up. But there was no sign of him. He asked at reception, but nobody had seen him. He called up to Oakes's room: no answer. He went up and banged on the door: ditto.

He was back in reception, ready to demand a duplicate key, when Cary Oakes came walking in through the hotel door.

'Where the hell have you been?' Stevens asked, feeling almost dizzy with relief.

'No caffeine for you this morning, Jim,' Oakes said. 'Look at you, you've got the shakes already.'

'I asked where you'd been.'

'Got up early. Guess I'm still on US time. Walked down by the docks.'

'Nobody here saw you leave.'

Oakes looked over towards the reception desk, then

back to Stevens. 'Is there a problem? I'm here now, aren't I?' He opened his arms wide. 'Isn't that what counts?' He placed a hand on Stevens' shoulder. 'Come on, let's eat.' Started leading them towards the dining room. 'Have I got some great stuff for you this morning. Your editor's going to offer to blow you when he reads it . . .'

'Just another day at the office then,' Stevens said, wiping sweat from his brow.

18

The businessman who owned the Clipper Night-Ship asked Rebus if he wanted to make him an offer.

'I'm serious. I'd be happy to make a loss, only no one wants to buy her.'

He explained that the Clipper had brought him little but headaches. Licensing hassles, complaints from local residents, a council investigation, police visits . . .

'All that so punters can have a piss-up on a boat. I could run a pub with less grief and bigger takings.'

'So why don't you?'

'I used to: the Apple Tree in Morningside. But at that time it seemed like every pub had to have a gimmick. God knows what it's all about with Irish pubs: whoever came up with the notion they're any better than Scottish ones? Then there's the other theme pubs – Sherlock Holmes or Jekyll and Hyde, or pubs for Australians and South Africans.' He shook his head. 'I took one look at the Clipper and thought I was on a winner. Maybe I am, only sometimes it seems like a lot of hard work and sweet FA to show for it.'

They were seated in the offices of PJP: Preston-James Promotions. Rebus and Janice Mee were one side of the desk, Billy Preston the other side. Rebus didn't think Preston would appreciate being informed that his name-sake used to play keyboards for the Beatles and the Stones.

Billy Preston was in his mid-thirties, immaculately turned out in a grey collarless suit with a metallic shine to it. You got the feeling nothing would stick to him, a regular Teflon Man. His head was shaved, but his long square chin sported a Frank Zappa beard. The offices of PJP took up two rooms on the first floor of a building halfway down Canongate. Below was a shop specialising in antiquarian maps.

'We'd move,' Preston had told them, 'find somewhere bigger, somewhere with parking, only my partner says to hold fire.'

'Why?' Rebus had asked.

'The Parliament.' Preston had pointed out of the window. 'Two hundred yards that way. Property around here is rocketing. We'd be mugs to sell.' He kept playing with his computer mouse, running it over its mat, clicking and double-clicking. It annoyed Rebus, who couldn't see the screen. 'Now if they'd chosen Leith instead of Holyrood . . .' Preston rolled his eyes.

'The Clipper wouldn't be causing you this grief?' Rebus guessed.

'Bingo. We'd have bided our time, waited for the MPs and their staff, all on healthy salaries and looking to spend.'

'The Clipper's like a private club?' Janice asked.

'Not exactly. She's for hire. If you guarantee me a minimum of forty punters on a week day, sixty at weekends, she's yours gratis, so long as they're drinking at the ship's bar. You pay for the disco, that's it.'

'You say a minimum of forty. What's the maximum?'

'Public Safety regulations stipulate seventy-five.'

'But forty guarantees you a profit?'

'Just barely,' Preston said. 'I've got staff, overheads, power . . .'

'So some nights you don't open?'

'It comes in waves, if you'll pardon the pun. We've had good times. Now we're in . . .'

'The doldrums?' Rebus offered.

Preston snorted, reached into a drawer for a ledger book. 'So what date is it you're interested in?'

Janice told him. She had both hands cupped around a

mug of coffee. It had been tepid and stewed on delivery. Rebus wondered at the qualifications of the tall blonde secretary in the outer office. Paperwork all over the floor, unopened mail . . . If Preston wasn't helpful, Rebus could foresee a phone call to the VAT inspectors.

But in fact he flicked quickly through the ledger. 'Found this here when we moved in,' he explained. 'Thought I'd try to find a use for it.' He looked up. 'You know, a continuity kind of thing.'

His finger found the date, ran along the line.

'Booking that night, private party. Fancy dress.' He looked up at Janice. 'Sure your son was headed for the Clipper?'

She shrugged. 'It's possible.'

'Whose party was it?' Rebus asked. He was already out of his chair. Preston, eyes on the ledger, didn't seem to notice Rebus coming around the side of the desk. Rebus's first impulse: look at the screen. A game of patience, sitting waiting for the player to start.

'Amanda Petrie,' Preston said. 'I was there that night. I remember it. There was a theme . . . pirates or something.' He rubbed his chin. 'No, it was *Treasure Island*. Some arsehole turned up dressed as a parrot. By the end of the night, he was as sick as one.' He looked at Janice. 'Can I see those photos again?'

She handed them over: Damon and the blonde from the security cameras; then Damon in a holiday snap.

'They weren't in fancy dress?' Preston asked.

Janice shook her head.

Preston's hands were busy with the ledger and the photos. Rebus, leaning over to examine the ledger, found that his elbow had nudged the mouse up the screen, to where it could close the game. Slight pressure on the mouse, and the screen changed. From a game of patience to the image of a woman on all fours. The photo had been taken from behind, the model turning her head to pout at the photographer. She was wearing white stockings and

158

suspenders, nothing else. The pout was exaggerated. On the floor nearby, an empty champagne bottle. Rebus looked up to the windowsill, where an empty champagne bottle sat.

'But is she any good at shorthand?' Rebus said. Preston saw what he was looking at, switched the screen off. Rebus took the opportunity to lift the heavy ledger from the desk, walk back around to his chair with it.

'So you were there that night?' he asked.

Preston looked flustered. 'Keeping an eye on things.'

'And you didn't see either Damon or the blonde?'

'I don't remember seeing them.'

Rebus glanced up. 'Not quite the same thing, is it?'

'Look, Inspector, I'm trying to help . . .'

'Amanda Petrie,' Rebus said. Then he saw her address, recognised it. He looked up at Preston again.

'The judge's daughter?'

Preston was nodding. 'Ama Petrie.'

'Ama Petrie,' Rebus echoed. He turned to Janice, saw the question in her eyes. 'Edinburgh's original wild child.' Back to Preston: 'I see you didn't charge her for the boat.'

'Ama always brings a good crowd.'

'She uses the Clipper a lot?'

'Maybe once a month, usually fancy dress of some kind.'

'Does everyone play along?'

Preston saw what he was getting at. 'Not all the time.'

'So this night, there'd have been guests in normal clothes?'

'Some, yes.'

'And they wouldn't have been quite as eye-catching as pirates and parrots?'

'Agreed.'

'So it's possible . . . ?'

'It's possible,' Preston said with a sigh. 'Look, what do you want me to say? Want me to lie and say I saw them there?'

'No, sir.'

'Best person to talk to is Ama herself.'

'Yes,' Rebus said thoughtfully. Thinking of Amanda Petrie, her reputation. Thinking too of her father, Lord Justice Petrie.

'She runs with a pretty fast bunch,' Preston said.

Rebus nodded. 'Pretty rich too.'

'Oh yes.'

'The kind of customers you could do with more of.'

Preston glared at him. 'I wouldn't lie for her. Besides, I'm not sure the old ticker could cope with more than one Ama. Takes an age to clean up after her – more expense for me. And I always seem to get the bulk of complaints after Ama's parties. God knows, they're loud enough when they arrive . . .'

'Anything out of the ordinary that night?'

Preston stared at Rebus. 'Inspector, this was *Ama Petrie*. With her, there *is* no "ordinary".'

Rebus was copying her phone number from the ledger into his notebook. His eyes ran down other bookings, saw nothing to interest him.

'Well, thanks for your time, Mr Preston.' A final glance towards the computer. 'We'll let you get back to your game.'

Outside, Janice turned to him. 'I get the feeling I missed something back there.'

Rebus shrugged, shook his head. The car was parked on a sideroad. Drizzle was being blown into their faces as they walked.

'Ama Petrie,' Rebus said, keeping his head bowed. 'She doesn't fit my picture of Damon.'

'The mystery blonde,' Janice stated.

'Friend of hers, you reckon?'

'Let's ask Ms Petrie.'

Rebus tried the number from his cellphone: got an answering machine, and didn't leave a message. Janice looked at him.

'Sometimes it helps not to give too much advance warning,' he explained.

'Gives people time to concoct a story?'

He nodded. 'Something like that.'

She was still looking at him. 'You're good at this, aren't you?'

'I used to be.' He thought of Alan Archibald: all those years on the force, all that persistence, pursuing Deirdre Campbell's killer . . . It might be a kind of madness, but you had to admire it. It was what Rebus liked about cops. Only thing was, most of them weren't like that at all . . .

'Back to Arden Street,' he told Janice. There were calls she still had to make; his flat was still her base.

'What about you?' she asked.

'Things to do, people to see.'

She took his hand, squeezed it. 'Thanks, John.' Then reached up to touch his face. 'You look tired.' Rebus removed her fingers from his cheek, held them to his mouth, kissed them. Reached down with his free hand to turn the ignition.

The first instalment of Cary Oakes's 'Lifer Story' was perfunctory: a couple of paragraphs about his return to Scotland, a couple more about his incarceration, and then early biography. Rebus noted that place-names were kept to a minimum. Oakes's explanation: 'I don't want anywhere getting a bad rep just because Cary Oakes once spent a wet winter there.'

Thoughtful of him.

Several times, revelations were hinted at – teasers to keep the audience coming back for more – but on the whole it looked like whatever the paper had paid Oakes, they'd got themselves a pig in a poke. Rebus doubted Stevens' editor would be chuffed. There were photos: Oakes at the airport; Oakes on his release from the penitentiary; Oakes as a baby. A small photo too of 'reporter James Stevens', alongside his byline. Rebus noted that the photographs took up more space than the actual story. Looked like the reporter would be struggling to get a book's worth.

He folded the paper and looked out of his car window. He was parked at the gateway to a Do-It-Yourself superstore, one of those thinly disguised warehouses which, cheaply and quickly built, seemed to surround the city. There were only four cars in the capacious car park. He didn't know this part of the city well: Brunstane. Just to the west was The Jewel, with its mandatory shopping centre; to the east stood Jewel and Esk College. The message Jane Barbour had left for him at the office had been perfunctory: time and place, telling him to meet her. Rebus lit another cigarette, wondering if she was ever coming. Then a car pulled up alongside him, sounded its horn, and proceeded into the car park. Rebus started his engine and followed.

DI Jane Barbour drove a cream-coloured Ford Mondeo. She was getting out as Rebus parked alongside her. She reached back into the car for an A4 envelope.

'Nice car,' Rebus said.

'Thanks for coming.'

Rebus closed the car door for her. 'What's up? Run out of rawl-plugs?'

'Have you been here before?'

'Can't say that I have.'

The wind blew her hair across her face. 'Come on,' she said, all businesslike, verging on the hostile.

He let himself be led round the side of the building. This was where staff parked their cars and bikes. There were two fire-exit doors, painted a green as drab as the grey of the corrugated walls. The back of the warehouse was a waste and delivery area. Skips spilled out flattened cardboard boxes. A dozen terracotta pots waited to be taken inside and displayed for sale. A low brick wall surrounded the area.

'Is this where you mug me?' Rebus asked, sticking his hands in his pockets.

'Why have you got it in for Darren Rough?'

'What's it to you?'

'Just tell me.'

He tried for eye contact, but she wasn't playing. 'Because of what he is, what he was doing at the zoo. Because he slandered a fellow officer. Because of . . .'

'Shiellion?' she guessed, her eyes meeting his at last. 'You couldn't touch Ince and Marshall, but suddenly there was *someone* you could replace them with.'

'It wasn't like that.'

Barbour reached into the envelope, lifted out a black and white photograph. It looked old, showed a three-storey Georgian house. A family posed in front of it, proud of their new motor car. The car was a 1920s model.

'They knocked it down six years ago,' Barbour explained. 'It was either that or wait for it to disintegrate of its own accord.'

'Nice-looking house.'

'The patriarch there,' Barbour said, tapping the man with one foot on the car's running-board, 'he went bankrupt. Mr Callstone, he was called. Worked in jute or something. The family home had to be sold. Church of Scotland snapped it up. But part of the deal was, they had to retain the family's name. So it stayed Callstone House.'

She waited for him to get the name. 'Children's home,' he said at last, watching her nod.

'Ramsay Marshall worked there, prior to his transfer to Shiellion. He already knew Harold Ince before the move.' She handed him more photos.

Rebus looked through them. Callstone House as a children's home, run by the Church of Scotland. Kids grouped outside the same front door, kids photographed inside, seated at long tables, looking hungry. Dormitory beds. Some photos of stern-looking staff. Rebus's mind was working now. 'Darren Rough spent some time at Call-stone . . .'

'Yes, he did.'

'During Ramsay Marshall's reign?'

She nodded again.

'You . . .' he said, suddenly getting it. 'It was you that wanted Darren Rough back here.'

'That's right.'

'For the trial?'

She nodded. 'Arranged a flat for him, wanted him amenable. Worked on him for weeks.'

'He was abused?' Rebus frowned. 'He's not on the list.'

'The Procurator Fiscal didn't think he'd make a good witness.'

Rebus nodded. 'Criminal record. Couldn't risk cross-examination.'

'That's right.'

Rebus handed back the photographs. He knew where this was leading now. 'So what happened to him?'

She busied herself putting the photos back in their envelope. 'One night, Marshall went into the dorm. Darren wasn't asleep. Marshall said they were going on a drive. He took Darren to Shiellion.'

'Proving that Marshall and Ince were already in cahoots?'

'That's how it looks. The two of them and a third man took turns.'

'Christ.' Rebus stared at the warehouse, imagining it as a children's home, a supposed refuge. He wondered what Mr Callstone's ghost would be making of it. 'Who was the third man?'

Barbour shrugged. 'They had Darren in a blindfold.'

'How come?'

'The thing is, John, I made certain promises to him.'

'To a convicted paedophile,' Rebus felt bound to add.

'Ever heard of environment working on character?'

'The abused becoming the abuser? You think that's a reasonable excuse?'

'I think it's a reason.' She was calmer now. 'Professor Calder in Glasgow, he has this test. It shows how likely it is someone will reoffend. Darren came out low-risk. All his time inside, he went to the meetings, kept the therapy going.'

Rebus wrinkled his nose. 'How come he's not registered?' He'd checked: forty-nine sex offenders registered with police in Edinburgh; Rough wasn't among them.

'That was part of the deal. He's terrified they'll get him.'

'"They"?'

'Ince and Marshall. I know they're locked up, but he still has nightmares about them.' She waited for him to say something, but Rebus was thoughtful. 'What's happening down at Greenfield,' she pressed on, 'it's not right. Is that your answer: hound them, chase them out? They'll end up *somewhere*, John. We need to deal with them, not hand them to the mob.'

Rebus looked down at his shoes. As ever, they needed a clean. 'Did Rough tell you?'

She shook her head. 'When I saw the paper, I tried to find him. Then I spoke to his social worker. Andy Davies is pretty sure it was you.'

'You believe him?'

She shrugged. They were walking back towards their cars. 'So what do you want?' Rebus asked. 'An apology?'

'I just want you to understand.'

'Well, thanks for the therapy. I think I'm ready to be released back into the community.'

'I'm glad you can make a joke of it,' she said coldly.

He turned to her. 'Rough comes back to Edinburgh, and Jim Margolies, the cop he accused of beating him up, decides to take a walk from Salisbury Crags. I think there might be a connection. *That's* why I'm interested in ...' He saw her face change at Jim Margolies' name. 'What?' he asked. She shook her head. Rebus narrowed his eyes.

165

'You spoke to Jim, didn't you? Had the same conversation we've just had?'

She hesitated, then nodded. 'I was bringing Darren back to Edinburgh. He was reluctant, wanted to know if DI Margolies was still around.'

'So you met with Jim, explained it all?'

'I wanted to know there'd be no . . . conflict, I suppose.'

'So Margolies knew Rough was coming back?' Rebus was thoughtful. A mobile phone sounded: hers. She lifted it from her pocket, listened for a moment.

'I'll head straight there,' she said, terminating the call. Then to Rebus: 'You'd better come too.'

He looked at her. 'What is it?'

She opened her car door. 'Ugly scenes in Greenfield. Looks like Darren's finally gone home.'

19

There was a mob on the landing outside Darren Rough's flat, and the only thing standing between them and it was PC Tom Jackson. Van Brady was at the front of the queue, brandishing a crowbar. Other women crowded behind her. A local TV crew jockeyed for position. A news photographer was snapping a cluster of kids holding up a banner. The banner was homemade: half a bedsheet and black spray-paint. The message read: SAVE US FROM THE BEAST.

'Lovely,' Jane Barbour said.

People in the other blocks were watching from their windows, or had opened them to shout encouragement. Rebus saw that paint had been daubed on the door of the flat. Eggs and grease had been smeared on the window. The crowd was baying for blood, and more people seemed to be joining in all the time.

Rebus thought: *What in God's name have I done?*

Tom Jackson glanced in Rebus's direction. His face was red, lines of sweat trickling from both temples. Jane Barbour was pushing her way to the front.

'What's going on here?' she shouted.

'Just bring the bastard out here,' Van Brady yelled back. 'We'll bloody well lynch him!'

There were cries of agreement – 'String him up!'; 'Hanging's too good!' Barbour held up both hands, appealing for quiet. She saw that most of the protestors were wearing white sticky labels on their jackets and jumpers. Plain labels on which had been written three letters – GAP.

'What's that?' she asked.

'Greenfield Against Perverts,' Van Brady told her.

Rebus saw a kid handing the labels out. Recognised him as Jamie Brady, Van's youngest.

'Since when was it your job to stick up for sick bastards like him?' one woman asked.

'Everybody's got certain rights,' Barbour replied.

'Even sickos?'

'Darren Rough served his sentence,' Barbour went on. 'He's now on a rehab programme.' She saw the film crew getting close, whispered something to Tom Jackson. He pushed his way to the camera, held a hand in front of it.

'We want answers,' Van Brady was shouting. 'Why was he put here? Who knew about it? Why weren't we told?'

'And we want him out!' a male voice called. A newcomer, the sea of bodies parting to let him through. A young man, chiselled face, bare-armed. He stood shoulder to shoulder with Van Brady, ignoring Barbour and directing his comments towards the film crew.

'This is our community here, not the police's.' Applause and cheers. 'If they can't deal with scum,' jerking his thumb back towards Rough's front door, 'no problem – we'll deal with it ourselves. We've always been tidy that way in Greenfield.'

More cheers; nods of agreement.

One protestor: 'You said it, Cal.'

Cal Brady, standing next to his mum, who looked on with pride at her son's oratory. Cal Brady: Rebus's first sighting in the flesh.

Well, not exactly: first sighting with the knowledge of who he was. But Rebus had seen Cal Brady before. At Gaitano's nightclub, standing at the bar with the under-manager, Archie Frost. Frost with his pigtail and bad manners; his friend saying nothing, then making himself scarce . . .

'Could we talk about it?' Jane Barbour asked.

168

'What's there to talk about?' Van Brady asked, folding her arms.

'This whole situation.'

Cal Brady ignored her, spoke to his mother. 'Is he in there?'

'One of his neighbours heard sounds.'

Cal Brady thumped on the window, then had to wipe grease off on his jeans.

'Look,' Jane Barbour was saying, 'if we could all—'

'Right you are,' Cal Brady said. Then, swiping the crowbar from his mother, he swung it at the window, shattering the glass. Grabbed at the soiled sheet, pulling it down from where drawing-pins held it in place. He was halfway over the windowsill and into the room, crowbar still in his hand. Rebus grabbed him by the feet, pulled him back. Glass shards ripped the front from Brady's T-shirt.

'Hey, you!' Van Brady yelled, swinging a punch at Rebus. Cal Brady wriggled free, pulled himself up and got into Rebus's face.

'You want it, do you?' Brandishing the crowbar. Not recognising the policeman.

'I want you to calm down,' Rebus said quietly. He turned to Van. 'And you, behave yourself.'

The crowd had formed around the window, keen for a view of the flat's interior. It looked much like any other: emulsioned walls, sofa, chair, bookcase. No TV, no hi-fi. Books piled on the sofa: photography texts; fiction titles. Newspapers on the floor, empty pot noodle containers, a pizza box. Cans and lemonade bottles on the bookcase. They all looked disappointed with this haul.

'He's polis,' Van warned her son.

'Listen to your mother, Cal,' Rebus said.

Cal Brady was lowering the crowbar as half a dozen uniforms came out of the stairwell.

First thing they did was disperse the crowd. Van Brady

shouted that there'd be a GAP meeting in her flat. The TV crew looked ready to follow. The photographer lingered to take shots of Darren Rough's living room, until uniforms moved him on too. Barbour was on her mobile, calling for someone to come and board up the window.

'And pronto, before someone tips a can of petrol into the place.'

Tom Jackson, mopping his brow, came over to where Rebus was standing.

'Christ almighty,' he said. 'I think I preferred it the way it was before.'

When Rebus looked up, Jackson's eyes were on him.

'You're blaming me for this?' Rebus asked.

'Did I say that?' Jackson was still busy with his handkerchief. 'I don't remember saying that.' He turned and walked away.

Rebus looked in through the window. There was a musty smell from the room; hardly surprising, when it got neither fresh air nor sunlight. In for a penny, he thought to himself, lifting a foot on to the sill and pulling himself up.

Broken glass crunched underfoot. No sign of Darren Rough.

This is what you wanted, John. The voice in his head: not his own, but Jack Morton's. *This is what you wanted, and now you've got it . . .*

No, he thought, I didn't want *this.*

But Jack was right to a degree: here it was anyway.

A narrow archway from the living room led into the kitchenette. Rebus felt the electric kettle: a trace of warmth. Looked in the fridge: bread, marge, jam. No milk. In the swing-top bin: empty milk carton, baked bean tins.

Jane Barbour looked in at him. 'Anything?'

'Nothing much.'

'How about opening the door?'

'Sure.' He opened the door to the hall, which was in darkness. Fumbled and found a light switch. Bare forty-watt bulb. He tried opening the door, but the mortice had been locked, no sign of a key anywhere. The letterbox was protected by a block of wood. Not that Rough would get much mail. He went back to the window, let Barbour know she'd have to climb in if she wanted the tour.

'No thanks,' she said. 'Once was enough.' Rebus looked at her. 'When I first brought him here.'

Rebus nodded, went back into the hall. Just the two bedrooms, plus bathroom and separate toilet. The first bedroom contained a sleeping bag on the floor. Bedtime reading: the Bible, Good News version. Empty crisp packets. Rebus picked them up. There was a used condom inside one. Curtain across the window: Rebus pulled it open, looked down on to a roadway. Second bedroom was empty, not even a lightbulb. Same view as bedroom one. The bathroom needed a clean. There was mould on the walls. The only towel was a pitifully small and frayed affair, hospital knock-off or similar. Rebus tried the toilet door. It was locked. He pushed harder, definitely locked. He tapped on the wood.

'Rough? You in there?' No way of locking the door from the outside. 'Police,' Rebus called. 'Look, we're about to move out, and your front window's smashed. Minute we're gone, the barbarians will be back.' Silence. 'Fine and dandy,' Rebus said, turning away. 'By the way, DI Barbour's outside. Cheers, Darren.'

Rebus was half out of the window when he heard the noise behind him. Turned and saw Darren Rough standing in the doorway, face gaunt, eyes flickering in terrified expectation. Looking both haunted and hunted. He held shivering hands up to his chest, like they'd protect him from a crowbar's blows.

Rebus, immune to most things, felt a sudden stab of pity. Jane Barbour was out on the walkway, talking to Tom Jackson. She saw Rebus's look, broke off the conversation.

'DI Barbour,' he called. 'One of yours, I believe.'

*

171

Jim Stevens tried to put from his mind the sight of Cary Oakes urinating in the church. Now that he had Oakes, he needed the story, needed it to be *big*. His boss had complained about the first instalment, called it a 'cock-tease', hoped there was better to come. Stevens had given him his word.

Oakes had a Bible beside his bed. Yet in the church . . . Stevens didn't want to think about what it might mean. There was something about Oakes . . . you looked into his eyes sometimes and saw it, and if he caught you watching, he was able to blink it away. But for seconds at a time, his mind would be somewhere else, somewhere the reporter didn't want to be.

Just do your job, he kept telling himself. A few more days, plenty of time to score maximum brownie points with his boss, show the other rags that he could still cut it, and put together a proposal for whichever publisher made the highest bid. He was already in negotiation with two London houses, but four more had turned the idea down.

'Killers' life stories,' one editor had said dismissively, 'been there, done that.'

To get a bidding war going, he needed more offers. Two interested parties barely qualified as a tiff.

And now this.

Oakes had said he was going to his room for half an hour after lunch. The morning session had been good; not brilliant, but all right. Enough nuggets for the next instalment. But Oakes had complained of a headache, said he wanted to soak in a bath. After half an hour, Stevens had tried his room: no one answering. Reception hadn't seen him. Stevens had thought about going out and asking the surveillance, but that would have been rash. He persuaded the manager that he was worried about his colleague's health. A skeleton key got them into the room. No one there, no one at all. Stevens had apologised to the manager, gone back to his own room. Where he now sat, nipping at his fingernails and wondering where his story had gone.

It had to be bravado.

Caught snivelling and shivering like that by the police ... The only way for Darren Rough to scrape together any self-esteem was to turn down Barbour's offer of a move. She could offer a police cell until something better came up; could no longer guarantee his safety in Greenfield.

Rough had smiled as she said 'no longer', both of them knowing she was playing with words.

'I'm staying,' he'd said. 'Got to stop running some time, might as well be here and now.' And he'd chuckled. 'Like some old Western, isn't it? Whatsisface, John Wayne.' He made his fingers into a six-shooter, blasted the air. Then he looked around and sniffed, his face losing its animation.

'I don't think it's a good idea,' Barbour said.

'I agree,' Andy Davies said. It was the first time Rebus had met Darren Rough's social worker. He was tall and thin and bearded, red hair going bald at the dome. Laughter lines around his eyes; small pink mouth.

'There *is* something you could do for me,' Rough said. Davies leaning forward on the sofa, hands pressed between his knees. 'What's that, Darren?'

'A dustpan and brush, so I can clear up all this shit.' Kicking at a fragment of glass.

A council workman had arrived to put boards across the window. There was a dull loathing in his eyes. Someone down below had pressed a GAP label on to his toolbox. He used a cordless screwdriver, saw and hammer to fix the sheets of board to the windowframe, blotting out the last of the daylight.

When Rough went into the kitchenette, Rebus made to follow. The social worker stood up.

'It's OK,' Rebus told him, 'I just want a word.' The two men fixed one another with a stare. Rebus motioned for

173

Davies to sit back down, but instead Davies walked to the window. Rebus made his way to the kitchenette's archway. Rough was opening and closing cupboards, not really sure what he was doing or why. He knew Rebus was there, but wouldn't look at him.

'Got what you wanted,' he muttered.

'What I want are some answers.'

'Funny way to go about it.'

Rebus slid his hands into his pockets. 'How long have you been back?'

'Three, four weeks.'

'I don't suppose you've seen DI Margolies?'

'He's dead. I saw it in the paper.'

'Yes, but before then.'

Rough slammed shut one of the doors, turned on Rebus, voice shaking. 'Christ, what now? He topped himself, didn't he?'

'Maybe.'

Rough rubbed a hand over his forehead. 'You think I . . . ?'

Andy Davies had come over. 'What the hell is it now?'

'He's trying to set me up,' Rough blurted out.

'Look, Inspector, I don't know what you think—'

'That's right,' Rebus snapped back, 'you don't. So why don't you just keep out of it?'

'I can't handle this,' Rough bawled, on the verge of tears.

Jane Barbour came in from the hall. Rebus read her look: four parts accusation to one part disappointment. He remembered what she'd told him about Rough. The man was sniffing now, rubbing the back of his hand beneath his nose. His knees looked like they were about to give way. The workman was nearly finished, leaving the room in twilight. Each screw that went home was like fixing the lid on a coffin.

'Did DI Margolies come to see you?' Rebus persisted.

Rough fixed him with a defiant look. 'No.'

Rebus stared him out. 'I think you're lying.'

'So slap me around a bit.'

Rebus took a step towards him. The social worker was pleading with Barbour.

'DI Rebus,' Barbour warned.

Rebus got right up into Rough's face. Rough had backed all the way into the kitchenette, nowhere else to go.

'Did he come to see you?'

Rough looked away, bit his lip.

'Did he?'

'Yes!' Darren Rough screamed. He bowed his head, pulled a hand through his hair. Incessant hammering of nails into wood. He pushed both palms against his ears. Rebus pulled them away, using as little force as possible. Kept his voice quiet when he spoke.

'What did he want?'

'Shiellion,' Rough groaned. 'It's always been Shiellion.'

Rebus frowned. 'DI Rebus . . .' Barbour's voice growing taut, breaking point almost reached.

'What about Shiellion?'

Rough looked to Jane Barbour, his words directed at her. 'You told him what happened to me.'

'And?' Rebus probed.

'He wanted to know why they'd blindfolded me . . . kept asking who else was there.'

'Who else *was* there, Darren?'

Through gritted teeth: 'I don't know.'

'That what you told him?'

A slow nod. 'Could have been anyone.'

'Someone they didn't want you to see. Maybe you knew them.'

Rough nodded. His voice was calmer. 'I've often wondered. Maybe I'd have recognised . . . I don't know, a uniform or something. Priest's dog collar.' He looked up. 'Maybe even one of your lot.'

But Rebus had stopped listening. 'Priest?' he said.

'Callstone and Shiellion were run by the Church of Scotland. They don't have priests.'

But Rough nodded. 'We had one.'

Barbour, looking intrigued now, frowned. 'You had a priest?'

'Visited for a while, then stopped coming. I liked him. Father Leary, his name was.' A weak smile. 'Told us to call him Conor.'

When Rebus headed downstairs, Jane Barbour followed.

'What do you make of it?' she asked.

Rebus shrugged. 'Why was Jim Margolies interested in Shiellion?'

Her turn to shrug.

'You told Jim that Rough was abused there?'

She nodded. 'You think it has something to do with his suicide?'

'If it *was* suicide.'

She blew air from her cheeks. 'I'd better talk to the vigilantes,' she told him. 'Keep the lid on the pressure cooker.'

'Tom Jackson's already had a word.'

They turned, hearing footsteps behind them on the stairwell: Andy Davies.

'We should move him,' Davies said. 'It's not safe for him to stay here.'

'He doesn't want to leave.'

'We could insist.'

'If that mob up there couldn't make him leave, what chance have *we* got?'

'You could arrest him.'

Rebus burst out laughing. 'A couple of days back—'

Davies turned on him. 'I'm talking about *protecting* him, not harassment.'

'We'll keep someone in the vicinity,' Barbour said.

'Tom Jackson's got to go home some time,' Rebus commented.

'I'll do guard duty myself if need be.' She turned to Davies. 'At the moment, I'm not sure what more we can be expected to do.'

'And if he'd proved useful to you in court . . . ?'

'I'll ignore that remark, Mr Davies.' Said with ice in her voice, and eyes like weaponry.

'They'll kill him,' the social worker said. 'And I don't suppose you'll be shedding too many tears.'

Barbour looked to Rebus, wondering if he would respond. All Rebus did was shake his head and light up a cigarette.

Rebus had known Father Conor Leary for years. For a time, he'd visited the priest regularly, sharing conversation and cans of Guinness. But when Rebus called Leary's number, another priest answered.

'Conor's in hospital,' the young priest explained.

'Since when?'

'A few days ago. We think it was a heart attack. Fairly mild, I think he'll be fine.'

So Rebus drove to the hospital. Last time he'd visited Leary, there'd been a fridge full of medicine. The priest had explained that they were for minor ailments.

'How long have you known?' Rebus asked, drawing a chair over to his friend's bedside. Conor Leary looked old and pale, his skin slack.

'No grapes, I notice,' Leary said, his voice lacking its usual gruff power. He was sitting up in the bed, surrounded by flowers and get-well cards. On the wall above his head Christ on the cross gazed down.

'I only heard half an hour ago.'

'Nice of you to drop by. Can't offer you a drink, I'm afraid.'

Rebus smiled. 'They say you'll be out in no time.'

'Ah, but did they say whether I'd be leaving in a box?'

Rebus managed a smile. Inside, he saw a carpenter, hammering home nails.

'I've a favour to ask,' he said. 'If you're up to it.'

'You want to turn Catholic?' Leary joked.

'Think the confessional could cope?'

'True enough. We'd need a relay team of priests for a sinner like yourself.' He rested his eyes. 'So what is it then?'

'Sure you're up to it? I could come back . . .'

'Cut it out, John. You know you're going to ask me anyway.'

Rebus leaned forward in his chair. His old friend had flecks of white at the corners of his mouth. 'A name you might remember,' he said. 'Darren Rough.'

Leary thought for a moment. 'No,' he said. 'You'll need to give me a clue.'

'Callstone House.'

'Now that was a while back.'

'You spent time there?'

Leary nodded. 'One of those multi-faith things. God knows whose idea it was, but it wasn't mine. A minister would visit Catholic homes, and I got to spend time in Callstone.' He paused. 'Was Darren one of the kids?'

'He was.'

'The name doesn't mean anything. I spoke with a lot of them.'

'He remembers you. Says you told him to call you Conor.'

'I'm sure he's right. Is he in trouble, this Darren?'

'You haven't heard?'

'This place tends to swaddle you. No newspapers, no news.'

'He's a paedophile, released into the community. Only the community doesn't want him.'

Conor Leary nodded, eyes still closed. 'Did he abuse another child?'

'When he was twelve. The victim was six.'

'I remember him now. Whey-faced, wouldn't say boo to a goose. The man who ran Callstone . . .'

'Ramsay Marshall.'

'He's on trial, isn't he?'

'Yes.'

'Did he . . . ? With Darren?'

'Afraid so.'

'Ah, dear Lord. Probably going on under my very nose.' He opened his eyes. 'Maybe the boys . . . maybe they tried to tell me, and I couldn't hear what they were saying.' When the priest's eyes closed again, a tear escaped from one and trickled down his cheek.

Rebus felt bad, which hadn't been his intention in coming here. He squeezed his friend's hand. 'We'll talk again, Conor. But you need to rest now.'

'John, when do the likes of you and me ever rest?'

Rebus got up, looked down at the figure on the bed. *Priest's dog collar* . . . Maybe, but never Conor Leary. *Even one of your lot* . . . Someone in uniform. Rebus didn't want to think about it, but Jim Margolies had put some thought into it. And soon afterwards, he'd died.

'John,' the priest was saying, 'remember me in your prayers, eh?'

'Always, Conor.'

Hadn't the heart to admit he'd stopped praying long ago.

20

Back at his flat, he made two mugs of coffee and took them through to the living room. Janice was on the phone to yet another charity, giving them details of Damon. Rebus sat at the dining table. It was a big room, twenty-two feet by fourteen. Bay window (still with the original shutters). High ceiling – maybe eleven feet – with cornicing. Rhona, his ex-wife, had loved the room, even with the original wallpaper from when they'd bought it (purple wavy lines which made Rebus feel seasick whenever he walked past). The wallpaper had gone, as had the brown carpet with matching paintwork.

He thought of Darren Rough's flat. He'd seen worse in his time, of course, but not much worse. Janice put down the receiver and scratched at her hair with a pen, before scribbling a note on a pad of paper. Having scored a line through the charity's phone number, she threw the pen on to the table.

'Coffee,' Rebus told her. She took the mug with a smile of thanks.

'You look glum.'

'My natural disposition,' he said. 'Mind if I use the phone?'

She shook her head, so he moved over to the chair, sat down and picked it up. A cordless model; he'd only had it a few months. He called Ama Petrie's number again. A flustered male voice told him to try one of the function rooms at the Marquess Hotel, told him what he'd find there.

'You got a message from Damon's bank manager,' Janice told him, when the call was finished.

'Oh yes?'

'Head office approval. If there are any debits from Damon's account, he'll let you know.'

'Nothing so far?'

'No.'

'Night he vanished, he took out a hundred.'

'How far does that go these days?'

'If he's sleeping rough, quite a way.'

'We're talking as if he's a runaway.'

'Until proved otherwise, that's what he is.'

'But why would he . . . ?' She broke off, smiled. 'Same old questions. You must be sick of hearing them.'

'The only one who can explain is Damon himself. Doing your head in isn't going to help in the interim.'

She looked at him. 'Right as ever, Johnny.'

He shrugged. 'Pleased to be of service.'

When Janice had finished her coffee, using the last mouthfuls to wash down two paracetamol tablets, he told her they were going out.

'Where?' she asked, looking around for her jacket.

'A beauty contest,' Rebus told her. Then he winked. 'Brought your swimsuit with you?'

'No.'

'Doesn't matter, you wouldn't be eligible anyway: too old.'

'Thanks very much.'

'You'll see,' he said, leading her to the door.

Cary Oakes had a newspaper cutting. It was old and fragile. These days, he didn't look at it much for fear that it would crumble between his fingers. But today was a special occasion, sort of, so in the café he withdrew it from his pocket and read it through. Faded words on grey paper. A report of his trial and verdict, clipped from one

British tabloid. And words of hate: 'He should have had the electric chair.' A simple statement of belief.

But they hadn't given him 'Old Sparky', and here he was, back in the same town as the person who'd wanted them to fry him. The anger rising in him again, his hands trembled a little as he folded the cutting along its well-creased lines, slipping it back into his pocket. One day very soon, he'd make someone eat those words. He'd sit there watching them chew, seeing fear and knowledge in their eyes.

And then he'd spark out *their* life.

Leaving the café, he headed uphill, wandering past bungalows, along quiet pavements. Until he reached his destination. Stared at the building.

He was in there. Oakes could almost taste and smell him. Maybe he was alone in his room, resting or asleep. Or reading the newspaper, catching up on the exploits of Cary Oakes.

'Soon,' Oakes said quietly to himself, turning away, not wanting to seem conspicuous. 'Soon,' he repeated, beginning to walk back down the hill towards the town.

The hotel was a 1930s design, next to a roundabout on the western edge of Edinburgh.

'Looks like the Rex, doesn't it?' Janice said.

She had a point. The Rex had been one of Cardenden's three cinemas, perched on a prominent site on the town's main street. As a kid, it had looked to Rebus like one of those state buildings you saw in films about the Iron Curtain: forbidding, all straight lines and right angles. This hotel was an elongated version of the Rex, as though someone had gripped its sides and pulled. The spaces in the car park were taken, so Rebus did what others before him had done: bumped the Saab up on to the grass verge so that its nose touched the flower beds.

There was a large noticeboard in the middle of the hotel lobby. It told them that Our Little Angels could be found in the Devonshire Suite. Through a double set of doors and along a corridor, hearing a smattering of applause. At the door to the Devonshire Suite was a large woman in a fuchsia two-piece. She sat behind a small table with half a dozen name-tags left lying on it. She asked them their names.

'We're not expected,' Rebus told her, taking out his warrant card. Her eyes widened, and stayed that way as Rebus led Janice into the room.

There was a temporary stage at one end, rows of chairs arranged in front of it, pink and blue drapes hanging behind it. Burgeoning vases of flowers sat along the front of the stage and at the ends of each row of chairs. The room was about half-full. Around the walls sat bags and coats. Mothers and daughters were busy at work, primping and preening. Hair was brushed and teased, make-up perfected, a dress straightened or a ribbon retied. The daughters looked around the room, studying the competition nervously – or occasionally with a hint of contempt. None of them could have been older than eight or nine.

'It's like a dog show,' Janice whispered to Rebus.

A man at a microphone was reading from a prompt-card, introducing the next contestant.

'Molly comes from Burntisland and attends the local primary school. Her hobbies are pony-trekking and dress-designing. She designed her own dress for today's competition.' He looked up at his audience. 'How about that, eh, folks? The next Dior. Please welcome Molly.'

The mother patted her daughter on the shoulder, and with hesitant tread Molly made her way up the three wooden steps to the stage. The compère crouched down, microphone in hand. Fake tan and hair-weave – or maybe Rebus was just jealous. The judges were in the front row, trying to hide their voting papers from prying eyes.

'And how old are you, Molly?'

'Seven and three-quarters.'

'Seven and three-quarters? You're sure it's not

seven-eighths?' The compère was smiling, but Molly's face had turned panicky, unsure how to respond. 'Not to worry, my darling,' the compère went on. 'So tell us about that lovely dress you're wearing.'

Rebus looked around him. Make-up applied to faces not yet ready for it, so that the girls looked like clowns. Hair spun into grown-up shapes. Mothers fussing, looking fraught and expectant. The mothers wore make-up too, and bright clothes. Some of them had dyed hair. A few had probably been under the knife. Nobody was paying any attention to Rebus and Janice: there were plenty of couples in evidence. But this was a mother-and-daughter show, no doubt about that.

No sign of Ama Petrie, and he'd no idea what she'd be doing here anyway. The voice on the phone hadn't had time to explain. Then he saw two figures he recognised. Hannah Margolies, long blonde hair curling past her shoulders. At her father's funeral she'd worn white lace. Today she was in a pale-blue dress with white tights and glossy red shoes. There were blue bows in her hair, her mouth a glistening crimson button. Her mother, Katherine Margolies, was kneeling in front of her, giving a final pep-talk. Hannah kept her eyes on her mother's, nodding slightly from time to time. Katherine took her hands and squeezed them, then stood up.

Jim Margolies' widow had looked composed at the funeral; she looked more nervous now. She was still wearing black – skirt and jacket over a white silk blouse. She glanced towards the stage where Molly, aided by tape-recorded backing, was singing 'Sailor', a song Rebus associated with Petula Clark. Janice, who had found a seat at the end of a row, turned to look up at Rebus with disbelieving eyes. When he looked back at Hannah, he saw Katherine Margolies studying him, as if trying to work out where she'd met him before. Molly was finishing her act, taking the applause with a curtsey. She fairly skipped off the stage, grinning to show wide-spaced teeth.

'Our next contestant,' the compère was saying, 'is Hannah, who lives right here in Edinburgh . . .'

When Hannah had taken the stage, Rebus wandered across to her mother.

'Hello, Mrs Margolies.'

She put a finger to her lips, her concentration focused on the stage. She pressed her hands together in something like prayer as she watched Hannah's performance, her mouth twisting when the compère asked what seemed to her a tricky question. Finally, the mother reached down into one of her bags and walked to the stage with a recorder, handing it to her daughter with a smile. Unaccompanied, Hannah played a tune which Rebus suspected was classical. He'd heard it on an advert somewhere, couldn't think what the advert was for. Looking towards Janice, Rebus saw that seated next to her were an elderly couple, beaming at the stage. They held hands. In the man's free hand was a walking stick. Rebus recognised them: Jim Margolies' parents.

Finally: applause, and Hannah came back to her mother, who kissed her hair.

'You were perfect,' Katherine Margolies said. 'Just perfect.'

'I played a wrong note.'

'I didn't hear it.'

Hannah turned to Rebus. 'Did you hear it?'

Rebus shook his head. 'Sounded fine to me.'

Hannah's face relaxed a little. She whispered something to her mother.

'Off you go then.'

As Hannah made her way to her grandparents, Katherine Margolies got slowly to her feet, watching her leave.

'We haven't actually met, Mrs Margolies,' Rebus said, 'but I was at Jim's funeral. I used to work with him. My name's John Rebus.'

She nodded distractedly. 'You must think I'm . . .' She

sought the words. 'I mean, so soon after Jim's accident. But I thought it might take Hannah's mind off things.'

'Of course.'

'She's been so upset.'

'I'm sure.' He noticed that she was now studying the judges, the members of the audience, as if looking for some clue as to Hannah's success. 'You think Jim fell?' he asked.

She looked at him. 'What?'

'People seem to think it was suicide.'

'Let them think what they like,' she snapped. Then she turned to him. 'You want me to tell Hannah her father took his own life?'

'Of course not . . .'

'He was out walking, got too close to the edge. It was dark . . . a gust of wind maybe.'

'Is that what you believe?' She didn't reply. 'Did Jim often go out walking at night?'

'What business is it of yours?'

He looked down at the carpet. 'Frankly, none.'

'Well then.'

'It's just that I've been trying to make sense of it.'

She looked at him again. 'Why?'

'For my own satisfaction.' He held her stare. She was beautiful. Black hair pulled back to show the geometry of her face. Thin arched eyebrows, good cheekbones. Hannah's eyes were blue, same as her father's, but Katherine Margolies' were hazel. 'And because,' Rebus went on, 'I thought it might have something to do with Darren Rough.'

'Who's he?'

'Didn't Jim mention him?'

She shook her head, sighed with impatience, and turned her gaze towards the judges again. One of them was having a conversation with the compère, who had switched his microphone off.

Rebus thought she was about to say something. When she didn't, he tried another question.

'He didn't take his car, did he?'

'What?'

'It was raining that night.'

'When you go for a walk, do you take *your* car?'

'I wouldn't head up Salisbury Crags in a downpour, day or night.'

'Well, Jim did, didn't he?'

'Yes, he did . . . and I still don't understand why.'

'Well, Mr Rebus, I've enough to worry about, so if you'll excuse me . . .' She looked over his shoulder and her face brightened.

'Amanda, darling!'

A young woman had breezed through the door, completely ignoring the woman at the desk. She now came forward with arms open, shopping bags swinging from both hands, and embraced Katherine Margolies.

'Sorry I'm late, Katy. Traffic was murder. Tell me I haven't missed her.'

'Afraid so.'

'Oh, fuck it!' Loud enough for heads to turn. From a distance of four feet, Rebus could smell the cigarettes and booze. The shopping bags: Jenners, Cruise, Body Shop. 'How was she? I'll bet she was brilliant . . .' Looking around. 'Where is she anyway?'

Hannah was coming towards them, leading her grandmother by the hand, her grandfather following. Her face lit up at the sight of her new visitor. Amanda crouched down and opened her arms again, and Hannah ran into them.

'Careful with her make-up, Ama,' Katherine Margolies warned.

'You look like an angel,' Amanda told Hannah. 'Not that angels ever wore lipstick.'

Katherine Margolies was looking at Rebus. 'I'm sorry, I thought we'd finished chatting.' A polite dismissal.

187

'We had,' Rebus said. 'But it's Miss Petrie I've come here to see.'

Amanda Petrie stood up. She was wearing a clinging black mini-dress and black leather jacket with zips to spare. Black high heels and bare legs. She looked Rebus up and down.

'Who do I owe money to?' she asked. Her attention shifted to Dr and Mrs Margolies. 'Hello, you two.' She kissed and embraced both of them. 'How are you bearing up?'

'Well, you know, dear,' Mrs Margolies said.

'Hannah was *splendid*,' Dr Margolies said. 'We haven't been introduced.' He held a hand towards Rebus.

'DI Rebus,' Rebus said, watching the old man's face fall. And now Ama Petrie was studying him. He smiled. 'I've been taken for worse things than a loan-shark's muscle,' he told her. 'Maybe we could have a drink at the bar . . . ?'

But Amanda Petrie wasn't that stupid. Rebus's thinking: a couple more drinks would loosen her up even more. Amanda, however, had insisted on a pot of tea and several glasses of orange juice. Rebus, Janice and Ama Petrie: just the three of them, seated in the hotel lounge. Ama tucking a strand of blonde hair behind one ear. Rebus looking at her, knowing what Janice was thinking: could she be the mystery blonde? He didn't think so; her build was different, not so tall, narrower at the shoulders. He couldn't see any resemblance to her father . . .

She played with one of the shoulders of her dress. Her eyes kept scanning the lounge, looking for anyone more interesting, more glamorous, anyone she should know.

'I want to be back for the judging,' she reminded them. 'Hannah's bound to win.'

'Why do you say that?'

'She's got breeding. It's not something you can paint on to a face or run up with a sewing-machine.'

'Ever done any sewing yourself?' Rebus asked.

She pulled her attention back to him. 'Needlework and home economics. My school wanted to make little women of us.' She lit a cigarette, tucked her legs under her. Since she hadn't offered, Rebus made a show of taking out his own pack, lighting one for himself and offering another to Janice.

'Sorry,' Ama Petrie said, offering them her pack. Rebus waved his already lit cigarette at her. 'How did you find me?' she asked.

'Phoned your number.'

'You probably spoke to Nick.' She blew out smoke. 'He's my brother. Always ready to shop his sis to the filth.'

Rebus let that one go. 'How do you know Hannah?' he asked.

'We're cousins or something. Twice removed, you know how it is with families.'

Rebus knew Jim Margolies had married someone with 'society connections'. He hadn't known Katherine was related to Lord Justice Petrie.

'Not that I'd have anything to do with most of my family,' Ama Petrie went on, 'but Hannah's just adorable, don't you think?' She asked the question of Janice, who nodded.

'I'm not sure about these shows, though,' Janice said.

Ama seemed to agree. 'Yes, but Katy loves them, and I think Hannah does too.'

'All those mothers . . .' Janice mused. 'Pushing their daughters.'

'Yes, well . . .' Ama tapped her cigarette against the ashtray. 'What is it you want, anyway?'

Rebus explained the situation. As he talked, Ama's attention moved to Janice. At one point, she leaned forward and took her hand, squeezing it.

'You poor dear.'

An agony aunt's look on her face; someone who'd been touched by loss only at one remove.

'I did have a party that night,' she agreed. 'Not that I

189

remember it too well. Bit too much to drink, too many people ... as per. Word gets around, I do get the occasional gatecrasher. I don't mind, so long as they're interesting, but the boat's owner goes on about over-crowding. He's always asking me if I know this or that person, did I invite them?' She drained her second glass of orange. 'Christ knows why I bother.'

'Why do you bother?'

A smirk. 'Because it's fun, I suppose. And because while I'm doing it, I'm *somebody*.' She thought about this, shrugged the thought aside as if it were the wrong jacket. 'You're sure he was coming to *my* party?'

'It's the last time he was seen,' Janice confirmed.

Rebus got out the photographs: Damon; Damon and the mystery blonde. As Ama studied them, he asked casually if she'd ever been to Gaitano's.

'Do people call it Guiser's?' He nodded confirmation. 'Yes, once or twice. Lots of sweaty job-creation-schemers and dole-fiddlers. Off their faces on happy-hour cocktails, dropping E in the lavs.' She smiled. 'Not my scene, I'm afraid.' She handed back the photos. 'Sorry, don't mean a thing to me.'

'Not even the woman?'

She wrinkled her nose. 'Looks a bit tarty.'

'It couldn't be someone you know?'

'Inspector.' A throaty laugh. 'That's hardly narrowing things down. I know *everybody*.'

'But you don't know my son,' Janice said grimly.

'No,' Ama said, face making a show of contrition. 'I'm very much afraid I don't.' She sprang to her feet. 'I'd better get back. They'll have started the judging.'

Rebus and Janice followed her, stood in the doorway as the prizes were handed out. Hannah was runner-up. As the winner was announced, and went forward to receive a sparkling tiara, everyone clapped and cheered. Everyone except Ama Petrie, who bounced on her toes, booing at the top of her voice as she gave an enthusiastic thumbs-down to the little girl with voluminous black hair, shimmering with glitter.

Katherine Margolies tried to stop Ama making a scene, but to Rebus's eyes she didn't try very hard . . .

'Where the hell have you been?'

Stevens found Cary Oakes in the bar, where he was drinking orange juice and talking to the staff.

'Walking, thinking.' Oakes looked at him. 'Want to make sure I don't forget anything.'

Stevens picked up Oakes's glass. 'Then don't forget this: that's *my* juice you're drinking, *my* money paying for it. We've lost a whole session.'

'I'll make it up to you.' Oakes blew Stevens a kiss, grinned and winked at the barman. Turned back to Stevens. 'Look at you, man, all trembling and sweating. A cardiac arrest's having your name paged as we speak. You got to slow down, Jim. Go with the flow.'

'My editor wants better copy.'

'You could give him Kennedy's assassin, he'd say he wanted better copy. You and I know, Jim, the best stuff has to wait for the book, right? The book's what's going to make us rich.'

'If I find a publisher.'

'It'll happen, trust me. Now sit down here beside me and let me buy you one. Hell, I don't mind putting my hand in my pocket for a friend.' He wrapped an arm around Stevens' shoulders. 'You're with Cary now, Jim. You're part of my exclusive circle. Nothing bad's going to happen.' Oakes made eye contact, held it. 'You can depend on that,' he said. 'Cross my heart.'

'Just drop me off at Haymarket,' Janice said. They were back in the car, heading into town.

'You sure? I could drive you—'

She was shaking her head.

'Look, Janice, a trail like this . . . we're bound to run

191

into dead ends. Maybe a lot of them. It's something you'll have to accept.'

She shook her head. 'I was thinking of all those kids . . . wondering what they'll be like when they grow up. If I'd had a daughter . . .' She shook her head again.

'It was pretty ghastly,' Rebus agreed.

She looked at him. 'Did you think so? I thought so too, at first. But then I kept looking . . . and they all looked so beautiful.' She took out a handkerchief, dabbed at her eyes.

'I think I'd better drive you home,' he said.

'No, I don't want that.' She paused, put a hand on his arm. 'I just mean . . . I don't want to put you . . . Oh Christ, I don't know what I want any more.'

'You want Damon back.'

'Yes, I want that.'

'What else?'

She seemed to consider the question. But in the end she made no answer, just turned to him again and smiled, eyes shiny from crying.

'In a funny way, it's like you've never been away,' she told him.

He nodded. 'Just the thirty-odd years. What's that between friends?'

They shared the laughter; he touched the back of her hand with his fingers. Parked outside Haymarket station, they sat in silence for a while. Then she opened the door, got out. Smiled one last time and walked away.

Rebus sat for another minute or two, imagining himself running down to the platform, seeking her amongst the crowds . . . Like in a film. Real life was never like that. In films, there was nothing you couldn't do; in the real world . . . in the real world it always got messy.

He went back to Oxford Terrace. Patience wasn't home. They'd passed beyond the stage of leaving notes. He soaked in a bath for half an hour, drifting off to sleep, startling himself awake as his chin dipped beneath the water. He saw the headline: dog-tired cop in bathtime tragedy. One for Jim Stevens to relish.

He lay on the sofa, put some music on. Pete Hammill: 'Two or Three Spectres'. He knew they were there, his ghosts, settling around him, getting comfortable. More comfortable than he could ever be. Patience, Sammy, Janice ... A point was coming, between Patience and him. A crisis point maybe, but then they'd been there before. But was there some point coming between Janice and him too? Something very different ... ? He picked up a book, covered his eyes with it.

Slept.

21

Ama Petrie wasn't the only one who'd thought the mystery blonde looked 'tarty' or a bit like a pro. On his way down to The Shore that evening, Rebus decided on a slight detour.

A few of the working girls still plied their trade dockside. Most of the city's prostitutes worked in licensed premises masquerading as saunas, but a few still took risks by walking the streets. Sometimes it was because they were desperate or unemployable – which meant they had an obvious drug habit – while others just liked to do their own thing, despite the dangers. Over in Glasgow, there were fewer saunas and more girls on the street. Result: seven murders in as many years.

Rebus's thinking: street girls worked Leith; the blonde looked 'tarty'; the taxi had brought her and Damon to Leith. It was another possibility. Say they hadn't been making for the Clipper. Say they'd been heading for her room.

Her room, or maybe a hotel . . .

There were only three women out this evening on Coburg Street, but he knew one of them. Stopped the car and called her over. She got into the passenger seat, bringing waves of perfume with her.

'Long time no see,' she said. Her name was Fern. Punters assumed it was made up, but Rebus knew from her records that she'd been born Fern Bogot. He knew too that she worked the streets because she liked to be her own boss. In saunas, the proprietor was always taking a cut. She had her regulars; didn't often go with strangers.

Mature gentlemen preferred. She found them less aggressive.

Her mane of red hair was a wig, though it looked natural enough. Rebus put the car into gear and signalled to move off. She took her punters to some waste ground in Granton. If Rebus stuck around, he wasn't a punter, and that made everyone uneasy. Looking in his rearview, he saw one of the remaining women peering at the car, then turning to scrawl something on a wall.

'What's she doing?' he asked.

Fern turned back. 'Good old Lesley,' she said. 'She's taking your registration. That way, if my body turns up, there's something for the cops to go on. We call it our insurance policy. Can't be too careful these days.'

Rebus nodded agreement, drove them around the streets, asking his questions. She studied the photographs in detail, but was forced to shake her head.

'Nobody like that works down here.'

'What about the lad?'

'Sorry.' She handed the photos back. Rebus exchanged them for one of Janice's flyers.

'Just in case,' he said.

When he dropped her back at her patch, he got out of the car and went to look at the wall. Sure enough, there were rows of car registration numbers scrawled there, most of them in various shadings of lipstick, some worn away by the elements. His own was at the bottom of the last column. He looked up the column, started to frown. At the top was a number he thought he recognised. Where did he know it from . . . ?

Suddenly it dawned on him: he'd seen it in a file at Leith police station. Leith: where Jim Margolies had been stationed. It was mentioned in the file on Jim's suicide.

It was the registration number of his car.

'What is it?' Fern asked.

Rebus tapped the wall. 'This one. Belongs to a guy called Jim. A cop.'

She frowned in concentration, then shrugged. 'Not one of mine,' she said. 'But it's orange lipstick.'

'So?'

'Lesley has a code, her way of telling who's gone in which car.'

'And who does orange lipstick mean?'

She was shaking her head. 'Not a who so much as a what. Orange means whoever it was, he liked them young . . .'

Roy Frazer wasn't the only one waiting for Rebus down at The Shore. Sitting in the car alongside him was the Farmer.

'Checking up on us, sir?' said Rebus, getting into the back seat. As he got in, Frazer got out, closing the door after him.

'Where the hell have you been?' the Farmer said. 'I've spent half the day trying to find you.' He handed Rebus the day's surveillance notes. 'First entry,' he snapped.

Rebus looked. Bill Pryde recorded himself taking over from Rebus at 0600. His next entry: 'Cary Oakes entered hotel at 0745.'

'Which means,' the Farmer said, 'he left the hotel at some point, and one of you missed him.'

'I saw his bedroom light go off,' Rebus said.

'That's right, you did. It's in the log.'

'Which means he sneaked out on my shift?' Rebus's fingernails dug into his palms.

'Or during the first hour of Bill Pryde's.'

'Either's possible. We're only covering the front of the building. Plenty of access points at the rear.'

The Farmer turned to face him. 'Access isn't our problem, John. Our problem is that he seems to be able to leave whenever he likes.'

'Yes, sir. But a single-officer surveillance . . .'

'Is no bloody use at all if we're not keeping tabs on him.'

'I thought the point was to needle him, let him know we can make things difficult.'

'And does it look to you like we're succeeding, Inspector?'

'No, sir,' Rebus conceded. 'Thing is, if he's got a way of getting out undetected, why not go back the same way?'

'Because the doors at the back can only be opened from within.'

'That's one possibility, sir.'

'And the other?'

'He's playing with us, having a little joke at our expense. He *wants* us to know what he's been doing.'

'And what has he been doing, all the time he's been out roaming?'

Rebus shook his head. 'I don't know, sir. Why don't we ask him?'

When Frazer and the Farmer had left, Rebus decided to follow his own advice. He found Cary Oakes in the bar: no sign of Jim Stevens. Oakes was sitting on a stool, chatting with the two barmen. There were a few other drinkers scattered round the tables, business types, discussing deals even in their cups.

Oakes waved for Rebus to join him, asked him what he was drinking.

'Whisky,' Rebus said. 'A malt.'

'Take your pick, Mr Stevens is paying.' Oakes allowed himself a little chuckle, chin tucked into his neck. He looked like he'd had a few, but Rebus saw he was drinking cola. 'What about something to chase it down?'

Rebus shook his head. 'And I pay for my own,' he said.

There was plenty of choice behind the bar. Rebus decided on something fiery: Laphroaig, with a splash of water to damp the flames. Cary Oakes tried signing for the drink, but Rebus was insistent.

'Your good health then,' Oakes said, lifting his own glass.

'You like playing games, don't you?' Rebus asked.

'Not much else to do in jail. I taught myself chess.'

'I don't mean board games.'

'What then?' Oakes' eyes were heavy-lidded.

'Well, you're playing a game right now.'

'Am I?'

'Bar-room raconteur. A couple too many, telling stories to anyone who'll listen.' He nodded towards the barmen, who'd moved to the far end to wash glasses. 'Just another piece of play-acting.'

'You could go on TV with this stuff. No, I mean it. You're *so* shrewd. Guess you have to be in your profession.'

'Is Jim Stevens falling for it?'

'For what?'

'The stories you're telling him. How much of the truth are you giving him?'

Oakes narrowed his eyes. 'How much truth do you think he can take? If I went into details, think his newspaper would publish them?' He shook his head slowly. 'People can only take so much truth, John.' He leaned towards Rebus. 'Want me to tell *you* about it, John? Want me to tell you how many I really did kill?'

'Tell me about Deirdre Campbell.'

Oakes sat back, took a sip of his drink. 'Alan Archibald thinks I killed her.'

'And did you?' Rebus tried to keep the question casual. Lifted his glass to his lips.

'Does it matter?' Oakes smiled. 'It matters to Alan, doesn't it? Why else would he have come running when I called?'

'He wants the truth – all of it.'

'Maybe you're right. And what do you want, John? What brought *you* running in here? Shall I tell you?' He made himself comfortable on the stool. 'The morning shift saw me coming back. I wasn't sure he was awake: arms folded, head over on one shoulder. I thought he'd nodded off.' He tutted. 'I'm not sure his heart's in it. The job, I mean, police work. He looks the type who's coasting to retirement.'

Which just about summed up Bill Pryde; not that Rebus was about to admit it.

'I think you have problems with your job, too, but not in the same way.'

'Taught yourself psychology along with the chess?'

'When there were no new books to read, I started reading people.'

'You killed Deirdre Campbell, didn't you?'

Oakes put a finger to his lips. Then: 'Did *you* kill Gordon Reeve?'

Gordon Reeve: another ghost; a case from years back . . . Jim Stevens had been shooting his mouth off.

'Tell me,' Rebus said, 'do you trade with Stevens? You tell him a story, he has to tell you one?'

'I'm just interested in you.'

'Then you'll know I killed Gordon Reeve.'

'Did you mean to?'

'No.'

'Are you sure about that? You stabbed a drug-dealer . . . he died.'

'Self-defence.'

'Yes, but did you want him dead?'

'Let's talk about you, Oakes. What made you pick Deirdre Campbell?'

Oakes gave another wry smile. Rebus wanted to rip his lips from his face. 'See, John? See how easy it is to play the game? Stories, that's all they are. Way back in the past, things we'd like to think we can forget.' He slipped off the stool. 'I'm going to my room now. A nice hot bath, I think, then maybe one of the in-room movies. I might call down for a sandwich later. Would you like something sent out to the car?'

'I don't know, what's the menu like?'

'No menu, you just order what you like.'

'Then I'll have your head on a plate, no garnish required.'

Cary Oakes was laughing as he left the bar.

There was someone in the car.

Rebus started forward, saw they were in the passenger seat. As he got close, he saw it was Alan Archibald. Rebus opened the driver's-side door and got in.

'Car wasn't locked,' Archibald said.

'No.'

'Didn't think you'd mind.'

Rebus shrugged, lit a cigarette.

'Have you been talking to him?' Archibald needed no confirmation. 'What did he say?'

'He's playing a game with you, Alan. That's all it is to him.'

'He told you that?'

'He didn't need to. It's what he does. Stevens, you, me . . . we're how he gets his kicks.'

'You're wrong there, John. I've seen how he gets his kicks.' He leaned down to the floor, brought out a green folder. 'Thought you might like something to read.'

Alan Archibald's file on Cary Dennis Oakes.

Cary Oakes had travelled to the USA on a tourist visa. His biography prior to this time was sketchy: a father who'd died when he was young; a mother who'd had psychological problems. Cary had been born in Nairn, where his father had worked as a green-keeper at one of the local golf courses, and his mother as a maid at a hotel in the town. Rebus knew Nairn as a windswept coastal resort, the kind of destination that had lost out as cheap foreign holidays had prospered.

When Oakes's father had died following a stroke, the mother had experienced a breakdown. Her employers had let her go, and she'd headed south with her son, finally stopping in Edinburgh, where she had a half-sister. They'd never been particularly close, but there was no one else, no other family, so mother and son had been squeezed into a room in the house in Gilmerton. Soon afterwards, Cary had started running away. His school had notified his mother that his attendance was irregular at best. There were nights and weekends when he just didn't bother going home at all. His mother was beyond caring, and her half-sister preferred him out of the house anyway, since her husband had taken a furious dislike to the boy.

Where did the money come from for his trip to the States? Alan Archibald had done some digging, uncovering a series of muggings and break-ins in Edinburgh, unsolved, but tailing off at about the time Cary Oakes made his trip. The mystery of his niece's murder made for a file in itself. Archibald had interviewed Oakes's mother and half-sister (both now deceased) and the husband (still alive; living alone in sheltered accommodation in East Craigs). They hadn't remembered anything specific about the night of the murder, couldn't even be sure that Cary had been near the house that day or the next.

Deirdre Campbell had been out dancing in town, ending up at a club on the corner of Rose Street – not a hundred yards from where Gaitano's was now sited. She'd been picked by one particular man, had danced the last four or five dances with him. She'd introduced him to her friends. She had exams coming up, shouldn't have been there in the first place. The club was for over-twenty-ones only, and Deirdre had been underage. The owner had got into trouble afterwards. His defence: 'If she hadn't come in here, they'd have let her in someplace else.' Which was true: make-up, choice of clothes and hairstyle could add half a dozen years to a teenage girl. After the club, the group had headed out to Lothian Road, trying hard not to let the night die. A pizza restaurant, and then taxis. Deirdre had said she'd walk. She lived in Dalry, it would only take her twenty minutes.

Police questioned the young man who'd been with her,

the one she'd danced with. He'd asked if he could see her home, but she'd shaken her head. He lived way out at Comiston, so had accepted a ride in one of the taxis. Deirdre had started walking home.

Only to end up murdered on a hillside. Clothing interfered with, but no sign of rape or assault. A blow to the head, then strangulation.

Three days later, Cary Oakes had been heading out of Scotland, taking with him a rucksack and sports holdall. None of his family knew what he was up to. First they'd heard was when he'd been arrested, over two months later.

They hadn't bothered contacting police, registering him as missing.

'He was old enough to make his mind up what he wanted to do,' his uncle had told Alan Archibald. 'We knew he'd taken some clothes and stuff, figured he'd just took off.'

Archibald had used police reports and trial evidence to piece together Cary Oakes's American travels. From New York he'd taken a bus cross-country. At his trial, Oakes stated that he did this 'because it's what all the pioneers did: headed west'. He spent a week in Chicago, just criss-crossing the city on foot and by means of public transport. Then, hitching rides west, he stopped at Minneapolis, where he decided he needed more money and tried his hand at mugging. A couple of minor successes, and one major setback: picked on a woman with Mace in her coat pocket and a lethal left hook. He left Minneapolis with a swollen left eye and the right bloodshot and stinging. He ate at truck stops along I-94, passing through Fargo and Billings, making it as far as Spokane before his need for dollars became desperate. He broke into a couple of houses, tried pawning his meagre findings. The brokers knew swag when they saw it, offered him a few dollars, then, when he bad-mouthed them, called his description in to the police.

He'd taken to sleeping rough, finding like-minded individuals. Joined a little shoplifting gang. With his 'funny accent', he'd keep the staff busy and interested while the others went about their work undetected. Already, he was boasting that he was on the run, that he'd 'offed' someone back in Scotland. No details, the assertion taken for bravado. Everyone on the street hid behind a shield of lies and fantasies. They'd all tasted the good life; all fallen from a state of grace.

In Spokane, he'd murdered Dorothy Anne Wreiss, a forty-two-year-old divorcee who taught kindergarten three days a week. She lived in a sprawling suburban tract. It was thought Oakes had spotted her at the mall, followed her home or trawled the neighbourhood until he'd spotted her station wagon parked in the drive.

She was found in her kitchen, groceries still in their bags on the breakfast bar. Her two cats had curled up on her back and were sleeping. She'd been beaten with a rock, then strangled with a dishtowel. Her purse had been emptied, as had the jewellery box in her bedroom. Next day, Oakes had tried pawning her watch. At the trial, he'd say it had been gifted to him by one of his drifter friends, the one called Otis. But no one who'd known him had known anyone called Otis.

He ran towards Seattle, stayed there over a week. There was one unsolved they'd tried pinning on him: man found unconscious in the car park of the King Dome. He'd been beaten around the head, his car stolen. Died in hospital of his injuries. The car turned up in Ballard, as did Cary Oakes. By now, the police forces of several states were interested in the 'Scottish drifter'. A couple of serious assaults in Chicago; a known homosexual found dead in his car in the La Grange district of the city. A woman attacked and left for dead in a mall on the outskirts of Bloomington, Minneapolis. The death of a seventy-eight-year-old following a break-in at her home in Tacoma, Washington. Sometimes, police had physical descriptions of someone at or near the scene; sometimes all they had was an MO. No useful fingerprints, no positive IDs of Cary Oakes.

The final killing: another homosexual, Willis Chadaran, age sixty. The attack had taken place in the master bedroom of his home in Bellevue. A heavy statuette, which Chadaran had won for his editing work on a documentary film back in 1982, was the weapon. He'd been beaten senseless with it, then finished off with the belt from his red silk *yakuta*. Cary Oakes's fingerprints were found on the headboard. When arrested and presented with the fingerprint match-up, he admitted he'd been to Chadaran's home, but denied killing him. Detectives had asked how his prints had ended up on the headboard. Oakes said he'd sneaked into the room looking for stuff to steal, maybe he'd touched it then.

He was finally arrested at Pike Place Market. Traders had complained that he'd looked ready to swipe something. Police had asked for his ID. He'd offered his passport, with its invalid tourist visa, then made a run for it. They'd caught him, taken him in, and someone had connected him to various descriptions which had been coming in from all across the country.

At the trial, the prosecution's summing-up had been succinct.

'This is a man for whom brutal murder has become a way of life, a commonplace. If he needs something, wants something, covets something . . . he kills for it. He sees us all as potential victims. We're not fellow humans to him; he's ceased to think of us in those terms, the terms by which we co-ordinate and validate our society, terms without which we cannot call ourselves *civilised*. His soul has shrivelled to the size of a walnut, maybe not even that big. Cary Oakes, ladies and gentlemen of the jury, has stepped outside our society, our laws, our civilisation, and he must pay the price.'

The price being two life sentences.

Rebus put down the file. 'Lots of circumstantial evidence,' he mused.

'It all adds up though. More than enough to make a case.'

Rebus nodded agreement. 'But I can see where he found his loopholes.' He tapped the folder, thought of the summing-up. 'Wonder how big a soul usually is . . .' He turned to Archibald. 'He plays games.'

'I know that. The version Jim Stevens' paper is printing . . . Oakes is spinning them a line.'

'He told me one of his victims was the same age as my daughter. Nobody in here fits with that.'

Alan Archibald shrugged. 'Your daughter's mid-twenties, Deirdre was eighteen.' He paused. 'Maybe there are others we don't know about.'

Yes, thought Rebus, and maybe it had been just another lie. 'So what are you going to do?' he asked.

'Keep at him.'

'Play along with him?'

'I don't see it that way.'

'I know you don't; that's what worries me.'

'She wasn't *your* niece.'

Rebus looked into Alan Archibald's eyes; saw courage and grit, the vital energies which had stayed with him all his working years, not about to be jettisoned now.

'How can I help?'

'What makes you think I want any help?'

'Because you came back tonight. Not to talk to him, but to see me.'

Alan Archibald smiled. 'I know a bit about you, John. I know we're not so very different.'

'So how can I help?'

'Help me make him come to Hillend.'

'What good do you think it would do?'

'He ran from the crime, John. Ran as far as he could from the memory of it. Take him back there, back to his

205

first killing . . . I think it would bring it all back: the terror, the uncertainty. I think he'd start to unravel.'

'Is that what we want?' Rebus thinking: *He'll kill again* . . .

'It's what I want. I just need to know if I'll have your help.'

Rebus rubbed his hands over the steering-wheel. 'I'll need to think.'

'Well, don't be too long about it. I get the feeling maybe you need this as much as I do.'

Rebus looked at him.

'We can't always live by faith alone,' Archibald went on. 'Now and then, there has to be something more.'

22

After a further hour of conversation, Archibald left, saying he'd find himself a taxi. He'd talked about his niece, his memories of her, the way her murder had affected the family.

'We disintegrated,' he'd said. 'So slowly, I don't think anybody noticed. I think we felt guilty whenever we met, like we were to blame. Because when we got together, there was only one possible subject, one thing on our minds, and we didn't want that.'

He'd talked too about his work on the case: weeks spent in police archives; months spent piecing together Cary Oakes's history; trips to the US.

'It must all have cost a lot,' Rebus had said.

'Worth every penny, John.'

Rebus hadn't added that money wasn't his point. He knew all about obsession, knew how it could rob you of everything. He'd been given a jigsaw one year as a Christmas present, back when Sammy was just a kid. He'd cleared a table and started work on it, found he worked late into the night, even though he knew the picture he was making – knew because it was right there on the box. Only he tried not to look at it, wanting to complete the puzzle without any help.

And one piece was missing. He'd asked Rhona, questioned Sammy: had she taken it? Rhona told him maybe it wasn't in the box to start with, but he couldn't accept that. He'd stripped the sofa and chairs, pulled up the carpet, gone over the room inch by inch, then the rest of the flat – just in case Sammy *had* put it somewhere. Never found it. Even years later, he would find himself wondering if maybe it had slipped between the floorboards, or under the skirting-board . . .

Police work could affect you like that, if you let it. Unsolved cases; questions that niggled; people you *knew* were the culprits but couldn't incriminate . . . He'd had more than his fair share of those. But eventually he let them go, even if it meant drinking them into oblivion. Alan Archibald didn't look capable of putting Cary Oakes behind him. Rebus got the feeling that even if Oakes were proved innocent, Archibald would go on believing in his guilt. It was in the nature of obsession.

Alone with his thoughts, Rebus reached into his pocket for the quarter-bottle, drained it dry.

Proved innocent . . . He thought of Darren Rough, shaking with fear, holed up in his locked toilet. All because Social Work had put him in a flat above a kids' playground. And because John Rebus had placed on Rough's shoulders the sins of others – the sins of men who had themselves abused Rough.

Rebus rubbed at his eyes. It wasn't unusual for him to feel a weight of guilt. He carried Jack Morton's death with him. But something had changed. In the old days, he wouldn't have given much thought to Darren Rough. He'd have told himself Rough deserved what he got, for being what he so evidently was. But go back further . . . back to the cop he had once been, so long ago now, and he wouldn't have taken Rough's story to the tabloids. Maybe Mairie Henderson was right: *something's gone bad inside you.*

He admired Alan Archibald's persistence, but wondered what would happen if he were proved *wrong*. Would he still pursue Cary Oakes? Would he take things further than mere pursuit . . . ? Rebus stared out at the night sky.

It's all pretty tricky down here, isn't it, Big Man?

He wondered what point the surveillance was serving. Oakes seemed to be turning it to his own advantage, coming and going as he pleased, letting them know he could do it. So that all their efforts seemed so much waste. He closed his eyes, listened to the occasional message on the police radio, his thoughts turning to Damon Mee. The boat looked like another dead end. Damon had walked out of the world, given his life the slip. Thoughts of Damon took him to Janice, and from there to his schooldays, when everything had just started to get complicated in his life.

Alec Chisholm had disappeared one day; never found. Rebus had gone to the school leaving dance, with something he wanted to tell Mitch.

Then Janice had knocked him cold, a gang had descended on Mitch, and suddenly Rebus's whole life was decided . . .

A noise brought him out of his reverie. He thought it had come from the back of the hotel. He decided to investigate. The car park and service entrance in darkness, but he swept his torch around. Looked up at the hotel windows. You could tell the corridors: lights still burned in those windows. One of the windows was open, curtains flapping. Rebus moved his torch in a downward arc, its beam landing on the roof of a lock-up garage, one of a row of three. They were separated from the hotel property by a wall. Rebus pulled himself up and over it. A narrow alley, puddles and rubbish underfoot. No sign of life, but footprints in the mud. He followed the path. It led him around the back of a factory unit and tenement, then up on to the busy thoroughfare of Bernard Street, where late-night cars and taxis idled at traffic lights. Where drunks stumbled their way home. One man was doing an elaborate dance and providing his own musical accompaniment. The woman with him thought he was hilarious. Can: 'Tango Whiskyman'.

There was no sign of Cary Oakes, no sign at all, but Rebus got the feeling he was out there. He retraced his steps, stopped at a rubbish skip parked next to one of the service doors, took the empty bottle from his pocket and tossed it in,

Felt his head jerk forward as a blow hit him from behind. Searing pain, his eyes screwing shut. He raised a hand, half-turned. A second blow laid him out cold.

It was pitch black, and when he moved there was a dull steel echo.

And a smell.

He was lying on something soft. Voices above him, then blinding light.

'Dear oh dear.'

Second voice, amused: 'Sleeping it off, sir?'

Rebus shielded his eyes, peered up at sheer walls. Two heads bobbing over the rim. He pulled his knees up, slithered as he tried to stand. His hands were tingling. His head pulsed with pain.

He was . . . he knew where he was. In a rubbish skip, the one behind the hotel. Wet cardboard boxes beneath him, and Christ knew what else. Hands were helping him to his feet.

'Come on then, sir. Let's . . .' The voice died as the torch found his face again. Two uniforms, probably from Leith cop shop. And one of them had recognised him.

'DI Rebus?'

Rebus: dishevelled, whisky on his breath, being helped from a skip. Supposedly on surveillance. He knew how it must look.

'Christ, sir, what happened to you?'

'Get that torch out of my face, son.' Their faces were shadows to him, no way to tell if he knew them. He asked the time, worked out that he'd been unconscious only ten or fifteen minutes.

'Call from a public box on Bernard Street,' one of the uniforms was explaining. 'Said there was a fight going on at the back of the hotel.'

Rebus examined the back of his head: no blood on his

palm. Hands still tingling. He rubbed at the fingers. They hurt when he worked them. Lifted them into the torch-light. One of the uniforms whistled.

The knuckles were grazed, bruised. A couple of the joints seemed to be swelling.

'Gave him a sore one, whoever he was,' the uniform said.

Rebus studied the scrapes. Like he'd been punching concrete. 'I didn't hit anyone,' he said. The uniforms shared a glance.

'If you say so, sir.'

'I suppose it's asking too much to tell you to keep this to yourselves.'

'We won't breathe a word, sir.'

An outright lie; it didn't do to beg favours from uniforms.

'Anything else we can do, sir?'

Rebus started to shake his head, felt a wave of nausea as the pain slammed in. Steadied himself with a hand on the skip.

'My car's round the corner,' he said, voice brittle.

'You'll want a shower when you get home.'

'Thank you, Sherlock.'

'Only trying to help,' the uniform muttered.

Rebus walked slowly around the building. The reception-ist looked ready to call security until Rebus produced ID and asked her to buzz Oakes's room. There was no reply.

'Will there be anything else, sir?'

Rebus was looking in his wallet. His cards were there, but the cash had gone.

'Any idea where Mr Oakes is?' he asked.

She shook her head. 'I didn't see him leave.'

Rebus thanked her and walked over to a sofa, fell down on to it. A little later, he asked for aspirin. When she brought them, she had to shake his shoulder to wake him up.

*

He headed for Patience's: sod the surveillance. Oakes wasn't in his room. He was out on the streets. Rebus needed clean clothes, a shower, and more painkillers. As he stumbled through the door, Patience came into the hall, blinking her eyes sleepily. He held up both hands to pacify her.

'It's not what you think,' he said.

She came forward, held his hands, looking at the swelling.

'Explain,' she said. So Rebus did just that.

He lay in the bath, a cold compress on the back of his skull. Patience had rigged it up from a sandwich bag, some ice cubes, and a bandage. She was treating his hands with antiseptic cream, having cleaned them and established nothing was broken.

'This man Oakes,' she said, 'I'm still not sure why he'd do it.'

Rebus adjusted the ice-pack. 'To humiliate me. He made sure I'd be found by uniforms, out cold in a rubbish skip.'

'Yes?' She dabbed on more ointment.

'Knuckles bruised like I'd been fighting. And whoever I'd fought had whipped me. Found like that at the back of the hotel, there's only one real candidate. By morning, it'll be round every station in the city.'

'Why would he do that?'

'To show me he can. Why else?' He tried not to flinch as she rubbed cream into a cut.

'I don't know,' she said. 'Maybe to distract you.'

He looked at her. 'From what?'

She shrugged. 'You're the detective here.' She examined her handiwork. 'I need to wrap your hands.'

'So long as I can still drive.'

'John . . .' Knowing he'd pay no attention.

'Patience, if I go round with hands looking like a mummy's, he's won this round.'

'Not if you refuse to play.'

He saw the depth of concern in her eyes, brushed her

212

cheek with the back of his hand. Saw Janice doing the self-same thing to him, and withdrew his hand guiltily.

'Hurts, does it?' Patience asked, misreading the gesture. He nodded, not trusting himself to speak.

Later, he sat on the sofa with a mug of weak tea. He'd washed down two more painkillers, prescription-strength. His soiled clothes had been bundled into a black bin-liner, ready for a trip to the cleaner's. Such a shame, he thought, that his soiled thoughts couldn't be steam-pressed so easily.

When his mobile phone sounded, he stared at it hard. It lay on the coffee table in front of him, alongside his keys and small change. Patience was standing in the doorway as he finally picked the phone up. There was a little smile on her lips, but no humour in her eyes. She'd known all along he would answer it.

Cal Brady came home from Guiser's feeling pretty good. The buzz lasted all of ten seconds. As he flopped on to his bed, he remembered about the pervert. His mum was in her bedroom with some bloke; walls were so thin they'd have been as well having it off in front of him. All the flats were like that, so that things you wanted done in secrecy you had to do quietly. He put his ear to one wall, then another: his mum and her bloke; a couple of television stations – Jamie was still awake, watching the box in the living room, and the portable was on in Van's room, a weak attempt to mask other sounds. He put his ear to the floor. He could still hear all of it, plus the people below's movements, coughs and conversations. He'd gone to the doctor a while back, asked if maybe he had ears that were more sensitive than the norm.

'I keep hearing things I don't want to.'

When he'd explained that he lived in one of the high-rises in Greenfield, the doctor had suggested a personal stereo.

But it was the same on the street: he overheard snippets

of conversation, stuff the talkers didn't think he could hear. Sometimes he thought it was getting worse, thought he could hear people's hearts beating, the quick flow of blood around their bodies. He thought he could hear their *thoughts*. Like at Guiser's, when girls looked at him and he smiled back. They were thinking: he might not look much, but he's with Archie Frost, so he must be important in some way. They'd think: if I dance with him, let him buy me a drink, I'll be closer to the *power*.

Which was why he seldom did anything, just stayed by the bar, affecting a cool poise and saying nothing. But listening, always listening.

Always hearing things ... Things about Charmer, things about the clients – Ama Petrie, her brother and the rest. His own version of the *power*.

It had been quiet in the club tonight. If it hadn't been for a busload from Tranent, the place would have been dead. They hadn't looked too impressed: nobody to dance with but themselves. Archie doubted they'd be back. Archie was already looking for other work: plenty more clubs in the city. Cal hadn't started looking though. Cal believed in loyalty.

'I know Charmer's trying to collect on some debts,' Archie had said, 'but the problem is, he's got debts of his own. Only a matter of time before people come calling ...'

Cal had straightened his back, as if to say: fine by me.

He wanted to think things through, get them straight in his head, which was why he'd come into his bedroom rather than sitting up with Jamie. But even before he'd reached that sanctuary, his thoughts had turned to Darren Rough. The hall was half-full of placards. They sat against the wall, still smelling of fresh paint. Cardboard boxes had been cut up flat, messages written on their blank sides. DESTROY ALL MONSTERS; KEEP AWAY FROM OUR KIDS; LET'S PLAY HANG THE PERV.

Destroy all monsters, Cal was thinking, lying on his bed,

smoking a cigarette. He got up abruptly, thumped on the far wall.

'Will you fucking well shut up, the pair of you!'

Silence, then muffled laughter. For a moment, Cal was ready to burst in on them, but he knew what his mum would do to him. And besides, last thing he wanted was to see her like that.

Destroy all monsters.

The doorbell. Who the fuck at this time of night . . . ? Cal went to see. Recognised the woman. She looked agitated, rubbing her hands like she was doing the washing-up.

'You haven't seen our Billy, have you?' She was Joanna Horman, Billy's mum. Billy was one of Jamie's pals. Cal called for him and Jamie came out of the living room.

'Have you seen Billy Boy?' Cal asked. Jamie shook his head. He had a packet of crisps in his hand. Cal turned back to Joanna Horman. Some of his friends reckoned she looked all right. Right now, though, she looked a mess.

'What's up?' he asked.

'He went out to play about seven, I haven't seen him since. I thought maybe he'd gone to his gran's, but when I checked she hadn't clapped eyes on him.'

'I'm just in. Hold on a minute.' He went and banged on Van's door: as good an excuse as any to break things up in there. 'Hiy, Maw, has Billy Horman been round here the night?'

Noises from within. Joanna Horman was leaning against the door, looking ready to fall down. Not a bad body, Cal decided. Bit squishy, but he didn't like them all skin and bones. His mother's bedroom door opened. Van was wearing her dress, arranging it over her. Nothing on underneath, he'd bet. She closed the door quickly behind her; no way to tell who else was in the room.

'Something the matter, Joanna?' Pushing past Cal, ignoring him altogether.

'It's wee Billy, Van. He's disappeared.'

215

'Aw, Christ. Come into the living room.'

'I just don't know what to do.'

'Where have you looked?'

Cal followed the two women into the living room.

'Everywhere. I think maybe it's time I called the police.'

Van snorted. 'Oh aye, they'd be round here like a shot. Only thing those buggers are interested in is protecting perverts . . .' Her voice died away; for the first time, she looked at her son. They knew one another so well, no words were needed.

'Joanna, pet,' Van said quietly, 'you stay there. I'm going to round up the troops. If your Billy's anywhere on the estate, we'll find him, don't you worry.'

Within half an hour, Van Brady had the search parties organised. People were going from door to door, asking questions, getting new volunteers. Jamie had been sent to bed, but wasn't asleep, and Joanna Horman was in the living room with a tumbler of rum and Coke. Cal had offered to keep an eye on her. She was on the sofa, and he was in the chair. He couldn't think of anything to say. Wasn't normally this tongue-tied. He found himself aroused by her grief, the way it softened her. But he felt ashamed to be so affected by her, and his brain was spinning the way it did when he'd drunk too much or taken some speed.

He got up, opened the door to Jamie's room.

'Get up, you, and keep an eye on Billy's mum. I've got to go out.'

Then he opened the main door and stalked down the hallway. Down the stairwell and out into the night. There were some lock-ups across the way. He had the key to one of them. He was keeping some stuff there. Jerry Langham's lock-up it was, but Jerry was serving three-to-five in Saughton, another six months before he'd have even a whiff of roly-paroley. He kept his car in the lock-up. It was a 1970s Merc with rusty sills and a custard-yellow paint job, but Jerry loved it.

'I don't keep my missus under lock and key, but no way am I letting any bastard near my Merc.'

This was by way of a warning: use the lock-up, keep an eye on the motor, but never think of touching it. Not that Cal had heeded the advice. He unlocked the car sometimes and sat in it, pretending to be driving. And he'd opened the boot once, too, so he knew what was inside.

He unlocked it now, lifted out the jerrycan and gave it a shake. He was sure there'd been more than that; it was barely half-full now. Evaporation or something. He supposed petrol could do that. On a stack of shelves he found some oily rags. Stuffed them into his pockets and he was ready.

Back to the block of flats, taking the steps two at a time. He had a purpose now, jerrycan making quiet sloshing sounds. Close your eyes, you could almost be at the seaside. Crept along to Darren Rough's flat. Fresh lengths of board across his window. The kids had already been busy with their aerosols. GAP had made the flat their first stop tonight: no answer, nobody home. Cal opened the mouth of the can, held it high so the petrol trickled out of it, running it the length of the boarded window, then across the door. Took a ball of rag from his pocket and doused it in petrol. Stuffed it into the narrow gap between board and wall. Then another and another. Chucked the empty can over the balcony, then cursed to himself: there'd be prints on it. And besides, Jerry might want it. He'd go retrieve it in a minute.

Took out his cigarette lighter, the one Jamie had given him for Christmas. Jamie . . . he was doing this for Jamie and his pals, for all the kids. Jamie was bright. Didn't like school, but then who did? Didn't make him thick. He could go places, do things with his life: a couple of times when drunk, Cal had tried to tell him as much. He got the feeling it hadn't come out right, had come out like he was

217

envious. Maybe he was, just a little. A kid like Jamie, the world was his oyster. Cal looked at the lighter. Another thing about his wee brother: he had shoplifting down to an art.

23

When Rebus got to Greenfield, half the estate was out watching the fire, or what was left of it.

Rebus knew one of the firemen, guy called Eddie Dickson. Dickson nodded a greeting. He was in full uniform, standing guard by his engine.

'If I move, they'll be in about it.' Meaning the local kids; meaning they'd strip it of anything they could find. 'We got bottled coming in.'

'Who by?'

Dickson shrugged. 'Came flying out of the dark. I get the feeling we weren't wanted.'

Uniforms from St Leonard's were trying to get the spectators to go back to bed.

'Any casualties?'

Dickson shrugged again. 'You mean from the bottles?'

Rebus stared at him. 'I mean in there.' Pointing towards Darren Rough's flat.

'Place was empty when we got here.'

'Door open?'

Dickson shook his head. 'Had to kick in what was left of it. Grudge thing, is it?'

'Don't you read the papers?'

'When do I get the time, John?'

'Paedophile.'

Dickson nodded. 'Remember it now. Frying's too good for them, eh?'

Rebus left him to his guard duty, headed for Cragside Court. The uniform in the lobby told him not to bother with the lifts.

'One's buggered, the other's a toilet.'

Rebus would have taken the stairs anyway. Nothing left of the boards across Rough's window but a few charred scraps clinging to their screws. The door had been torched, too. DC Grant Hood was standing in the hallway of the flat. Rebus toed open the toilet door: nobody home.

'Your pal,' Hood said. He was young, bright. Followed Glasgow Rangers with a passion, but nobody was perfect.

'Wasn't me,' Rebus commented. 'But thanks for the call.'

Hood shrugged. 'Thought you might be interested.' He nodded towards Rebus's bandaged hands. 'Had an accident yourself?'

Rebus ignored the question. 'No chance *this* was an accident, I suppose?'

'Bits of rag hanging from the windowframe. Petrol spilt on the walkway . . .'

'No sign of the occupier?'

Hood shook his head. 'Any ideas?'

'Look around, Grant. It's the Wild West out here. Any one of them's capable.' Rebus had walked back through what remained of the door, was leaning over the balcony. 'But if it was me, I'd be asking Van Brady and her eldest son.'

Hood jotted the names down. 'I don't suppose Mr Rough will be coming back.'

'No,' Rebus said. Which had been the point all along. But now that they'd come to that point, Rebus wondered why he felt so lousy inside . . . Jane Barbour's words came back to him: low chance of reoffending . . . abused as a child himself . . . need to give him a chance.

Then he saw Cal Brady, down amongst the thinning crowd. He was fully clothed, looked like he hadn't yet been to bed. Rebus went back downstairs. Cal was handing out GAP stickers to anyone who didn't have one. Women with coats thrown over their nighties were getting them. Cal placed each one on its recipient with exaggerated gentleness, causing some of the women – not exactly coy maidens – to blush.

'All right, Cal?' Rebus said. Cal looked round at him, peeled off a sticker and slapped it on Rebus's jacket.

'I hope you're with us, Inspector.'

Rebus started removing the sticker. Cal put out a hand to stop him, and Rebus caught it, lifted it to his nose. Cal pulled away quickly, but not quickly enough.

'Soap and water's usually a good idea,' Rebus told him.

'I haven't done anything.'

'You stink of petrol.'

'Not guilty, Your Honour.'

'I'm not one to prejudge, Cal—'

'Not what I hear.'

'But in your case I'll definitely make an exception.' Thinking: who had Cal been talking to? Who'd been telling him about Rebus? 'DC Hood's going to want to ask you some questions. Be nice to him.'

'Fuck the lot of you.'

'Think your dick's long enough?' Said with a smile.

Cal stared him out; then broke off and laughed. 'You're a clown. Go home to your circus.'

'What do you think *you* are, Cal? The ringmaster?' Rebus shook his head. 'No, son, you'll do tricks for whoever's cracking the whip.' Rebus turned away. 'Whether it's your mum or Charmer Mackenzie.'

'What do you mean?'

'You work for him, don't you?'

'What's it to do with you?'

Rebus just shrugged and went back to his car. He'd parked it right next to the fire engine: didn't want to find it up on bricks.

'Hey, John,' Eddie Dickson said, 'won't it be perfect?'

'What?'

'When they build the Parliament.' He swept an arm before him. 'Right next door to all this.'

Rebus looked up, saw the dark form of Salisbury Crags.

221

Once more he felt like he was in a canyon of some kind, sheer walls affording no escape. Your fingers would be raw and bleeding from trying.

Either that or stained with four-star.

Hood came running up as Rebus was flexing his hands. 'I think we've got a problem.'

'Be a miracle if we didn't.'

'There's a kid missing. They weren't even going to tell us.'

Rebus was thoughtful. 'It's UDI,' he said. Hood looked puzzled. 'A Unilateral Declaration of Independence, son. So who spilt the beans?'

'I went to Van Brady's flat. Door was open, young woman in the lounge.' He checked his notebook. 'Name's Joanna Horman. Kid's name is Billy.'

Rebus remembered his first visit to Greenfield, Van Brady leaning out of her window: *I saw you, Billy Horman!* He couldn't remember much about the kid, only that he'd been playing with Jamie Brady.

'Now we know why they torched the flat,' Hood went on.

'A brilliant deduction, Grant. Maybe we better go talk to the lady in question.'

'The kid's mum?'

Rebus shook his head. 'Van Brady.'

Having opened negotiations with Van Brady, her kitchen providing an unpromising table for such a high-powered summit, Rebus called for reinforcements. They'd organise more search parties, police and residents working together.

'This is your patch,' Rebus had conceded, washing down more pills with a mug of cheap chicory coffee. 'You know the place better than any of us: any hidey-holes, gang huts, anywhere he might stop the night. If his mum gives us a list of his school pals, we can contact their parents, see if he's maybe staying with one of them. There are things we can do best, and things you can do.' He'd kept his voice level, and maintained eye-contact throughout. There were eight bodies in the kitchen, and more in the hallway and living room.

'What about the pervert?' Van Brady had asked.

'We'll find him, don't worry. But right now, I think we should concentrate on Billy, don't you?'

'What if he's the one who's *got* Billy?'

'Let's wait and see, eh? First thing is to get the search going again. We're not going to find anyone sitting here.'

Meeting over, Rebus had sought out Grant Hood.

'This is yours, Grant,' he said. 'I shouldn't even be here.'

Hood nodded. 'Sorry I got you involved.'

'Don't be. But keep yourself straight: wake up DI Barbour and let her know the score.'

'What happens if they find him first?' Meaning Darren Rough rather than the kid.

'Then he's dead,' Rebus said. 'It's as simple as that.'

He drove out of Greenfield, wondering at what point Darren Rough had vacated his flat. Wondering where the young man would go. Holyrood Park: once, centuries back, it had been sanctuary for convicts. As long as you didn't cross the boundary, you were on Crown Estate and couldn't be touched by the law. Debtors would flee there, live there for years, existing on charity, fish from the lochs and wild rabbits. When their debts were finally paid or written off, they'd cross the boundary, step back into society. The park had provided them with an illusion of freedom; in reality, they'd merely been in an open prison.

Holyrood Park: a road wound its way around the base of Salisbury Crags and Arthur's Seat. There were car parks near the lochs, popular with families and dog-owners during the day. At night, couples drove there for sex. The Royal Parks Police made irregular patrols. There had been talk of their disbanding, of the park falling

223

within Lothian and Borders jurisdiction. It hadn't happened yet.

Rebus made three circuits of the park. Driving slowly, not really interested in the few parked cars he passed. Then, by St Margaret's Loch, just as he was readying to exit at Royal Park Terrace, he thought he caught shadow play at the edge of his vision. Decided to stop the car. Maybe just the headache and the pills, tricking his vision. He kept the engine running, wound down the window and lit a cigarette. Foxes, maybe even badgers . . . he could have been mistaken. There were all kinds of shadows in the city.

But then a face appeared at the open window.

'Any chance of a ciggie?'

'No problem.' Rebus averted his face as he searched his pockets.

'Eh . . . look, I'm not sure . . .' A clearing of the throat. 'I mean, you're not looking for company, are you?'

'As a matter of fact, I am.' Now Rebus looked up. 'Get in, Darren.'

Shock hit Darren Rough's face as he recognised Rebus. His face was blackened. He coughed again, doubling over.

'Smoke inhalation,' Rebus observed. 'You left it pretty late getting out.'

Rough wiped his mouth. The sleeves of his green raincoat were singed where he'd held them in front of his face.

'I thought they'd be waiting for me outside. I kept listening for a fire engine.'

'Somebody called one eventually.'

He snorted. 'Probably afraid it would spread to their flat.'

'Nobody was waiting outside?'

Rough shook his head. No, Rebus thought, because they'd all been out searching for Billy Horman. Cal Brady had torched the flat alone, and hadn't stuck around to be spotted.

It had started to rain; sudden gobbets which bounced off Rough's shoulders. He lifted his face to the sky, opened his scorched mouth to the drops.

'You better get in,' Rebus told him.

He angled his head, stared at Rebus. 'What am I charged with?'

'A kid's gone missing.'

Rough lowered his eyes. Said something like 'I see', but so quietly Rebus didn't catch it. 'They think I . . . ?' He stopped. 'Of course they think I did it. In their shoes, I'd think the same.'

'But it wasn't you?'

Rough shook his head. 'I don't do that any more. That's not me.' He was getting soaked.

'Get in,' Rebus repeated. Rough got into the passenger seat. 'But you still think about it,' Rebus said, watching for a response.

Rough stared at the windscreen, his eyes glinting. 'I'd be a liar if I said I didn't.'

'So what's changed?'

Rough turned to him. 'Are you charging me?'

'No charge,' Rebus said, putting the car into gear. 'Tonight, you ride for free.'

24

Rebus took Darren Rough to St Leonard's.

'Don't worry,' he said. 'Call it protective custody. I just want to make your answers on the missing kid official.'

They sat in an interview room with the recording machine running and a uniform on the door, drinking watery tea and with the rest of the station practically empty. All the spare bodies were down at Greenfield, looking for Billy Horman.

'So you don't know anything about a missing child?' Rebus asked. Because there was no one around to tell him not to, he'd lit himself a cigarette. Rough didn't want one, but then changed his mind.

'Cancer's probably the least of my problems right now,' he surmised. Then he told Rebus that all he knew was what he'd heard from the detective himself.

'But the locals warned you off, and you stayed put. There must have been a reason.'

'Nowhere else to go. I'm a marked man.' Glancing up. 'Thanks to you.' Rebus stood up. Rough flinched, but all Rebus did was lean against the wall, so he was facing the video camera. Not that it mattered: the camera wasn't on.

'You're a marked man because of what you are, Mr Rough.'

'I'm a paedophile, Inspector. I suppose I'll always be one. But I have ceased to be a *practising* paedophile.' A shrug. 'Society's going to have to get used to it.'

'I don't think your neighbours would agree.'

Rough allowed himself a condemned man's smile. 'I think you're right.'

'What about friends?'

'Friends?'

'Others who share your interests.' Rebus flicked ash on to the carpet; the cleaners would be in before morning. 'Had any of them round to the flat?'

Rough was shaking his head.

'Sure about that, Mr Rough?'

'Nobody knew I was there till the papers splashed me across a double-page spread.'

'But afterwards . . . nobody from the old days got in touch?'

Rough didn't answer. He was staring into space, still thinking of newspapers. 'Ince and Marshall . . . I see the stories about them. Where they are . . . in the cells . . . do they get to see the news?'

'Sometimes,' Rebus admitted.

'So they'll know about me?'

Rebus nodded. 'Don't worry about them. They're on remand in Saughton Prison.' He paused. 'You were going to testify against them.'

'I wanted to.' He stared into space again, his face tightening with memories. Rebus knew the story: the abused became abusers themselves. He'd always found it easy to discard. Not every victim turned abuser.

'That time they took you to Shiellion . . .' Rebus began.

'Marshall took me. Ince told him to.' His voice was trembling. 'Didn't pick on me specially or anything – could have been any one of us. Only I think I was the quietest, the least likely to do anything about it. Marshall was right under Ince's thumb at that time, loved the way Ince ordered him about. I saw a photo of Ince, he hasn't changed. Marshall's got a lot tougher-looking, like he's grown an extra skin.'

'And the third man?'

'I told you, could have been anybody.'

'But he was already there, waiting at Shiellion when you arrived.'

227

'Yes.'

'So probably a friend of Ince, rather than Marshall.'

'They took it in turns.' Rough's hands were holding the edge of the desk. 'Afterwards, I tried telling people, but nobody would listen. It was: "You mustn't say that"; "Don't tell such stories." Like it was all *my* fault. I'd touched up a neighbour's kid, so I deserved everything I got . . . Even worse, some of them thought I was lying, and I never lied . . . never.' He closed his eyes, rested his forehead on his hands. He muttered something that might have been 'Bastards.' And then he started to cry.

Rebus knew he had choices. Phone Social Work and have them take Rough somewhere. Put him in a cell. Or drop him off somewhere . . . anywhere. But when he tried the Social Work emergency number, no one answered. They'd be out on a call. The recorded message told him to keep trying the number every ten minutes or so. It told him not to panic.

There were empty cells in the station, but Rebus knew word would get out, and when it came time to release Darren Rough, there'd be a crowd waiting. So he lit another cigarette and went back to the interview room.

'Right,' he said, opening the door, 'you're coming with me.'

'Nice room,' Darren Rough said. He looked around, examining the high cornicing. 'Big,' he added, nodding to himself. He was trying to be pleasant, make conversation. He was wondering what Rebus was going to do with him, here in Rebus's own flat.

Rebus handed over a mug of tea and told him to sit down. He offered Rough another cigarette, the offer refused this time. Rough was sitting on the sofa. Rebus wanted to tell him to move on to one of the dining chairs. It was as if Rough could contaminate everything he touched.

'Your social worker better find you something in the morning,' Rebus said. 'Something far from Edinburgh.'

Rough looked at him. His eyes were dark-ringed, his hair needing a wash. The green raincoat was draped over the back of the sofa. He wore a check suit-jacket with jeans and baseball boots, white nylon shirt. He looked like he'd won a ninety-second dash through an Oxfam shop.

'Keep moving, eh?'

'A moving target's harder to hit,' Rebus told him.

Rough smiled tiredly. 'I see you've been hitting a target yourself.'

Rebus flexed his fingers again, trying to stop them seizing up.

Rough sipped his tea. 'He did beat me up, you know.'

'Who?'

'Your friend.'

'Jim Margolies?'

Rough nodded. 'All of a sudden he got this look in his eyes. Next thing the fists were flying.' He shook his head. 'When he killed himself, I read the obituaries. They all said he was a "fine officer", a "loving father". Attended church regularly.' A half-smile. 'When he laid into me, he must have been demonstrating muscular Christianity.'

'Careful what you say,'

'Yes, he was your friend, you worked with him. But I wonder if you *knew* him.'

He didn't say as much, but Rebus was beginning to wonder the same thing. Orange lipstick, meaning he liked them young. He'd asked Fern how young. Nothing illegal, she'd told him.

'Why do you think he died?' Rebus asked.

'How should I know?'

'When the two of you talked . . . how did he seem?'

Rough was thoughtful. 'Not angry with me or anything. Just wanting to know about Shiellion. How often I'd been . . . you know. And who by.' He glanced towards

229

Rebus. 'Some people get a kick that way, listening to stories.'

'You think that's why he was asking?'

'Why are *you* asking all these questions, Inspector? Outing me to the papers, then coming to the rescue. I think maybe that's how *you* get your kicks, fucking with people's heads.'

Rebus thought of Cary Oakes and his games. 'I think you had something to do with Jim Margolies' death,' he said. 'Whether you know it or not.'

They sat in silence after that, until Rough asked if there was anything he could eat. Rebus went through to the kitchen, stared at one of the cupboard doors, wanting to punch it. But his knuckles wouldn't thank him for that. He looked at them. He knew what Oakes had done, rubbed them hard over the floor of the car park, maybe bunched them into fists and driven them into the steel skip. Twisted little bastard that he was. And Patience wondered if it was all a blind, some way of diverting Rebus from some other scheme. His head seemed full of diversions. How could he trust what Rough was telling him? He didn't see Rough as a schemer; too weak. But Jim Margolies . . . had *he* been playing some game?

And had it killed him?

Rebus opened the cupboard door, called out that he could do beans on toast. Rough said that would be fine. There was no marge for the toast, but Rebus reckoned the tomato sauce would soften it up. He emptied the beans into a pot, stuck the bread under the grill, and went to sort out the sleeping accommodation.

Not his own room; definitely not his own room. He opened the door to what had been the guest room, and – long before that – Sammy's room. Her single bed was still there; posters on the walls; teenage girls' annuals on a bookshelf. One of the last people to use the room had been Jack Morton. No way was Darren Rough sleeping there.

230

Rebus opened the wardrobe, found an old blanket and pillow, took them through to the living room.

'You can have the sofa,' he said.

'Fine. Whatever.' Rough was standing at the window. Rebus crossed over to him. A couple of kids lived across the street, but their shutters were closed, no peep-show available.

'It's so quiet here,' Rough said. 'In Greenfield, there always seems to be a row going on. Either that or a party, and most of the parties turn into a row.'

'But you're a good neighbour, eh?' Rebus said. 'Quiet, keep yourself to yourself?'

'I try to.'

'What about when the kids are noisy: don't you want to do something about them?'

Rough closed his eyes, pressed his forehead to the glass. 'I won't make any excuses,' he whispered.

'And no apologies either?'

Another smile, eyes still shut. 'I can apologise until the cows come home. It doesn't change anything. It doesn't change how I feel.' He opened his eyes, turned to Rebus. 'But you don't want to hear about that, do you?'

Rebus stared at him. 'The toast's burning,' he said, turning away.

At five o'clock, with Rough hidden under the blanket on the sofa, Rebus telephoned Bill Pryde.

'Sorry to wake you, Bill.'

'The alarm was about to go off anyway. What's up?'

'The surveillance car.'

'What about it?'

'It's not at The Shore.' He explained where it was.

'Christ, John, what about Oakes?'

'He comes and goes as he likes, Bill. The only thing we were doing there was keeping him amused.'

'You better tell that to the Farmer.'

'I will.'

231

'Meantime, you want me to pick up the car from your flat?'

'I've filled in the log, explained everything.'

'What about the keys?'

'Under the front seat, same place the log is. I've left it unlocked.'

'And now you're about to get your head down?'

'Something like that.' He stared at Darren Rough, watching the rise and fall of the blanket. He looked about as dangerous as pastry dough. Rebus cut the connection, tried the station. There was still no sign of Billy Horman. They'd looked everywhere. The search was being called off until daylight. Rebus called the hotel, asked for Cary Oakes's room: still no answer. He put down the phone, went into his bedroom. Lay on his bed – a mattress on the floor. He'd thought about going back to Patience's, but didn't like the thought of Rough being here by himself. He might explore, find Sammy's room. Pull open drawers, touch things. As soon as feasible, Rebus wanted him out.

You brought him here, a voice in his head seemed to say. *You brought him to this.* Sticks and crowbars and angry voices. The residents of Greenfield roused to a mob. Cal Brady with his petrol and denials. He worked for Charmer Mackenzie, worked the door at Guiser's. Damon Mee had left there, got into a taxi with a blonde. Last seen in the vicinity of the Clipper, the night of one of Ama Petrie's parties. Her father was presiding over Shiellion, where Darren Rough should have given evidence, where Rebus had been steamrollered by Richard Cordover. Lord Justice Petrie . . . who was related to Katherine Margolies.

Ama, Hannah, Katherine . . . Sammy, Patience, Janice . . . The never-ending dance of relationships and criss-crossings which took up so much space in his head. The party that never stopped, the invitations guilt-edged.

Life and death in Edinburgh. And space still left over for a few ghosts, their numbers increasing.

If I'd stuck around Fife, he thought, *not joined the army ... what would I be thinking now? Who would I be?*

The voice in his head again – was it Jack Morton's? *It was never going to happen. This is where you were always headed.* He looked around the room for whisky, but he was all cleaned out. Closed his eyes instead. Still that dull pain at the back of his skull. *Please, Lord, let my sleep be dreamless.*

His first prayer in a while.

Cary Oakes had been in Arden Street for Rebus's return, had seen him get out of his car with another man, lead the man into his tenement. He wondered who this stranger was, wondered where Rebus had met him. He'd been standing across the road, hidden in the shadow of a tenement doorway. He had a plastic bag with him, a paperback book inside to give it weight. If anyone saw him, he had his story ready: working shifts, waiting for his lift to turn up. They were late, he'd say.

Only no one saw him. No one entered or left the building. But he saw the lights come on in Rebus's living room. Saw the stranger approach the window, put his head to it. Saw Rebus over the man's shoulder, staring down. Oakes stood his ground, felt he hadn't been spotted. The beauty was, even if Rebus *did* see him, well, that was all right too. Then Rebus had come out of the tenement, gone to his car to fetch something: a book of some kind. Way he was moving, acting, Oakes hadn't done too much damage. Rebus took the book upstairs with him, then came back down half an hour later, put it back in the car. When he'd gone back up again, Oakes crossed to where the car was parked, tried the driver's door. It wasn't locked. He got in, felt on the floor for where Rebus had put the book. Found it. And the car keys. Smiled to himself. He turned the ignition, powered up the police radio: easy listening while he perused the surveillance notes. Rebus hadn't put in anything about Alan Archibald. That was interesting.

Fifty minutes later, when the tenement door rattled open, he slid down in his seat, rose up again to watch the stranger walk away from the building. He looked dirty and dishevelled. Some secret little vice of Rebus's? Oakes didn't think so. But it intrigued him all the same. He waited till the man had rounded the corner, then started the engine and began to follow . . .

At six o'clock, Rebus was wakened by the front buzzer. He went to the door, pushed the intercom.

'Who is it?'

'It's me.' Bill Pryde, not sounding happy.

'What's the matter?'

'This car I'm supposed to pick up. Just where exactly have you hidden it?'

'Hang on.'

Rebus walked into the living room, glanced at the sofa. Saw the blanket had been folded neatly; no sign of Darren Rough. Peered out of the window. A space where the car had been. He cursed under his breath. Put his shoes on and headed downstairs.

'I think someone took it,' he told Bill Pryde.

'This isn't my fuck-up, John.' Pryde: ticking off the days till retirement.

'I know,' Rebus said, unwilling to add that he might know who'd taken it: Darren Rough.

Pryde pointed at his hands. 'Word's out you lost the punch-up. How does Oakes look?'

'That's not what happened,' Rebus said.

'You were found KO'd in a skip, way I heard it.'

Rebus stared at him. 'You want to walk to work, Bill?'

Pryde shook his head. 'I want to be ringside for the main bout: you telling the Farmer how you came to lose the car.'

Rebus stared up and down the road again. 'Better slip a horseshoe into my glove for that one,' he said, turning back into the tenement.

25

Rebus drove them to St Leonard's in his Saab and reported the theft, cheering up the day shift who'd just come on. At quarter to nine, he was in the Farmer's office, explaining the whole thing yet again, including the scrapes on his hands. The Farmer busied himself at his coffee machine all the time Rebus was making his report. It was an espresso-maker with a spout for steamed milk. He hadn't offered Rebus a cup. When Rebus stopped talking, the Farmer poured the foamy milk into his mug, switched off the machine, and sat behind his desk. Holding the mug in both hands, he looked at Rebus.

'I always thought surveillance was a fairly simple procedure. Once more, you've managed to prove me wrong.'

'It wasn't going anywhere, sir.'

'Unlike the missing car.'

Rebus looked down at the floor.

'So let me see where we stand,' the Farmer continued, taking another sip. 'I tell you to lay off Darren Rough. You go out looking for him. I tell you to keep an eye on a man whom experts say may murder someone. You end up unconscious in a rubbish skip.' The Farmer's voice was rising. 'You find Darren Rough and take him to your flat. He then leaves, taking one of our cars with him, along with the surveillance log. Does that just about cover it?' His face was growing red with anger.

'Clear and concise, sir.'

'*Don't you dare be amused!*' The Farmer slapped a hand down on the desk.

'I'm anything but, sir.' Rebus gritted his teeth. 'But I thought I was doing the right thing at the time.'

'No, Inspector. As usual, what you were doing was following your own agenda, and to hell with the rest of us. Isn't that nearer the mark?'

'With respect, sir—'

'Don't give me that. You've no respect for me, no respect for the job we're supposed to be doing here!'

'Maybe you're right, sir,' Rebus said quietly, his head beginning to throb again.

The Farmer looked at him, leaned back in his chair and took another mouthful of coffee. 'So what are we going to do about that?'

'I don't know, sir. I mean, you're right: I've been having doubts about the job for months. Ever since Jack Morton . . .'

'Maybe even before then?' Sounding calmer now.

'Maybe, sir. More than once, I've thought about chucking it.' He looked at his boss. 'Make your life a bit easier.'

'But you haven't chucked it.'

'No, sir.'

'Must be a reason.'

'Maybe a bit of me still believes, sir. And funnily enough, that part's been growing.'

'Oh?'

Alan Archibald; Darren Rough: he hadn't mentioned Archibald to the Farmer, hadn't seen the point.

'I was wrong about Rough, I admit that. Well . . . I'm not sure I was wrong, to tell you the truth. But I know now why he's in Edinburgh. I know a bit more about his background.'

'What are you saying?' The Farmer narrowed his eyes. 'You *understand* him, is that it?' A smile with an edge of cruelty to it. 'Compassion? *You*, John? I didn't know dinosaurs could evolve.'

'Either that or the species dies,' Rebus said, pressing his

237

hands to his knees. How could he explain it, explain what he was learning: that the past shapes the present, that free will is a fantasy, that a force we could call Fate or God controls the paths we take? Janice throwing a punch . . . young Darren Rough in a car on the way to Shiellion . . . Alan Archibald and his niece. All seemed connected in some strange and intricate way.

'You'll want a full report,' Rebus said, straightening in his chair.

The Farmer nodded. 'I was about to pull the surveillance anyway.' He put down his mug. 'Do you think Cary Oakes is dangerous?'

'Definitely. But I think he's changed.'

'Changed how?'

'His spree in the States, it wasn't planned. There was a lack of deliberation, and it always seemed to be part of some other strategy.'

'Explain.'

'He killed because he needed things: money, a car, whatever. But towards the end, I think he was really getting a taste for it. Then he got caught. He's been all these years in jail, remembering that buzz.'

'So now he might kill for no other reason than the buzz?'

'I'm not sure. I think he has some sort of plan, something that involves Edinburgh.' And Alan Archibald, he might have added. 'I think he's getting all sorts of tingly feelings just planning it.'

'Maybe he'll put it off indefinitely.'

Rebus smiled. 'I don't think so. This is foreplay to him.'

The Farmer seemed embarrassed by the image, relieved when his phone sounded. He picked up the receiver, listened.

'Good,' he said at last. 'I'll let him know.'

He put down the receiver, looked up at Rebus. 'The car's turned up.'

'Great.'

238

'Handily parked, too.'

Rebus asked what the Farmer meant. The answer gave him the shock of his life.

A couple of uniforms were already on the scene when Rebus, the Farmer and Bill Pryde arrived at The Shore. The Rover was sitting in its usual spot, opposite the hotel.

'I don't believe it,' Rebus said for the fifth or sixth time.

'This isn't some joke of yours?' Bill Pryde asked.

The Farmer looked inside. 'Where's the log?'

'It was under the seat, sir.'

The Farmer reached in, pulled out the log and a set of car keys.

'Did you say anything to Rough about the surveillance?' he asked. Rebus shook his head. 'So can we assume Rough did *not* take the car?' Rebus shrugged.

'Looks like it was someone who knew what we were up to,' Bill Pryde admitted.

'Or simply read about it in the log,' Rebus said. 'Anyone finding the keys would have found the log.'

'True,' Pryde conceded.

'Which might put Rough back in the frame,' the Farmer said. 'Thing is, it also means whoever stole the car read the surveillance notes.'

'Red faces all round, sir,' Pryde said.

'More than that if Fettes get to hear about it.'

'Who's going to tell them?'

The Farmer had flipped through the notes, coming to Rebus's final section – or what should have been the final section. He opened the book wide, held it out so Rebus and Pryde could see it.

'What's this?'

Rebus looked. Written in big capitals, red felt pen. Someone had added a postscript to Rebus's thoughts on the case:

NAUGHTY, NAUGHTY. WHERE'S MR ARCHIBALD????

The Farmer was staring at him.

'Who's Mr Archibald?'

Pryde was shrugging. 'Search me.'

But the Farmer had eyes only for John Rebus.

'Who's Mr Archibald?' he repeated, red rising to his cheeks. Rebus said nothing, crossed the street and looked in through the large windows of the restaurant. They were serving late breakfasts, tables half-hidden behind potted plants and hanging baskets. But there, at a window table and enjoying the show, sat Cary Oakes. He waved a fork at Rebus, sat beaming a grin as he lifted a glass of orange juice and toasted him. Rebus made for the hotel door, pushed it open, strode inside. Cooking smells were wafting from the restaurant. A waiter asked if he wanted a table for one. Rebus ignored him, walked straight up to the table where Cary Oakes was seated.

'Care to join me, Inspector?'

'Not even if you were coming apart at the seams.' Rebus pushed his knuckles into Oakes's face. 'Remember these?'

'Looks nasty,' Oakes said. 'I'd get a doctor to look at them. Lucky you already know one.'

'You know where I live,' Rebus hissed. 'Jim Stevens told you.'

'Did he?' Oakes started cutting up a sausage. Rebus noticed that he sliced it lengthwise first, as though dissecting it.

'You took the car.'

'Bit early for riddles.' Oakes lifted a morsel of meat to his lips. Rebus flung out a hand, sent fork and sausage flying. Then he hoisted Cary Oakes to his feet.

'What the fuck are you up to?'

'Shouldn't that be my line?' Oakes said, grinning. There was a sudden explosion of light. Rebus half-turned his head. Jim Stevens was behind him. Next to him stood a photographer.

'Now,' Stevens was saying, 'if we could have the two of

you shaking hands in the next one.' He winked at Rebus. 'Told you I wanted some pictures.'

Rebus dropped Oakes, flew towards the journalist.

'Inspector!'

The Farmer's voice. He was in the restaurant doorway, face like fury. 'A word with you outside, if you don't mind.' A voice not to be disobeyed. Rebus stared hard at Jim Stevens, letting him know this wasn't the end of anything. Then he walked out of the dining room and into reception. The Farmer was after him.

'I'm still waiting for an answer. Who is Mr Archibald?'

'A man with a mission,' Rebus told him. In his mind, he could still see the grin on Oakes's face. 'Problem is, he's not the only one.'

Rebus spent till lunchtime 'in conference' with the Farmer. Just before midday, Archibald himself joined them, the Farmer having dispatched a squad car to Corstorphine to pick him up. The two men knew one another of old.

'Thought you'd have had the gold watch by now,' Archibald said, shaking the Farmer's hand. But the Farmer was not to be mollified.

'Sit down, Alan. For a retired copper, you haven't half been busy.'

Archibald glanced at Rebus, who was staring at the window-blind.

'I'm going to nail him, that's all.'

'Oh, that's all, is it?' The Farmer looked mock-astonished. 'John tells me you've seen the files on Cary Oakes. In fact, you've got more gen on him than we have. So you should know who you're dealing with.'

'I know *what* I'm dealing with.'

The Farmer's gaze went from Archibald to Rebus and back again. 'It's bad enough I'm lumbered with this one,' he said, nodding towards Rebus. 'Last thing I need is yet another headcase out there trying to take the law into his own hands. You think Oakes killed your niece, show me the evidence.'

'Come on, man . . .'

'Show me the evidence!'

'I would if I could.'

'Would you, Alan?' The Farmer paused. 'Or would you want to keep it personal, right to the bitter end?' He turned to Rebus. 'What about you, John? Were you going to lend a hand burying the body?'

'If I'd wanted him dead,' Archibald said, 'he'd be in the ground by now.'

'But what if he confesses, Alan? Just you and him, no third party.' The Farmer shook his head. 'Wouldn't be enough to go to court with, so what would you do?'

'It'd be enough,' Archibald said quietly.

'For what?'

'For me. For Deirdre's memory.'

The Farmer waited, turned to Rebus. 'Do you buy that? You think Alan here would listen to Oakes's confession and then just walk away?'

'I don't know him well enough to comment.' Rebus still seemed mesmerised by the window-blind.

'Two peas in a pod,' the Farmer said. Rebus glanced at Archibald, who was looking at him. There was a knock at the door. The Farmer barked an order to enter. It was Siobhan Clarke.

'Come to intercede?' the Farmer asked.

'No, sir.' She seemed unwilling to come in; stood with only her head showing round the door.

'Well?'

'Suspicious death, sir. Up on Salisbury Crags.'

'How suspicious?'

'First reports say very.'

The Farmer pinched the bridge of his nose. 'This is one of those weeks that seem to last a fortnight.'

'Thing is, sir, from the description, I'd say we have an ID.'

He looked at her, hearing something in her tone. 'Someone we know?'

Clarke was looking towards Rebus. 'I'd say so, sir.'

'This isn't a parlour game, DC Clarke.'

She cleared her throat. 'I think it might be Darren Rough.'

26

'Start any time you're ready.'

Jim Stevens' room was beginning to look messy and lived-in, just the way he liked. But they weren't in Stevens' room, they were in Oakes's, and it looked like its occupant hadn't spent any time there at all. There were two chairs at a small circular table by the window. The complimentary book of matches still sat folded open in its ashtray. Two magazines of interest to visitors to Edinburgh sat beside it, and lying on top of them was the guests' comment card, yet to be filled in, or even perused.

Most people, Stevens guessed, even people who'd spent a third of their life enjoying the facilities of a foreign country's prison service, would do what he'd done in his own room: explore it, try out and touch everything, flick through every piece of literature.

But not Cary Oakes, who now cleared his throat.

'Aren't you curious about what Rebus wanted?'

Stevens looked at him. 'I just want this finished.'

'Lost the old vigour and vim, eh, Jim?'

'You have that effect on people.'

'Tracked down any of my old teenage gang?' Oakes laughed at the look on Stevens' face. 'Thought not. Probably scattered to the four winds by now.'

'Last time we broke off,' Stevens said coldly, checking the spools were turning, 'you were crossing America.'

Oakes nodded. 'I got to a place called, believe it or not, Opportunity, a ratty little truck-stop on the Washington-Idaho border. That's where I met the trucker, Fat Boy. I never learned his real name; I think even the ID he carried was fake.'

'What name was on the ID?'

Oakes ignored the question. 'Fat Boy had these notions about a government conspiracy, told me he kept his home booby-trapped whenever he was working long-distance. He said truckers got a real good view of the world – by which he meant the USA; that's as far as his world stretched – a real good view from behind the wheel of a truck. He knew a trucker would make a damned good President.

'So that was Fat Boy. My introduction to him. Opportunity, Washington. Lots of names like that in the States. Lots of Fat Boys, too. We got talking about murder. The radio was on, and every other station had news flashes about unlawful killing. He said the word "unlawful" was a misnomer. There was "wrong" killing and "right" killing, and which was which was down to the individual, not the lawmakers.'

'And what kind did you do?'

Oakes didn't like his flow being interrupted. 'I'm talking about Fat Boy, not me.'

'How long did you travel with him?' Stevens was trying to keep the chronology right.

'Three, four days. We headed south to make a delivery, then back up on to I-90.'

'What was he carrying?'

'Electrical goods. He worked for General Electric. Meant he travelled all over. He said that was good, considering his hobby. His hobby was killing people.' Oakes looked to Stevens. 'It was supposed to unnerve me, him saying something like that while we're travelling fifty-five on an interstate. Maybe if it had, that would have been it: he'd have tried skinning me. But I just looked at him, told him that was interesting.' A laugh. 'Mild understatement, right? Someone tells you they're a serial killer and you say "Mm, that's interesting."'

'But you believed him?'

'After a while, yes. And I thought: all this stuff he's telling me, no way is he letting me go. Every time we stopped, I thought he was about to whack me.'

'You were ready for him?' Stevens was staring at Oakes, trying to gauge how much of the story was true. Did it relate in some way to the relationship between Oakes and the reporter himself?

'You know the strange part? I just let myself relax into it. Like, if he was going to kill me, OK, that's what was going to happen. It was as if I didn't care; I could have died right then, and it would have been poetic justice or something.'

'Did he kill anyone while you were on the road?'

'No.'

'But he convinced you he wasn't lying?'

'You think he was lying, Jim?'

'When they arrested you, did you tell the police about him?'

'Why the hell would I do that?'

'Might have scored you some points.'

'Truth is, I never thought about it.'

'But he made you think about killing?'

'He knew what he was talking about. I mean, you can always tell when someone's making it up, can't you?' Oakes beamed a smile. '"Can the world really be like this?" I remember asking myself that as I listened to him. And the answer came back: yes, of course. Why should it be any different?'

'You're saying Fat Boy made you feel all right about killing?'

'Am I?'

'Then what are you saying?'

'Just telling you my story, Jim. It's up to you how you read it.'

'What about in jail, Cary? All that time to yourself, thoughts that you're thinking . . . ?'

'Jim, you get no time to yourself. There's always noise, disruption, routine. You sit there trying to think, they send you for psychiatric evaluation.' Oakes took a final sip of orange juice. 'But I see what you're getting at.' He examined his empty glass. 'How's the background check going, by the way? Spoken to anyone at Walla Walla?' Turned the empty glass in his hand. 'Take away the juice and the ice, you're left with a lethal weapon.' He pretended to smash the glass against the edge of the table, and then laughed a laugh which sent a shiver right along Jim Stevens' arms.

Climbing back up Salisbury Crags, Rebus kept his hands in his pockets and his thoughts to himself. He knew what the Farmer was thinking, This morning, Darren Rough had been in Rebus's flat. As far as they knew, Rebus was the last person to have seen him alive.

And Rebus had been his tormentor, his nemesis. The Farmer wouldn't make anything of it, but others might: Jane Barbour; Rough's social worker.

Radical Road was a stony footpath which led around the Crags. You could start near the student residences at Pollock Halls and end up at Holyrood. Along the way, you had the city skyline for company, stretching from the south and west to the city centre and beyond. All spires and crenellations. Manfred Mann: 'Cubist Town'. With Greenfield almost directly below.

'You picked him up here, didn't you?' the Farmer asked as they walked.

Rebus shook his head. 'St Margaret's Loch.' Which lay around a long curve in the rock and down an impossibly steep bank. 'Tell you what, though,' he added. 'Jim Margolies jumped from up there.' And he pointed with his finger, way up to where the rock-face ended in something akin to a clifftop. People took their dogs for walks across the plateau, not straying too close to the edge. Edinburgh was prone to sudden, malevolent gusts, any one of which could have you over the side.

The Farmer was breathing hard. 'You still see a connection between Rough and Jim Margolies?'

'Now more than ever, sir.'

The body lay a little further along the path, cordoned off by warning tape. A few walkers, wrapped up against the weather, had gathered at the cordon, stretching their necks for a view. A white plastic contraption like a windbreak had been placed around the body, so that only those who needed to see it would. A woman with a black springer spaniel was being interviewed: she'd been the one to find the body. Out walking the dog, a daily ritual which both had looked forward to. From now on, she'd find another route, a long way from Salisbury Crags.

'Hard to believe they're putting our Parliament there,' the Farmer commented, looking down towards Holyrood Road. 'A real old backwater. Traffic's going to be a nightmare.'

'And it's on our patch.'

'Not my problem, thank God.' The Farmer sniffed. 'I'll have that gold watch on one hand and a golfing glove on the other.'

They passed through the cordon. The scene-of-crime team was at work, securing the *locus* and ensuring what they liked to call its 'purity'. This meant Rebus and the Farmer had to don coveralls and overshoes, so they'd leave no trace elements at the scene.

'The wind up here will probably have scattered them to the four corners anyway,' Rebus said. But it was a half-hearted grouch: he knew the worth of scene-of-crime work, knew that science and forensics were his friends. A police doctor had declared the victim deceased. Dr Curt was the usual pathologist, but he was in Miami to give a paper at some convention. His superior, Professor Gates, had stepped in, and was examining the body *in situ*. He was a large man with thick brown hair slicked back from his forehead. He carried a hand-held tape recorder, talking into it as he moved around. He was forced to jostle for space: a photographer and video cameraman both wanted shots of the corpse.

DS George Silvers came over. He nodded a greeting to his Chief Superintendent, but took it further, so that it turned into something more akin to a ceremonial bow. That was typical of Silvers, whose station nickname was 'Hi-Ho'. He was in his late thirties, always smartly dressed and coiffed, always on the eye for promotion without the necessary concomitant of hard work. His black hair and deep-set eyes gave him the look of football pundit Alan Hansen.

'We think we've got the murder weapon, sir. A rock with some blood and hair on it.' He pointed up the path. 'Forty yards or so that way.'

'Who found it?'

'A dog, sir.' One eye twitching. 'Licked most of the blood off before we could get to it.'

Professor Gates looked up from his work. 'So if the lab gets a match,' he said, 'and tells you the victim had a lovely shiny coat, you'll know what the problem is.'

He laughed, and Rebus laughed with him. It was like that at the *locus*, everyone pretending nothing was out of the ordinary, erecting barriers to separate them from the glaring fact that *everything* was out of the ordinary.

'I'm told you might manage an informal ID,' Gates said. Rebus nodded, took a deep breath and stepped forward. The body was lying where it had fallen, the back of the skull smashed open and caked with blood. The face rested against the jagged path, one leg bent at the knee, the other straight. One arm was trapped beneath the body, the other stretching so the fingers could claw at the cold earth. Rebus could tell from the clothes, but crouched down to study what could be seen of the face. Gates lifted it a little to help. Light had died behind the eyes; the three-day growth of beard would need to be shaved by the undertaker. Rebus nodded.

'Darren Rough,' he said, his voice growing thick.

Having taken a break from recording, Jim Stevens sat naked on the edge of his bed, discarded clothes strewn around him, two empty miniatures of whisky on his bedside cabinet. The empty glass was clutched in one hand, and he stared at it and through it, focusing on things the world couldn't see ...

Part Two
Found

I invite you to examine more closely your duty and the obligations of your earthly service because that is something which all of us are only dimly aware of, and we scarcely . . .

27

One of Rough's shoes had come off at some point, about halfway between the spot where his body had fallen and where the rock had been found. One early theory: someone had thumped him hard. He'd stumbled, staggered on, trying to get away from his attacker. His shoe had come off and been discarded. Finally, he'd fallen to the ground, where he'd died from the earlier blows. A barking dog approaching had alerted the attacker to the need to flee.

Another theory: after being hit, Rough had died instantly. His attacker had then dragged him along the path, the shoe coming free. Maybe intending to set things up so it looked like Rough had jumped or fallen from the Crags. But the dog-walker had come along, scaring off the killer.

'What was he doing up there anyway?' someone back at the station asked.

'I think he liked it there,' Rebus said. He was now officially the St Leonard's expert on Darren Rough. 'It was like a sanctuary, somewhere he felt safe. And he could look down on Greenfield from there, see what was happening.'

'So someone followed him? Sneaked up on him?'

'Or persuaded him to go there.'

'Why?'

'To make it look like suicide. Maybe they read about Jim Margolies in the paper.'

'It's a thought . . .'

There were plenty of thoughts, plenty of theories. One

thought was: good riddance to the bastard. A week ago, it would have been Rebus's view, too.

The murder room was being prepared, computers moved from other parts of the building into the room set aside for such work. The Farmer had put Chief Inspector Gill Templer in charge. Rebus had been her lover for a time, so long ago now it might have been in some past life. Her hair was a dark-streaked feather-cut. Her eyes were emerald green. She moved confidently across the room, checking preparations.

'Good luck,' Rebus told her.

'I want you on the team,' she said.

Rebus thought he could understand. She was circling the wagons, and it was better to have him in the ring shooting out, than outside shooting in.

'And I want a report on my desk: everything you can tell me about you and the deceased.'

Rebus nodded, got to work on one of the computers. *Everything you can tell me*: Rebus liked her wording, it gave him an escape clause – not everything he *knew* necessarily, but all he felt able to divulge. He looked across to where Siobhan Clarke was compiling a wall-mounted duty roster. She saw him and made a T sign with her hands. He nodded, and five minutes later she was back with two scalding beakers.

'Here you go.'

'Thanks,' he said. She was looking over his shoulder at the screen.

'Nothing but the truth?' she asked.

'What do you think?'

She blew on her cup. 'Any idea who'd want him dead?'

'I can't think of many who didn't. We've got half the population of Greenfield to start with.' Especially Cal Brady, with his previous convictions; and not forgetting his mother . . .

'Chasing him out and killing him aren't quite in the same league.'

'No, but something like that can escalate. Maybe Billy Horman was all it took.'

She rested against the corner of the desk. 'Hit with a rock . . . doesn't sound premeditated, does it?'

Hit with a rock . . . Deirdre, Alan Archibald's niece, had been killed in a similar way: smashed over the head with a rock and then strangled. Clarke could read his mind.

'Cary Oakes?'

'Have we got a time of death yet?' Rebus asked, reaching for a telephone.

'Not that I know of. Body was found at eleven thirty.'

'And we're guessing the killer heard someone coming and ran for it.' Rebus had pressed the digits and was waiting. Connected. 'Hello, could you put me through to James Stevens, please?'

Clarke looked at him. He put his hand over the mouthpiece. 'I want to know what happened after breakfast.' He listened again, took his hand away. 'Could you try Cary Oakes's room for me?' Shook his head to let Clarke know Stevens wasn't in his own room. This time the call was answered.

'Oakes, is that you? It's Rebus here, put Stevens on.' He waited a moment. 'One question: what happened after breakfast?' Listened again. 'Was he out of your sight? You've been there all morning?' Listened. 'No, it's all right. You'll find out soon enough.'

Replaced the receiver.

'They've been working all morning.'

'No chance it was Oakes then.' She looked at the computer screen. 'What would be his motive anyway?'

'Christ knows. But he was at my flat. He took the patrol car. Maybe he saw Rough leave, worked out he was connected to me.'

'Can you prove that?'

'No.'

'Then all he has to do is deny it.'

Rebus exhaled noisily. 'It's all games with him.'

Gill Templer was staring at them from across the room.

'I'd better get back to work,' Clarke said, taking her tea with her. Rebus finished his report, printed it out, handed it personally to Gill Templer.

'When's the post-mortem?'

She checked her watch. 'I was just about to head over there.'

'Need a driver?'

She studied him. 'Has your driving improved?'

'I'll let you be the judge, ma'am.'

The city mortuary wasn't in business. Health and Safety; changes needed to be made. Meantime, they were using the Western General Hospital. Because they couldn't find any relatives or friends, Andy Davies had been called to verify Rebus's identification. The social worker was waiting when Rebus and Gill Templer arrived. He made the ID, said nothing to Rebus but shot him a cold look before leaving.

'Bad blood?' Templer asked.

'Better than none at all, Gill.'

Professor Gates was already at work by the time they'd got their gowns and masks on. For the official ID, Rough's corpse had worn a shroud. Now, lying on the stainless-steel bench, it wore nothing at all. Prominent ribs, Rebus noted. He was thinking of the meal he'd made for Rough. Grudgingly made. Beans on toast. Probably the man's last meal ever. And eventually, Gates would reveal it to the world again. Rebus half-turned his face.

'Seasick, Inspector?' Gates asked.

'I'll be fine so long as we keep out of the bilges.'

Gates chuckled. 'But below decks is the most interesting part.' He was measuring, muttering his findings to his assistant, a young man with a face the colour of a cancer bed.

'And how are you, Gill?' he asked at last.

'Overworked.'

Gates glanced up. 'Fine lassie like you should be at home, bringing up strong healthy bairns.'

'Thanks for the vote of confidence.'

Gates chuckled again. 'Don't tell me you lack suitors?'

She chose to ignore the remark.

'What about you, John?' Gates persisted. 'Love life satisfactory? Maybe I should play Cupid, put the two of you together. What do you say to that now, eh?'

Rebus and Templer shared a look.

'Professions like ours,' Gates drawled on, 'aren't the same as being a lawyer or a novelist, are they? Not much of an ice-breaker at parties.' He nodded towards his assistant. 'Bear that in mind, Jerry. No nookie unless you lie about what you do.' Gates's final chuckle turned into a choking bark, a bronchial cough which almost doubled him over. He wiped his eyes afterwards.

'Time to stop smoking,' Templer warned him.

'I can't do that. It would spoil the bet.'

'What bet?'

'Dr Curt and myself: who'll live the longer on twenty a day.'

'That's . . .' Templer had been about to say 'sick', but then she saw that the body had been opened up almost without her noticing, and she realised why Gates kept the conversation going: it was to take everyone's mind off the task at hand. And for a few moments, it had worked.

'I'll tell you one thing straight off,' the pathologist said. 'His clothes were damp, and to me that means rain. I've checked: we had a short shower early this morning and nothing since.'

'Could he have got wet lying on the path?'

'He was lying on his front. The back of his clothing was damp. So he was out in that shower, whether alive or dead I can't say. But his hair was wet, too. Now, if you're caught in a sudden downpour, wouldn't you usually pull your jacket up over your head?'

'Depends on your state of mind,' Rebus said.

Gates shrugged. 'I'm only surmising. But one thing I'm sure of.' He ran a finger along the body, tracing patches of pale bluish markings. '*Livor mortis*. It was present at the scene. I arrived forty-five minutes after the body was discovered.'

'But lividity starts . . . ?'

'Well, it starts from the moment the heart stops pumping, but it becomes visible somewhere between half an hour and an hour after death. This was well-established by the time I arrived.'

'What about rigor mortis?'

'Eyelids had stiffened, as had the jaw. I'll take a potassium sample from the eye, to get a better idea of timing, but right now I'd guess the body had been lying there for three hours, maybe more.'

Rebus took a step forward. If Gates was right – and he invariably was – the dog-walker had not disturbed the killer. The killer had been long gone by the time the spaniel and its owner had arrived, and Darren Rough had died around seven or eight in the morning. At five he'd been asleep on Rebus's couch; by six he'd gone . . .

'Did he die where we found him?' Rebus asked, wanting to be sure.

'Judging by the patterns of lividity, I'd say it's a racing certainty.' The pathologist paused. 'Of course, I've lost a few pounds on horses in my time.'

'We need a more specific time of death.'

'I know you do, Inspector. You *always* do. I'll do what tests the budget will stretch to.'

'And ASAP.'

Gates nodded. He was about ready to begin removing the inner organs. Jerry was fussing with the necessary tools.

Rebus was thinking: three, maybe four hours.

Thinking: Cary Oakes was back in the running.

28

They took him in for questioning, Rebus keeping out of
the way, listening to the tapes afterwards. Stevens' paper
had provided their client with a solicitor from one of the
city's top firms, despite Templer's insistence that all they
had were a few questions, easily cleared up. But Oakes
was saying nothing. Templer was good, and she had
Pryde with her: their routine was well-honed, but Rebus
got the feeling Oakes had seen all the moves before. He'd
been examined and cross-examined and called to the
stand again, he'd been through all that in an American
courtroom. He just sat there and said he knew nothing
about the patrol car, nothing about where Rebus lived,
and nothing about any dead paedophile. His final comment:

'What's all the fuss about a kiddie-fucker?'

Pryde, listening to the tape, folded his arms at that and
puckered his lips, most of him agreeing with the senti-
ment. When Pryde asked if Rebus was heading outside for
a smoke, Rebus, inwardly gasping for one, shook his head.
Later, he went out into the car park alone, pacing as he
sucked hungrily on first one Silk Cut and then a second.
Ten a day, he was keeping to ten a day. And if he went as
high as twelve today, that meant only eight tomorrow.
Eight was fine, he could handle that. It gave him a margin
for today, a margin he reckoned he'd need.

Only thing was, he was already in arrears for the week;
for the whole month, truth be told.

Tom Jackson came out, lit one of his own. They didn't

speak for the first couple of minutes. Jackson scuffed his shoes on the tarmac and broke the silence.

'I hear you took him in.'

Rebus blew smoke from his nose. 'That's right.'

'Rescue act, let him stay the night.'

'So?'

'So not everyone would have been so charitable.'

'I'm not sure it was charity.'

'What then?'

What then? It was a good question.

'Thing is,' Jackson went on, 'a few days back, you were all for stringing him up.'

'Don't exaggerate.'

'You set that pack of wild dogs on him.'

'You mean the papers or his neighbours?'

'Both.'

'Careful, Tom. You're their community officer. That's your flock you're talking about.'

'I'm talking about *you*: what happened?'

'He only slept on my couch, Tom. It's not like I gave him a gam or anything.' Rebus flicked his third cigarette on to the ground, stubbed it out. Only half-smoked, so he'd count two and a half; round it down to two.

'We still haven't turned up the kid.'

'How's his mother doing?'

Jackson knew the question's subtext, answered accordingly. 'Nobody seems to think she's a suspect.'

'What's her history?'

'Billy's her only kid. Had him at nineteen.'

'Is the father around?'

'Did the usual vanishing act before the baby was born. Ran off to Ulster to join the paramilitaries.'

'He'll be running for office now then.'

Jackson snorted. 'She's had half a dozen blokes since; been living with the latest for the past few weeks.'

'The three of them in the flat together?'

Jackson nodded. 'He's being interviewed. We're digging into his history.'

'A fiver says he's got form.'

'What? Living in Greenfield?' Jackson smiled. 'Keep your money in your pocket.' He paused. 'You really don't think this connects to our deceased friend?'

'It might do, Tom. But just maybe not in the way we think.'

'What do you mean?'

'Be seeing you,' Rebus said, moving away.

Thinking of an old Gravy Train song: 'Won't Talk About It'.

He told Patience he wouldn't be seeing her. There must have been something in his tone of voice.

'Out on the ran-dan?' she said.

'You know me too well.' He put the receiver down before she could say anything else. He started at The Maltings, headed up Causewayside to Swany's, then took a taxi to the Ox. His car was back at St Leonard's: no problem, he could walk into work next morning. Salty Dougary, one of the Young Street regulars, had just been in hospital: a coronary; they'd operated, angioplasty or something like that. He was telling the bar all about it. For some reason Rebus couldn't fathom, the operation had apparently started at Dougary's groin.

'Way to a man's heart,' Rebus commented, sinking another whisky. He was diluting them with water, but not overly so. He felt fine, as in not drunk; mellow, kind of. But he knew if he walked out of the bar, he'd start to feel the alcohol. A good excuse to stay put, like that character in *Apocalypse Now*: 'Never get out of the boat.' It was only when you left the boat that you got into trouble. The same thing, in Rebus's experience, was true of pubs, which was why he was still in the Ox at half past midnight. The back room had been taken over by musicians, a dozen or more

261

of them; guitars mostly, twelve-bar blues. One guy with a beard was playing the harmonica like he was in front of a Madison Garden crowd. Janis Joplin: 'Buried Alive in the Blues'.

Rebus was talking with George Klasser, a doctor at the Infirmary. Klasser usually left early – sevenish or a little after. When he stayed late, it was a sign things were fraught at home. He'd started the evening advising Salty Dougary to regulate his alcohol intake.

'The pot calling the kettle black,' had been Dougary's riposte. Dougary looking like he'd just been on holiday rather than in surgery: face tanned, ciggies cut down from forty a day to ten. Klasser with dark shadows under his eyes, a slight trembling to the hand when he picked up his glass. Rebus had had an uncle who'd smoked a pack of cigarettes every day of his life and lived to be eighty. His own father had died younger, having given up cigarettes two decades previously.

You never could tell.

There were only four of them in the front bar, five including Harry. Dougary, who'd drunk in every pub in the city, reckoned Harry was Edinburgh's rudest barman, which was quite a feat, considering the competition.

'I wish youse lot would bugger off home,' Harry said, not for the first time that evening.

'Night's young yet, Harry,' Dougary said.

'How come they let you out of intensive care?'

Dougary winked. 'Intensive care's what I come in here for.' He toasted them with his glass and raised it to his lips. Twenty minutes before, Rebus had told Klasser about Darren Rough. Now Klasser turned to him, eyes heavy-lidded.

'There was a famous murder case. Turn of the century, I think it was. German couple came here on their honeymoon, only it turned out he wanted her money rather than love. He planned to kill her, make it look like suicide. So they went for a walk up on Arthur's Seat, and he pushed her off the Crags.'

'But he didn't get away with it?'

'Obviously not, or there'd be no story to tell.'

'So how was he caught?'

Klasser stared into his glass. 'I can't recall.'

Dougary laughed. 'Don't let him start telling any jokes, he always forgets the punchline.'

'I'll punch *you* in a minute, Salty.'

'Get in the queue,' Harry commented.

Some nights it was like that in the Oxford Bar. When the guitar-players packed up, Rebus put his coat on. There was a stiff breeze outside, and it had been raining again, the streets black and shiny as a beetle's back. He'd meant to phone Janice, but what would he have said? There was no news of Damon. He walked along Princes Street, deciding he liked the city best like this: all the visitors tucked up in bed. Outside the Balmoral Hotel, a line of Jags and Rovers sat, their chauffeurs waiting for some function to finish. A young couple walked past, sharing a bottle of cheap cider. The male wore a jacket with a badge on it. The badge said Stockholm Film Festival. Rebus had never heard of it. Maybe it was the name of a band: you couldn't be sure these days.

He walked up the Bridges, stopped at some railings so he could look down on to the Cowgate. There were clubs still open down there, teenagers spilling on to the road. The police had names for the Cowgate when it got like this: Little Saigon; the blood bank; hell on earth. Even the patrol cars went in twos. Whoops and yells: a couple of girls in short dresses. One lad was down on his knees in the road, begging to be noticed.

Pretty Things: 'Cries from the Midnight Circus'.

In Edinburgh, sometimes it could be midnight in the middle of the day . . .

He didn't know where he was going, what he was doing. If he was going home, he was doing so only by degrees. When a taxi came, he flagged it down. On sudden impulse, he named his destination.

'The Shore.'

29

The idea was . . .

The idea was to stand in the freezing cold outside the hotel, call up to Oakes's room on the mobile. Get him downstairs . . . no crack to the back of the head this time. Face to face. But it was the drink, that was all. Rebus knew he wouldn't do it; knew Oakes wouldn't fall for it anyway. Looking across from The Shore, he saw there were lights from the Clipper, and a minder on the door. So Rebus crossed the bridge, introduced himself. The minder was wiping sweat from his face. From within, Rebus could hear raised voices, laughter.

'Party?' he asked.

'Don't tell me there've been complaints,' the minder growled. His accent was Liverpudlian. From his size, Rebus would bet his family had worked dockside. 'That's all I need right now.'

'What's up?'

'Buggers don't want to leave, do they?'

'Have you tried asking nicely?'

The man snorted.

'Nobody here to help you?'

'When we turned the music off, looked like they weren't going to stick around. DJ packed up and sodded off home. So did Mr Frost – my boss. Told me all I had to do was switch off the lights and lock up after me.'

'You're new to this game.'

The bouncer smiled. 'Does it show?'

'I take it you've got a mobile about your person. Why not call Mr Frost?'

'Don't have his home number.'

Rebus rubbed his chin. 'Is that as in Archie Frost?'

'That's him.'

Rebus was thoughtful for a moment. 'Want me to talk to them?' He nodded towards the boat. 'See if I can get them to pack up?'

The minder stared at him. He was well-educated in the relationship that should exist between his profession and Rebus's: a favour done now might mean a favour asked later. He turned towards a noise. One of the revellers had come up on deck and was preparing to urinate off the side. He sighed.

'Why not?' he said.

And Rebus was in.

One guy had pegged out on the deck, champagne bottle held to his chest. His bow tie was hanging from his neck; his watch was a gold Rolex. The guest using the Albert Basin as his own private loo rocked to and fro on his heels. He was humming the chorus of some pop song. Seeing Rebus, he beamed a smile. Rebus ignored him, headed down the steps into the main body of the boat. It was set up for a party: chairs and tables around a long narrow dancefloor. Bar at one end, makeshift stage at the other. There was a lighting rig, a mirror-ball over the dancefloor. Shutters had been brought down across the bar and fixed with a padlock, which another drunk was trying to pick with a plastic toothpick. A couple of the tables had been knocked over, along with a dozen or so chairs. There were forgotten items of clothing strewn across the floor, along with crisps, peanuts, empty bottles, and bits of sandwich and squashed quiche. The main action was centred on two tables which had been pushed together. Fourteen or fifteen people sat here. Women sat on men's laps, kissing deeply. A few couples were indulging in muted conversations. One or two individuals were fast asleep. A hard core of five – three men, two women – were telling slurred stories, detailing the party highlights, mostly involving drink, vomit and snogging.

'Hello again,' Rebus said to Ama Petrie. 'This your do, is it?'

She had her head on the shoulder of the young man next to her. Her mascara was smeared, making her look tired. Her short dress was a meshing of black gauzy layers. Her bare feet were in the lap of the man on the other side of her. He was playing with her toes.

'Oh, Christ,' this man said, eyes drooping, 'they've sent in the heavy brigade. Look, my good man, we've paid for this evening – cash, and upfront. So kindly bugger off and—'

'Oscar, you arse, he's a policeman,' Ama Petrie said. Then, to Rebus: 'Nice to see you again.' It was an automatic greeting, something she couldn't help but say, even though her eyes told a different story. Her eyes told Rebus she wasn't in the least pleased to see him.

'Well,' Oscar said, smiling to the assembly, 'in that case, it's a fair cop, guv, but society's to blame. I never had a chance.' He slipped into the role effortlessly, drawing smiles and laughter from his audience. Rebus looked at the faces around him: the faces of Edinburgh's rich young things. They'd have their own flats in the New Town, gifts from indulgent parents. They had their parties and their nights out. Maybe by day they shopped or lunched or attended a couple of lectures at the university. Maybe they drove their sports cars out to the country. Their lives were predestined: a job in the family business, or something 'arranged' – a position they could cope with, something requiring inbred charm and minimal effort. Everything would fall into their laps, because that's the way the world was.

'Shame he's not in uniform, eh, Nicky?'

'What have we done, Officer?' another of the men asked.

'Well, you've overstayed your welcome,' Rebus said.

267

'But that doesn't really concern me. Might I ask whose party this is?' He was looking at Ama.

'Mine, actually,' the man with the toothpick said, turning away from the bar. He pushed his thick fair hair back from his forehead. A thin face, soft-featured. 'I'm Nicol Petrie, Ama's brother.' Rebus guessed this was 'Nicky': *Shame he's not in uniform, eh, Nicky?*

He was in his early twenties, fashionably unshaven so his face shone a spiky gold. 'Look,' he said, 'I'll move this lot off the boat, promise.' And to his friends: 'We'll go back to my place. Plenty of drink there.'

'I want to go to a casino,' one woman complained. 'You *said* we'd go.'

'Darling, he only said that so you'd give him a blow job.'

Hoots of laughter, pointed fingers. Ama had her eyes closed but was chuckling, her feet grinding against her companion's groin.

Everyone seemed to have forgotten Rebus. The conversations were starting up again. He reached into his pocket, handed two photographs to Nicol Petrie.

'His name's Damon Mee. He left a nightclub with the blonde woman. We think they were on their way to a party on this boat, hosted by your sister.'

'Yes,' Nicol Petrie said, 'Ama told me.' He studied the photos, shook his head. 'Sorry.' Handed them back.

'You were at the party in question?' Petrie nodded. 'All of you?'

They looked to Ama, who told them which party it had been. A couple hadn't been present – previous commitments. Rebus handed the photos out anyway. Nobody paid much attention to them; they kept talking to each other as they passed them round.

'I could just go some smoked salmon.'

'Alison's bash next Friday: are you going?'

'Hair extensions, they change your whole face instantly . . .'

'Thought about putting a consortium together, buy a racehorse . . .'

Ama Petrie didn't even glance at the pictures, just passed them along.

'Sorry,' the last of the group said, handing them back to Rebus before continuing a conversation. Nicol Petrie looked apologetic.

'I promise we'll leave soon, assemble some taxis.'

'Right, sir.'

'And I'm sorry we couldn't be more help.'

'Not to worry.'

'I ran away from home once . . .'

'Nick, you were only *twelve*,' Ama Petrie drawled.

'All the same, I know how much it hurt our mother and father.'

Ama disagreed. 'They hardly noticed you were gone.' She looked up at him. 'It was me who called the police.'

'What happened?' Rebus asked.

'I'd been staying at a friend's house,' Nicol Petrie explained. 'When his parents heard I was supposed to be missing, they drove me home.' He shrugged. A couple of his friends laughed.

'Right,' he said, raising his voice slightly. 'Back to my place. The night is still young, and so are we!'

There were cheers at this. Rebus got the feeling Nicol had roused the troops like this before.

'Where's Alfie?' Ama asked.

'Taking a leak,' she was told.

Rebus made for the stairs. 'Thanks anyway,' he said to her brother. Nicol Petrie shot out a hand, which Rebus shook.

Shame he's not in uniform . . . What the hell had that meant? Some private joke? Rebus climbed back up into fresh air. The man who'd been relieving himself – Alfie – was sitting on the floor of the boat, legs splayed. He'd forgotten to button his flies.

'Leaving so soon?' he asked.

'Everyone's going back to Nicky's,' Rebus said, like he was one of the gang.

'Good old Nicky,' Alfie said.

'You're Alfie, aren't you?'

The young man looked up, trying to place Rebus. 'Sorry,' he said, 'can't seem to . . .'

'John,' Rebus said.

'Of course, John.' Nodding briskly. 'Never forget a face. You're in the finance sector?'

'Securities.'

'Never forget a face.' Alfie started to get up. Rebus helped him. He still had his photos in one hand.

'Here,' he said. 'Take a look.' Didn't say any more than that, just handed them over.

'Photographer must have been pissed,' Alfie said.

'Not very good, are they?'

'Bloody awful. I've got a friend who's a photographer. Let me give you his number.' Reaching into his jacket.

'You'll know his face, though,' Rebus said, tapping the holiday snap of Damon.

Alfie squinted at the photo, brought it close to his nose, moved it to pick up the available light.

'I pride myself,' he said, 'on never forgetting a face. But in this chap's case, I'll make an exception.' Smiled crookedly at his own little joke. 'Now the lady, on the other hand . . .'

'Alfie!' Ama Petrie was standing at the top of the stairs, arms folded against the chill. 'Come on, we're getting ready to go.'

'Super idea, Ama.' Alfie blinked so slowly, Rebus thought he'd nodded off.

'About the blonde . . .' Rebus persisted.

Ama had come up to them, was tugging on Alfie's sleeve. Alfie patted Rebus's arm. 'See you at Nicky's, old boy.'

'Come on, Alfie.' Ama pecked his cheek, led him to the stairs. A quick backward glance towards Rebus. Looking

270

. . . angry? Relieved? A mix of the two? When they disappeared from view, Rebus walked off the boat.

'They're on their way,' he told the minder.

'Cheers.'

'That's one you owe me,' Rebus said, waiting till the minder had nodded. 'To square things, I want you to tell me what Archie Frost has to do with Billy Preston.'

'He just works for him, same as I do.'

'But he runs Gaitano's for Charmer Mackenzie.'

The minder was nodding. 'That's right.'

'No conflict of interests?'

'Should there be?'

Rebus narrowed his eyes. 'Mackenzie owns this boat?'

The minder licked his lips. 'Part-owns. Mr Preston has the other half.'

Charmer Mackenzie had a half-share in the Clipper. And he owned Gaitano's. Damon had been at Gaitano's, and was last seen near the Clipper. Rebus was beginning to wonder . . .

'That's us quits,' the minder said, as the party-goers did a conga towards the gangway.

He went back to his flat but couldn't sleep. The blanket Darren Rough had slept under was still folded on the sofa. He couldn't bring himself to move it. Instead, he sat in his chair, waiting for the ghosts to come. Maybe Darren would be with them, or maybe he'd have other souls to haunt.

But no ghosts came. Rebus dozed, came awake with a start. Decided he'd be better off out of doors. He cut through The Meadows, past the Infirmary. It was due to move out of town, south to Little France. There was talk the old Infirmary site would be turned into upmarket flats, or maybe a hotel. Prime city-centre site, but who'd want a flat where a hospital ward had been?

He paused at the statue of Greyfriars Bobby. When you thought of it, Bobby was just a dog with nowhere better to go, nothing better to be doing. Rebus reached out and patted the statue's head.

'Stay,' he said, heading down George IV Bridge. A couple of taxis slowed beside him, touting for custom, but he waved them on, took the Playfair Steps down to the National Gallery and Royal Academy. He passed a couple of people sleeping rough, watched the Castle beginning to assume shape again against the sky as night segued into morning. He thought of his grandfathers, whose names were buried somewhere in the Castle's Books of Remembrance. He couldn't even recall what regiments they'd served in. Both had died in the 1914–18 campaign, long before Rebus's parents had even met.

Princes Street had the usual haphazard look to it. The pavements seemed plenty wide when there was no one else about. He nipped up the side of Burger King and into the Penny Black, which opened for business at five. There were a couple of drinkers already in. Rebus ordered a whisky, added plenty of water.

'Man, you're drowning it,' one drinker commented.

Rebus just smiled; didn't tell the man that water was his lifeline. An early edition of the *Scotsman* sat on the bar. Rebus flicked through it. A report of the previous day's doings in the Shiellion trial, plus the 'suspicious death' of Darren Rough and the disappearance of Billy Horman. There was an anonymous quote from a member of GAP, to the effect that they blamed Rough for the boy's disappearance.

'And we're just glad and relieved that one piece of vermin has departed this earth. May all the others do the same.'

Van Brady in preaching mode. There was talk of a residents' committee, of new arrivals in Greenfield being vetted by their neighbours. There was going to be discussion of neighbourhood patrols, spot checks, and even some kind of barrier to stop 'undesirables' from entering Greenfield and 'defacing' it.

Rebus knew Scotland was gearing up for self-rule, but this was taking it to extremes.

'We've got a computer in the community centre,' the spokesperson said, 'and now we want to get hooked up to the Internet so we can ask the Guardian Angels for advice. We're hoping a lottery grant will get us the software. This community deserves no less.'

If there was going to be a private police force in Greenfield, Rebus wondered who'd be best placed to operate it. The name Cal Brady came readily to mind . . .

He finished his drink and decided to have breakfast down in Leith, where there was a café open at six with huge portions and little fuss. He walked the length of Leith Walk, found the café and settled down. With the paper already read, he'd nothing to do but chew on a half-slice of fried bread and stare out of the window. When a taxi stopped at the lights outside the café, Rebus caught a glimpse of the passenger. He tried for a better look, but the taxi was already on the move, taking Cary Oakes back to his hotel. He got the licence number, jotted it on the back of his hand. A mouthful of scalding tea helped him wash down the bread, then he asked to use the owner's phone. Called a cab company and asked about the reg.

'You kidding? Know how many cabs we've got?'

'Do your best, eh?' He gave them his mobile number, then tried the other companies in the city. They all seemed to think he was asking a lot, but by the time he got to St Leonard's, he had a result. The cabbie was actually back at base, his shift over. Rebus spoke to him.

'You took a fare down to Leith, I'm guessing The Shore. About an hour ago.'

'Yeah, last pick-up I had.'

'Where exactly did you pick him up?'

'Out Corstorphine way, just before the Maybury round-about. What's he done?'

Corstorphine: where Alan Archibald lived. Rebus thanked the driver and terminated the call. He went to the toilets for a wash and shave, swallowed two paracetamol with some coffee. The murder room was empty, no one yet at work. He examined the photos on the wall. Archibald's niece had been murdered on a hillside; Darren Rough had been murdered on a hillside. Was it a connection? He thought of Cary Oakes, roaming freely through the city. Picked up one of the phones and called Patience.

'Morning,' she said sleepily.

'This is your alarm call.'

He could hear her stretch her back, sitting up in bed. 'What time is it?'

He told her. 'I couldn't get back for breakfast, thought I'd phone instead.'

'Where are you?'

'St Leonard's.'

'Did you sleep at Arden Street?'

'I managed a nap.'

'I don't know how you do it.' She was probably pushing hair out of her eyes. 'I need eight hours minimum.'

'They say it's the sign of a clear conscience.'

'What does that say about you?' She knew he wasn't going to answer that, asked instead if she'd see him for dinner.

'Sure,' he told her. 'Unless you don't, of course.'

'Of course,' she said. Then: 'How's the head?'

'Fine.'

'You liar. Try one day off the booze, John, just for me. One day, and tell me you don't feel better in the morning.'

'I know I'll feel better in the morning. Problem is, as soon as I have a drink, I forget.'

'Bye, John.'

'Bye, Patience.'

Patience: more than living up to her name . . .

30

Rebus and Gill Templer, in Interview Room B with Cal Brady.

Interview Room B: same room Rebus had taken Darren Rough. Same room he'd first met Harold Ince during the Shiellion inquiry. They were talking to Cal Brady again because Templer had a few things to clear up.

'You started that fire,' she said.

'Did I?' Brady looked around, wide-eyed. 'Maybe we better get a solicitor in here then.'

'Don't try to be funny, Mr Brady.'

'Only jokers I see around here are you lot.'

'Billy Horman is reported missing, next thing you're out torching Darren Rough's flat. If I was of a mind, I might think *you* had something to gain from that.' She paused, shifting the paperwork in front of her. 'Or something to hide.'

'Such as?' Brady sat back in his chair, arms folded.

'That's what I'm wondering.'

Brady snorted, looked to where Rebus was standing. 'Lost your voice or what?'

Rebus didn't rise to it. Gill Templer was quite capable of dealing with the likes of Cal Brady.

'Everyone else went out looking for Billy,' she continued, 'but you held back. Why's that, Mr Brady?'

Brady shifted in his seat. 'Kept an eye on Billy Boy's mum.'

Templer made a show of checking her notes. 'Joanna Horman?' She waited for Brady to nod agreement. 'That's women's work, isn't it, Calumn? Holding the mother's

275

hand, offering sympathy and a rum and Coke. Thought you were more of an Action Man.'

'Someone had to do it.'

'But why *you*, that's what I'm getting at? Maybe you fancied her. Maybe the two of you know one another . . . ?' She paused. 'Or could it be that you already knew there was no point looking for Billy Horman . . . ?'

Brady thumped the desk. 'Don't you start on this!' Quick to ignite. 'Everybody knows what happened to Billy Boy. He got snatched by Rough or one of his cronies.'

'Then where is he?'

'How the hell should I know?'

'And who killed Darren Rough?'

'If it had been me, he'd've been missing some bits.'

'What if I tell you he was?' Templer playing a little game.

Brady looked surprised. 'Was he? Nobody said . . .'

Templer looked at her notes. Then: 'DI Rebus, I believe you have a few more questions for Mr Brady.'

Rebus having cleared things with her first, explaining his interest. He moved towards the desk, rested his knuckles on it.

'How do you come to know Archie Frost?'

'Archie?' Brady looked at Templer. 'What's this got to do with anything?'

'Another inquiry, Mr Brady. Unconnected to the other two, except, perhaps, by you.'

'I don't get it.'

'You want that solicitor now?'

He thought about it, shrugged his shoulders. 'I do some work for him.'

'For Mr Frost?'

'That's right. I work on the door some nights.'

'You're a bouncer?'

'I keep an eye out for trouble.'

Rebus produced the photographs again. They had

276

curled and creased at the edges, and were smeared with fingerprints.

'Do you remember me asking about these people?'

Brady looked at the photos, nodded. 'I wasn't on the door that night.'

'And which night is that?' Brady looked up from the photos. Rebus was smiling. 'I don't recall giving Mr Frost any particular night.'

'If I'd been working that night I'd have spotted him. I had a run-in with him once before. No way he would have got past the door with me there.'

Rebus narrowed his eyes. 'What sort of run-in?'

Brady shrugged. 'Nothing much. He was just a bit pissed, making too much noise. I told him to calm down and he didn't, so a couple of us escorted him off the premises.'

Brady liked this last phrase; smiled at it. A nice official ring to it: 'escorted', 'premises'.

'You ever do any door work at the Clipper?'

Brady shook his head.

'But you work for its owner.'

'Mr Mackenzie has a share of the boat, that's all.'

'But he provides the bouncers too.'

'I tried it once, didn't like it.'

'Why not?'

'All these stuck-up tarts and Hooray Henries, thinking they could walk all over you because they had a bit of cash.'

'I know what you mean.' Brady looked at him. 'No, really. I've seen them for myself.' Rebus was still thinking about Brady's run-in with Damon Mee. He'd thought it was Damon's first visit to Gaitano's; no one had told him any different. 'Thing is, Cal, Damon's a missing person, and I'm a bit like Gulliver in one of Lilliput's toilets.'

'Eh?'

'I've not got much to go on.' Gill Templer groaned at the joke, while Rebus counted off on his fingers. 'I've got

Damon going missing, last seen with a blonde being dropped by taxi outside the Clipper. The boat's part-owned by Charmer Mackenzie, who also owns Guiser's, which is where Damon and the blonde seemed to meet. See, there's a connection there. Right now, it's the only thing I've got, which is why I'm going to keep working away at it until I've got some answers.' He paused. 'Only you don't have any of the answers, do you?'

Brady stared at him. Rebus turned to Templer.

'No further questions, m'lud.'

'All right, Mr Brady,' she said. 'You can go now.'

Brady walked to the door, opened it, turned his head back towards Rebus.

'Gulliver,' he said. 'Is he the one in the cartoon with the little people?'

'That's him,' Rebus acknowledged.

Brady nodded thoughtfully. 'I still don't get it,' he said, closing the door after him.

At lunchtime, Rebus sat in his car and slept for half an hour, before heading back to the office with a beaker of tomato soup and a cheese and Branston sandwich.

'We've got something,' Roy Frazer informed him. 'Sighting of a white saloon car, exiting Holyrood Park at the Dalkeith Road end. Someone from maintenance at the Commonwealth Pool noticed it. Early morning, no traffic about. This car was doing a fair lick, went through a red light. He's a cyclist, pays attention to that sort of thing.'

'And a model citizen too, I'll bet. Never sneaks through a red on his bike when nobody's watching.' Rebus thought for a moment. 'Any surveillance cameras that might have caught it?'

'I'll check.'

'Clear it with DCI Templer first. She's in charge.'

'Yes, sir.' Frazer bounded off in search of her. He reminded Rebus of a pet spaniel, always ready for attention and praise. White saloon car . . . Something was niggling Rebus. He put in a call to Bobby Hogan at Leith police station.

'If I say the words "white saloon car" to you, what would you say to me?'

'I'd say my brother's got one, a Ford Orion.'

'I'm thinking of Jim Margolies.'

'Something in the notes?'

'Yes. I'm sure there was a white saloon.'

'Can I call you back?'

'Soon as poss.' He put down the receiver, scribbled circles within circles on his pad, then sent lines radiating out from the centre. He couldn't decide if it looked more like a spider's web or a dartboard, came to the answer: neither. The telescopic sight from a warplane maybe? Or a section through a tree-trunk? All possibilities, but really all it was in the end was a meaningless squiggle. And when he ran over it a few times with the pen, it became clotted past interpretation.

His phone rang and he picked up.

'Is it important?' Bobby Hogan asked.

'I don't know. Might connect to something else.'

'Want to tell me what?'

'You go first.'

He seemed to be considering the offer, then began to recite from the case-notes. 'Light-coloured saloon car, possibly white or cream. Seen parked on Queen's Drive.'

'Where on Queen's Drive?' Queen's Drive being the roadway that wound around Holyrood Park.

'You know The Hawse?'

'Not by name.'

'It's at the foot of the Crags, near where the path starts. This car was parked there, lights on, apparently nobody in it. Someone came forward when they heard about the suicide. But the timing was wrong. They spotted it at around ten thirty that night. It was gone by the time a patrol went past at midnight. Margolies didn't head up there until later.'

'According to his widow.'

'Well, she should know, shouldn't she? So are you going to tell me what this is all about?'

'Another sighting of a white saloon, the morning Darren Rough was killed. Seen haring out of Holyrood Park.'

'What's that got to do with Jim's suicide?'

'Probably nothing,' Rebus said, thinking of the doodle again. 'Maybe I'm just seeing things.' He saw the Farmer standing in the doorway, beckoning. 'Thanks anyway,' he said.

'Any other fantasies you get, they've got special phone numbers these days.'

Rebus put down the receiver, started towards the door.

'My office,' the Farmer said, moving away before Rebus could reach him. There was a mug of coffee already sitting on the Farmer's desk. He poured Rebus one, handed it over.

'What have I done this time?' Rebus asked.

The Farmer motioned for him to sit. 'It's Darren Rough's social worker. He's made an official complaint.'

'About me?'

'He reckons you "outed" his client, and brought this whole thing on. He's asking questions about how closely you tie in to Rough's death.'

Rebus rubbed his eyes, managed a tired smile. 'He's welcome to his opinions.'

'No danger he can back them up with hard proof?'

'Not a chance in hell, sir.'

'It's still not going to look good. You were the last person Rough had any contact with.'

'Only if you discount the killer. Have forensics turned up anything?'

'Only that the killer probably got some of Rough's blood on him.'

'What if I put forward a proposal?'

280

The Farmer picked up a pen, studied it. 'What sort of proposal?'

'That we bring in Cary Oakes again. I'm positive he nicked my car, which puts him in Arden Street around the time Darren Rough was leaving. What was he doing there in the first place? Staking the place out? In which case, he'd been there a while, maybe saw us going in, took Rough for a friend of mine . . .'

The Farmer was shaking his head. 'We can't bring in Oakes, not without something solid.'

'How about a mallet?'

It was the Farmer's turn to smile. 'Stevens' paper has lawyers, John. And you've said yourself, Oakes is a pro. He'll sit there keeping schtum till they spring him. At which point, the daily rags have got themselves another story about police harassment.'

'I thought we were *trying* to harass him?'

The Farmer dropped the pen on the floor, stooped to pick it up. 'We've been through all this.'

'I know.'

'So now we're going in circles. Bottom line, a complaint from Social Work has to be followed up.'

'And meantime, I can't work the investigation.'

'It would look bloody odd under the circumstances. What other work have you got?'

'Officially, not a lot.'

'I heard you had a MisPer.'

'I was working it in my own time.'

'So spend a bit more time on it. But – and this is off the record, mind – keep close to Gill and the team. You seem to know more about Rough and Greenfield than most.'

'In other words, you need me, but can't afford to be seen with me?'

'You always had a way with words, John. Off you go now. POETS day, you know, weekend coming up. Go and enjoy yourself.'

Janice Mee turned up at Arden Street for want of anything more constructive to do. She had all this time to herself, and over in Fife she felt she was accomplishing nothing. If she sat at home, the patterns on the wallpaper started swirling, and the clock's tick seemed amplified beyond all enduring. But if she went out, there were questions to be answered by neighbours and passers-by – 'Is he no' back yet?'; 'Where do you think he'd have went?' – and comments to be fielded – usually to do with having patience or keeping fingers crossed. Besides, she had a feeling whenever she stepped off the train at Waverley that Damon was nearby. It was true people had a sixth sense: you could feel when someone was creeping up behind you. And every time she stepped on to the platform, stopping there while the workers and shoppers made to pass her, hurried lives they had to be getting on with ... when she stopped there, it was as if her world stopped turning, and everything became still and peaceful. In those moments, with the city hushed and the blood singing in her heart, she could almost hear him, smell him – everything but reach out and touch his arm. She saw herself pulling him to her, scolding him as she poured kisses on his face, and him all grown-up and trying to resist, but pleased, too, to be wanted like this and loved like this, loved the way no one in the universe would ever love him.

Since he'd gone missing, she'd been sleeping in his room. At first, she'd reasoned to Brian that Damon might sneak back in the night for his things. This way, she'd be there to confront him, to snare him. But then Brian had said he'd move into the room too, and she'd pointed out there was just the single bed, and he'd countered that he'd sleep on the floor. On and on the discussion had gone, until she'd lost it and blurted out that she'd rather be on her own.

The first time she'd spoken the words.

'Frankly, Brian, I'd much rather be on my own . . .'

His face had lost all rigidity, had folded in on itself, and she'd felt sick in her stomach. But she'd been right to say the words, wrong to keep them inside the past months and years.

'It's Johnny, isn't it?' Brian, face averted, had plucked up the courage to ask.

And in a way it was, though not quite the way Brian meant. It was that Johnny had shown her another road she might have taken, and in doing so had opened up the possibility of all the other roads left untravelled, all the places she'd never been. Places like Emotion and High and Elation. Places like Myself and Free and Aware. She knew she'd never say these things to anyone; they sounded too much like stuff from the magazines. But that didn't stop her feeling they were true. Born and bred in the town, lived most of her days there: did she really want to die there? Did she want it that thirty-odd years of her life could be summarised in five minutes to a friend she hadn't seen since secondary school?

She wanted more.

She wanted out.

Of course, she knew what people would say: you're just emotional, dear. It's bound to be upsetting, something like this. And it was. Oh, Jesus sweet Christ almighty, it was. Yet she felt more powerless and aimless than ever. She'd told her story to all the charities, she'd done her bit talking to the taxi drivers, but what was left? She knew there must be something she hadn't tried, but couldn't think what. All she knew was, this was where she had to be.

Now that she had a feel for the city, she enjoyed the walk to Marchmont. The steep climb up Cockburn Street, full of 'alternative' shops – some of them had even taken her flyers. Then up the High Street to George IV Bridge, and down past libraries and bookshops to Greyfriars Bobby. Past the university and the milling students, carrying books with them or pushing their bicycles. Then The Meadows, flat and green and with Marchmont rising in the distance. She liked the shops near Johnny's flat; liked the tenement itself and all the streets around it. The roofs seemed to her like castle turrets. Johnny said the area was full of students. She'd always imagined students living in poorer places.

She opened the main door and climbed to Johnny's landing. There was mail behind his door. She picked it up, took it through to the living room. It looked like bills and junk; no real letters. No photos in his living room; gaps in the wall-units which she would have filled with ornaments. Books tidied away into piles: before she moved them, they'd been lying everywhere. There was a time Brian wouldn't have stood for it if she'd moved his stuff around; these days, he probably wouldn't even notice. Johnny had noticed when she'd tidied up, but she wasn't sure he'd been pleased, even though he'd said 'Thanks.'

She took mugs, plate and ashtray through to the kitchen. Took a blanket from the sofa and put it on the bed in the spare room. When everything was to her satisfaction, she wondered what to do next. Clean the windows? With what? Make herself a cup of something? Listen to some music . . . when had she last sat down and listened to music? When had she last had time? She looked through Johnny's collection. Pulled out an album – one of the first by the Rolling Stones. It looked the same copy he'd had when they'd been going out together. On the back she found an ink doodle: JLJ – Janice Loves Johnny. She'd put it there one night, wondering if he'd notice. He always liked to study his LP sleeves. And when he had noticed, he hadn't been too thrilled, had tried taking a rubber to it. You could still see the smudge . . .

Summers in the café, long evenings with the Coke machine and the jukebox. Then a bag of chips, salt and vinegar. Maybe a film some nights, or just a stroll in the park. The youth club was run by the local church. Johnny hadn't liked that; hadn't been churchy. Yet here was a copy of the Bible, sitting alone on the mantelpiece. And other books that looked religious: *The Confessions of St Augustine; The Cloud of Unknowing.* She liked the sound of that last one. Lots of books, yet he didn't seem much of a reader, and the books looked brand new, most of them.

His bedroom . . . she'd sneaked a peek in there. Not the most inviting of rooms: mattress on the floor, clothes in piles in a corner, waiting to be decanted into the chest of drawers. Odd socks: what was it with men and odd socks? The whole flat had an unloved feel to it, despite some redecoration in the living room. His chair, positioned next to the bay window, phone on the floor next to it – the whole flat seemed to revolve around that one space. Kitchen cupboards: bottles of whisky and brandy and vodka and gin. More vodka in the freezer; beer in the fridge, along with cheese, marge, and an unpromising quarter of corned beef. Jars of beetroot and raspberry jam on the worktop, breadbin with two stale rolls and the heel of a loaf.

They said you could tell a lot about a man from his home. She got the feeling Johnny was lonely, but how could that be when he had the doctor, Patience whatser-name?

The doorbell. She wondered who it could be. Went and opened the door, not even bothering with the spy-hole. A man standing there, smiling.

'Hiya,' he said. 'Is John in?'

'No, I'm afraid not.'

The smile disappeared; the man checked his watch. 'I hope he's not going to stand me up again.'

'Well, in his job . . .'

'Oh, that's true enough. You'll know all about it, I suppose.'

She felt herself blushing under his gaze. 'I'm not his girlfriend or anything.'

'No? And here I was thinking he'd struck lucky, the old devil.'

'No, I'm just a friend.'

'Just good friends, eh?' He tapped his nose. 'You can trust me, I won't tell Patience.'

Her blush spread. 'We were at school, Johnny and me. Met up again recently.' She was babbling, and knew it, but somehow couldn't stop herself.

'That's nice: old friends getting together. Plenty to catch up on, eh?'

'Plenty.'

'I know the feeling. I was out of touch with John for years too.'

'Really?'

'Working in the States.'

'How interesting. Were you there long . . . ?' She caught herself. 'Sorry, I can't keep you standing out there, can I?'

'I was beginning to wonder.'

She opened the door wider, took a step back. 'You better come in. My name's Janice, by the way.'

'You'll laugh when I tell you my name. All I can say is, nobody consulted *me*.'

'Why, what's your name?' Laughing now as he stepped past her into the hall.

'Cary,' he told her. 'After the actor. Only I've never managed to be quite so suave.'

He was winking at her as she closed the door.

The flat was empty when Rebus got home, but he sensed someone had been there: things moved, things tidied. Janice again. He looked for a note, but she hadn't left one. He took a beer from the fridge, then turned on the hi-fi.

The Stones: 'Goat's Head Soup'. On the album cover, David Bailey had photographed them with their made-up faces covered by some diaphanous material, making Jagger look more feminine than ever. Rebus turned the volume down and called Alan Archibald's number. Nobody home but the answering machine. Archibald's voice sounded clipped and distant.

'It's John Rebus here. A simple message: ca' canny. A taxi driver picked Oakes up near your home. I can't think of any other reason he'd have been in the neighbourhood. He's also been in my street. I don't know what his thinking is, maybe he just wants to rattle us. Anyway, consider yourself forewarned.'

He put down the phone. Forewarned is forearmed, he thought, wondering how Alan Archibald would arm himself.

He turned up the volume, sat by the window and stared out at the opposite tenement. The kids were home from school, playing at their living room table. Some card game, it looked like. Happy Families maybe. Rebus had never been much good at that. When he turned from the window, he saw a shape in the doorway.

'Christ,' he said, putting a hand to his chest, 'don't do that to me.'

'Sorry,' Janice said, smiling. She raised a carton of milk for him to see. 'You were running out.'

'Thanks.' He followed her through to the kitchen, watched her put the milk in the fridge.

'Did you forget your appointment?' she asked.

'Appointment?' Rebus was thinking: doctor? Dentist?

'You stood your friend up. He was round here an hour ago. I went with him for a coffee.' She tutted at Rebus's fecklessness.

'You've lost me,' he said.

'Cary,' she told him. 'The two of you were going out for a drink.'

Rebus felt his spine turn cold. 'He came here?'

287

'Looking for you, yes.'

'And you went out with him?'

She'd been wiping the worktop, but turned towards him, saw the look on his face.

'What is it?' she asked.

He looked towards the cupboards, made a show of opening one to check for something. He couldn't tell her. She'd have a fit. He closed the cupboard door.

'Have a nice chat, the two of you?'

'He told me about his job in the States.'

'Which one? I think he had a couple.'

'Did he?' She frowned. 'Well, the only one he told me about was being a prison guard.'

'Oh, right.' Rebus nodded. 'I suppose you told him about us?'

She gave him a sly glance. There were spots of red on her cheeks. 'What's to tell?'

'I mean, told him about yourself, how we know one another . . . ?'

'Oh, yes, all that.'

'And Fife?'

'He seemed really interested in Cardenden. I told him off, thought he was taking the mickey.'

'No, Cary's always interested in people.'

'That's exactly what he said.' She paused. 'Sure you're all right?'

'Fine. It's just . . . work-related problems.' Namely, Cary Oakes, who had now pulled Janice into his game. And Rebus, himself in the middle of the board, had yet to be told the rules.

'Want some coffee or something?'

Rebus shook his head. 'We're going somewhere.' *We?* If Cary Oakes had gone to Fife, it was safer for Janice to stay in Edinburgh. But stay where? Rebus's flat was proving no sanctuary. She was safer with Rebus, and Rebus had somewhere he needed to be.

'Where?'

'Back to Fife. I've a few more questions for Damon's friends.' And terrain to scout, seeking signs of contamination by Oakes.

She stared at him. 'Have you ... are you on to something?'

'Hard to tell.'

'Try me.'

He was shaking his head. 'I don't want to raise your hopes. It might turn out to be nothing.' He started to move out of the kitchen. 'Give me a minute to do some packing.'

'Packing?'

'Weekend's coming, Janice. Thought I might stay over till tomorrow. Is there still a hotel in town?'

She hesitated for a moment. 'You can stay with us.'

'A hotel will be fine.'

But she shook her head. 'You'll understand, I couldn't let you have Damon's room, but there's always the couch.'

Rebus pretended to be torn. 'OK then,' he said at last. Thinking: I want to be there overnight; I want to be close to her. Not for any obvious reasons – reasons he might have put to himself a day or two ago – but because he wanted to know if Cary Oakes would travel to Cardenden, stake out her home. Whatever Oakes was planning, it was moving apace. If he was going to move on Janice, Rebus reckoned it would be at the weekend.

If anything happened, Rebus needed to be there.

'I'll just throw some stuff in a bag,' he said, heading for his bedroom.

32

Rebus took Janice to Sammy's first of all. He just wanted to check on her. She was doing pull-ups with the help of her parallel bars, hoisting herself to standing, locking her knees, then easing herself back into the wheelchair. The front door was unlocked: she kept it that way when Ned wasn't home. Rebus had been worried, until she'd explained her reasoning.

'I had to weigh up the chances, Dad: me needing help, versus someone breaking in. If I'm lying paralysed on my back, I want any Good Samaritans to be able to get in.'

She wore a grey sleeveless T-shirt, its back turned a darker grey by sweat. There was a towel around her shoulders, and her hair was matted to her forehead.

'God knows if this is helping my legs,' she said, 'but I'm getting a shot-putter's biceps.'

'And not an anabolic steroid in sight,' he said, leaning down to kiss her. 'This is Janice, old school-pal of mine.'

'Hello, Janice,' Sammy said. When she looked back at her father, he felt embarrassed, and wasn't sure why.

'Her son's disappeared,' he explained. 'I'm trying to help.'

Sammy wiped her face with the towel.

'I'm sorry,' she said. Janice smiled and shrugged.

'Janice still lives in Cardenden,' Rebus went on. 'We're headed back there, in case you were thinking of phoning me tonight.'

'Right,' Sammy said, her face still busy in the towel. Now that he was here, he knew he'd made some kind of mistake, knew Sammy was jumping to all the wrong conclusions, and couldn't think of a way out without embarrassing Janice.

'So I'll see you some time,' he said.

'I'm not going anywhere.' She had finished with the towel; was studying the bars, the extent of her current universe.

'We'll have to go through there some day. I can show you my old hunting-ground.'

She nodded. 'We can take Patience, too. I'm sure she wouldn't want to be left out.'

'Have a nice weekend, Sammy,' he said, making for the door.

She neglected to tell him to do the same.

'I'll just phone Patience,' he said, easing his mobile out of his pocket. They were back in the car, heading for the A90. Patience sometimes went out with friends on a Friday night; it was a regular thing – drinks and a meal, maybe a play or concert. Three other women doctors: two of them divorced, one still apparently happily married. She answered on the fourth ring.

'It's me,' he said.

'What have I told you about using that thing when you're driving?'

'I'm stalled at lights,' he lied, giving Janice a conspirator's wink. She looked uncomfortable.

'Got plans?'

'I have to go to Fife, couple of interviews I want to get out of the way. I'll probably stay the night. Are you going out?'

'In about twenty minutes.'

'Say hello to the gang from me.'

'John . . . when are we going to see one another?'

'Soon.'

'This weekend?'

'Almost certainly.'

'I'm going over to Sammy's tomorrow.'

'Right,' he said. Sammy would tell Patience about Janice. Patience would know Janice had been in the car when he'd called her. 'I'm staying the night with some friends: Janice and Brian.'

'The ones you were at school with?'

'That's right. I didn't realise I'd mentioned them.'

'You hadn't. Thing is, as far as I'm aware you haven't *made* any friends since school.'

'Bye, Patience,' he said, easing into the outside lane and putting his foot down.

Dr Patience Aitken had a taxi ordered. When it arrived, the driver pushed open her gate, headed down the steep and winding set of stone steps which led to her garden flat. He rang the doorbell and waited, scuffing his feet on the flagstones. He liked the New Town's garden flats, the way they were below street level at the front, but had gardens at the back. And they had these little courtyards at the front, with cellars built into the facing wall. Not that you'd use the cellars for much; too damp. Certainly not for keeping wine in. He'd taken the wife to the Loire the previous summer, learned all about the wines. He had three mixed cases now, stored in the cupboard beneath his stairs. Far from ideal conditions: a modern two-storey semi out at Fairmilehead. Too dry, too warm. What he needed was a flat like this one – he'd bet there'd be cupboards inside just right for laying down wine, cool and dryish with thick stone walls.

He noticed that the doctor had tried for a sort of garden feel in the courtyard: hanging baskets, terracotta pots. Nothing down here would get too much light, that was the thing. First thing he'd done with his front garden when he'd moved in: put flagstones over most of it, leaving just a square of earth in the middle, couple of roses planted in there. Minimum maintenance.

The door opened and the doctor stepped out, pulling a

shawl around her shoulders. Perfume wafted out with her: nothing too overbearing.

'Sorry I've kept you,' she said, pulling the door closed and making for the steps.

'I'd double-lock it if I were you,' he suggested.

'What?'

'Yales,' he explained, shaking his head. 'A kid could be inside in ten seconds flat.'

She thought about it, shrugged her shoulders. 'What's life without a bit of a risk?'

'As long as you're insured,' he said, studying her ankles as he climbed the steps after her.

Jim Stevens lay on his bed, one hand covering his eyes, the other holding the telephone receiver to his ear. He was listening to Matt Lewin, who had just told him how good the weather was in Seattle. Stevens had faxed him portions of Cary Oakes's 'confession', and Lewin was giving his views.

'Well, Jim, bits of it seem to tally all right. The truck driver story is new, and frankly, I don't think it's worth chasing.'

'You think he made it up?'

'Not my problem, thank God. I tell you, Jim, no disrespect, but I wouldn't trust anything that bastard told me, and I sure as hell wouldn't give him the satisfaction of seeing it in print.'

Which seemed to be Stevens' boss's view, too. The projected eight-parter had been cut to just five.

'I'm sure as hell glad he's your problem now and not ours,' Lewin went on.

'Thanks.'

'He giving you any trouble?'

Stevens didn't see the point in telling Lewin that Oakes was proving more awkward by the day. He'd slipped away from the hotel again that afternoon, stayed out the best part of three hours and wouldn't say where he'd been.

'It's nearly over anyway,' Stevens said, rubbing his hand over his brow.

'Good riddance, that's my advice.'

'Yes.' But Stevens couldn't help but worry. He worried about what Oakes would do with himself afterwards, once he was out on the street. No way was Stevens' paper going to come up with ten K, not for the scraps Oakes had given them. Stevens still had to break that news to Oakes.

He worried for himself too. He was part of Oakes's sphere now, and was just hoping Oakes would let him go.

He got the feeling, God help him, that it might not be all that easy . . .

Cary Oakes watched the taxi leave. Dr P, he presumed. Getting on a bit, but then the state Rebus was in, he doubted he'd be complaining. Basement apartment too: perfect for what he had in mind. He came out from behind the parked car and looked up and down the street. The place was dead. Half of Edinburgh seemed dead to him: you could wander around for ages and not go noticed, never mind raise suspicion.

Jim Stevens had been in a foul mood, watching the Cary Oakes story relegated as the editor decided to run a special on vigilanteism. Stevens blamed the paedophile murder.

'Bloody Rebus again,' he'd muttered, and Oakes had asked him to explain.

Stevens' theory: Rebus had outed Darren Rough, raised the mob against him. And now one of them had taken it too far. Everything Oakes learned about the detective made Rebus seem more interesting, more complicated.

'What sort of code does he live by, do you think?' he'd asked.

Stevens had snorted. 'Could be Morse or Highway for all I know.'

'Some people make up their own rules,' Oakes had mused.

'You mean like the serial killer?'

'Hmm?'

'The one who picked you up in his truck.'

'Oh, him . . . Well, yes, of course.'

And Stevens had looked at him. And Cary Oakes had stared back.

He crossed the road now. No houses across the street from where he'd be working, just a wrought-iron fence, a bank of grass behind it. No neighbours to spot him as he went about his business.

He expected no interruptions at all.

The batteries were fading anyway, Rebus rationalised, and he didn't have the recharger with him. So he switched off his mobile.

'The weekend starts here,' he said, as they crossed the Forth Road Bridge into Fife.

Later: 'Roads have changed,' as they came off the dual carriageway outside Kirkcaldy. But the old Kirkcaldy–Cardenden road seemed much the same, same twists and turns, potholes and bumps.

'Remember we walked to Kirkcaldy once to go to the pictures?' Janice said.

Rebus smiled. 'I'd forgotten that. Why didn't we just take the bus?'

'I think we didn't have enough money.'

He frowned. 'Was it just us?'

'Mitch and his girlfriend too. Can't remember who he was dating at the time.'

'He went through them, all right.'

'Maybe *they* got fed up of *him*.'

'Maybe.' They sat in silence for a minute. 'What was the film?'

'Which film?'

'The one we walked six miles to see.'

'I don't recall watching much of it.'

They glanced at one another, burst out laughing.

Brian Mee heard the car, came out to meet them.

'This is a surprise,' he said, shaking Rebus's hand.

'I need to talk to Damon's pals,' Rebus explained.

Janice touched her husband's arm. 'He said he wanted to go to the hotel.'

'Rubbish, you can stay with us. Damon's room's . . .'

'I thought maybe the sofa,' Janice interjected.

Brian recovered well. 'Oh aye, it's not that old. Comfy too. I should know: I nod off on it most nights myself.'

'That's settled then,' Janice said. She had a man on either arm as she walked up the front path.

They ordered Chinese from the takeaway, opened a couple of bottles of wine. Old stories, rekindled memories. Half-remembered names; the exploits of those who'd grown old in the town; changes to the fabric of the place. Rebus had phoned Damon's friends, the ones who'd been with him at Gaitano's, but neither of them was in. He'd left messages, saying he had to see them in the morning.

'We could go out for a drink,' he told his hosts. His eyes were on Janice as he spoke. 'Be the first time we had a drink together in the Goth without being underage.'

'The Goth's shut, John,' Brian said.

'Since when?'

'They're turning it into a centre for the unemployed.'

'Isn't that what it always was?'

They smiled at that. The Goth closed: his dad's watering-hole; the first place John Rebus had ever bought a round.

'Railway Tavern's still going,' Brian added. 'We'll be there tomorrow night for the karaoke.'

'You'll stay for that, won't you?' Janice asked.

'I'm kind of allergic to karaokes, actually.' Rebus was once again in the 'seat by the fire', the one he'd been made to sit in on his first visit. The TV was playing, sound turned down. It was like a magnet, their eyes sliding towards it throughout the conversation. Janice cleared away the dishes – they'd eaten with the plates on their laps. He helped her take the things through to the kitchen,

saw it was too small for three people to eat in. There was a
dining table in front of the living room window, but set
with ornaments, its leaves folded. Used for special occasions only. With the leaves opened, it would all but fill the
room. They ate all their meals on their laps, in front of the
TV. He imagined the three of them – mother, father, son –
staring at the screen, using it to excuse the lengthening
gaps in conversation.

After coffee, Janice said she was going up to bed. Brian
said he'd be up in a while. She brought down blankets and
a pillow for Rebus, told him where the bathroom was.
Told him where the light-switch was in the hall. Told him
there was plenty of hot water if he wanted a bath.

'See you in the morning.'

Brian reached for the remote, switched off the TV, then
caught himself.

'There wasn't something you wanted to . . . ?'

Rebus shook his head. 'I'm not a big fan.'

'And what would you say to a wee whisky?'

'More my cup of tea altogether,' Rebus acknowledged
with a smile.

They sipped the whisky in silence. It wasn't a malt:
maybe Teacher's or Grant's. Brian had added a dollop of
water to his, but Rebus hadn't bothered.

'Where do you think he is?' Brian asked at last, swirling
the drink around the rim of his glass. 'Just between us,
like.'

As if Janice couldn't take it; as if he were stronger than
her.

'I don't know, Brian. I wish I did.'

'They normally go to London, though.'

'Yes.'

'And most of them do OK for themselves?'

Rebus nodded, not wanting any of this, wishing of a
sudden that he was back in his flat with his own whisky,
his music and books. But Brian had a need to talk.

'I blame us, you know.'

'I'd guess most parents do.'

'I think he picked up on the atmosphere, and it drove him away.' He sat on the edge of the sofa, hands squeezing his glass. He was looking at the floor as he spoke. 'I got the feeling Janice was just waiting for Damon to go. You know, get a place of his own. That's what she was waiting for.'

'And then what?'

Brian glanced up at him. 'Then she'd have no reason to stay. Every time she goes to Edinburgh, I think that's it: she won't be back.'

'But she always comes back.'

He nodded. 'But it's different now. She comes back in case Damon's here. Nothing to do with me.' He coughed, cleared his throat, drained the whisky. 'Want a refill?' Rebus shook his head. 'No, suppose not. Time for kip, eh?' Brian got to his feet, managed a smile. 'Schooldays, eh, Johnny?'

'Schooldays, Brian,' Rebus agreed. He watched something brighten behind Brian Mee's eyes, then die again.

Rebus brushed his teeth in the kitchen – didn't want to intrude upstairs, not with Brian readying for bed. He laid the blankets out on the sofa. Sat there with the lights out, then got up and went to the window. Peered through the curtains. Outside, the street-lamps cast a faint orange glow. The street itself was empty. He crept into the hall, opened the front door quietly, leaving it on the latch. Five minutes outside told him Cary Oakes wasn't in the vicinity. He headed back indoors, needed the toilet. The kitchen sink seemed inappropriate, so he listened at the foot of the stairs then headed up. He knew the bathroom door, went in and did his business. One bedroom door was closed, the other slightly open. The open door had a football scarf pinned to it, and half a dozen used concert tickets from a few years before. Rebus pushed his head around the door: saw the outlines of posters, a wardrobe and chest of drawers. Saw the window with the curtains

drawn. Saw the single bed, and Janice sleeping in it, her
breathing regular.

Crept downstairs again feeling like a housebreaker.

33

Next morning after breakfast, he had a meeting with Damon's friends.

They came round to the house, while Janice and Brian were out shopping. Joey Haldane was tall and skinny with closely cropped bleached hair and dark bushy eyebrows. He wore all denim – jeans, shirt, jacket – with black Dr Marten shoes. Rebus noticed that his mouth hung open most of the time, as though he had trouble breathing through his nose.

Pete Mathieson was as tall as Joey but a lot broader, the kind of son a farmer would be proud of (and probably exploit). He wore red jogging pants and a blue sweatshirt, Nike trainers with the soles almost rubbed away. They sat on the sofa. Rebus's sheets and pillow had disappeared upstairs before breakfast, while he'd been soaking in the bath.

'Thanks for coming,' Rebus began. Instead of one of the overstuffed armchairs, he was seated on a straight-backed dining chair, planted in the middle of the room. Below him, the boys sank into the sofa. He'd turned his chair so he could straddle it, leaning his arms on its back.

'I know we've talked before, Joey, but I've got a couple of back-up questions. So-called because when I think someone's not playing straight with me, it tends to get my back up.'

Joey wet his lips with his tongue, Pete twitched a shoulder, angled his head and tried to look bored.

'See,' Rebus went on, 'I was told the three of you had gone just that once to Edinburgh for your night out. But now I think I know differently. I think you'd been there before. I think maybe it was a regular thing, which makes me wonder why you'd lie. What is it you're trying to hide? Remember, this is a missing person investigation. No way you're not going to be found out.'

'We haven't done nothing.' This from Joey, his voice a hoarse local accent, the sound of carpentry work.

'Know what a double negative is, Joey?'

'Should I?' Holding Rebus's stare for the briefest of moments.

'If you say you haven't done nothing, it means you've done *something*.'

'I've told you, we haven't done nothing.'

'You haven't lied about that night? You hadn't been to Edinburgh for a night out before . . . ?'

'We'd been before,' Pete Mathieson said.

'Hello there, Pete,' Rebus said. 'Thought you'd lost the power of speech for a minute there.'

'Pete,' Joey spat, 'for fuck's—'

Mathieson gave his friend a look, but when he spoke it was for Rebus's benefit.

'We'd been before.'

'To Guiser's?'

'And other places – pubs, clubs.'

'How often?'

'Four, five nights.'

'Without telling your girlfriends?'

'They thought we were down Kirkcaldy, same as always.'

'Why not tell them?'

'That would have spoiled it,' Joey said, folding his arms. Rebus thought he knew what he meant. It was only an adventure if it was furtive. Men liked to have their little secrets and tell their little lies. They liked a sense of the illicit. All the same, he got the feeling it went further. It was the way Joey was leaning back in the sofa, crossing one ankle over the other. He was thinking of something,

301

something about the nights out, and the thought was making him feel good . . .

'Was it just you that was cheating, Joey, or was it all of you?'

Joey's face grew darker. He turned to his friend.

'I never said nothing!' Pete blurted out.

'He didn't need to, Joey,' Rebus said. 'It's written on your face.'

Joey wriggled in his seat, less comfortable by the second. Eventually he sat forward, arms on knees. 'If Alice finds out she'll kill me.'

So much for the thrill of the illicit.

'Your secret's safe with me, Joey. I just need to know what happened that night.'

Joey glanced towards Pete, as though giving him permission to do the talking.

'Joey met a girl,' Pete began. 'Three weeks before. So every time we went across, he hooked up with her.'

'You weren't in Guiser's?'

Joey shook his head. 'Went back to her flat for an hour.'

'The plan was,' Pete explained, 'we'd all meet up later at Guiser's.'

'You weren't there either?'

Pete shook his head. 'We were in a pub beforehand, I got chatting to this lassie. I think Damon was a bit bored.'

'More likely jealous,' Joey added.

'So he headed off to Guiser's on his own?' Rebus asked.

'By the time I got there,' Pete said, 'there was no sign of him.'

'So he wasn't at the bar for a round of drinks? You made that up so nobody would know you were busy elsewhere?' He was looking at Joey.

'That's about it,' Pete answered. 'Didn't think it made any difference.'

Rebus was thoughtful. 'What about Damon? Did he ever hook up with anyone?'

'Never seemed to get lucky.'

302

'It wasn't because he was thinking of Helen?'

Joey shook his head. 'He was just useless with birds.'

And he'd gone off to Guiser's on his own . . . thinking what? Thinking about how of the three, he was the only one who couldn't pick up a girl for the night. Thinking he was 'useless'. Yet somehow he'd ended up sharing a taxi with the mystery blonde . . .

'Does it matter?' Pete asked.

. 'It might. I'll have to think about it.' It mattered because Damon had been there alone. It mattered because now Rebus had no idea what had happened to him between leaving Pete in the pub and standing at the bar in Guiser's waiting to be served, with a blonde at his shoulder. They might have met en route. Something might have happened. And Rebus couldn't know. Just when the picture should have been becoming clearer, it had been torn apart.

When Janice and Brian started bringing bags in from the car, Rebus dismissed Pete and Joey. Something else they'd said: Damon wouldn't have minded finding a girl for the night. What did that say about his relationship with Helen?

'All right, John?' Janice said, smiling.

'Fine,' he replied.

After lunch, Brian invited him to the pub. It was a regular thing – Saturday afternoon, football commentary on the radio or TV. A few drinks with the lads. But Rebus declined. He had the excuse that Janice had offered to take a walk around the town with him. Rebus didn't want to be out drinking with Brian, a time when bonds could be made or tightened, secrets could dribble out 'in confidence'. Now that he'd seen Janice sleeping in a separate room, Rebus felt he knew things he shouldn't.

Of course, she might be sleeping there because of Damon, because she missed him. But Rebus didn't think that was it.

303

So Brian went off to the pub, and Janice and Rebus went walking. Rain was falling, but lightly. She wore a red duffel coat with a hood. She offered Rebus an umbrella, but he declined, explaining that ever since he'd seen someone almost get their eye taken out with one on Princes Street, he'd regarded them as offensive weapons.

'Where we're walking won't be quite so crowded,' she told him.

And it was true. The streets were empty. Locals went to Kirkcaldy or Edinburgh for their shopping. When Rebus had been young his family hadn't owned a car. The shops on the main street had catered for all their needs. The needs these days seemed to be videos and takeaway food. The Goth was indeed closed, its windows boarded up, reminding Rebus of Darren Rough's flat. The flats on Craigside Road had been demolished, new houses replacing them. Some of them were owned by the local housing association, the others were private.

'Nobody owned their own house when we were growing up,' Janice stated. Then she laughed. 'I must sound about seventy-eight.'

'The good old days,' Rebus agreed. 'Places do change, though.'

'Yes.'

'And people are allowed to change too.'

She looked at him, but didn't ask what he meant. Maybe she already knew.

They climbed up to The Craigs, a high ridge of wilderness above Auchterderran, and walked along it until they could see the old school.

'Not that it's used as a school any more,' Janice explained. 'Kids these days go to Lochgelly. Remember the school badge?'

'I remember it.' Auchterderran Secondary School: ASS. Kids from other schools used to bray at them, poking fun.

'Why do you keep looking round?' she asked. 'Think someone's following us?'

'No.'

'Brian's not like that, if that's what you're thinking.'

'No, no, nothing—'

'Sometimes I wish he was.' She strode ahead of him. He took his time catching up.

They walked back into town past the Auld Hoose pub. Cardenden as it now was had at one time been four distinct parishes known as the ABCD – Auchterderran, Bowhill, Cardenden and Dundonald. When they'd been going out together, Rebus had lived in Bowhill, Janice in Dundonald. He would take this route walking her home, going the longest way round they could think of. Crossing the River Ore at the old humpbacked bridge – now long replaced by a tarmac road. Sometimes, in summer, say, cutting through the park, crossing the river further up at one of the wide-diameter pipes. Those pipes had provided a test for the local kids. Rebus had known boys freeze halfway across, until their parents had to be fetched. He'd known one boy pee in his trousers with fear, but keep on moving his feet inch by inch along the pipe, while the river surged below him. Others took the crossing at a canter, hands in their pockets, needing no help with balancing.

Rebus had been one of the cautious ones.

The same pipe ran the length of the park before disappearing into the undergrowth beyond. You could follow it all the way to the bing – the hill-sized mound of dross and coal-shavings which the local colliery had deposited. Fires started on the bing could smoulder for months, wisps of smoke rising from the surface as from a volcano. In time, trees and grass had grown on the slopes, so that more than ever the bing came to resemble a natural hill. But if you climbed to the top, there was a plateau, an alien landscape, wired off for safety's sake. It was like a small loch, its surface oily, thick-looking, and black. Nobody knew what it was, but they respected it –

kept their distance and threw stones, watching them sink slowly from view as they were sucked beneath the surface.

Boys and girls went into the wild areas behind the park and found secret places, flattened areas of fields which they could call their own. And that had been Janice and Johnny, too, once upon a time . . .

The Kinks: 'Young and Innocent Days'.

Now, the place had changed. The bing had gone, the whole area landscaped. The colliery had been demolished. Cardenden had grown up around coal, hurried streets constructed in the twenties and thirties to house the incoming miners. These streets hadn't even been given names, just numbers. Rebus's family had moved into 13th Street. Relocation had taken the family to a pre-fab in Cardenden, and from there to a terraced house in a cul-de-sac in Bowhill. But by the time Rebus had been at secondary school, the coal was proving difficult to mine: fractured strata, so that a face might yield low tonnage. The colliery had become uneconomic. The daily siren signalling the change of shifts had been silenced. Schoolfriends of Rebus, boys whose fathers and grandfathers had been miners, were left wondering what to do.

And Rebus too had been asking himself questions. But with Mitch's help he'd come to a decision. They'd both join the army. It had seemed so simple back then . . .

'Is Mickey still around?' Janice asked.

'Lives in Kirkcaldy.'

'He was a pest, your wee brother. Remember him charging into the bedroom? Or opening the bowley-hole all of a sudden so he could catch us?'

Rebus laughed. *Bowley-hole*: a word he hadn't heard in years. The serving-hatch between kitchen and living room. He could see Mickey now. He'd be up on the worktop in the kitchen, trying to spy on Rebus and Janice while they were alone in the living room.

Rebus looked around again. He didn't think Cary Oakes was in town. A place this size, where everyone knew everyone, it was hard to hide. He'd already had a couple of people come up and say hello, like they'd seen him just the other day, rather than a dozen or more years ago. And Janice had been stopped by half a dozen people – neighbours or the plain curious – and asked about Damon. It was hard to escape him: every wall, lamp-post and window seemed to have his picture stuck to it.

'I was here a few years back,' he told Janice. 'Hutchy's betting shop.'

'You were after Tommy Greenwood?'

He nodded. 'And I bumped into Cranny.' Their old nickname for Heather Cranston.

'She's still around. So's her son.'

Rebus sought the name. 'Shug?'

'That's it,' Janice said. 'If you're lucky, you might see Heather tonight.'

'Oh?'

'She often comes to the karaoke.'

Rebus asked Janice if they could turn back. 'I want to see the cemetery,' he explained. And backtracking, he might have added, as he'd learned in the army, was a good way to find if you were being followed. So they headed back through Bowhill, and up the cemetery brae. He was thinking of all the stories buried in the graveyard: mining tragedies; a girl found drowned in the Ore; a holiday car crash which had wiped out a family. Then there was Johnny Thomson, Celtic goalkeeper, fatally injured during an Old Firm derby, only in his twenties when he died.

Rebus's mother had been cremated, but his father had insisted on a 'proper burial'. His headstone was over by the end wall. Loving husband to . . . and father of . . . And at the bottom, the words *Not Dead, But at Rest in the Arms of the Lord*. But as they approached, Rebus saw that something was wrong.

'Oh, John,' Janice gasped.

White paint had been poured down the headstone, covering most of the lettering.

'Bloody kids,' Janice said.

Rebus saw tracks of paint on the grass, but no sign of the empty tin.

'This wasn't kids,' he said. Too much of a coincidence.

'Who then?'

He touched his finger to the headstone: the paint was still viscous. Oakes *had* been in town. Janice was squeezing his arm.

'I'm so sorry.'

'It's only a bit of stone,' he said quietly. 'It can be fixed.'

They drank tea in the living room. Rebus had tried Oakes's hotel – Stevens' room, the bar, no one was there.

'We've had phone calls,' Janice told him.

'Cranks?' he guessed.

She nodded. 'Telling us Damon's dead, or we killed him. Thing is, the callers . . . their voices sound local.'

'Probably are local then.'

She offered him a cigarette. 'It's pretty sick, isn't it?'

Rebus, looking around, nodded his agreement.

They were still sitting in the living room when Brian came back from the pub.

'I'll just take a shower,' he said.

Janice explained that he always did this. 'Clothes in the washing basket, and a good wash. I think it's the cigarette smoke.'

'He doesn't like it?'

'Hates it,' she said. 'Maybe that's why I started.' The front door was opened again. It was Janice's mum. 'I'll fetch a cup,' Janice said, getting to her feet.

Mrs Playfair nodded a greeting towards Rebus and sat down opposite him.

'You haven't found him yet?'

'Not for want of trying, Mrs Playfair.'

'Ach, I'm sure you're doing your best, son. He's our only grandchild, you know.'

Rebus nodded.

'A good laddie, wouldn't harm a fly. I can't believe he'd get into trouble.'

'What makes you think he's in trouble?'

'He wouldn't do this to us otherwise.' She was studying him. 'So what happened to you, son?'

'How do you mean?' Wondering if she'd read his thoughts.

'I don't know . . . the way your life's gone. Are you happy enough?'

'I never really think about it.'

'Why not?'

He shrugged his shoulders. 'I like looking into people's lives. That's what detective work is.'

'The army didn't work out?'

'No,' he said simply.

'Sometimes things don't work out,' she said, as Janice came back into the room. She watched her daughter pour the tea. 'A lot of marriages break up round here.'

'Do you think Damon and Helen would have made a go of it?'

She took a long time thinking about it, accepted the cup from Janice. 'They're young, who knows?'

'What odds would you give them?'

'You're talking to Damon's gran, John,' Janice said. 'No girl in the world's good enough for Damon, eh, Mum?' She smiled to let him know she was half-joking. Then, to her mother again: 'Johnny's had a shock.' Describing the vandalised grave. Brian came in rubbing his hair. He'd changed his clothes. Janice repeated the story for him.

'Wee bastards,' Brian said. 'It's happened before. They push the stones over, break them.'

'I'll fetch you a mug,' Janice said, making to get up again.

'I'm fine,' Brian said, waving her back. He looked

towards Rebus. 'Probably don't feel like eating out then? Only we were going to treat you.'

After a moment's thought, Rebus said, 'I'd like to get out. But I should be paying.'

'You can pay next time,' Brian said.

'Judging on past history,' Rebus said, 'that'll be roughly thirty years from now.'

Rebus drank nothing but mineral water with his curry. Brian was on the beers, and Janice managed two large glasses of white wine. Mr and Mrs Playfair had been invited, but had declined.

'We'll let you young things get on with it,' Mrs Playfair had said.

From time to time, when Janice wasn't looking, Brian would glance in her direction. Rebus thought he was worried: worried his wife was going to leave him, and wondering what he was doing wrong. His life was falling apart, and he was on the lookout for clues as to why.

Rebus considered himself something of an expert on break-ups. He knew sometimes a perspective could shift, one partner could start wanting things that seemed outwith their reach as long as they stayed married. It hadn't been that way with his own marriage. There, it had been down to the fact that he never should have married in the first place. When work had begun to consume him, there hadn't been much left to sustain Rhona.

'Penny for them,' Janice said at one point, tearing apart a nan bread.

'I'm wondering about getting the headstone clean.'

Brian said he knew a man who could do it: worked for the council, took graffiti off walls.

'I'll send you the money,' Rebus told him. Brian nodded.

After the meal, he drove them back to Cardenden. The karaoke night was held in a back room at the Railway

Tavern. The equipment sat on a stage, but the singers stayed on the dancefloor, eyes on the TV monitor with its syrupy videos and the words appearing along the bottom of the screen. Sheets came round, printed with all the songs. You wrote your choice on a slip of paper and handed it to the compère. A skinhead got up and did 'My Way'. A middle-aged woman had a go at 'You to Me are Everything'. Janice said she always took 'Baker Street'. Brian switched between 'Satisfaction' and 'Space Oddity', depending on his mood.

'So most people sing the same song every week?' Rebus asked.

'That guy getting up just now,' she said, nodding towards the corner of the room, where people were shifting their seats to allow someone out, 'he always chooses REM.'

'So he's probably pretty good at it by now?'

'Not bad,' she agreed. The song was 'Losing My Religion'.

Drinkers were wandering through from the front bar, standing in the doorway to watch. There was a small bar specially for the karaoke: a hatch, manned by a teenager who kept testing the acne on his cheeks. People seemed to have their regular tables. Rebus, Janice and Brian were seated near one of the loudspeakers. Brian's mum was there, alongside Mr and Mrs Playfair. An elderly man came over to talk to them. Brian leaned towards Rebus.

'That's Alec Chisholm's dad,' he said.

'I wouldn't have known him,' Rebus admitted.

'They don't like talking to him. He's always on about how long Alec's been gone.'

It was true that the Playfairs and Mrs Mee sat stony-faced as they listened to Chisholm. Rebus got up to get a round in. He felt numb, remembering the scene which had greeted him in the cemetery, Oakes letting him know he was one step ahead, making it *personal*. Rebus saw it as another part of the test, knew Oakes was trying to break him. Rebus was more determined than ever not to let that happen.

Janice's mum was drinking Bacardi Breezes, watermelon flavour. Rebus doubted she'd ever seen a watermelon in her life. He saw Helen Cousins standing in the doorway with a couple of friends, went up to say hello.

'Any news?' she asked.

He shook his head, and she just shrugged, like she'd already given up on Damon. So much for the big romance. She was holding a bottle of Hooch, lemon flavour. All these sugary drinks, perfect for Scotland: a sweet tooth and a kick. Through in the saloon, he'd noticed they kept the bottles of mixers – lemonade and Irn Bru – on the bar, to be used freely by the punters. Not many pubs did that any more. Another thing: cheap beer. A lesson in economics: where you had a depressed area, you had to make your beer affordable. He'd spotted Heather Cranston through in the bar, seated on a stool, eyes drooping as some man talked into her ear and rested his hand on the back of her neck.

Helen handed her bottle to one of her friends, said she was off to the loo. Rebus hung around. The two girls were staring at him, wondering who he was.

'She must be taking it hard,' he said.

'What?' the one chewing gum asked, face creasing into puzzlement.

'Damon disappearing.'

The girl shrugged.

'More embarrassed than anything,' her friend commented. 'Doesn't do much for your morale, does it, your boyfriend doing a runner?'

'I suppose not,' Rebus said. 'I'm John, by the way.'

'Corinne,' the gum-chewer said. She had long black hair crimped with curling-tongs. Her pal was called Jacky and was tiny with dyed platinum hair.

'So what do you think of Damon?' he asked. He meant

about Damon disappearing, but they didn't take it that way.

'Ach, he's all right,' Jacky said.

'Just all right?'

'Well, you know,' Corinne said. 'Damon's heart's in the right place, but he's a bit thick. A bit slow, like.'

Rebus nodded, as if this were his impression too. But the way Damon's family had spoken of him, he'd been more of a genius in waiting. Rebus realised suddenly just how superficial his own portrait of Damon was. So far, he'd heard only one side of the story.

'Helen likes him, though?' he asked.

'I suppose so.'

'They're engaged.'

'It happens, doesn't it?' Jacky said. 'I've got girlfriends who got engaged just so they could throw a party.' She looked at her pal for support, then leaned towards Rebus to utter a confidentiality. 'They used to have some mega arguments.'

'What about?'

'Jealousy, I suppose.' She waited till Corinne had nodded confirmation. 'She'd see him notice someone, or he'd say she'd been letting some guy chat her up. Just the usual.' She looked at him. 'You think he's gone off with someone?' Rebus saw behind her eyeliner to a sharp intelligence.

'It's possible,' he said.

But Corinne was shaking her head. 'He wouldn't have had the guts.'

Looking along the corridor, Rebus saw that Helen hadn't made it to the toilets. She was chatting to some guy, her back to the wall, hands behind her. Rebus asked Corinne and Jacky what they were drinking. Two Bacardi-Cokes. He added them to the shopping list.

When he got back to his table, Janice was taking the floor. She sang 'Baker Street' with real emotion, eyes closed, knowing the words by heart. Brian watched her, his face giving away little. He probably didn't realise he spent the whole song tearing a beer-mat into tinier and tinier pieces, piling them on the table before sweeping them on to the floor as the number finished.

Rebus stepped outside, took deep gulps of the crisp night air. He was sticking to whisky, heavily watered. There were shouts in the distance, football chants. UVF spray-painted on the side wall of the pub. A man was urinating there. Afterwards, he reeled towards Rebus, asked if he could borrow a cigarette. Rebus gave him one, lit it.

'Cheers, Jimmy,' the drunk said. Then he studied Rebus's face. 'I knew your father,' he said, walking away before Rebus could quiz him further.

Rebus stood there. This wasn't where he belonged, he knew that now. The past was a place you could visit, but it didn't do to linger there. He'd drunk too much to drive, but first thing . . . first thing he would head back. Cary Oakes wasn't here. He'd visited only long enough to leave a message. Rebus felt sorry for Janice and Brian, the way things had gone for them. But right now they were the least important of his many problems. He'd allowed his perspective to skew, and Oakes had made far too much capital from that.

Back indoors, no one tried to press the microphone on him. By now they all knew who he was, knew about the act of desecration. Stories passed quickly through a town the size of Cardenden. What else was history made up of?

34

It was still dark when he awoke. He dressed, folded the blankets, left a note on the dining table. Then headed out to his car, drove through the quiet streets and quieter countryside, hitting dual carriageway and giving the Saab's engine a proper work-out as he sped south towards Edinburgh.

He found a space round the corner from Oxford Terrace and walked back to Patience's flat. It was still too dark to see the door; he ran his fingers over it, found the lock and keyed it open. The hall was in darkness too. He walked on tiptoe, headed for the kitchen, poured water into the kettle. When he turned round, Patience was standing in the doorway.

'Where the hell have you been?' she said, tiredness failing to dampen her irritation.

'Fife.'

'You didn't call.'

'I told you I was going.'

'I tried your mobile.'

He switched the kettle on. 'I had it turned off.' He saw pain suddenly crease her face. Took her by the arms. 'What is it, Patience?'

She shook her head. There were tears in her eyes. She sniffed them back, took him by the hand into the hallway, where she switched on the light. He saw marks on the floor, a trail of them leading to the front door.

'What happened?' he asked.

'Paint,' she said. 'It was dark, I didn't see I was treading it in. I've tried cleaning it off.'

A white snail's trail of footprints . . . Rebus thought of the white tracks leading to his father's grave. He stared at her, then went to the front door and opened it. Behind him, she reached for the light-switch, illuminating the patio. Rebus saw the paint. Words daubed in foot-long letters on the paving-stones. He angled his head to read them.

YOUR COP LOVER KILLED DARREN.

The whole message underlined.

'Christ,' he gasped.

'Is that all you can say?' Her voice trembled. 'I've been trying to get you all weekend!'

'I was . . . When did it happen?' He was walking around the message.

'Friday night. I came home late, went to bed. About three, I woke up with a headache. Went to get some water, put the hall light on . . .' She was pulling back her hair with her hands, her face stretching, tightening. 'I saw the paint, came out here, and . . .'

'I'm sorry, Patience.'

'What does it mean?'

'I'm not sure.' Oakes again. All the time Rebus had been in Fife, Oakes had been right here, making his next move. He didn't just know about Janice, he knew about Patience too. And had told Rebus as much, telling him it was lucky he knew a doctor.

He'd telegraphed the move, and Rebus hadn't read it.

'You're lying,' Patience said. 'You know damned well. It's *him*, isn't it?'

Rebus tried putting his arms round her, but she shrugged him off.

'I called St Leonard's,' she said. 'They sent someone round. Two kids in uniform. In the morning, Siobhan turned up.' She smiled. 'She took me out for breakfast. I think she knew I hadn't been to sleep. It made me realise how vulnerable this place is. Garden at the back: anyone could scale the wall, get in through the conservatory. Or

316

break down the front door: who's going to notice?' She looked at him. 'Who am I going to call?'

He made again to put his arms around her. This time she allowed it, but he could feel resistance.

'I'm sorry,' he repeated. 'If I'd known . . . if there'd been any way . . .' Friday night he'd switched off his mobile. Now he asked himself why. To conserve the battery? It was what he'd told himself back then, but maybe he'd been trying to block Fife off from everything else in his life; so busy thinking about Janice, he'd ignored Oakes's more obvious move. He kissed Patience's hair. Skewed perspectives, not thinking straight. Oakes was winning every fucking round. The bond Rebus felt with Janice was undeniable, but was all about failed chances. In the here and now, Patience was his lover. Patience was the one he was holding and kissing.

'It'll be all right,' he told her. 'Everything's going to be OK.'

She pulled away from him, wiped her eyes with the sleeve of her gown. 'Something funny's happened to your voice. You've gone all Fife.'

He smiled. 'I'll make us some tea. You go back to bed. If you need me, you know where I'll be.'

'And where's that?'

'Ben the scullery, hen.'

'It's got to be Oakes,' he said.

He'd called Siobhan to thank her. Patience had told him to ask her to lunch. So now, with the sun overhead, they were seated at the table in the conservatory. The Sunday papers lay unread in a pile in the corner. They ate Scotch broth, cooked ham and salad. A couple of bottles of wine had taken a pasting.

'Know what she did last night?' Patience had said – meaning Siobhan; talking to Rebus. 'Phoned to check I was all right. Said if I wasn't, I could sleep round at her place.' A lazy half-drunken smile, and she got up to make

317

the coffee. It was then that Rebus voiced his suspicions to Siobhan.

'Evidence?' she replied, before finishing her wine: just the two glasses – she was driving.

'Gut feeling. He's been watching my flat. He knows I was the last person to see Rough alive. He took Janice out, and now it's Patience's turn.'

'What has he got against you?'

'I don't know. Maybe it could have been any one of us; just so happens I got the short straw.'

'From what you say, he's more calculating than that.'

'Yes.' Rebus pushed a cherry tomato around the bed of lettuce on his plate. 'Patience said something a while back. She said it all could be some kind of tactic to keep us from seeing what he's really up to.'

'And what might that be?'

Rebus sighed. 'I wish to God I knew.' He studied the salad again. 'Remember when you could only get one kind of lettuce? One kind of tomato?'

'I'm too young.'

Rebus nodded thoughtfully. 'Do you think she'll be OK?' Meaning Patience.

'She'll be fine.'

'I should have been here.'

'She said you were in Fife. What were you doing there?'

'Living in the past,' he said, finally stabbing the tomato with his fork.

He spent the rest of the day with Patience. They took a walk in the Botanic Gardens, then dropped in on Sammy. Patience hadn't gone to see her on Saturday – had phoned to say something had come up, not elaborating. She had a lie prepared for their visit, briefed Rebus so he'd back her up. Another walk: this time with Sammy in the wheelchair. Rebus still felt awkward, going out with her in public. She teased him about it.

'Ashamed to be seen with a cripple?'

'Don't talk like that.'

'What is it then?'

But he had no answer for her. What was it? He didn't know himself. Maybe it was other people, the way they stared. He wanted to say: she's going to get better, she won't be in this thing forever. He wanted to explain how it had happened and how well she'd taken it. He wanted to tell them she was *normal*.

With Sammy in a wheelchair . . . it was like she was a toddler again, and he felt himself watching for bumps and dips in the pavement, for awkward kerbs and safe crossing-places. He was insistent they wait for the green man, even when there was no traffic in sight.

'Dad,' she would say, 'what are the odds of me getting hit again?'

'Don't forget, the bookies had us odds-on for Culloden.'

And she would laugh.

Her boyfriend Ned was with them, but Sammy insisted on pushing herself, leaning back to do wheelies and show her mastery of the vehicle. Ned laughed with her, walked alongside with hands in pockets. Patience slipped her hand into Rebus's.

A Sunday outing: that's what it was.

And afterwards, back at the flat there were cream cakes and mugs of Darjeeling, football highlights on the TV with the sound turned down. Sammy talking to Patience about her latest exercise regime. Ned talking to Rebus. Rebus not listening, his eyes half-turned to the window, wondering if Cary Oakes was out there . . .

That evening, he told Patience he had to go home. 'Couple of things I need. I'll be back later.' He kissed her. 'You all right here, or do you want to come with me?'

'I'll stay,' she said.

So Rebus got into his car and drove. Not to Arden Street but down to Leith. He walked into the hotel and asked to speak to Cary Oakes. Reception tried his room: no answer.

'Maybe he's in the bar,' the woman said.

But Cary Oakes was not in the bar – Jim Stevens was.

'Let me get you a drink,' he said. Rebus shook his head, noticed Stevens was on large G and Ts.

'Where's your boy?'

Stevens just shrugged.

'I thought you'd want to keep tabs on him,' Rebus said, trying to control his anger.

'I do, believe me. But he's a slippery little bugger.'

'How much more can you milk out of him?'

Stevens smiled, shaking his head. 'Something strange and wonderful has happened. You know me, Rebus, I'm what they call a seasoned hack, meaning I'm tough and I'm relentless and I don't take shit.'

'And?'

'And I think he's been giving me shit.' Stevens shrugged. 'It's not bad stuff, don't get me wrong. But where's the corroboration?'

'Since when has that stopped you?'

Stevens bowed his head, acknowledging the point. 'For my own satisfaction,' he added, 'I'd like to know. And along the way, dear old Cary seems to have managed to weasel almost as many stories out of me as I've had from him.'

'Oh, you've always been known for your reticence.'

'I don't mind telling stories . . . bit of repartee at the bar. But Oakes . . . I don't know. It's not the stories themselves that interest him so much as what they say about the people involved.' He picked up his drink. There were three empty glasses beside it. He'd decanted all the lemon slices into the most recent arrival. 'That probably makes no sense. I don't care: I'm off duty.'

'So are you finished with him?'

Stevens smacked his lips. 'I'd say we're getting there. The question is: is *he* finished with *me*?'

Rebus took out a cigarette and lit it, offered one to the reporter. 'He's been tailing me, people I know.'

'What for?'

'Maybe he wants another story for you.' Rebus moved closer. 'Listen, off the record, just two old bastards talking . . .'

Stevens blinked away some of the alcohol. 'Yes?'

'Has he said *anything* about Deirdre Campbell?' Stevens couldn't place the name. 'Alan Archibald's niece.'

'Oh, right.' An exaggerated nod, face dipping towards the gin glass, then a frown of concentration. 'He did say something about clear-up rates. Said that's what happened when they pinned you for something: they tried to tidy away a few unsolveds by sweeping them into your case-file.'

Rebus had eased himself on to a stool. 'He didn't mention specifics?'

'You think there's something I've missed?'

Rebus was thoughtful. 'You've said it yourself: you think he's using you.'

'By putting clues in his story that I'm not going to get? Give me a bit of credit.'

'He likes *games*,' Rebus hissed. 'That's all we are to him.'

'Not me, pal. I'm his sugar daddy.'

'Sugar daddies get cheated on.'

'John . . .' Stevens sat up straight, took a reviving lungful of air. 'This story's put me back on the map. *I* got to him first. Me, washed-up old Jim Stevens, gold-watch contestant. Even if he buggered off tonight, I'd have the best part of a book's-worth.' He nodded to himself, eyes on the glass he was picking up. Rebus found himself not believing the reporter. 'See, when I make a toast these days,' Stevens went on, raising his glass, 'it's only ever to Number One. As far as I'm concerned, pal, the rest of you can go straight to hell, no Just Visiting and no Free Parking.' He drank, drained the glass dry.

He was ordering another as Rebus made for the door.

35

When Rebus left Patience's next morning, she was out on the patio, discussing with two workmen how best to clean the paint off the flagstones. As he walked into St Leonard's and made for the CID suite, he could feel that something had happened. There was activity around him and the air felt charged. Siobhan Clarke was first with the news.

'Joanna Horman's lover.' She handed Rebus a report. 'He's dirty.'

Rebus glanced down the sheet. The lover's name was Ray Heggie. He'd done time for housebreaking and assorted acts of drunken violence. He was ten years older than Joanna. He'd been living with her for six weeks.

'Roy Frazer's got him in the interview room.'

'How come?' Rebus handed back the report.

'A previous girlfriend of Heggie's. She read about the kid going missing, phoned to tell us he'd abused her little girl. That was why they broke up.'

'She didn't think to tell us before?'

Clarke shrugged. 'She's told us now.'

Rebus twitched his nose. 'How old's the girl?'

'Eleven. Someone from Sex Offences is talking to her at home.' She looked at him. 'You're not buying it, are you?'

'*Caveat emptor*, Siobhan. I'll decide after the test drive.' He winked, moved away. An old girlfriend with a grudge, probably all it was. Saw a chance to make mischief . . . All the same, if Heggie was an abuser, maybe he'd known Darren Rough. Rebus knocked on the interview room door.

'Detective Inspector Rebus enters the room,' Frazer said,

for the benefit of the recording tape. He was following procedure: audio- *and* video-taping. 'Hi-Ho' Silvers sat beside him at one side of the table, arms folded, looking unimpressed by everything he'd heard. That was Silvers's role: say nothing, but make the suspect uncomfortable. Across the table sat a man in his forties, black curly hair with a pronounced bald spot. He hadn't shaved for a couple of days. His eyes were dark-ringed. He wore a black T-shirt, and ran his hands over thickly haired arms.

'Join the party,' was his comment to Rebus. The room was so small, Rebus stood by the wall, folding his own arms and preparing to listen.

'The locals organised a search party,' Frazer went on, 'you weren't part of it. How come?'

'I wasn't there.'

'Where were you?'

'Glasgow. I went out drinking with a mate, stayed the night at his place. Ask him, he'll tell you.'

'I'm sure he will. Mates are good that way, aren't they?'

'It's the truth.'

Frazer scribbled a note to himself. 'You went out drinking, that means there'll be witnesses.' He looked up from his notebook. 'So name me some.'

'Give me a break. Look, the pubs were all dead, so we got a carry-out and went back to his flat. Sat watching some videos.'

'Anything good?'

'Top-shelf stuff.' Heggie winked. Frazer just glared back.

'Porn?'

'That's what I said.'

'Straight?'

'I'm not a poof.' Heggie stopped rubbing his arms.

'I meant, was there any lezzie action?'

'Might have been.'

'Bondage? Animals? Kids?'

Heggie saw where this was leading. 'I'm not into any of that, I've told you.'

'Your ex says different.'

'That slut'd say anything. Wait till I see her . . .'

'Anything happens to her, Mr Heggie, if she so much as catches a cold, I'll have you back in here. Understood?'

'I didn't mean anything. It's just a saying, isn't it? But she's been slagging me off, telling people I've got AIDS, you name it. Vindictive, she is. Any chance of a cuppa?'

Frazer made a show of checking his watch. 'We'll take a break in five minutes.' Rebus had to stifle a smile, knowing they'd only break when Frazer was good and ready. 'You've got a record of violence, Mr Heggie. My thinking is: you lost patience with the kid, didn't mean to hurt him. But a valve blew, and next thing you knew he was dead.'

'No.'

'So you had to hide him somewhere.'

'No. I keep telling you—'

'Where is he then? How come he goes missing and you turn out to have a record of hurting kids?'

'All you've got is Belinda's word for it!' Belinda: the ex. 'I'm telling you, get a doctor to look at Fliss.' Fliss: the ex's daughter. 'And even if it turns out someone's been poking her, no way it was me. No fucking way. Ask her.' He scratched at his hair with one hand.

'We're doing that, Mr Heggie.'

'And if she says I did anything, her mum's put her up to it.' He was growing more agitated. 'I don't believe this, really I don't.' He shook his head. 'You lot told Joanna. Now what's she going to think?'

'Why do you always shack up with single mothers?'

Heggie raised his eyes to the ceiling. 'Tell me this is a bad dream.'

Frazer, who'd been resting his arms on the table, now sat back, glanced towards Rebus. It was the signal Rebus had been waiting for. It meant Frazer was finished for the moment.

'Did you know Darren Rough, Mr Heggie?' Rebus asked.

'He's the one that got topped?' He waited for Rebus to nod confirmation. 'Never knew him.'

'Never spoke to him?'

'We weren't in the same block.'

'You knew where he lived then?'

'It's been all over the papers. Perverted little bastard, whoever did it deserves a medal.'

'Why do you say he was "little"? He was, by the way. Not tall, at any rate. But it wasn't in the papers.'

'It's just . . . it's something you say, isn't it?'

'It's certainly something *you* say. Makes me think you'd seen him.'

'Maybe I had. It's not that big a scheme.'

'No, it's not,' Rebus said quietly. 'Everyone knows everyone else.'

'Until the council move in bastards they can't put anywhere else.'

Rebus nodded. 'So you might have seen Darren Rough around?'

'What difference does it make?'

'It's just that he liked young kids too. Paedophiles seem to be good at recognising one another.'

'I'm not a paedophile!' Losing it. His voice was trembling as he got to his feet. 'I'd kill every last one of them.'

'Did you start with Darren?'

'What?'

'Get rid of him, you'd be a hero.'

A burst of nervous laughter. 'So now I didn't just do in Billy, I topped the pervert as well?'

'Is that what you're telling us?' Rebus asked.

'I haven't killed anyone!'

'How did you get on with Billy, by the way? Must've been awkward, having him around, you wanting Joanna all to yourself.'

'He's a nice kid.'

'Sit down, Mr Heggie,' Frazer commanded.

Eventually Heggie sat down, but then leapt up again, his finger pointing at Rebus. 'He's trying to set me up!'

Rebus shook his head, gave a wry smile. He pushed off from the wall.

'I'm just after the truth,' he said, making to leave the room.

'Inspector Rebus leaving the interview room,' he could hear Frazer saying behind him.

Later, Frazer stopped off at Rebus's desk. 'You don't really make him for Darren Rough, do you?'

Rebus shrugged. 'Do you make him for the kid?'

'Maybe if Sex Offences come up with something. From what I hear, her mum's sticking to her like glue, answering for her, putting words in her mouth.'

'Doesn't mean she's lying.'

'No.' Frazer was thoughtful. 'Heggie doesn't give a shit about Billy Horman. All he's worried about is that Joanna will boot him out.' He shook his head slowly. 'People like him, you never get through to them, do you?'

'No.'

'And you can't get them to change.' He looked at Rebus. 'That's what you think too, isn't it?'

'Welcome to my world, Roy,' Rebus said, reaching for the telephone.

He had to keep working; had to stop letting thoughts of Cary Oakes consume him. So Rebus phoned Phyllida Hawes at Gayfield station.

'Has your MisPer turned up?' she asked.

'Not a bloody sign of him.'

'Well, that can be good news too, can't it? Means he's probably still alive.'

'Or the body's been well-hidden.'

'I do like an optimist.'

Another time, Rebus might have kept the banter going. 'You know Gaitano's?' he said instead, getting to the point.

'Yes.' Sounding curious, wondering what he was after.

'As owned by Charmer Mackenzie?'

'The same.'

'What have you got on him?'

Silence for a moment. 'Is he connected to your MisPer?'

'I'm not sure.' Rebus told her about the boat.

'Yes, I knew about that,' she said. 'But it's strictly a money thing. I mean, Mackenzie has a share, but he doesn't interfere with the business. You've met Billy Preston?' Rebus admitted he had. 'Charmer leaves him to get on with it.'

'Not quite. The under manager at Gaitano's, young guy called Archie Frost, he keeps an eye on the Clipper. Plus provides muscle for the door.'

'Is that so?' Rebus could hear her scribbling a note to herself.

'Does he have any other interests?' he asked.

'You might want to take this conversation to NCIS.'

NCIS: the National Criminal Intelligence Service. Rebus leaned forward in his chair. 'They have something on Mackenzie?'

'They have a file, yes.'

'So he's got dirt under his fingernails: what is it exactly?'

'Farmyard mud for all I know. Go talk to NCIS.'

'I will.' Rebus put the phone down, logged on at one of the computer terminals and entered Mackenzie's details. At the bottom of the screen there was a reference number and an officer's name. Rebus called NCIS and asked to speak to the name: Detective Sergeant Paul Carnett.

'That's a misprint,' the switchboard told him. 'It's not Paul, it's Pauline.' She put him through anyway, where a male voice told Rebus DS Carnett would be in a meeting for another hour, maybe an hour and a half. Rebus checked his watch.

'Has she anything after that?'

'Not that I can see.'

'Then I'd like to make a reservation: table for two, the name's DI Rebus.'

36

The Scottish office of NCIS was based at Osprey House in Paisley, not far off the M8. Last time Rebus had been this way had been to drop his ex-wife off at Glasgow Airport. She'd come up from London to see Sammy, and all the Edinburgh flights had been full. He couldn't remember what they'd talked about on the drive.

Osprey House was supposed to be the future of high-profile policing in Scotland, housing as it did the Scottish Crime Squad and Customs and Excise as well as NCIS and the Scottish Criminal Intelligence Office. Its remit was intelligence-gathering. Having started with just the two officers, NCIS now had a staff of ten. There had been bad feeling when the office had opened, due to the fact that the Scottish NCIS team reported not to a Scottish chief constable but to the London-based director of the whole UK operation, who in turn reported to the Scottish Secretary. NCIS dealt with counterfeiting, money-laundering, organised drug and vehicle crime, and, if Rebus remembered correctly, paedophile gangs. Rebus had heard the officers at NCIS called 'anoraks' and 'computer nerds', but not by anyone who'd actually met them.

'It's fairly irregular,' Pauline Carnett said, as Rebus explained why he was there.

They were seated in an open-plan office, around them the incessant humming of computer fans and quiet telephone conversations. The occasional flurry of key-board strokes. Young men in shirtsleeves and ties; two women, both dressed for business. Pauline's desk was at the opposite end of the room from the other woman officer. Rebus wondered if there was any significance in this.

Pauline Carnett was in her mid-thirties with short blonde hair brushed out from a centre parting. Tall and broad-shouldered, she had offered a handshake firmer than most Masons Rebus knew. She had a gap between her two front teeth and seemed overly conscious of the fact, which made Rebus want to make her smile.

Like all the others, her desk was L-shaped, with one surface given over to a computer, the other to paperwork. The office shared a printer. It was churning out work, a young man standing beside it, looking bored.

'So this is the heart of the machine,' had been Rebus's comment on entering the room.

Carnett put her cup down on a mouse pad stained with dozens of coffee rings. Rebus set his own cup on the worktop.

'Irregular,' she said again, as if he might be persuaded to leave. Instead, he just shrugged. 'Information is usually requested by telephone or fax.'

'I've always preferred the personal touch,' Rebus said. He handed her a scrap of paper on which he'd jotted the reference number concerning Charmer Mackenzie. She slid her chair closer to the desk and hammered on the keys, as if meaning to do violence to the keyboard. Then she slid the mouse around the pad, expertly avoiding the coffee cup, and double-clicked.

Charmer Mackenzie's file came up. Rebus saw straight away that there was a lot of stuff there. He moved his own chair closer to hers.

'Initially,' she said, 'it looks like we got on to him because Crime Squad had him hosting private parties for someone called Thomas Telford.'

'I know Telford,' Rebus said. 'I helped put him away.'

'Good for you. Telford used Mackenzie's club for meetings, and also rented a boat part-owned by Mackenzie. The boat was used for parties. Crime Squad kept tabs on it because you never knew who might turn up. Didn't get much joy, though: operation suspended.' She hit the return key, bringing up another page. 'Ah, here we go,' she said, leaning in towards the screen. 'Money-lending.'

'Mackenzie?'

She nodded. Rebus read over her shoulder. NCIS suspected Mackenzie of running a little business on the side, fronting money for criminal schemes – guaranteed payback, one way or another – but also loaning cash sums to people who either couldn't get the money elsewhere or had reasons not to go walking into a bank or building society.

'How accurate is this?' Rebus asked.

'It wouldn't be here if it wasn't one hundred per cent.'

'All the same . . .'

'All the same, there's obviously not enough to go on, or we'd have had him in court.' She pointed to an icon at the foot of the screen. 'Case-notes went to the Procurator Fiscal, who decided there wasn't enough for a prosecution.'

'So is the case ongoing?'

She shook her head. 'We have patience, we can wait. We'll see what else filters down to us, decide when the time's right to try again.' She glanced at him. 'Robert the Bruce and all that.'

Rebus was still studying the screen. 'Have you got names?'

'You mean people who've borrowed from him?'

'Yes.'

'Hang on.' She hit more keys, studied the information as it came up on the screen. 'Hard copies,' she mumbled at last. Then she got up from her seat and told him to follow her. They went to a storeroom filled with filing cabinets.

'So much for the paperless office,' Rebus said.

'I'm with you on that.' She found the cabinet she was looking for, pulled out the top drawer and started riffling through the file-holders, found the one she was looking for and pulled it out.

Inside the green file were about three dozen sheets of paper. Two of the sheets listed 'suspected' users of Charmer Mackenzie's loan scheme.

'No statements,' Rebus said, sifting the sheets.

'Case probably didn't get that far.'

'I thought it was your case.'

She shrugged. 'We get sent a lot of stuff from Crime Squad, Customs, wherever. It goes into the computer and into a drawer – that's my job.'

'You're a filing clerk?' Rebus suggested. Her eyes narrowed aggressively. 'Sorry,' he said. 'Trying to make a joke.' He went back to the file. 'So how did you come by these names?'

'Probably one or two people talked.'

'But didn't make reliable witnesses?'

She nodded. 'People who need to go to a loan shark, we're not talking public-minded citizens here.'

Rebus recognised a couple of names: known house-breakers. Maybe looking to finance some bigger scheme.

'Others on the list,' Carnett was saying, 'could be they got thumped by Mackenzie or his men, and Crime Squad got wind of it.'

'And nobody would talk?' Rebus guessed. She nodded again. He'd come across this before; they both had. It was fine to have seven bells knocked out of you, but a black mark to talk to the filth about it. You'd get 'GRASS' sprayed on your front door. People would cross the road to avoid you. Rebus started jotting down names and addresses, sure none of it was going to be any use. But he'd come all this way, after all.

'I can make copies,' Carnett suggested.

Rebus nodded. 'I'm a bit of a dinosaur, need to have the gist in my wee book.' He tapped one entry. No name, just a series of numbers. 'Is this what we're supposed to call Prince now?'

She smiled, covered it quickly with her hand. 'Looks like another reference,' she said. 'I'll check it back at my desk.'

So they went back there, and while Rebus finished his cold coffee, he watched her work.

'Interesting,' she said at last, leaning back in her chair. 'It's our way of keeping certain names quiet. Computers aren't always safe from prowlers.'

'Hackers.'

She looked at him. 'Not quite a dinosaur,' she commented. 'Wait here a minute.'

She was actually gone three minutes, long enough for her screen-saver to activate. When she returned, she had a single sheet of paper with her, which she handed to Rebus.

'We use numbers as codes when a name is judged too hot: that means someone we don't want everyone knowing about. Any idea who he is?'

Rebus was looking at the name on the sheet. There was nothing else printed there.

'Yes,' he said at last. 'He's a judge's son.'

'That would explain it then,' Pauline Carnett said, lifting her cup.

The name on the sheet was Nicol Petrie.

When they delved a little deeper, they found a Crime Squad report detailing a mugging attack. Nicol Petrie had been found unconscious in one of the shadowy back lanes off Rose Street – about a hundred yards from Gaitano's nightclub. Petrie had been taken by ambulance to hospital, a uniformed officer waiting to talk to him. But when he'd regained consciousness, he had had nothing to say.

'I can't remember,' had been his refrain. He couldn't even say if anything had been stolen from him. But a couple of eye-witnesses gave descriptions of two men leaving the lane. They were laughing, lighting cigarettes. One of them even complained that he'd scraped his knuckles. Police got as far as holding an ID parade for the witnesses, but by then they'd long since sobered up and wanted nothing to do with it, refused to identify anyone.

Two bouncers from Gaitano's had been in the parade: one of them was named as Calumn Brady.

Rebus went through the witness statements. The descriptions of the attackers were vague. He could just about see one of them – the shorter of the two – as Cal Brady. But it didn't matter. Nicol Petrie wasn't about to say anything, and the witnesses had either been warned off, paid off, or had just come to their senses.

Crime Squad put it down to a 'warning' from Mackenzie, and let it go at that. Speculation: that's all it was. But Rebus was willing to go along with it. All the same . . . something refused to click into place.

'Nicol's dad's a judge, plenty of money. Why didn't he just borrow from him?'

Pauline Carnett didn't have an answer for that.

Later, he asked if he could speak to someone from the paedophile unit. He was introduced to a woman officer called DS Whyte. He asked her about Darren Rough. She brought the details up on her screen.

'What about him?' she said.

'Known associates.'

She hammered keys, shook her head. 'He was a loner. NKA.'

NKA: No Known Associates. Rebus scratched his chin. 'How about Ray Heggie.'

She hit more keys. 'No record,' she said at last. 'Is he someone I should know about?'

Rebus shrugged.

'In that case . . .' she said, adding the name to her screen. Rebus's name went there too. 'Just so I know where I first heard of him.'

Rebus nodded. 'Have you been following Shiellion?'

'I hear the jury's out. Looking good for guilty.'

'Not if Richie Cordover has anything to do with it.'

'He's good, but I've come across Lord Justice Petrie before, and if there's one thing he can't stand, it's a paedophile. The way Petrie summed up, Ince and Marshall are fucked.'

'Not before time,' Rebus added, getting up to go.

37

Back in Edinburgh, he was wanted at Fettes – by the ACC, no less.

The Assistant Chief Constable (Crime) was known to be scrupulous, fair, and to have no record of suffering fools gladly. He had a nice fat file on Rebus which told him the officer was 'difficult but useful'. Rebus had made a career out of making enemies. The ACC, whose name was Colin Carswell, liked to think of himself as not among them.

There was an identifying plaque on the door, and the room number below it: 278. The room itself was large, with institutional carpet and curtains, and a bowl of flowers on the windowsill. There was little other decoration. Carswell, tall and thin with a good head of salt-and-pepper hair and moustache to match, rose from his chair just long enough to shake Rebus's hand. Typically, he didn't sit behind his desk for interviews, but conducted them in two chairs by the window. The chairs were swivel designs and sat on castors, so that unwary officers could find themselves spinning a hundred and eighty degrees or sliding backwards towards Carswell's desk. After an interview like that, most agreed they'd have settled for the old-fashioned kind.

Which, the ACC might have told them, was the whole point of the exercise.

The dark eyes spoke of lost sleep. Despite his advancing years, the ACC had recently become a father for the fourth time. As his other kids were all grown-up, the conclusion reached by every station in the city was that the new addition was an accident, which would make it practically the only thing in the ACC's life that he'd not been able to orchestrate or control.

'How are you, John?' he asked.

'Not bad, sir. How's the wee one?'

'Fit as a fiddle. Look, John . . .' Carswell never wasted time on preliminaries. 'I've been asked to look into this murder case.'

'Darren Rough?'

'That's the one.'

'Social Work, was it, sir?' Rebus settled his hands on the arm rests.

'Fellow called Andrew Davies. Made a sort of complaint.'

'Sort of?'

'Couched fairly ambiguously.'

'He's probably got a point, sir.'

The ACC held his breath for a second. 'Am I hearing you right?'

'I chased Rough through the zoo without probable cause, giving our poisoner the chance to strike again. Then when I found out Rough was living upstairs from a playground, I put word out on the street.'

Carswell put his hands together, as if in prayer. Knowing Rebus's reputation, a confession was the last thing he'd been expecting. 'You outed him?'

'Yes, sir. I wanted him off my patch. At the time . . .' Rebus paused. 'I didn't work through the consequences. Later on, I helped him get away from Greenfield – at least, that was the plan. Only he left my flat and got himself murdered. Right at the end, though . . . I think I did try to make amends.'

'I see. You want me to take this to Social Work?'

'That's up to you, sir.'

'Then what *do* you want?'

Rebus looked at him. It was bright outside: another ploy of the ACC's – he tended to use the chair trick when it was sunny. All Rebus could see of his superior was a haze of light.

'For a while, I thought I wanted out, sir. Maybe that was in my mind when I went after Rough: if I went after him hard, I might end up kicked off the force, but still feel all right about it.'

'But that didn't happen.'

'It hasn't happened yet, sir, no.'

Carswell was thoughtful. 'How do you feel now?'

Rebus squinted into the light. 'I'm not sure. Tired, mostly.' He managed a smile.

'A long time back, John – I know you all like to think I've spent my whole life behind a desk – but a long time back there was this man got himself into a fight down in Leith. Clean-cut type, suit and everything. Wife and kids at home. And he'd walked into a pub by the dockside, looked for the biggest, meanest-looking bugger he could find, and started having a go at him. I was young back then, they sent me to interview him in hospital. Turned out he'd been trying to commit suicide, hadn't had the guts. So he'd gone looking for someone to do the job for him. Sounds a bit like what you were up to with Darren Rough: assisted career suicide.'

Rebus smiled again, but he was thinking: *Suicide again . . . like with Jim Margolies. Assisted career suicide . . .*

'I don't think I'm going to give this to our friends in Social Work,' the ACC said finally. 'I think I'm going to sit on it for a while. Maybe there's room for some sort of apology . . . that'll be up to you.'

'Thank you, sir.'

'And John,' rising to his feet, taking Rebus's hand again, 'I appreciate you not trying to spin me some yarn.'

'Yes, sir.' Rebus was on his feet, too. 'And maybe, with respect, sir, there's a way you could show your appreciation . . .'

Nicol Petrie lived in a West End flat, sprawling over the

338

top two floors of a Georgian pile. There was a shared entrance hall with occasional tables and rugs. The tables had vases and things on them. It was a far cry from the tenement stairwells Rebus was used to.

And there was a lift, its mirrored interior highly polished, the wooden surrounds gleaming. Beside the buttons for each floor were printed labels listing the occupants. There were two Petries: N and A. Rebus guessed that A stood for Amanda.

The lift brought Rebus out on to a landing, glass cupola above. Pot plants surrounded him. And more carpeting. Nicol Petrie opened the door and gave a little nod, leading Rebus inside.

Rebus had been expecting antiquity, but was disappointed. The flat's walls were painted an almost luminous white and were devoid of paintings or posters. The floors had been stripped and varnished. It was like stepping into an Ikea catalogue. An internal stairway led up to the top floor, but Nicol led Rebus past it and into the living room, fully thirty-five feet long and twelve high, and with double sash windows giving uninterrupted views across Dean Valley and the Water of Leith. The Fife coastline was visible in the distance. Walking into the room, taking it all in, Rebus missed the doll on the floor and ended up giving it a kick, sending it flying towards its owner.

'Jessica!' the little girl squealed, moving on hands and knees to pick up her property and nurse it to her bosom. Then she slid back across the floor to where a toys' tea-party was in progress. Rebus apologised, but Hannah Margolies wasn't listening.

'Hello again,' Hannah's mother said. She was seated on a white sofa. 'Sorry about that. Hannah's toys get everywhere.' She sounded tired. Rebus noted that she still wore black, albeit a short black dress with black tights. Mourning as fashion statement.

'Sorry,' he said to Nicol Petrie, 'I didn't know you had company.'

'You know one another?' Petrie bowed his head at the stupidity of the question. 'Through Jim, of course. Sorry.'

It seemed to Rebus that all anyone had done so far was make apologies. Katherine Margolies got to her feet in a sudden elegant movement.

'Come on, Han-Han. Time to go.'

Hannah didn't argue or complain, just rose to her feet and joined her mother.

'Nicky,' Katherine said, kissing both his cheeks, 'thanks as ever for listening.'

Nicol Petrie embraced her, then crouched down for a kiss from Hannah. Katherine Margolies lifted Hannah's coat from the back of the sofa.

'Goodbye, Inspector.'

'Bye, Mrs Margolies. Bye, Hannah.'

Hannah gave him a look. 'You think I should have won, don't you?'

Katherine stroked her daughter's hair. 'Everyone knows you were robbed, sweetheart.'

Hannah was still staring at Rebus. 'Someone stole my father,' she said.

Nicol Petrie made a fuss of her as he showed mother and daughter to the door. When he returned to the room, Rebus was standing at one of the windows, looking down into the street immediately below. Petrie began tidying the toys into a cardboard box.

'Sorry again if I disturbed you, sir,' Rebus said, not managing much enthusiasm for the lie.

'That's all right. Katy often pops in unannounced. Especially since . . . well, you know.'

'Do you make a good listener, Mr Petrie?'

'No more than most, I don't suppose. Usually it's because I can't think of anything helpful to say, so all I do is fill the gaps with questions.'

'You'd make a good detective then.'

Petrie laughed. 'I rather doubt that, Inspector.' He opened one of the doors leading off the living room. It led

340

to a walk-in cupboard. There were shelves inside, and he placed the box of toys on one of them. Everything tidied away. Rebus would bet the box always went back on the same shelf, always the same spot. He'd known people like that, people who managed their lives by compartments. Siobhan Clarke was just the same: if you wanted to annoy her, you only had to move something of hers from one desk-drawer to its neighbour.

Below him, Katherine Margolies and her daughter emerged from the building. Their car had remote locking. It was a Mercedes saloon, new-looking. The number plate was the same one he'd seen lipsticked on the wall in Leith.

It was a white Mercedes.

White . . .

'Has it hit her hard?' he asked, still watching from the window.

'Devastated, I should think.'

'And the little one?'

'I'm not sure Han-Han's taken it in yet. Like she said, she thinks he's been stolen from her.'

'She's right in a way.'

'I suppose so.' Petrie came to the window, watched with Rebus as the car drove off. 'Nobody could fail to be shocked by something like that.'

'Why do you think he did it?'

Petrie looked at him. 'I haven't the faintest idea.'

'His widow hasn't said anything?'

'That's between her and me.'

'Sorry,' Rebus said. 'It's just curiosity. I mean, someone like Jim Margolies . . . it makes you ask questions of yourself, doesn't it?'

'I think I know what you mean.' Petrie turned back into the room. 'If you've got it all and you're still unhappy, what's the point of everything?' He slumped into a chair. 'Maybe it's a Scottish thing.'

Rebus took a seat on the sofa. 'What is?'

'We're just not supposed to have it all, are we? We're

341

supposed to fail gloriously. Anything we succeed at, we keep low-profile. It's our failures we're allowed to trumpet.'

Rebus smiled. 'Might be something in that.'

'It runs right through our history.'

'And ends at the national football team.'

It was Petrie's turn to smile. 'I've been very rude: can I offer you something to drink?'

'What are you having?'

'I thought maybe a glass of wine. I'd opened a bottle for Katy, thinking she'd come by taxi. Parking around here is hellish.' He left the room, Rebus following. The kitchen was long and narrow and spotless. The hob looked like it had never been used. Petrie went to the fridge, lifted out a bottle of Sancerre.

'Lovely flat,' Rebus said, as Petrie reached into a cupboard for two glasses.

'Thank you. I like it.'

'What do you work at, Mr Petrie?'

Petrie glanced at him. 'I'm a student, second year into my PhD.'

'Was your first degree at Edinburgh?'

'No, St Andrews.' Pouring now.

'Not many students with flats as grand as this – or am I behind the times?'

'It's not mine.'

'Your father's?' Rebus guessed.

'That's right.' Pouring the second glass; looking a little less serene now.

'He must like you.'

'He loves his children, Inspector. I'd assume most parents do.'

Rebus thought of himself and Sammy. 'Not always a two-way thing, though, is it?'

'I don't know what you mean.'

Rebus shrugged, accepted the glass. 'Cheers.' He took a sip. Petrie was at the end of the narrow kitchen: no way out of there except past Rebus. And Rebus wasn't moving. 'Funny thing is, if I'd a father who loved me, who'd spent a fortune on a flat for me, any time I got into trouble I'd probably turn to him to bail me out.'

'Look, what's—'

'Say, if I needed money. I wouldn't go to a loan shark.' Rebus paused, took another sip. 'How about you, Mr Petrie?'

'Christ, is that what this is about? Those two thugs giving me a kicking?'

'Maybe it wasn't about money. Maybe they just didn't like your looks.' Nicol Petrie: face unblemished, thin dark eyebrows, high cheekbones. A face so perfect you might just want to damage it.

'I don't know what they wanted.'

Rebus smiled. 'Yes you do. That handy amnesia of yours, you let it slip. You shouldn't have known there were two of them.'

'The police said as much at the time.'

'Two men employed by Charmer Mackenzie. We call them "frighteners", and believe me, I'd have been frightened too. He's a hard bastard, Cal Brady, isn't he?'

'Who?'

'Cal Brady. You must have come across him.'

Petrie shook his head. 'I don't think so.'

'How much was it you owed? I'm assuming you've paid it off by now. And why didn't you tap your dad for a loan in the first place? See, I'm curious, Mr Petrie, and when I start asking questions, I tend not to give up till I've found answers.'

Petrie put his glass down on the worktop. He wasn't looking at Rebus when he spoke. 'This is strictly between us? No way I'm taking this any further.'

'Fair enough,' Rebus said.

Petrie folded his arms around himself, looking skinnier than ever. 'I did borrow money from Mackenzie. We knew, those of us who frequented the Clipper, knew he'd lend money. And I found myself needing some. My father can be generous when it suits him, Inspector, but I'd managed to fritter away a good deal of his money. I didn't want him knowing. So I went to Mackenzie instead.'

'Surely you could have arranged an overdraft?'

'I dare say I could.' Petrie looked away. 'But there was something . . . the idea of dealing with Mackenzie was so much more appealing.'

'How so?'

'The danger, the whiff of the illicit.' He turned back towards Rebus. 'You know Edinburgh society loves that sort of thing. Deacon Brodie didn't need to break into people's houses, but that didn't stop him. Strait-laced old town, how else are we going to get our thrills?'

Rebus stared at him. 'Know something, Nicky? I almost believe you. Almost, but not quite.' He raised a hand towards Petrie, who flinched. But all Rebus did was place a fingertip against the young man's temple. It came away with a bead of perspiration clinging to it. The droplet fell, splashed onto the worktop.

'Better wipe that up,' Rebus said, turning away. 'You wouldn't want anything marking that stainless surface of yours, would you?'

38

There was still no sign of Billy Horman.

His mother Joanna had cried at the press conference, ensuring TV coverage. Ray Heggie, Joanna's lover, had sat beside her, saying nothing. When the crying started, he'd tried to comfort her, but she'd pushed him away. Rebus knew he'd drift away eventually, as long as he was innocent.

GAP was as active as ever. They were holding a vigil outside the High Court while the jury retired to reach a verdict in the Shiellion case. They'd lit candles and tied placards to the railings. The placards detailed child-killers and paedophiles and their victims. The police were instructed not to move the protesters on. Meantime, there were fresh news reports of paedophiles being released from prison. GAP sent members to the relevant towns. It had become a movement now, Van Brady its unlikely figure-head. She hosted her own news conferences, blown-up photos of Billy Horman and Darren Rough on the wall behind her.

'The world,' she'd said at one meeting, 'should be a green field without limits, where our children can play free from harm, and where parents can leave their children without fear. That is the purpose and intention of the Green Field Project.'

Rebus wondered who was writing her speeches for her. GFP was a departure for GAP, a funding application to set up patrolled play areas with security cameras and the like. To Rebus, it sounded less like the world as green field, more like the world as prison camp. They were applying to the Lottery and the EC for cash. Other housing schemes had made successful bids in the past, and were lending a hand to Greenfield. They wanted something like two million quid. Rebus shuddered to think of Van and Cal Brady in charge of such a fund.

But then it wasn't his problem, was it?

His immediate problem, as he knew when he picked up the ringing phone, was Cary Oakes.

The voice on the line belonged to Alan Archibald. 'He's agreed.'

'Agreed to what?'

'To go out to Hillend with me. To walk across the hills.'

'He's admitted it?'

'As good as.' Archibald's voice shook with excitement.

'But has he said anything *specific*?'

'Once we get out there, John, I know he'll tell me, one way or the other.'

'You're going to torture him, are you?'

'I don't mean it like that. I mean once he's there, the scene of the crime, I think he'll crack.'

'I wouldn't be so sure. What if it's a trap?'

'John, we've been through this.'

'I know.' Rebus paused. 'And you're still going.'

The voice quiet now, calm. 'I've got to, whatever happens.'

'Yes,' Rebus said. Of course Archibald would go. It was his destiny. 'Well, count me in.'

'I'll ask him—'

'No, Alan, you'll *tell* him. It's both of us or no go.'

'What if he—'

'He won't. Trust me on this. I think he'll want me out there too.'

The tape was still running, but Cary Oakes hadn't spoken for a couple of minutes. Jim Stevens was used to it, used to long pauses as Oakes gathered his thoughts. He let another sixty seconds spool on before asking: 'Anything else, Cary?'

Oakes looked surprised. 'Should there be?'

'That's it then?' Still Stevens left the tape running. Oakes only nodded, and reached his hands behind his head, job done. Stevens checked his watch, spoke the time into the machine, then squeezed the Stop button. He slipped the recorder into the breast pocket of his pale mauve shirt. It was pale because it had been through about three hundred washes in the five years since Stevens had bought it. He knew the other reporters thought he'd filled out in the past half-decade. The shirt could have proved them wrong, but would also have proved how seldom he bought new clothes.

'Satisfied?' Oakes said, getting to his feet, stretching as if after a long day at the coal-face.

'Not really. Journalists never are.'

'Why's that?'

'Because no matter how much we're told, we *know* we're not getting everything.'

Oakes held his hands out. 'I've given you blood, Jim. I feel like you've taken a transfusion from me.' That unnerving grin again; so lacking in humour. Stevens wrote date and time on a sticker, peeled it off and placed it down one edge of the cassette case. He made this tape number eleven. Eleven hours of Cary Oakes. It wasn't enough for a book, but it might get him the contract, and the rest of the book could be padded: trial reports, interviews, photographs.

Only thing was, he didn't think he was going to find a publisher. He wasn't even going to try.

'What are you thinking, big man?' Oakes asked. He'd taken to calling Stevens 'big man'. Stevens wasn't naive enough to take it as a compliment; at best it was weighted with irony.

'I'm ... not really thinking at all.' Stevens shrugged. 'Just that it's over, that's all.'

'So now it's pay-off time for old Cary.'

'You'll get your cheque.'

'What good's a cheque? I said cash.'

Stevens shook his head. 'A cheque, has to be or our accounts department would have a breakdown. You can use it to open a bank account.'

'And sit around how long waiting for it to clear?' Oakes had been pacing the room. Now he came to Stevens' chair and leaned down over him, staring him out. Stevens blinked first, which seemed victory enough for Oakes. He propelled himself back upright and angled his head to the ceiling, letting out a whoop of laughter. Then he leaned down again long enough to pat one of Stevens' resilient cheeks.

'It's OK, Jim, really it is. I never really needed the money anyway. What I needed was for you to think you had me by the balls.'

'I never ever thought that, Oakes.'

'No more first names, huh? Did I upset you or something?'

Stevens shook the tape box. 'How much of this is crap?'

Oakes grinned again. 'How much do you think, partner?'

'I don't know. That's why I'm asking.' He saw Oakes glance towards the clock by the bed. 'Going somewhere?'

'My work here's finished. Nothing to keep me.'

'Where are you going?' Stevens didn't know why, but while Oakes had been laughing, he'd switched the recorder back on. Situated as it was in his shirt pocket, he didn't know how much it would pick up. He could hear its small motor working, feel it grinding against his chest.

'Why should you care?'

'I'm a reporter. You're still a story.'

'You haven't seen the best of it, Jimmy baby.'

Stevens ran a dry tongue over his lips.

'Do I scare you, Jim?'

'Sometimes,' Stevens admitted.

'You're bigger than me, heavier anyway. You could take me, couldn't you?'

'It's not always down to size.'

'True, true. Sometimes it's down to just how rip-roaring crazy and ferocious your opponent is. Is there a touch of madness in me, Jimbo?'

Stevens nodded slowly. 'And ferocity too,' he added.

'You better believe it.' Oakes was examining himself in the wall-mirror, running a hand over his cropped head. 'And it's a hungry madness, Jim. It wants me to eat people up.' A sly sideways look. 'Not you, though, don't worry on that score.'

'What score should I worry on?'

'You'll find out soon enough.' He studied himself in the mirror again. 'I have a date with my past, Jim. A date with destiny, as you and your fellow hacks might put it. With someone who never listened to me.' He was nodding to himself. 'Just one last thing, Jim.' Turning towards the journalist. 'I knew when I came out I'd be telling my story. I've had a long time to get it straight.'

' "Straight" rather than true?'

'You're smarter than you look, Jimbo.' Oakes laughed.

Stevens' heart beat a little faster. It was what he'd suspected for some days, but that didn't make it any easier to hear.

'Some of it must have been accurate,' he managed to utter.

'Scots are a nation of storytellers, Jim, isn't that right?' He patted Stevens' cheek again, then headed for the door. 'It was all shit, Jim. Remember that till the day you die.'

After the door had closed on Oakes, Stevens put his head in his hands and sat there for a few moments, relieved it was all over, whatever the outcome. When his phone rang, he remembered the recorder in his pocket. Removed it and switched it off, rewound and hit Play.

Oakes's voice had grown small and tinny, but no less devilish. *It was all shit, Jim.* He turned off the tape and went to answer the phone. Cleared his throat first, sat down on the edge of the bed.

'Hello?' he said into the receiver.

'Jim, is that you? Peter Barclay here.'

Barclay worked for a rival tabloid. 'What do you want, Peter?'

'Caught you at a bad time?' Barclay chuckled. He always spoke with a cigarette in his mouth. It made him sound like a bad ventriloquist.

'You might say that.'

'I do say that. Your boy's been telling tales out of school.'

'What?' Stevens stopped rubbing the back of his neck.

'He's sent a letter to all your lovely competitors, saying his "autobiography" is complete bollocks. Any comment to make, Jim? On the record, naturally.'

Stevens slammed the receiver back into its cradle, then swiped the apparatus off the bedside table and on to the floor.

'Number disconnected,' he said, giving it a kick for good measure.

39

There was mist on the Pentland Hills, leaching colour from the landscape and threatening to cut Hillend and Swanston off from the city just north of them.

'I don't like it,' Rebus said as they parked.

'Afraid we'll get lost?' Cary Oakes smiled. 'Wouldn't that be a blow to humanity?'

He was sitting in the passenger seat, Alan Archibald in the back. Rebus hadn't wanted Oakes in the back; had wanted him where he could see him. Before setting off, he'd insisted on patting Oakes down. Oakes had asked if Rebus would reciprocate.

'I'm not the killer here,' Rebus had said.

'I'll take that as a no.' Oakes had turned to Archibald. 'I thought it would just be the two of us. More intimate that way.' Nodding towards Rebus. 'No need for outsiders, Mr Archibald.'

'You're going nowhere without me,' Rebus had said.

And here they were. Archibald seemed nervous. Getting out of the car, he dropped his Ordnance Survey map. Oakes picked it up for him.

'Maybe we should leave a little trail of breadcrumbs,' he suggested.

'Let's just get on with it,' Archibald answered, nerves lending his voice an edge of irritation.

Rebus was looking around. No other cars in the vicinity; no hill-walkers; no sounds of dogs being exercised.

'Creepy, isn't it?' Oakes said. He was donning a cheap green kagoul.

Rebus's jacket had an integral hood. He rolled it out but didn't put it over his head. He knew it would work like a pair of blinkers, and didn't want to be deprived of his peripheral vision. Archibald had a flat tweed cap with him, and was wearing hiking boots. Cap and boots looked brand new: they'd been waiting on this day for a while.

'Drinkie anyone?' Oakes said, taking out a hip flask. Rebus stared at him. 'You going to be scowling like that all day?' Oakes laughed. 'Got something you want to get off your mind, maybe?'

'Plenty.' Rebus's fists were clenched.

'Not here, John,' Archibald pleaded. 'Not now.'

Eyes on Rebus, Oakes held out the flask to Archibald, who shook his head. Oakes tipped the flask to his own mouth, showing them the liquid trickling in. He swallowed noisily.

'See,' he said, 'it's not poisoned.' He made the offer again, and this time Archibald took a sip. 'I had them fill it at the hotel bar.' He took the flask back from Archibald. 'And yourself, Inspector?'

Rebus took the flask, sniffed its contents. Christ, it did smell good, but he handed it back untouched.

'Balvenie,' he said. 'If I'm not mistaken.'

Oakes laughed again; Archibald forced a smile.

'I thought you didn't drink,' Rebus said.

'I don't, but this is in the nature of a special occasion, wouldn't you say?'

Then Archibald started unfolding the map, and it became business, Oakes studying the area intently, aware of Rebus immediately behind him, and finally saying: 'I'm not sure this is going to be much use.' He looked around. 'I think I'm going to have to follow my nose.' He glanced at Archibald. 'Sorry about that.'

'Just take me to where she was killed,' the older man said.

'Maybe you should lead the way,' Oakes said. 'After all, I've never been here before.' And he gave a wink.

They started walking.

Eventually Rebus said: 'Another game, Oakes?'

Oakes stopped walking, caught his breath. 'You know how the song goes, Inspector: we can't go on together, if you're going to have a suspicious mind. Far as I'm concerned, we're just out for a breath of country air. Besides, I'm curious to see where the body was found.'

'You know damned well where the body was found!' Alan Archibald snapped.

Oakes turned his lips into a pout. Rebus wanted to see blood there, wanted teeth dislodged and a gushing nose. Instead, his fingernails bit more deeply into his palms.

'Did you kill her?' he asked.

'Kill her when?'

Rebus felt his voice rising. 'Did you kill her?'

Oakes wagged a finger. 'I might not have been back that long, but don't think I don't know how it's played. There are two of you. Anything I admit, you've got corroboration.'

'This is between ourselves,' Alan Archibald said. 'It's gone beyond anything I'd take to the police.'

Oakes smiled. 'How long have you been chasing ghosts? If I say I killed her, will you rest easy in your bed?' Archibald didn't answer. 'How about you, Inspector: any ghosts keeping *you* awake at night?'

As if he knew. Rebus tried not to show anything, but Oakes was nodding, smiling to himself. 'A career littered with bodies, man,' Oakes went on, 'and I'm the one they lock up.' He paused. 'Tell me something,' folding his arms, eyes on Archibald now, 'how did the killer get her up here? Long way to bring a victim.'

'She was terrified.'

'What if she wasn't? What if she was willing? She'd been out drinking, right? Feeling a bit horny . . .'

'Shut up, Oakes.'

'I thought you *wanted* me to talk?' He opened his arms wide. 'I might just be speculating here, but say he picked her up, drove her up here. Say it's exactly what she wanted. I mean, this is a complete stranger she's in the car with, but tonight she's in the mood for *danger*. She feels reckless. Who knows, maybe she even *wants* it to happen.'

Archibald turned on him, waving his fist. 'Don't talk about her like that.'

'I'm just—'

'You abducted her. Knocked her cold and dragged her up here.'

'Any signs of a struggle, Al? Huh? Did the post-mortem show she'd been dragged anywhere?'

Archibald looked at him. 'You know it didn't.'

More laughter. 'No, Al, I don't know jack-shit. I'm just guessing, that's all. Same as you are.'

Oakes started walking again. The wind was rising, a fine rain blowing into their faces, threatening to drench them. Rebus looked back. Already the car was lost to view.

'It's OK,' Archibald assured him. 'I'm marking our route as we go.' He had the map folded, tapped a pen against one of the contour lines.

Rebus took the map from him, wanting to be sure. He'd done map-reading in the army. It looked like Archibald knew what he was doing. Rebus nodded and handed the map back. But the look in Archibald's eyes, that mix of fear and expectation . . . Rebus patted his shoulder.

'Come on, slowcoaches,' Oakes said, waiting till they caught up.

'You took it too far,' Rebus told him.

'Huh?'

'Your little joke with the skip, I didn't mind that so much. But the cemetery, the patio . . . no way you're getting away with those.'

'You're forgetting your old flame.' Oakes turned towards him. There wasn't more than a foot or two between them. 'I talked to her, remember? How come

354

she's not on your little hit-list? She told me the two of you might be hooking up again.' He tutted. 'Don't tell me you're going to let her down? Does she know?'

Rebus caught Oakes a glancing blow. Fist barely connected with cheek, Oakes arching back on the balls of his feet. Fast, he was hellish fast. Didn't change his stance, so confident, so sure of his opponent. Archibald's arms wrapped themselves around Rebus, but Rebus shrugged them off.

'I'm fine,' he said, voice lacking emotion.

'Want some more?' Oakes threw open his arms. 'I'm right here, man.' There was a graze on his cheek, but he paid it no notice.

Rebus *knew* he couldn't afford to lose it; had to stay calm. But Oakes had crawled all the way under his skin. Laughing at him now, putting a theatrical hand to his face.

'Ouch! That *stings*.' Laughing all the time. Then walking away, and now it was Archibald's turn to pat Rebus's shoulder.

'I'm OK,' Rebus told him, making after Oakes.

A little later, Oakes stopped. Visibility was down to a hundred yards, maybe less. 'Where's Swanston Village from here?' he asked. He seemed to have forgotten all about Rebus. Archibald checked the map, pointed with his finger. He was pointing into swirling smoke, pointing into nothingness.

'It's like bloody *Brigadoon*,' Rebus said, lighting a cigarette. Oakes took a bar of chocolate from his pocket, offered it around.

'You know,' he said, 'I'm amazed you're trusting me. Not you, Mr Archibald, you've got no choice. But the Inspector here.' Oakes fixed Rebus with his dark, peering eyes. 'You're a hard man to figure.'

'And you're full of shite.'

'Please, John . . .' Archibald had a hand on Rebus's shoulder. Despite his clothing, he looked cold and tired and suddenly so very old. Rebus realised what this meant to him: an answer, one way or another. Either Oakes had killed his niece – in which case there could be proper grieving – or someone else had, in which case he'd wasted these years with his pet theory, and her killer was still out there somewhere . . .

'OK, Alan,' Rebus said. The three of them out here: an old man, a nutter with shorn head and piercing eyes, and John bloody Rebus. Oakes enjoying every moment, Archibald looking as brittle as the chocolate bar.

And Rebus? Trying hard not to add another body to the hill's death toll.

Oakes offered Archibald his flask, and Archibald took a grateful drink. Rebus declined, and Oakes screwed the top back on.

'Not having one yourself?' Rebus asked.

Oakes ignored him, offered him chocolate instead. Rebus again refused.

'So where exactly are we going?' Oakes asked.

'It's not far now,' Archibald told him.

Oakes saw Rebus studying him. 'Got any questions for me yourself, John? Any unsolveds you want to pin on me?'

'Anything in particular you want me to ask?'

'Nicely put, sir. I see someone killed Darren Rough.'

'You were outside my flat that night.'

'Was I?'

'You took the car.' Rebus paused. 'You saw Rough leave.'

'Man, I was busy that night, wasn't I?' Rebus stared him out. Oakes came close, leaned in towards him as if to speak confidentially. Rebus moved away. 'I'm not going to bite,' Oakes said.

'Say what you were going to say.'

Oakes put on a wounded look. 'I don't know if I want to now.' Then he grinned. 'But I will anyway. I saw him leave your place, even followed him for a while. I wondered who he was, only found out later when I saw his picture in the paper.'

'What happened?'

'You tell me. I lost him.' Oakes shrugged. 'He cut across The Meadows. No way to follow in a car.' He gave another wink.

'This is all just another part of your little—'

'Don't say it!' Alan Archibald screeched. 'Don't say it's a game! It's not a game, not to me!' He was shaking.

Rebus pointed to Oakes, but spoke to Archibald. 'This is what he wants. You thought by bringing him up here you'd have the upper hand. Don't you think he knew that, played on it? Look at him, Alan, he's laughing at you. He's laughing at all of us!'

'I'm not laughing.' And it was true: Oakes was stony-faced, his eyes on Archibald. He walked up to him, touched his arm. 'Sorry,' he said. 'Come on, you're right – we've got work to do.'

He started walking again. Archibald made to apologise to Rebus, but Rebus waved it aside. Oakes was moving off at a brisk pace, as if determined to finish things. That look on his face . . . Rebus couldn't read it. There had been something there, a gloss of sympathy. But beneath it he thought he detected something more feral, itself mixed with something like the curiosity of the scientist when faced with some unexpected result.

Visibility was decreasing as they climbed.

'You've been playing a little game with *me*, haven't you, Al?'

'What do you mean?'

'Come on, Al, the route you've brought us, we've already been past the spot where she was killed. I bet you've got it all planned so we'll end up circling it. You want me rattled, don't you, Al? It's not going to happen.'

'How do you know where she was killed?' Rebus asked.

'I got all the newspapers. Plus Al kept sending me stuff, didn't you, Al?'

'You said you never read any of it,' Archibald said, trying to catch his breath.

'So I lied. Thing is, I'm getting a picture in my head . . . They had sex further up the slope. Then she panicked, ran back down. That's when he hit her. But where they had sex . . . he left something behind.'

'What?'

'Hidden.'

'What?'

'Alan, he's—'

Archibald turned on Rebus. 'Shut up!' he hissed.

'I'm seeing three hillocks,' Oakes called back. 'If there's a line of hillocks anywhere nearby, I'd be interested to see them.'

'Hillocks . . . ?' Archibald broke into a trot, trying to reach Oakes. He had the map in front of his face, seeking the corresponding contours. 'Maybe just to the west.'

Rebus hadn't seen him mark anything on the map with his pen, not for a while.

'How's our position, Alan?'

But Archibald wasn't listening, not to Rebus.

'Maybe three-quarters of the way up the slope,' Oakes was saying. 'A line of three . . . maybe four . . . but three distinct outcrops, similar heights.'

'Hang on a second,' Archibald said. His finger scratched over the map. He folded it smaller, brought it closer to his face, blinked so as to focus better. 'Yes, just to the west. That way, about a hundred yards.'

He started to climb. Oakes was already on his way, Rebus bringing up the rear. He looked behind him: couldn't see a damned thing. It was a landscape out of time. Kilted warriors might have emerged from that mist and he wouldn't have been surprised. He rounded some bracken and kept moving, his joints aching, a slight burning in his chest. Archibald was moving faster, moving with the zeal of the possessed.

Rebus wanted to tell him: *you've* got a map, what's to

say Oakes didn't buy one too? What's to say he didn't study it, looking for certain features? He might even have been here already on a recce – he'd given his minders the slip plenty of times.

'Hang on!' he called, quickening his pace.

'John!' Archibald called back, his form ghostlike up ahead. 'You try that way, we'll take the other two!' Meaning Rebus was to explore the easternmost outcrop.

'Will I need to dig?' he called out. Receiving laughter in reply: Oakes's laughter. The more unsettling for the fact he could barely be seen.

'Will we?' he heard Archibald asking Oakes.

'Oh, I don't think so,' Oakes answered. 'We'll just leave the bodies where they fall.'

Rebus was still wondering if he'd misheard when he heard the dull sound of an impact, and a distant groan.

'Oakes!' he roared, upping his pace. He could make out the shadowy silhouette: Oakes standing over the fallen Archibald, a rock in his hand, raised to strike again.

'Oakes!' he repeated.

'I hear you!' Oakes yelled back, bringing the rock down on to Archibald's head.

By now Rebus was almost upon him. Oakes tossed the rock on to the ground and was licking his lips as Rebus reached him. 'You'll never know the satisfaction,' he said. 'A flea's been biting me for years, and now I've squashed it.' He slipped a hand into his waistband and brought out a folding knife.

'Amazing what the human body can hide,' Oakes said, grinning now. 'A rock was good enough for the old man, but I thought maybe you deserved something with a bit more bite.' He lunged. Rebus jumped back, lost his footing and was skidding back down the slope. Above him, he saw Oakes in pursuit, bounding like a mountain goat.

'I'm going to enjoy this!' Oakes called. 'You'll never know how much!'

Rebus kept himself rolling until bracken stopped him.

He clambered to his feet, picking up a stone and hurling it. His aim was wild. Oakes dodged it easily, only ten yards away now and slowing his descent.

'Ever skinned a rabbit?' Oakes said, breathing heavily, sweat glistening on his skull.

'You're just where I want you,' Rebus hissed.

Oakes gave a look of mock surprise. 'And where's that?'

'Committing an offence. Now I get to arrest you, and it's clean.'

'You get to *arrest* me?' Spluttering laughter. He was so close, his saliva hit Rebus's face. 'Man, you've got balls.' Moving the knife. 'Enjoy them while you can.'

'All these games,' Rebus was saying. 'There's something else, isn't there? Something you don't want us to know. Keeping us all busy so we don't go looking.'

'No shit?'

'What is it?'

But Oakes was shaking his head, working the knife. Rebus turned and ran. Oakes was after him, whooping, bounding through bracken. Rebus looking around, seeing nothing but hillside and a killer with a knife. He stumbled, came to a stop and turned to face Oakes.

'Gotcha,' Oakes called out.

Rebus, almost out of breath, just nodded.

'Know what you are, man?' Oakes asked. 'You're my spot of R&R, that's all.'

Rebus, walking backwards, started tugging his shirt out of his waistband. Oakes looked puzzled, until Rebus pulled the shirt up, revealing a tiny mike taped to his chest. Oakes looked at him, Rebus holding the stare. Then looked around, seeking shapes.

Voices approaching at speed.

'Thanks for all that shouting,' Rebus said. 'Better than a trail of breadcrumbs any day.'

With a roar, Oakes took a final lunge at him. Rebus sidestepped it, and Oakes was past him and running. Downhill to start with, then changing his mind and making an arc, climbing now, further into the hills. The first uniforms appeared out of the mist. Rebus pointed after Oakes.

'Get him!' he called. Then he started climbing too, making his way back to where Alan Archibald lay, still conscious but with blood pouring from his wounds. Rebus crouched beside him as more uniforms ran past.

'Radio down for help!' Rebus called out to them. One of the uniforms turned back to him.

'Don't need to, sir. You've already done it.'

Rebus looked at the mike on his chest and realised this was true.

'Where did the cavalry come from?' Archibald asked, his voice faint.

'I got them from the ACC,' Rebus told him. 'He promised me a chopper too, but it would have needed X-ray eyes.'

Archibald managed a smile. 'Do you think . . . ?'

'I'm sorry, Alan,' Rebus said. 'It was all crap, that's what I think. He just wanted a couple more scalps.'

Archibald touched shaking fingers to his head. 'He nearly got one,' he said, closing his eyes to rest.

Alan Archibald went to hospital, and Rebus went in search of Jim Stevens. He'd already checked out of the hotel, and wasn't at the newspaper office. Eventually, Rebus tracked him down to The Hebrides, a furtive little bar behind Waverley station. Stevens was sitting alone in a corner with only a full ashtray and glass of whisky for company.

Rebus got himself a whisky and water, gulped it down, ordered another and went to join him.

'Come to gloat?' Stevens asked.

'About what?'

'That wee shite set me up.' He told Rebus what had happened.

'Then I'm an angel straight from heaven,' Rebus said.

Stevens blinked. 'How do you make that out?'

'I bring glad tidings. Or more accurately, a news story, and I'd say you're ahead of the pack.'

Rebus had never seen a man sober up so quickly. Stevens pulled a notebook from his pocket and folded it open. His pen ready, he looked up at Rebus.

'It'll have to be a trade,' Rebus told him.

'I need this,' Stevens said.

Rebus nodded, told him the story. 'And I'd have been next if he got his way.'

'Jesus Christ.' Stevens exhaled, took a gulp of whisky. 'There are probably dozens of questions I should be asking you, but right now I can't think of any.' He took out a mobile phone. 'Mind if I call this in?'

Rebus shook his head. 'Then we talk,' he said.

While Stevens read from his notes, turning them into sentences and paragraphs, Rebus listened, nodding confirmation when it was demanded of him. Stevens listened while the story was read back to him. He made a few changes, then finished the call.

'I owe you,' he said, putting the phone on the table. 'What'll it be?'

'Another whisky,' Rebus said, 'and the answers to some questions.'

Half an hour later he had a pair of headphones on and was listening to the tape of Oakes's last interview.

' "A date with my past",' he recited, slipping the headphones off his ears. ' "A date with destiny".'

'That's Archibald, isn't it? Archibald's been hassling him for years.'

Rebus thought back to Alan Archibald . . . the way he'd looked as they'd lifted him into the ambulance. He'd looked spent and stunned, as if his dearest possession had been torn from him. Easy to steal away a dream, a hope . . . Cary Oakes had done that.

And had gotten away.

'They didn't catch him then?' Stevens asked, not for the first time.

'He ran into the hills, could be anywhere.'

'It's a hell of an area to search,' Stevens conceded. 'What made you take reinforcements?'

Rebus shrugged.

'You know, John, once upon a time you wouldn't have thought you needed them.'

'I know, Jim. Things change.'

Stevens nodded. 'I suppose they do.'

Rebus rewound the tape, listened to the last half again. *'A date with destiny, as you and your fellow hacks might put it. With someone who never listened to me . . .'* This time, he was frowning when he finished.

'You know,' he said, 'I'm not sure he means Archibald and me. He called us his spot of R&R.'

Stevens had drained his glass. 'What else could it be?'

Rebus shook his head slowly. 'There was some reason for him coming back here.'

'Yes, me and my chequebook.'

'Something more than that. More than the chance to play games with Alan Archibald . . .'

'What?'

'I don't know.' He looked at Stevens. 'You could find out.'

'Me?'

'You know the city inside out. It has to be something from his past, something from before he went to America.'

'I'm not an archaeologist.'

'No? Think of all the years you've spent digging dirt. And Alan Archibald has a lot of stuff on Oakes, better than anything the bastard gave you.'

Stevens snorted, then smiled. 'Maybe . . .' he said to himself. 'It would be a way of getting back at him.'

Rebus was nodding. 'He's given you a tissue of lies, you bounce back with a whole boxful of truth.'

'The truth about Cary Oakes,' Stevens said, measuring it up for a headline. 'I'll do it,' he said at last.

'And anything you find, you share with me.' Rebus reached for Stevens' notepad. 'I'll give you my mobile number.'

'Jim Stevens and John Rebus, working together.' Stevens grinned.

'I won't tell if you don't.'

40

There were messages for Rebus. Janice had called three times; Damon's bank manager once. Rebus spoke to the bank manager first.

'We have a transaction,' the man said.

'What, when and where?' Rebus reached for paper and pen.

'Edinburgh. A cash machine on George Street. Withdrawal of one hundred pounds.'

'Today?'

'Yesterday afternoon at one forty precisely. It's good news, isn't it?'

'I hope so.'

'I mean, it proves he's still alive.'

'It proves someone's used his card. Not quite the same thing.'

'I see.' The manager sounded a little dispirited. 'I suppose you have to be cautious.'

Rebus had a thought. 'This cash machine, it wouldn't be under surveillance, would it?'

'I can check for you.'

'If you wouldn't mind.' Rebus wound up the call and phoned Janice.

'What's up?' he asked.

'Nothing.' She paused. 'It's just you ran off so early that morning. I wondered if it was something we'd . . .'

'Nothing to do with you, Janice.'

'No?'

'I just needed to get back here.'

'Oh.' Another pause. 'Well, I was just worried.'

'About me?'

'That you were disappearing from my life again.'

'Would I do that?'

'I don't know, John: would you?'

'Janice, I know things are a bit rocky between you and Brian . . .'

'Yes?'

He smiled, eyes closed. 'That's it really. I'm not exactly an expert on marriage guidance.'

'I'm not in the market for one.'

'Look,' he said, rubbing his eyes, 'there's a bit of news about Damon.'

A longer pause. 'Were you planning on telling me?'

'I just did tell you.'

'Only so you could change the subject.'

Rebus felt like he was in the boxing-ring, cornered on the ropes. 'It's just that his bank account's been used.'

'He's taken out?'

'Someone's used his card.'

Her voice was rising, filling with hope. 'But nobody else knows his number. It has to be him.'

'There are ways of using cards . . .'

'John, don't you *dare* take this away from me!'

'I just don't want you getting hurt.' He saw Alan Archibald again, saw that look of final inescapable defeat.

'When was this?' Janice said; she was barely listening to him now.

'Yesterday afternoon. I got word about ten minutes ago. It was a bank on George Street.'

'He's still in Edinburgh.' A statement of belief.

'Janice . . .'

'I can feel it, John. He's there, I know he's there. What time's the next train?'

'I doubt he's still hanging around George Street. The withdrawal was a hundred pounds. Might have been travelling money.'

'I'm coming anyway.'

'I can't stop you.'

'That's right, you can't.' She put down the telephone. Seconds later, it rang again. Damon's bank manager.

'Yes,' he said, 'there's a camera.'

'Trained on the machine?'

'Yes. I've already asked: the tape's waiting for you. Talk to a Miss Georgeson.'

As Rebus finished the call, George Silvers brought him a cup of coffee. 'Thought you'd have gone home,' he said: Hi-Ho's way of showing he cared.

'Thanks, George. No sign of him yet?'

Silvers shook his head. Rebus stared at the paperwork on his desk. There were cases to write up, he could barely recall them. Names swimming in front of him. All of them demanding an ending.

'We'll catch him,' Silvers said. 'Don't you worry about that.'

'You've always been a comfort to me, George,' Rebus said. He handed back the cup. 'And one of these days you'll remember that I don't take sugar.'

He went to talk to Miss Georgeson. She was plump and fiftyish and reminded Rebus of a school dinner-lady he'd once dated. She had the videotape ready for him.

'Would you like to view it here?' she asked.

Rebus shook his head. 'I'll take it back to the station, if you've no objection.'

'Well, really I should make you a copy . . .'

'I don't intend losing it, Miss Georgeson. And I *will* bring it back.'

He left the bank with the tape held tightly in one hand. Checked his watch, then headed down to Waverley. He sat on one of the benches on the concourse, drinking a milky coffee – or *caffe latte* as the vendor had called it – and keeping an eye open. He had the tape in his raincoat pocket; no way he was leaving it in the car. He flicked through the evening paper. Nothing about Cary Oakes – it would be an exclusive in Stevens' paper first thing in the morning, and Stevens would have answered his detractors with one mighty two-fingered salute.

A date with destiny . . .

What the hell did that mean? Was Oakes laying yet another false trail? Rebus would put nothing past him. He'd sold Stevens, Archibald, and himself dummies like he was vintage George Best and they were Sunday league.

Finally he saw her. Late-afternoon trains into Edinburgh weren't busy; the traffic was all the other way. She was walking against the crowds as she came off the platform. He got into step beside her before she'd noticed him.

'Needing a taxi?' he said.

She looked surprised, then bemused. 'John,' she said. 'What brings you here?'

For answer, he took the video out and held it in front of her.

'A peace offering,' he said, leading her back to his car.

They sat in the CID suite. It too was quiet. Most people had gone home for the day. Those who were left were trying to finish reports or catch up with themselves. No one was in the mood to dawdle. The video monitor sat in one corner. Rebus pulled two chairs over. He'd fetched them coffee. Janice was looking excited and fearful at the same time. Again, he was reminded of Alan Archibald on the hillside.

'Look, Janice,' he warned her, 'if it's not him . . .'

She shrugged. 'If it's not him, it's not him. I won't blame you.' She flashed him a momentary smile. He started the tape. Miss Georgeson had explained that the camera was motion-sensitive, and would only begin recording when someone approached the machine. Back at the bank, Rebus had taken a look at the cash machine. The camera was above it, shooting from behind one of the bank's glass windows. When the first face came on the tape, Rebus and Janice were looking at it from above. The time-counter said 08.10. Rebus used the remote to fast forward.

'We're looking for one forty,' he explained. Janice was sitting on the edge of her chair, the coffee cup held in both hands.

This, Rebus thought, was the way it had started: with security footage, grainy pictures. Towards the middle of the day, more people were using the machine. There was a lot of tape to get through. Lunchtime queues built up, but by one thirty it was a little quieter.

The time-counter said 13.40.

'Oh, dear Lord, there he is,' Janice said. She'd placed her cup on the floor, clapped her hands to her face.

Rebus looked. The face was angled down, looking at the machine's keypad. Then it turned away, as if staring down the street. Fingers were tapped impatiently against the screen of the cash machine. The card was retrieved, a hand went to the slot to extract the notes. Didn't linger; didn't wait for a receipt. The next customer was already moving forward.

'Are you sure?' he asked.

A tear was falling from Janice's cheek. 'Positive,' she said, nodding.

Rebus found it hard to tell. All he had were photos of Damon and the footage from Gaitano's; he'd never met him. The hair looked similar . . . maybe the nose too, the shape of the chin. But it wasn't as though they were unusual. The person on view now, they looked much like the customer who'd just left. But Janice was blowing her nose. She was satisfied.

'It's him, I'd swear to it.' She saw uncertainty on his face. 'I wouldn't say it was if it wasn't.'

'Of course not.'

'It's not just the face or hair or clothes . . . it's the way he stood, the way he held himself. And those little twitches of impatience.' She used a corner of the hankie to wipe her eyes. 'It was him, John. It was him.'

'OK,' Rebus said. He rewound the tape, played the minutes leading up to 13.40. He was studying the background to see if he could spot Damon making for the machine. He wanted to know if he'd been alone. But he entered the picture suddenly, and from the side. That look again, towards where he'd just come from. Was there a slight nod of the head . . . some signal to another person just out of shot . . . ? Rebus rewound and watched again.

'What are you looking for?' Janice asked.

'Anyone who might have been with him.'

But there was nothing. So he let the tape play on, and was rewarded a minute or two later by legs moving across the top of the picture, just behind the person at the machine. Two pairs, one male, one female. Rebus pressed freeze-frame, but couldn't get the picture to stay absolutely still and focused. So instead, he rewound and played it again, following the feet with his finger.

'Recognise the trousers, the shoes?'

But Janice shook her head. 'They're just a blur.'

And so they were.

'Could be anybody,' she added.

And so it could.

She got to her feet. 'I'm going to George Street.' He made to say something but she cut him off. 'I know he won't be there, but there are shops, pubs – I can show them his picture at least.'

Rebus nodded. She gripped his forearm.

'He's still here, John. That's *something*.'

As she left, she held the door open to someone just coming in: Siobhan Clarke.

'Any sign of him?' Rebus asked.

Siobhan slumped into a chair. 'Billy Horman?'

Rebus shook his head. 'Cary Oakes.'

She stretched her neck. He heard the snap. 'Another day down,' he told her.

She nodded. 'I'm not working Oakes. I'm on Billy Boy.'

'No progress?'

She shook her head. 'We need another dozen officers. Maybe a couple of dozen.'

'I can see the budget stretching to that.'

'Maybe if we got rid of a few of the bean-counters.'

'Careful, Siobhan. That's anarchist talk.'

She smiled. 'How are you? I hear Oakes was ready to kill the pair of you.'

'The tremors have stopped,' he told her. 'Buy you a drink?'

'Not tonight. I've a date with a hot bath and a takeaway. What about you?'

'Straight home, same as yourself.'

'Well . . .' She stood up as though the effort was costing her. 'See you tomorrow.'

'Night, Siobhan.'

She waved fingers over her shoulder as she left.

Rebus was almost as good as his word – just the one stop-off to make beforehand. He climbed the stairwell of Cragside Court. Darkness was falling, but there were still children out playing, albeit supervised by a member of GAP. They'd had T-shirts printed up with a logo on the front, getting more organised by the day. The woman in the T-shirt had studied Rebus, knowing she'd seen him somewhere before, but not recognising him as a resident.

He stood looking out over Greenfield. On one side, Holyrood Park; on the other, the Old Town, and the site of the new Parliament. He wondered if the estate would be allowed to survive. He knew that if the council wanted it run down, they would work by stealth. Repairs would not be carried out, or would be botched. Flats would be found to be uninhabitable, tenants rehoused, windows and doors blocked and padlocked. Things would slowly deteriorate, causing residents to rethink their options. More of them would move out. The state of the high-rises would become a 'cause for concern'. There'd be a media outcry about conditions. The council would move in with offers of help – meaning relocation: cheaper than shoring up the estate. And eventually it would be deserted, a demolition site from which new buildings could rise. Expensive *pieds-à-terre* for parliamentarians, perhaps. Or offices and select shops. It was a prime site, no doubt about it.

As for Salisbury Crags . . . he didn't doubt there'd be people who would build on it too, given the chance. But that chance would be a long time coming. All the centuries of change, and the park was much as it ever had been. It made no judgements on the work around it, but merely sat there, above it all. And the people who tramped over it were minor irritations, dead by the age of seventy if not before. They made no impression on it, not when measured in millennia.

Rebus was outside Darren Rough's flat now. Darren had come home to give evidence against two evil men. As recompense, he'd been harried, cursed and eventually killed. Rebus didn't feel proud that he'd been the first player. He hoped Darren might one day forgive him. He almost said as much to the ghostly shape at the end of the walkway, but when it came towards him, he saw it was flesh and blood, very much alive.

It was Cal Brady, his face an angry scowl.

'What do you want?'

'Just taking a look.'

'I thought you were another pervert.'

Rebus nodded towards the mobile phone in Brady's hand. 'Did the playground guard tell you?' He nodded to himself. 'Nice little operation you've got here, Cal. Anything in it for you?'

'It's my public duty,' Brady said, puffing out his chest.

Rebus took a step closer, hands in coat pockets. 'Cal, the day people like you are deciding what's right and what's wrong, we're all in Queer Street.'

'You calling me a poof?' Cal Brady yelled, but Rebus was already past him and heading for the stairs.

41

'Tell me about Janice,' Patience said.

They were seated in the living room, a bottle of red wine open on the carpet between them. Patience was lying along the sofa. There was a paperback novel folded open on her chest. She had placed it there some time ago; had been staring into space, listening to the music on the hi-fi. Nick Drake, 'Pink Moon'. Rebus was in the armchair, legs hanging over its side. He had kicked off his shoes and socks, was catching up with the football news in that day's paper.

'What?'

'Janice, I'd like to know about her.'

'We were at school together.' Rebus stopped reading. 'She's married with just the one son. She used to work as a teacher. I was at school with her husband, too. His name's Brian.'

'You went out with her?'

'At school, yes.'

'Sleep together?'

Rebus looked at her. 'Didn't quite get that far.'

She nodded to herself. 'Are you curious about what it would have been like?'

He shrugged.

'I think I would be,' she went on. Her glass was empty, and she leaned over to refill it. The book slid on to the floor, but she paid it no heed. Rebus was still on his first helping of the Rioja. The bottle was nearly empty.

'Anyone would think you were the one with the drink

problem,' he said, making sure he was smiling as he spoke.

She was getting comfortable again. A splash of wine fell on to the back of her hand, and she put her mouth to it.

'No, I just like a little bit too much now and again. So, have you thought about sleeping with her?'

'Christ, Patience . . .'

'I'm interested, that's all. Sammy says Janice had a look about her.'

'What sort of look?'

Patience frowned, as if trying to recall the exact words. 'Hungry. Hungry and a little desperate, I think. How's the marriage?'

'Rocky,' Rebus admitted.

'And you going to Fife . . . did that help?'

'I didn't sleep with her.'

Patience wagged a finger. 'Don't go defending yourself before an accusation's made. You're a detective, you know how it looks.'

He glared at her. 'Am I a suspect?'

'No, John, you're a man. That's all.' She took another sip of wine.

'I wouldn't hurt you, Patience.'

She smiled, stretched out a hand as if to squeeze his, but he was too far away. 'I know that, sweetheart. But the thing is, you wouldn't even be thinking of me at the time, so the idea of hurting me or not hurting me wouldn't enter into it.'

'You're so sure.'

'John, I get it every single day. Wives coming into the surgery, wanting anti-depressants. Wanting *anything* that'll help them get through the bloody awful marriages they've found themselves in. They tell me things. It all spills out. Some of them turn to drink or drugs, some slash their wrists. It's bizarre how seldom they just walk out. And the ones who do walk out are usually the ones married to the violent cases.' She looked at him. 'Do you know what *they* do?'

'End up going back?' he guessed.

She focused on him. 'How do you know?'

'I get them too, Patience. The domestics, the neighbours who complain of screams and punches. The same wives *you* get, only further down the road. They won't press charges. They get put into a hostel. And later, they walk back to the only life they really know.'

She blinked away a tear. 'Why does it have to be like that, John?'

'I wish I knew.'

'What's in it for us?'

He smiled. 'A paycheque.'

She had stopped looking at him. Picked her book off the floor, put down her wine glass. 'The man who painted that message . . . What was he trying to do?'

'I'm not sure. Maybe he wanted me to know he'd been here.'

She had found her page, stared at the words without moving her eyes. 'Where is he now?'

'Lost on the hills and freezing to death.'

'You really think so?'

'No,' he admitted. 'Someone like Oakes . . . that would be too easy.'

'Will he come after you?'

'I'm not at the top of his list.' No, because Alan Archibald was still alive. X-rays had shown a skull fracture; Archibald would be in hospital a little longer. There was a police guard on his bed.

'Will he come here?' Patience asked.

The CD had finished; there was silence in the room. 'I don't know.'

'If he tries painting my flagstones again, I'll give him a bloody good kicking.'

Rebus looked at her, then began laughing.

'What's so funny?' she said.

Rebus was shaking his head. 'Nothing really. I'm just glad you're on my side, that's all.'

She raised the wine glass to her lips again. 'What makes you so sure of that, Inspector?'

Rebus raised his own glass to her, pleased that until Patience had mentioned her, he hadn't thought once that evening of Janice Mee. He hit 'Replay' on the CD remote. 'This guy sounds like he needs help,' Patience said.

'He did,' Rebus told her. 'He OD'd.' She looked at him and he shrugged. 'Just another casualty,' he said.

Later, he headed outside for a cigarette. The message was still there on the patio: YOUR COP LOVER KILLED DARREN. The workmen would start cleaning it off tomorrow. Oakes said he'd followed Darren but lost him. Well, someone had found him. Rebus wasn't going to take the blame for that. Cigarette lit, he climbed the steps. There was a marked patrol car parked directly outside, a message to Cary Oakes should he think about paying a visit. Rebus had a word with the two officers inside, finished his cigarette and headed back indoors.

42

'Fancy a run?' Siobhan Clarke offered.

'I trust you mean "run" as in "drive"?'

'Don't worry, I don't have you down as the jogging type.'

'Perceptive as ever. Where are you going?'

It was morning in St Leonard's. The weather up on the Pentlands had cleared, and Rebus had made sure the helicopter would be out scanning the area for signs of Cary Oakes. Villages and farms in the foothills had been warned to be on the look out.

'Don't try to corner him,' the message had gone. 'Just let us know if you see him.'

So far, no one had called in.

Rebus felt like dead weight. He'd made breakfast for Patience – orange juice and two sachets of Resolve – and had been complimented on both his diagnosis and his bedside manner. She'd said she'd make the surgery OK.

'I just hope no one expects me to do my Agony Aunt bit today.'

And now Rebus was in the CID suite with his coffee and a Mars Bar.

'Breakfast of coronaries,' he said, noting Siobhan's distaste.

'We've had a sighting of Billy Boy. It'll probably turn out to be a waste of time . . .'

'And you'd rather waste it with me?' Rebus smiled. 'Isn't that thoughtful?'

'Never mind,' she said, turning away.

'Whoa, hold on. What side of the bed did you fall out of?'

'I didn't quite reach bed last night,' she snapped. Then she melted a little. 'It's a long story.'

'Just right for a car-ride then,' he said. 'Come on, you've got me hooked.'

The story was, her upstairs neighbours' washing-machine had sprung a leak. They'd been out, and hadn't noticed. And she'd only found out when she'd gone into her bedroom.

'Their washing-machine's above your bedroom?' Rebus asked.

'That's another bone of contention. Anyway, I noticed this stain on the ceiling, and when I touched the bed it was soaked through. So I ended up on the couch in a smelly old sleeping-bag.'

'Poor you.' Rebus was thinking of all the times he'd slept in his chair – but that had been voluntary. He looked in the wing mirror as they crawled westwards out of town. 'Tell me something: why are we going to Grangemouth? Couldn't the locals handle it?'

'I'm reluctant to delegate.'

Rebus smiled: she'd stolen one of his lines. 'What you mean is, you don't trust anyone to do the job thoroughly.'

'Something like that,' she said, glancing at him. 'I had a good teacher.'

'Siobhan, it's been quite some time since I could teach you anything.'

'Thanks.'

'But that's because you've stopped listening.'

'We are not amused.' She craned her neck. 'What is with this traffic?'

The vehicles ahead were barely moving.

'It's part of the new council initiative. Make things bloody awful for drivers, and they'll stop coming into town and making everything look untidy.'

'They want a conservation village.'

Rebus nodded. 'And just the half a million villagers.'

Eventually they got moving. Grangemouth lay out to the west along the Forth estuary. Rebus hadn't been to the town in years. As they approached, Rebus's first impression was that they'd wandered on to the set of *Blade Runner*. A vast petrochemical complex dominated the skyline, throwing up jagged chimneys and weird configurations of pipes. The complex looked like some encroaching alien life-form, about to throw its many mechanical arms around the town and squeeze the life out of it.

In fact, the contrary was true: the complex and all that went with it had brought employment to Grangemouth. The streets they eventually drove through were dark and narrow, with architecture from much earlier in the century.

'Two worlds collide,' Rebus muttered, taking it all in.

'I feel they've spoiled their chances in the conservation village stakes.'

'I'm sure the townsfolk are grieving.' He was peering at the street names. 'Here we go.' They parked outside a row of cottage-type houses, all of which had added bedrooms and windows to their roof-space.

'Number eleven,' Siobhan said. 'Woman's name is Wilkie.'

Mrs Wilkie had been waiting for them. She seemed the type of neighbour every street has: interested to the point of nosiness. Her kind could be a distinct asset, but Rebus would bet some of her neighbours didn't see it that way.

Her living room was a tiny box, overheated and with pride of place given to a large and ornate doll's-house. When Siobhan, out of politeness, showed interest in it, Mrs Wilkie delivered a ten-minute speech concerning its history. Rebus could swear she didn't once draw breath, giving neither of her prisoners the chance to jump in and take the conversation elsewhere.

'Well, isn't that lovely?' Siobhan said, glancing towards

Rebus. The look on his face had her sucking in her cheeks to stop from laughing. 'Now, about this boy you saw, Mrs Wilkie . . . ?'

They all sat down, and Mrs Wilkie told her story. She'd seen the laddie's picture in the paper, and as she was coming back from the shops around two, caught him playing football in the street.

'Kicking the ball against the wall of Montefiore's Garage. There's this low stone wall around the . . .' She made motions with her hands. 'What do you call it?'

'Forecourt?' Siobhan suggested.

'That's the word.' She smiled at Siobhan. 'I'll bet you're a dab hand at crosswords, brain like that.'

'Did you say anything to the boy, Mrs Wilkie?'

'It's Miss Wilkie actually. I never married.'

'Really?' Rebus managed to put on a surprised look. Siobhan coughed into her hand, then handed some snaps of Billy Horman over to Miss Wilkie.

'Well, these certainly look like him,' the old woman said, sorting through the photos. She lifted one out. 'Except for this, that is.'

Siobhan took the proffered photo, stuck it back in her folder. Rebus knew she'd sneaked in a picture of a different kid to assess how alert her witness actually was. Miss Wilkie had passed.

'To answer your question,' Miss Wilkie said, 'no, I didn't say anything. I came back here and took another look at the paper. Then I phoned the number it said to call. Spoke to a very nice young man at the police station.'

'This was yesterday?'

'That's right, and I haven't seen the laddie today.'

'And you just saw him the once?'

Miss Wilkie nodded. 'Playing all by himself. He looked so lonely.' She had handed back the photos, and got up to look out of her window. 'You notice strangers on a street like this.'

'I'm sure not much gets past you,' Rebus said.

'All these cars nowadays . . . I'm surprised you found a space.'

Rebus and Siobhan looked at one another, thanked Miss Wilkie for her time, and left.

Outside, they looked to left and right. There was a garage on the corner at the far end of the street. They walked towards it.

'What did she mean about the cars?' Siobhan asked.

'My guess is, there's always someone parked outside her window. Makes it harder for her to see everything that's going on.'

'I'm impressed.'

'Not that I speak from experience, you understand.'

But back in the cottage, Rebus had felt a sudden depression. He, too, was a watcher. All the nights he sat in his flat, lights off, watching from the window . . . As he got older, would he turn into a Miss Wilkie: the street's nosy neighbour?

Montefiore's Garage consisted of a single line of petrol pumps, a shop, and a double work-bay. A man in blue overalls was in one of the work-bays, his head just visible as he stood in the pit, a blue Volkswagen Polo above him. There was another, older man behind the counter in the shop. Rebus and Siobhan stopped on the pavement.

'Might as well ask if they saw him,' Siobhan said.

'Suppose so,' Rebus replied, with little enthusiasm.

'I told you it was a wild shot.'

'Could be a neighbourhood kid. New family moved in, hasn't had time to make friends.'

'It was two o'clock she saw him. He should have been at school.'

'True,' Rebus said. 'She seemed so certain, didn't she?'

'Some people do. They want to be helpful, even if it means making up a story.'

Rebus tutted. 'You didn't learn cynicism like that from me.' He looked around at the bumper-to-bumper parking. 'I wonder . . .'

'What?'

'He was kicking the ball off the forecourt wall.'

'Yes.'

'Not much of a game if all these cars were here. Pavement's not wide enough.'

Siobhan looked at the wall, the pavement. 'Maybe the cars weren't here.'

'According to Miss Wilkie, that would be unusual.'

'I can't see what you're getting at.'

Rebus pointed to the forecourt. 'What if he was in there? Plenty of space so long as no cars are using the pumps.'

'They'd chase him off.' She looked at him. 'Wouldn't they?'

'Let's go ask them.'

They went to the shop first, identified themselves to the man behind the counter.

'I'm not the owner,' he said. 'I'm his brother.'

'Were you here yesterday?'

'Been here the past ten days. Eddie and Flo are on their hols.'

'Somewhere nice?' Siobhan asked, making out they were just having a normal conversation.

'Jamaica.'

'Do you remember a young boy?' Rebus asked. Siobhan held up one of the photographs. 'Playing kickabout in the forecourt?'

The owner's brother nodded. 'Gordon's nephew.'

Rebus tried to keep his voice level. 'Gordon who?'

The man laughed. 'Gordon Howe, actually.' He spelt the name for them, and they laughed along with him.

'Bet he gets jokes about that,' Siobhan said, wiping an imaginary tear from her eye. 'Any idea where we could find Mr Howe?'

'Jock will know.'

Siobhan nodded. 'And who's Jock?'

'Sorry,' the man said. 'Jock's the other mechanic.'

'Under the Polo?' Rebus asked. The man nodded.

'So Mr Howe works for the garage?'

'Yes, he's a mechanic. He's got the day off today. Well, we're not busy, and with him looking after young Billy . . .' He waved the picture of Billy Horman.

'Billy?' Siobhan said.

Sixty seconds later they were out on the forecourt again and Siobhan was using Rebus's mobile. She got through to St Leonard's and asked if Billy Horman had an uncle called Gordon Howe. Listening to the answer, she shook her head to let Rebus know what she was hearing. They walked towards the work-bay.

'Could we have a word?' Rebus called. They had their IDs ready as the mechanic called Jock crawled out from under the Polo and started wiping his hands on an impossibly oil-blackened rag.

'What have I done?' He had ginger hair, curling to the nape of his neck, and a long earring dangling from one ear. The backs of his hands were tattooed, and Rebus noticed he was missing the pinkie on his left hand.

'Where can we find Gordon Howe?' Siobhan asked.

'Lives on Adamson Street. What's the matter?'

'Will he be there just now, do you think?'

'How should I know?'

'He's got the day off,' Rebus said, taking a step closer. 'Maybe he told you how he planned to spend it?'

'Taking Billy out.' The mechanic's eyes flicked from one detective to the other.

'Billy being . . .?'

'His sister's kid. She's been poorly, one-parent family and that. Billy either went into care for the duration or Gordy looked after him. Is it Billy? Has he been up to something?'

'Do you think he's the type?'

'Not at all.' The mechanic smiled. 'Very quiet kid, actually. Didn't want to talk about his mum . . .'

*

'Didn't want to talk about his mum,' Siobhan repeated, as they walked up the path to the house in Adamson Street. It was a sixties-built semi in an estate on the edge of town. Council-owned for the most part. You could tell the homes that had been purchased by their tenants: replacement windows and better doors. But they all had the same grey harled walls.

'Uncle Gordon's orders, no doubt.'

They rang the bell and waited. Rebus thought he detected movement at an upstairs window. Took a step back to look, but couldn't see anything.

'Try again,' he said, opening the letterbox while Siobhan pushed the doorbell. There was a door at the end of the corridor, half-open. He saw shadows beyond it, snapped the letterbox shut.

'Round the back,' he said, heading for the side of the house. As they entered the back garden, a man was disappearing over a high bark fence.

'Mr Howe!' Rebus shouted.

By way of response, the man called out, 'Run for it!' to the boy who was with him. Rebus let Siobhan climb the fence. He headed back round to the front, ran down the road, wondering where the two would appear.

Suddenly they were ahead of him. Howe was limping, clawing at one leg. The boy was off like a shot, Howe spurring him on. But when the boy looked back, saw the distance widening between himself and Howe, his pace slowed.

'No! Keep running, Billy! Keep running!'

But the boy wasn't listening to Howe. He came to a dead stop, waited for the man to catch up. Siobhan came into view, a rip in the knee of her trousers. Howe saw he was going nowhere and put up his hands.

'All right,' he said, 'all right.'

He looked despairingly at Billy, who was walking back towards him.

'Billy, will you never listen?'

As Gordon Howe dropped to his knees, Billy slid his arms around his neck, man and boy embracing.

'I'll tell them,' Billy was wailing. 'I'll tell them it's all right.'

Rebus looked down at them, saw the tattoos on Gordon Howe's bare arms: No Surrender; UDA; the Red Hand of Ulster. He recalled Tom Jackson's story: *ran off to Ulster to join the paramilitaries* . . .

'You'll be Billy's dad then,' Rebus guessed. 'Welcome back to Scotland.'

43

On the way back into Edinburgh, Rebus sat in the back with Howe, while Billy sat in the front with Siobhan.

'You read about Greenfield in the paper?' Rebus guessed. Gordon Howe nodded. 'What's your real name?'

'Eddie Mearn.'

'How long have you been back from Northern Ireland?' Siobhan asked.

'Three months.' He reached out a hand to ruffle his son's hair. 'I wanted Billy back.'

'Did his mother know?'

'That cow? It was our secret, wasn't it, Billy?'

'Aye, Dad,' Billy said.

Mearn turned to Rebus. 'I used to visit him on the quiet. If his mum had found out, she'd've put a stop to it. But we kept it hush-hush.'

'Then you read about Darren Rough?' Rebus added.

Mearn nodded. 'Looked too good to be true. I knew if I snatched Billy, they'd just assume that wanker had him – at least for a while. Give us a chance to get settled. We were getting on fine, weren't we, Billy?'

'Grand,' his son agreed.

'Your mum's been at her wits' end, Billy,' Siobhan said.

'I hate Ray,' Billy said, tucking his chin into his neck. Ray Heggie: Joanna Horman's lover. 'He hits her.'

'Why do you think I wanted Billy out of there?' Mearn said. 'It's not right for a kid to have to deal with. It's not right.' He bent forward to kiss the top of his son's head. 'We were all fixed up, though, weren't we, Billy Boy? We'd've managed.'

Billy turned in his seat, tried to hug his father, the seatbelt restricting him. Looking in the rearview, Siobhan fixed her eyes on Rebus's. Both knew what would happen: Billy would go back to Greenfield; Mearn would probably be charged. Neither officer felt especially great about it.

As they headed into central Edinburgh, Rebus asked Siobhan to make a detour along George Street. There was no sign of Janice . . .

'You know something?' Rebus asked Mearn.

They were in an interview room at St Leonard's. Mearn had a cup of tea in front of him. A doctor had looked at his leg: just a sprain.

'What?'

'You said you knew they'd all blame Billy's disappearance on Darren Rough, and that would give you some time to get settled.'

'That's right.'

'But I can think of a better way, a plan that would mean they'd *give up* looking for Billy.'

Mearn looked interested. 'What's that then?'

'If Rough was dead,' Rebus said quietly. 'I mean, we'd look for Billy for a while, even if all we expected to find was a body hidden somewhere. But we'd call a halt eventually.'

'I thought of that.'

Rebus sat down. 'You did?'

Mearn was nodding. 'You know, after I read about him being topped. I thought it was the answer to our prayers.'

Rebus was nodding. 'And that's why you did it?'

Mearn frowned. 'Did what?'

'Killed Darren Rough.'

The two men stared at one another. Then a look of horror spread across Mearn's face. 'N-n-no,' he stammered. 'No way, no way . . .' His hands gripped the edge of the table. 'Not me, I didn't do it.'

388

'No?' Rebus looked surprised. 'But you've got the perfect motive.'

'Christ, I was starting a *new* life. How could I contemplate *that* if I'd topped someone?'

'Lots of people do it, Eddie. I see them in here several times a year. I'd've thought it would be easy for someone with paramilitary training.'

Mearn laughed. 'Where did you get that idea?'

'It's what they're saying on the estate. When Joanna got pregnant with Billy, you ran off to join the terrorists.'

Mearn calmed down, looked around. 'I think I want a solicitor,' he said quietly.

'One's on its way,' Rebus explained.

'What about Billy?'

'They've phoned his mum. She's on her way too. Probably smartening herself up for the press conference.'

Mearn squeezed his eyes shut. 'Shit,' he whispered. Then: 'Sorry, Billy.' He was blinking back tears as he looked towards Rebus. 'What gave us away?'

A nosy old lady and a line of parked cars, Rebus could have told him. But he hadn't the heart.

There were cameras and microphones outside St Leonard's; so many that the journalists were spilling on to the road. Cars and vans were sounding their horns, making it hard to hear Joanna Horman speaking of her emotional reunion with her son. No sign of Ray Heggie: Rebus wondered if she'd given him the push. And not much sign of emotion from young Billy Boy. His mother kept hugging him to her, almost smothering him as the cameramen bayed for another shot. She pockmarked his face with lipstick kisses. As she made to answer another question, Rebus noticed Billy trying to wipe his face clean.

There were civilians mixed in with the reporters: passers-by and the curious. A woman in a GAP T-shirt was trying to hand out leaflets: Van Brady. Across the road, a kid sat balanced on his bike, one hand touching a lamp-post for support. Rebus recognised him: Van's youngest. No leaflets; no T-shirt – Rebus wondered about that. Was the boy less easily swayed than those around him?

'And I'd like to thank the police for all their hard work,' Joanna Horman was saying. You're welcome, Rebus thought to himself, pushing through the scrum and crossing the road. 'But most of all, I'd like to thank everyone at GAP for their support.'

A loud roar of agreement went up from Van Brady . . .

'It's Jamie, isn't it?'

The boy on the bike nodded. 'And you're the cop who came looking for Darren.'

Darren: first name only. Rebus took out a cigarette, offered one to Jamie, who shook his head. Rebus lit up, exhaled.

'I suppose you saw Darren around a bit?'

'He's dead.'

'But before then. Before the story got out.'

Jamie nodded, eyes guarded.

'Did he ever try anything?'

Now Jamie shook his head. 'He just said hello, that's all.'

'Did he hang around the playground?'

'Not that I saw.' He was staring at the scene across the road.

'Looks like Billy's the centre of attention, eh?' Rebus got the feeling Jamie was jealous, but trying not to let it show.

'Yeah.'

'I bet you're glad he's back.'

Jamie looked at him. 'Cal's moved in with his mum.'

Rebus took another draw on his cigarette. 'She's booted Ray out then?' Jamie nodded again.

'And moved your brother in?' Rebus looked impressed. 'That's fast work.'

Jamie just grunted. Rebus saw an opening.

'You don't sound too chuffed: are you going to miss him?'

Jamie shrugged. 'Not bothered.' But he was. His brother had moved out; his mother was busy with GAP; and now Billy Boy Horman was getting all the attention.

'You ever see Darren with anyone? I don't mean kids, I mean visitors.'

'Not really.'

Rebus angled his face so Jamie had little choice but to look at him. 'You don't sound too sure.'

'Someone came looking for him.'

'When?'

'When all the stuff about GAP started.'

'Friend of Darren's?'

Another shrug. 'He didn't say.'

'Well, what did he say, Jamie?'

'Said he was looking for the guy from the newspaper. He had the paper with him.' The paper: the story outing Darren Rough.

'Were those his exact words: "the guy from the newspaper"?'

Jamie smiled. 'I think he said "chap".'

'Chap?'

Jamie put on a posh voice. ' "The chap who was in the newspaper." '

'Not a local then?'

Now Jamie let out a stuttering laugh.

'What did he look like?'

'Old, quite tall. He had a moustache. His hair was grey, but the moustache was black.'

'You'd make a good detective, Jamie.'

Jamie wrinkled his nose in distaste. His mother had spotted the conversation, was making to cross the road towards them.

'Jamie!' she called, trying to weave between traffic.

'What did you tell him, Jamie?'

'I pointed to Darren's flat. Told him I knew Darren wasn't in.'

'What did the man do?'

'Gave me a fiver.' He looked around, almost furtively. 'I followed him back to his car.'

Rebus smiled. 'You really would make a detective.'

Another shrug. 'It was a big white car. I think it was a Merc.'

Rebus backed off as Van Brady reached them.

'What's he been saying, Jamie?' she asked, staring daggers at Rebus. But Jamie looked at her defiantly.

'Nothing,' he said.

She looked at Rebus, who just shrugged. When she turned back to her son, Rebus winked at him. Jamie gave the flicker of a smile. For a few moments, *he'd* been the centre of someone's attention.

'I was just asking about Cal,' Rebus told Van Brady. 'I've heard he's moving in with Joanna.'

She turned on him. 'What's it to you?'

He nodded towards the leaflet in her hand. 'Got one of those for me?'

'If you did your job right,' she sneered, 'we wouldn't need GAP.'

'What makes you think we need it anyway?' Rebus asked her, turning to walk away.

Rebus got on the computer, and decided to cover his bets by talking to the area's Merc dealerships. He already knew one person who drove a white Merc: the widow Margolies. Rebus tapped his pen against his desk, started calling. He got lucky with the first number he tried.

'Oh, yes, Dr Margolies is a regular customer. He's been buying nothing but Mercedes for donkey's years.'

'Sorry, I'm talking about a Mrs Margolies.'

'Yes, his daughter-in-law. Dr Margolies bought that car, too.'

Dr Joseph Margolies . . . 'He bought one for his son and daughter-in-law?'

'That's right. Last year, was it?'

'And for himself?'

'He likes to part-ex: keeps the model a year or two, then trades for something brand new. That way you don't get the same scale of depreciation.'

'So what's he driving just now?'

The sales manager turned cautious. 'Why don't you ask him yourself?'

'Maybe I'll do that,' Rebus said. 'And I'll be sure to tell him you could have saved me the trouble.'

Rebus listened to the receiver making a sighing sound. Then: 'Hang on a sec.' He heard fingers on a keyboard. A pause, then: 'An E200, purchased six months ago. Happy?'

'As a kid on Christmas morning.' Rebus scribbled the details down. 'And the colour?'

Another sigh. 'White, Inspector. Dr Margolies always buys white.'

As Rebus put down the phone, Siobhan Clarke came over. She rested against the corner of his desk.

'Looks like someone got lazy,' she said.

'How do you mean?'

'Eddie Mearn. As far as the inquiry was concerned, he was still in Northern Ireland. Someone made a phone call to Lisburn, and took it as gospel when he was told Mearn was still around.'

'Who made the call?'

'Roy Frazer, I'm sorry to say.'

'It's the only way he'll learn.'

'Sure, like you've learned from past mistakes.'

He smiled. 'That's why I never make the same one twice.'

She folded her arms. 'You think Mearn had this planned all along?'

Rebus nodded slowly. 'I'd say it's likely. Moved back

from Lisburn, maybe it's true he didn't tell anyone there he was leaving. Sets up a new identity for himself in Grangemouth – striking distance of Edinburgh. Why lie about who he was? Only reason I can think of is, he was going to snatch Billy. New life for both of them.'

'Would that have been so bad?' Siobhan asked.

'No worse than where Billy is now,' Rebus admitted. He looked at her. 'Careful there, Siobhan. You're in danger of thinking the law's an ass. That's only one step away from making up your own rules.'

'The way you've done.' It was statement rather than question.

'The way I've done,' Rebus was forced to agree. 'And look where it's got me.'

'Where's that?'

He tapped his sheet of notes. 'Seeing white cars everywhere.'

44

A white car had been spotted the night Jim Margolies had
flown from Salisbury Crags. Fair enough, Jim himself
owned a white car, but according to his wife the car had
stayed in the garage. He'd walked all the way to the
Crags. How likely was that? Rebus didn't know.

Another white car had been spotted in Holyrood Park
around the time Darren Rough was bludgeoned to death.

And prior to this, someone in a white car had been
looking for Darren.

Rebus told the story to Siobhan, and she pulled over a
chair so they could work through some theories.

'You're thinking they're all the same car?' she asked.

'All I know is, they're in the park when two apparently
unconnected deaths occur.'

She scratched her head. 'I'm not seeing anything. Any
other owners of white Mercs?'

'You mean, have any serial killers bought or hired one
lately?' She smiled at this. 'I'm checking,' Rebus went on.
'So far, the only name I have is Margolies.' He was
thinking: Jane Barbour drove a cream-coloured car, a
Ford Mondeo . . .

'But there are more white Mercs than that out there?'

Rebus nodded. 'But Jamie's description of the man
sounds awfully like Jim's father.'

'You saw him at the funeral?'

Rebus nodded. And at a children's beauty show, he
might have added. 'He's a retired doctor.'

'Racked with grief at his son's suicide, he decides to
become a vigilante?'

'Ridding the world of corruption to protest at the iniquity of life.'

Her smile broadened. 'You don't see it, do you?'

'No, I don't.' He tossed his pen on to the desk. 'To tell you the truth, I'm not seeing anything at all. Which must make it time for a break.'

'Coffee?' she suggested.

'I was thinking of something stronger.' He saw the look on her face. 'But coffee will do in the meantime.'

He went out to the car park for a cigarette, but ended up jumping into the Saab and heading down The Pleasance, across the High Street and past Waverley station. He drove west along George Street, then made an illegal turn to head back east along it. Janice was sitting on the kerb, head in her hands. People were looking at her, but no one stopped to ask if they could help. Rebus pulled up alongside and got her into the car.

'I know he's here,' she kept repeating. 'I know it.'

'Janice, this isn't doing either of you any good.'

Her eyes were bloodshot, looking sore from all the crying. 'What would you know about it? Have you ever lost a child?'

'I nearly lost Sammy.'

'But you didn't!' She turned away from him. 'You've never been any good, John. Christ, you couldn't even help Mitch, and he was supposed to be your best friend. They nearly blinded him!'

She had plenty left to say, plenty of poison. He let her talk, resting his hands lightly on the steering-wheel. At one point, she tried to get out, but he pulled her back into the car.

'Come on,' he said. 'Give me more. I'm listening to you.'

'No!' she spat. 'Know why? Because so help me, I think you're enjoying it!' This time when she opened the door, he didn't try to stop her. She took a left at the corner, heading down into the New Town. Rebus turned the car again, took a right into Castle Street and a left into Young Street. Stopped outside the Oxford Bar and walked in. Doc Klasser was standing in his usual spot. The afternoon drinkers were in: most of them would clear out by five or six, when the place filled with office workers. Harry the barman saw Rebus and lifted a pint glass. Rebus shook his head.

'A nip, Harry,' he said. 'Better make it a large one.'

He sat in the back room. Nobody there but the writer, the one with the big bag of books. He seemed to use the place as an office. A couple of times Rebus had asked him what books he should be reading. He'd bought the suggestions, but hadn't read them. Today, neither man seemed in need of company. Rebus sat with his drink and his thoughts. He was thinking back over thirty years, back to the last school party. His own version of the story . . .

Mitch and Johnny had a plan. They'd join the army, see some action. Mitch had sent away for the literature, then had dropped into the Army Careers Office in Kirkcaldy. The following week, he'd taken Johnny with him. The recruiting sergeant told them jokes and stories from his time 'in the field'. He told them they'd breeze through basic training. He had a moustache and a paunch and told them there'd be 'shagging and boozing galore': 'two good-looking lads like you, it'll be dripping out of your ears'.

Johnny Rebus hadn't been sure what that meant exactly, but Mitch had rubbed his hands together and chuckled with the Sarge.

So that was that. All Johnny had to do was tell his dad and Janice.

His dad, it turned out, wasn't keen. He'd done some time in the Far East in World War II. He had some photographs and a black silk scarf with the Taj Mahal sewn into it. He had a scar on his knee that wasn't really a bullet wound, even though he said it was.

'You don't want that,' Johnny's dad said. 'You want a

proper job.' They kicked it back and forth between them. His dad's final shot at goal: 'What will Janice say?'

Janice didn't say anything; Rebus kept putting off telling her. And then one day she learned from her mum, who'd been talking to Johnny's dad, learned Johnny was thinking of leaving.

'It's not like I'm going for good,' he argued. 'I'll have plenty of home visits.'

She folded her arms, the way her mother did when she had right on her side. 'And am I supposed to just wait for you?'

'Please yourself,' Johnny said, kicking a stone.

'That's the plan,' she said, walking off.

Later, they made it up. He went to her house, went up to her bedroom with her: it was the only place they could talk. Her mum brought up juice and biscuits; gave them ten minutes then came up again to check they didn't need anything. Johnny said he was sorry.

'Does that mean you've changed your mind?' Janice asked.

He shrugged. He wasn't sure. Who did he want to let down: Janice or Mitch?

By the night of the dance, he'd made his mind up. Mitch could go alone. Johnny would stay behind, get a job of some kind and marry Janice. It wouldn't be a bad life. Plenty before him had done the same thing. He would tell Janice, tell her at the dance. And Mitch too, of course.

But first they had a drink. Mitch had got some bottles and an opener. They sneaked into the churchyard next to the school, drank a couple each, lay there in the grass, the headstones rising all around them. And it felt good, felt comfortable. Johnny swallowed back his confession. It could wait; he couldn't spoil this moment. It was like their whole lives had been sorted out, and everything was going to be fine. Mitch talked about the countries they'd visit, the things they'd see and do.

'And they'll all be gutted, just you wait.' Meaning

everyone who stayed in Bowhill, all their friends who were going off to college or down the pit or into the dockyard. 'We'll see the whole fucking world, Johnny. And all they'll ever see is this place.' And Mitch stretched his arms out until his fingertips brushed the rough surfaces of two headstones. 'All they'll ever have to look forward to is this . . .'

They were untouchable as they marched into the playground. A teacher and the deputy head were on the door, collecting tickets.

'I smell beer,' the deputy head said, catching them off guard. Then he winked. 'You might have saved one for me.'

Johnny and Mitch were laughing, all grown-up now, as they walked into the assembly hall. There was music playing, people up dancing. Soft drinks and sandwiches on trellis tables in the dining hall. Chairs around the perimeter of the assembly hall; huddles of conversation, eyes darting everywhere. It felt – just for a moment – as if everyone was looking at the new arrivals . . . looking at them, *envying* them. Mitch slapped Johnny's arm, headed towards his girlfriend Myra. Johnny knew he'd tell him at the end of the dance.

He looked for Janice, couldn't see her. He had to tell her . . . had to find the words. Then someone told him there was whisky in the toilets, and he decided to stop there first. Two cubicles, side by side. Three boys in each, passing the bottle back and forth over the partition. Keeping silent so they wouldn't be caught. The stuff tasted like fire. Its fumes came rolling down Johnny's nostrils. He felt drunk; elated; unstoppable.

Back in the hall, it was ladies' choice. A girl called Mary McCutcheon asked him up. They danced well together. But the reel made Johnny light-headed. He had to sit down. He hadn't noticed some recent arrivals – three boys from his year; boys who had over time become Mitch's implacable enemies. The leader of the three, Alan Protheroe, had gone one-on-one with Mitch. Mitch had pulverised him, eventually. Johnny didn't see them eyeing up Mitch. Didn't think that the last dance of schooldays might be a time for settling scores, for ending things as well as beginning them.

Because now Janice was in the hall. Seated next to him. And they were kissing, even when Miss Dysart stood in front of them clearing her throat in warning. When Janice drew away eventually, Johnny stood up, pulling her to her feet.

'I've something to tell you,' he said. 'But not here. Come on.'

And had led her outside, round the back of the old building to where the bike-sheds – now largely unused – still stood. Smokers' Corner, they called it. But it was a place for lovers too, for quick snogs at lunchtime. Johnny sat Janice down on a bench.

'Aren't you going to tell me how lovely I look?'

He drank her in. She did look lovely. Light from the school windows made her skin seem to glow. Her eyes were dark invitations, her dress rustled with layers waiting to be unpeeled. He kissed her again. She tried to break away, asked him what it was he wanted to tell her. But now he knew that could wait. He was light-headed and full of dreams and desire. He touched her neck where it was bare at the shoulders. He ran his hand down her back, slipping it beneath the material. Her mum had made the dress; he knew it had taken hours. When he pressed harder, he felt the stitching in the zip give way. Janice gave a gasp and pushed him away.

'Johnny . . .' Craning her neck to try to assess the damage. 'You silly bugger, see what you've done.'

His hands on her legs, sliding the dress up past the knee. 'Janice.'

She was standing now. He stood, too, pressing in on her for another kiss. She turned her face away. He seemed all limbs, sliding up her legs, slithering around her neck and down her back . . . She knew he tasted of beer and whisky. Knew she didn't like it. When she felt his hand trying to prise her legs apart, she pushed him away again, and he stumbled. Regaining balance, he wasn't so much smiling as leering as he moved in on her again.

And she swung back her hand, made a fist of it, and hit him a solid blow, almost dislocating her wrist in the process. She rubbed her knuckles, mouthing silent words of pain. He was flat out on the ground; knocked cold. She sat down again on the bench and waited for him to get up. Then heard what sounded like a commotion, and felt she'd much rather investigate than stay out here . . .

It was a fight. Slaughter might have been nearer the mark. The gang of three had somehow got Mitch on his own. They were at the edge of the playing-field, The Craigs silhouetted behind them. The sky was dark blue, bruise-coloured. Maybe Mitch had felt that tonight of all nights, he could take all three. Maybe they'd offered him a rematch, promising one-on-one. But it was three against one, and Mitch was on his hands and knees as the kicks rained in on his face and ribs. Janice was running forward, but a small, wiry figure beat her to it, legs and arms working like a windmill, head smashing into an unprotected nose, teeth bared with determination. She was amazed to identify the figure as Barney Mee, everyone's joker. What he lacked in elegance and precision, he more than made up for in sheer bloody-mindedness. He was like a machine. It only lasted a minute, maybe less, and at the end he was exhausted, but three figures were slouching off into the encroaching darkness as Barney slumped to the ground and lay on his back, staring up at the moon and the stars.

Mitch had pulled himself into a sitting position, one hand on his chest, the other covering an eye. Both hands were smeared with his own blood. His lip was split, and his nose was dripping red. When he spat, half a tooth was attached to the string of thick saliva. Janice stood above Barney Mee. He didn't seem so small, lying stretched out like that. He seemed . . . compact, but heroic. He opened his eyes and saw her, gave her one of his toothy grins.

'Lie down here,' he told her. 'There's something you should see.'

'What?'

'You won't see it standing up. You've got to lie down.'

She didn't believe him, but she lay down anyway. What did it matter if her dress got mucky: it was already split at the back. Her face was inches from his.

'What am I supposed to be looking at?' she asked.

'Up there,' he said, pointing.

And she looked. The sky wasn't black, that was the first strange thing. It was dark, certainly, but streaked with seams of white stars and clouds. And the moon seemed huge and orange rather than yellow.

'Isn't it amazing?' Barney Mee said. 'Every time I look at it, I can't help saying that.'

She turned to him. '*You're* amazing,' she said.

He smiled at the compliment. 'What are you going to do?'

'You mean when I leave?' She shrugged. 'Don't know. Look for a job, I suppose.'

'You should go to college.'

She looked at him more closely. 'Why?'

'You'd make a good teacher.'

She laughed out loud, but only for a second. 'What makes you say that?'

'I watch you in class. You'd be good, I know you would. Kids would listen to you.' He was looking at her now. 'I know I would,' he said.

Mitch cleared some blood from the back of his throat. 'Where's Johnny?' he asked.

Janice shrugged. Mitch eased his hand away from his eye. 'I'm fucking blind,' he said. 'And it hurts.' He bent over and began to cry. 'It hurts inside my head.'

Janice and Barney got up, helped him to his feet. They got one of the teachers to drive him to hospital. By the time Johnny Rebus came round, the show was over. He didn't even notice Janice dancing with Barney Mee. He just wanted a lift to the hospital.

'There's something I need to tell him.'

Eventually Mitch's parents came, and gave Johnny a lift to Kirkcaldy.

'What in God's name happened?' Mitch's mum asked. 'I don't know. I wasn't there.'

She turned to look at him. 'Weren't there?' He shook his head, ashamed. 'Then how did you get that bruise . . . ?'

His cheekbone, all the way down to his chin: a long purple trail. And he couldn't tell anyone how he'd come by it.

They had a long wait at the hospital. X-rays were mentioned. Cracked ribs.

'When I find whoever did this . . .' Mitch's dad said, balling his fists.

And then later, the bad news: a retina had been dislodged, maybe even worse. Mitch would lose the sight in one eye.

And by the time Johnny was allowed in to see him – with warnings not to stay too long, not to wear him out – Mitch had heard the news and was in tears.

'Christ, Johnny. Blind in one eye, how about that?'

There was a gauze patch over the eye in question.

'Long John fucking Silver and no mistake.' One of the patients on the ward coughed at the swear-word. 'And you can fuck off too!' Mitch yelled at him.

'Jesus, Mitch,' Johnny whispered. Mitch grabbed his wrist, squeezed it hard.

'It's you now. For both of us.'

Johnny licked his lips. 'How do you mean?'

'They won't take me, not blind in one eye. I'm sorry, pal. You know I am.'

Johnny was shaking, trying to think his way out.

'Right,' he said, nodding. It was all he could say, and he kept repeating it.

'You'll come back and see us, though, eh?' Mitch was saying. 'Tell me all about it. That's what I'd like . . . as if I was there with you.'

'Right, right.'

'You're going to have to live it for me, Johnny.'

'Sure, right.'

A smile from Mitch. 'Thanks, pal.'

'Least I can do,' said Johnny.

So he'd joined up. Janice hadn't seemed to mind. Mitch had waved him off at the station. And that was that. He sent Mitch and Janice letters; received none in return. By the time of his first leave, Mitch was nowhere to be found, and Janice was on holiday with her parents. Later, he found out Mitch had run off somewhere, no one seemed to know why or where. Johnny had half an idea: those letters, the visits home – reminders of the life Mitch could now never have . . .

Then his brother Mickey wrote to him, told him Janice had said to tell him she was going out with Barney Mee. And Johnny hadn't gone home after that for a while, had found other places to be when he was on leave, writing lies home so his father and brother wouldn't suspect, coming to think of the army as his home now . . . the only place he could be understood.

Drifting further in his mind from Cardenden and the friends he'd once had, and the dreams he'd once thought were within his reach . . .

45

It was dark and Cary Oakes was hungry and the game still wasn't over.

In prison, he'd been given lots of good advice about evading capture, all of it from men who'd been caught. He knew he needed to change his appearance: easily achieved with a visit to a charity shop. A new outfit of jacket, shirt and trousers for less than £20, topped off with a flat tweed cap. After all, he couldn't suddenly make his hair grow. When he saw his likeness in the newspaper, he made further adjustments, shaving himself scrupulously in a public convenience. He found a few stray carrier bags and filled them with rubbish. Examining himself in a shop window, he saw an unemployed man, a little bitter but still with enough money to buy the shopping.

He found the places where the down-and-outs spent their days: drop-in centres in the Grassmarket; the bench beside the toilets at the Tron Kirk; the foot of The Mound. These were safe places for him. People shared a can and a cigarette and didn't ask questions he couldn't make up answers to.

He was shivery and achy, made soft from his stay in the hotel. The windswept night on the hills had skimmed off some of his strength. It hadn't played the way he'd wanted it to. Archibald was still alive. Two spirits needed cleansing from his life: both were still to be dealt with.

And Rebus . . . Rebus had turned out to be something more than the 'wild operator' described by Jim Stevens. The way the reporter had talked, Oakes had expected Rebus to turn up naked to do battle. But Rebus had brought a whole goddamned army with him. Oakes had escaped by dint of good fortune and the weather. Or because the gods wanted his mission to succeed.

He knew things now would be difficult. In the centre of the city, he could remain anonymous, but further out there'd be more danger of discovery. The suburbs of Edinburgh remained places where strangers did not go undetected for long. It was as if people sat with their chairs at their windows in a constant state of alert. Yet one such suburb was his ultimate destination, as it had been all along.

He could have taken a bus, but in the end he walked. It took him well over an hour. He passed Alan Archibald's bungalow: 1930s styling with a bow window and white harled walls. There was no sign of life within. Archibald was in a hospital bed, and – according to one newspaper – under police guard. For the moment, Oakes had scratched him from his plans. Maybe the old bastard would die in hospital anyway. No, he was heading uphill and along another winding road into East Craigs. He'd been here just twice before, knowing people would get suspicious if he suddenly started frequenting the area. Two trips, one at night, one in the daytime. Both times he'd taken taxis from the foot of Leith Walk, making sure he was dropped off a few streets from his destination, not wanting the cabbies to know. In the dead of night, he'd walked right up to the walls of the building and touched trembling fingers to the stonework, trying to feel for a single life-force within.

He knew he was in there.

Couldn't stop shaking.

Knew he was in there, because he'd called to ask, identifying himself as the son of a friend. Asked if he could keep his call a secret: he wanted his visit to be a surprise.

He wondered if it *would* be a surprise . . .

Now, he was level with the car park. He sauntered past, just another tired worker on his way home. From the corner of his eye, he checked for police cars. Not that he thought they'd have guessed, but he wasn't going to underestimate Rebus again.

And saw instead a car he thought he recognised. Stopped and put his bags down, making to change hands, making out they were heavier than they were. And studied the car. A Vauxhall Astra. Numberplate the same. Oakes bared his teeth and let out a hiss of air. This was too much, the bastards were determined to wreck his plans.

Only one thing for it. He fingered the knife in his pocket, knowing he'd have to do some killing.

He had ditched the carrier bags and was lying beneath the car when he heard footsteps. Turned his head to watch them coming closer. He reckoned he'd been lying on the ground for a good hour and a half. His back was chilled, and the shivers were starting again. When he heard the clunk of the locks disengaging, he slid out from his hiding-place and tugged open the passenger door. Seeing him, the driver made to get out again, but Cary Oakes had the knife in his right hand while his left grabbed at Jim Stevens's sleeve.

'Thought you'd be pleased to see me again, Jimbo,' Oakes said. 'Now close the door and get this thing moving.' He took off his jacket, tossed it on to the back seat.

'Where are we going?'

'Just drive, man.' His shirt followed.

'What are you doing?' Stevens asked. But Oakes ignored him, loosed his trousers and threw them into the back too.

'This is all a bit sudden for me, Cary.'

'A man who likes a joke, huh?' As they left the car park, Oakes realised he was sitting on something. Pulled out the reporter's notebook and pen.

'Been working, Jim?' He opened the notebook, and was disappointed to see Stevens had used shorthand.

407

'Why'd you go see him?' Oakes asked, beginning to tear each page of the notebook into four.

'See who? I was visiting an old neighbour of mine, and—'

The knife arced into Stevens's side. He took his hands off the wheel, and the car veered towards the kerb. Oakes straightened it up.

'Keep your foot down, Jim! If this car stops, you're a dead man!'

Stevens examined his palm. It was wet with blood. 'Hospital,' he croaked, face twisted with pain.

'You'll get a hospital *after* I've had my answers! What made you go to see him?'

Stevens hunched over the wheel, taking control again. Oakes thought he was going to pass out, but it was just the pain.

'I was checking details.'

'That all?' Ripping at the notebook.

'What else would I be doing?'

'Well, that's why I'm asking, Jim-Bob. And if you don't want knifing again, you'll convince me.' Oakes reached for the heater switch, slid it to full.

'It's for the book.'

'The book?' Oakes narrowed his eyes.

'I don't have enough material with just the interviews.'

'You should have asked me first.' Oakes was silent for a minute.

'Where are we going?' Stevens had one hand on the steering-wheel, one pressed to his side.

'Turn right at the roundabout, head out of town.'

'The Glasgow road? I need a hospital.'

Oakes wasn't listening. 'What did he say?'

'What?'

'What did he say about me?'

'Probably what you'd expect.'

'He's *compos mentis* then?'

'Pretty much.'

408

Oakes wound down the window, scattering the scraps of paper. When he turned round again, Stevens was scrabbling on the floor with his hand.

'What are you doing?' Oakes brandished the knife.

'Paper hankies. I thought I'd a box somewhere.'

Oakes examined his handiwork. 'Just between you and me, Jim, I don't think paper tissues are going to do the job.'

'I feel faint. I've got to stop.'

'Keep going!'

Stevens' eyelids looked heavy. 'See if they're in the back.'

'What?'

'The box of hankies.'

So Oakes turned in his seat, pushed his clothes around. 'Nothing here.'

Stevens was rooting in his pockets. 'Must be something . . .' Eventually he found a large cotton handkerchief, eased it inside his shirt.

'Take the airport exit,' Oakes commanded.

'You leaving us, Cary?'

'Me?' Oakes grinned. 'When I'm just beginning to enjoy myself?' He sneezed, spraying the windscreen with spittle.

'Bless you,' Stevens said. There was silence in the car for a moment, then both men laughed.

'That's funny,' Oakes said, wiping an eye. 'You blessing me.'

'Cary, I'm losing a lot of blood.'

'It's all right, Jimbo. I've seen people bleed to death before. You've got hours left in you.' He sat back in his seat. 'So you were out there all by yourself, checking background . . . ? Who knew you were going?'

'Nobody.'

'Not your editor?'

'No.'

'And John Rebus?'

Stevens snorted. 'Why would I tell him?'

'Because I made you mad.' Oakes pushed out his bottom lip. 'Sorry about that, by the way.'

'Was it really all lies?'

'That's between me and my conscience, man.'

The car hit a bump and Stevens grimaced.

'Know what they say about pain, Jim? They say it makes you see colour for the very first time. Makes everything really *vivid*.'

'The blood certainly looks vivid.'

'There's nothing like it,' Oakes said quietly, 'not in the whole world.'

They were coming to another roundabout. Off to their left sat Ingliston Showground, unused for the most part of the year. Unused tonight.

'Airport?' Stevens asked.

'No, take a left.'

So Stevens did, and found himself approaching a building site. Another new hotel was being thrown up, to complement the one at the airport exit. Around it lay farmland, the dwellings few and far between. There were no visible lights at all, not even from planes landing and taking off.

'No hospitals near here,' Stevens said, dread overcoming him.

'Pull over.'

Stevens did as he was told.

'They'll have a doctor at the airport,' Oakes told him. 'I'll need your car, but you can walk it.'

'Better still, you could drop me off.' Jim Stevens licked his dry lips.

'Or better yet . . .' Cary Oakes said. And his hand flew, and the knife went into Stevens' side again.

And again and again, as the journalist's words became twisted sounds, finding a new vocabulary of terror, resignation and pain.

Oakes dragged the corpse out and dumped it behind a

mound of earth. Searched in the pockets and found Stevens' cassette recorder. There wasn't much light, but he was able to prise it open, remove the tape. Left the recorder behind; took the tape. Little money in Stevens' wallet: credit cards, but he wanted neither to use them nor be caught with them in his possession. He bent down again, wiped the recorder on Stevens' jacket, getting rid of prints.

The wind was cutting through him. If he tried concealing the body, he might die of hypothermia. He raced back to the car, got into the driver's seat and headed off. The heater wouldn't go any higher. The blood was sticking his underpants to the seat. He could feel it against his skin. Couldn't put his clothes on yet: had to keep them clean. Couldn't go wandering around Edinburgh with blood-stained clothes.

Another trick from prison. Maybe his fellow inmates hadn't been so stupid after all.

On the way back into town, he stopped in a deserted supermarket car park, threw the tape into a bin.

Then he was on his way. Knew he had at least one night before the body was found. One night when he'd have some shelter, courtesy of Jim Stevens' car.

46

Anything out west was a Torphichen call, but news travelled fast. Roy Frazer drove Rebus out to the scene. The whole drive, Rebus only said one thing to the young man.

'You screwed up about Eddie Mearn. It happens. Best to have it happen young when you can still learn from it. Otherwise you get intimations of infallibility, which translates to your colleagues as "smart-arse".'

'Yes, sir,' Frazer said, frowning as though trying to memorise the advice. Then he reached into his pocket. 'Message from DS Clarke.' He handed over the note. Rebus unfolded the piece of paper. At first he didn't take it in. His brain was overloaded as it was. But eventually the words hit him with the force of electricity.

I did a bit of digging. Joseph Margolies wasn't just a doctor. He worked for the council for a time, had special responsibility for children's homes. Don't know if it means anything, but I get the feeling you had him down as a GP. Cheers, S.

He read the note half a dozen times. He wasn't sure if it *did* mean anything. But he could see definite connections beginning to appear. And connections could always be exploited . . .

The DI from Torphichen was Shug Davidson. He offered a brief smile as Rebus got out of the car.

'They say the culprit always returns to the scene of the crime.'

'That's not funny, Shug.'

'Way I hear it, you and the deceased weren't exactly bosom buddies.'

'Maybe towards the end,' Rebus said. 'Have they moved him yet?'

Davidson shook his head. Work on the construction site had stopped. There were faces at the portakabin windows. Other workers milled around outside, wearing hard hats, drinking tea from their flasks. Their gaffer was complaining that work was a fortnight behind as it was.

'Then a few more hours isn't going to make much of a dent, is it?' Davidson said.

Rebus had ducked beneath the *locus* tape. The victim had been pronounced dead. They were photographing the body. Forensics had already completed taping it. Uniforms were spreading out from the *locus*, seeking clues. Davidson had the whole situation under control.

'Any ideas?' Davidson asked Rebus.

'One fairly big one.'

'Oakes?' Rebus looked at Davidson, who smiled. 'I read the papers too, John. Friend of a friend told me Oakes had dumped on Stevens. Next thing, Oakes is on the run after the attack on Alan Archibald.' He broke off. 'How is he, by the way?'

'Doing better than this poor bugger,' Rebus said, moving closer to the body. Professor Gates was crouched – or as Gates himself liked to say, on his 'cuddy-hunkers' – at Stevens' head. He nodded a greeting towards Rebus, but carried on with his initial appraisal of the scene. One of the forensics team held out a clear plastic bag, into which Jim Stevens' possessions were being dropped.

'No car keys?' Rebus asked. The forensics woman shook her head.

'No car either,' Davidson added.

'Stevens drives a Vauxhall Astra.'

'I know, John. It's being hunted.'

'Must have been brought here in a car. Oakes doesn't have one.'

'Probably lost a lot of blood en route,' Gates said. 'His

413

shirt and trousers are soaked, but there's not that much lying beneath him.'

'You think he was stabbed somewhere else?'

'That would be my guess.' Gates turned to the forensics officer. 'Let Inspector Rebus see the machine.'

She lifted a small metal box from the bag. Rebus looked at it closely, but knew better than to touch.

'It's his recorder.'

'Yes,' Gates said. 'And in his right-hand pocket, well away from the wounds and the blood.'

'But there's blood on it,' Rebus said.

Gates nodded. 'And no tape inside.'

'The killer took the tape?'

'Or it was important enough for the deceased to take time to remove it, even though by that time he'd already been stabbed and was probably entering a state of shock.'

Rebus turned to Davidson. 'Any sign of it?'

'That's what they're looking for.' Davidson motioned towards the uniforms. 'John, have you any idea what Stevens was up to?'

'Last time I spoke to him, he was going to look into Oakes's past.'

'Wonder what he found.'

Rebus shrugged. 'Bringing in Oakes *has* to be the priority.'

'After his attack on you, it already was.'

Rebus stared down at the lifeless body of Jim Stevens. Stevens, who had been Rebus's shadow for so long, and who had come back into his life only recently.

'I'd only just started liking him,' Rebus said. 'That's the funny thing.' He looked at Davidson. 'I get the feeling the game's not over, Shug. Not by a long chalk.'

One of Davidson's officers sprinted towards them. 'Car's been found,' he called.

'Where?' Rebus was first to ask.

The officer blinked, shook his head. 'You're not going to like it . . .'

*

414

Jim Stevens' Astra sat on a single yellow line on a street called St Leonard's Bank, just round the corner from St Leonard's cop shop. St Leonard's Bank boasted a single row of higgledy-piggledy houses, all of them facing a wrought-iron fence behind which sat Holyrood Park and Salisbury Crags. The car was parked outside a double-fronted three-storey house painted a vivid pink. The key was in the ignition. This was what had first alerted one of the neighbours. They'd gone next door to ask if anyone there had left their keys in their car. Heading out to investigate, they'd found the doors to be unlocked. On opening the driver's side, they'd noticed how wet and stained the seat seemed to be. Pressing fingers down into the fabric, lifting them away to find them stained viscous red . . .

'Is he taking the piss or what?' Roy Frazer said. A crowd from St Leonard's had gathered, though more, it seemed, out of curiosity than from a desire to help. Rebus started shooing most of them away. He'd brought three of the forensics team with him; the rest would follow when they'd finished at the construction site. Chief Superintendent Watson came to gawp, and to make sure everything was 'under control'.

'It's Shug Davidson's call really, sir,' Rebus informed him. 'He's on his way.'

The Farmer nodded. 'Fair enough, John. But let's get the car moved ASAP, even if only into our car park. It's already been on Lowland Radio. Leave it much longer, we can start selling tickets.'

It was true that the crowd around the car was swelling. Rebus recognised a few faces from Greenfield. The estate was only a short walk away.

Roy Frazer was repeating his question.

'He's taunting us,' Rebus answered. He went to see how the forensics team was doing.

'Found this on the floor under the driver's seat,' one of them said. Inside a plastic bag he had a cassette tape, unlabelled. There was a single bloody thumb print clearly visible on its casing.

'I need this,' Rebus said.

'We need to print it.'

Rebus shook his head. 'The print belongs to the victim.' He was managing to smile. *You clever bugger, Jim*, he was thinking. *He didn't get your tape . . .*

At least, that was what he hoped.

'Something else,' another of the team said, pointing to show Rebus a spread of tiny spots on the windscreen. 'These are on the inside. The way the pattern is . . . it's like someone coughed or sneezed. If it was the killer . . .'

'Is there enough for DNA?'

'It's a hell of a long shot, but you never know. Don't know if this is relevant.' Now he pointed to a notebook on the floor of the passenger side. It had a tin spiral holding the loose-leaf pages in place. Shreds of paper clung to the spiral, showing where pages had been torn out.

Rebus patted the man's shoulder. He didn't like to say *It doesn't matter. I know who killed him . . . I may even know why . . .* When he turned away, he was carrying the cassette tape in its little poly-bag, for all the world like a solemn kid who'd won a goldfish at the fair.

Because it was quieter there, Rebus used one of the interview rooms. He'd slotted the tape into one of the recorders, being careful to hold it by its edges. No point destroying trace evidence. He had a pair of Sennheiser headphones on, and spread out in front of him the contents of Cary Oakes's file, as well as cuttings of his recent newspaper interviews. He'd telephoned Stevens' old employer, and they were faxing over the unused portions of transcript. Every now and then, a uniform would stick his or her head round the door and hand him the latest fax sheets, so that the table became covered.

Siobhan Clarke went so far as to bring him a mug of coffee and a BLT, but otherwise left him to it, which was just what he wanted. His mind was on nothing but the interview he was listening to.

'Little bugger came to us with his mum . . . my wife's sister, she was. Right little runt he was.' The man's voice sounded old, wheezy.

'You didn't get on with him?' Jim Stevens' voice, making the hairs rise on Rebus's arms. He looked around but Stevens' ghost was nowhere to be seen; not yet . . . Occasional background noises: coughs, voices, a television playing. An audience . . . no, spectators. Spectators at what sounded like a football match. Rebus went through to CID and dug in bins, looked through the papers sitting folded and forgotten on window ledges, until he found one for the previous day. Seven thirty: UEFA Cup action. That seemed to fit the bill. He tore out the TV page, took it back with him to the interview room, turned the tape on again.

'I hated him, to be frank with you. Bloody disruption, that's all it was. I mean, we had ourselves sorted out, everything going smoothly, everything just so . . . and then the two of them come waltzing in. Couldn't very well kick them out, being family and all, but I made sure they knew I wasn't happy. Oi, I'm watching that!'

Someone had changed channels. Studio laughter. Rebus checked the paper: a sitcom on the BBC.

Back to the sound of crowd and commentator.

'We had some high old ding-dongs, him and me.'

'What about?'

'Everything: him staying out, him thieving. Money kept disappearing. I laid a few traps, but I never caught him, he was too canny for that.'

'Did your fights ever become physical?'

'I should say so. Tough little runt, I'll give him that. You see me the way I am now, but back then I was fighting fit.' He coughed loudly; sounded like his lungs were being turned inside out. 'Give me that water, will you?' The old man took a drink, then broke wind. 'Anyway,' he went on, not bothering to apologise, 'I made

sure he knew who was boss. It was my house, remember.'
As if Stevens were accusing him.

'You were the boss,' Stevens reassured him.

'I was and all. Take my word for it.'

'And if you thumped him, it was just so he'd understand.'

'That's what I'm telling you. And he was no angel, believe you me. Mind you, try telling the women that.'

'His mother and her sister?'

'My wife, aye. She never saw any harm in anyone, did Aggie. But I'd have to say, even back then I knew there was badness in him. Deep-rooted badness.'

'You tried knocking it out of him.'

'I'd have needed a sledgehammer, son. Did use a hammer on him once, as it happens. Bastard was tough by then, ready to give as good as he got.' Rebus thinking: *The poison passed from one generation to the next. As with abuse, so with violence.*

'Did he run with a gang?'

'Gang? Nobody would have him, son. What did you say your name was?'

'Jim.'

'And you're with the papers? I spoke to some of your lot when he was put away.'

'What did you tell them?'

'That he should've had the electric chair. We could do a lot worse ourselves than bring back hanging.'

'You think it's a deterrent?'

'Once they're dead, son, they don't do it again, do they? What more proof do you want?'

There were sounds of someone bringing Stevens a cup of coffee or tea.

'Aye, they're good to me in here.'

Nursing home . . . Cary Oakes's uncle . . . What was his name? Rebus found it in the notes: Andrew Castle. Alongside it, the name of his nursing home. Rebus got on the phone, found a number for the home and rang them.

'You've got a resident called Andrew Castle.'

'Yes?'

'He had a visitor last night.'

'He did, yes.'

'Did you see him leave?'

'I'm sorry, who is this?'

'My name's Detective Inspector Rebus. Only Mr Castle's visitor has turned up dead, and we're trying to trace his last movements.'

There was a tapping at the door. Shug Davidson came in. Rebus nodded for him to sit.

'Gracious,' the woman at the nursing home was saying. 'You mean the reporter?'

'That's who I mean. What time did he leave?'

'It must have been . . .' She broke off. 'How did he die?'

'He was stabbed, madam. Now, what time did he leave?'

Davidson, seated across the table from Rebus, turned some of the fax sheets round so he could read them.

'Just before bedtime . . . say, nine o'clock.'

'Did he have a car with him?'

'I think so, yes. He parked it outside.'

'Was anyone seen hanging around?'

She sounded puzzled. 'No, I don't think so.'

'Any suspicious sightings the past day or two?'

'Gracious me, Inspector, what's this about?'

Rebus thanked her for her time, said someone would be coming to get her statement. Then he put down the phone, checked the home's address against an A–Z.

'Shug,' he said, 'I've got Stevens at a nursing home near the Maybury roundabout, probably from around seven thirty last night till nine.'

'Maybury's on the road out to the airport.'

Rebus nodded. 'I think Oakes was already there.'

'Where?'

'The nursing home.'

'Who was Stevens seeing there?'

'Oakes's uncle. The questions Jim used on the tape . . . I think he'd already talked to the uncle, already made up his mind about him.'

'How do you mean?'

'The questions were angled a certain way, letting the uncle show himself as a sadist.'

'You're going to tell me this uncle turned Cary Oakes into a psychopath?'

Rebus shrugged. 'That's you talking, not me. What I *do* think is, Oakes has a grudge.' He thought for a moment. *I have a date with my past. A date with destiny . . . with someone who wouldn't listen . . .* Oakes's words to Stevens at the end of their last interview . . . 'Alan Archibald lives out that way.' He opened the *A–Z* again, pointed to Archibald's street, then the cul-de-sac which housed the nursing home. They were barely half a dozen streets apart. 'I thought Oakes went there to scope out Alan Archibald.'

'Now you think different?'

'He came back to Edinburgh to settle old scores. There's none older than his uncle.' He looked up at Davidson. 'I think he'll try to kill him.'

Davidson rubbed a palm over his jaw. 'And Jim Stevens?'

'Was in the wrong place at the wrong time. If Oakes thought Jim was on to his plan, he'd have to deal with him. Oakes took the tape from Jim's recorder, only Jim had switched tapes. Then Oakes tore out the pages from Jim's notebook. He didn't want us knowing.'

'But we were bound to find out where Stevens had been.'

'Eventually, yes.' Rebus tapped the tape machine. 'But without this, it would have taken a while.'

Davidson was starting to rise. 'Long enough to let him carry out his plan?'

'Which means it's got to be soon.' Rebus was on his feet too.

As Davidson reached for the phone, Rebus sprinted from the room.

47

They had undercover officers on the scene. It was difficult
to blend in: most of the staff were middle-aged women.
Young, wary-looking men with CID haircuts looked out of
place. The officers came from the Scottish Crime Squad.
Andrew Castle was confined to his room. There were two
men in there with him: one participating in a game of
cards – twopenny bets – while the other sat in the corner,
affording the best view of door and window. The window
was curtained. There was another man in a parked car
outside.

'Would he try a sniper shot?' had been one of the
questions at the briefing. Rebus had doubted it: he'd no
known access to guns, and besides, it was personal with
him. His uncle would have to know the why and the who
before any killing could be done.

One of the other officers was pushing a mop up and
down the corridor outside. Rebus and Davidson were
satisfied.

Another question from the briefing: 'What if all we do is
scare him off?'

Rebus's response: 'Then we've saved an old man's life
. . . for now.'

He'd listened once more to the whole tape, and didn't
doubt that Oakes's uncle had been – and probably still
was – rotten to the marrow, despite his senility and frailty.
Now he had questions.

If Cary had ended up in a home where he'd been loved,
would everything have been changed? Were people
programmed from birth to become killers, or did other

people – and sets of circumstances – conspire to make killers of them, turning the potential that was in most people into something more tangible?

They weren't new questions, certainly not to him. He thought of Darren Rough, the abused becoming abuser. Not all abuse victims took that road, but plenty did . . . And what about Damon Mee? What *had* made him leave home? His parents' failing marriage? Fear of getting married himself? Or had he been coerced away, forcibly stopped from returning?

And why had Jim Margolies died?

And would Cary Oakes walk into the trap?

My, my, my, said the spider to the fly . . .

Oakes had been the spider for far too long.

Rebus dropped into hospital to check on Alan Archibald. There was nothing for him to do at the nursing home. In fact, as one of the Crime Squad officers had succinctly put it, he was 'a positive hindrance'. Meaning that because Oakes knew Rebus, his presence on the scene could spoil everything.

'Soon as anything happens, we'll call.'

Rebus had made the officer write his mobile number on the back of his hand. Then had handed him a business card anyway: 'Just in case you wash it off by mistake.'

Archibald was at the far end of an open ward, with a screen around his bed. Bobby Hogan from Leith CID was sitting bedside, flicking through a copy of *Mass Hibsteria*.

'Your team's going down, Bobby,' Rebus told him.

Hogan looked up. 'It's not mine.' He waved the football fanzine at Rebus. 'Someone left it on the ward.'

The two men shook hands, and Rebus went to fetch another chair. Alan Archibald was snoring gently, head propped up on three pillows.

'How is he?' Rebus asked. Archibald's head was bandaged and there was a gauze compress taped to one ear.

'Thumping headache.'

'Well, his head *did* take a thumping.'

'They did some tests, say he'll be fine.' Hogan smiled. 'They tried testing his memory, but as Alan said, at his age he's lucky to remember which day it is, dunt on the heid or no'.'

Rebus smiled too. 'You know him then?'

'Worked together years ago. That's why I asked for this detail.'

'Were you with him when his niece was murdered?'

Hogan stared at the sleeping figure. 'It took all the juice out of him, like his batteries were flat after that.'

'He wanted it to be Cary Oakes.'

Hogan nodded. 'I think anyone would have done as far as Alan was concerned, but Oakes was the obvious choice.'

'Still could be.'

Hogan looked at him. 'Not according to Alan.'

'I wouldn't trust anything Oakes said. Everything in his world has to be twisted round.'

'But he thought he was going to kill Alan . . . why bother lying to him?'

'To amuse himself.' Rebus crossed one leg over the other. 'That seems to be what he's been doing ever since he hit town, spinning stories . . .' And now Rebus was surplus to requirements; other officers would bring in Cary Oakes.

'Did you ever get anywhere with Jim's suicide?'

Rebus looked at Hogan. 'I was beginning to. I got sidetracked.'

'So what can you tell me?'

Alan Archibald grunted, and his lips started moving as though savouring something. Slowly his eyes opened. He looked to his left and saw his two visitors.

'Any sign of him?' he asked, voice dry and brittle. Hogan poured him some water.

'Do you want any more tablets, Alan?'

Archibald made to shake his head, then screwed shut his eyes with the sudden pain. 'No,' he said instead. As Hogan trickled the water into his mouth, it dribbled either side of the plastic cup and down his chin. Hogan dabbed it with a napkin.

'He'd make a great nurse.' Archibald winked at Rebus. His eyes looked unfocused; Rebus wondered what kind of painkillers they had him on. 'They haven't caught him?'

'Not yet,' Rebus admitted.

'But he's been busy, hasn't he?'

Rebus didn't know if it was pure instinct or whether something in his voice had alerted Archibald. He nodded, told Archibald about Jim Stevens, about the nursing home and Oakes's uncle.

'I remember the uncle,' Archibald said. 'I interviewed him a while back. I think he hated Oakes almost more than I did.'

'You didn't happen to mention him to Oakes, did you?'

Archibald was thoughtful for a moment. 'Not for a while. He might have been in one of the letters I sent.' His eyes widened. 'How did Oakes know where he was? You think I . . . ?' Pain coursed across his face. 'I should have twigged. But I wasn't thinking like a copper, that's the bottom line. I had my own motives. I wasn't really interested in the uncle, only in what he could tell me about Oakes. There was that one question always at the back of my mind . . . that one question I needed the answer to.'

'Yes,' Rebus agreed.

'Everything I'd learned went out the window.' Tears were welling in Archibald's eyes.

'Don't blame yourself,' Hogan said, touching his shoulder.

Archibald was looking past him, towards the seated figure of John Rebus. 'Whether he killed her or not . . . I'll never know for sure, will I?'

Tears dropped on to Archibald's cheeks and down his

chin. Bobby Hogan dabbed at them with the already damp napkin.

'All these years not knowing . . . damned fool to think I could . . .' He closed his eyes, crying softly. In the other beds, no one stirred. Crying in the night maybe wasn't so unusual here. Bobby Hogan had taken hold of both the old man's hands. It looked like Archibald was squeezing with all his might.

Alan Archibald was in hospital because he'd become obsessed with an idea. Rebus, knowing what he knew now, was wondering if Jim Margolies had become obsessed too. With nothing else to do, he headed back to St Leonard's. It took a couple of hours, several phone calls, and a lot of grudging help before Rebus got what he wanted.

He sat at his desk scoring through points on his notepad. The people he'd spoken to from the Health Board and Social Work had all asked if it couldn't wait till morning. Rebus had insisted it could not.

'It's a murder inquiry,' had been his only line of attack. When pressed for details, he'd said he couldn't add anything 'at the present moment in time', trying to sound like the sort of detective they'd expect him to be: a bureaucrat, a man following a preordained path of investigation where no overnight rest-stops could be taken.

In the end, he'd had to drive to the various offices himself to pick up the information he'd asked for. On each occasion, he'd been met by the official he'd spoken to on the phone. They'd all stared at him with ill-will and irritation. But they'd all handed over the documents. Which gave Rebus little to do but head back to St Leonard's and plough through the field of information on Dr Joseph Margolies.

Dr Margolies had been born in Selkirk, and educated in the Borders and at Fettes. His medical degree was completed at the University of Edinburgh, with stints working in Africa for a Christian charity. He'd become a general practitioner, then had taken to lecturing, specialising in paediatrics. And eventually, as Siobhan's note had said, he'd been employed to 'look after' the council-run children's homes in Lothian, a job which also took him into private homes licensed by the council – such as those owned and operated by churches and charities.

What his job meant in effect was that he checked the children for signs of abuse, and would be brought in to make a physical examination should any accusations of abuse be made. Also, some of the kids were classed as 'difficult cases', and a medical prognosis would be part of their ongoing record. Dr Margolies might recommend psychiatric consultation, or a move to some other type of institution. He could prescribe treatments and medication. His powers, in effect, were almost without limit. His word was law.

About halfway through his reading, Rebus began to get a queasy feeling in his gut. He hadn't eaten for hours, but didn't think that had anything to do with it. Nevertheless, he forced himself to get some fresh air, visited Brattisani's for a fish supper with buttered bread and tea. Afterwards, he knew he'd been away from the station for the best part of an hour, but couldn't recall any of that time: no faces, no voices. Brain busy with other things.

He remembered a recent case, a priest who'd abused children for years. The children had been in the care of nuns, and when any of them complained they were thrashed by the nuns, told they were liars, and made to attend confession – where, listening to them, would be the same priest they'd just accused of abuse.

He knew that oftentimes paedophiles were well able to hide their true natures for months and years as they trained for positions in children's homes and the like. They would pass all the checks and psychological tests, only later for the mask to slip. Their need was so great, they would go to extraordinary lengths to fulfil it. And sometimes it might have remained latent had they not encountered at some point a fellow traveller, each spurring the other on . . .

Like Harold Ince and Ramsay Marshall. Rebus could believe that either one, left in isolation, would never have found the strength to begin their eventual programme of systematic abuse. But together, working as a team, the effect had been to intensify their lusts and desires, making the eventual abuse so much more appalling.

Rebus looked back through all the paperwork on Dr Joseph Margolies, until he was sure of what he saw.

That Margolies had been attached to the city's children's homes at the time of the Shiellion scandal.

That he had retired soon afterwards – and prematurely – on 'health grounds'.

That he was considered courageous by those he worked with for the way he'd kept going following his daughter's suicide.

Rebus didn't find much about the daughter. She'd killed herself at fifteen, hadn't left a note. She'd been a quiet child, withdrawn. Adolescence had done her few favours. She'd been worried about upcoming exams. Her brother Jim had been devastated by her death . . .

She hadn't leapt from some high spot. She'd slashed her wrists in the bathroom of her home. Her father had kicked open the door and found her there. It was believed she'd done the deed in the dead of night. Her father was always the first to rise in the morning.

Rebus put a call through to Jane Barbour. By dint of white lies and stubbornness, he secured her mobile number. When she picked up, he could hear loud music and cheering in the background.

'Good party, is it?'

'Who's this?'

'DI Rebus.'

Another wave of cheering behind her. 'Hang on, I'll just

take this outside.' The sounds died away. Barbour exhaled noisily. She sounded drunk. 'We're at the Police Club.'

'What's the celebration?'

'Take a guess.'

'Guilty verdicts?'

'On both the bastards. Not a single juror went against us.'

Rebus sat back in his chair. 'Congratulations.'

'Thanks.'

'Cordover must be seething.'

'Bugger Cordover. Petrie pronounces tomorrow. He'll stick them away for ever and a day.'

'Well, congratulations again. It's a hell of a result.'

'Why don't you come down? We've enough booze here—'

'Thanks all the same. But it's a coincidence, I'm phoning about Ince and Marshall.'

'Oh?'

'Indirectly anyway. Dr Joseph Margolies.'

'Yes?'

'You know who he is?'

'Yes.'

'Was he called to give evidence?'

'No, he wasn't. Christ, it's so mild out here tonight.'

Rebus wondered if she was on anything other than a natural high. 'Why wasn't he called?'

'Because of the facts of the case. It's true a few of the Shiellion kids made accusations at the time, but they weren't believed.'

'There'd be a medical check, though.'

'Of course, carried out by Dr Margolies. I interviewed him several times. But the boys were known to be gay, insofar as they worked as occasional rent boys around Calton Hill. If they ran from Shiellion, that's where everyone knew to find them. So you see, evidence of anal sex was not in itself evidence of abuse – I'm quoting the

Procurator Fiscal's line. To my mind, these kids were underage and in care, and anyone who had sex with them was guilty of abuse.' She paused. 'End of rant.'

'Sooner you're free of this case the better.'

'So why are you dragging it all up again?'

'I'm trying to get a fix on Dr Margolies.'

'Why?'

'When you talked to him, was he helpful?'

'As much as he could be. He said himself the kids had been caught lying before, so who was going to believe them next time? And a lot of the abuse claims referred to oral sex and masturbation . . . not many medical tests for those, Inspector.'

'No,' Rebus said thoughtfully. 'So he didn't give evidence?'

'Not in court. Fiscal said it would be a waste of time. Might even have harmed our case by casting doubt in the jury's mind.'

'In which case Cordover might have wanted the doctor as a witness.'

'Yes, but he didn't, and I wasn't about to give him a hand.' She paused. 'You think Margolies was involved in a cover-up?'

'What makes you ask?'

'I wondered about it myself. I mean, chances are there were people working at Shiellion who had a good idea what was happening. But nobody stuck their head above the parapet.'

'Afraid to cause trouble?'

'Or warned off by the Church. It's not been unknown in the past. Of course, there's an even worse scenario.'

Rebus dreaded to think what it might be. But he asked anyway.

'Just this,' she said. 'People knew it was happening, but they just didn't care. Now if you'll excuse me, I'm heading back indoors to get blisteringly drunk.'

430

Rebus thanked her and rang off. Sat with his head in his hands, staring at his desk.

People knew ... they just didn't care ...

48

Just as during their actual trial, Ince and Marshall were being held in Saughton Prison. The difference was, now they'd been found guilty they were no longer on remand. As remand prisoners, they'd been able to wear their own clothes, phone out for food, and go about their business. Now they'd be getting used to prison garb and all the other comforts of the prison regime proper.

They were being held in separate cells, with an empty cell between so there was less chance of them communicating. Rebus didn't know why anyone bothered: they'd probably end up in the same sex offender programme.

He had a difficult choice to make: Ince or Marshall? Of course, if one failed him, there was nothing to stop him trying the other. But that would mean going through the same process again, asking the same questions, playing the same games. The right choice might save him all that grief.

He chose Ince. His reasoning: Ince was the elder, with the higher IQ. And though early on in the relationship, there was no doubt that he'd been the leader, the pupil had soon become the master. In the courtroom, Marshall had been the one who'd scowled and grunted and played to the gallery; the one who'd looked as though the trial had nothing to do with him.

The one with no visible show of shame, even as his victims told their stories.

The one who'd fallen down the stairs a couple of times on his way back to the cells.

Yes, Marshall had learned a lot from Harold Ince, but

he'd added ingredients of his own. He was the more savage, the more amoral, the less penitent. He was the one who thought it was the world's problem, not his. At the trial, he'd tried quoting Aleister Crowley, to the effect that only *he* had the right to judge his actions right or wrong.

The court hadn't thought much of that.

Rebus sat in the visitors' room and smoked a cigarette. He'd called Patience, got the machine: a message telling callers to try her mobile. He did so, found she was at a friend's. Another woman doctor, off on prenatal leave.

'I might stay the night,' Patience told him. 'Ursula's offered.'

'How is she?'

'Sick.'

'Oh dear.'

'You misunderstand: she's sick she can't drink. Never mind, I'm drinking for two.'

Rebus smiled. 'I'll go to Arden Street,' he said. 'If you're going home, let me know.'

'You think I should stay away?'

'It might be an idea.' He meant until Cary Oakes was caught. When he rang off, he got through to St Leonard's, who confirmed that the patrol car was now stationed outside Patience's friend's.

'Safe as houses, John.'

So he sat in the visitors' room and smoked a cigarette, defying the sign on the wall, flicking ash on to the carpet. The uniform brought Harold Ince in. Rebus thanked him, told him to wait just outside. Not that Rebus expected anything from Ince: no violence, no escape attempt. He looked resigned to his fate. Since Rebus had seen him at the trial, his face had grown longer and thinner, the pallid skin hanging from it. His stomach bulged, but his chest seemed to have caved in, as though the heart had been removed. Rebus knew that at least one of Ince's victims had committed suicide. There was a smell from the man: sulphur mixed with Germolene.

Rebus offered him a cigarette. Ince, slumping into a chair, shook his head.

'You gave evidence, didn't you?' The voice was thin and reedy.

Rebus nodded, flicked ash. 'Your lawyer tried carving me up.'

The brief flicker of a smile. 'I remember now. Didn't work, did it?'

'And now you've been found guilty.'

'Come to rub it in?' Ince's eyes found Rebus's for the briefest moment.

'No, Mr Ince, I've come to ask for your help.'

Ince snorted, folded his arms. 'Yeah, I'm well in the mood to help the police.'

'I wonder if he's already made up his mind?' Rebus asked, as if wondering aloud.

Ince's forehead creased. 'Who?'

'Lord Justice Petrie. He's a tough old buzzard.'

'So I've heard.'

But soft on his kids, Rebus thought to himself. *Or is he . . .?*

'My money's on Peterhead for the pair of you,' he said. 'You'll be there a long time. That's where they take the sex offenders.' Rebus sat forward. 'It's also where a lot of the real hard cases are kept, the ones who rate kiddie-fuckers slightly lower than the amoeba on the evolutionary ladder.'

'Ahh . . .' Ince sat back, nodded. 'So that's it: you've come to scare me. Let me save you the effort: the guards at the trial told me what I could expect, whichever jail I'm sent to. A couple of them said they'd be coming to see me themselves.' Another glance at Rebus. 'Isn't that thoughtful?'

Behind the show of bravado, Rebus could tell Ince was terrified. Terrified of the unknown. Every bit as scared as the kids must have been, every time they heard him approaching ...

'I don't want to scare you, Mr Ince. I want you to help me. But I'm not stupid, I know I have to offer something in return.'

'And what would that be, Inspector?'

Rebus stood up, walked over to where the video camera covered the room.

'You'll notice I'm not taping this,' he said. 'Good reason for that. This stays off the record, Mr Ince. Anything you tell me, it's for my own satisfaction only. Nothing to do with building a case. If I ever tried using it, it would be my word against yours: inadmissible.'

'I know the law, Inspector.'

Rebus turned towards him. 'Me too. What I'm saying is, this is strictly between us. I could get into trouble just for making you an offer.'

'What offer?' Sounding interested now.

'Peterhead, I know a few of the villains up there. I'm owed favours.'

There was silence while Ince digested this. 'You'd put in a word on my behalf?'

'That's right.'

'But they might choose not to heed it.'

Rebus shrugged, sat down again, arms resting along the edge of the desk. 'It's the best I can do.'

'And I only have your word that you'd do it anyway.'

Rebus nodded slowly. 'That's right, you do.'

Ince was studying the backs of his own hands, his fingers gripping the desk.

'Well, I must say, that's a very generous offer.' A touch of humour in the voice.

'It could save your life, Harold.'

'Or it could be totally meaningless.' He paused. 'What is it you want to ask me?'

'I need to know who the third man was.'

'Wasn't it Orson Welles?'

Rebus made himself smile. 'I mean the night Ramsay Marshall brought Darren Rough to Shiellion.'

'Long time ago. I was on the drink back then.'

'You made Darren wear a mask.'

'Did we?'

'Because of the other man. Maybe it was his idea. Didn't want Darren recognising him.' Rebus lit another cigarette. 'You'd been drinking. Maybe with this man. Chatting about this and that. Eventually telling him your secret.' Rebus studied Ince. 'Because you thought you could see something . . .'

Ince licked his lips. 'What?' Said so quietly it was barely above a whisper. Rebus lowered his own voice.

'You thought he was like you. You could see a potential. The more you talked, the clearer you saw it. You told him Marshall was bringing some kid along. Maybe you suggested he stay.'

'You're making this up, aren't you?'

Rebus nodded. 'Insofar as I can't prove any of it, yes, I'm making it up.'

'This potential you speak of . . . I'd contend it's in every one of us.' Now Ince looked at Rebus, and his eyes seemed harder. He held Rebus's gaze, returned it. 'Do you have any children, Inspector?'

'I've a daughter,' Rebus admitted, knowing the danger of letting Ince into his personal life, letting him inside his head. But Ince was no Cary Oakes. 'She's grown up now.'

'I bet at some point in your relationship you've thought about what it would be like to bed her, to have sex with her. Haven't you?'

Rebus could feel the pressure behind his eyes: anger and revulsion. Strong enough to make him blink away the smoke.

'I don't think so.'

Ince grinned. 'That's what you tell yourself. But I think you're lying, even if you don't know it. It's human *instinct*, nothing to be ashamed of. She might have been fifteen, or twelve, or ten.'

Rebus got to his feet. Had to keep moving, otherwise he'd pound Ince's head into the desk. He wanted to light another cigarette, but was only halfway through the current one.

'This isn't about me,' he said. Even to his ears, it sounded weak.

'No? Perhaps . . .'

'It's about Darren Rough.'

'Ah . . .' Ince leaned back on his chair. 'Poor Darren. They had him down on the list of witnesses, but didn't use him. I'd have liked to see him again.'

'Not possible. Someone murdered him.'

'What? Before the trial?'

Rebus shook his head. 'During it. I've been trying to find a motive, only now I think I was looking in all the wrong places.' He rested a hand on the desk, leaned down over Ince. 'I had a look at the charge sheets, the evidence. Just you and Marshall; none of the other victims mention a third abuser. Was it just that one night? Someone who tried it just the once . . . ?' Rebus sat back down in his seat. He'd finished the cigarette at last; lit himself another from its stub, chain-smoking now. 'I found Darren at the zoo. Found out where he lived. It leaked to the newspapers. This third man . . . he knew you weren't going to mention him in court. I don't know why, but I can guess. But the one thing he was scared of was Darren. Which was fine – as far as he knew, Darren Rough was well out of things. Then suddenly he reads that Darren's here, and he can guess why: Darren's helping with Shiellion. There's half a chance he saw something or heard something, maybe without knowing it. There's half a chance our third man's picture might end up in the paper after the trial, and Darren will recognise it.

'Suddenly there's danger. So he has to strike.' Rebus blew a thin column of smoke at Ince. 'We both know who

I'm talking about. But for my own satisfaction, I'd be happier to hear a name.'

'That's why Darren died?'

Rebus nodded. 'I think so.'

'But you've no proof?'

Rebus shook his head. 'And I'm unlikely to find it. With you or without you.'

'I'd like a mug of coffee,' Harold Ince said. 'Milk, two sugars. If you order it, it might come *sans* saliva.'

Rebus looked at him. 'Anything to eat?'

'I'm partial to a chicken korma curry. Nan bread, no rice. Sag aloo as a side dish.'

'I can phone out for it.'

'Again, I'd prefer it unadulterated.' There was confidence in Ince's voice now. He'd made a decision.

'And meantime we'll talk?' Rebus asked.

'For your own peace of mind, Inspector ... yes, we'll talk.'

49

Rebus sat in the darkness of his living room, sipping from a glass of whisky and water. The street outside was night-time quiet, interrupted by the occasional dull crunching sound of car tyres passing over the setts. He didn't know how long he'd been sitting there, maybe a couple of hours. He'd put a CD on, but hadn't bothered getting up to change it. It had been on the repeat function for three or four plays. 'Stray Cat Blues' had never felt so sordid. It affected him more than the literate and well-mannered 'Sympathy for the Devil', which had an air of desperation to it. There was no desperation in 'Stray Cat Blues', just the certainty of underage sex . . .

When the phone rang, he was slow to answer. It was Siobhan, relaying a message. Patience's flat had been broken into.

'Did they get anyone?'

'No. A couple of uniforms are still there. They're waiting for someone who can deal with the alarm . . .'

Rebus called St Leonard's, and a patrol car arrived to take him to Oxford Terrace. The driver could smell whisky on Rebus's breath.

'Been out partying, sir?'

'Your basic party animal, that's me.' Rebus's tone ensured no more questions came from the front of the car.

The alarm was still ringing. Rebus went down the steps and pushed open the front door. The two uniforms were in the kitchen, far away from the noise. They'd made themselves tea, and were searching the cupboards for biscuits.

'Milk, no sugar,' Rebus told them. Then he went back into the hall and used his key to disable the alarm. One of the uniforms handed him a mug.

'Thank God for that. It was driving us mental.'

Rebus was at the front door, examining it.

'Clean job,' the uniform said. 'Looks like they had a key.'

'More likely he picked it.' Rebus went back into the hall. 'But he couldn't pick the alarm box . . .' He walked from room to room.

'Anything missing, sir?'

'Yes, son: some hot water from the kettle, two tea-bags and a spot of milk.'

'Maybe the alarm scared him off.'

'If he picked one lock, why not another?' Rebus thought he knew the answer: because the very fact the alarm was set had told the intruder something.

Told him no one was home.

And he wanted *someone* to be home – Rebus or Patience – that was the whole point of the exercise. Cary Oakes hadn't broken in with the intention of stealing anything. He'd had other plans altogether . . .

When they left, Rebus reset the alarm and made sure the mortice lock was engaged as well as the Yale.

In the trade, it was known as shutting the stable door.

He got the patrol car to take him home by way of Sammy's. Not that he went into her flat – he just wanted to see everything was OK. She wouldn't be on her own; Ned would be sleeping beside her. Not that Ned would give Oakes many problems . . .

'Do me a favour, will you?' Rebus asked the driver. 'Arrange for a car to come past here once an hour until morning.'

'Will do, sir. You think he'll try it again?'

Rebus didn't even know if Oakes knew Sammy's address. He didn't know if Stevens had known it. He used the car's two-way to talk to the nursing home.

440

'Quiet as the grave here,' he was told.

Then he tried the hospital, got one of the night staff, who assured him there was someone with Mr Archibald and, yes, they were wide awake. From her description, Rebus guessed it was still Bobby Hogan.

Everyone was safe. Everyone was covered.

The patrol car dropped him off, and he climbed the stairs to his flat. Unlocking the door, he thought he heard a sound on the stairwell below him. He peered over the banister, but couldn't see anything. Mrs Cochrane's tabby probably, rattling the cat-flap as it went in or out.

He closed the door after him, didn't bother with the light in the hallway. He knew it well enough in the dark. Switched the light on in the kitchen and boiled the kettle. His head was thick from the whisky. He made tea, took it through to the living room. Too late for music, really. He walked over to the window and stood there, blowing on the tea.

Saw a shape move. On the pavement across the road. The outline of a man. He cupped his hands to the window, put his face between them, trying to block out the light from the streetlamp.

It was Cary Oakes. He was swaying slightly, like he could hear music. And he had a huge smile on his face. Rebus turned from the window, looked for his phone. Couldn't see it anywhere. He kicked books across the floor. Where the hell was it?

His mobile then: where was that? He'd forgotten to take it with him: probably in a coat pocket. He went to the hall cupboard: no sign of it. Kitchen? No. Bedroom? Not there either.

Cursing, he ran back to the window to check if Oakes had gone. No, he was still there, only now he had his hands raised, as though in surrender. Then Rebus saw he was holding two small dark objects. He knew what they were.

His cordless phone and his mobile.

'Bastard!' Rebus roared. Oakes had been in the flat; picked the stairwell Yale and the front door.

'Bastard,' Rebus hissed. He ran to the door, yanked it open. He was halfway down the stairs when he heard the main door creaking open. Had it been locked? If so, Oakes had dealt with it quickly.

Suddenly Oakes was there at the foot of the stairwell, backlit by a single bulb on the wall. All the walls were painted a weak-custard yellow, making his face seem jaundiced. His teeth were bared, mouth open to expose his tongue. He dropped the phones on the stone floor, reached into his waistband.

'Remember this?'

He was holding the knife. Purposefully, eyes on Rebus, he started climbing the steps, his feet making the sound of sandpaper on wood.

Rebus turned and ran.

'Where you going, Rebus?' He was laughing, not worried about keeping his voice down. The neighbours were students and old-age pensioners: he probably fancied his luck against the whole lot of them.

Mrs Cochrane had a telephone. Rebus thumped on her door as he passed, knowing it to be a futile gesture. She was stone deaf. The students on his landing: would they have a phone? Would they even be home? He ran in through his own door, shut it after him. The Yale clicked, but he knew it would take more than that to keep Oakes out. He slid the chain across, knew a good kick would probably smash it and the Yale both. Where was the key for the mortice? It was usually in its lock. He looked on the floor, then realised Oakes must have taken it. He'd studied the locks, known the mortice would keep him out ... Rebus put his eye to the spy-hole. Oakes's face appeared from nowhere. Rebus could hear what he was saying.

'Little pigs, little pigs, let me in.'

Lines from *The Shining*.

Rebus went into the kitchen, opened the cutlery

drawer. He found a twelve-inch-long Sabatier with a riveted black handle. He didn't think it had ever been used. He ran his thumb over its blade and cut himself.

It would do.

Rebus had come up against knife attackers before. But he'd been able to reason with most of them. The others, he'd been able to deal with . . . But that was then and this was altogether different. Back out in the hall, he decided to take the fight to Oakes. With the carving-knife in his fist, he slid the chain off, threw open the door. He was expecting an immediate attack, but none came. He craned his neck, couldn't see Oakes on the landing.

'Piggy going walkies.'

Oakes's voice: halfway down to the first landing. Rebus was out of the door, not hurrying, trying to keep calm. Eyes boring into Oakes's, peripheral vision fixed on Oakes's knife.

'Ooh, that *is* a big one,' Oakes mocked. He was moving backwards down the stairs, seeming sure of himself. 'Let's take it outside, Rebus. Let's give it some air.'

He turned and jogged out of the tenement. Rebus thought for a moment. His telephones were lying there. He should pick up his mobile and call in, get officers here pronto. Then he thought of Alan Archibald and Patience and Janice . . . and of his parents' grave. Of Jim Stevens. Time to end it. He had to keep Oakes in his sight, couldn't let him slip away again.

He reached down, pocketed the mobile, and headed for the door.

Oakes was standing on the pavement, nodding.

'That's right. Just the two of us.'

He started walking. Rebus followed. The pace was brisk, without either man ever breaking into a jog. Oakes kept his head angled back towards his pursuer. He looked pleased that things were turning out this way. Rebus couldn't see the logic, but he was wary. So far, Oakes had done nothing without good reason. Bouncing around Rebus's head, the words *Finish it! This is the last round . . .*

'Good for the arteries, an early-morning constitutional. Helps make up for the Scottish diet. I looked in your fridge, man. I had more food in my fucking cell back in Walla Walla. Whisky by the chair in the lounge, though: I have to give you credit for that.' He laughed. 'What are you, Sam Spade or something?'

Rebus said nothing. Oakes was a lot younger than him, and fitter too. Last thing Rebus wanted was to tire himself out yapping.

They were crossing Marchmont Road, heading along Sciennes and past the Sick Kids Hospital. Rebus cursed himself for living in such a quiet area. The pubs had all emptied; the chip shops were closed. There were no clubs, not so much as a massage parlour. Then, on the other side of the road: two young men walking home, knees just locking and no more – the end of a good night's drinking. One of them was demolishing a kebab. They looked at the strange pursuit. Oakes's knife was in his pocket, but Rebus brandished his.

'Call the police!' he called out.

Oakes just laughed, as if his buddy was drunk and joking, waving his rubber dagger around.

One man grinned; the other, the one with kebab sauce on his chin, stared, still chewing.

'I'm not joking!' Rebus shouted, not caring who he woke up. 'Call the cops!'

He couldn't stop to show them ID, couldn't risk letting Oakes out of his sight: there were too many potential victims out there. And he couldn't take his eyes off Oakes for a second.

So they kept moving, leaving the two young men far behind.

'By the time they get home,' Oakes said, 'they'll have forgotten the whole thing. It'll be drinks from the fridge

444

and Jerry Springer on TV. That's how it is these days, Rebus. Nobody gives a shit.'

'Nobody but me.'

'Nobody but you. Ever wondered why that is?'

Rebus shook his head. He didn't mind Oakes talking: while Oakes was talking, he was using up energy.

'You never think about it? It's because you're a fucking dinosaur, man. Everyone knows it – you, your bosses, the people you work with. Probably even your doctor friend. What's with her: she likes to screw prehistoric things?' Oakes laughed again. 'In case you're wondering, I kept fit in the pen. I can bench-press your ass. I can keep this pace up all day and night. How about you? You look about as fit as something extinct.'

'Sometimes all you need is attitude.'

They were cutting through narrow passageways now, coming out on Causewayside.

'Where are we going?'

'Nearly there, Rebus. Wouldn't want to tire you out . . . what's the Scots word again: puggle?' He laughed. There were cars on Causewayside. Rebus made sure they saw him holding the knife. Maybe they'd stop at a phone box or flag down a patrol car. But he knew the odds weren't good – not many patrol cars round here. Probably no foot patrols either. They'd drive home, and then *maybe* they'd phone to report it.

And *maybe* someone from St Leonard's would come to investigate.

It would be too late. Whatever was being played out, he got the feeling it was coming to its conclusion right now. For some reason, it had to do with . . . no . . . he knew where they were. The far end of Salisbury Place: they were at the junction with Minto Street.

'It was here, wasn't it?' Oakes asked, stopping because Rebus had stopped too. 'She was crossing the road or something?'

445

Sammy . . . crossing the road when the driver hit her. Twenty yards down Minto Street.

Rebus stared at Oakes. 'Why?'

Oakes just shrugged. Rebus was trying to focus again on *this* moment. This was what counted; he could think about Sammy later. He had to stop letting Oakes *play* with him.

'He sent her flying, huh?' Oakes was saying. He had his hands in his pockets, as if they were just stopping to chat. Rebus couldn't remember which pocket the knife was in. His own weapon hung from his right hand, useless for the moment. Crossing the road and she . . . she never had a chance.

He realised he hadn't been here since the day after the collision. He'd been avoiding the place.

And somehow Oakes had known the effect this place would have on him. Rebus blinked a few times, tried clearing his head.

'You've been to check on her, haven't you?' Oakes asked.

'What?' Rebus narrowed his eyes.

'You went to your girlfriend's flat, knew I'd been there. Next thing you did was go to your daughter's. But you didn't go in, did you?'

It was like staring into a devil's eyes. 'How do you know?'

'You wouldn't be here otherwise.'

'Why not?'

'Because I've *been* there, Rebus. Earlier tonight.'

'You're lying.' Rebus's voice was dry, his throat acrid. *Trying to get you off your guard, same trick worked with Archibald . . .*

Oakes just shrugged. They were at the corner. Diagonally across from them, two cars had drawn up side by side at a red light. Taxi on the inside lane; boy racer revving beside him. The taxi driver was watching what looked like a fight about to break out: nothing he hadn't seen before.

'You're lying,' Rebus repeated. He slipped his free hand into his pocket, brought out the mobile. Used his thumb to press the digits, holding the phone to his face so he could watch it and Oakes at the same time.

'She didn't need her legs anyway,' Oakes was saying. The phone was ringing. 'There's no answer, is there?'

Sweat was trickling into Rebus's eyes. But if he shook his head to clear the drops, Oakes would think he was answering his question.

The phone stopped ringing.

'Hello?' Ned Farlowe's voice.

'Ned! Is Sammy there? Is she all right?'

'What? Is that you, John?'

'*Is she all right?*' Knowing the answer; needing to hear it anyway.

'Of course she's—'

Oakes flew at him, the knife emerging from his right-hand pocket. Missing Rebus's chest by centimetres. Rebus stepped back, dropped the phone. He had the longer reach. The taxi driver had his window down.

'Cut that out, the pair of you!'

'I'll cut it out all right,' Oakes hissed. 'I'll dice it and slice it.' He made another sweep with the knife. Rebus tried to kick it away, almost lost his footing. Oakes laughed at him. 'You're no Nureyev, pal.' A quick thrust took the knife into Rebus's arm. Rebus felt his nerves go dull: prelude to agony. *Finish it.*

Rebus took a step forward, feinted with the knife, so that Oakes had to move position. On the edge of the pavement now. Rebus saw the traffic lights behind Oakes were changing. Oakes leaned forward, slashed at his chest. Thin whistling sound as Rebus's shirt split. Blood warm on his arm, more blood trickling from the fresh wound. Red to red/amber.

To green.

Rebus charged in with his foot up and hit Oakes solid in the chest with his sole. Oakes got in a swipe before he was propelled back into the road, where the boy racer, oblivious to the fight, radio on full-blast and his girl with her arm around him, was showing off his car's acceleration from a flat start. The car clipped Oakes, sent him flying, breaking his hip and, Rebus hoped, a few more bones to boot. The car screeched to a halt, the young man's head appeared through the window. He saw knives. He pulled his foot off the clutch and roared off.

Rebus didn't bother to catch the licence plate. He stood on Oakes's knife-hand, forcing the fingers open, then lifted the knife and pocketed it. The taxi driver was still at the lights.

'Phone for police assistance!' Rebus called to him. He held his injured arm to his chest.

Oakes was rolling on the ground, hand to his thigh and side, teeth bared not in a grin now but in a grimace of pain.

Rebus stood up, took a step back, and kicked him in the groin. As Oakes groaned and retched, Rebus gave him another kick, then crouched down again.

'I'd like to say that was for Jim Stevens,' he said. 'But if I'm being entirely honest with you, really it was for me.'

Rebus spent an hour in the casualty department – four stitches to his arm, eight to his chest. The arm wound was deepest, but both were clean. Oakes was somewhere nearby, being treated for breaks and fractures. Six of Crime Squad's finest on guard detail.

A patrol car took Rebus back to his flat, where he retrieved his cordless phone – didn't want any of the students pocketing it – and had a mouthful of whisky. Then another after that.

The rest of the night he spent at St Leonard's, typing his report one-handed, giving an additional verbal briefing to Chief Superintendent Watson, who'd been summoned from bed and whose hair sported a cow's-lick which flapped when he moved his head.

There was little certainty that Oakes could be charged with Jim Stevens' murder. It would depend on forensic evidence: fingerprints, fibres, saliva. Stevens' cassette had been bagged and handed over to the white-coat brigade.

'But he'll go down for the attack on me and Alan Archibald?' Rebus asked his superior.

Farmer Watson nodded. 'For the Pentland attack, yes.'

'What about the attempted murder of three hours ago?'

The Farmer shuffled paperwork. 'You've said yourself, most of the witnesses will have seen *you* with the knife, not him.'

'But the taxi driver . . .'

The Farmer nodded. 'He'll be crucial. Let's hope he gets his story straight.'

Rebus saw what his boss was getting at. 'Sir, you do believe I acted in self-defence?'

'Of course, John. Goes without saying.' But the Farmer wouldn't meet his eyes.

Rebus tried to think of something to say; decided it wasn't worth his breath.

'Crime Squad are pissed off,' the Farmer added with a smile. 'They hate an anti-climax.'

'I might not look it, but inside I'm crying for them.' Rebus turned to leave the room.

'No going back to the hospital, John,' the Farmer warned. 'Don't want him falling out of bed and saying he was pushed.'

Rebus snorted, went downstairs and into the car park. It would be growing light soon. He dry-swallowed some more painkillers, lit a cigarette and stared in the direction of Holyrood Park. They were there – Arthur's Seat, Salisbury Crags – it was just, you couldn't always see them. It didn't mean they weren't there.

Easy to lose your footing in the dark . . . Easy for someone to come up behind you . . .

Rebus left the car park and headed into St Leonard's Bank. Stevens' car had been taken away for examination at Howdenhall. At the end of the road, there was a gap in the fence, allowing passage into the park itself. Rebus headed down the slope towards Queen's Drive. Once across it, he started to climb. Away from the street-lighting now, his steps were more tentative. He sensed more than saw the starting-point of Radical Road, above which loomed the irregular rockface of the Crags them-selves. Rebus ignored the path, kept climbing until he was on top of the Crags, the city spread out below him in a grid of orange sodium and yellow-white halogen. The beast was definitely beginning to awake: cars heading into the city. Turning round, he saw that the sky was a lighter shade of black than the mass of rock below it. Some people said Arthur's Seat looked like a crouched lion, ready to pounce. It never did pounce, though. There was a lion on the Scottish flag too – not crouched but rampant . . .

Had Jim Margolies come up here with the express intention of leaping off? Rebus thought he knew the answer now. And he knew because of the Margolies' dinner engagement that evening, across the park from where they lived.

That, and the fact of a white saloon car . . .

50

Dr Joseph Margolies lived with his wife in a detached house in Gullane, with an uninterrupted view of Muirfield golf course. Rebus didn't play golf. He'd tried a few times as a kid, dragging a half-set of clubs around his local course, losing half a dozen balls in Jamphlars Pond. He knew some of his colleagues had taken up the game thinking it would help their careers, making sure to concede defeat to their superiors.

That didn't sound like a game to Rebus.

Siobhan Clarke parked the car, and switched off the radio news. It was ten in the morning. Rebus had managed a couple of hours' shut-eye in his Arden Street flat, and had phoned Patience to let her know Cary Oakes was behind bars.

'Stay in the car,' he told Clarke, manoeuvring himself out of the door. Not easy with one arm strapped up and his chest giving him grief every time he stretched.

Mrs Margolies answered the door. Close up, she resembled her son. Same flat chin, same narrow eyes. She even had the same smile.

Rebus introduced himself and asked if he could have a word with her husband.

'He's in the greenhouse. Is there a problem, Inspector?'

He smiled at her. 'No problem, madam. Just a couple of questions, that's all.'

'I'll show you the way,' she said, standing back to let him in. She'd glanced at his arm, but wasn't going to comment on it. Some people were like that: didn't like to ask questions . . . As he followed her down the corridor, he glanced through open doorways, seeing domestic order everywhere: knitting on a chair; magazines in a paper-rack; dusted ornaments; gleaming windows. The house dated from the 1930s. From the outside, it seemed to be all eaves and gables. Rebus asked her how long they'd lived there.

'Over forty years,' Mrs Margolies replied, proud of the fact.

So this was the house Jim Margolies had grown up in. And his sister too. From the notes, Rebus knew she'd committed suicide in the family bathroom. Often, in a situation like that, the families elected to sell up and move somewhere new. But he knew other families would elect to stay, because something of their loved one still remained in the home, and would be lost forever if they abandoned it.

The kitchen was tidy too, not so much as a cup and saucer drying on the draining-board. A message-list had been fixed to the fridge with a magnet in the shape of a teapot. But the list remained blank. Mrs Margolies asked him if he'd like some tea. He shook his head.

'I'm fine, thanks anyway.' Still smiling, but studying her. Thinking: *The wife often knows* ... Thinking: *Some people just don't ask questions* ...

Outside the kitchen door was a short hall with two walk-in cupboards – both open to display garden tools – and the back door, which also stood open. They stepped outside and into a walled garden, obviously much worked-on. There was a rockery, and next to it some flowerbeds. These were separated by a trimmed lawn from a long, narrow vegetable bed. Towards the bottom of the garden were trees and bushes, and tucked away in one corner a small greenhouse with a figure moving around inside.

Rebus turned to his guide. 'Thank you, I'll be fine.'

And he walked across the lawn. It was like walking across luxury Wilton. He looked back once, saw Mrs

Margolies watching him from the doorway. In a neigh-bouring garden, someone was having a bonfire. Smoke crackled over the wall, white and pungent. Rebus walked through it as he neared the greenhouse. A black labrador pricked up its ears at his approach, then pushed itself up to sitting and gave a half-hearted bark. Its nose and whiskers were grey, and it had about it a pampered look: overfed and, in its declining years, underexercised. The door of the greenhouse slid open and an elderly man peered through half-moon glasses at his visitor. Tall, grey hair, black moustache – just the way Jamie Brady had described him: the man who'd gone to Greenfield looking for Darren Rough.

'Yes? Can I help you?'

'Dr Margolies, I'm Detective Inspector John Rebus.'

Margolies held up his hands. 'You'll forgive me for not shaking.' The hands were blackened with soil.

'Me too,' Rebus said, gesturing to his arm.

'Looks nasty. What happened?' Not sharing his wife's reticence. But then maybe she'd had half a lifetime of biting back questions. Rebus leaned down to rub the labrador's head. Its heavy tail thumped the ground in appreciation.

'Got into a fight,' Rebus explained.

'Line of duty, eh? We've met before, I think.'

'Hannah's competition.'

'Ah, yes.' Nodding slowly. 'You wanted to speak to Ama.'

'I did then, yes.'

'Is this something to do with her?' Margolies was retreating back into the greenhouse. Rebus followed, and saw that the old man was potting seedlings. It was warm in the greenhouse, despite the day being overcast. Margolies asked Rebus to close the door.

'Keep the heat in,' he explained.

Rebus slid the door shut. Most of the available space was taken up with work surfaces, trays of seedlings laid along them in rows. A bag of potting compost lay open on the ground. Dr Margolies was scooping a black plastic flowerpot into it.

'How does it feel to get away with murder?' Rebus asked.

'I'm sorry?' Margolies took a seedling, pushed it into its new pot.

'You murdered Darren Rough.'

'Who?'

Rebus took the pot from Margolies' fingers. 'It's going to be a devil trying to prove it. In fact, I don't think it will happen. I really do think you've got away with it.'

Margolies met his eyes, reached to take his pot back.

'I'm sorry,' he said. 'I haven't the faintest idea what you're talking about.'

'You were seen in Greenfield. You were asking about Darren Rough. Then off you drove in your white Mercedes. A white saloon car was seen in Holyrood Park around the time Darren was killed. I think he went there for sanctuary, but you found it an ideal site for a murder.'

'These riddles, Inspector . . . Do you know who I am?'

'I know exactly who you are. I know both your children committed suicide. I know you were part of the Shiellion set-up.'

'I beg your pardon?' A slight trembling in the voice now. A seedling slipped from parchment fingers.

'Don't worry, Harold Ince is going to keep his side of the bargain. He talked to me, but it wouldn't be admissible, and he won't tell anyone else. He told me you were at Shiellion that night. Ince had talked with you often, had come to know you. He'd told you what he did to the kids in his care. He *knew* you wouldn't say anything, because the two of you were alike. He knew how useful it would be to him if a doctor, the man responsible for examining the children, were part of the whole enterprise.' Rebus leaned close to Margolies' ear. 'He told me *all* of it, Dr Margolies.'

The after-hours drinking, loosening up the doctor. Then

the arrival of Ramsay Marshall with a fresh new kid, Darren Rough. Making the kid wear a blindfold so he wouldn't recognise Margolies – this at the doctor's insistence. Sweating and trembling . . . knowing this night changed everything . . .

And afterwards: self-loathing perhaps; or maybe just fear of exposure. He hadn't been able to cope, had feigned ill-health, opting for early retirement.

'But you could never loose Ince's grip on you. He'd been blackmailing you, him and Marshall both.' Rebus's voice was little more than a whisper, his lips almost touching the old man's ear. 'Know what? I'm so fucking *glad* he's been sucking you dry all these years.' Rebus stood back.

'You don't know anything.' Margolies' face was blood-red. Beneath the checked shirt, he was breathing hard.

'I can't *prove* anything, but that's not quite the same thing. I *know*, and that's what matters. I think your daughter found out. The shame of it killed her. You were always the first one awake in the morning; she knew *you'd* be the one to find her. And then somehow Jim found out, and he couldn't live with it either. How come *you* can live with it, Dr Margolies? How come you can live with the deaths of both your children, and the murder of Darren Rough?'

Margolies lifted a gardening fork, held it to Rebus's throat. His face was squeezed into a mask of anger and frustration. Beads of perspiration dripped from his forehead. And outside, the billowing smoke seemed to be cutting them off from everything.

Margolies didn't say anything, just made sounds from behind gritted teeth. Rebus stood there, hand in pocket.

'What?' he said. 'You're going to kill me too?' He shook his head. 'Think about it. Your wife's seen me. There's another officer waiting for me out front. How will you talk your way out of it? No, Dr Margolies, you're not going to kill me. Like I say, I can't prove anything I've just said. It's between you and me.' Rebus lifted the hand from his pocket, pushed the fork aside. The black lab was watching through the door, seemed to sense all was not well. It frowned at Rebus, looking disappointed in him.

'What do you want?' Margolies spluttered, gripping the work-bench with both hands.

'I want you to live the rest of your life knowing that I know.' Rebus shrugged. 'That's all.'

'You want me to kill myself?'

Rebus laughed. 'I don't think you've got it in you. You're an old man, you're going to die soon enough. Once you're dead, maybe Ince and Marshall will rethink their loyalty to you. You won't be left with any reputation at all.'

Margolies turned towards him, and now there was clear, focused hatred in his eyes.

'Of course,' Rebus said, 'if any evidence does turn up, you can be assured I'll be back here at the double. You might be celebrating the millennium, you might be getting your card from the Queen, and then you'll see me walking through the door.' He smiled. 'I'll never be very far away, Dr Margolies.'

He slid open the greenhouse door, manoeuvred his way past the dog. Walked away.

It didn't feel like any sort of victory. Unless something turned up, there'd be no justice for Darren Rough, no public trial. But Rebus knew he'd done what he could. Mrs Margolies was in the kitchen, making no pretence of doing anything other than waiting for him to return.

'Everything all right?' she asked.

'Fine, Mrs Margolies.' He headed down the hall, making for the front door. She was right behind him.

'Well, I just was wondering . . .'

Rebus opened the door, turned to her. 'Why not ask your husband, Mrs Margolies?'

The wife often knows, never brings herself to ask.

'Just one thing, Mrs Margolies . . . ?'

'Yes?'

Your husband's a cold-blooded murderer. His mouth opened and closed, but no words came. He shook his head, started down the garden path.

Clarke drove him to Katherine Margolies' house, in the Grange area of Edinburgh. It was a three-storey Georgian semi in a street half of whose homes had been turned into bed-and-breakfast establishments. The white Merc was parked in front of the gate. Rebus turned to Clarke.

'I know,' she said: 'stay in the car.'

Katherine Margolies looked less than thrilled to see him.

'What do you want?' She seemed ready to keep him on the doorstep.

'It's about your husband's suicide.'

'What about it?' Her face was narrow and hard, hands long and thin like butcher's knives.

'I think I know why he did it.'

'And what makes you think I'd want to know?'

'You already do know, Mrs Margolies.' Rebus took a deep breath. Well, if she didn't mind them talking like this on her doorstep . . . 'When did he find out his father was a paedophile?'

Her eyes widened. A woman emerged from the neighbouring house, preparing to walk her Jack Russell terrier. 'You better come in,' Katherine Margolies said sharply, eyes darting up and down the street. After he walked in, she closed the door and stood with her back to it, arms folded.

'Well?' she said.

Rebus looked around. The hall had a grey marble floor veined with black lines. A stone staircase swept upwards. There were paintings on the walls: Rebus got the feeling they weren't prints. She didn't seem to have noticed his arm, had no interest in him that way.

'Hannah not home?' he asked.

'She's at school. Look, I don't know what it is—'

'Then I'll tell you. It's been gnawing at me, Jim's death.

457

And I'll tell you why. I've been there myself, standing at the top of a very high place, wondering if I'd have the guts to jump off.'

Her face softened a little.

'Usually it was the booze doing it,' he went on. 'These days, I think I've got that under control. But I learned two things. One, you have to be incredibly brave to pull it off. Two, there's got to be some crunch reason for you not to go on living. See, when it comes to it, going on living is the easier of the two options. I couldn't see any reason why Jim would take his life, no reason at all. But there had to be one. That's what got to me. There *had* to be one.'

'And now you think you've found it?' Her eyes were liquid in the cool dimness of the hall.

'Yes.'

'And you felt it worth sharing with me?'

He shook his head. 'All I need from you is confirmation that I'm right.'

'And then you'll have contentment?' She waited till he'd nodded. 'And what right do you have to that, Inspector Rebus? What gives you the right to sleep easy?'

'I never find sleep very easy, Mrs Margolies.' It seemed to him then – and maybe it was a trick of the light – that he was seeing her at the end of a long dark tunnel, so that while she stood out clearly, everything between and around them was a blur of indistinct shading. And things were moving and gathering on the periphery: the ghosts. They were all here, providing a ready-made audience. Jack Morton, Jim Stevens, Darren Rough ... even Jim Margolies. They felt so alive to him he could scarcely believe Katherine Margolies couldn't make them out.

'The night Jim died,' Rebus went on, 'you'd been out to dinner with friends in Royal Park Terrace. I wondered about that ... Royal Park Terrace to The Grange.'

'What about it?' Looking bored now more than anything. Rebus thought it was bravado.

'Easiest route is to cut through Holyrood Park. Is that the way you drove home?'

'I suppose so.'

'In your white Mercedes?'

'Yes.'

'And Jim stopped the car, got out . . .'

'No.'

'Someone saw the car.'

'No.'

'Because something had been making his life hell, something he'd maybe just discovered about his father . . .'

'No.'

Rebus took a step towards her. 'It was bucketing down that night. He wouldn't have gone out walking. That's your version, Mrs Margolies: in the middle of the night he got up, got dressed, and went out walking. He walked all the way to Salisbury Crags in the rain, just so he could throw himself off.' Rebus was shaking his head. 'My version makes more sense.'

'Maybe to you.'

'I'm not about to go shouting from the chimney-pots, Mrs Margolies. I just need to know that that's how it happened. He'd been talking to one of the Shiellion victims. He found out his father was involved in the Shiellion abuse and he was afraid it would come out, afraid the shame would rebound on to him.'

She exploded. 'Christ, you couldn't be more wrong! It had nothing to do with that. What's any of this got to do with Shiellion?'

Rebus collected himself. 'You tell me.'

'Don't you see?' She was crying now. 'It was Hannah . . .'

Rebus frowned. 'Hannah?'

'Hannah was his sister's name. Our Hannah was named after her. Jim did it to get back at his father.'

459

'Because Dr Margolies had . . .' Rebus couldn't bring himself to say the word. 'With Hannah?'

She rubbed the back of her hand across her face, smudging mascara. 'He interfered with his own daughter. God knows whether it was just once. It might have been going on for years. When she killed herself . . .'

'She did so knowing who'd be first to find her?'

She nodded. 'Jim knew what had happened . . . knew why she'd done it. But of course nobody ever talks about it.' She looked at him. 'You just don't, do you? Not in polite society. Instead he tried shutting it out, accepting that there was no remedy.'

'I'm not sure I understand.' But he understood something, knew now why Jim had beaten up Darren Rough. Displaced anger: he hadn't been hitting Rough; he'd been hitting his father.

She slid down the door until she was crouching, arms hugging her knees. Rebus lowered himself on to the bottom step of the staircase, tried to make sense of it: Joseph Margolies had abused his own daughter . . . what would have made him turn to a boy like Darren Rough? Ince's insistence, perhaps; or simple lust and curiosity, the thought of more forbidden fruit . . .

Katherine Margolies' voice was calm again. 'I think Jim joined the police as another way of telling his father something, telling him he'd never forget, never forgive.'

'But if he knew all along about his father, why did he kill himself?'

'I've told you! Because of Hannah.'

'His sister?'

She gave a wild, humourless laugh. 'Of course not.' Paused for breath. 'Our daughter, Inspector. I mean Hannah, our daughter. Jim had . . . he'd been worried for some time.' She took a deep breath. 'I'd noticed he wasn't sleeping. I'd wake in the night and he'd be lying there in the darkness, eyes open, staring at the ceiling. One night he told me. He felt I ought to know.'

'What was he worried about?'

'That he was turning into his father. That there was some genetic component, something he had no control over.'

'You mean Hannah?'

She nodded. 'He said he tried not to have the thoughts, but they came anyway. He looked at her and no longer saw his daughter.' Her eyes were on the pattern in the floor. 'He saw something else, something to be desired . . .'

Finally Rebus saw it. Saw all Jim Margolies' fears, saw the past which had haunted him and the expectation of recurrence. Saw why the man had turned to young-looking prostitutes. Saw the dread of history. *Not in polite society.* If families like the Margolies and the Petries represented polite society, Rebus wanted nothing to do with it.

'He'd been quiet all evening,' Katherine Margolies went on. 'Once or twice I caught him looking at Hannah, and I could see how scared he was.' She rubbed the palm of either hand over her eyes, looked up to the ceiling, demanding something more from it than the comfort of cornice and chandelier. The noise that escaped from her throat was like something from a caged animal.

'On the way home, he stopped the car and ran. I went after him, and he was just standing there. At first, I didn't realise he was at the very edge of the Crags. He must have heard me. Next thing, he'd vanished. It was like a stunt, something a stage magician would do. Then I realised what it was. He'd jumped. I felt . . . well, I don't know what I felt. Numb, betrayed, shocked.' She shook her head, unsure even now what her feelings were towards the man who had killed himself rather than give in to his most feral craving. 'I walked back to the car. Hannah was asking where her daddy was. I said he'd gone for a walk. I drove us home. I didn't go down to help him. I didn't do anything. Christ knows why.' Now she ran her hands through her hair.

461

Rebus got up, pushed open a door. It led into a formal dining room. Decanters on a polished sideboard. He sniffed one, poured a large glass of whisky. Took it through to the hall and handed it to Katherine Margolies. Went back to fetch another for himself. He saw the sequence now: Jane Barbour telling Jim that Rough was coming back to town; Jim dusting off the case, becoming intrigued by the third man. Knowing his father had been working in children's homes. Wanting to know, quizzing Darren Rough, his world collapsing in on him . . .

'You know,' his widow was saying, 'Jim wasn't scared of dying. He said there was a coachman.'

'Coachman?'

'He took you to wherever it was you went when you died.' She looked up at him. 'Do you know that story?'

Rebus nodded. 'An old Edinburgh ghost story, that's all it is.'

'You don't believe in ghosts then?'

'I wouldn't say that necessarily.' He raised his glass. 'Here's to Jim,' he said. When he looked around, there wasn't a ghost to be seen.

51

A week later, Rebus received a phone call from Brian Mee.

'What's up, Brian?' Rebus already guessing from the tone of voice.

'Ah, shite, John, she's left me.'

'I'm sorry to hear that, Brian.'

'Are you?' There was a hint of disbelief in the laugh that followed.

'I really am, I'm sorry.'

'She told you, though?'

'In a roundabout sort of way.' Rebus paused. 'So do you know where she is?'

'Cut the crap, John. She's at your flat.'

'What?'

'You heard me. She's biding with you.'

'First I've heard of it.'

'She doesn't know anybody else over there.'

'There are bed and breakfasts, rooms to rent . . .'

'You're not putting her up?'

'You've got my word for it.'

There was a long silence on the line. 'Christ, man, I'm sorry. I'm off my head with worry here.'

'Only to be expected, Brian.'

'Think it's worth my while coming to look for her?'

Rebus exhaled. 'What do you think?'

'I think she used to love me.'

'But not any more?'

'She wouldn't have left otherwise.'

'True enough.'

'Even if she finds Damon, I don't think she's coming back.'

'Give her some time, Brian.'

'Aye, sure.' Brian Mee sniffed. 'Know something? I used to like it that folk called me Barney. I know how I got the name, you know.'

'I thought you said you didn't?'

'Oh aye, but I know all the same. Barney Rubble. Because folk thought I was like him. Somebody said it to me once, not just "Barney" but "Barney Rubble".'

Rebus smiled. 'But you liked the name anyway?'

'I didn't say that. I said I liked that I had a nickname. It was a sort of identity, wasn't it? And that's better than nothing.'

Rebus's smile stretched. He was seeing Barney Mee, the tough little battler, wading in to save Mitch. The years separating the present from that long-ago event seemed to fall away. It was as if the two could live side by side, the past a ghostly presence forever of the here and now. Nothing lost; nothing forgotten; redemption always a possibility.

But if that was true, how could he explain that Dr Margolies would never see a court of law, his crimes known only to the few? And how to explain that the Procurator Fiscal seemed able to prosecute Cary Oakes only for the attempted murder of Alan Archibald? All the forensic evidence connecting him to Jim Stevens could be explained away: fingerprints and fibres in Stevens' car – Oakes had ridden in it before. Hell, three police officers had watched him being driven away from the airport in it. The Stevens file would be kept open, but no one would be investigating. Everyone knew who'd done it. But short of a confession, there was nothing they could do.

'Let's stick to our strongest suit,' the fiscal depute had said. This meant discarding the attack on Rebus, too, even though the taxi driver had been willing to testify.

'Too many possible arguments for the defence,' the

fiscal depute had said. Rebus tried not to take it personally. He knew prosecution was a game all to itself, where the best player might lose, the cheat prosper. He knew it was the job of the police to investigate and present the facts. It was the job of lawyers like Richie Cordover to then twist everything around until they could persuade juries and witnesses that Celtic fans sang 'The Sash' and Cowdenbeath was an ideal holiday location.

'Hey, John?' Brian Mee was saying.

'Yes, Barney?'

Brian laughed at that. 'What about coming through some weekend, just you and me, eh? Double-act at the karaoke, and see if we can dust off some chat-up lines.'

'Sounds tempting, Barney. I'll give you a bell some time.' Both men knowing he wouldn't.

'Right then, that's you on a promise.'

'Cheers, Barney.'

'Bye, John. It was good to catch up with you . . .'

Another paedophile had been released from prison, this time in Glasgow. GAP had organised a bus and headed off for Renfrew, where he was rumoured to be holed up. Some of the younger males in the company had gone for a night on the town, which had ended with a full-scale battle raging through the streets.

It was hoped, at least in some quarters, that the resulting negative publicity would sound the organisation's death knell. But Van Brady was still giving interviews and getting her picture in the papers, still applying to the Lottery for funding. Journalists liked that she talked almost exclusively in sound-bites, even if half of them had to be toned down for publication.

There was a memorial service for Jim Stevens. Rebus went along. He suspected that in his day Stevens had probably fallen out with at least three-quarters of the mourners. But there were eulogies and sombre faces, and Rebus couldn't help feeling that Jim wouldn't have wanted it that way. Afterwards, he held a little wake of his own in the Oxford Bar's back room with three or four of the loudest, rudest, and funniest hacks around. They drank till well after midnight, their laughter almost drowning out the music from the ceilidh band in the corner.

Rebus stumbled down the road to Oxford Terrace, dumped his clothes in the washing basket and had a shower.

'You still reek,' Patience told him as he climbed into bed.

'I'm keeping up traditions,' Rebus said. 'Edinburgh's not called "Auld Reekie" for nothing.'

He thought it curious that Cal Brady should want to speak to him. Cal was out on bail, awaiting trial for various offences against the person on the night of the Renfrew stramash. The morning phone call was so unexpected, Rebus walked out of the station without telling anyone where he was going. They met up on Radical Road. Cal had wanted somewhere not too far from home, but not a cop-shop, somewhere they could talk without anyone hearing.

The wind was flying, stinging Rebus's ears. There were occasional blasts of sunshine as the fast-moving clouds broke, only to blot out the sun again moments later. Cal Brady had deep bruises beneath both eyes, and a burst lip. His left hand sported a bandage and he seemed to limp ever so slightly as he walked.

'Bad one, was it?' Rebus asked.

'Those weegies . . .' Cal shook his head.

'I thought it was Renfrew?'

'Renfrew, Glasgow . . . all the same, man. Mad bastards, each and every one. Their idea of a square go is to rip your face off with their teeth.' He shivered, pulled his denim jacket tighter around him.

'You could button it up,' Rebus told him.

'Eh?'

'The jacket . . . if you're cold.'

'Aye, but it looks stupid when you do that. Levi jackets are only cool when they're open.' Rebus had no answer to that. 'I hear you got a bit of a scrape yourself.'

Rebus looked at his arm. No sling now, just a taped compress. Another week or so, the stitches would dissolve. 'What did you want to see me for, Cal?'

'These fucking charges.'

'What about them?'

'I'll probably end up going down, record I've got.'

'So?'

'So, I could do without it.' He twitched a shoulder. 'Gonny help me out?'

'You mean put in a good word?'

'Aye.'

Rebus stuck his hands in his pockets, as if relaxing. In truth, he'd been on his guard ever since arriving at the meeting-point five minutes before Brady: on the lookout for traps or a possible ambush. Lessons learned from Cary Oakes. 'Why should I do that?' he asked.

'Look, I'm no fucking snitch, right?'

Rebus nodded agreement, as seemed to be expected.

'But I hear things.' He paused. 'Try not to, but sometimes I can't help it.'

'Such as?'

'So you'll put a word in?'

Rebus stopped walking. He seemed to be admiring the vista. 'I could tell them you're one of mine. I could make you sound important.'

'But I wouldn't *be* your grass, right? That's the crux.'

Rebus nodded. 'But you've got something to trade?'

Cal looked around, as if even here he might be overheard. When he lowered his voice, Rebus had to move close to him to hear what he was saying over the noise of the wind.

'You know I work for Mr Mackenzie?'

'You're his enforcer.'

Brady prickled at that. 'Sometimes he's owed money. Happens to a lot of businesses.'

'Sure.'

'I make sure his debtors know the risks they're taking.'

Rebus smiled. 'A nice way of putting it.'

Brady looked around again. 'Petrie,' he said, like this would explain everything.

'I know,' Rebus said. 'Nicky Petrie owed Charmer money, got beaten up in lieu of a final reminder.'

But Brady was shaking his head. 'It was his sister owed the money.'

'Ama?' Brady nodded. 'So why thump Nicky?'

Brady snorted. 'She's a cold, hard bitch. Maybe you haven't noticed. But she likes her little brother. She *loves* little Nicky . . .'

'So you were sending the message to her?' Rebus thought about it, remembered something Ama had said to him at the beauty contest: *Who do I owe money to?* 'Why didn't she get the money from her father?'

'Story is, she wouldn't ask him for the time of day, and he wouldn't give it to her if he'd a watch on either arm.'

'I still don't know what this has to do with me.'

'That flat of theirs.'

'What about it?'

'*She* lives there. The blonde you were looking for.'

Rebus stared at Brady. 'She's in that flat?' Brady was nodding. 'What's her name?'

'I think it's Nicola.'

'How do you know all this?'

Brady shrugged. 'They can't help talking, that little gang.'

Rebus thought of the scene on the boat . . . the way the drunk had been about to say something until warned off by Ama Petrie . . .

'They know about this Nicola?'

'They *all* know.'

Which meant they'd all lied to Rebus . . . including the brother and sister, Nicky and Ama.

'Is she Nicky's girlfriend?'

Brady shrugged again.

'Or Ama's maybe?'

'I don't get involved,' Brady said, waving his hand as though to cut the discussion dead.

'How about you, Cal? Still living with Joanna?'

'Nothing to do with you.'

'How's Billy Boy? Don't you think he'd be better off with his dad?'

'That's not what Joanna wants.'

'Has anyone asked Billy what *he* wants?'

Brady's voice rose. 'He's just a kid. How's he supposed to know what's best for him?'

'I bet when you were his age you knew what you wanted.'

'Maybe,' Brady conceded after a moment's thought. 'But I'll give you odds-on I didn't get it.' He laughed. 'Maybe I'm *still* not getting it. Know what I think about that?'

'What?'

'Just watch.'

And Rebus did watch, as Cal Brady unzipped his fly, took out his penis, and began to urinate off the edge of Radical Road. Standing well back from the performance, it seemed to Rebus that he was pissing on Holyrood and Greenfield and St Leonard's, pissing in a giant arc over the whole city.

And if Rebus had been able, at that exact moment he might have joined him.

52

Returning to St Leonard's with Siobhan Clarke after a call-out, Rebus made a detour to the New Town. Clarke knew better than to ask why: he'd tell her in his own good time and not before.

It was late afternoon, and he sat kerbside, indicators flashing, wondering about Nicky Petrie. To pay a visit, or not to pay a visit? Would the girlfriend be there? Would Petrie string together another series of lies and half-truths? Clarke was about to open her mouth to say something when she saw his hands tighten on the steering-wheel.

A woman was coming down the steps from Petrie's building. Rebus saw for the first time that a taxi was waiting. She stepped into it. He'd caught only a glimpse of her: tall, willowy. A blonde pageboy cut. Black dress and tights beneath a billowing black wool coat. Rebus switched off the indicators, made to follow the cab, started explaining the situation to Clarke.

'Where do you think she's going?'

'Only one way to find out.'

The taxi headed towards Princes Street, crossed it and crawled up The Mound. Through traffic lights at the top and took a right down Victoria Street. Grassmarket was the destination. Nicola paid the driver, got out. She looked around, somewhat uncertainly. Her face was like a mask.

'Bit heavy on the make-up,' Clarke commented. Rebus was trying to find a parking space. Finding none, he left the car on a single yellow line. If he got a ticket, it could join the others in the glove compartment.

'Where did she go?' he asked, getting out of the car.

'Down Cowgate, I think,' Clarke said.

'Hell does she want down there?'

While Grassmarket itself had been gentrified, the area immediately to the east was still Hostel City: a place the city's dispossessed could, for the moment, call its own. Things would doubtless be different once the politicians moved in down the road.

They stood on street corners, or sat on the steps of disused churches – baggy-trousered and grim-bearded, with too few teeth, and stooped backs. As Rebus and Clarke rounded the corner, they saw that the woman was walking with exaggerated slowness through a phalanx of admirers, only a smattering of whom bothered asking her for spare change and cigarettes.

'Likes to show off,' Clarke said.

'And not too fussy with it.'

'Just one thing bothering me, sir . . .'

But Nicola had turned to acknowledge a wolf-whistle, and as she did so she saw them. She turned again quickly and upped her pace, keeping a tight hold of her zebra-skin shoulder-bag.

'Not the world's greatest surveillance,' Clarke said.

'She knows us,' Rebus hissed. They broke into a trot, ran along the pavement below George IV Bridge. She wore flat-heeled shoes, ran well despite the tangle of her long coat. She found a gap in the traffic and darted across the road. Cowgate was horrible: a narrow canyon, with high-sided buildings. When traffic built up, the carbon monoxide had no place to go. The stitches in Rebus's chest slowed him down.

'Guthrie Street,' Clarke said. That was where Nicola was headed. It would bring her up on to Chambers Street, where she could more easily lose her pursuers. But as she turned into the steep wynd, she bumped into someone. The collision sent her spinning. Something fell to the ground, but she kept running. Rebus paused to scoop it up. A short blonde wig.

'What the hell?'

'That's what I was trying to tell you, sir,' Clarke said. Ahead of them, Nicola was tiring, holding the wall for support as she hauled herself up the incline. Limping, too, an ankle twisted in the collision. Eventually, just as she reached Chambers Street, her hair short and merely fair now rather than blonde, she gave up, stood with her back to the wall, panting noisily. Perspiration was streaking the make-up. Behind the mask, Rebus saw someone he knew only too well.

Not Nicola, Nicky. Nicky Petrie.

Petrie's words: *Straitlaced old town, how else are we going to get our thrills . . . ?*

Rebus's heart was on fire as he stopped in front of him. He could hardly get the words out.

'It's story time, Mr Petrie.' He slapped the wig down on Nicky Petrie's head. Petrie, with a show of disgust, removed the wig, held it to his face. It was hard to make out now what was sweat and what was tears.

'Oh God, oh God, oh God,' he kept saying.

'Where's Damon Mee?'

'Oh God, oh God, oh God.'

'I don't think He's in a position to help you, Nicky.'

Rebus looked at the clothes. They could belong to Ama Petrie: brother and sister were of similar build, Nicky slightly taller and broader. The black dress looked tight on him.

'This is what you like to do, Nicky? Dress up as a woman?'

'No harm in it,' Clarke added quickly. 'We're all different.'

Nicky looked at her, blinking to refocus his eyes.

'You could do with a makeover, sweetheart,' he said. She smiled. 'You're probably right.'

'Who does your make-up, Nicky?' Rebus asked. 'Ama?'

He straightened up. 'All my own work.'

'And then you head for this side of town? Walk up and down and soak up the admiration?'

'I don't expect you to—'

'Nobody's asking what you expect, Mr Petrie.' He turned to Clarke. 'Go fetch the car.' Handed her the keys. 'We'll need to take Mr Petrie here to the station.'

Petrie's eyes widened with fear. 'Why?'

'To answer a few questions about Damon Mee. And to explain why you've been lying to us all along.'

Petrie made to say something, then bit his lip.

'Suit yourself,' Rebus told him. Then, to Clarke: 'Go get the car.'

Rebus questioned Nicky Petrie for half an hour. He made sure that anyone who wanted to gawp had the chance to come into the interview room. Petrie sat there with his head in his hands, not looking up, while a parade of CID and uniforms commented on his shoes, tights and dress.

'I can get you some trousers and a shirt,' Rebus offered.

'I know what you're trying to do,' Petrie said when they were alone. 'Humiliate me all you like, this lady's *not* for talking.' He managed a small defiant smile.

'I'm sure your dad will come riding to the rescue anyway,' Rebus commented, pleased to see some of the colour leave the young man's lips.

'I don't need my father.'

'That's as may be, but we'll need to contact him. Best for us to do it rather than the papers.'

'Papers?'

Rebus barked a laugh. 'Think they'll let something like this pass them by? No, sir, you're going to be cover-boy for a day, Nicky. Congratulations. Bit of pan-stick and a wig, they might even pay you for the privilege.'

'They don't need to know,' Petrie said quietly.

Rebus shrugged. 'Cop-shops are like sieves, Nicky. All

these people who've seen you here . . . I can't promise they won't talk.'

'Bastard.'

'If you like, Nicky.' Rebus leaned forward. 'All I want to know is where I can find Damon Mee.'

'Then I can't help you,' Nicky Petrie said, with all the defiance he could muster.

Plan Two: Ama Petrie.

She flew into the station like a whirlwind. Cal Brady was right: she had a soft spot for her little brother.

'Where is he? What have you done with him?'

Rebus looked at her with a façade of utter calm. 'Shouldn't those be *my* questions?'

She didn't seem to understand.

'Damon Mee,' Rebus explained. 'Nicky met him at Gaitano's, took him to the boat where you were having one of your parties. That's the last time he was seen alive, Ms Petrie.'

'It's got nothing to do with Nicky.'

They were seated in the same interview room, Nicky Petrie having been taken down to the cells. It was also the same interview room where Harold Ince had first been questioned. Ince had been sentenced to twelve years, Marshall to eight, the bulk of both sentences to be served at Peterhead. Had Rebus known anyone there, he might have put in a word for Ince. But he didn't know a single damned soul . . .

'What's got nothing to do with Nicky?' he asked.

'It's my fault, not his.'

Rebus understood: she thought Nicky had talked, had somehow incriminated himself. She was underestimating him. The chink in her armour which Cal Brady had detected: she loved her brother too much.

Rebus sat back, knew how to play this. He asked her if she wanted anything to drink. She shook her head violently.

'I want to make a statement,' she blurted out.

'You'll probably want a solicitor, Ms Petrie.'

'Bugger that.' She stopped suddenly. 'Is Nicky here? In this station?'

'Safely in the cells.'

'Safely?' Her voice trembled. 'Poor Nicky . . .' She was dry-eyed but her face was tense.

'Did Damon Mee know Nicky wasn't really a woman?'

'How could he not?'

Rebus shrugged. 'Your brother's pretty convincing.'

She allowed herself a brief smile. 'He always said he should have been the girl and I the boy.'

Rebus knew Nicky had run away from home aged twelve. He'd been running ever since . . .

'So what happened on the boat?'

'We'd all been drinking.' She looked at him. 'You know what parties are like.'

She was trying to win him round to her side. Too late for that, but he nodded anyway.

'Then Nicky brought this piece of rough below decks.'

'Piece of rough?'

'As in rough and ready. I'm not being a snob, Inspector.'

'Of course not. I take it all of you knew Nicky's . . . preferences?'

'The gang of us, yes. A few couples were up dancing. Nicky and this Damon joined them.' Her eyes went unfocused; she was picturing the scene. 'Nicky had his head on Damon's shoulder, and just for a moment our eyes met . . . and he looked so *happy*.' She screwed shut her eyes.

'Then what happened?'

She opened her eyes again, staring at the desk. 'Alfie and Cherie were one of the other couples. Alfie was as drunk as I've ever seen him. For a joke, he leaned over and snatched Nicky's wig. Nicky chased him round the room. And Damon just stood there, like he was thunder-struck. He looked ... it really seemed hilarious at the time. His face was a picture. Then he ran for the stairs. Nicky saw what was happening and went after him ...'

'They had a fight?'

She looked at him. 'Is that what he told you?' She smiled. 'Dear Nicky ... You've seen him, Inspector. He couldn't hurt a fly. No, by the time I came up on deck, this Damon person had Nicky down on the ground. He was strangling the life out of him, at the same time thumping his head against the deck. Lifting it ... thudding it back down. I grabbed an empty wine bottle, swung it at the side of his head. It didn't knock him cold or anything. The bottle didn't even break, not like in the films. But he let go of Nicky, staggered to his feet.'

'And?'

'And seemed to lose his balance. He fell over the side and into the water. It's funny ... the deck's not that high above the water line ... he hardly made a sound as he fell.'

'What did you do?'

'I had to make sure Nicky was all right. I took him back down below. His throat hurt, but I got a brandy down him.'

'I meant, what did you do about Damon?'

'Oh, him ...' She thought it over. 'Well, by the time I went back up, there was no sign of him. I assumed he'd swum ashore.'

Rebus stared at her. 'Are you quite sure that's what you assumed?'

'To be honest ... I'm not sure I thought anything at all. He was gone, and he couldn't hurt Nicky, that was all that mattered. That's all that ever matters to me. So you see, whatever Nicky's told you, he only did in order to protect me. I'm the one you should put in the cell. Nicky should go home.'

'Thanks for the advice.'

'You will let him go, won't you?'

He stood up, leaned across the desk towards her. 'I know Damon's family. I've seen the way they've been suffering. Your precious brother doesn't know the half of it.'

She glowered at him. 'And why should he?'

He thought of a thousand answers, knew she'd rebut every one of them. Instead, he told her he'd need a written statement. He'd send someone in to take it. He made for the door.

'And then you'll let Nicky out, won't you, Inspector?'

His one little victory: he left without saying a word.

Epilogue

Later that night, he found himself in Cowgate again, further to the east this time, past the mothballed mortuary, walking towards the building site on Holyrood. Behind it, he could make out a couple of the Greenfield tower-blocks, and behind those Salisbury Crags. The sun had set, but it wasn't quite dark. The twilight could last an age at this time of year. Demolition work had stopped for the day. He couldn't be sure where everything would go, but he knew there'd be a newspaper building, a theme park, and the Parliament building. They'd all be ready for the twenty-first century, or so the predictions went. Taking Scotland into the new millennium. Rebus tried to raise within himself a tiny cheer of hope, but found it stifled by his old cynicism.

No longer twilight now. Darkness had fallen. Shadows seemed to rise all around him as a bell tolled in the distance. The blood that had seeped into stone, the bones that lay twisting in their eternity, the stories and horrors of the city's past and present . . . he knew they'd all come rising in the digger's steel jaws, bubbling to the surface as the city began its slow ascent towards being a nation's capital once again.

Forget it, John, he told himself. It's the Old Town, that's all.

Cary Oakes sat in the visitors' room at Saughton Prison. They hadn't put any cuffs on him, and there was just the one guard. One guard was almost demeaning. Then the door opened and his solicitor walked in. That's what they were called here – solicitors. Cary smiled, bowed his head in greeting. The lawyer was young, looked eager but flustered. First time, probably, but that was OK. Youngsters, working hard to make the grade . . . they'd put in the hours for you, go the extra yard. Cary had nothing against fresh blood.

He waited till the guy was seated and ready, notepad out, pen held in his right hand. Then he began his spiel.

'I'm innocent, man, so help me. And you've got to do that: you've got to help me. Between us, we can prove I didn't do anything.' He leaned forward, rested his elbows on the table. 'It'll make your career. You're my man, I can sense it.'

Gave a big open smile.

1

'Then why are you here?'

'Depends what you mean,' Rebus said.

'Mean?' The woman frowned behind her glasses.

'Mean by "here",' he explained. 'Here in this room? Here in this career? Here on the planet?'

She smiled. Her name was Andrea Thomson. She wasn't a doctor – she'd made that clear at their first meeting. Nor was she a 'shrink' or a 'therapist'. 'Career Analysis' was what it had said on Rebus's daily sheet.

2.30–3.15: Career Analysis, Rm 3.16.

With *Ms* Thomson. Which had become Andrea at the moment of introduction. Which was yesterday, Tuesday. A 'get to know' session, she'd called it.

She was in her late thirties, short and large-hipped. Her hair was a thick mop of blond with some darker streaks showing through. Her teeth were slightly oversized. She was self-employed, didn't work for the police full-time.

'Do any of us?' Rebus had asked yesterday. She'd looked a bit puzzled. 'I mean, do any of us work full-time . . . that's why we're here, isn't it?' He'd waved a hand in the direction of the closed door. 'We're not pulling our weight. We need a smack on the wrists.'

'Is that what you think you need, Detective Inspector?'

He'd wagged a finger. 'Keep calling me that and I'll keep calling you "Doc".'

'I'm not a doctor,' she'd said. 'Nor am I a shrink, a therapist, or any other word you've probably been thinking in connection with me.'

'Then what are you?'

1

'I deal with Career Analysis.'

Rebus had snorted. 'Then you should be wearing a seat-belt.'

She'd stared at him. 'Am I in for a bumpy ride?'

'You could say that, seeing how my *career*, as you call it, has just careered out of control.'

So much for yesterday.

Now she wanted to know about his feelings. How did he feel about being a detective?

'I like it.'

'Which parts?'

'All of me.' Fixing her with a smile.

She smiled back. 'I meant—'

'I know what you meant.' He looked around the room. It was small, utilitarian. Two chrome-framed chairs either side of a teak-veneered desk. The chairs were covered in some lime-coloured material. Nothing on the desk itself but her A4-sized lined pad and her pen. There was a heavy-looking satchel in the corner; Rebus wondered if his file was in there. A clock on the wall, calendar below it. The calendar had come from the local fire brigade. A length of net curtaining across the window.

It wasn't her room. It was a room she could use on those occasions when her services were required. Not quite the same thing.

'I like my job,' he said at last, folding his arms. Then, wondering if she'd read anything into the action – defensiveness, say – he unfolded them again. Couldn't seem to find anything to do with them except bunch his fists into his jacket pockets. 'I like every aspect of it, right down to the added paperwork each time the office runs out of staples for the staple-gun.'

'Then why did you blow up at Detective Chief Superintendent Templer?'

'I don't know.'

'She thinks maybe it has something to do with professional jealousy.'

2

The laugh burst from him. 'She said that?'

'You don't agree?'

'Of course not.'

'You've known her some years, haven't you?'

'More than I care to count.'

'And she's always been senior to you?'

'It's never bothered me, if that's what you're thinking.'

'It's only recently that she's become your commanding officer.'

'So?'

'You've been at DI level for quite some time. No thoughts of improvement?' She caught his look. 'Maybe "improvement" is the wrong word. You've not wanted promotion?'

'No.'

'Why not?'

'Might be I'm afraid of responsibility.'

She stared at him. 'That smacks of a prepared answer.'

'Be prepared, that's my motto.'

'Oh, you were a Boy Scout?'

'No,' he said. She stayed quiet, picking up her pen and studying it. It was one of those cheap yellow Bics. 'Look,' he said into the silence, 'I've got no quarrel with Gill Templer. Good luck to her as a DCS. It's not a job I could do. I like being where I am.' He glanced up. 'Which doesn't mean here in this room, it means out on the street, solving crimes. The reason I lost it is . . . well, the way the whole inquiry's being handled.'

'You must have had similar feelings before in the middle of a case?' She had taken her glasses off so she could rub the reddened skin either side of her nose.

'Many a time,' he admitted.

She slid the glasses back on. 'But this is the first time you've thrown a mug?'

'I wasn't aiming for her.'

'She had to duck. A full mug, too.'

'Ever tasted cop-shop tea?'

3

She smiled again. 'So you've no problem then?'

'None.' He folded his arms in what he hoped was a sign of confidence.

'Then why are you here?'

Time up, Rebus walked back along the corridor and straight into the men's toilets, where he splashed water on his face, dried off with a paper towel. Watched himself in the mirror above the sink as he pulled a cigarette from his packet and lit it, blowing the smoke ceilingwards.

One of the lavatories flushed; a door clicked its lock off. Jazz McCullough came out.

'Thought that might be you,' he said, turning on the tap.

'How could you tell?'

'One long sigh followed by the lighting of a cigarette. Had to be a shrink session finishing.'

'She's not a shrink.'

'Size of her, she looks like she's shrunk.' McCullough reached for a towel. Tossed it in the bin when he'd finished. Straightened his tie. His real name was James, but those who knew him seemed never to call him that. He was Jamesy, or more often Jazz. Tall, mid-forties, cropped black hair with just a few touches of grey at the temples. He was thin. Patted his stomach now, just above the belt, as if to emphasise his lack of a gut. Rebus could barely see his own belt, even in the mirror.

Jazz didn't smoke. Had a family back home in Broughty Ferry: wife and two sons about his only topic of conversation. Examining himself in the mirror, he tucked a stray hair back behind one ear.

'What the hell are we doing here, John?'

'Andrea was just asking me the same thing.'

'That's because she knows it's a waste of time. Thing is, we're paying her wages.'

'We're doing some good then.'

4

Jazz glanced at him. 'You dog! You think you're in there!'

Rebus winced. 'Give me a break. All I meant was . . .' But what was the point? Jazz was already laughing. He slapped Rebus on the shoulder.

'Back into the fray,' he said, pulling open the door. 'Three thirty, "Dealing with the Public".'

It was their third day at Tulliallan: the Scottish Police College. The place was mostly full of recent recruits, learning their lessons before being allowed out on to public streets. But there were other officers there, older and wiser. They were on refresher courses, or learning new skills.

And then there were the Resurrection Men.

The college was based at Tulliallan Castle, not in itself a castle but a mock-baronial home to which had been added a series of modern buildings, connected by corridors. The whole edifice sat in huge leafy grounds on the outskirts of the village of Kincardine, to the northern side of the Firth of Forth, almost equidistant between Glasgow and Edinburgh. It could have been mistaken for a university campus, and to some extent that was its function. You came here to learn.

Or, in Rebus's case, as punishment.

There were four other officers in the seminar room when Rebus and McCullough arrived. 'The Wild Bunch', DI Francis Gray had called them, first time they'd been gathered together. A couple of faces Rebus knew – DS Stu Sutherland from Livingston; DI Tam Barclay from Falkirk. Gray himself was from Glasgow, and Jazz worked out of Dundee, while the final member of the party, DC Allan Ward, was based in Dumfries. 'A gathering of nations,' as Gray had put it. But to Rebus they acted more like spokesmen for their tribes, sharing the same language but with different outlooks. They were wary of each other. It was especially awkward with officers from the same region. Rebus and Sutherland were both Lothian and Borders, but the town of Livingston was F Division, known to anyone in Edinburgh as 'F Troop'. Sutherland was just waiting for Rebus to say something to the others, something disparaging. He had the look of a haunted man.

The six men shared only one characteristic: they were at Tulliallan because they'd failed in some way. Mostly it was an issue with authority. Much of their free time the previous two days had been spent sharing war stories. Rebus's tale was milder than most. If a young officer, fresh out of uniform, had made the mistakes they had made, he or she would probably not have been given the Tulliallan life-line. But these were lifers, men who'd been in the force an average of twenty years. Most were nearing the point where they could leave on full pension. Tulliallan was their last-chance saloon. They were here to atone, to be resurrected.

As Rebus and McCullough took their seats, a uniformed officer walked in and marched briskly to the head of the oval table where his chair was waiting. He was in his mid-fifties and was here to remind them of their obligation to the public at large. He was here to train them to mind their p's and q's.

Five minutes into the lecture, Rebus let his eyes and mind drift out of focus. He was back on the Marber case . . .

Edward Marber had been an Edinburgh art and antique dealer. Past tense, because Marber was now dead, bludgeoned outside his home by assailant or assailants unknown. The weapon had not yet been found. A brick or rock was the best guess offered by the city pathologist, Professor Gates, who had been called to the scene for a PLE: Pronouncement of Life Extinct. Brain haemorrhage brought on by the blow. Marber had died on the steps of his Duddingston Village home, front-door keys in his hand. He had been dropped off by taxi after the private

6

viewing night of his latest exhibition: New Scottish Colourists. Marber owned two small, exclusive galleries in the New Town, plus antique shops in Dundas Street, Glasgow and Perth. Rebus had asked someone why Perth, rather than oil-rich Aberdeen.

'Because Perthshire's where the wealth goes to play.'

The taxi-driver had been interviewed. Marber didn't drive, but his house was at the end of an eighty-metre driveway, the gates to which had been open. The taxi had pulled up at the door, activating a halogen light to one side of the steps. Marber had paid and tipped, asking for a receipt, and the taxi-driver had U-turned away, not bothering to look in his mirror.

'I didn't see a thing,' he'd told the police.

The taxi receipt had been found in Marber's pocket, along with a list of the sales he'd made that evening, totalling just over £16,000. His cut, Rebus learned, would have been twenty per cent, £3,200. Not a bad night's work.

It was morning before the body was found by the postman. Professor Gates had given an estimated time of death of between nine and eleven the previous evening. The taxi had picked Marber up from his gallery at eight thirty, so must have dropped him home around eight forty-five, a time the driver accepted with a shrug.

The immediate police instinct had screamed robbery, but problems and niggles soon became apparent. Would someone have clobbered the victim with the taxi still in sight, the scene lit by halogen? It seemed unlikely, and yet by the time the taxi turned out of the driveway, Marber should have been safely on the other side of his door. And though Marber's pockets had been turned out, cash and credit cards evidently taken, the attacker had failed to use the keys to unlock the front door and trawl the house itself. Scared off perhaps, but it still didn't make sense.

Muggings tended to be spontaneous. You were attacked on the street, maybe just after using a cash machine. The mugger didn't hang around your door waiting for you to come home. Marber's house was relatively isolated: Duddingston Village was a wealthy enclave on the edge of Edinburgh, semi-rural, with the mass of Arthur's Seat as its neighbour. The houses hid behind walls, quiet and secure. Anyone approaching Marber's home on foot would have triggered the same halogen security light. They would then have had to hide – in the undergrowth, say, or behind one of the trees. After a couple of minutes, the lamp's timer would finish its cycle and go off. But any movement would trigger the sensor once again.

The Scene of Crime officers had looked for possible hiding places, finding several. But no traces of anyone, no footprints or fibres.

Another scenario, proposed by DCS Gill Templer:

'Say the assailant was already inside the house. Heard the door being unlocked and ran towards it. Smashed the victim on the head and ran.'

But the house was high-tech: alarms and sensors everywhere. There was no sign of a break-in, no indication that anything was missing. Marber's best friend, another art dealer called Cynthia Bessant, had toured the house and pronounced that she could see nothing missing or out of place, except that much of the deceased's art collection had been removed from the walls and, each painting neatly packaged in bubble-wrap, was stacked against the wall in the dining room. Bessant had been unable to offer an explanation.

'Perhaps he was about to re-frame them, or move them to different rooms. One *does* get tired of the same paintings in the same spots . . .'

She'd toured every room, paying particular attention to Marber's bedroom, not having seen inside it before. She called it his 'inner sanctum'.

The victim himself had never been married, and was quickly assumed by the investigating officers to have been gay.

'Eddie's sexuality,' Cynthia Bessant had said, 'can have no bearing on this case.'

But that would be something for the inquiry to decide.

Rebus had felt himself side-lined in the investigation, working the telephones mostly. Cold calls to friends and associates. The same questions eliciting almost identical responses. The bubble-wrapped paintings had been checked for fingerprints, from which it became apparent that Marber himself had packaged them up. Still no one – neither his secretary nor his friends – could give an explanation.

Then, towards the end of one briefing, Rebus had picked up a mug of tea – someone else's tea, milky grey – and hurled it in the general direction of Gill Templer.

The briefing had started much as any other, Rebus washing down three aspirin caplets with his morning latte. The coffee came in a cardboard beaker. It was from a concession on the corner of The Meadows. Usually his first and last decent cup of the day.

'Bit too much to drink last night?' DS Siobhan Clarke had asked. She'd run her eyes over him: same suit, shirt and tie as the day before. Probably wondering if he'd bothered to take any of it off between times. The morning shave erratic, a lazy run-over with an electric. Hair that needed washing and cutting.

She'd seen just what Rebus had wanted her to see.

'And a good morning to you too, Siobhan,' he'd muttered to himself, crushing the empty beaker.

Usually he stood towards the back of the room at briefings, but today he was nearer the front. Sat there at a desk, rubbing his forehead, loosening his shoulders, as Gill Templer spelt out the day's mission.

More door-to-door; more interviews; more phone calls.

His fingers were around the mug by now. He didn't know whose it was, the glaze cold to the touch – could even have been left from the day before. The room was stifling and already smelt of sweat.

'More bloody phone calls,' he found himself saying, loud enough to be heard at the front. Templer looked up.

'Something to say, John?'

'No, no . . . nothing.'

Her back straightening. 'Only if you've anything to add – maybe one of your famous deductions – I'm all ears.'

'With respect, ma'am, you're not all ears – you're all talk.' Noises around him: gasps and looks. Rebus rising slowly to his feet.

'We're getting nowhere fast.' His voice was loud. 'There's nobody left to talk to, and nothing worth them saying!'

The blood had risen to Templer's cheeks. The sheet of paper she was holding – the day's duties – had become a cylinder which her fingers threatened to crush.

'Well, I'm sure we can all learn something from *you*, DI Rebus.' Not 'John' any more. Her voice rising to match his. Her eyes scanned the room: thirteen officers, not quite the full complement. Templer was working under pressure: much of it fiscal. Each investigation had a ticket attached to it, a costing she daren't overstep. Then there were the illnesses and holidays, the latecomers . . . 'Maybe you'd like to come up here,' she was saying, 'and give us the benefit of your thoughts on the subject of just exactly *how* we should be proceeding with this inquiry.' She stretched an arm out, as if to introduce him to an audience. 'Ladies and gentlemen . . .'

Which was the moment he chose to throw the mug. It travelled in a lazy arc, spinning as it went, dispensing cold tea. Templer ducked instinctively, though the mug would have sailed over her head in any case. It hit the back wall just above floor level, bouncing off and failing to break. There was silence in the room as people rose to their feet, checking their clothes for spillage.

Rebus sat down then, one finger punching the desk as if trying to find the rewind on life's remote control.

*

'DI Rebus?' The uniform was talking to him.

'Yes, sir?'

'Glad you've decided to join us.' Smiles all around the table. How much had he missed? He didn't dare look at his watch.

'Sorry about that, sir.'

'I was asking if you'd be our member of the public.' Nodding to the opposite side of the table to Rebus. 'DI Gray will be the officer. And you, DI Rebus, will be coming into the station with what could turn out to be some vital information pertaining to a case.' The teacher paused. 'Or you could be a crank.' Laughter from a couple of the men. Francis Gray was beaming at Rebus, nodding encouragement.

'Whenever you're ready, DI Gray.'

Gray leaned forward on the table. 'So, Mrs Ditchwater, you say you saw something that night?'

The laughter was louder. The teacher waved them quiet. 'Let's try to keep this serious, shall we?'

Gray nodded, turned his eyes to Rebus again. 'You definitely saw something?'

'Yes,' Rebus announced, coarsening his voice. 'I saw the whole thing, Officer.'

'Though you've been registered blind these past eleven years?'

Gales of laughter in the room, the teacher thumping the table-top, trying to restore order. Gray sitting back, joining the laughter, winking across at Rebus, whose shoulders were rocking.

Francis Gray was fighting hard against resurrection.

'I thought I was going to wet myself,' Tam Barclay said, lowering the tray of glasses on to the table. They were in the larger of Kincardine's two pubs, lessons finished for the day. Six of them forming a tight circle: Rebus, Francis Gray, Jazz McCullough, plus Tam Barclay, Stu Sutherland and Allan Ward. At thirty-four, Ward was the youngest of the group and the lowest-ranking officer on the course. He had a tough, spoilt look to him. Maybe it came from working in the south-west.

Five pints, one cola: McCullough was driving home afterwards, wanted to see his wife and kids.

'I do my damnedest to *avoid* mine,' Gray had said.

'No joking,' Barclay said, squeezing into his seat, 'near wet myself.' Grinning at Gray. '"Blind these past eleven years".'

Gray picked up his pint, raised it. 'Here's tae us, wha's like us?'

'Nobody,' Rebus commented. 'Or they'd be stuck on this damned course.'

'Just got to grin and bear it,' Barclay said. He was late thirties, thickening around the waist. Salt-and-pepper hair brushed back from the forehead. Rebus knew him from a couple of cases: Falkirk and Edinburgh were only thirty minutes apart.

'I wonder if Wee Andrea grins when she bares it,' Stu Sutherland said.

'No sexism, please.' Francis Gray was wagging a finger.

'Besides,' McCullough added, 'we don't want to stoke John's fantasies.'

Gray raised an eyebrow. 'That right, John? Got the hots for your counsellor? Better watch, you might make Allan jealous.'

Allan Ward looked up from the cigarette he was lighting, just glowered.

'That your sheep-frightening look, Allan?' Gray said. 'Not much to do down in Dumfries, is there, except round up the usual ewes?'

More laughter. It wasn't that Francis Gray had made himself the centre of attention; it seemed to happen naturally. He'd been first into his seat, and the others had congregated around him, Rebus sitting directly opposite. Gray was a big man, and the years told on his face. And because he said everything with a smile, a wink or a glint

12

in his eye, he got away with it. Rebus hadn't heard anyone making a joke about Gray himself yet, though they'd all been his target. It was as if he were challenging them, testing them. The way they took his comments would tell him everything he needed to know about them. Rebus wondered how the big man would react to a jibe or joke directed against him.

Maybe he'd have to find out.

McCullough's mobile sounded, and he got up, moving away.

'His wife, odds-on,' Gray stated. He was halfway down his pint of lager. Didn't smoke, told Rebus he'd given up a decade back. The two of them had been outside during a break, Rebus offering the packet. Ward and Barclay smoked too. Three out of six: it meant Rebus could feel comfortable lighting up.

'She's keeping tabs on him?' Stu Sutherland was saying.

'Proof of a deep and loving relationship,' Gray commented, tipping the glass to his mouth again. He was one of those drinkers, you never saw them swallow: it was as if they could hold their throat open and just pour the stuff down.

'You two know each other?' Sutherland asked. Gray glanced over his shoulder to where McCullough was standing, his head bowed towards the mobile phone.

'I know the type,' was all Gray said by way of answer.

Rebus knew better. He rose to his feet. 'Same again?'

Two lagers, three IPAs. On his way to the bar, Rebus pointed towards McCullough, who shook his head. He still had most of his cola, didn't want another. Rebus heard the words 'I'll be on the road in ten minutes . . .' Yes, he was on the phone to his wife. Rebus had a call he wanted to make too. Jean was probably finishing work right around now. Rush hour, the journey from the museum to her home in Portobello might take half an hour.

The barman knew the order: this was their third round of the evening. The previous two nights, they'd stuck to the college premises. First night, Gray had produced a good bottle of malt, and they'd sat in the common room, getting to know each other. Tuesday, they'd met in the college's own bar for an after-dinner session, McCullough sticking to soft drinks and then heading out for his car.

But at lunchtime today, Tam Barclay had mentioned a bar in the village, good rep.

'No trouble with the locals,' was the way he'd put it. So here they were. The barman looked comfortable, which told Rebus he'd dealt with intakes from the college before. He was efficient, not over-friendly. Midweek, only half a dozen regulars in the place. Three at one table, two at one end of the bar, another standing alone next to Rebus. The man turned to him.

'Up at the cop school, are you?'

Rebus nodded.

'Bit old for recruits.'

Rebus glanced at the man. He was tall, completely bald, his head shining. Grey moustache, eyes which seemed to be retracting into the skull. He was drinking a bottle of beer with what looked like a dark rum in the glass next to it.

'Force is desperate these days,' Rebus explained. 'Next thing, they'll be press-ganging.'

The man smiled. 'I think you're having me on.'

Rebus shrugged. 'We're here on a refresher course,' he admitted.

'Teaching old dogs new tricks, eh?' The man lifted his beer.

'Get you one?' Rebus offered. The man shook his head. So Rebus paid the barman and, deciding against a tray, hoisted three of the pints, making a triangle of them between his hands. Went to the table, came back for the last two, including his own. Thinking: best not leave it too late to phone Jean. He didn't want her to hear him drunk. Not that he was planning on getting drunk, but you could never tell . . .

'This you celebrating the end of the course?' the man asked.

'Just the beginning,' Rebus told him.

St Leonard's police station was mid-evening quiet. There were prisoners in the holding cells waiting for next morning's court appearance, and two teenagers being booked for shoplifting. Upstairs, the CID offices were almost empty. The Marber inquiry had wound down for the day, and only Siobhan Clarke was left, in front of a computer, staring at a screen-saver in the form of a banner message: WHAT WILL SIOBHAN DO WITHOUT HER SUGAR DADDY? She didn't know who had written it: one of the team, having a bit of a laugh. She surmised it referred to John Rebus, but couldn't quite work out the meaning. Did the author know what a sugar daddy was? Or did it just mean that Rebus looked after her, watched out for her? She was annoyed to find herself so irritated by the message.

She went into the screen-saver options and clicked on 'banner', erased the present message and replaced it with one of her own: I KNOW WHO YOU ARE, SUCKER. Then she checked a couple of other terminals, but their screen-savers were asteroids and wavy lines. When the phone on her desk started ringing, she considered not answering. Probably another crank wanting to confess, or ready with spurious information. A respectable middle-aged gent had called yesterday and accused his upstairs neighbours of the crime. Turned out they were students, played their music too loud and too often. The man had been warned that wasting police time was a serious matter.

'Mind you,' one of the uniforms had commented afterwards, 'if I'd to listen to Slipknot all day, I'd probably do worse.'

Siobhan sat down in front of her computer, lifted the receiver.

'CID, DS Clarke speaking.'

'One thing they teach at Tulliallan,' the voice said, 'is the importance of the quick pick-up.'

She smiled. 'I prefer to be wooed.'

'A quick pick-up,' Rebus explained, 'means picking up the phone within half a dozen rings.'

'How did you know I was here?'

'I didn't. Tried your flat first, got the answering machine.'

'And somehow sensed I wasn't out on the town?' She settled back in her chair. 'Sounds like you're in a bar.'

'In beautiful downtown Kincardine.'

'And yet you've dragged yourself from your pint to call me?'

'I called Jean first. Had a spare twenty-pence piece . . .'

'I'm flattered. A whole twenty pee?' She listened to him snort.

'So . . . how's it going?' he asked.

'Never mind that, how's Tulliallan?'

'As some of the teachers would say, we have a new tricks–old dog interface scenario.'

She laughed. 'They don't talk like that, do they?'

'Some of them do. We're being taught crime *management* and victim *empathy response*.'

'And yet you still have time for a drink?'

Silence on the line; she wondered if she'd touched a nerve.

'How do you know I'm not on fresh orange?' he said at last.

'I just do.'

'Go on then, impress me with your detective skills.'

'It's just that your voice gets slightly nasal.'

'After how many?'

'I'll guess four.'

'The girl's a marvel.' The pips started sounding. 'Hang on,' he said, putting in more money.

'Another spare twenty pee?'

'A fifty, actually. Which gives you plenty of time to update me on Marber.'

'Well, it's all been very quiet since the coffee incident.'

'I think it was tea.'

'Whatever it was, the stain's not budging. For what it's worth, I think they over-reacted, sending you into purdah.'

'I'm wasting money here.'

She sighed, sat forward. The screen-saver had just kicked in: I KNOW WHO YOU ARE, SUCKER scrolling right to left across the screen. 'We're still looking at friends and associates. Couple of interesting stories: an artist Marber had fallings-out with. Not unusual in the business, apparently, but this came to blows. Turns out the artist is one of these New Scottish Colourists, and leaving him out of the exhibition was a definite snub.'

'Maybe he whacked Marber with his easel.'

'Maybe.'

'And the second story?'

'That one I've been saving up to tell you. Did you ever see the guest list for the preview?'

'Yes.'

'Turns out not everyone who turned up was on the list. What we had were people who'd signed Marber's guest book. But now we've printed off a list of the people who actually got invites. Some of them were at the exhibition, hadn't bothered to RSVP or sign the book.'

'This artist was one of them?' Rebus guessed.

'God, no. But a certain M. G. Cafferty was.'

She heard Rebus whistle. Morris Gerald Cafferty – Big Ger, to those in the know – was the east coast's biggest gangster, or the biggest one they knew about. Cafferty and Rebus went back a long way.

'Big Ger a patron of the arts?' Rebus mused.

'He collects paintings, apparently.'

'What he doesn't do is smack people over the head on their doorsteps.'

'I bow to your superior knowledge.'

There was a pause on the line. 'How's Gill doing?'

'Much better since you left. Is she going to take it any further?'

'Not if I finish this course – that was the deal. How about the L-plate?'

Siobhan smiled. By L-plate Rebus meant the latest addition to CID, a detective constable called Davie Hynds. 'He's quiet, studious, industrious,' she recited. 'Not your type at all.'

'But is he any good?'

'Don't worry, I'll slap him into shape.'

'That's one of the prerogatives, now you've been promoted.'

The pips were sounding again. 'Do I get to go now?'

'A concise and helpful report, DS Clarke. Seven out of ten.'

'Only seven?'

'I'm deducting three for sarcasm. You need to address this attitudinal problem of yours, or—'

The sudden hum on the line told her his time was up. It was taking some getting used to, being addressed as 'DS'. She sometimes still introduced herself as Detective Constable Clarke, forgetting that the recent round of promotions had been kind to her. Could jealousy be behind the message on her screen? Silvers and Hood had stayed the same rank – as had most of the rest of CID.

'Narrowing the field nicely, girl,' she told herself, reaching for her coat.

Back at the table, Barclay lifted a mobile phone and told Rebus he could have borrowed it.

'Thanks, Tam. I've actually got one.'

'Are the batteries flat?'

Rebus lifted his glass, shook his head slowly.

'I think,' Francis Gray said, 'John just prefers things done the old-fashioned way. Isn't that right, John?'

Rebus shrugged, tipped the glass to his lips. Above the rim, he could see the bald man standing sideways on to the bar, watching the group intently . . .